THE NORTON BOOK OF
THE SEA

THE NORTON BOOK OF
THE SEA

Edited by CAPTAIN JOHN O. COOTE

Introduction by HAMMOND INNES

W · W · NORTON & COMPANY · NEW YORK · LONDON

First Edition

Library of Congress Cataloging-in-Publication Data

The Norton book of the sea: an anthology/edited with
commentary by John Coote.—1st ed.
p.   cm.
British ed. published in 1989 under title:
The Faber book of the sea:
Bibliography: p.
Includes index.
1. Ocean.   2. Sea in literature.   I. Coote, J. O. (John O.)
GC28.N67 1989   89-3136
551.46—dc19

ISBN 0-393-02778-3

W. W. Norton & Company, Inc., 500 Fifth Avenue, New York, N.Y. 10110
W. W. Norton & Company Ltd., 37 Great Russell Street, London WC1B 3NU

1   2   3   4   5   6   7   8   9   0

Contents

Preface

In the vast literature of the sea, ranging back through all its moods to the sagas and the Christian voyages, right back to the African adventures of the Phoenicians and the ocean wanderings of Polynesian and Eskimo peoples, the choices for an anthology are infinite. The person who makes this choice must therefore be not only an experienced sailor but in love with his subject.

The two do not necessarily go together, for there are many hardened sailors who hate the sea, and almost always with reason.

"...But we do be afraid of the sea, and we do only be drownded now and again."

Anyone who quotes this passage from Synge at the outset of his selection of sea writings is my sort of man. The Fastnet '79 was raced by quite a few who had never read *The Arran Islands,* or if they had, they chose to ignore the warning. He who lets the sea lull him into a false sense of security is in very grave danger, for the sea is an element governed by natural forces so powerful that our warheads are toys by comparison.

This, and the fact that from very early times water was man's easiest mode of transport in a swamp-filled, densely forested world, is what gives the sea its endless fascination. The vehicles by which man ventured onto its surface are a subject in themselves. Clashes of interest occurred over territory and over the goods that were carried; so vessels of war were developed—the Viking longships a prime example, enabling the Scandinavians to reach out to all the western world.

The *Norton Book of the Sea* is not the first anthology of the sea. Nor will it be the last. Indeed, Villiers and Hough have both found ample material for a whole book in the waters off one single cape: the Horn. Do not be surprised, therefore, if you have a real knowledge of sea literature, to find gaps in the present work.

Mysteries, for instance. Gavin Maxwell had a chapter marvelously titled *There Be Dragons.* There do be mysteries, endless mysteries. The Prologue touches on two of the most publicized: the *Marie Celeste* and the Bermuda Triangle. Also the *Waratah.* But a whole section would not have been amiss, for there are always new sea mysteries to capture our imagination. A man living in Fiji, who wrote *Raft* for the survival of those whose ships had been sunk under them during World War II, had a beauty, and if he hadn't died when he did he was going to present me with all the details.

And there are old mysteries that one can still unravel—or believe one has unraveled. Scylla, for instance.

Homer in the *Odyssey* begins his description of Scylla with an account of the clouds hanging over the higher of the two peaks Odysseus has to sail past on his way from the Wandering Rocks (of Stromboli) to the now-defunct hazard of the Charybdis whirlpool in the Messina Straits. And when Scylla strikes he describes the monster as having "twelve feet, all dangling in the air, and six long necks, each ending in a grisly head with triple rows of teeth. . . ." And when he loses half a dozen of his men, they are not drawn into the sea as they would be if Scylla were a sea monster, a giant squid, but are lifted skyward so that their arms and legs "dangled high in the air above my head."

One morning, sheltering in the old port of Ventotene with *Mary Deare* moored to bollards hacked out of the tufa rock by the Romans and still showing the deep marks of their chafing hawsers, I saw Scylla, or I think I did.

The Italian Navy was exercising offshore and far away we saw what looked like a shell burst. But the shell burst stayed there, and then from the inky cloud layer two thousand feet above a black finger protruded, growing longer and longer, and twisting grotesquely as though in search of prey, until at last it struck the sea at the spot where the white spray of the "explosion" was still suspended in the air. Other fingers appeared and struck down into the sea, and the Italian Navy retreated at speed.

There were two Napoli trawlers also sheltering in Ventotene; one of the skippers called this phenomenon a *"trompo marina,"* said he had been caught by one once in a boat about the size of *Mary Deare* and had been lifted 100 meters into the air and then slammed down and thrust below the level of the sea to a depth of about 10 meters. He estimated the distance between the cloud layer and the "shell burst" in the sea as 1,000 meters and the depth of the underwater disturbance as about 100 meters.

Since he was still alive he must have been exaggerating a little, but the speed with which the Navy ships retreated was significant and I had no hesitation in writing afterwards that I had seen the most probable solution to one of the oldest of all the sea's mysteries.

There are really only two ways of compiling a sea anthology: choose short excerpts, which of course involves the hard work of linkage and explanation, or pick your favorite passages and run them at sufficient length for each of them to stand on its own.

Somewhere in a bottom drawer I have an as-yet-uncompleted sea anthology of the second type. But then I am a storyteller. The publishers, I think rightly, have chosen an ex-naval officer as editor. He uses the first technique, and because of his background the early part of this book is much taken up with naval matters: the people involved, from admiral to rating, the conditions on board fighting vessels in the days of sail, the hard discipline and the training. And then, right at the end, a whole section on war at sea.

But besides being a retired captain RN married to an admiral's daughter, John Coote is an experienced sailing man, a member of the Royal Yacht Squadron who has written a great deal about the sea and has recently been sailing a boat in Venezuelan waters. So in total the excerpts are very wide ranging. He has not been concerned that each passage should tell a story; his concern has been to work a much larger canvas, so that what he gives us is a picture of the sea in all its facets, and in particular of the people who go down to it in their manifold craft.

This involves an immense amount of research and many hours of hard writing to fill in the gaps and to give the whole anthology continuity and sense for the reader. This he has done so successfully, in my opinion, that what we have got is something as vivid as a Turner.

It is not my intention to pick out any particular piece or section, though my eye went immediately to that headed "Far Horizons." And of course one looks for one's friends, eager to see what particular passage of theirs has caught the editor's fancy.

He quotes the *Odyssey*, Noah, and the Brendan voyage. He has taken a few passages from fiction, too—Hornblower, of course, Monsarrat, Conrad, *The Caine Mutiny*. And for a classic of small boat voyages he has picked my own choice, Shackleton's voyage from Elephant Island to South Georgia—except that I prefer Worsley's account of it. There's laughter, too, with Richard Gordon and W. W. Jacob.

I could go on and on, for this is a wonderfully dippy book and there is infinite choice in the contents. But as you read this splendid hotchpotch with its glimpses of the sea you never dreamed of, spare a thought for the immense amount of reading John Coote has done. And then to select and fine it all down to give a very broad picture of an element that occupies nine-tenths of the world's surface...a lot of work, for which I personally am grateful to him. I think you will be, too.

Hammond Innes
Kersey, 1989

Introduction

Stories about the sea have an enduring fascination for all manner of people. That landlubbers enjoy their vicarious hardships and dangers is as incomprehensible as trying to explain to someone who is dizzy looking over Waterloo Bridge that others get their kicks hanging from spikes driven into the north face of the Eiger in a one-man bivouac over a sheer drop of 2,000 feet.

For sailors these yarns are evocative of good times and rough ones; moments of farce, boredom or blind terror. Any retired sea-captain takes a perverse pleasure in listening to gale warnings on the radio as his windows rattle and the bedside light flickers with another impending power cut. Then is the moment for him to roll over and drift into sleep, snug in the certainty that there will be no rough shake at seven bells advising maximum foul-weather gear, no call of 'All hands on deck' or hooter sending him to action stations.

During their lives at sea most captains had time on their hands, when they kept detailed logs or journals, some of them of high literary merit, for most sailors acquire the manner of making themselves clearly understood.

The process of selecting material for this book – known appropriately in the publishing world as 'trawling' – drew me back through the ages to Noah and his ark, Ulysses' raft and the bay in Malta named after the missionary Paul when his prison-ship was cast ashore by the gregale. But on the whole I have avoided quoting verbatim from books written before the eighteenth century, as their language, spelling and idiom are tedious to modern readers. So I have turned to more recent historians' accounts of events in Elizabethan days and before. It has to be said that the most vivid first-hand recollections of life at sea have been recorded during the last century, from the Golden Age of Sail down to solo circumnavigators of recent times. These appeal most to sailors because they tell of men and ships not too dissimilar to those which have sailed within our lifetime.

Apart from Winston Churchill and others refighting the Battle of Jutland in pursuit of a verdict, the First World War, 1914–18, did not endow us with too many contemporary accounts of the struggle at sea, although latter-day naval historians are now filling that gap on our bookshelves.

But the Second World War, 1939–45, was a very different matter.

Possibly for fear of libel, many of the best books about it were written in the third person thinly veiled as fiction – not the Hornblower variety stretching facts for box-office appeal, but readily identifiable as the real thing. So I have no hesitation here and now declaring my choice of the three greatest books ever written about war at sea – all of them fiction. Nicholas Monsarrat's *The Cruel Sea* is a chillingly authentic story of life in corvettes on the Western Approaches, manned mostly by young conscripts who two years previously would have thought twice about taking the paddlewheel ferry from Southend to Ramsgate.

Even without seeing Humphrey Bogart in the movie of *The Caine Mutiny* it is possible to believe that a paranoid like Captain Queeg might have been serving somewhere in the vast armadas supporting Admiral Halsey's strike carriers in the Pacific. The book was closely based on the disaster which overwhelmed Task Force 38 in December 1944 when they were unwittingly manoeuvred into the dangerous quarter of an advancing typhoon for an urgently needed replenishment rendezvous.

The third finest book about war at sea, in my opinion, was by a German war correspondent who sailed in one of Doenitz's U-boats at the height of the Battle of the Atlantic. His life expectation was 1.6 war patrols, at which point he would join the 27,000 other German submariners who perished out of fewer than 40,000. But Lothar-Gunther Buchheim and his camera safely returned from three patrols. His experiences were encapsulated in the best-selling novel *U-boat*, which inspired the cult movie *Das Boot*, with its haunting music and the lonely sensitive Kapitan wearing the only badge of submarine command at sea – a dirty white cap cover.

Although my selection pays due respect to the literary merits of such master wordsmiths as John Masefield, Joseph Conrad and Rudyard Kipling, nothing in my estimation equals first-person reporting of high achievements to the very limit of human endurance. Many of them were by one-off authors whose work has sadly been allowed to got out of print for all time, yet they deserve a permanent memorial, even if only as a few paragraphs in this book. Captain Richard England's *Schoonerman* is one such; in it he tells the poignant story of the inevitable but tragic end to a lifetime spent with his young family fighting a losing battle to survive in the coastal trade under sail. Another is Captain H. K. Oram's *Ready for Sea* vividly recalling his early training under sail and the rough life in the gunrooms of the Grand Fleet down to the moment when he witnessed the surrender of the German High Seas Fleet as first lieutenant of a steam-driven K-Class submarine.

Many classic sea stories are difficult to come by now, such as Joshua Slocum's *Sailing Alone Around the World* and Robin Knox-Johnston's *A World of My Own* describing how he sailed his primitive 44–foot ketch *Suhaili* into the history books by making the first non-stop solo circumnavigation. Tim Severin stands high on my list, not only for the quality of his writing and scholarship when following in the wake of St Brendan's leather boat from Ireland to North America a thousand years before Columbus, but as a record of ultimate endurance and fine seamanship. His later books, retracing voyages by Sinbad and Ulysses, were not so memorable, as they were conducted from the relative comfort of sedate, well-manned craft.

In putting the selected material into relevant sections, there has been some blurred distinction between events and people. I must also apologize for seemingly being biased towards the Royal Navy in making a subjective choice of which great sea-captains and battles I have given prominence to. The pieces about admirals are chosen for the degree to which they illuminate their personalities and qualities of leadership, rather than dwelling on their most glorious victories – as has so often been done in the past. Lack of space alone has obliged me to overlook the many fine leaders who had added lustre to the battle honours of other navies, particularly the United States Navy.

There is one category of book which I have deliberately omitted: lurid accounts of lonely voyages to impossible destinations, which are suspect on many important points, but seem to be lapped up as gospel by paperback publishers. These books are rightly designated 'faction', to be given the same treatment as other modern apocrypha, like estate agents' descriptions of houses for sale and any party manifesto before a General Election.

Two other objectives have sustained my enthusiasm in putting together this anthology: I hope to preserve something from the hundreds of excellent new books which have been submitted to the judges of the King George's Fund for Sailors Best Book of the Sea Award during the last twenty years. Otherwise, like several of those mentioned above, they would long since have disappeared on to the shelves of second-hand booksellers, along with most of the 48,000 new titles published annually in the British Isles. And I hope to whet the appetite of all those who are fascinated by the sea to share something of the pleasure I have found in reading for the first time so many wonderful books by forgotten authors.

In my quest I have received help and encouragement from many enthusiasts: John Munday, Curator Emeritus of the National Maritime Museum at Greenwich; Sohei Hohri, Librarian of the New York Yacht Club; Kingsley Amis, who introduced me to Stephen Leacock; Mick Delap of the BBC World Service who produced some vintage treats from his own bookshelves; the staff of my local library at Midhurst and the helpful ladies at the London Library who went to endless trouble tracking down rare sources; Eric Swenson of W. W. Norton, unflappable shipmate, stylish wit and a fellow *aficionado* for the mysterious sea and the eccentric dilettante characters it breeds; and, finally, Will Sulkin, my editor, conscience and time-keeper at Faber and Faber.

John Coote
Iping, West Sussex
June 1988

PROLOGUE

A man who is not afraid of the sea will soon be drowned, for he'll be going out on a day when he shouldn't. But we do be afraid of the sea, and we do only be drownded now and again.

The Arran Islands by J. M. Synge

What It Is All About

Alone on the deck on a clear starlit night miles from land even the most hard-bitten cynical unbeliever must pause to ponder the meaning of eternity – the other worlds beyond those we can see millions of light years away.

There has to be a purpose and some higher power beyond it.

'What is it in the sea life which is so powerful in its influence? . . .

'It whispers in the wind of the veldt, it hums in the music of the tropical night. To some it is borne on the booming night-notes of the deep forest, to others it speaks on the silent snow-peaks. But above all it is there to the man who holds the night-watch alone at sea. It is the sense of things done, of things endured, of meanings not understood; the secret of the Deep Silence, which is of eternity, which the heart cannot speak.

'It is the same to Ulysses and Columbus as it is to-day to the barge's skipper or the young fourth officer of a Liverpool tramp. The Northland fisherman, the Arab, the Malay, have felt its extraordinary depth and intensity, and many a black-coated city man is the happier and sounder for having heard its silent eloquence. He has felt the tie that binds all seamen of different nationalities and climes and ages; he has looked on the same mysteries, has heard the same music of the deeps; and he has found the rest to his soul which the great silence of Nature brings to the seeker at all times, whatever his race or creed.

'There is nothing sordid, cramped, or unhealty for body or mind in what a man may learn from sailing boats. It is a subject, beyond most, shrouded about by the immensities which are the "vesture of the Eternal."

'Apart from mere physical triumph which man has in handling tackle, there is for the sailing men the additional glory which is known to the explorer, the soldier, and the huntsman, which has made the wild nature life of the great continents exercise the enduring attraction which it does to the men who have lived the life – the glory, namely, of the pathfinder, the man who must seek the road, dare the experiment, keep a clear head, and understand a map more clearly than a picture – which things are hidden for ever from the man "who is carried." '

from *Mast and Sail* by H. Warington Smyth

Those who live on planet earth need to remind themselves that they inhabit only a small part of it, for over nine-tenths of its surface is sea. So it is important to have a broad understanding of the forces which govern its behaviour.

The sea, in general, may be divided into the principal oceans and the lesser seas. The oceans, of course, are the Pacific, the Atlantic and the Indian.

3

They have areas, respectively of about sixty-four, thirty-two, and twenty-eight million square miles. The Arctic, while commmonly known as an ocean, is more logically grouped with the seas, for its area is only five and a half million square miles. Of the remaining seas, the Mediterranean and Caribbean are next largest in extent, each having an area of a million square miles. The other seas, ranged in order of size, are: the Bering Sea, Gulf of Mexico, Okhotsk Sea, East China Sea, Hudson Bay, Japan Sea, North Sea, Red Sea, Baltic Sea and the Persian Gulf. The three oceans make up 90 per cent of the total area of the earth covered by water, while the thirteen seas constitute the remaining 10 per cent.

. . . It is estimated that the average depth is somewhat less than twelve thousand five hundred feet (2.36 miles). Knowing the area, this gives a basis for estimating the volume of water in the sea. It figures about three hundred and twenty-nine million cubic miles, as compared with a volume of thirty million cubic miles for the land above sea-level, using 2,750 feet (approximately half a mile) for the average height of land. These figures indicate, then, that the total volume of water on the earth is eleven times as great as the volume of land above sea-level. It is estimated that if all the inequalities in the height of land and depressions in the sea bottom were to be levelled off, the entire earth would be covered by a uniform layer of water one and a half miles in depth.

*

. . . it is on the . . . continental shelves that the world's largest fisheries are located, for the shallow waters permit light to penetrate to the bottom with the result that marine plants grow here in great abundance. Here, too, the rivers discharge their heavy deposits of natural fish food.

At the seaward edge of the continental shelf we find the beginning of a steeper descent, known as the continental slope. This, on an average, extends out as far as the 1,000-fathom line. An idea of the gradient on this slope may be obtained from a consideration of conditions obtaining along the Atlantic Coast. Here the continental shelf has a width of about fifty miles, defined by the 100-fathom curve. The 1,000-fathom line, delimiting the continental slope, is found at a distance of about one hundred miles from shore, so that the slope is no wider than the shelf, despite the great differences in depth at their seaward edges.

Seven per cent of the bottom of the sea lies at depths of more than three thousand fathoms. To these abysses are given the name of deeps. From soundings taken up to the present time, fifty-seven of these great depressions in the floor of the sea have been discovered. Two of these, one in the North Pacific and one lying partly in the Atlantic and partly in the Indian Ocean, each cover an area of more than a million square miles.

By plotting sounded depths on a chart the navigator is often able to get a good idea of his position when working along the coast in thick weather.

*

The most common characteristic of sea water . . . is its saltiness. Striking

4

a general average . . . every 1,000 pounds of sea water carries in solution 35 pounds of solid matter, of which more than 27 pounds is sodium chloride, or common salt. The remaining percentage is composed of various chemical compounds such as chlorides, sulphates, bromides and carbonates. Actually, the sea is the ultimate source of all salt, for the origin of salt deposits can invariably be traced back to the drying up of various seas. Analysis of the salt content of certain bodies of water shows that the total volume of all salts varies greatly, depending on a number of factors, but in each case the percentages of the separate salts making up the total content are identical. Thus it is found that each 1,000 pounds of water from the Red Sea contains 40 pounds of salts, while a similar quantity from the Baltic would contain but eight. The relative proportions of the separate salts, however, remain the same.

As both air and sea receive their heat from the rays of the sun, these great differences in the range of temperature are explained by the fact that . . . it takes 3,000 times as much heat to change the temperature of a given volume of water one degree as would be required to effect a similar change in the same volume of air. Consequently, the sea tends to store its heat and maintain it at a constant temperature, responding slowly to external changes. As might be expected, the temperature varies almost directly with the latitude. Starting with water at the freezing-point in polar regions, the temperature of the surface waters raises about half a degree with each change of one degree in latitude going towards the equator.

In the depths of the ocean the temperature of the great mass of sea water is little above freezing, even at the equator. This is brought about by a slow bottom current which is constantly bringing cold water from polar regions down towards the equator. In tropical regions, starting from the very warm waters of the surface, the temperature drops about forty degrees within a distance of 400 or 500 fathoms. Averaging the temperatures of the entire volume of sea water from bottom to surface in the various latitudes, there is a difference of only about ten degrees between tropical and polar regions. The sea, as a whole, is cold, averaging about forty degrees even in the tropics.

*

The subject of ice in the sea is one of vital importance to navigation. Ever since the loss of the liner *Titanic* in 1912, a close watch has been kept upon the movements of the great bergs and ice-fields each year in the North Atlantic by means of the International Ice Patrol. Through their efforts ships to-day are kept in constant touch by radio with the daily positions of all icebergs in dangerous proximity to the shipping lanes.

Tremendous volumes of ice are formed each year in the polar regions of both hemispheres as a result of the prolonged periods of extremely low temperature. Even in lower latitudes great quantities of ice are found in the form of bergs brought down by the drift of the major ocean currents. This ice in the sea is of two forms – the great fields formed by the freezing of sea water and the bergs born of the disintegration of glaciers as they push down from the land into the sea . . . After they have found their way into the warmer waters of the Gulf Stream, they last only a week or two before they have completely disintegrated.

Waves are a common phenomenon of the sea . . . The size of waves in the open sea, where there is sufficient depth to prevent any hampering of free wave movement, depends upon a number of factors – the strength of the wind, duration of the blow, and the stretch of open water over which the wind has a free sweep. As a rough rule, it may be stated that sea waves attain a height in feet one half the velocity of the wind in miles per hour. Waves higher than forty feet are rare, since it would take an eighty-mile wind to produce such waves. Fifty feet may be considered a maximum height, resulting from prolonged and severe storm conditions.

No specific rule can be formulated for the length of a wave, as the formation differs in various cases. However, as a general rule, a sea wave will measure in length from fifteen to thirty times its height. Accurate measurements of storm waves 500 feet long have been recorded and instances are cited of unusual cases where the wave length attained the remarkable proportions of 2,500 feet.

*

Besides the irregular movement of the sea in response to wind, it is subject also to a periodic vertical movement – the constant rising and falling of the tide in regular and definite cycles. This generally manifests itself in successive periods of six hours rise and six hours fall, although at certain points there will be but one high and one low water during the course of a day.

This phenomenon of the sea results directly from the gravitational influence which the moon and sun exert on both the earth and the sea. As the moon sweeps over a given point, it tends to draw the water up to it, producing at that point a high tide. Similarly a high tide is created on the side of the earth opposite the moon as the earth is attracted with greater intensity than the more distant waters. As the earth rotates, then, the moon seems to draw the waters behind it in the form of a rising wave, each point on the earth experiencing ordinarily two high and two low waters each day.

While the tides primarily follow the moon, the sun also exerts a powerful influence, but of approximately only two-fifths the intensity of that of the moon. Thus it is that the tide experienced at any point varies during the month depending on the relative positions of sun and moon. When the three bodies are nearly in line, as they are at the time of new and full moon, the tides respond to the combined pull of both bodies in the form of higher high tides and lower lows. At first quarter and third quarter, these forces tend to oppose each other and we have lower highs and higher lows.

*

6

The periodic tidal rise and fall of the sea is translated into a horizontal flow along the coasts of the continents as the water runs in and out of bays and sounds and other indentations along the shore. The shoreward motion is called the flood and the receding seaward current is known as the ebb tide. These tidal currents, periodically changing their direction of flow roughly every six hours, must be distinguished from the non-tidal currents found in streams which always flow in one direction due to the force of gravity, that is, dropping from a higher to a lower level. Winds may also set up non-tidal currents which have nothing in common with the ebb and flow resulting from the influence of the moon's gravitation.

Tidal currents are generally of greatest strength near the coasts and in narrow entrances to bays, sounds and rivers. Like the tide (that is, the vertical movement of the sea), the tidal currents vary greatly from day to day, flowing with greatest velocity at the times of new and full moon, and being subject also to variations in wind conditions.

Unlike the tidal current, the great ocean currents move always in one direction . . .

*

. . . In each ocean the surface waters tend to travel in two complete circles, one in the Northern Hemisphere and one in the Southern. In the Northern one the movement of water is clockwise and in the Southern counter-clockwise. Between these two great currents there is a movement eastward through a very narrow belt near the equator. The velocity of these currents is generally low – with a few exceptions it amounts to about half a mile an hour or less.

from *The Seas and the Oceans* by William H. Koelbel

Few sailors realize that the oft-quoted Naval Prayer, which is the creed of the Royal Navy, was written in 1662, although it has been updated during every reign since. Note the addition of the threat from the air in the 1962 version:

O Eternal Lord God, who alone spreadest out the heavens and rulest the raging of the sea; who has compassed the waters with bounds until day and night come to an end. Be pleased to receive into thy Almighty and most gracious protection the persons of us thy servants, and the Fleet in which we serve. Preserve us from the dangers of the sea, and of the air, and from the violence of the enemy; that we may be a safeguard unto our most gracious Sovereign Lady, Queen ELIZABETH, and her Dominions, and a security for such as pass on the seas upon their lawful occasions; that the inhabitants of our Island and Commonwealth may in peace and quietness serve thee our God; and that we may return in safety to enjoy the blessings of the land, with the fruits of our labours, and with a thankful

7

remembrance of thy mercies to praise and glorify thy holy Name; through Jesus Christ our Lord. Amen

The Naval Prayer by Bishop Sanderson

In the original version 'the fruits of our labours' may have referred to prize-money.

Wind and Waves

To this day sailors in the snug of waterfront taverns all over the world argue the size of monster waves they have survived, as they have done since men first ventured across the open oceans. Surprisingly, there is little to support popular belief that the biggest waves are to be found in the Southern Ocean. A 'normal' gale will be accompanied by waves 25 feet high, but they may be more than double that if there is a long fetch of open ocean and the gale has persisted for some time. Of all the oceans I have sailed in, the one I would least care to face again in its worst mood is the stretch running from the Denmark Strait north of Iceland towards Bear Island off the North Cape of Norway. Seen from the bridge of a destroyer with a height of eye of 45 feet we encountered waves with an average height of 60 feet. And every sailor knows from personal experience that each storm carries a fair percentage of rogue waves which tower over all others. To set the scene, the official inquiry into the 1979 Fastnet Race storm between the south coast of Ireland and Cornwall accepted that at least some yachts had to face waves over 40 feet high in winds gusting up to 60 knots.

Throughout the century that has followed the report of Dumont d'Urville that he encountered a wave 100 feet high off the Cape of Good Hope, science generally has viewed such figures with skepticism. Yet there is one record of a giant wave which, because of the method of measurement, seems to be accepted as reliable.

In February 1933 the U.S.S. *Ramapo*, while proceeding from Manila to San Diego, encountered seven days of stormy weather. The storm was part of a weather disturbance that extended all the way from Kamchatka to New York and permitted the winds an unbroken fetch of thousands of miles. During the height of the storm the *Ramapo* maintained a course running down the wind and with the sea. On 6 February the gale reached

8

its fiercest intensity. Winds of 68 knots came in gusts and squalls, and the seas reached mountainous height. While standing watch on the bridge during the early hours of that day, one of the officers of the *Ramapo* saw, in the moonlight, a great sea rising astern at a level above an iron strap on the crow's nest of the mainmast. The Ramapo was on even keel and her stern was in the trough of the sea. These circumstances made possible an exact line of sight from the bridge to the crest of the wave, and simple mathematical calculations based on the dimensions of the ship gave the height of the wave. It was 112 feet.

*

. . . All the feeling and the fury of such a storm, couched almost in Conradian prose, are contained in the usually prosaic *British Islands Pilot*:

'In the terrific gales which usually occur four or five times in every year all distinction between air and water is lost, the nearest objects are obscured by spray, and everything seems enveloped in a thick smoke; upon the open coast the sea rises at once, and striking upon the rocky shores rises in foam for several hundred feet and spreads over the whole country.

'The sea, however, is not so heavy in the violent gales of short continuance as when an ordinary gale has been blowing for many days; the whole force of the Atlantic is then beating against the shores of the Orkneys, rocks of many tons in weight are lifted from their beds, and the roar of the surge may be heard for twenty miles; the breakers rise to the height of 60 feet, and the broken sea on the North Shoal, which lies 12 miles northwestward of Costa Head, is visible at Skail and Birsay.'

The first man who ever measured the force of an ocean wave was Thomas Stevenson, father of Robert Louis. Stevenson developed the instrument known as a wave dynamometer and with it studied the waves that battered the coast of his native Scotland. He found that in winter gales the force of a wave might be as great as 6,000 pounds to the square foot . . .

*

A list of the perverse and freakish doings of the sea can easily be compiled from the records of the keepers of lights on lonely ledges at sea, or on rocky headlands exposed to the full strength of storm surf. At Unst, the most northern of the Shetland Islands, a door in the lighthouse was broken open 195 feet above the sea. At the Bishop Rock Light during a winter gale a bell was torn away from its place of attachment 100 feet above high water. About the Bell Rock Light on the coast of Scotland one November day a heavy ground swell was running, although there was no wind. Suddenly one of the swells rose about the tower, mounted to the gilded ball atop the lantern, 117 feet above the rock, and tore away a ladder that was attached to the tower 86 feet above the water. There have been happenings that, to some minds, are tinged with the supernatural, like that at the Eddystone Light in 1840. The entrance door of the tower had been made fast by strong bolts, as usual. During a night of heavy seas the door was broken open from within, and all its iron bolts and hinges were torn loose. Engineers say that such a thing happens as a result of pneumatic action – the sudden back draught created by the recession of a heavy wave combined with an abrupt release of pressure on the outside of the door.

*

Along a rocky coast, the waves of a severe storm are likely to be armed with stones and rock fragments, which greatly increase their destructive power. Once a rock weighing 135 pounds was hurled high above the lightkeeper's house on Tillamook Rock, 100 feet above sea level. In falling, it tore a 20-foot hole through the roof. The same day showers of smaller rocks broke many panes of glass in the lantern, 132 feet above the sea. The most amazing of such stories concerns the lighthouse at Dunnet Head, which stands on the summit of a 300-foot cliff at the southwestern entrance to Pentland Firth. The windows of this light have been broken repeatedly by stones swept from the cliff and tossed aloft by waves.

For millennia beyond computation, the sea's waves have battered the coastlines of the world with erosive effect . . . The high clay cliff of Cape Cod, rising at Eastham and running north until it is lost in the sand dunes near Peaked Hill, is wearing back so fast that half of the ten acres which the Government acquired as a site for the Highland Light has disappeared, and the cliffs are said to be receding about three feet a year. Cape Cod is not old, in geologic terms, being the product of the glaciers of the most recent ice age, but apparently the waves have cut away, since its formation, a strip of land some two miles wide. At the present rate of erosion, the disappearance of the outer cape is foredoomed; it will presumably occur in another 4000 or 5000 years.

The cliffs on the south shore of Nantucket are said to be retreating as much as six feet a year under the grinding attack of rock-laden waves. The sea's method on a rocky coast is to wear it down by grinding . . .

And yet we owe some of the most beautiful and interesting shoreline scenery to the sculpturing effect of moving water. Sea caves are almost literally blasted out of the cliffs by waves, which pour into crevices in the rocks and force them apart by hydraulic pressure.

from *The Sea Around Us* by Rachel Carson

The incidence of freak waves has been studied by Laurence Draper at the National Institute of Oceanography. Their probability of occurrence can be predicted by a calculation with the esoteric title of a Stationary Random Process. The end-result is that one wave in twenty-three is over twice the height of the average wave running, which disposes of the old salt's belief that it is liable to be every seventh wave. If you care to count, one wave in 1,175 is over three times the average height, whilst one in 300,000 comes along four times the size of its neighbours. Sometimes it occurs as an extra deep trough, as in the examples quoted from the south-east of South Africa:

Reports of freak waves usually concern waves with unexpectedly high crests, as in most of the instances described in previous chapters, but there is just as much chance of an unusually low trough occurring. The reason why they are not often reported must be that a high crest can be seen from a large distance, but a vessel would have to be on the very edge of a deep trough to notice it. Two reports of deep troughs (at least, that is what we believe them to have been) were described in the *Marine Observer* under the heading 'The one from nowhere'. The following is an extract from the report of Commodore W. S. Byles, R. D., master of the *Edinburgh Castle*:

Ever since the *Waratah* was lost without trace, having sailed from Durban to Cape Town on 26th July 1909, Cape coastal waters have been suspect and especially in the vicinity of Port St. Johns. There was a report that she had been 'spoken' and reported 'all well' off Port Shepstone; she had a morse lamp but no wireless.

On 21st August 1964 in 31° 39' S, 29° 46' E the *Edinburgh Castle* was experiencing a strong south-west wind and a heavy south-west swell, but, being 750 ft. long and of 28,600 gross tonnage, these conditions presented no serious problem to her. As she dipped into the swell she was spraying forward a little, and (on the big ones) shovelling up a little water through the hawse pipes. The reputation of the coast, my previous experience and my desire to avoid damage of any sort, decided me to abandon the benefit of the Agulhas current, put up with a later arrival and close the coast. To further ensure that no untoward incident should occur, I took a knot off her speed and, to close the coast I had, of course, put the swell cosily on the bow instead of driving into it head-on. Under these conditions she was very comfortable for three-quarters of an hour or so. The distance from one wave top to the next was about 150 ft. and the ship was pitching and scending about 10–15 degrees to the horizontal. And then it happened. Suddenly, having scended normally, the wave length appeared to be double the normal, about 300 ft., so that when she pitched she charged, as it were, into a hole in the ocean at an angle of 30 degrees or more, shovelling the next wave on board to a height of 15 or 20 ft. before she could recover, as she was 'out of step'.

*

The conditions in which the 'holes' appeared were those of a fairly heavy swell, the familiar characteristics of which are groups of large waves followed by an interval of relatively low waves. It seems possible that the holes were caused by the chance coincidence, already explained, of a large number of wave components in exactly the same way as high crests are formed. If the depth of the 'hole' were, say, more than five times the average trough depth, the chance of it occurring to one vessel would require the time equivalent of scores of lifetimes at sea, so perhaps there is no wonder that such things are rarely seen.

. . . It seems possible that the cause of these problems in this area is that the 60 to 100 mile wide Agulhas current sweeps south westward at a speed of 4 or 5 knots along the coast, often meeting a heavy swell coming up from the Antarctic. At the interface where the swell meets the current, the swell reacts by slowing down and by increasing its wave height. In extreme cases the wave heights may try to increase beyond the limits of steepness (ratio of height over length) within which a progressive wave can exist. The excess energy must then be dissipated almost instantly by wave breaking presenting a barrier which must be impenetrable by virtually any vessel.

*

For example, the race off Portland Bill is an example of the ferocity of the battle between waves and current, and few prudent small-boat sailors would venture near it with waves running into an opposing current.

On many occasions a freak wave is not just alone – sometimes two or three waves, all much bigger than the general run of large waves, are seen to occur together, and, of course, in such cases they have deep troughs between them. Many a vessel must have been lost when the first wave laid her over on her side and she did not have time to right herself before another and possibly larger wave crashed down on her exposed side. In those conditions no one survives to tell what happened. Recent figures from Lloyds show that over a ten-year period an average of 77 sea-going vessels, each of over 100 tons displacement, were lost every year due to overwhelming by the sea itself, without the aid of rocks, reefs or collision. One of these was a vessel of 20,000 tons displacement.

from Heavy Weather Sailing by K. Adlard Coles

The Sea's Mysteries

Sea lore abounds in mysterious ghost-ships, giant amphibian monsters and freak natural phenomena which are suspected of having over-whelmed ships and their crews. There have certainly been instances of big ships disappearing without trace. Even today half a dozen ships go that way every year without satisfactory explanation, although structural failure in exceptionally heavy weather may often be suspected. The disappearance of the 10,000-ton immigrant ship *Waratah* reported in the preceding extract was most likely due to her suffering from a design deficiency, in that she was not only known to be tender but seems to have developed that most alarming of all ships' tantrums, a 'loll'. That is when a ship hangs briefly at the end of a heavy roll and then goes further over. From that moment it only takes cargo to shift or an exceptional wave to come inboard, adding to the free surface water in the bilges, for the ship to go all the way, in the manner of the 1987 ferry disaster off Zeebrugge.

Even in recent times it is not unknown for crews to abandon ship in order to collect their insurance value. Sometimes a passing ship has managed to board them before the scuttling arrangements have taken effect. Then everything is found to be in place except the crew. So we turn to the most famous 'mystery' of them all. The 99-foot brig *Marie Celeste* had been trading uneventfully all over the North Atlantic for twelve years before she sailed from New York in 1872, bound for Genoa with a cargo of 1,700 barrels of industrial alcohol. A month later the brig *Dei Gratia* came across her north-east of the Azores, drifting along in fair weather with only storm canvas spread.

The story goes that she was then boarded and found to be deserted, but with every appearance of the crew having been on board only hours before. The galley-stove was warm, a half-eaten meal was on the captain's table, clothes were neatly stowed. The truth is that there was evidence she had suffered a knockdown during heavy weather, shipped an alarming amount of water through open hatches and skylights and that the crew had then panicked and taken to the one boat they could launch. Significantly, the captain had taken his sextant, chronometer and ship's papers with him, but not before marking his last position on the chart, which showed that she had sailed 600 miles on her own before being sighted.

A boarding-party of four hands from *Dei Gratia* had no difficulty in sailing her to Gibraltar, where the Admiralty Court official smelt a king-sized rat, suspecting he had an open-and-shut case of barratry on his hands. The world's press seized on the evidence presented in court and created the legend which persists to this day.

Eventually she was released and went on trading for another thirteen years, pursued everywhere by superstitious waterfront gossip that she was a hoodoo ship with a jinx on her. There is little mystery about how she met her end, wrecked on a reef off Haiti, sufficiently close to the beach for her cargo to be salvaged and sold to a corrupt local official for $500. At the same time $3,000 was collected from underwriters in New York.

The most enduring mystery of them all concerns the Bermuda Triangle which has, according to legend fostered by scriptwriters and investigative journalists, claimed over thirty aircraft and fifty ships, including the nuclear submarine USS *Scorpion*, in unexplained circumstances. Even its precise area is in dispute, but a general consensus puts the island of Bermuda near its northern apex, with its southern base stretching from Antigua to the Florida cays. Any way you look at it, the suspect area is over one million square miles of the North Atlantic. Yet each year hundreds of small yachts sail through it to avoid the New England winter in perfect safety and return without so much as a sea serpent to report. True, it lies in the path of young hurricanes whizzing towards the Florida coast, whilst the turbulent Gulf Stream forms its western boundary. In the days before reliable hurricane-reporting and tracking it is small wonder that many ships were overwhelmed in the area, but more recent research indicates that the incidence of disasters there has not been out of the ordinary.

The squadron of US Navy bombers which flew out from Fort Lauderdale Naval Air Station, never to return, are now reckoned to have flown on a reciprocal course from a beacon and simply spluttered out of fuel one by one over the Gulf of Mexico. The man responsible for putting it in perspective is Lawrence Kusche, himself a commercial pilot and instructor in the area.

Many theories have been proposed to solve the mystery of the Bermuda Triangle. Time warps, reverse gravity fields, even witchcraft have been suggested as possible causes of the disappearances. Atmospheric aberrations. Magnetic and gravitational anomalies. Strange forces that silence radios, block radar, and affect compasses.

Seaquakes. Waterspouts. Tidal waves. Freak seas. Death rays from Atlantis. Black holes in space. Underwater signaling devices to guide invaders from other planets. UFOs collecting earthlings and their vehicles for study in other galaxies, or to save them from an approaching holocaust.

The area has been described as a 'Vile Vortex', or an anomaly, a place where events and objects do not behave as they normally would. It has been said that a murky mantle of death, or a jinx, lurks about the Triangle.

*

My research, which began as an attempt to find as much information as possible about the Bermuda Triangle, had an unexpected result. After examining all the evidence I have reached the following conclusion: *There is no theory that solves the mystery.* It is no more logical to try to find a common cause for all the disappearances in the Triangle than, for example, to try to find one cause for all the automobile accidents in Arizona. By abandoning the search for an overall theory and investigating each incident independently, the mystery began to unravel.

The findings of my research were consistent.

1. Once sufficient information was found, logical explanations appeared for most of the incidents. It is difficult, for example, to consider the *Rubicon* a mystery when it is known that a hurricane struck the harbor where it had been moored. It is similarly difficult to be baffled by the loss of the *Marine Sulphur Queen* after learning of the ship's weakened structure and the weather conditions as described in the report of the Coast Guard investigation.

2. With only a few exceptions, the mishaps that remain unsolved are those for which no information can be found. In several cases important details of the incident, and in other cases, entire incidents, are fictional.

3. Disappearances occur in all ports of the ocean and even over land. During my research I found nearly two hundred vessels that disappeared or were found abandoned between the New England states and northern Europe since 1850.

Although the disappearances that took place in the Bermuda Triangle are the ones that have been widely publicized, some losses that occurred elsewhere have been 'credited' to the Triangle. The most notable of these are the *Freya*, which was found abandoned in the Pacific Ocean in 1902, and the Globemaster that crashed near Ireland in 1951. If all the locations of 'Bermuda Triangle incidents' were plotted on a globe it would be found that they had taken place in an area that included the Caribbean Sea, the Gulf of Mexico, and most of the North Atlantic Ocean. The Bermuda Triangle is hardly unique.

4. Some of the lost vessels passed through the Bermuda Triangle but it is not known that they vanished there. The *Atalanta*, for example, may have sunk anywhere between Bermuda and England.

5. In many cases the place where a vessel met its end was almost completely unknown and searchers were required to spread themselves thinly over vast areas. The only information known about the British airliner *Star Ariel* is that it went down somewhere between Bermuda and Jamaica.

6. Many incidents were not considered mysterious when they occurred, but became so many years later when writers seeking reports of additional incidents in the Bermuda Triangle, found reference to them. It is often difficult to find complete information (even when one wants it) on an event that occurred many years before.

7. Contrary to the Legend, the weather was bad when many of the incidents occurred. In several cases highly publicized hurricanes were responsible.

8. Many of the mishaps occurred late in the afternoon or at night, making it impossible for searchers to attempt visual sightings until the next morning

and thus giving the sea many additional hours to disperse whatever debris there might have been.

9. Many of the writers who publicized the events did no original research but merely rephrased the articles of previous writers, thereby perpetuating the errors and embellishments in earlier accounts.

10. In a number of incidents writers withheld information that provided an obvious solution to the disappearance.

With the exception of point 9, the above statements also apply to the region known as the Limbo of the Lost. Moreover, the fact that the Limbo of the Lost encompasses an area at least half as large as the North Atlantic Ocean makes it difficult to sustain the point that it, like the Bermuda Triangle, is somehow unique.

The Legend of the Bermuda Triangle is a manufactured mystery. It began because of careless research and was elaborated upon and perpetuated by writers who either purposely or unknowingly made use of misconceptions, faulty reasoning, and sensationalism. It was repeated so many times that it began to take on the aura of truth.

I, like everyone else, like a good mystery, an enigma that stretches the mind. We all seem to have an innate desire to remain in awe of those phenomena for which there appears to be no logical, scientific explanation. Yet we also exult in seeking and in finding legitimate answers to these same puzzles.

Perhaps we are beginning to grow a bit weary of being constantly bombarded by spectacular unsolved mysteries. It is satisfying to know that we need not remain forever baffled by all phenomena that seem to be beyond explanation.

from *The Bermuda Triangle Mystery – Solved* by Lawrence David Kusche

CAPTAINS AND CREWS

No man will be a sailor who has contrivance enough to get him into jail: for being in a ship is being in a jail, with the chance of being drowned . . . a man in jail has more room, better food and commonly better company . . .

When a man come to like a sea life, they are not fit to live on land.

Dr Samuel Johnson

The wonder is always new that any sane man can be a sailor.

Ralph Waldo Emerson

Oh was there ever a sailor free to choose that didn't settle somewhere near the sea?

Rudyard Kipling

Jolly Jack – Ashore and Afloat

For all their faults sailors have always been welcomed with open arms, which is exactly what they had in mind on setting foot ashore, with or without permission. The following profile by Ned Ward in his 1744 book *Wooden World Dissected* might have been written 150 years later. Pub signs have preserved the legend of big-spending tars on a run ashore. The Sailor's Return or the Jolly Sailor may be found just around any corner, but I do not know of any Laughing Fusilier or Rollicking Royal Marine. Gilbert and Sullivan caught the mood, whilst music-halls insisted the 'Every Nice Girl Loves a Sailor'.

The old-time sailor, again, was essentially a creature of contradictions. Notorious for a 'swearing rogue,' who punctuated his strange sea-lingo with horrid oaths and appalling blasphemies, he made the responses required by the services of his Church with all the superstitious awe and tender piety of a child. Inconspicuous for his thrift or 'forehandedness,' it was nevertheless a common circumstance with him to have hundreds of pounds, in pay and prize-money, to his credit at his bankers, the Navy Pay-Office; and though during a voyage he earned his money as hardly as a horse, and was as poor as a church mouse, yet the moment he stepped ashore he made it fly by the handful and squandered it, as the saying went, like an ass. When he was sober, which was seldom enough provided he could obtain a drink, he possessed scarcely a rag to his back; but when he was drunk he was himself the first to acknowledge that he had 'too many cloths in the wind.' According to his own showing, his wishes in life were limited to three: 'An island of tobacco, a river of rum, and – more rum'; but according to those who knew him better than he knew himself, he would at any time sacrifice all three, together with everything else he possessed, for the gratification of a fourth and unconfessed desire, the dearest wish of his life, woman. Ward's description of him, slightly paraphrased, fits him to a hair: 'A salt-water vagabond, who is never at home but when he is at sea, and never contented but when he is ashore; never at ease until he has drawn his pay, and never satisfied until he has spent it; and when his pocket is empty he is just as much respected as a father-in-law is when he has beggarded himself to give a good portion with his daughter.' With all this he is brave beyond belief on the deck of a ship, timid to the point of cowardice on the back of a horse; and although he fought to a victorious finish many of his country's most desperate fights, and did more than any other man of his time to make her the great nation she became, yet his roving life robbed him of his patriotism and made it necessary to wring from him by violent means the allegiance he shirked. It was at this point that he came in contact with what he hated most in life, yet dearly loved to dodge – the press gang.

from *The Press Gang* by J. R. Hutchinson

A much earlier portrait of our sailors survives in an essay introducing the final volume of Hakluyt's *Voyages*, in which the Spanish ambassador reported during Columbus's days:

'The English sailors,' wrote Ferdinand's ambassador at the Court of King Henry VII, 'are generally savages.' They were unchanged since the days of Chaucer, and picked up a living, without loss of temper, from a precarious coasting trade and adventures not easily distinguishable from piracy. The character of the English sailor is the most inalterable and valuable of national assets; while the British Constitution has moved from precedent to precedent, he has remained the same. His life is a hard one, but he takes it as it comes. He is untouched by the formal punctilios of the cavalier and the cankered scruples of the puritan. He is careless of the graces and ornaments of life. Though he has a warm heart, he is no humanitarian. Danger is his daily companion, and he has learned the lesson of Sir Edward Howard, that a seaman is useless unless he is resolute to the degree of madness. Above all, he is alert and serious in what concerns his craft. Of all professions, the sailor is habituated to subordinate himself most completely to the necessities of the work to be done.

from essay by Professor Walter Raleigh introducing volume XII of *Hakluyt's Voyages*

Especially amidst the harsh regime afloat for those on the lower deck in the Royal Navy during the eighteenth, enlightened leadership paid dividends. The captains concerned were not necessarily drawn from privileged backgrounds, as the following example shows:

How the mariners loved and appreciated a good sea officer is shown by their grief at the death of Sir Christopher Myngs, who had died of his wounds received in the Four Day's Battle, as recorded by Pepys, and it must be remembered that this occurred at a time when men were clamouring for pay, and in a state of great distress. Pepys describes the episode as 'one of the most romantique that ever I heard in my life, and could not have believed, but that I did see it.' He was in a coach with Sir William Coventry. 'About a dozen able, lusty, proper men come to the coach-side with tears in their eyes, and one of them that spoke for the rest begun and said to Sir W. Coventry, "We are here a dozen of us, that have long known and loved, and served our dead commander, Sir Christopehr Myngs, and have now done the last office of laying him in the ground. We would be glad we had any other to offer after him, and in revenge of him. All we have is our lives; if you will please to get his Royal Highness to give us a fire-ship among us all, here are a dozen of us, out of all which choose you one to be commander, and the rest of us, whoever he is, will serve him; and if possible, do that which shall show our memory of our dead commander, and our revenge." ' Captains then and earlier came from various classes of society. Sir Christopher Myngs is said to have boasted that he was a shoemaker's son, but the story is probably apocryphal. Edward Montagu, Earl of Sandwich, represented the aristocracy.

Even in those day there were those who perceived the better qualities which distinguished Jack from his counterparts ashore. One such was a doctor, Charles Fletcher, who wrote to the Admiralty in 1800:

> Touching the character of seamen, Fletcher tells us that if there should be mutinous conduct on board there would be more on shore. 'Nay, I shall go further, and repeat what I have advanced in my preface to the book, that the *Royal George*, with a complement of one thousand men (provided she be well disciplined) abounds less in vice, if not more in virtue, than most villages in England with the same number of souls. . . . If they get drunk, it can only be when on shore upon leave; and should they appear on board in that state, they are punished.' He goes on to remark that he cannot bear to hear seamen spoken of with disparagement or contempt, whether they be officers or men. 'It was only a captain of a man-of-war who was killed!' 'You shall be sent, sirrah, into a man-of-war, says a mother to her child, for there you'll be whipp'd into good manners! And again, of the men, – the scum of the earth! – the sweepings of gaols! – the excrescences of the people! with such like epithets.' Such sneers made the writer's gorge rise, and he speaks scornfully of those who uttered them.
>
> The hilarity of the seaman, his zest for life, and his high spirits, occupy a large space in Fletcher's pages. He gives us the humours of the midshipmen's berth. A young Irish gentleman, a native of Tipperary, comes to his captain with a complaint that he has been contumeliously treated by his shipmates. They had said the Irish were a nation of Hottentots and supplied two-thirds of the Newgate calendar, and that there never was a Tipperary man who had not a piece of potato in his brain!

About this time an anonymous chronicler of life on the Lower Deck at the time of Trafalgar emerged.

> Captain Hall goes on to show how well disciplined in work and efficiency is a ship under a good officer, and he adds, 'It has been well observed that the simple fact of Lord Nelson's joining the fleet off Trafalgar, double-manned every ship in the line.'
>
> And now, from this contemplation of the officers of the Nelson time, let us glance at the remarks of a pamphleteer – a sailor who, as he says on his title-page, was 'politely called by the officers of the Navy, Jack Nasty-Face.' His 'Nautical Economy, or Forecastle Recollections of Events during

the last War,' was not published until 1836, but it relates to the period of Trafalgar, and was dedicated 'To the Brave Tars of Old England,' and addressed to 'My Brother Seamen and Old Shipmates.' It gives what may be described as a plain, unvarnished story – a story with a purpose, being a protest against the old but necessary evil of impressment, of which so much has been said, and against the punishments, of which a good deal of the severity still remained.

Jack Nasty-Face was himself impressed, and seems to have been sent on board the receiving ship, in the Thames, in May, 1805, with some of the Lord Mayor's men, who had been committed by magistrates for their offences, and therefore he met with rather rough treatment. He was sent round to Portsmouth and drafted on board a line-of-battle ship, fitting out to join Nelson's flag. Here he says he met with discipline 'with all its horrors.' He describes the daily routine on board, beginning with the cleaning of the deck, 'with holy-stones or hand-bibles, as they are called by the crew.' He tells us that the breakfast usually consisted of 'burgoo,' made of coarse oatmeal and water. There was also 'Scotch coffee,' made by boiling burnt bread in water and adding sugar, and generally cooked in a hook-pot in the galley. Usually eight persons formed a mess, in a berth between two guns on the lower deck, where a board swung which served for a table. Jack asserts that men were flogged for most trifling offences. At eight bells, or twelve o'clock, came the most pleasant part of the day, when the fiddlers played 'Nancy Dawson' or some other lively tune, being the signal that the grog was ready to be served out. Jack says he became inured to the life, made up his mind to be obedient, and soon began to pick up a knowledge of seamanship.

*

Jack speaks of a tyrannical midshipman, who delighted to torture the men, and who was killed in the battle, and not lamented. He gives incidents which show the humanity of the seaman. A young Frenchwoman, he says, unwilling to leave her husband at Cadiz, disguised herself as a seaman, remained on board his ship, and was engaged in the battle. Her husband was killed, the ship took fire, and a few survivors, among them the unfortunate woman, stripped themselves naked and swam for their lives. She was picked up half dead in this condition, taken on board, provided with material for clothing, and officers and men vied with one another in doing all they could for her. Finally, the unfortunate woman was sent across from Gibraltar to Algeciras. The pamphleteer shows the pride the men had in their ships. Nelson had painted the sides of his vessels in chequers, and they became famous, so that it would be said of a ship, 'Oh! she is one of Nelson's chequer-players.' A new captain came and replaced the chequers with stripes, whereat the men were indignant, thinking they were robbed of the badge of their glory. They were proportionately gratified, therefore, when a new captain came who 'Nelsonified' them again.

London theatre audiences in the eighteenth century lapped up heroic melodramas about the Royal Navy's victories at sea. They tell us much about the officers and men who fought under their heroes. Captain Charles Shadwell's *The Fair Quaker of Deal* was the *Rainbow's End* of its day: first produced in 1710 it was rewritten at David Garrick's instigation in 1773 by Captain Edward Thompson and had a huge success at Drury Lane. The plot had all the twists and turns of a libretto for a Mozart opera, featuring Commodore Flip and Captain Worthy, just returned from Virginia and straightway into unbelievable matrimonial muddles:

> '*Worthy*. Since you love your common sailors so well, what reason can you have for using your lieutenant so like a dog?
>
> *Flip*. Because he sets up for a fine gentleman, and lies in gloves to make his hands white, and tho' 'tis his watch, when I ring my bell, the rogue is above coming to my cabin. I sent him ashore yesterday to the post house with a letter to the Admiralty, and I ordered him to buy me a quarter of mutton and threescore cabbages for my own use; the landlubber (for he is no sailor) had the impudence to tell me he would not be my boy. I told him I would bring him to a court-martial, and he threatened to throw up his commission and cut my throat.
>
> *Rovewell*. Ha, ha, I am glad thou hast met with a young fellow of life and vigour, that knows how to use you according to your deserts.'

As a contrast to this picture of the old commodore (who, by the way, may be compared with Smollett's Trunnion), we have those of Captain Worthy and the lieutenants Sir Charles Pleasant and Cribidge, whom we are obviously to regard as representatives of the majority of the officers and gentlemen of the period, both when Shadwell wrote and Thompson revised the play. On the other hand, Captain Mizen (who has his counterpart in Smollett's time in Captain Whiffle), if a caricature, must certainly have been representative of a class, probably small and exceptional, but not less well known in the reign of George II than in that of Queen Anne. In the earlier edition Flip thus describes him:

'I value myself for not being a coxcomb, that is what you call a gentleman captain; which is a new name for our sea fops, who, forsooth, must wear white linen, have fixed beds, lie in holland sheets, and load their noddles with thirty ounces of horse hair, which makes them hate the sight of an enemy for fear bullets and gunpowder should spoil the beau wig and lac'd jacket. They are indeed pretty fellows at single rapier, and can, with a little drink in their heads, cut the throats of their best friends; but catch them yardarm and yardarm with a Frenchman, and down goes the colours. Oh! it was not so in the Dutch wars, then we valued ourselves upon wooden legs, and stumps of arms, and fought as if heaven and earth was coming together.

23

Rovewell. Yes, yes, you fought very gloriously when you let the Dutch burn the fleet at Chatham.

Flip. That act was owing to the treachery of some rogues at land, and not to us seafaring folks.'

from *The British Tar in Fact and Fiction* by Commander C. N. Robinson

William Hickey was a late eighteenth-century diarist, perhaps better known for his name having been adopted over a century after his death by the gossip column of the *Daily Express*. As the eighth son of an Irish lawyer he had few expectations. Ultimately he acceded to his father's wishes and qualified in his profession, but not before he had been run out of town at the age of nineteen by his own father, despairing of his profligacy, gambling and debauchery. He was shipped out to Madras as a junior purser in the East India Company's *Plassey*. He was fortunate in finding an agreeable Captain to serve under . . .

Captain Waddell, then about forty years of age, naturally grave, with an appearance of shyness or reserve, possessed one of the mildest and most equal tempers that ever man was blessed with, nor did I during a voyage out and home which I made in his ship, ever once see him angry, or hear him utter a single oath or hasty expression. He loved to set the young people at some gambol or other, and was constantly promoting it. He was himself wonderfully active and strong, amongst various proofs of which, he did one feat that amazed the whole ship's company, and which I never knew any other person come at all near. It was this:– Standing upon the Quarter deck, under the main shroud he laid hold of the first ratline with his right hand, then sprung to the second, with his left, and so on alternately, right and left, up to the last, close to the Futtock shrouds. The exertion in accomplishing this must have been prodigious, nor was there another man in the ship, and we had many fine, active fellows on board, that could get beyond the third ratline, and only two that reached even the third.

Later he served with less congenial shipmates, still in the service of the East India Company in the *Nassau*, in which Mr Greer the chief mate was always drunk. On passage to Madras they were celebrating the King's birthday in the captain's cabin when they were hit by a sudden storm . . .

As the night approached the gale increased so much that we could scarcely bear close-reefed topsails with the wind upon the beam. This did not prevent our filling some bumpers to George the Third's health and being very merry. It drawing towards midnight we were beginning to talk of retiring to our cots, when Mr. Larkins sent a quartermaster to request Captain Gore would come upon deck, a summons that created some alarm amongst us, which was not a little increased by hearing a general uproar immediately afterwards and the people all in confusion. Upon going under the awning, I found land had been discovered close to us, extending from the lee bow to abaft the beam.

Captain Gore, panicstruck, knew not what he was about, giving orders and counter orders in the same breath, and crying out to put the ship about. In the midst of the bustle Mr. Greer crawled from his cabin, desiring that an anchor might be let go, whereupon Mr. Larkins exclaimed, 'An anchor, Mr. Greer! In the name of God what can be expected from an anchor in such a sea as we are now encountering? Our only chance of escape is by making sail and endeavouring to clear the land that has so unexpectedly come in our way.' Every person on board competent to judge felt the force of what Mr. Larkins said, and all were equally ready to testify to the very extraordinary skill and exertions of the boatswain, Jerry Griffin, who, when the men hesitated to perform a requisite duty from the risk attending it, himself set them an example, going out to the weather yardarm of the main topsail and succeeding in handing the sail, the whole time using the most extraordinary and out-of-the-way expressions. A reef was forthwith let out of each of the topsails, the courses reefed and set, and the ship hauled close to the wind. And this she bore admirably, though we had before thought too much sail was set, and that something was giving way every half-hour.

We perceptibly passed the land rapidly, which when nearest to us appeared towering above the mastheads, it seeming that we must inevitably be upon it. The night was uncommonly dark, with a tremendous sea running, rendering our situation truly alarming, indeed absolutely desperate.

In two hours we had cleared the land sufficiently to consider the danger over, and congratulated each other upon our miraculous escape. At four in the morning the day dawned, showing us the land that had caused our danger within a short distance upon our lee quarter, but as we had no ground with sixty fathoms of line and all clear ahead we had no further apprehensions.

Mr. Larkins then told us that at nine o'clock, when summoned to supper he had for some time been looking steadily at a black spot nearly right ahead which he could no way account for, that he had made the man at the helm keep the ship half a point nearer the wind in consequence. Still the spot seemed fixed. He called the fifth mate, who was upon the watch with him, pointing out the object that engaged his attention, but this officer pronounced it to be a cloud, as did some of the seamen. Larkins, however, still thought it had all the appearance of land; he ordered a cast of the lead directly. The line being accordingly passed forward and hove in a few minutes, was instantly declared to have struck the bottom with only a few fathoms of line out, and this in a part of the ocean where by all the charts we should not have been upon soundings. Mr. Larkins conjectured that at the first cast there was about fifteen fathoms, after which the soundings varied from fourteen fathoms (the least water we had) to thirty-five, hard rocky bottom.

It is a most extraordinary circumstance that in a passage so much frequented as that of the Sombrere Channel was, and had been for a great number of years, by all ships bound from Madras to China, there should be almost in the middle of it an island totally unknown, or, at least, unnoticed, in the charts of those seas. Yet such indubitably was the fact.

Captains at sea are nothing if not individuals, many mildly eccentric. When William Hickey shipped home in a Dutch ship, he found a rare case . . .

On the 9th March, 1780, I took leave of Captains Gore and Lenox, as well as my other *Nassau* companions, and on the morning of the 10th, with my little pet boy, Nabob, went on board the *Held Woltemade*. I felt rejoiced at leaving the Cape in the hope that my health would mend from the pure air at sea . . .

Upon rising the first morning I saw breakfast upon table, a clean cloth and every article as neat as could be. There was coffee, tea, as good rolls as ever were baked on shore, and what was more extraordinary, admirable fresh butter, toast, eggs, ham, sausages, smoked beef rasped, and lastly an immense cheese. The tea and coffee I found were exclusively for me, my messmate not touching either, but eating heartily of the solids, qualifying the same with two or three draughts of cline (small) beer, as the Captain called it, but which was, in fact, as strong as our porter. He finished by chucking down a glass of the favourite liquor gin, then called for his pipe. Indeed, it was scarcely ever out of his mouth except when eating or asleep. I will not venture to say how many *sopekys* he took between breakfast and dinner. It appeared to me that his servant was in perpetual motion with the gin bottle and glass. True, the latter was small, but the repetition rendered the quantity considerable, and yet I never saw him intoxicated.

Everything was very comfortable on board, and Captain Paardakoper's attentions to me most marked. Observing that I was low-spirited, he tried various ways to correct it, and amongst his good-natured endeavours was that of teaching me trick-track, a game I became exceedingly fond of.

*

About a week after we had been at sea, the Captain, after dinner, said to me, 'Come, sir, I perceive that I must be your doctor. Follow my advice and you'll be a stout man very soon.' I replied that I was ready to do whatever he recommended. 'Well then,' added the Captain, 'as I know you have good claret on board, let you and I take a bottle of it, instead of that vile sweet stuff you daily drink.' I acceded, a bottle of claret was produced which we emptied, took a second, and I never slept better than the ensuing night. His prescription proved so congenial to my stomach that I improved under it every day, soon feeling as well as ever I was in my life.

from the *Memoirs of William Hickey* ed. by Alfred Spencer

Admirals

Francis Drake, in many respects a typical Englishman of his time, acquired a unique position both then and in later history. He did so because of an altogether special assortment of gifts.

Like most other English boys, born into a poor, large family, at that time, he was ill-educated, although not illiterate, so far as can be judged from the remarks of those who wished to denigrate him and those, more patronising, who were astounded that one who started with so few advantages should have his readiness of address, fertility of ideas and native eloquence. He may have been conscious of this himself.

*

. . . He, a man of the new kind – the supreme example of the new man – wished to make sure of his place in the old establishment. He was also a pious Protestant, a Puritan, with the prickly, proselytizing zeal of one whose family had been persecuted for their faith and who was warily conscious that the shiversome terrors depicted in his friend John Foxe's *Book of Martyrs* were not necessarily abolished for ever. But all this could have been said of a hundred English sea officers of the time. Why was Drake picked out from among them so that the reign of Queen Elizabeth I is almost synonymous with the age of Drake?

The answer can surely not be in doubt. Because of personal qualities which exerted a strong influence upon the youth of the time. A youth which was unusually restless, acquisitive and ungovernable, but which was also filled with wild and – as we should say – romantic dreams of discovery and adventure. And plunder, too. Wealth won by running dreadful dangers but involving no tedious labour. That, of course, was an element in Drake's appeal. He was the most spectacular freebooter of his time. And if the name 'pirate' was one that he himself resented, it carried a lighter weight of moral obloquy than it might have done with many of his contemporaries. He was, as he insisted, a privateer. And that was – what exactly? A pirate with a licence more or less valid, or a patriot fighting his country's battles while sparing his sovereign any embarrassment his deeds might bring? But there were scores of privateering captains sailing out of Plymouth, Weymouth and the Thames. Drake was neither the first nor the last of them. True, he worked on a bigger scale than most. There was an element of

27

the thunderclap about his exploits. But this was true of Hawkins, Frobisher, Cavendish, Cumberland and, in later years, the dazzling Essex. Yet Drake possessed in a singular degree the power to stamp his image on the time and draw its young men to his ships.

*

Only two other leaders of the age, Henry of Navarre and Essex, seem to have had a comparable power to command men's hearts. But Henry was a king, Essex a great nobleman. In truth, Drake, who was neither the one nor the other, may have owed the special quality of his magnetism to his origins among the Thames-side people, the mudlarks.

He had defied one entrenched power and elbowed his way into another, and they felt in a confused way that he had done so as their representative. He had sailed round the world, a heroic feat, and had plundered the rich, a praiseworthy form of crime in the eyes of the poor. And, if he had become rich himself . . .

from *Sir Francis Drake* by George Malcolm Thomson

On 13 October 1805 Lord Nelson spent his last night at his country home near Wimbledon with Emma, his slatternly mistress and mother of his only child. He was under orders to join his flagship HMS *Victory* off Southsea and then take command of the fleet being assembled outside Cadiz for the decisive encounter with the French and Spanish combined fleets. His departure was typical of any naval officer leaving his family in wartime, knowing that he might not return, although few nowadays would compose a valedictory prayer in his diary during a stopover at Guildford.

Nelson's hours at Merton were now numbered. The last of the dramatic high-tensioned twenty-five days was come. The summer was waning. There was early mist, driven away by hot sun at midday, and in the kitchens of Merton talk of mushroom ketchup. On the morning of the 13th, when he presented himself for his accustomed before-breakfast tour of his property, Thomas Cribb made so bold as to impart, 'some private family news'. The Admiral congratulated an anxious dependant, and gave him an extra tip, 'to buy a Christening frock', adding his favourite, 'If it's a boy, call him Horatio, if a girl, Emma.' Cribb's future son-in-law, Hudson, with some of the garden lads, watched, with the realization that he was witnessing something he would remember all his life, a post-chaise summoned from the 'King's Head' dash up to the front door, and the master embark, 'To get his final sailing orders from the Admiralty', the boy believed.

Nelson returned to dine with Lady Hamilton, and with the Matchams, who had stayed to the last in a house suddenly and noticeably quiet. Seated in the drawing-room, his relatives listened to the arrival of the vehicle which was to carry the Admiral through the night to Portsmouth. When they heard him coming downstairs alone, George Matcham arose, and prepared to attend him, in dreadful silence, to the front door. The heart of the accomplished civilian was too full for words, but Nelson, up to the moment that they grasped hands, was speaking cheerfully, only regretting that he had not, so far, been able to repay the £4,000 which he had borrowed from his brother-in-law, to buy Axe's field. George Matcham found his voice, to reply, 'My dear Lord, I have no other wish than to see you return home in safety. As to myself, I am not in want of anything.'

One of Nelson's last acts before this scene had been a visit of farewell to the bedside of Horatia. The country September night was advanced; a child in its fifth year had been deeply asleep for hours. Touched by a sight always awe-inspiring, even to a happy parent, he fell upon his knees, and prayed that the life of Horatia might be happy. A prayer which he entered in his private diary, later that night, while horses were being changed, probably at Guildford, was copied by Dr. Scott:

'Friday night, at half-past ten, drove from dear, dear Merton, where I left all which I hold dear in this world, to go to serve my king and country. May the great God whom I adore, enable me to fulfill the expectations of my country; and if it is His good pleasure that I should return, my thanks will never cease being offered up to the throne of His mercy. If it is His good Providence to cut short my days upon earth, I bow with the greatest submission, relying that He will protect those so dear to me, that I may leave behind. His will be done. Amen. Amen. Amen.'

But Emma was still very much on his mind a week later in the Great Cabin of his flagship waiting for battle to commence. He asked his faithful flag captain, Thomas Hardy, and the senior frigate captain (who had reported on board for orders) to witness his signature on a codicil to his will. He could never have envisaged then that his 'Bequest to the Nation' would one day be the theme of a powerful play by Terence Rattigan – or that Emma would quickly be reduced to penury in Calais, on the run from her creditors.

'. . . I leave Emma Lady Hamilton, therefore, a Legacy to my King and Country, that they will give her an ample provision to maintain her rank in life. I also leave to the beneficence of my Country my adopted daughter, Horatia Nelson Thompson; and I desire she will use in future the name of Nelson only.

'These are the only favours I ask of my King and Country at this moment when I am going to fight their Battle. May God Bless my King and Country, and all those who I hold dear. My relations it is needless to mention; they will of course be amply provided for.

'Nelson and Brontë.'

The Captains signed their names, and Blackwood seized the chance, before his juniors arrived, to suggest that the Chief should shift his flag to the *Euryalus*, and conduct the battle from her; but 'he would not hear of it, and gave as his reason the force of example'. The only visible result of the suggestion was an order for more sail to be made upon the *Victory*. After receiving their instructions, the four frigate Captains stalked behind the Chief and his Flag Captain as he went the rounds of the ship. The Admiral praised the manner in which the hawse holes had been barricaded, and reminded gun crews not to waste a shot. The word 'Victory' was continually on his lips, and he appealed to Blackwood several times for an opinion as to the number of prizes they would take to-day, always adding that person-ally he would not be satisfied by anything less than twenty. Blackwood, in reply, was 'careful not to hold the enemy light', and suggested that the capture of fourteen ships would be 'a glorious result'. A feature of the picture which did not surprise any contemporary was that the ship's company thus invoked included Frenchmen, Spaniards, Scandinavians, Hindus, Germans, Italians, Portuguese, Swiss, Dutch, Kanakas and Amer-icans, and in spite of the efforts of press-gangs, the *Victory* was underm-anned. On the other hand, the name of Nelson had brought to his flagship nearly two hundred volunteers.

At about 9.30, Blackwood, having failed to get Nelson to shift his flag to the *Euryalus*, suggested that one or two other ships might precede the *Victory* into action. 'I ventured to give it as the joint opinion of Captain Hardy and myself how advantageous it would be for the Fleet for his Lordship to keep as long as possible out of the Battle.' Nelson answered briefly, 'Let them go', and Blackwood departed, allowed to hail the *Temeraire* to go ahead. 'On returning to the *Victory*, I found him doing all he could to increase rather than diminish sail.' Blackwood got the ear of Hardy, and pointed out that unless the swift-sailing *Victory* gave way, the labouring *Temeraire* could not pass, but Hardy would take no action, and when, half an hour before the *Victory* opened fire, the *Temeraire*, having been signalled at 12.15 to take her place astern, ranged up on the *Victory*'s quarter, Nelson (speaking as he always did, with a slight nasal intonation) said, 'I'll thank you, Captain Harvey, to keep in your proper station, which is astern of the *Victory*.'

The approach to action was at a rate which promised a heavy casualty list for the leading ships when the enemy opened fire. The advance of the British fleet, though all possible sail was set, fell from three knots to a mile and a half an hour. 'About 10 o'clock, Lord Nelson's anxiety to close with the enemy became very apparent.' He remarked again and again, 'They put a good face upon it', always adding quickly, 'I'll give them such a dressing as they never had before.' A little before 11 he went below to his cabin for the last time.

Bulkheads throughout the fleet were down, and the Admiral's quarters were scarcely recognizable, having been cleared of all fixtures. Nearly all the furniture had gone into the hold, and Dr. Scott, while upon the poop, had heard him giving particular instructions to the men engaged in unhanging his pictures, using the words, 'Take care of my Guardian Angel.' His desk had been left with his pocket-book lying upon it, and he now added a paragraph to the few professional notes which he had entered earlier, under date 'Monday, October 21st, 1805'. His last writing was a prayer:

'May the Great God, whom I worship, grant to my Country, and for the benefit of Europe in general, a great and glorious Victory; and may no misconduct in anyone tarnish it; and may humanity after Victory be the predominant feature in the British Fleet. For myself, individually, I commit my life to Him who made me, and may His blessing light upon my endeavours for serving my Country faithfully. To Him I resign myself and the just cause which is entrusted to me to defend. Amen. Amen. Amen.'

from *Nelson* by Carola Oman

What followed is a familiar story. Signal Lieutenant John Pascoe briefly took centre stage with his amendment to the Commander-in-Chief's last general signal, substituting the word 'expects' in the message dictated to him as : 'England confides that every man will do his duty.' It was not the last time that a flag lieutenant improved upon an admiral's draft for the sake of using the vocabulary of the Fleet Signal Book, rather than hoist a string of substitutes.

Less than two hours later Nelson was mortally wounded by a sniper firing from the mizzen-top of the seventy-four gun *Redoubtable* whilst she was locked alongside *Victory*. The Commander-in-Chief would not be persuaded by his staff to wear a plain coat, so the four glittering stars of Orders to which he had been appointed provided a perfect aiming point, besides identifying the prime target on the French hit-list. The musket ball which was later extracted from his spine lies in Windsor Castle to this day, with traces of gold filament picked up as it passed through his left epaulette on its fatal path.

Although he did not live long enough to realize it, the victory was complete and marked the beginning of a century of peace in European waters. The combined enemy fleets lost 20,000 as prisoners besides the 6,000 killed or wounded in the action, over three times as many as the Royal Navy. The defeated Commander-in-Chief, Villeneuve, did not last long – he committed suicide in a hotel bedroom in Rennes. Only eleven of the thirty-three ships-of-the-line which formed the Combined Fleet reached harbour, never to go to sea again.

The debonair, good-looking David Beatty was born of Irish fox-hunting stock in 1871 and had a meteoric rise to flag rank at the age of thirty-eight. He had attracted notice and been decorated early in his career for gallantry on the Nile during the Sudan War and again at the Taku forts during the 1900 Boxer rebellion in China. From the outset he was the sort of toff beloved by the lower deck and followed with blinding loyalty by officers from less privileged backgrounds. On cue he married an American heiress and thereafter seemed to be more interested in the company of pretty women or hunting with the Quorn than in furthering his career. This dilettante façade belied the fact that he was well read, *au courant* with political affairs and deeply immersed in the development of naval science and tactics.

Inevitably Winston Churchill was attracted by him and had him appointed to command the cavalry of the Royal Navy, the dashing Battlecruiser Squadron. He got the better of his German opposite number, Admiral Hipper, at the Heligoland and Dogger Bank actions, yet failed to land the knock-out punch at Jutland. All these disappointments were compounded by failures in signal communications. He believed that the simplest way to get over that problem

would be for the admiral to make as few signals as possible, relying on his Flag Officers and captains to understand his intentions through personal knowledge of their chief.

It came naturally to Beatty, like Nelson, to trust his subordinates, and he took care to impress upon them individually in walks ashore his views on tactics and his intentions in battle. Senior officers who had served under his command long enough to learn his ways soon came to know what they were expected to do. Hence at Jutland Beatty made comparatively few signals. His tactics were based always on the principle of the offensive, and no captain could go wrong if he sought out and engaged the enemy. Some critics may say why then did he tell the Admiralty, in January 1918, that he did not intend to seek action with the High Seas Fleet until the submarine menace had been mastered? Beatty made this decision after characteristic deliberation. As we have seen, he had correctly regarded the High Seas Fleet as the bulwark behind which the enemy could build up their submarine strength, and while their fleet remained in being, Beatty had to keep the Grand Fleet concentrated and ready for battle. Towards the end of 1917, it became clear, through Admiralty intelligence, that the pick of the German officers and men had been transferred from the High Seas Fleet to their submarine service for unrestricted attack on British trade. Beatty then came to the conclusion that Germany had no intention of seeking another fleet action except as a last resort, so he released many of his light forces from the Grand Fleet for offensive operations against the greater menace. In fact, he took the offensive in the right direction at the right moment.

Beatty had studied closely the life of Nelson and drew inspiration from him. Mahan was his favourite authority, but the book that he prized most was an account of Nelson's death written by the surgeon of the *Victory* whose name was Beatty. The walls of the Admiral's cabins in the *Lion* and *Queen Elizabeth* carried a fine selection of old prints of Nelson and his battles. A neatly framed copy of Nelson's prayer for victory before Trafalgar lay on Beatty's desk, and another copy hung above the pillow in his sleeping cabin.

Those who served at sea with him were fired by the thought that their chief was endowed with the immortal spirit of the world's greatest naval commander, and Winston Churchill has recorded how that gallant old warrior Pakenham once whispered in his ear: 'First Lord – Nelson has come again.'

It would be invidious to stretch the parallel too far. Circumstances have changed with the century and their achievements were different, but it can be truly said that Nelson and Beatty each in his day symbolized to the people of all nations the fighting spirit of the British Navy.

In religion, Beatty held the 'honest to God' belief of the sailor. He always attended Divine Service on board. Like Drake, Duncan, Nelson, and many another of our greatest leaders, he had a simple faith in the guiding hand of Providence, which explains, not only his phenomenal courage, but his splendid habit of being always ready to take a risk if the occasion required it. He was often heard to say, 'Oh, well, *le bon Dieu* will see to that'.

*

His first act after the surrender of the German Fleet was to order a massed service of thanksgiving to be held simultaneously in all ships of the Grand Fleet.

After the war his religion took the practical form of supporting the needy, and taking an active interest in such schemes as the Dockland Settlements and Seamen's Institutions.

Yet he was no saint. He loved the joys of life and was intensely human. He was attractive to women and enjoyed their company. He was a good husband and devoted father, and never happier than when at home with his family.

He died in March 1936 after having ignored his doctor's orders and marched behind the cortège of his friend, King George V. He now lies near Nelson's tomb.

He would have chosen to be buried beside his wife at Dingley Hall, and had caused a space to be left for his own name on her memorial stone, but the nation claimed him as one of her most distinguished sons, so on 16th March, 1936, amidst the solemn pageantry that England reserves for her great, Beatty was borne through the streets of London to St. Paul's

Cathedral. The union flag that covered the coffin was the same flag that had flown so proudly at the main-mast head of his Flagship when he reached the zenith of his career.

In the hallowed atmosphere of the great Cathedral, as the congregation sang 'Crossing the bar', the coffin was lowered gently into the crypt. In a moving address the Archbishop of Canterbury said:

'It may not be unfitting that one voice should try to express the admiration and gratitude of the great body of his fellow-countrymen. To them as to his comrades he was, as one of these comrades has said, "the very embodiment of the fighting spirit of the Navy". In him something of the spirit of Nelson seemed to have come back. As with Nelson – to use the words of the old Psalm – his was the ministry of a flaming fire.

from *The Life and Letters of David, Earl Beatty*, by Rear-Admiral W. S. Chalmers

A generation after Beatty there emerged within the Royal Navy another who seemed to model himself on the dashing leader of the Battlecruiser Squadron. Unfortunately, Dickie Mountbatten's courage and flamboyant style, so admirable in the hunting field, driving sports cars or playing polo, was not built on a solid base of tactical skills, let alone seamanlike qualities. He made enemies, many of them jealous of his Royal connections and immensely rich wayward wife. However, nothing seemed to stand in the way of securing the place in history he had in mind for himself, let alone the more immediate career plan of avenging his father's humiliation of having been hounded out of office as First Sea Lord at the outset of the First World War because he was a German – as indeed was the King.

The establishment of society and the Royal Navy would have none of Mountbatten, as was apparent in March 1940 when HMS *Kelly* leading the 5th Destroyer Flotilla was crippled by E-boat torpedoes in the North Sea in an encounter that should never have happened:

The *Kelly* should not have been where she was when the attack took place. The purpose of the expedition had been to harass enemy mine-layers. Mountbatten allowed himself to be diverted in fruitless search of a U-boat. He then dallied too long in pursuit – 'One should never lose visual contact with one's own forces at night' was an axiom for destroyer commanders which Robson, at least, held sacred. Finally, he had compounded his errors by making conspicuous and unnecessary signals. A report prepared for the benefit of the Commander-in-Chief, Home Fleet concluded that Mountbatten had blundered into a trap. Even if that attributes too much cunning to the Germans, it is evident that he contributed largely to his own undoing.

34

From the ensuing disaster he won glory. The return of the *Kelly* in circumstances of almost impossible difficulty was an epic of skill and heroism. In economic terms it might have been as cheap to scuttle the ship and rebuild from scratch; for the morale of the crew, of the Navy, even of the nation, the difference was inestimable. Mountbatten's feat caught the imagination of the public; it also caught the imagination of Winston Churchill. When Mountbatten was mentioned in despatches in recognition of his achievement, Churchill minuted that surely this gallant young officer was worth a D.S.O. The First Sea Lord referred the matter to the Commander-in-Chief, Home Fleet, who replied that many other destroyer captains were more worthy of the honour. The Duke of Kent also intervened with no more result. 'If the King's brother cannot get his cousin the same decoration as every other Captain (D) has been given, then the powers working against me must be very strong indeed,' wrote Mountbatten bitterly. From Beaverbrook came the sinister message: 'Tell Dickie that Winston warned me that Forbes means to break him.'

Forbes was the Commander-in-Chief of the Home Fleet, and he did not mean to break Mountbatten; indeed, it would be more true to say that Churchill meant to break Forbes. He did, however, think that Mountbatten's reputation was inflated and accepted Hughes Hallett's verdict that the heroism would not have been necessary but for the initial blunder. When the First Lord argued that Mountbatten's feat in bringing back the *Kelly* was sufficiently remarkable to deserve a decoration, Forbes replied 'that owing to a series of misfortunes – mine, collision, torpedo – *Kelly* had only been to sea 57 days during the war, and that any other captain would have done the same in bringing the ship home'. In this he was less than fair. Mountbatten's achievement had indeed been extraordinary; but Forbes's reluctance to recommend a man for an award when the justification for it stemmed from his own misjudgement does not seem unreasonable. Certainly it did not amount to victimization. This Mountbatten found hard to accept. 'There is never smoke without fire,' he told his wife darkly in a letter describing the resentment felt by everyone in *Kelly* at this slight to their Captain. 'Please promise me *not* to show my letter to anyone – not even . . . Lady Pound. If you like to learn up the arguments by heart and make out you got them from any of my officers direct – I cannot see there is any harm in that.'

Though Mountbatten did not know it, the interest taken in his career by Winston Churchill was to prove to be worth a dozen D.S.O.s. The Prime Minister believed that this dashing and courageous young officer was being unfairly held down by stick-in-the-mud admirals who had no idea how to fight a contemporary war. That belief was to stand Mountbatten in good stead when his career took its next and decisive turn.

At the end of the year, after Admiral Forbes had been relieved as Commander-in-Chief Home Fleet and taken his opinion of the accident-prone destroyer leader with him to Plymouth, Mountbatten quietly got his DSO. He attributed it to his wife's 'large blue eyes' having persuaded the civilian First Lord of the Admiralty. In April 1941 he sailed with his flotilla to reinforce the hard-pressed Mediterranean under the steadfast unflappable command of the austere ABC (Admiral Sir Andrew B. Cunningham). In his 500–page post-war autobiography spanning a career of forty years he only mentions Mountbatten in four inconsequential sentences. In her first major engagement with the enemy off Crete HMS *Kelly* was predictably sunk, with all guns blazing and the engine-room telegraphs set at Full Ahead. On being landed at Alexandria with the other survivors, he was accommodated in the commander-in-chief's residence. In a rare moment of indiscretion he passed a harsh judgement on Mountbatten, saying that his flotilla had been 'thoroughly badly led'. He shared the views of many senior officers that Mountbatten was

something of a puppy, and, like all puppies, needed to be kept in check. Yet this resentment does not invalidate Cunningham's conclusion. Mountbatten was not a good flotilla leader, or wartime commander of destroyers. It is perhaps not too fanciful to equate his performance on the bridge with his prowess behind the wheel of a car. He was a fast and dangerous driver. His maxim was that, if you were shaping up to pass and saw another car approaching, it was always better to accelerate and press on. Usually this worked, but if it did not the casualty list was likely to be formidable. His daughter Pamela remembered how, driving up from Adsdean in the staff bus, the servants would point out black stains on the road: 'Look, his Lordship's skid-marks!'

If a destroyer could leave skid-marks, *Kelly* would have disfigured every sea in which she sailed. Mountbatten was impetuous. He pushed the ship fast for little reason except his love of speed and imposed unnecessary strain on his own officers and the other ships in the flotilla. He allowed himself to be distracted from his main purpose by the lure of attractive adventures. Above all he lacked that mysterious quality of 'sea sense', the ability to ensure that one's ship is in the right place at the right time. Mountbatten was as good a captain as most and better than many of his contemporaries but among all his peers who have expressed an opinion the unanimous feeling is that, by the highest standards, he was no better than second-rate.

To say this is in no way to disparage his qualities of leadership, the loyalty and devotion he inspired among all who sailed with him. His farewell address to what was left of his crew showed him at his best.

I have always tried to crack a joke or two before, and you have been friendly and laughed at them. But today I am afraid I have run out of jokes, and I don't suppose any of us feel much like laughing. The *Kelly* has been in one scrap after another, but even after we have had men killed the majority survived and brought the old ship back. Now she lies in fifteen hundred fathoms and with her more than half our shipmates. If they had to die, what a grand way to go, for now they all lie together in the ship we loved . . . We have lost her, but they are still with her. There may be less than half the *Kelly* left, but I feel that each of us will take up the battle with even stronger heart . . . You will all be sent to replace men who have been killed in other ships, and the next time you are in action remember the *Kelly*. As you ram each shell home into the gun, shout 'Kelly!' and so her spirit will go on inspiring us until victory is won. I should like to add that there isn't one of you I wouldn't be proud and honoured to serve with again. Goodbye, good luck, and thank you all from the bottom of my heart.

The night before Mountbatten left Alexandria, what was left of the *Kelly*'s officers gave him a farewell dinner – 'but with more gaps than places it was a sad affair'.

from *Mountbatten* by Philip Ziegler

Kelly turned out to be his last command in the front line of the battle at sea, for Churchill had singled him out for a series of higher appointments, culminating in Vice-Regal Lodge, New Delhi. If anyone still doubts Noel Coward's assertion that his film *In Which We Serve* was not based on Mountbatten and his beloved *Kelly*, let him read the moving farewell speech to her survivors quoted above by his unusually candid official biographer. It is almost verbatim from the screenplay of the movie which did more than anything to establish Mountbatten as a national hero.

Captains and Masters

On top of their round-the-clock responsibility for the conflicting claims of making safe, fast passages, masters of sailing-ships had to share all the dangers and most of the discomfort of their crews. Many had no security or even homes of their own, so they served until they dropped. Not unnaturally some of their wives could not endure the life. The following passage also recounts how prolonged calm could be just as great a threat to a tall-rigged ship as any gale:

In the first decade of the twentieth century, many British merchant ship-masters were very badly treated by any standards, especially in sailing

37

ships. Poorly paid, without security of any kind or hope of earning enough to provide their own, they were members of an oppressed class, and so of course were their officers and crews. The results are obvious in a study of the records, particularly of the surviving official logs, the reports of inquiries, and the general tidings reported in Lloyd's messages, and the contemporary shipping newspapers. Many masters write 'the ship' in the space provided in the log for their homes, having no other. Many were younger sons with no inheritance. When the master's wife of the *Fifeshire* dies as the ship puts into the Falklands to get medical attention for her, and her husband has to record the fact in the heartless log, the poor man cries out on the cold page. Her home 'was on board the barque *Fifeshire* for the past ten years,' for she also had no other. Many masters' wives die, by no means all of them old women. (Mrs. Caddell of the *Fifeshire* was thirty-eight.) Another far from old wife died in the *Port Elgin* on passage from Antwerp toward San Francisco in '04–'05. She was Frances Hand, aged thirty-seven. 'My dearly loved wife passed away after an illness of 34 days,' the master had written. 'As far as my opinion goes, cause of death was lung infection. I have caused the body to be preserved in spirits and, God willing, I intend sending her back to her friends in Australia. I followed the treatment for acute pulmonary consumption.'

The poor man wrote 'affection,' not infection. It certainly was the sick woman's love for her husband which killed her. A sailing ship off the Horn was no place for the consumptive.

Far more masters died: how old they were nobody but themselves knew, for many went by fictitious ages for years. Who cared, so long as they sailed with their cargoes aboard and the ships came in again, in due course, to the ports to which they were bound? Seamen were not documented before the First World War, and not overmuch then. They required no passports, for they went with their ships and the ship's papers covered them. So long as they could stand up they went to sea.

In a sailing ship, the traditional organization – indeed the only practical effective means of control – was that the master was (or should be) the brains, the ship-handler, the sailor, the decision-maker. He had assistants (mates, usually two, of whom the first was much senior to the second: tradesmen in their own departments: a steward for the important matter of food) but he had no substitute. The others were his temporary eyes as watchkeepers, his specialized supervisors of detail. Traditionally he kept no watch, but the conscientious were in fact on watch all the time: and so the strain on them could be tremendous. He could not really learn to be a master while he was a mate. Command was flung at him suddenly. He had to rise to it and live with it (in those days) so long as he had a ship, with such respite as his own efficiency, skill and capacity to create and maintain harmony in his ship might make possible. Nobody had *all* the desirable qualities; not many had even the essentials on the twenty-four-hours-a-day basis the sailing ship demanded. The low emoluments kept many fine men too long at sea until they were quite worn out.

There was, for instance, old Captain Thomas England Parker of the four-masted bark *Holt Hill* of 2,400 tons, who suddenly dropped dead in the saloon of that vessel while preparing data for longitude sights one morning. How old he was no one knew: his age is penciled in as seventy-three on the record of his death in the official log. But he had celebrated his eightieth birthday some years before and the event was publicized, for he was a fine, tough old shipmaster, well known. In 1885, he had had the odd experience of having his ship, the *Ellenbank*, destroyed when in ballast off Cape Horn in a calm. Apparently she was caught in *two* heavy swells left by recent storms, one westerly, the other southerly, and with no wind in her sails to steady her, the bewildered ship flung this way and that, rolled right over. After some days – no one knew how many – a passing ship picked up the sole survivor. This was Captain Parker, sitting on the upturned keel. He was well past sixty then.

Calm destroyed several other fine ships in the same area, but not by rolling them over. They got ashore, like the *Bidston Hill*, or were dismasted by the violent rolling, like the *Fitzjames* when she was the German *Pinnas*: nobody sat on her keels. But the oddest loss in calm was probably that of the Norwegian bark *Alexandra* which was stuck in calm and current around the Galapagos Islands for so long that her crew of twenty had to abandon her just before she put herself, slowly but finally and very firmly, on the rocks of Iguana Cove at Albemarle Island. The *Alexandra* was bound with bunker coal from Newcastle, New South Wales, toward Panama and was then over six months out. She had been drifting about for weeks in a windless backwater of the Humboldt current, and had run out of food. The crew took to the boats, and some of them rowed and sailed to the coast of Ecuador, over 600 miles away. The sluggard bark broke up and sank.

from *War with Cape Horn* by Alan Villiers

In battle no ship was better than her captain. In Nelson's day his authority was sustained by absolute powers – far greater than the King's – with the unquestioned right to make his officers and men's lives a misery or order them to face certain death in battle. Flogging was a matter of daily occurrence, with five dozen lashes not being an unusual sentence. In 1860 there were 1,000 floggings by warrant (officially approved by an admiral) in a Royal Navy of 54,000 men. Not long afterwards it became a 'suspended' punishment, but remained in the Queen's Regulations and Articles of War as an effective reminder with the cat-o'-nine-tails left hanging in a prominent place, like a gibbet on a nearby hilltop intended to deter highwaymen.

Some tyrants drove their men to mutiny. When Captain Bligh was cut loose in HMS *Bounty*'s longboat none of the mutineers believed he would ever see civilization again. Mutineers in the frigate *Hermione* on the West Indies station took no chances. They murdered Captain Hugh Pigot and made off with the ship.

Pigot got his command through being the son of an Admiral sent to relieve the triumphant Rodney and nephew of a wealthy nabob.

Sometimes when a man who was perfectly balanced as a lieutenant was given command of a frigate and moved up from the casual *bonhomie* of the wardroom, he found himself overwhelmed by the loneliness represented by the great cabin. Unless he invited officers – which he could not do too frequently – he ate every meal alone; when he walked the quarterdeck the officers and men left the windward side clear for him. He was the captain; no one joked with him, no one chatted, always there was an invisible wall between him and his officers, a wall which represented discipline but one that shut out the captain. It was a wall which vanished the moment a captain tried to make himself popular, currying favour among his subordinates. From then on he was no longer the captain; he was an object of derision among the men he was supposed to lead.

The loneliness of command was something that a good leader accepted; but with an inadequate man it led to drinking or brooding and introversion; a healthy attitude towards the Church could become a religious mania; a normal strictness could warp itself into sadism. Obsessions seemed to be lying around waiting to be claimed – having the decks scrubbed half a dozen times, having the ship's company dressed in a particular way (at a time when there was no uniform). Some captains judged the ship's efficiency by the sail handling and gave not a damn about gunnery; others were more concerned in the number of broadsides that could be fired in a given time.

A successful captain fitted no pattern. One thinks of Nelson – small, narrow-chested, fretful, with a whining voice, and as a captain inclined to meddle in matters it would have been wiser to ignore (as the merchants in Antigua found when the young captain of the *Boreas* frigate started invoking the Navigation Laws against the Yankee traders). These was Collingwood, quiet, firm, thoughtful, who rarely flogged a man, but had a reputation for coldness. There was Sir John Jervis, later Earl St Vincent, a dour and ruthless disciplinarian. There was Thomas Cochrane, a daredevil captain who cared little for orders (if he was receiving them) and even less for the enemy, fighting actions which almost defied belief. In every case the men followed them through thick and thin. Edward Hamilton, commanding the *Surprise* frigate, was such a harsh disciplinarian that his ship's company were terrified of him – yet when it came to cutting out a frigate from a port on the Spanish Main defended by three castles and more than 200 guns they succeeded with casualties which are unbelievable unless one has examined the official Spanish figures and list of names in the archives. The

Surprise had four men seriously wounded and seven slightly, and no one killed. The Spanish lost 119 killed and 291 taken prisoner (97 wounded). Hamilton received a knighthood for his bravery and was later court-martialled for cruelty to a seaman, with no one pointing out the contradiction of a man so planning a desperate operation that none of his men were killed – and yet being harsh.

There was, then, no pattern. One captain commanded his ship with a joke on his lips and a gentle hand on the rein; another rarely spoke and even more rarely smiled. Yet each commanded successfully. There was, however, one type of captain detested by both seamen and officers – the easygoing, slack captain. The men hated him because it left the way open for bullying officers; the officers hated him because it meant they received no backing in enforcing discipline.

Discipline was based only on the Articles of War, thirty-six numbered paragraphs, each of between fifty and one hundred and fifty words, which laid down in broad terms the rules and regulations and penalties. The Articles covered the shortcomings of admirals and captains rather more than seamen, and several gave death as the punishment, taking the penalty out of the hands of the court, once a man was found guilty.

from *Life in Nelson's Navy* by Dudley Pope

The owner of the 85-ton *Foam* might have been regarded as something of an eccentric himself by his mid-Victorian contemporaries in the Royal Yacht Squadron, when he cruised to the most northerly point of Spitzbergen in 1856. But the professional skipper he engaged an hour before sailing had unusual qualifications to match his music-hall appearance:

On his head he wore a queer kind of smoking cap, with the peak cocked over his left ear; then came a green shooting jacket, and flashy silk tartan waistcoat, set off by a gold chain, hung about in innumerable festoons, – while light trowsers and knotty Wellington boots completed his costume, and made the wearer look as little like a seaman as need be. It appeared, nevertheless, that the individual in question was Mr. Ebenezer Wyse, my new sailing-master; so I accepted Captain C.'s strong recommendation as a set-off against the silk tartan; explained to the new comer the position he was to occupy on board, and gave orders for sailing in an hour. The multitudinous chain, moreover, so lavishly displayed, turned out to be an ornament of which Mr. Wyse might well be proud; and the following history of its acquisition reconciled me more than anything else to my Master's unnautical appearance.

Some time ago there was a great demand in Australia for small river steamers, which certain Scotch companies undertook to supply. The difficulty, however, was to get such fragile tea-kettles across the ocean; five started one after another in murderous succession, and each came to grief before it got halfway to the equator; the sixth alone remained with which to try a last experiment; should she arrive, her price would more than compensate the pecuniary loss already sustained, though it could not bring to life the hands sacrificed in the mad speculation; by this time, however, even the proverbial recklessness of the seamen of the port was daunted, and the hearts of two crews had already failed them at the last moment of starting, when my friend of the chain volunteered to take the command. At the outset of his voyage everything went well – a fair wind (her machinery was stowed away, and she sailed under canvas) carried the little craft in an incredible short time a thousand miles to the southward of the Cape, when one day, as she was running before the gale, the man at the wheel – startled at a sea, which he thought was going to poop her, let go the helm, – the vessel broached to – and tons of water tumbled in on the top of the deck. As soon as the confusion of the moment had subsided, it became evident that the shock had broken some of the iron plates, and that the ship was in a fair way of foundering. So frightened were the crew, that after consultation with each other, they determined to take to the boats, and all hands came aft, to know whether there was anything the skipper would wish to carry off with him. Comprehending the madness of attempting to reach land in open boats at a distance of a thousand miles from any shore, Wyse pretended to go into the cabin to get his compass, chronometer, &c., but returning immediately with a revolver in each hand, swore he would shoot the first man who attempted to touch the boats. This timely exhibition of spirit saved their lives; soon after the weather moderated; by undergirding the ship with chains, St. Paul fashion, the leaks were partially stopped, the steamer reached her destination, and was sold for 7,000*l.* a few days after her arrival. In token of their gratitude for the good service he had done them, the Company presented Mr. Wyse on his return with a gold watch and . . . chain . . .

from *Letters from High Latitudes* by Lord Dufferin

Selection and Training

In Nelson's day, and for a generation afterwards, there was no discernible plan governing the selection and training of midshipmen. If they had connections, or 'interests' as their patrons were referred to, they might rise to command and even a flag. But many served on well into middle age without even being presented for examination to the rank of lieutenant. This had its effect on the style and manners prevailing amongst the 'young gentlemen' who messed in the gunrooms of the fleet.

Things were very different in the navy at the period under consideration, than now. I doubt much if, in 1809, there could be a greater change in a boy's life than being launched from his comfortable home at thirteen years of age into the stormy elements of a midshipman's berth; for in those days the company was not quite so select as at present; people of all sorts and all descriptions became midshipmen. A shoemaker, who had a long outstanding bill against a captain, cancelled the bill and the obligation by having his son placed on the quarter-deck: hence some of the very objectionable characters, who have in after life so completely disgraced the navy, and men in good society too, who have accidentally met some of these intruders, have formed their ideas of the whole profession by the blundering remarks of a hatter's son and by the awkward demeanour of a tinker's brat.

from *The Life of a Sailor* by a captain in the Navy

If I were desired to point out the root of all evil in the navy, the secret spring of that tyrannical sway, which has in all societies cast such a stigma on our nautical defenders, I should pronounce it most indubitably to be the result of sending such striplings to sea – mere children.

. . . it is . . . an admitted point, that the proper age to commence a naval life is *thirteen*! This is the extreme verge of propriety with the old school . . . They are of that age, when suddenly freed from the restraint of school, they long to start into manhood at once; and whatever they see or hear in others older than themselves, that they do instantly imitate. Thus their education, as relates to the practical part of it, and their bent and disposition in after-life, is necessarily formed and moulded on board a ship. What, let us inquire, is the picture from which they have to copy in a midshipman's berth? In nine cases out of ten – or more – licentiousness and profanity in every shape. No one refinement is indigenous. Here then he learns to swear and drink. He next goes on deck, and meets a first lieutenant of the old school, treating men like hogs, and officers like felons: using language, which many a poor creature whom necessity has driven to live by prostitution, would hold in scorn. He is kept in one continued forced and false dread of punishment . . . Thus, then, we will say the first three years of a midshipman's life generally passes in skulking his watch, and shirking his duty; and were you to examine ten youngsters at this period, they would be almost wholly ignorant of how to go through the necessary directions in reefing or shifting a topsail, or mooring a ship, or, in fact, of any of these primary and important duties of a sailor; and out of that ten, four at least would be unable to put a vessel about, and to weigh an anchor, and cast the ship's head. Then what can they do? They can drink half a pint of rum, and can carry on 'a blackguarding match' with any of the mess; they can cut out to perfection, weather the lieutenant of the watch in a dark night, break their leave, and then spin the first lieutenant a yarn as tough as most folks. But as to their use in any case of emergency, they are no more fit to be entrusted with the lives of the men under their command than a quaker would be . . .

from *Cavendish, or the Patrician at Sea* by a captain in the Navy

In those days in the navy, before we had been polished by the society of females, or enjoyed the benefits of peace, the dinner-service in a midshipman's berth was not quite so costly as a nobleman's. Glass, a brittle material, and one which shows dirt both in the liquid and on its sides, was too expensive and too easily expended to be much used in the navy. Cups would answer this purpose, and therefore cups were used. The soup-tureen, a heavy, lumbering piece of block tin, pounded into shape, was, for want of a ladle, emptied with an everlasting teacup; the knives were invariably black, both on the handles and on the blades; and the forks were wiped in the tablecloth by the persons about to use them, and who, to save eating more than was requisite of actual dirt, always plunged them through the tablecloth to clean between the prongs. Of course, as only one tablecloth was used during the week, on the Saturday it was voted always dirty enough to be put in a bag to await its ablution. The rest of the furniture was not much cleaner: now and then an empty bottle served as a candlestick; and I have known both a shoe and a quadrant-case used as a soupplate. The sides of the berth were adorned with dirks; and cocked-hats, belonging to no particular member of the community, were placed à *cheval*, like the little wooden god Thor at Upsala, on a ten-penny nail. It was in a habitation like this, 'a prison,' as Dr. Johnson says, 'with the chance of being drowned,' and with only one plank between man and eternity that the sons of the highest nobility were placed . . .

from *The Life of a Sailor* by a captain in the Navy

The hero in C. S. Forester's series of novels about the Royal Navy in the war against the French 1793–1815 is that paragon of all naval virtues, Horatio Hornblower. Most of the books were written in California after the Second World War, but the masterly grasp of detail betrays the author's British background, including wartime service in the RNVR. Every step of Hornblower's career is recorded, from midshipman to Admiral of the Fleet. At the outset he is a midshipman (acting lieutenant) serving in HMS *Indefatigable* under Captain Pellew. On the ship's arrival at Gibraltar he is ordered to report for his overdue oral examination for the rank of lieutenant. The board is convened on board the hulk *Santa Barbara*, a prize taken from Cadiz in 1780 and now the home for 2,000 Spanish prisoners. Forty midshipmen were crammed into the port after-cabin awaiting their ordeal. The examining board was seen to arrive from their own ships. There were some hard cases amongst them, so Hornblower dreaded his summons to the after-cabin.

Facing his examiners, the left-hand face suddenly spoke. 'You are close-hauled on the port tack, Mr. Hornblower, beating up channel with a nor-easterly wind blowing hard, with Dover bearing north two miles. Is that clear?'

'Yes, sir.'

'Now the wind veers four points and takes you flat aback. What do you do, sir? What do you do?'

Hornblower's mind, if it was thinking about anything at all at that moment, was thinking about rhumb lines; this question took him as much aback as the situation it envisaged. His mouth opened and shut, but there was no word he could say.

'By now you're dismasted' said the middle face – a swarthy face; Hornblower was making the deduction that it must belong to Black Charlie Hammond. He could think about that even if he could not force his mind to think at all about his examination.

'Dismasted' said the left-hand face, with a smile like Nero enjoying a Christian's death agony. 'With Dover cliffs under your lee. You are in serious trouble, Mr. – ah – Hornblower.'

Serious indeed. Hornblower's mouth opened and shut again. His dulled mind heard, without paying special attention to it, the thud of a cannon shot somewhere not too far off. The board passed no remark on it either, but a moment later there came a series of further cannon shots which brought the three captains to their feet. Unceremoniously they rushed out of the cabin, sweeping out of the way the sentry at the door. Hornblower followed them . . .

'See there!' said a voice.

Across half a mile of dark water a yellow light grew until the ship there was wrapped in flame. She had every sail set and was heading straight into the crowded anchorage.

'Fire ships!'

'Officer of the watch! Call my gig!' bellowed Foster.

A line of fire ships was running before the wind, straight at the crowd of anchored ships. The *Santa Barbara* was full of the wildest bustle as the seamen and marines came pouring on deck, and as captains and candidates shouted for boats to take them back to their ships. A line of orange flame lit up the water, followed at once by the roar of a broadside; some ship was firing her guns in the endeavour to sink a fire ship. Let one of those blazing hulls make contact with one of the anchored ships, even for a few seconds, and the fire would be transmitted to the dry, painted timber, to the tarred cordage, to the inflammable sails, so that nothing would put it out. To men in highly combustible ships filled with explosives fire was the deadliest and most dreaded peril of the sea.

'You shore boat, there!' bellowed Hammond suddenly. 'You shore boat! Come alongside! Come alongside, blast you!'

His eye had been quick to sight the pair-oar rowing by.

'Come alongside or I'll fire into you!' supplemented Foster. 'Sentry, there, make ready to give them a shot!'

At the threat the wherry turned and glided towards the mizzen chains. 'Here you are, gentlemen' said Hammond.

The three captains rushed to the mizzen chains and flung themselves down into the boat. Hornblower was at their heels . . .

'There's one of them' said Harvey.

Just ahead, a small brig was bearing down on them under topsails; they could see the glow of the fire, and as they watched the fire suddenly burst into roaring fury, wrapping the whole vessel in flames in a moment, like a set piece in a fireworks display. Flames spouted out of the holes in her sides and roared up through her hatchways. The very water around her glowed vivid red. They saw her halt in her career and begin to swing slowly around.

'She's across *Santa Barbara*'s cable' said Foster.

'She's nearly clear' added Hammond. 'God help 'em on board there. She'll be alongside her in a minute.'

Hornblower thought of two thousand Spanish and French prisoners battened down below decks in the hulk.

'With a man at her wheel she could be steered clear' said Foster. 'We ought to do it!'

At last Hornblower found his tongue. 'Let me go, sir. I'll handle her.'

'Come with me, if you like' replied Foster. 'It may need two of us.'

His nickname of Dreadnought Foster may have had its origin in the name of his ship, but it was appropriate enough in all circumstances. Harvey swung the boat under the fire ship's stern; she was before the wind again now, and just gathering way, just heading down upon the *Santa Barbara*.

For a moment, Hornblower was the nearest man in the boat to the brig and there was no time to be lost. He stood up on the thwart and jumped; his hands gripped something, and with a kick and a struggle he dragged his ungainly body up onto the deck. With the brig before the wind, the flames were blown forward; right aft here it was merely frightfully hot, but Hornblower's ears were filled with the roar of the flames and the crackling and banging of the burning wood. He stepped forward to the wheel and seized the spokes, the wheel was lashed with a loop of line, and as he cast this off and took hold of the wheel again he could feel the rudder below him bite into the water. He flung his weight on the spoke and spun the wheel over. The brig was about to collide with the *Santa Barbara*, starboard bow to starboard bow, and the flames lit an anxious gesticulating crowd on the *Santa Barbara*'s forecastle.

'Hard over!' roared Foster's voice in Hornblower's ear.

'Hard over it is!' said Hornblower, and the brig answered her wheel at that moment, and her bow turned away, avoiding the collision.

At a distance of only two or three yards the fire ship passed on down the *Santa Barbara*'s side . . .

*

'Tiller ropes burned away, sir' reported Hornblower.

Flames roared up beside them. His coat sleeve was smouldering.

'Jump!' said Foster.

Hornblower felt Foster shoving him – everything was insane. He heaved himself over, gasped with fright as he hung in the air, and then felt the breath knocked out of his body as he hit the water. The water closed over him, and he knew panic as he struggled back to the surface. It was cold – the Mediterranean in December is cold. For the moment the air in his clothes supported him, despite the weight of the sword at his side, but he could see nothing in the darkness, with his eyes still dazzled by the roaring flames. Somebody splashed beside him.

'They were following us in the boat to take us off' said Foster's voice. 'Can you swim?'

'Yes, sir. Not very well.'

'That might describe me' said Foster; and then he lifted his voice to hail, 'Ahoy! Ahoy! Hammond! Harvey! Ahoy!'

*

It was then that he heard the splashing and grinding of oars and loud voices, and he saw the dark shape of the approaching boat, and he uttered a spluttering cry. In a second or two the boat was up to them, and he was clutching the gunwale in panic.

They were lifting Foster in over the stern, and Hornblower knew he must keep still and make no effort to climb in, but it called for all his resolution to make himself hang quietly onto the side of the boat and wait his turn . . . Then they dragged him in and he fell face downward in the bottom of the boat, on the verge of fainting. Then somebody spoke in the boat, and Hornblower felt a cold shiver pass over his skin, and his feeble muscles tensed themselves, for the words spoken were Spanish – at any rate an unknown tongue, and Spanish presumably.

. . . Foster was sitting doubled up, in the bottom of the boat, and now he lifted his face from his knees and stared round him.

'Who are these fellows?' he asked feebly – his struggle in the water had left him as weak as Hornblower.

'Spanish fire ship's crew, I fancy, sir' said Hornblower. 'We're prisoners.'

'Are we indeed!'

The knowledge galvanized him into activity just as it had Hornblower. He tried to get to his feet, and the Spaniard at the tiller thrust him down with a hand on his shoulder. Foster tried to put his hand away, and raised his voice in a feeble cry, but the man at the tiller was standing no nonsense. He brought out, in a lightning gesture, a knife from his belt . . .

'How are we heading?' he asked Hornblower, sufficiently quietly not to irritate their captors.

47

'North, sir. maybe they're going to land on the Neutral Ground and make for the Line.'

'That's their best chance' agreed Foster.

'Boat ahoy!' came a hail across the water; there was a dark nucleus in the night over there. The Spaniard in the sternsheets instantly dragged the tiller over, heading the boat directly away from it, while the two at the oars redoubled their exertions.

'Guard boat –' said Foster, but cut his explanation short at a further threat from the knife.

*

'Boat ahoy!' came the hail again. 'Lay on your oars or I'll fire into you!'

The Spaniard made no reply, and a second later came the flash and report of a musket shot . . .

'Boat ahoy!'

This was another hail, from a boat right ahead of them. The Spaniards at the oars ceased their efforts in dismay, but a roar from the steersman set them instantly to work again.

The Spaniards' intention was to ram and capsize the approaching Royal Navy guard-boat, but they were too late. They were overpowered. At first Captain Foster and Hornblower were taken to be Spanish and were roughed up accordingly. Then another boat hailed. It was Hammond in the guard boat who recovered them.

When it was all over Captain Foster addressed Hornblower:

'And you, my fire-breathing friend. May I offer you my thanks? You did well. Should I live beyond tomorrow, I shall see that authority is informed of your actions.'

'Thank you, sir.' A question trembled on Hornblower's lips. It called for a little resolution to thrust it out, 'And my examination, sir? My certificate?'

Foster shook his head. 'That particular examining board will never reassemble, I fancy. You must wait your opportunity to go before another one.'

'Aye aye, sir' said Hornblower, with despondency apparent in his tone.

'Now lookee here, Mr. Hornblower' said Foster, turning upon him. 'To the best of my recollection, you were flat aback, about to lose your spars and with Dover cliffs under your lee. In one more minute you would have been failed – it was the warning gun that saved you. Is not that so?'

'I suppose it is, sir.'

'Then be thankful for small mercies. And even more thankful for big ones.'

from *Mr Midshipman Hornblower* by C. S. Forrester

Midshipmen

Whereas flogging was discontinued in the Royal Navy in the 1880s, corporal punishment for seaman boys and midshipmen continued until the Second World War. This account of life in a gunroom in a cruiser just before the First World War could just as easily be describing the events of twenty years later. Everything depended on the personality of the sub-lieutenant in charge of the mess – the sub of the gunroom. In this case he appears to have given the senior group of midshipmen unlimited licence to make life unbearable for their juniors through 'evolutions' of the sort Charles Morgan here describes:

On his right stood Elstone with a jug of water, on his left Howdray, clutching an armful of ship's biscuits.

'Now, first Wart forward. At the run!'

Sentley, who was on the right of the line, hurried from his place and stood at attention before Krame.

'On the knee! . . .'Shun! . . . On the knee!' The spectators roared to see Sentley clambering from one position to the other. Howdray picked up a thick cane from the sideboard and hit Sentley as he knelt.

'Come on,' he said, 'get a move on. 'Shun! Now, at the order "Kneeling position – place," you'll drop on your knees – understand? – drop, not let yourself down like an old woman . . . Kneeling position – place!'

Sentley went down. His knees brought up hard against the deck. He kept his body and head erect, his hands to his sides. Banford-Smith and Tintern climbed out of their places on the settee; one perched himself on the edge of the table behind Howdray, the other found a convenient seat by the piano.

'The child,' said Krame, after the manner of a gunnery instructor, 'will incline the 'ead forward in a reverent attitood and assoom a mournful aspect. 'E will now repeat the Warts' Creed.'

Sentley repeated that parody of the Apostles' Creed which had been given to each junior midshipman earlier in the day. 'I believe in the Sub Almightly, master of every Wart, and in Peter Krame, 'is noble 'elp, our Lord . . .' and so on to the end. No senior midshipman protested against this Creed, no junior midshipman refused to repeat it.

When he was silent, a ship's biscuit, thick and tough, was beaten and beaten on Sentley's head until the biscuit broke. Howdray was about to pour water from the jug when Banford-Smith restrained him. 'Cut out the water,' he said, 'it will make such a damned mess on the deck.'

Each junior midshipman came forward in turn, dropped on his knees, was struck with Howdray's stick if he dropped not fast enough, bowed his head, repeated the Creed, and had a biscuit broken upon him. John, because he stood on the left of the line, came last. When the ceremony was over, Krame glanced behind him.

'Now let's have a hymn,' he said to Tintern.

'What hymn?'

'Any old hymn – something to celebrate the young gentlemen's regeneration. Lynwood will lead the singing. All Warts will support him.'

Tintern emptied a glass of port, squared himself to the piano, and beat out the first chords of No. 165. Not only the Warts sang it; the senior midshipmen, tired of the many repetitions of the christening ceremony, were glad of a chance to make a noise.

'*O Gawd, our 'elp in ages pa-ha-hast.*' This prolongation was in response to Tintern's improvised chords and runs. '*Our 'ope for years to come.*' The voices swelled to a roar, and paused for breath. In the momentary silence the ship rolled deeply; the sea came surging over a scuttle and receded, leaving wisps of luminous foam. '*Our shelter from the stormy bla-ha-hast, And our eternal –*'

Tintern was beating the keyboard with his doubled fists as a kind of desperate finale. The wild discords screamed under the steel bars overhead. A locker flew open, and by a lurch of the ship all it contained was shot across the Gunroom. A Manual of Seamanship, a 'Child's Guide,' a writing-case, a Gunnery Drill-Book, and a box of instruments, lay scattered on the table amid a pile of crumpled letters. An Oxford Bible was open and face downwards on the deck. Near it a bottle of ink, streaming its contents, rolled to and fro. Finally, there fell from the locker a photograph of Driss's mother. He started forward to gather up his possessions.

'Fall in, damn you!' Krame shouted. 'Who told you to fall out?'

Driss went on.

Krame stood up. 'Come here, Driss. Did you hear me tell you to fall in?'

'Yes.'

'Well?'

'I am going to pick up my things before they are spoilt.'

'Why don't you keep your locker properly shut? Look at the ink on the deck. I've a damned good mind – by God, you shall lick it up!'

Driss's face was pale, his Irish eyes dangerous. Tintern leaned sideways in his seat and took Krame by the arm.

'Dry up, you fool!' he said in an undertone, and turned back to the piano. He had tact, moreover.

'*O Gawd, our 'elp in ages pa-ha-hast . . .*'

Before the chorus was ended Driss had secured his locker and quietly fallen in again.

The next Evolution was known alternatively to two names – one, 'The Angostura Hunt'; the other, which was sometimes attached in other Gunrooms to an Evolution slightly different, 'Creeping for Jesus.' John was the first taken. Thrust on his knees near the serving slab, he was blindfolded with two handkerchiefs. He could hear the senior midshipmen's voices.

'Lay it here . . . No, not under the table. We can't get at him under the table . . . There, that will do. Replace the bitters, Elstone.'

'Can you see?' asked Krame.

'No.'

'Can you smell?'

'Yes.'

'Can you feel?'

'Yes.'

'Well, that's what is wanted – a good scent, and probably a bit of feeling before you're through with it.' He cleared his throat. 'Now, Lynwood, somewhere in the Gunroom is a piece of bread on the deck. Between you and the bread is a trail of Angostura bitters – pungent, so as to make it easy. You've got to find the bread by scent and pick it up with your mouth. No feeling with your hands, mind you. Put his nose on the trail, someone.'

Hands seized John's head and thrust it downwards. 'Got it? Smell it?'

'Not yet.'

'Give him a sniff at the bottle . . . Got it now?'

'Yes.'

'Right. Wait for the order to commence . . . Stand by. Go!'

John began to crawl along the floor. They were shouting at him to go faster. 'Get a move on. Good dog. Good dog. – – ! the beggar isn't trying. Let him have it, Howdray.'

A cane sang through the air and fell upon John's legs, sang and fell again. The blood ran to his head. The smell of corticine and dust sickened him. The blows were falling rapidly now. Someone other than Howdray seized a stick and sent the pain shooting through John's body. He saw now the reason for this creeping position – the excellence of the target it provided. If he could but regain the scent and get to the end of it! But the scent was gone, and he could not steady himself. The weight of his body on his hands was making his wrists ache. The noise was deafening. On his palms the dust seemed inches thick. When he tried to rise, they thrust him down again . . .

Behind the bandage on his eyes was scarlet blindness, and he was visited by a sense of the desperate impotence of the blind. The words of those shouting above him conveyed no clear meaning to him now. They were giving him guidance, he thought. There was a medley of cries: 'Port! Starboard! . . . He doesn't know his port from his starboard hand.' A stick fell again.

'Give him a chance, Howdray. Still a moment; I'll put him on the trail.' This was Tintern's voice.

But help was unavailing. Perhaps some foot had extinguished the trail; at any rate, even with Tintern's guidance, John could not detect the scent. He groped forward to no purpose. Banford-Smith, sliding from the table, stood unintentionally on his fingers, causing him so much pain that, though he was now too bitter to cry out, he reeled from his track. A moment later

51

his hand touched something wet – perhaps the blood from beneath his crushed finger-nail, perhaps no more than Driss's ink. He neither knew nor cared. In his head, which he dared not raise from the ground, it seemed that fire was burning. His temples and his eyes were throbbing as if they would burst. He paused bewildered, and instantly sticks fell on him again . . . It would never, never end. Perhaps he was going to faint. He wished he might. That might end it for the evening at least. That might end it all.

Shouts, forcing themselves upon his consciousness, suggested that he was near the bread he was seeking. He groped in the dust with his teeth and tongue, hoping he might end his quest. The grit was about his lips and in his nostrils.

Then the bandage shifted, and he saw the bread. He did not dare to seize it immediately lest they should guess that he could see, but he worked slowly towards it and picked it up between his teeth. A great burst of cheering followed, vague cheering, such as he remembered having heard when, down and out in a boxing competition, he had been dragged by his seconds to his corner. Presently he found himself leaning against the table, the bandage having been pulled away. The sweat was dripping from his forehead and stinging his eyes. His whole body ached. He stooped, brushed the dust mechanically from the knees of his trousers, and tried to smile to show that he was 'taking it well.'

*

'Fall in again!' Krame said. 'Fall in, I say!'

Evolution followed Evolution: the obstacle race in reverse order; an affair called Torpedoes, that consisted essentially in hurling the junior midshipmen's bodies along the table against the for'ard bulkhead; and half a dozen other, the product of Krame's ingenuity. Even the flame in Driss died down. There comes a time when resistance, even mental resistance, disappears. The limbs move as they are told.

At ten o'clock a ship's corporal tapped at the door and announced that it was time to close the Gunroom.

'Last drinks,' said Krame, and rang the bell. 'Warts fall out!'

from The Gunroom by Charles Morgan

Service in the Royal Navy – and most others – in the eighteenth century was not sufficiently attractive for its ships to be manned by volunteers. In 1664, four years after the Restoration, it was noted by the Admiralty that the Navy needed 30,000 men to keep its battle fleet in commission, yet only had 4,000 on the books. The balance of 26,000 were found by an uncompromising recruiting service known as the press-gangs. The word is derived from the French *prêt*, meaning 'ready' money – the forerunner of the King's shilling. It survives to this day as Cockney rhyming slang. 'Nelson Eddies' means 'readies' (i.e. cash in hand).

Press-gangs were organized by areas with a Regulating Officer in charge, usually an officer without immediate hope of employment afloat. He ran his operation from a Rendezvous (or 'rondy' as it was known to sailors), which as often as not would be a waterfront dive in which sozzled candidates for the fleet were easily rounded up.

Land-gangs of the Impress Service had authority wherever suitable recruits might be found. In the countryside they were little better than legalized highwaymen, intercepting at gunpoint men travelling from seaports to their homes. All roads out of Bristol were notorious in this respect.

The officers employed in this service were not of the highest calibre, as the following letter from a lieutenant to his friend in another area makes clear when his superior officer is about to be transferred:

'At first you'll think him a Fine old Fellow, but if it's possible he will make you Quarrel with all your Acquaintance. Be very Careful not to Introduce him to any Family that you have a regard for, for although he is near Seventy Years of Age, he is the greatest Debauchee you ever met with – a Man of No Religion, a Man who is Capable of any Meanness, Arbitrary and Tyrannicall in his Disposition. This City has been several times just on the point of writing against him to the Board of Admiralty. He has a wife, and Children grown up to Man's Estate. The Woman he brings over with him is Bird the Builder's Daughter. To Conclude, there is not a House in Chester that he can go into but his own and the Rendezvous, after having been Six Months in one of the agreeablest Cities in England.'

Ignorant of the fact that his reputation had thus preceded him. Capt. P. found himself assailed, on his arrival at Waterford, by a 'most Infamous Epitaph,' emanating none knew whence, nor cared. This circumstance, accentuated by certain indiscretions of which the hectoring old officer was guilty shortly after his arrival, aroused strong hostility against him. A mob of fishwives, attacking his house at Passage, smashed the windows and were with difficulty restrained from levelling the place with the ground. His junior officers conspired against him. Piqued by the loss of certain perquisites which the newcomer remorselessly swept away, they denounced him to the Admiralty, who ordered an inquiry into his conduct. After a hearing of ten days it went heavily against him, practically every charge being proved. He was immediately superseded and never again employed – a sad ending to a career of forty years under such men as Anson, Boscawen, Hawke and Vernon. Yet such was the ultimate fate of many an impress officer.

The sea-gangs sought to impose a rigorous martial law around the coastal waters of the British Isles, using small wherries to board ships at anchor or seagoing cutters backed by warships to intercept them at

53

sea. The scale of the operation was impressive. At Dover, Deal and Folkestone there were no less then 450 fulltime men in the service afloat – enough to man a ship-of-the-line themselves.

When the officer led the press-gang on board he was met by the ship's company drawn up in two groups: those eligible to be pressed and those protected under a wide range of exemptions, all of them liable to be challenged or ignored. The gang-leader left them in no doubt:

> 'Now, my lads,' said the gang officer, addressing the pressable contingent in the terms of his instructions, 'I must tell you that you are at liberty, if you so choose, to enter His Majesty's service as volunteers. If you come in in that way, you will each receive the bounty now being paid, together with two months' advance wages before you go to sea. But if you don't choose to enter volunteerly, then I must take you against your wills.'

Top of the list of exemptions were, not surprisingly, members of the press-gangs. In theory foreigners were also in the clear, but if they made the mistake of marrying a British girl they would immediately be assumed to be naturalized and swooped upon, even during their honeymoon.

Those under eighteen or over fifty-five years of age were exempt by law, but few had ever heard of birth certificates, let alone possessed one, so the matter was judged entirely by appearances, with twelve-year-olds being picked up along with their grandfathers. In theory immunity was enjoyed by shipwrights in building yards, pilots, colliers, seamen in their first two years of service, those engaged in offshore fishing or whaling and crews of outward-bound ships. Any inward-bound ship was fair game, except for one category:

> The only inward-bound ship the gangsmen were forbidden to press from was the 'sick ship' or vessel undergoing quarantine because of the presence, or the suspected presence, on board of her of some 'catching' disease, and more particularly of that terrible scourge the plague. Dread of the plague in those days rode the country like a nightmare, and just as the earliest quarantine precautions had their origin in that fact, so those precautions were never more rigorously enforced than in the case of ships trading to countries known to be subject to plague or reported to be in the grip of it. The Levantine trader suffered most severely in this respect. In 1721 two vessels from Cyprus, where plague was then prevalent, were burned to the water's edge by order of the authorities, and as late as 1800 two others from Morocco, suspected of carrying the dread disease in the hides composing their cargo, were scuttled and sent to the bottom at the Nore. This was quarantine *in excelsis*. Ordinary preventive measures went no further than the withdrawal of 'pratique,' as communication with the shore

was called, for a period varying usually from ten to sixty-five days, and during this period no gang was allowed to board the ship.

The seamen belonging to such ships always got ashore if they could; for though the penalty for deserting a ship in quarantine was death, it might be death to remain, and the sailor was ever an opportunist careless of consequences.

Physical resistance to the press-gangs was resorted to whenever the odds seemed favourable, in much the same way that smugglers used to see off the excisemen when they were outgunned. In parts of Cornwall the locals' hostility to the press-gangs was so vehement that the regulation officer's operations chart showed them as no-go areas. Nearer the centre of affairs the fishermen of Brighton had long enjoyed immunity, which was shared by the whole town. Their lordships decided to take action. In July 1779 secret orders were issued to

> Capt. Alms, who, as regulating officer at Shoreham, was likewise in charge of the gang at Newhaven under Lieut. Bradley, and of the gang at Little-hampton under Lieut. Breedon. At Shoreham there was also a tender, manned by an able crew. With these three gangs and the tender's crew at his back, Alms determined to lay siege to Brighton and teach the fishermen there a lesson they should not soon forget. But first, in order to render the success of the project doubly sure, he enlisted the aid of Major-General Sloper, Commandant at Lewes, who readily consented to lend a company of soldiers to assist in the execution of the design.
>
> These preparations were some little time in the making, and it was not until the Thursday immediately preceding the 24th of July that all was in readiness. On the night of that day, by preconcerted arrangement, the allied forces took the road – for the Littlehampton gang, a matter of some twenty-miles – and at the first flush of dawn united on the outskirts of the sleeping town, where the soldiers were without loss of time so disposed as to cut off every avenue of escape. This done, the gangs split up and by devious ways, but with all expedition, concentrated their strength upon the quay, expecting to find there a large number of men making ready for the day's fishing. To their intense chagrin the quay was deserted. The night had been a tempestuous one, with heavy rain, and though the unfortunate gangsmen were soaked to the skin, the fishermen all lay dry in bed. Hearing the wind and rain, not a man turned out.
>
> By this time the few people who were abroad on necessary occasions had raised the alarm, and on every hand were heard loud cries of 'Press-gang!' and the hurried barricading of doors. For ten hours 'every man kept himself locked up and bolted.' For ten hours Alms waited in vain upon the local Justice of the Peace for power to break and enter the fishermen's cottages. His repeated requests being refused, he was at length 'under the necessity of quitting the town with only one man.' So ended the siege of Brighton;

but Bradley, on his way back to Newhaven, fell in with a gang of smugglers, of whom he pressed five. Brighton did not soon forget the terrors of that rain-swept morning. For many a long day her people were 'very shy, and cautious of appearing in public.' The salutary effects of the raid, however, did not extend to the fishermen it was intended to benefit. They became more insolent than ever, and a few years later marked their resentment of the attempt to press them by administering a sound thrashing to Mr. Midshipman Sealy, of the Shoreham rendezvous, whom they one day caught unawares.

*

Another town that gave the gang a hot reception was Whitby. As in the case of Chester the gang there was an importation, having been brought in from Tyneside by Lieuts. Atkinson and Oakes. As at Chester, too, a place of rendezvous had been procured with difficulty, for at first no landlord could be found courageous enough to let a house for so dangerous a purpose. At length, however, one Cooper was prevailed upon to take the risk, and the flag was hung out . . .

On Saturday the 23rd of February 1793, at the hour of half-past seven in the evening, a mob of a thousand persons, of whom many were women, suddenly appeared before the rendezvous. The first intimation of what was about to happen came in the shape of a furious volley of brickbats and stones, which instantly demolished every window in the house, to the utter consternation of its inmates. Worse, however, was in store for them. An attempt to rush the place was temporarily frustrated by the determined opposition of the gang, who, fearing that all in the house would be murdered, succeeded in holding the mob at bay for an hour and a half; but at nine o'clock, several of the gangsmen having been in the meantime struck down and incapacitated by stones, which were rained upon the devoted building without cessation, the door at length gave way before an onslaught with capstan-bars, and the mob swarmed in unchecked. A scene of indescribable confusion and fury ensued. Savagely assaulted and mercilessly beaten, the gangsmen and the unfortunate landlord were thrown into the street more dead than alive, every article of furniture on the premises was reduced to fragments, and when the mob at length drew off, hoarsely jubilant over the destruction it had wrought, nothing remained of His Majesty's rendezvous save bare walls and gaping windows. Even these were more than the townsfolk could endure the sight of. Next evening they reappeared upon the scene, intending to finish what they had begun by pulling the house down or burning it to ashes; but the timely arrival of troops frustrating their design, they regretfully dispersed.

On intercepting a likely customer at sea, the officer in charge of the press could only execute his orders by boarding the ship and producing his warrant. This did not always prove to be straightforward:

The first intimation the intended victim had of the fate in store for her was the shriek of the roundshot athwart her bows. This was the signal, universally known as such, for her to back her topsails and await the coming of the gang, already tumbling in ordered haste into the armed boat prepared for them under the tender's quarter. And yet it was not always easy for the sprat to catch the whale. A variety of factors entered into the problem and made for failure as often as for success. Sometimes the tender's powder was bad – so bad that in spite of an extra pound or so added to the charge, the shot could not be got to carry as far as a common musket ball. When this was the case her commander suffered a double mortification. His shot, the symbol of authority and coercion, took the water far short of its destined goal, whilst the vessel it was intended to check and intimidate surged by amid the derisive cat-calls and laughter of her crew.

Even with the powder beyond reproach, ships did not always obey the summons, peremptory though it was. One pretended not to hear it, or to misunderstand it, or to believe it was meant for some other craft, and so held stolidly on her course, vouchsafing no sign till a second shot, fired point-blank, but at a safe elevation, hurtled across her decks and brought her to her senses. Another, perhaps some well-armed Levantine trader or tall Indiaman whose crew had little mind to strike their colours submissively at the behest of a midget press-smack, would pipe to quarters and put up a stiff fight for liberty and the dear delights of London town – a fight from which the tender, supposing her to have accepted the gage of battle, rarely came off victor.

The last straw for the master of a ship boarded by the press was that he was required to pay the cost of the shot and powder expended before persuading her to heave to and submit to examination. This money was the perquisite of the gunner.

To avoid being pressed afloat, sailors would go to extreme lengths to escape detection by the boarding party. The ship in which one would-be evader hid with disastrous results is described as a 'snow' – a two-masted brig common in European waters at the time.

> About five o'clock in the afternoon of the 25th of June 1756, Capt. William Boys, from the quarterdeck of his ship the *Royal Sovereign*, then riding at anchor at the Nore, observed a snow on fire in the five-fathom channel, a little below the Spoil Buoy. He immediately sent his cutter to her assistance, but in spite of all efforts to save her she ran aground and burnt to the water's edge. Her cargo consisted of wine, and the loss of the vessel was occasioned by one of her crew, who was fearful of being pressed, hiding himself in the hold with a lighted candle. He was burnt with the ship.

There were many categories of sailors who made the press-gang's job easier. Smugglers had no chance – once intercepted. Nor did those with false protection papers, which could be obtained for a fee in many seaports, notably in North America.

From the smuggling vessels infesting the coasts the sea-going gangs drew sure returns and rich booty. In the south and east of England people who were 'in the know' could always buy tobacco, wines and silks for a mere song; and in Cumberland, in the coast towns there, and inland too, the very beggars are said to have regaled themselves on tea at sixpence or a shilling the pound. These commodities, as well as others dealt in by runners of contraband, were worth far more on the water than on land, and none was so keenly alive to the fact as the gangsman who prowled the coast. Animated by the prospect of double booty, he was by all odds the best 'preventive man' the country ever had.

There was certainty, too, about the pressing of a smuggler that was wanting in other cases. The sailor taken out of a merchant ship, or the fisherman out of a smack, might at the eleventh hour spring upon you a protection good for his discharge. Not so the smuggler. There was in his case no room for the unexpected. No form of protection could save him from the consequences of his trade. Once caught, his fate was a foregone conclusion, for he carried with him evidence enough to make him a pressed man twenty times over. Hence the gangsman and the naval officer loved the smuggler and lost no opportunity of showing their affection.

*

American protections were the Admiralty's pet bugbear. For many years after the successful issue of the War of Independence a bitter animosity characterized the attitude of the British naval officer towards the American sailor. Whenever he could be laid hold of he was pressed, and no matter what documents he produced in evidence of his American birth and citizenship, those documents were almost invariably pronounced false and fraudulent.

There were weighty reasons, however, for refusing to accept the claim of the alleged American sailor at its face value. No class of protection was so generally forged, so extensively bought and sold, as the American. Practically every British seaman who made the run to an American port took the precaution, during his sojourn in that land of liberty, to provide himself with spurious papers against his return to England, where he hoped, by means of them, to checkmate the gang. The process of obtaining such papers was simplicity itself. All the sailor had to do, at, say, New York, was to apply himself to one Riley, whose other name was Paddy. The sum of three dollars having changed hands, Riley and his client betook themselves to the retreat of some shady Notary Public, where the Irishman made ready oath that the British seaman was as much American born as himself. The business was now as good as done, for on the strength of this lying affidavit any Collector of Customs on the Atlantic coast would for a trifling fee grant the sailor a certificate of citizenship. Riley created American citizens in this way at the rate, it is said, of a dozen a day . . .

There were happier and less violent ways of commissioning a ship than resorting to the crude methods of the local regulating officer. If a popular captain was moving from one command to his next, without a delay that the Admiralty would refuse to finance by keeping the sailors on the books, they might volunteer *en bloc*.

Lord Dundonald asserts that he was only once obliged to resort to pressing – a statement so remarkable, considering the times he lived in, as to call for explanation. The occasion was when, returning from a year's 'exile in a tub,' a converted collier that 'sailed like a hay-stack,' he fitted out the *Pallas* at Portsmouth and could obtain no volunteers. Setting his gangs to work, he got together a scratch crew of the wretchedest description; yet so marvellous were the personality and disciplinary ability of the man, that with only this unpromising material ready to his hand he intercepted the Spanish trade off Cape Finisterre and captured four successive prizes of very great value. The *Pallas* returned to Portsmouth with 'three large golden candlesticks, each about five feet high, placed upon the mast-heads,' and from that time onward Dundonald's reputation as a 'lucky' commander was made. He never again had occasion to invoke the aid of the gang.

There were several reasons why the press-gangs were no longer needed soon after the beginning of the nineteenth century. After Trafalgar the fleet did not require so many ships or men. At about that time someone in the Admiralty must have realized that the average number of men raised by the press-gangs rarely exceeded the number of men employed in obtaining them.

While the average cost of 'listing a man 'volunteerly' rarely exceeded the modest sum of 30s., the expense entailed through recruiting him by means of the press-gang ranged from 3s. 9d. per head in 1570 to £114 in 1756. Between these extremes his cost fluctuated in the most extraordinary manner. At Weymouth, in 1762, it was at least £100; at Deal, in 1805, £32 odd; at Poole, in the same year, £80. From 1756 the average steadily declined until in 1795 it touched its eighteenth century minimum of about £6. A sharp upward tendency then developed, and in the short space of eight years it soared again to £20. It was at this figure that Nelson, perhaps the greatest naval authority of his time, put it in 1803.

Up to this point we have considered only the prime cost of the pressed man. A secondary factor must now be introduced, for when you had got your man at an initial cost of £20 – a cost in itself out of all proportion to his value – you could never be sure of keeping him. Nelson calculated that during the war immediately preceding 1803 forty-two thousand seamen deserted from the fleet. Assuming, with him, that every man of this enormous total was either a pressed man or had been procured at the cost of a pressed man, the loss entrailed upon the nation by their desertion represented an outlay of £840,000 for raising them in the first instance, and, in the second, a further outlay of £840,000 for replacing them.

In this estimate there is, however, a substantial error; for, approaching the question from another point of view, let us suppose, as we may safely do without overstraining the probabilities of the case, that out of every three men pressed at least one ran from his rating. Now the primary cost of pressing three men on the £20 basis being £60, it follows that in order to obtain their ultimate cost to the country we must add to that sum the outlay incurred in pressing another man in lieu of the one who ran. The total cost of the three men who ultimately remain to the fleet consequently works out at £80; the cost of each at £26, 13s. 4d. Hence Nelson's forty-two thousand deserters entailed upon the nation an actual expenditure, not of £1,680,000, but of nearly two and a quarter millions.

Writing a few years before the outbreak of the First World War, J. R. Hutchinson concludes his definitive history of the press-gang on an optimistic note:

Its memory still survives. Those who despair of military system, or of our lack of it, talk conscription. They alone forget. A people who for a hundred years patiently endured conscription in its most cruel form will never again suffer it to be lightly inflicted upon them.

from *The Press Gang* by J. R. Hutchinson

There were many devices for claiming exemption from the arbitrary methods of selection chosen by the press-gangs. But the odds were loaded against the victims:

I remember one night we wanted some men at the breaking out of the war in 1803 to man the *Victory*, and, as a pressgang was to be sent, I thought I'd go and see the fun. Accordingly, at the time the boat was to land at Gosport, I crossed over in a shore-boat and arrived just at the same time as a magistrate, who was appointed to accompany the gang, in order to prevent any row and to make people open their doors. It was dark and the men were armed with stretchers – pieces of wood just as well in their proper places as flourishing about a man's head, especially if he has not his hat on. The lieutenant who commanded the party was one of your steady kind of men who never makes a noise about anything, but who always gains his point. When we got near a small public-house and heard several voices, he directed his men to stand in such situations as to prevent any escapes; and said he, 'Take care you don't use any violence, my lads; but if the fellows won't stop, knock them down.' We were all in a regular cut-throat alley, and the magistrate, who said he was a peace-officer, did not like our preparations for war.

The lieutenant and two of the stoutest men entered the house, and the chaps inside soon stopped their singing.

'Who are you?' said the officer to one of the warblers.

'A barber,' said he, 'and I should like to know what business it is of yours?'

'You are just the shaver we want. Johnson, hand this fellow out!'

'I shan't go for you, or your Johnson either. I'm an apprentice and you can't take me.'

'Johnson,' said the officer and in a moment the barber was saved the trouble of paying his bill, and handed outside, where he would have called 'murder' had not one of the men stopped him by nearly committing the act.

'Who are you?' said the officer to another.

'A shoemaker, sir.' The affair of the barber had rendered him a little more civil.

'Just the very man we wanted to show our chaps how to cover the foremast-swifter with hide – Johnson – '

'I'm a married man with a family, sir, and I understand you only take seafaring men. My wife will be ruined, and the children left to starve, if you take me: they are dependent on my exertions. I hope, sir, you will consider this, and what she will suffer, poor soul! in her present situation, if you take me on board.'

'Ah, you are a civil, well-behaved man; but you have got too many children, and I shall be doing the parish a service by giving you employment elsewhere – Johnson – '

'Shame, shame!' said about a dozen ill-looking fellows. 'You shan't take Leathersoles without a fight for it! Come, my lads, one and all! Our only chance is a fair fight; for if that fellow takes one by one, we must go without resistance.'

Up they jumped, doused the lights, and made a rally. The boatswain's mate, who was with us, gave a pipe; all of our men crowded sail towards the house, when out went the lieutenant, Johnson, Peters, and myself, followed by these ragamuffins, who had nearly killed the officer, and split the head of Johnson by throwing a pewter-pot at him. Leathersoles fought like a demon; but he got a tap on the skull-cap from one of the *Victory's* men, which made him a bit of an astronomer: for he saw more stars flying about than any man who ever sailed on the Pacific. The rest got away, everyone of them but the barber and the shoemaker, and we were going towards the boat, when a woman, with about six children, came running after us. The little ones clung to the lieutenant, saying, 'Oh! save father! save father!' whilst the woman threw her arms round Leathersoles, and declared she would die if he was taken from her. The magistrate had topped his boom directly the scuffle began: he was gone, he said, for assistance, although he never rendered any.

The officer spoke kindly, but the woman would not listen to any reason.

'Give me my husband!' she said. 'Oh! what shall I do! I shall starve – I shall starve! Sir,' said she, as she knelt down to the lieutenant, holding him fast round the knees, 'if ever you knew what it was to leave your mother – to be torn from your wife – to be compelled to abandon your children to poverty and the poorhouse, do not be guilty of this cruelty! Leave me my Tom – it's only one man – and look at these dear little innocents, who will pray for you. See, sir, I shall shortly be a mother again. Oh! what shall I do, what shall I do!' and here she began twisting her hands and swabbing her eyes with her dress . . .

'It's very distressing,' said the lieutenant to the midshipman, 'very indeed; a most unpleasant service; and in this case, if we had taken the rest, we might have strained a point and released the shoemaker.'

'Oh! do, sir, do!' said the woman; and, as she extended her arms to clasp the officer and bless him, a large pillow dropped from under her dress. She saw that it was all over, so she caught up her burden and, having got a few yards distant, fired a volley of mud at us. She was one of your regular ladies who act as mothers every night of impressment.

from *Ben Brace, the Last of Nelson's Agamemnons* by Captain Frederick Chamier

After the era of the tea-clippers, sailing ships had to look for new fields in which they could compete for cargoes with steamers. Through the turn of the century profits could still be made by taking coal to Peru and bringing back nitrates. Their last viable trade on a big scale was to bring back wheat from Australia by way of Cape Horn, which continued until the outbreak of war in 1939. Some of those ships survive as training ships or museums.

The steel ships thus employed were very different from the racing clippers. Their task was to carry as much cargo as possible with a small crew backed by mechanical sail-handling. Grain was not perishable, so the notion of racing home the first of a new season's harvest was little but a publicity stunt. Most of them were more than three times the size of the old clippers, over 3,000 tons gross and 350 feet long. The most favoured rig was a four-masted barque carrying 45,000 square feet of sail. Captain Gustav Erikson of Mariehamn in Finland had thirteen of them in commission and actively trading throughout the 1930s. One of them was *Moshulu*, for which the author Eric Newby gave up his career in a smart West End advertising agency to sail before the mast as a totally inexperienced apprentice. He joined her in Belfast, where she was unloading the last of her cargo of 4,500 tons of wheat from her previous voyage. Rather like Evelyn Waugh's account of being outfitted for his assignment to Abyssinia as a war correspondent in *Scoop*, he got off the ferry from Heysham with Vuitton luggage and the smartest line in Gieves' foul-weather gear. Then he met the second mate with a hangover:

The Second Mate was thin, watery-eyed and bad-tempered. At sea he was to prove much better than he looked to me this morning. He did not like ports and he did not like to see the ship in her present state. My arrival did not seem propitious and after dressing me down for not reporting aft directly I had come on board, he suddenly shot at me: 'Ever been aloft before?'

'No, sir.'

We were standing amidships by the mainmast. He pointed to the lower main shrouds which supported the mast and said simply: 'Op you go then.' I could scarcely believe my ears. I had imagined that I should be allowed at least a day or two to become used to the ship and the feel of things, but this was my introduction to discipline. I looked at the Mate. He had a nasty glint in his eye and I decided I was more afraid of him than of the rigging. If I was killed it would be his fault, not mine, I said to myself with little satisfaction. Nevertheless I asked him if I could change my shoes which had slippery soles.

'Change your shoes? Op the rigging.' He was becoming impatient.

At this time *Moshulu* was the greatest sailing ship in commission, and probably the tallest. Her main mast cap was 198 feet above the keel. I started towards the main rigging on the starboard side nearest the quay but was brought back by a cry from the Mate.

'Babord, port side. If you fall you may fall in the dock. When we're at sea you will always use the weather rigging, that's the side from which the wind blows. Never the lee rigging. And when I give you an order you repeat it.'

'Op the rigging,' I said.

The first part of the climb seemed easy enough. The lower main shrouds supporting the mast were of heavy wire made from plough steel and the first five ratlines were iron bars seized across four shrouds to make a kind of ladder which several men could climb at once. Above them the ratlines were wooden bars seized to the two centre shrouds only, the space for the feet becoming narrower as they converged at the 'top', eighty feet up, where it was difficult to insert a foot as large as mine in the ratlines at all. Before reaching this point, however, I came abreast of the main yard. It was of tapered steel, ninety-five and a half feet from arm to arm, two and a half feet in diameter at the centre and weighed over five tons. It was trussed to the mainmast by an iron axle and preventer chain which allowed it to be swung horizontally from side to side by means of tackle to the yardarms; an operation know as 'bracing'.

Above me was the 'top', a roughly semi-circular platform with gratings in it. This was braced to the mast by steel struts called futtock shrouds. To get to the 'top' I had to climb outwards on the rope ratlines seized to

63

the futtock shrouds. There was a hole in the 'top' which it was considered unsporting to use. I only did so once for the experience and cut my ear badly on a sharp projection which was probably put there as a deterrent. I found difficulty in reaching the top this first time and remained transfixed, my back nearly parallel with the deck below, whilst I felt for a rope ratline with one foot. I found it at last and heaved myself, nearly sick with apprehension, on to the platform, where I stood for a moment, my heart thumping. There was only a moment's respite, in which I noticed that the mainmast and the topmast were in one piece – not doubled as in most sailing ships – before the dreadful voice of the Mate came rasping up at me:

'Get on op.'

The next part was nearly fifty feet of rope ratlines seized to the topmast shrouds. Almost vertical, they swayed violently as I went aloft; many of them were rotten and one broke underfoot when I was at the level of the topsail yards. Again the voice from the deck:

'If you want to live, hold on to those shrouds and leave the bloody ratlines alone.'

The lower topsail yard was slung from an iron crane but the upper topsail yard above it was attached to a track on the foreside of the topmast allowing the yard to be raised by means of a halliard more than twenty-five feet almost to the level of the crosstrees. The crosstrees formed an open frame of steel girdering about 130 feet up, at the heel of the topgallant mast. Originally the topsail had been a single sail, but to make it easier for the reduced crews to take in sail, it had been divided into two. At the moment the upper topsail yard was in its lowered position, immediately on top of the lower topsail yard. The crosstrees seemed flimsy when I reached them; two long arms extended aft from the triangle, spreading the backstays of the royal mast, the highest mast of all. I stood gingerly on this slippery construction; the soles of my shoes were like glass; all Belfast spread out below. I looked between my legs down to a deck as thin as a ruler and nearly fell from sheer funk.

'Op to the royal yard,' came the imperious voice, fainter now. Another forty feet or so of trembling topgallant shroud, past the lower and upper topgallant yards, the upper one, like the upper topsail yard, movable on its greased track. The ratlines were very narrow now and ceased altogether just below the level of the royal yard.

I was pretty well all in emotionally and physically but the by now expected cry of 'Out on the yard' helped me to heave myself on to it. In doing so I covered myself with grease from the mast track on which the royal yard moved up and down. It was fifty feet long and thinner than those below it. As on all the other yards, an iron rail ran along the top. This was the jackstay, to which the sail was bent. (In cadet training ships this rail would have had another parallel to hold on to, as, with the sail bent to the forward jackstay, there was little or no handhold. *Moshulu* had not been built for cadets and this refinement was lacking. With no sails bent what I had to do was easy, but I did not appreciate my good fortune at the time.) Underneath the yard was a wire rope which extended the length of it and was supported half-way between the mast and either yard-arm by vertical stirrups. This footrope was called the 'horse' and when I ventured out on it I found it slippery as well as slack so that both feet skidded in opposite directions, leaving me like a dancer about to do the splits, hanging on grimly to the jackstay.

'Out. Right out to the yardarm,' came the Mate's voice, fainter still. I hated him at this moment. There were none of the 'joosts' and 'ploddys' of the stylized Scandinavian to make me feel superior to this grim officer. He spoke excellent English.

Somehow I reached the yardarm. I tried to rest my stomach on it, and stick my legs out behind me but I was too tall; the footrope came very close up to the yard at this point, where it was shackled to the brace pendant, and my knees reached to the place on the yard where the riggers had intended my stomach to be, so that I had the sensation of pitching headlong over it. Fortunately there was a lift shackled to the yardarm band, a wire tackle which supported the yard in its lowered position, and to this I clung whilst I looked about me.

What I saw was very impressive and disagreeable. By now I had forgotten what the Mate had said about falling into the dock and I was right out at the starboard yardarm, 160 feet above the sheds into which *Moshulu's* 62,000 sacks of grain were being unloaded. The rooftops of these sheds were glass and I remember wondering what would happen it I fell. Would I avoid being cut to pieces by the maze of wires below, or miss them and make either a large expensive crater in the roof or a smaller one shaped like me? I also wondered what kind of technique the ambulance men employed to scoop up what was left of people who fell from such heights. I tried to dismiss these melancholy thoughts but the beetle-like figures on the dock below that were stevedores only accentuated my remoteness. The distant prospect was more supportable: a tremendous panorama beyond the city to the Antrim Hills and far up the Lough to the sea.

'Orlright,' called the Mate. 'Come in to the mast.' I did so with alacrity, but was not pleased when he told me to go to the truck on the very top of the mast. I knew that with these blasted shoes I could never climb the bare pole, so I took them off, and my socks too, and wedged them under the jackstay.

There were two or three very rotten ratlines seized across the royal backstays. The lowest broke under my weight so I used the backstays alone to climb up to the level of the royal halliard sheave to which the yard was raised when sail was set. Above this was nothing. Only six feet of bare pole to the truck. I was past caring whether I fell or not.

I embraced the royal mast and shinned up. The wind blew my hair over my nose and made me want to sneeze. I stretched out my arm and grasped

65

the round hardwood cap 198 feet above the keel and was surprised to find it was not loose or full of chocolate creams as a prize. Now the bloody man below me was telling me to sit on it, but I ignored him. I could think of no emergency that would make it necessary. So I slid down to the royal halliard and to the yard again.

'You can come down now,' shouted the Mate. I did. It was worse than going up and more agonizing as I was barefoot, with my shoes stuffed inside my shirt.

'You were a fool to take your shoes off,' said the Mate when I reached the deck. 'Now you can learn to clean the lavatories.'

from The Last Grain Race by Eric Newby

After a fast outward passage of eighty-two days *Moshulu* was the first of the thirteen grain ships to reach a European port when she called at Queenstown for orders at the end of a passage by way of Cape Horn in ninety-one days. Apart from the evidence that his sense of humour remained intact throughout, Eric Newby's enduring legacy of this voyage are the photographs in his book, many of them taken from aloft during gales in the Southern Ocean using the sort of camera then regarded as suitable for family picnics.

Selecting an Ocean-Racing Crew

The best writers who spin their magic against the background of the oceans are conscious that nothing has changed at sea since the Third Day of Creation, when the land emerged. Sailors need to be reminded that they have to answer the same questions today as those posed by Homer and Hakluyt.

No one realized this better than Bill Snaith, the industrial designer, *bon viveur* and fiercely competitive skipper in a succession of beautiful yawls all called *Figaro*, for he loved Mozart marginally more than J. S. Bach just as he preferred Montecristo No. 1s to 5–cent stogies and vintage clarets from the Medoc to anything bottled in the Napa Valley.

After he was placed second three times in the Fastnet Race and received only a cheap bronze medallion for his trophy-case, he designed a spectacular perpetual Royal Ocean Racing Club trophy for the runner-up – a seahorse set in an elliptical-section column of acrylic on a black plinth. His outright successes included the 1960 Transatlantic Race and the 1963 SORC (Southern Ocean Racing Conference, a winter series of inshore races sailed in Florida and the Bahamas, certainly the most prestigious achievement for any ocean-racer). *Figaro*'s appearances in the winner's enclosure were in no small measure due to his awareness that her performance was predetermined by those he chose to form her crew.

Unlike the raffish sweeping of Portsmouth and Plymouth waterfronts who willy-nilly gloried with Hawkins and Drake, and Nelson, modern ocean racers are gentlemen sailors who must meet rigorous standards.

1. *In the matter of race committee certification*: A crew must have demonstrable experience. If a ship is lost and everyone drowns, the papers will be filled with public wailings. The committees will be properly sad, of course, but, worse, it might endanger the sport. The drowning must, therefore, be on your own head. The committee cannot be placed in a position of blame as being lax and frivolous in certifying a boat ready to race.

2. *In the matter of crew's approval of one another*: To be locked up in a small, unprivate, jostling space capsule with strange people for several weeks is like being placed in a culture breeding flask in a laboratory. Any small infection is bound to wax, swell, and break out in epidemic proportions. The ideal crew member is a rare creature indeed. He has the coolness, courage, and derring-do of James Bond; the inventiveness and mechanical skills of Tom Swift; the agility and strength of an Olympic decathlon winner; and the winning ways and affableness of a graduate *summa cum laude* of the Dale Carnegie Institute of charm. He has a fund of new stories, is a good listener, and is as neat in his cabin habits as Mr. Clean.

You start with these requirments and settle for what you get. But you must be close. His crewmates must enjoy the pleasure of his company. Else who needs it? Do you go through all that palaver in convincing a wife and sweetheart that an absence of three and a half weeks will have salubrious effects on your idyll? Do you lay your career on the line convincing the boss that you can be absent for an amount of time beyond your regular vacation without injury to the flow of work and without giving him the idea that he might do without you altogether?

3. *In the matter of reassuring the captain-owner*: A crew should be skillful enough to reassure the captain in the secret fastness of his heart. The captain must know that when all hell breaks loose and he doesn't know what it's all about, someone aboard does and what's more will do something about it.

Few Sunday captains are equipped to make such personnel decisions, although training in decision making is built into our democratic society. It is the curse of a goal-oriented society; all parents apparently wish to bequeath this symbol of power and achievement to their children.

*

. . . there comes a time when one man must decide – as in choosing a crew. I have had minimal early training in the arts of command, having failed miserably with my square and round blocks and was therefore abandoned at the outset to the lesser cadres. I turned out to be a late bloomer, but no machinery existed in my day to bring this latent promise out. In my stumbling progress, I fell into yacht ownership, and in spite of the clear prerogatives that go with that estate, I share many of the same hesitations as my *beau ideal*, Horatio, Lord Hornblower. Like him, I kept my hesitations under an icy calm, except of course when I begin to holler and yell. Because of this underrunning uncertainty I am loath to switch around in the matter of crew, seeking for the bubble, quintessence. When I find a man who is capable, who knows what he is doing, does not feel demeaned by a turn in the galley, and above all is a delight to be with and who can tell stories, I bind him to me with bands of iron. All the men aboard are old friends. I am happy to call my young son MacLeod an old friend. We have all sailed the ocean together and know one another's ways. If I knowingly had to pick a crew with whom to be dismasted at sea in a boat equipped with leaking tanks, I could choose none better than these.

(My fingers are crossed. I hope this mention of dismasting remains an abstract. It is sheer carelessness to talk this way.)

This crew meets all the standards enumerated earlier, as well as certain further requirements of my own. There is the matter of age. In certain circles an average crew age above the midtwenties is considered over the hill, ready for the glue factory. In order for me to average out, I would need to take along my grandson, Colman. Besides, I don't always hold with the certain circles. I think them overly influenced by around the buoy racing – one all-out afternoon and then to the hot showers. Ocean racing is made up of many bad afternoons, ugly mornings, and hard nights. It calls for the long slog in conditions which, endured in other circumstances, would be considered as a sampling of the Grand Inquisitor's best. I find that the young tend to burn out early. They need more sleep and do not know how to husband their strength.

There is the hoary farmer's story of the bright young bull and his sage old companion at stud that makes the point succinctly. Says the young bull, noticing a break in the fence leading to the panting, virginal young heifers. 'Let's rush down there and ravish us one of them cuties apiece.' The old bull, first lifting a lid over a rheumy eye, then with a slight twitch of his muzzle, drawls 'Let's walk down and do the lot.'

from *On the Wind's Way* by William Snaith

68

Discipline

Since time immemorial the authority of the captain of a ship has been protected by savage disciplinary measures against any internal challenge. Until this century conviction for mutiny has meant either hanging from the yardarm or a bullet from a firing squad. In this century the odds swung in favour of the mutineers' survival, starting at Leningrad in the battleship *Potemkin*; then again at Invergordon, when the ugly word was never officially used to describe lower-deck action over which the officers temporarily lost control; likewise the Communist-inspired mutiny of the Royal Hellenic Navy for which none of the offenders paid the ultimate penalty.

In spite of this encouraging trend, few dared to take the final step of removing a naval captain from his command at sea, no matter to what extent he might have provoked his officers and men by tyranny, cowardice or dangerous incompetence. There was an American submarine in the Pacific whose commanding officer did not prosecute the war with sufficient zeal against some juicy targets of opportunity soon after Pearl Harbor. The executive officer confined the skipper to his cabin for the rest of the patrol. Fortunately he then sank several Japanese ships, so returned to base a hero, and nothing more was said about the captain.

A similar scenario developed on board the old First World War four-stacker *Caine* in Herman Wouk's classic novel set against the true story of three US Navy destroyers lost by capsizing in a typhoon, due to being ordered to replenish at sea on a downwind course. Lieutenant-Commander Queeg's handling of this situation, when all contact with his task force commander had been lost, was the last straw for the executive officer, Lieutenant Steve Maryk. He had been brooding over the captain's paranoia for months, keeping a detailed note of each incident which one day might justify any action he found necessary *in extremis*.

That night the executive officer wrote a long entry in his medical log. When he was through he put away the folder, locked his safe, and took down the fat blue-bound *Navy Regulations* volume. He opened the book, looked over his shoulder at the curtained doorway, then rose and slid shut the metal door, which was almost never used in the tropics. He turned to Article 184 and read aloud slowly, in a monotonous mutter: '*It is conceivable that most unusual and extraordinary circumstances may arise in which the relief from duty of a commanding officer by a subordinate becomes necessary, either by placing him under arrest or on the sick list; but such an action shall never by taken without the approval of the Navy Department or other appropriate higher authority, except when reference to such higher authority is undoubtedly impracticable because of the delay involved or for other clearly obvious reason . . .'*

USS *Caine* had just been ordered to make a 180° alteration of course when the typhoon was at its worst. The new course would put her in grave danger of broaching.

'Come left to 180'

'Sir, we can't ride stern to wind and save this ship,' said the exec.

'Left to 180 helmsman.'

'Hold it, Stilwell,' said Maryk.

'Mr. Maryk, fleet course is 180.' The captain's voice was faint, almost whispering. He was looking glassily ahead.

'Captain, we've lost contact with the formation – the radars are blacked out –'

'Well, then, we'll find them – I'm not disobeying orders on account of some bad weather –'

The helmsman said 'Steady on 000 –'

Maryk said, 'Sir, how do we know what the orders are now? The guide's antennas may be down – ours may be – call up Sunshine and tell him we're in trouble –'

Butting and plunging, the *Caine* was a riding ship again. Willie felt the normal vibration of the engines, the rhythm of seaworthiness in the pitching, coming up from the deck into the bones of his feet. Outside the pilothouse there was only the whitish darkness of the spray and the dismal whine of the wind, going up and down in shivery glissandos.

'We're not in trouble,' said Queeg. 'Come left to 180.'

'Steady as you go!' Maryk said at the same instant. The helmsman looked around from one officer to the other, his eyes popping in panic.

'Do as I say!' shouted the executive officer. He turned on the OOD.

'Willie, note the time.' He strode to the captain's side and saluted. 'Captain, I'm sorry, sir, you're a sick man. I am temporarily relieving you of command of this ship, under Article 184 of *Navy Regulations.*'

'I don't know what you're talking about,' said Queeg. 'Left to 180, helmsman.'

'Mr Keith, *you're* the OOD here, what the hell should I do?' cried Stilwell.

Willie was looking at the clock. It was fifteen minutes to ten. He was dumbfounded to think he had had the deck less than two hours. The import of what was taking place between Maryk and Queeg penetrated his mind slowly. He could not believe it was happening. It was as incredible as his own death.

'Never you mind about Mr. Keith,' said Queeg to Stilwell, a slight crankiness entering his voice, fantastically incongruous under the circum-

70

stances. It was a tone he might have used to complain of a chewing-gum wrapper on the deck. 'I told you to come left. That's an order. Now you come left, and fast –'

'Commander Queeg, you aren't issuing orders on this bridge any more,' said Maryk. 'I have relieved you, sir. You're on the sick list. I'm taking the responsibility. I know I'll be court-martialled. I've got the conn –'

'You're under arrest, Maryk. Get below to your room,' said Queeg. 'Left to 180, I say!'

'Christ, Mr. Keith!' exclaimed the helmsman, looking at Willie. Urban had backed into the farthest corner of the wheelhouse. He stared from the exec to Willie, his mouth open. Willie glanced at Queeg, glued to the telegraph, and at Maryk. He felt a surge of immense drunken gladness.

'Steady on ooo, Stilwell,' he said. 'Mr. Maryk has the responsibility. Captain Queeg is sick.'

'Call your relief, Mr. Keith,' the captain said at the same instant, with something like real anger. 'You're under arrest too.'

'You have no power to arrest me, Mr Queeg,' said Willie.

Later another officer makes his way to the bridge and finds that there has been a critical confrontation.

'What's the dope, Willie? What goes on?' yelled Keefer.

'Steve relieved the captain!'

'*What?*'

'Steve relieved the captain! He's got the conn! He's put the captain on the sick list!' The officers looked at each other and lunged for the wheelhouse. Willie edged to the rear bulkhead and peered around at the blurry barometer. He dropped to his hands and knees and crawled back to the pilothouse. 'Steve, it's up,' he cried, jumping to his feet as he came to the doorway. 'It's up! Twenty-eight ninety-nine, almost 29.00!'

'Good, maybe we'll be through the worst of it in a while.' Maryk stood beside the wheel, facing aft. All the officers except Paynter were grouped, dripping, against the bulkhead. Queeg was hanging to the telegraph again, glaring at the exec. 'Well, that's the story, gentlemen,' Maryk said, his voice pitched high over the roar of the wind and the rattle of spray on the windows. 'The responsibility is entirely mine. Captain Queeg will continue to be treated with the utmost courtesy, but I will give all command orders –'

'Don't kid yourself that the responsibility is all yours,' Queeg interposed sulkily. 'Young Mr. Keith here supported you in your mutinous conduct from the start and he'll pay just as you will. And you officers' – he turned, shaking his finger at them – 'if you know what's good for you, will advise Maryk and Keith to put themselves under arrest and restore command to me while the restoring is good. I may be induced to overlook what's happened in view of the circumstances, but –'

'It's out of the question, Captain,' said Maryk. 'You're sick, sir –'

71

'I'm no sicker than you are,' exclaimed Queeg with all his old irritation. 'You'll all hang for collusion in mutiny, I kid you not about that –' 'Nobody will hang but me,' said Maryk to the officers. 'This is my act, taken without anybody's advice, under Article 184, and if I've misapplied Article 184, I'll get hung for it. Meantime all of you take my orders. There's nothing else you can do. I've taken command, I've ballasted on my own responsibility, the ship is on the course I ordered –'

from *The Caine Mutiny* by Herman Wouk

To the end Queeg tries to reassert his authority, especially after the worst of the danger has past and the barometer is rising.

To this day commanding officers are required by the Queen's Regulations and Admiralty Instructions to read extracts from the Articles of War to the ship's company, usually as part of the ceremony of pronouncing a punishment approved by warrant (of a flag officer) for serious offences. There is still a range of offences which, in the immortal words of the Articles, are described as being 'punishable by death or such other punishments as may hereinafter be mentioned'. But in the days of George II the alternative did not always apply. Richard Parker paid the penalty for leading the mutiny at the Nore in 1797 by being strung up with full ceremonial. On another occasion the Royal Navy decided that pragmatism should rule the day:

The penalty for desertion, under a well-known statute of George I., was death by hanging. As time went on, however, discipline in this respect suffered a grave relapse, and fear of the halter no longer served to check the continual exodus from the fleet. If the runaway sailor were taken, 'it would only be a whipping bout.' So he openly boasted. The 'bout' it is true at times ran to six, or even seven hundred lashes – the latter being the heaviest dose of the cat ever administered in the British navy; but even this terrible ordeal had no power to hold the sailor to his duty, and although Admiral Lord St. Vincent, better known in his day as 'hanging Jervis,' did his utmost to revive the ancient custom of stretching the sailor's neck, the trend of the times was against him, and within twenty-five years of the reaffirming of the penalty, in the 22nd year of George II, hanging for desertion had become practically obsolete.

In the declining days of the practice a grim game at life and death was played upon the deck of a king's ship lying in the River St. Lawrence. The year was 1760. Quebec had only recently fallen before the British onslaught. A few days before the event, at a juncture when every man in the squadron was counted upon to play his part in the coming struggle, and to play it well, three seamen, James Mike, Thomas Wilkinson and William M'Millard by name, deserted from the *Vanguard*. Retaken some months later, they were brought to trial; but as men were not easy to replace in that latitude, the court, whilst sentencing all three to suffer the extreme penalty of the law, added to their verdict a rider to the effect that it would be good policy to spare two of them. Admiral Lord Colvill, then Commander-in-Chief, issued his orders accordingly, and at eleven o'clock on the morning of the 12th of July the condemned men, preceded to the scaffold by two chaplains, were led to the *Vanguard's* forecastle, where they drew lots to determine which of them should die. The fatal lot fell to James Mike, who, in presence of the assembled boats of the squadron, was immediately 'turned off' at the foreyard-arm.

from *The Press Gang* by J. R. Hutchinson

Flogging was rarely resorted to after the middle of the nineteenth century: in 1839, 2,007 men were flogged, but by 1847 the figure was down to 860. Officially any captain could award a punishment of up to twelve lashes, but this was often exceeded, especially on independent service, when there was the practical difficulty of obtaining a senior officer's approval (or warrant). This was always needed for the ultimate punishment of being flogged around the fleet. The cat-o'-nine-tails was made up of nine tarred hemp cords, each 18 inches long, hanging from a rope handle, like a fly-whisk. Generally there were three overhand knots tied into each tail. Some surviving specimens have many more knots in them, in order to inflict greater injury. Often ships reserved such 'Thieves' Tails' for punishing those convicted of theft on board, then regarded as the most serious crime short of deserving the noose from the yard-arm. At the time of a flogging the drummers would sound a peculiar cadence to draw attention to the severity of the punishment as a deterrent to others. 'The Rogue's Drum' as it was known survives in the expression describing dismissal from a regiment – being drummed out.

A man sentenced to be flogged around the fleet received an equal part of the whole number of lashes awarded, alongside each ship composing that fleet. For instance, if sentenced to three hundred lashes, in a fleet composed of ten sail, he will receive thirty alongside of each ship.

A launch is fitted up with a platform and sheers. It is occupied by the unfortunate individual, the provost marshal, the boatswain and his mates with their implements of office, and armed marines stationed at the bow and stern. When the signal is made for punishment, all the ships in the fleet send one or two boats each, with crews cleanly dressed, the officers

73

in full uniform, and marines under-arms. These boats collect at the side of the ship where the launch is lying, the hands are turned up, and the ship's company are ordered to mount the rigging, to witness that portion of the whole punishment which, after the sentence has been read, is inflicted upon the prisoner. When he has received the allotted number of lashes, he is, for the time being, released, and permitted to sit down, with a blanket over his shoulders, while the boats, which attend the execution of the sentence, make fast to the launch, and tow it to the next ship in the fleet, where the same number of lashes are inflicted with corresponding ceremonies; – and thus he is towed from one ship to another until he has received the whole of his punishment.

The severity of this punishment consists not only in the number of lashes, but in the peculiar manner in which they are inflicted; as, after the unfortunate wretch has received the first part of his sentence alongside of one ship, the blood is allowed to congeal, and the wounds partially to close, during the interval which takes place previously to his arrival alongside of the next, when the cat again subjects him to renewed and increased torture. During the latter part of the punishment the suffering is dreadful; and a man who has undergone this sentence is generally broken down in constitution, if not in spirits, for the remainder of his life.

from *The King's Own* by Captain Frederick Marryat

Historians vary in their accounts of Nelson's attitude to the standard shipboard punishment – flogging by the boatswain wielding a cat-o'-nine-tails. One contemporary account suggests that Nelson preferred discipline to be enforced by other means:

'Lord Nelson was loth to inflict punishment, and when he was obliged, as he termed it, "to endure the torture of seeing men flogged," he came out of his cabin with hurried steps, ran *into* the gangway, *made his bow to the marine-general*, and reading the Article of War the culprit had infringed, said, *"Boatswain*, do your duty." The lash was instantly applied, and, *consequently*, the sufferer exclaimed, "Forgive me, *Admiral*, forgive me!" – he would look round *with wild* anxiety, and, as all his officers kept silence (when the *fellow really merited* his punishment), he would say, "What! none of you speak for him? – Avast! cast him off! *Jack, in the day of battle remember me*, and be *a good fellow* in future!" – A poor devil was about to be flogged: he was a landsman, and few pitied him – his offence was drunkenness. As he was tying up, a *lovely* girl, contrary to all rules, rushed through officers, and falling on her knees, clasped Nelson's hands, in which were the Articles of War, "Pray forgive him, your honour, and he shall never offend again." – "Your *face*," said he, "is a security for his good behaviour – let *him* go; the *fellow* cannot be bad who has such a *lovely creature* in his care." The *man rose* to be a *lieutenant*; his name was William Pye.'

from *Naval Sketch-book* by Captain W. N. Glascock

Prize-Money

The *London Gazette* is best known nowadays as the journal listing honours and awards. But during Nelson's day it was avidly read by all ranks of the Royal Navy, past and present, for the advertisements inserted by prize agents giving details of captured enemy booty available for distribution.

The scale of shares paid out sounds like the way traffic fines imposed by the Guardia Civil are disposed of, with everyone from the local military governor down to the man on the beat taking his cut according to rank. Today, prize-money is confined to salvage carried out by HM Ships and paid in conformity with international law. So the likelihood of making more than a third dividend on the pools during one's naval career is remote. The only time any came my way was through some unremembered incident in which my submarine had played a bit part. The sum available was so trifling that the wardroom pooled theirs and put it on the wheel in the casino at Tripoli on the stroke of midnight, to be left to multiply until red came up three times. It disappeared into the croupier's bank at the third spin.

Not so in the eighteenth century. The value of a captured prize would first be established at a royal dockyard after survey by master shipwrights appointed by the local flag officer. Note that the final arbiter was the man who stood to gain the most after the captain of the ship which had made the snatch.

They would then list and value everything on board, ranging from sails to anchors, guns to watch glasses, roundshot to copper kettles. The survey report on the hull, masts and spars, and the inventory and valuations, would then be delivered to the Commander-in-Chief, with a suggested price for the ship based on her tonnage.

The Commander-in-Chief would then have to decide whether or not to buy the ship on behalf of the Admiralty (who had eventually to approve the transaction) and the total price. At this time a frigate was worth about £14 a ton, and a 32-gun frigate would total about 750 tons.

Her equipment would comprise hundreds of items and the values would be based on the prices *in Jamaica*. These were the prices charged to merchant ships wanting to buy anything from the naval store, which in turn was usually the price in England plus 60 per cent. Watch glasses (hour and four-hour glasses) would be listed at 2d each; a copper kettle in the galley, used for boiling the bags of meat or puddings, at about £12, which would also be about the price of a maintopgallant sail.

The actual valuations made for a particular captured frigate at this period were £10,038 for the 'hull, masts, yards, booms, rigging and fitted furniture', and £6,057 for the equipment, making a total of £16,095 prize money paid for the ship (providing the Admiralty, in consultation with the Navy Board, approved the prices).

Capturing an enemy merchant ship was a vastly different thing and financially much more dangerous for the captain because he had to produce bills of lading, charter parties and various other documents to get the ship and her cargo 'condemned' by an Admiralty court, a process which put money into the pockets of unscrupulous proctors and lawyers, who hung round courthouses like pimps and crimps lurking on the jetties. Providing ship and cargo were enemy-owned, all was well; but if the master, owners or shippers could prove that the ship was neutral they could – and usually did – sue the Royal Navy captain for damages, which he had to pay out of his own pocket.

Whereas 'head and gun money' was payment divided equally between every man on board the captor, prize money was shared out in a manner which in these more egalitarian days seems both scandalous and startling in its unfairness, although it should be recorded that at the time there was no great outcry.

The total prize money was divided into eighths and then shared out so that the admiral commanding the station or fleet received one-eighth and the captain of the ship two-eighths. The lieutenants, master surgeon and Marine captain shared an eighth; the principal warrant officers, master's mates, chaplain and admiral's secretary had an eighth, midshipmen, inferior warrant officers, mates of principal warrant officers and marine sergeants had an eighth, while the rest of the ship's company shared two-eighths. (This scale was changed in 1808, reducing the admiral's and captain's share.)

All of this meant that the admiral received £2,000 from the capture of the *Beta* frigate and the captain £4,000. There was £285 each for the four lieutenants, master, surgeon and Marine captain, while the next group's share could vary, but would be £222 if there were the boatswain, carpenter, gunner, admiral's secretary, and four master's mates (it was unlikely that a frigate carried a chaplain). The next group received well under £100 each, while there was £4,000 left to be shared among the remaining ship's company which, at this stage of the war, was unlikely to number more than 125, so they would receive £32 each.

The best way of assessing the value of such a prize payment is knowing that the capture of an enemy 32-gun frigate in good condition in the year 1801 was equal to more than thirty-five years' pay for the captain, four years for the lieutenants and master, and just under a year and a half for each able and ordinary seaman.

On top of that came the 'head and gun money', and because such an enemy frigate would have about 250 men on board each member of the ship's company would have more than £5.

These figures show that the man who became rich from prize money was the admiral, whose role usually was, on stations like the West Indies, making sure that his frigates were patrolling areas most likely to yield prizes. Sir Hyde Parker as Commander-in-Chief at Jamaica in the four years referred to earlier was reputed to have made £200,000.

from *Life in Nelson's Navy* by Dudley Pope

Taking Care of Jack

In the days before the ship's doctor's main problems were drunkenness or venereal disease – hence the name 'prick farrier' by which the Royal Navy's medical officers are affectionately known to this day – they had to deal with scurvy, tropical diseases and mangled limbs. Only HM ships and those carrying passengers had doctors, however imperfectly and distantly qualified. The rest had to rely on *The Ship's Captain's Medical Guide*, a long-running best-seller full of laconic advice on clearly recognizable set-piece situations, with a numbered inventory of pills and potions to meet every case which the master diagnosed. There was some straightforward advice about malingering:

> Medical Officers in Public Institutions of all kinds, and penal establishments in particular, have continually to face and deal with cunningly simulated diseases, and every shipmaster at times encounters trouble in this respect.
>
> It is a usual practice among Lascars once a voyage to complain of being sick and to claim 'Dawa' and the privilege of a day's exemption from duty, and to do them justice they are usually content with a day, and come to time the following morning. If they restrict themselves to this you are fortunate and will be wise to concede the point. The systematic shirker and loafer intent on lying up pursues different tactics. 'Pain in the back' is the usual complaint or 'a sort of all-overishness' when there is any special work to be done.
>
> These cases are difficult of detection even for trained medical observers. You have to take into consideration the temperature as shown by the clinical thermometer, the character of the man, his possible motives for simulating illness, and, not least of all, the opinion of his shipmates, who usually sympathize with genuine suffering. A man with a persistent back-

77

ache – a favourite device – is not necessarily a malingerer. You can't say he has not got a pain in his back. Rheumatism and Lumbago are common enough.

Should, however, he insist that the pain is worse when he is lying down or asleep, or supposing your lead pencil accidentally slips from your hand and he springs forward and readily bends to pick it up, you may be pretty sure there is not much amiss.

Many of these cases are an excellent test of your powers of observation and knowledge of human nature. Moreover, a man of sound physical power may honestly believe himself to be suffering acutely. Hysteria and overwrought nerves are by no means confined, as is commonly believed, to the weaker sex. Males are occasionally so affected, and then their morbid self-centred fancies run riot. In genuine shamming and shirking, rest in bed on slop diet, above all no tobacco and no companionship, will soon tire out a malingerer, though some men can do with a heap of such treatment. No hard and fast rule can be laid down for the captain's guidance. If in doubt let the patient have the benefit of it, always bearing in mind that it is better to allow the malingerer to escape than to incur risk of dealing harshly with any man who is really sick.

The Sick Report frequently listed drunkenness as a cause of absence from duty. The advice given by *The Ship's Captain's Medical Guide* on how to prevent it – by providing lots of newspapers and dice games in foreign ports – has not stood the test of time. But the recommended treatment seems a bit excessive:

> Give the patient 30 grains of Sulphate of Zinc [a near cousin to chloroform] in a glass of beer, or any other liquid, to make him vomit. Get everything clear about his neck and waist, rest his head, well raised, on a wet swab and put him in the open air, properly protected from the cold.

Or, as the chorus of the most famous sea shanty of all advises: 'Put him in the longboat till he's sober.' In the general preventive treatment recommended the 'hair of the dog' is endorsed as one of the shots in the physician's locker. The scale of medicinal alcohol carried was surprisingly generous, considering that there was plenty of rum on board and there were fallback stocks in the wardroom. For a merchantman with a crew of twenty-one to forty sailors, the surgeon could call on a case of port and half a dozen bottles of brandy.

> DRUNKENNESS is a fruitful cause of many diseases. Liver complaints, dysentery, dropsy, brain troubles, apoplexy, &c., may often be traced to this cause. Most ships now sail on teetotal principles, so that during the voyage there is no fear of this occurring. Whether in strict moderation, and at the proper times, alcoholic stimulants are useful as an article of diet, is

a matter on which opinions differ, and which it will be unnecessary to discuss; but if they are entirely withdrawn, an extra allowance of coffee or cocoa should be given in their place. It is on shore, and more especially at foreign ports, that drunkenness is most likely to prevail, and the bad quality of the liquor sold is as much to blame as the quantity consumed. Make the ship as comfortable as possible for the men so as to lessen the inducements for them to go on shore where they are liable to become drunk and useless, and to fall into the hands of undesirable persons. Give your men the opportunity of obtaining good tobacco on board, as well as any other extras they may wish to buy, and, at ports where newspapers are published or sold, let them have copies without stint. No ship ought to be without a supply of good books; and draughts, chess, dominoes, and any rational amusements should be encouraged as much as possible.

Every ship is obliged to carry a certain amount of wine and brandy for medical comforts, and it must be borne in mind that these are intended solely for the use of the sick men.

The *Medical Guide* includes a table to help the surgeon diagnose Concussion of the Brain, Intoxication, Opium Poisoning or Apoplexy. He could be forgiven for failing to notice any significant difference in the symptoms for the last two conditions, whilst the treatment recommended for them differs widely.

As the section on Cape Horn describes, frostbite was a widespread problem, but the treatment does not sound very encouraging:

This accident occurs most commonly to coloured seamen, and affects the fingers and toes. Urge your men, when the ship is in cold latitudes, to come to you as soon as their extremeties become red or at all shrunken.

Treatment – Rub gently the parts affected with snow or cold water, and afterwards apply rags wetted with cold water. Do not bring the patient into a warm cabin or near a fire, or the limb may be destroyed.

from *The Ship's Captain's Medical Guide* by Charles Burland

The *Medical Guide* ended with twenty-four listed 'recipes', ranging from the relatively harmless No. 1 – Saline Mixture ('2 tablespoonfuls of a mix of water, bicarbonate of potash and nitrate of potash') to the fiercer No. 19 – Clap Injection ('12 grains of Sulphate of Zinc, 1 drachm of Laudanum and 6 ounces of rain or distilled water'). The different type of water specified in the latter is presumably because the ship's water supply would be presumed to be tainted, at best. The extracts above came from the copy of the *Guide* found in the medicine chest of the royal cutter *Britannia* in daily use up to the end of her racing career in 1936. At the end of each day's racing the chest was taken ashore to Mr Beken's

79

chemist shop in Cowes where the inventory was checked and topped up overnight. It is in the possession of the Beken family to this day.

As often happened, even the most conscientious observance of the advice given in the *Guide* ended with a ceremony on the poop-deck, when the master read the appropriate sentences from the ship's Prayer Book and the weighted hammock was launched over the side, sewn around the body with the last stitch through the dead man's nose.

In the era of the clipper-ships, not long before the *Medical Guide* was first published, the master was already obliged to double as ship's doctor. He carried his own medical stores, which reflected the state of the art in those days. When the abandoned *Bird of Dawning* was boarded by the survivors from *Blackgauntlet* they took an inventory of the captain's medical stores:

All the stores were in excellent order, arranged in lockers on each side of the rudder shaft. The locker to port was the usual ship's medicine-chest with bandages, splints, dressings, and diagrams of men, clamped to cabin tables, undergoing simple operations; some thirty jars of drugs, and scales for weighing the same. The starboard locker at a first glance seemed to contain similar things, there were tins of arrowroot and of beef-jelly, a few tins of preserved milk, and a little ginger and camphor. The main bulk of the goods in this locker proved to be patent medicines for the Captain's private consumption. There were so many of these that Cruiser turned them out on to the cabin deck.

The first to come to hand was a box almost full of 'Dr. Jenkinson's Cholera Powders, the only known specific for this Fatal Complaint.' Next came a discreet bottle for Female Ailments, not otherwise described, and a large assortment of cheap medicines:

Doctor Hoborow's Mixture for the Blood.

Old Doctor Gubbins's Liver Remedy, with a picture of old Doctor Gubbins being told by an Eminent Scientist that the Remedy was essential to Health.

Rhubarb Pills, for use in the Spring.

Dr. Mainspring's Mariner's Joy, for the most obstinate cases.

Bile Pills.

Liver Pills.

Dr. Primrose's Kidney Pellets, as prescribed by the famous Dr. Primrose to the unfortunate Queen of the French.

Dr. Gubbins's Spring Mixture, for the Blood.

Dr. Gubbins's Autumn Mixture, for the Blood.

'These Sovereign specifics correct Nature in those difficult seasons when the Body politic is adjusting itself to changed conditions.'

Nature's Remedy, 'Vegetable Pills prepared from plants known to the

Red Indians, who by their daily use attain to the ages of 100: even 120 being not uncommon.'

Senna Tea, 'two tablets dissolved in the cup that cheers ensures a happy household.'

'The Sale of Life, being the active principle of Epson and Glauber Salts extracted by a new process.'

In addition to these, there were wrappers and empty boxes which marked where others had lain.

'Dr. Gubbins's Nutrient Corrective, being a Medical Food derived from Active Vegetable Principles by the World Famous Lemuel Gubbins.' There was a picture of Dr. Gubbins, who seemed to be a mixture of Euripides and the Duke of Wellington.

'Use Olopant and smile at Disease.' A Mother of seven wrote to say that she had and did.

from *The Bird of Dawning* by John Masefield

Even when professional surgeons were added to ships' complements their quality and experience did not improve matters greatly, as the following account of the early days of the Royal Navy's medical branch reveals:

In the Seven Years' War (1756–63), the Royal Navy lost 133,700 men by disease and desertion, but only 1,512 were killed in battle. In the Revolutionary and Napoleonic Wars, which lasted with a short break for twenty-two years, the Royal Navy lost 1,875 killed in the six major and four minor battles fought by its fleets and four by its squadrons, compared with more than 72,000 who died from disease or accident on board and another 13,600 who died in ships lost by accident or weather.

By 1799, in the sixth year of the war, when the Navy's strength was voted at 100,000 seamen and 20,000 marines, it had 634 surgeons, according to the Navy List published by Steel at the beginning of the year, and 646 ships in commission . . . though, only about 400 carried surgeons; the rest had surgeons' mates.

A surgeon was paid £5 a month, plus 2d per man per month for the ship he served in and £5 for every hundred men he treated for venereal disease. There was also a payment to surgeons made yearly 'or as often as they pass their accounts' called the 'Queen Anne's Free Gift to Surgeons', which depended on the size of the ships in which they served, ranging from £62 4s 5d in a first-rate to £25 16s 10d in a sixth. The gift was also made to surgeons' mates, who usually served in cutters and tenders – they received £18 18s 10d.

Before being employed, a surgeon or a surgeon's mate had to pass 'an examination in surgery, at Surgeons' Hall, Lincoln's Inn Fields. The Regulations laid down that a prospective surgeon or surgeon's mate had to apply to the Navy Commissioners of the Sick and Hurt at Somerset House for a letter to the Surgeons' Company. He then had to pass a second examination by the Surgeon's Company, and if successful he had to face a third one, by the Commissioners, who if satisfied then appointed him to a ship.

With a continual shortage of surgeons, the Commissioners were not very fussy and all too often a ship's surgeon was a disappointed man who could not make a living on land. James Gardner, in his opinions of his shipmates, found the surgeon of the *Salisbury* 'crabbed as the devil', while the surgeon's assistant in the *Orestes* was 'proud as the devil' and Thomas Trotter of the *Edgar* was 'a most excellent fellow with first rate abilities, an able writer and poet'. (Trotter, a former physician of the Fleet, did a great deal to improve the practice of medicine in the Navy.) The *Edgar*'s three assistant surgeons (the title after 1805 given to surgeon's mates) were described in order as being 'not very orthodox', 'much the gentleman', and 'drank like a fish'. In the *Brunswick* the surgeon was skilful 'but crabbed as the devil at times'. The ship's master was known as 'Pot Guts' while the surgeon was known as 'Bottle Belly', and 'used to eat very hearty and seemed to devour everything with his eyes on the table'.

The difference between a naval physician and a naval surgeon was considerable. The 1799 Navy List gives only three physicians of the fleets (Harness – who gave his name to a type of cask – Blair and Trotter, the man admired by James Gardner). The historians of *Medicine and the Navy* wrote: 'In the eighteenth century the physician was a gentleman, bound by an ethical code which did not even permit him to sue a defaulting patient for his legitimate fees, whereas the surgeon and the apothecary were regarded merely as craftsmen.' They point out that a physician had a medical degree, whereas the surgeon's qualifications were nominal, although changes made in 1805 meant that a physician had to serve as a ship's surgeon for five years before being appointed to a fleet or hospital.

All through the centuries the seaman's great enemy had not been rumbling broadsides ripping his ship to pieces with roundshot and grape, langridge and bar shot; nor had the great killer been storms and hurricanes and uncharted rocks. A musket ball, the shot and nails and scraps of metal fired from a privateer's musketoon, the slash of a cutlass or the jab of a pike – in war these took a negligible toll of men's lives compared with at first scurvy (a vile disease which, within a century, was to become almost unknown) and now typhus and yellow fever.

Scurvy killed more in war simply because there were more men at sea. Convoys sometimes arrived in England from the West Indies with the ships almost unmanageable because of men helpless and dying from disease. Yellow fever in the West Indies did its best to kill off the survivors. But typhus was by now the main enemy because of the vast number of men brought into the Navy by the Quota Act and the press gangs.

from *Life in Nelson's Navy* by Dudley Pope

In the eighteenth century scurvy was by far the biggest killer of sailors.

Its distressing symptoms and the deadly havoc it wreaked on Anson's crews must have made him think that he was up against a maritime version of the Black Death, as this account tells us:

Soon after our passing Streights *Le Maire*, the scurvy began to make its appearance amongst us; and our long continuance at sea, the fatigue we underwent, and the various disappointments we met with, had occasioned its spreading to such a degree, that at the latter end of *April* there were but few on board, who were not in some degree afflicted with it, and in that month no less than forty-three died of it on board the *Centurian*. But though we thought that the distemper had then risen to an extraordinary height, and were willing to hope, that as we advanced to the northward its malignity would abate, yet we found, on the contrary, that in the month of *May* we lost near double that number: And as we did not get to land till the middle of *June*, the mortality went on increasing, and the disease extended itself so prodigiously, that after the loss of about two hundred men, we could not at last muster more than six fore-mast men in a watch capable of duty.

This disease so frequently attending all long voyages, and so particularly destructive to us, is surely the most singular and unaccountable of any that affects the human body. For its symptoms are inconstant and innumerable, and its progress and effects extremely irregular; for scarcely any two persons have the same complaints, and where there hath been found some conformity in the symptoms, the order of their appearance has been totally different. However, though it frequently puts on the form of many other diseases, and is therefore not to be described by any exclusive and infallible criterions; yet there are some symptoms which are more general than the rest, and therefore, occurring the oftnest, deserve a more particular enumeration. These common appearances are large discoloured spots dispersed over the whole surface of the body, swelled legs, putrid gums, and above all, an extraordinary lassitude of the whole body, especially after any exercise, however inconsiderable; and this lassitude at last degenerates into a proneness to swoon on the least exertion of strength, or even on the least motion.

This disease is likewise usually attended with a strange dejection of the spirits, and with shiverings, tremblings, and a disposition to be seized with the most dreadful terrors on the slightest accident. Indeed it was most remarkable, in all our reiterated experience of this malady, that whatever discouraged our people or at any time damped their hopes, never failed to add new vigour to the distemper; for it usually killed those who were in the last stages of it, and confined those to their hammocks, who were before capable of some kind of duty, so that it seemed as if alacrity of mind, and sanguine thoughts, were no contemptible preservatives from its fatal malignity.

But it is not easy to compleat the long roll of the various concomitants of this disease; for it often produced putrid fevers, pleurisies, the jaundice, and violent rheumatick pains, and sometimes it occasioned an obstinate costiveness, which was generally attended with a difficulty of breathing; and this was esteemed the most deadly of all the scorbutick symptoms: At other times the whole body, but more especially the legs, were subject to ulcers of the worst kind, attended with rotten bones, and such a luxuriancy of fungous flesh, as yielded to no remedy. But a most extraordinary circumstance, and what would be scarcely credible upon any single evidence, is, that the scars of wounds which had been for many years healed, were forced open again by this virulent distemper: Of this, there was a remarkable instance in one of the invalids on board the *Centurion*, who had been wounded above fifty years before at the battle of the *Boyne*; for though he was cured soon after, and had continued well for a great number of years past, yet on his being attacked by the scurvy, his wounds, in the progress of his disease, broke out afresh, and appeared as if they had never been healed: Nay, what is still more astonishing, the callous of a broken bone, which had been compleatly formed for a long time, was found to be hereby dissolved, and the fracture seemed as if it had never been consolidated. Indeed, the effects of this disease were in almost every instance wonderful; for many of our people, though confined to their hammocks, appeared to have no inconsiderable share of health, for they eat and drank heartily, were chearful, and talked with much seeming vigour, and with a loud strong tone of voice; and yet on their being the least moved, though it was only from one part of the ship to the other, and that in their hammocks, they have immediately expired; and others, who have confided in their seeming strength, and have resolved to get out of their hammocks, have died before they could well reach the deck; and it was no uncommon thing for those who were able to walk the deck, and to do some kind of duty, to drop down dead in an instant, on any endeavours to act with their utmost vigour, many of our people having perished in this manner during the course of this voyage.

from *Anson's Voyage Round the World in the Years 1740–44* by Richard Walter

When Anson set out from England his ships were manned by 1,500 officers and men. Once in the Pacific he concentrated the 350 survivors in his flagship *Centurion*. By the time he reached Tinian in the Marianas – still a thousand miles east of his goal, the Spanish colonies in the Philippines – he had only seventy-one men left in a fit state to work the ship. It took five hours to furl the sails after reaching harbour.

At Canton he recruited extra seamen, but still had on board less than half his flagship's proper complement when he fell on a Spanish galleon bringing gold and silver from Mexico and took her as a prize.

Those who lived to see Spithead again after a voyage lasting three years and nine months had the consolation of knowing that there was prize-money to the tune of £1 million to be distributed.

But it was not until the nineteenth century that the simple remedy and cure for scurvy was known and understood. Lime juice was issued to ships' companies, from which sprang the term 'Limeys'.

Whilst Nelson was in the West Indies constantly in fear of yellow fever, other sailors in any waters were prone to be struck down by scurvy. William Hickey describes how it reduced an East Indiaman to impotence on passage home from Madras:

After being at sea three weeks many of the crew were so seriously attacked by the scurvy as to be rendered incapable of doing duty, our distress being magnified by the weather becoming very boisterous off the south end of Madagascar. We, however, proceeded until the 15th of January, at which time being in the latitude of thirty-nine and a half south in order to avoid the enemy's ships, a tremendous gale came on from the west-north-west, as adverse a wind as could blow. The ship was laid to under a balance mizen, tumbling about dreadfully. In three days we lost six of the hands from the scurvy, all of whom died suddenly, three of them dropping to rise no more whilst at the helm. Within the following twelve days our loss amounted to thirty-three, when we began really and truly to think we never should reach St. Helena or any port.

Captain Gore, terrified beyond measure at the forlorn state we were in, carried his weakness so far that at last he would not receive the sick list from the Doctor, also forbidding any tolling of the bell, as was customary, previous to performing the funeral service upon a corpse being committed to the deep. He shut himself up in his cabin, from which he never stirred except to attend at meals.

In the height of the bad weather, it becoming necessary to hand the fore-topsail (then close-reefed), the few men we had were so reduced and debilitated by illness that they remained two hours upon the yard in fruitless exertions and endeavours to do the duty they had been sent upon. This so enraged Jerry Griffin, the boatswain, that after a volley of the most blasphemous oaths, he dropped upon his knees, raising his hands as if in an act of devotion, and prayed to the Almighty that there might not be enough left living in the ship to bury the dead. Soon after uttering this impious and horrid wish, he observed the poor creatures upon the yard were likely to succeed in furling the sail. He in the instant clapped his hands, exultingly crying out to the men aloft, 'That's right, that's right. Well done, messmates, well done, my lads.'

The following morning Colonel Flint was talking to an invalid soldier whom he had often seen when serving with the army. As this man appeared to be free from scurvy, the Colonel congratulated him upon preserving his health amidst such general and fatal disease, asking if he had used any particular means to avoid infection, when the fellow bluntly replied, 'Grog, your honour, grog is your only. I'll be damned if scurvy or any other malady ever hurts me while I have plenty of grog, which possesses more virtues than all the contents of the Doctor's medical chest.' During the conversation we were summoned to dinner, and accordingly went into the cuddy where we were scarcely seated ere the Doctor was called out, but as that occurred daily nothing was said by any present. In a few minutes he returned, and to our inexpressible surprize and horror, announced that the man whom Colonel Flint had just before been talking with was dead! A shocking exit this.

The same author was homeward-bound in a ship of the East India Company in 1800 when they carried a supernumerary surgeon of odd behaviour . . .

On Friday the 29th the Surgeon's mate who had shipped himself for that station in Bengal, chiefly, as he said, with a view to obtaining a passage to Europe, which his finances would not allow him to pay for as a passenger, threw himself into the sea from the window of the larboard quarter gallery with the intent of drowning himself . . .

At the time the man was picked up and brought on board he was much exhausted and oppressed by the quantity of water he had taken into his stomach. He was immediately put to bed where the proper medicines were administered, which in twenty-four hours nearly restored him to health, the first use of which he made was to declare that there was no kindness in thus rescuing him from drowning, nor would he avail himself of it, being determined to quit a world in which he had met with nothing but misfortunes and ill-treatment, and die he certainly would in spite of all human endeavours to prevent it. The following night, while lying in his cot, he not only cut his throat, but wounded himself severely across both arms, with a surgical instrument he had secreted for the purpose, and such was his fortitude and determination that although his cot swung in the steerage, a very public part of the ship, and amidst a number of other persons, not the slightest groan or murmur of complaint was heard from him, nor was the rash act discovered until the blood having soaked through the bedding was seen running in streams along the deck. Mr. Powell being summoned to his assistance found him in nearly a fainting state from the great loss of blood. He, however, sewed up the neck and dressed the wounds in his arms, causing him to be removed to the lower deck close to the gunroom, where a space was divided off for the purpose, he being tied down and constantly watched, a sentry being placed over him, and relieved every two hours both day and night. In this dreary and dismal situation, the light of day never penetrating to that part of the ship, did the wretched creature remain during the remainder of the voyage, but to the extreme surprize of Mr. Powell, who had no expectation of his surviving the injury he had done himself, gradually recovered, and when the ship reached England, he was perfectly well in point of health, though raving mad. He was therefore landed and conveyed to a receptacle for lunatics, where I understand he has ever since remained.

There were other problems on the voyage . . .

In the evening our ship was in the utmost confusion owing to many of the crew being in a state of intoxication. An enquriy took place thereupon, when it was discovered that the sail-maker, aided by one of the foremast men, had contrived to break open the door of the lazaretto where the liquor was kept, from whence they supplied themselves and friends with a sufficient quantity of rum to make them excessively drunk: there were altogether twenty-one persons evidently inebriated. After an examination into the particulars, the two principal culprits, being the sail-maker and a foremast man, were immediately tied up to the main shrouds and severely flogged: four others were put into irons, the rest, expressing much contrition for the offence they had committed, were pardoned and order was restored.

On the 14th we met with a very serious loss and deprivation of comfort in the death of a remarkably fine Europe cow, which had come out in the ship and daily given an extraordinary quantity of milk. Without any apparent previous illness, she appeared about ten in the morning to be in great pain, and at twelve the poor animal died and was directly thrown overboard. Luckily we had another cow, a Bengallee one, on board, which with three fine Surat goats, yielded us a tolerable share of milk for morning and evening, besides an ample store for the children, who were, very properly, first considered.

from the *Memoirs of William Hickey* ed. by Alfred Spencer

In his capacity as ship's doctor, the Master often had to face injuries to his crew which would daunt a fully qualified surgeon with all the correct instruments. The following tells how it was even in the first decade of this century:

'Jerry' the Greek, whose leg had been smashed to pulp when caught in the washport on 13th September, was lashed into his own bunk in the forecastle, and was suffering immeasurable torments, as gangrene had set in.

The atmosphere in the forecastle had become so terrible that it is a wonder human beings could continue to live in it.

Since the port forecastle was stove in, fifteen men were bunked in the starboard forecastle, of whom seven, including the Greek, were unable to rise from their bunks. The portholes had been sealed for weeks, and the only fresh air admitted was when the door was opened for a second or two, as a man made a dash to get in or out. Smoke from the bogie-stove, mingled with tobacco smoke, stale breath, and the stink of unwashed bodies and clothes, made a thick fog, which was also pervaded by something sinister and dreadful – the vile, decayed stench of gangrene, a portent of death.

The gangrened leg of Jerry the Greek was the main source of the terrifying stench, but there was gangrene, too, in the toes of several of the men with frost-bitten feet.

In this horrible atmosphere, our six seamen, still on the active list, and the two partly incapacitated men, had to take such sleep and relaxation as they could, during their watches below.

In his delirium, the Greek cried and groaned loudly for hours, babbling in his own language, and at times screaming with the unbearable pain.

There were no medicaments on the ship for such a case as this. The sick men were given occasional tots of grog; but the many kinds of sedatives available to a later generation – evolved during two World Wars – were unknown to medical science in 1905, and beyond the imagining of a Captain whose medical knowledge was limited to first-aid treatment.

All that could be done to alleviate the injured men's sufferings was done by the Captain, the officers, the carpenter, and the steward, as opportunity to be absent from the poop or from duties on deck permitted. Their ship-mates in the forecastle naturally also did all they could to comfort the sufferers, by making tea for them, and in other ways acting as nurses; but, with the best that could be done, the forecastle had become a den of horror.

One morning, Gronberg, the carpenter, came aft, and reported to the Captain that Jerry the Greek was unconscious, and appeared to be dying.

Hurrying to the forecastle, the Captain examined the man, and saw that the gangrene was spreading in the injured leg.

'Dere ist only von t'ing to save him der life,' growled Gronberg. 'Cut him der leg off, or he die pretty quick!'

'What's that you say?' said Captain Barker, a man who never shirked a tough decision; and, after considering a moment: 'By heavens, I think you're right! I'll do it!'

There was no advice in the *Ship's Medical Guide-Book* on how to amputate a limb; nor were there in the medicine-chest any anaesthetics, or the surgical instruments necessary for such a major operation.

The prospects were enough to deter even a man of iron courage; but, having made his decision, Captain Barker characteristically swept aside all obstacles to his purpose, and set about the job with the crude tools which were at hand.

The cook's meat-saw and knife were hastily sharpened by the carpenter, and sterilized in a bucket of boiling water. An iron poker was fetched from the galley, and placed in the coals of the forecastle stove, to be used for cauterizing the wound.

The ship was rolling and tumbling in the heavy sea, as the Greek, deeply unconscious, was lifted from his bunk, and lashed down to the forecastle table.

The Mate was in charge on deck, while the operation was performed in the stinking, poorly lit forecastle, by the Captain, assisted by the Second

Mate, the senior apprentice (Paul Nelson); and the carpenter and the steward standing by; all in floor-wash up to their ankles.

The grisly scene was witnessed also by the six frost-bitten seamen lying in their bunks with a full view of it.

Ison, Love and I were at work on deck, and were later given a graphic account by Paul Nelson, who had the duty of standing by with a bottle of brandy, to sustain the courage of the surgeon and his assistants.

Overcoming nausea at the terrible stench of the gangrene, the Old Man, after binding and tightening ligatures on the thigh, cut through the living flesh, above the knee, and bared the bone.

Blood spurted from the severed arteries. With the red-hot poker the captain instantly cauterized the cut, and stopped the bleeding, as the stench of burning flesh filled the forecastle.

Then, seizing the meat-saw, he quickly cut through the thigh-bones, and applied the red-hot poker again, and again.

Gronberg, picking up the putrid severed leg, rushed out of the door and threw it overboard.

We on deck glimpsed him doing this, and realized that the operation was successful, as far as its main purpose was concerned.

Fortunately, Jerry the Greek remained in his deep coma during this butchery, and at the moment suffered no pain.

The ligatures were allowed to remain, the cords pressing deep into the flesh, and the cauterized stump was bandaged with cotton-wool dressings.

The patient was then lifted into his bunk, and chocked off and lashed there so securely that he would be unable to make any movement of his body or limbs when he 'came to'.

The operation took about half an hour, from start to finish. Strange to record, the patient survived. He came out of his coma, hours later, very pale in the face beneath his swarthy skin, and only his pain-filled eyes indicating the tortures he was enduring.

For the next three weeks, he continued in intense suffering – uttering loud groans at intervals when the pain became intolerable.

But the gangrene was arrested, and Jerry would live on. A few days after this remarkable operation, the Greybeards of Cape Horn claimed a victim.

On 9th October, at 4 a.m., the seaman, John West, who had sustained such terrible head injuries when he was dashed into the scuppers on 14th August, died.

For eight weeks, he had been lashed in his bunk, unconscious for most of the time, during the buffeting that the ship had received. There was practically nothing that could be done to relieve his sufferings. The Captain and the steward gave him whatever care they could. His shipmates at times looked into the cabin where he lay so helpless, pale, and yet obstinately clinging to the flicker of life that remained in him.

He had been a 'living corpse' for weeks, and now his end had come, without benefit of doctor or clergyman to soothe his dying.

He would have to be buried at sea. As a gale was blowing up, the Captain decided that this ceremony must be performed without undue delay. The sailmaker sewed the body into a canvas shroud, weighted with scrap-iron at the feet.

At 6 a.m., two hours after the man had died, all hands were mustered on the poop-deck, and the corpse was carried up by four of the elder seamen, and placed on a spare wooden hatch-board, resting under the lee taffrail.

In the grey light of the cold morning we bared our heads and stood by, while the Captain read, from a small prayer-book, the solemn words of the Church of England burial-service, for use at sea.

The words were carried away in the wind. We heard fragments, something about *the sure and certain hope of Resurrection . . . commit his body to the deep . . .*

The hatch-board was tilted up by Paddy Furlong and Otto Schmidt, and the body of John West, seaman, slid into the wild waters, to sink immediately from our sight.

The Captain closed the prayer-book and put it in his pocket. Then he eyed the weather and said brusquely to the Mate, 'Haul the mainsail up, Mister, before that squall hits us!'

All hands laid on to haul up the mainsail before the watch went below. Another shipmate was dead and gone, but the *British Isles* still lived . . .

Three days later the weather cleared.

from *The Cape Horn Breed* by Captain W. H. S. Jones

Incredibly Jerry the Greek lived. After a further amputation on arrival at Pisagua, he was shipped home with a wooden leg. Two of the Cape Horn casualties died in hospital, another also got a wooden leg, whilst three more were discharged with 'minor amputations' to arrest gangrene and lived to tell the tale.

Even by the standards of what was fit for human consumption ashore in the eighteenth and nineteenth centuries, the sailor's basic diet on board was disgusting and a contributory cause of ill health and indiscipline. Of interest in the following account is the word 'banyan' which survives in the Royal Navy to this day. Now it is associated with anchoring in a quiet bay off Beef Island or somewhere in the Aegean for the crew to have a day-long beach-party, with no holds barred on the food or drink.

In the matter of provisions, there can be little doubt that the sailor shared to the full the desire evinced by the surgeon of the *Seahorse* to take blood-vengeance upon someone on account of them. His 'belly-timber,' as old

Misson so aptly if indelicately describes it, was mostly worm-eaten or rotten, his drink indescribably nasty.

Charles II. is said to have made his breakfast off ship's diet the morning he left the *Naseby*, and to have pronounced it good; and Nelson in 1803 declared it 'could not possibly be improved upon.' Such, however, was not the opinion of the chaplain of the *Dartmouth*, for after dining with his captain on an occasion which deserves to become historic, he swore that 'although he liked that Sort of Living very well, as for the King's Allowance there was but a Sheat of Browne Paper between it and Hell.' Which of these opinions came nearest to the truth, the sequel will serve to show.

On the face of it the sailor's dietary was not so bad. A ship's stores, in 1719, included ostensibly such items as bread, wine, beef, pork, peas, oatmeal, butter, cheese, water and beer, and if Jack had but had his fair share of these commodities, and had it in decent condition, he would have had little reason to grumble about the king's allowance. Unhappily for him, the humanities of diet were little studied by the Victualling Board.

Taking beef, the staple article of consumption on shipboard, cooking caused it to shrink as much as 45 per cent., thus reducing the sailor's allowance by nearly one-half. The residuum was often 'mere carrion,' totally unfit for human consumption. 'Junk,' the sailor contemptuously called it, likening it, in point of texture, digestibility and nutritive properties, to the product of picked oakum, which it in many respects strongly resembled. The pork, though it lost less in the cooking, was rancid, putrid stuff, repellent in odour and colour – particulars in which it found close competitors in the butter and cheese, which had often to be thrown overboard because they 'stunk the ship.' The peas 'would not break.' Boiled for eight hours on end, they came through the ordeal 'almost as hard as shott.' Only the biscuit, apart from the butter and cheese, possessed the quality of softness. Damp, sea-water, mildew and weevil converted 'hard' into 'soft tack' and added another horror to the sailor's mess. The water he washed these varied abominations down with was frequently 'stuff that beasts would cough at.' His beer was no better. It would not keep, and was in consequence both 'stinking and sour.' Although the contractor was obliged to make oath that he had used both malt and hops in the brewing, it often consisted of nothing more stimulating that 'water coloured and bittered,' and sometimes the 'stingy dog of a brewer' even went so far as to omit the 'wormwood.'

Such a dietary as this made a meal only an unavoidable part of the day's punishment and inspired the sailor with profound loathing. 'Good Eating is an infallible Antidote against murmuring, as many a Big-Belly Place-Man can instance,' he says in one of his petitions. Poor fellow! his opportunities of putting it to the test were few enough. On Mondays, Wednesdays and Fridays, the so-called Banyan days of the service, when his hateful ration of meat was withheld and in its stead he regaled himself on plum-duff – the 'plums', according to an old regulation, 'not worse than Malaga' – he had a taste of it. Hence the banyan day, though in reality a fast-day, became indelibly associated in his simple mind and vocabulary with occasions of feasting and plenty, and so remains to this day.

If the sailor's only delicacy was duff, his only comforts were rum and tobacco, and to explore some unknown island, and discover therein a goodly river of the famous Jamaica spirit, flowing deep and fragrant between towering mountains of 'pig tail,' is commonly reputed to have been the cherished wish of his heart. With tobacco the navy Board did not provide him, nor afford dishonest pursers opportunity to 'make dead men chew,' until 1798; but rum they allowed him at a comparatively early date. when sickness prevailed on board, when beer ran short or had to be turned over the side to preserve a sweet ship, rum or wine was issued, and although the Admiralty at first looked askance at the innovation, and at times left commanders of ships to foot the bill for spirits thus served out, the practice made gradual headway, until at length it ousted beer altogether and received the stamp of official approval. Half a pint, dealt out each morning and evening in equal portions, was the regular allowance – a quantity often doubled were the weather unusually severe or the men engaged in the arduous duty of watering ship. At first the ration of rum was served neat and appreciated accordingly; but about 1740 the practice of adding water was introduced. This was Admiral Vernon's doing. Vernon was best known to his men as 'Old Grog,' a nickname originating in a famous grogram coat.

from *The Press Gang* by J. R. Hutchinson

THE DARK SIDE

Shipwrecks will not wait; the sea is a pressing creditor. An hour's delay may be irreparable.

Victor Hugo, on observing a sailing
barge cutting inside the rocks off Guernsey

Cape Horn

Cape Horn to the sailor is as the Alps must have seemed to one of Hannibal's soldiers waiting on the start-line west of the Rhône for the word to advance, with only the 15,000 foot Mont Cenis between him and the lush plunder of the Lombardy Plain: a bleak monochrome hell with its dangers mostly hidden by ugly black clouds, a treacherous unpredictable menace of sudden whiplash storms which could sweep him over the side at any time.

The sailor making his first – or for that matter any subsequent – voyage around Cape Horn would probably envy the lot of the soldier who, no matter whatever other danger lurked in his path, would not have to face those mountainous seas generated by prevailing westerly winds driving them 15,000 miles around the wastes of the Southern Ocean into the shallow gap between the Cape and the South Shetland Islands marking the northern extremity of the Antarctica, just 300 miles away.

The classic Admiralty publication *Ocean Passages for the World* appropriately carries an old Breton fisherman's prayer on its frontispiece:

Oh God be good to me.
Thy sea is so wide and my ship is so small.

No matter what size of ship one ventures to round the Cape in, it is as well to have the Almighty on your strength when the weather suddenly turns nasty. The cape lies at the extreme southern limit of the Roaring Forties. The anonymous writer of *Ocean Passages* comes straight to the point: 'South of latitude 40°S, even at midsummer, winds reach force 7 from 7 to 9 days a month, whilst (further south) the frequency rises to 15 days a month.' (On the Beaufort Scale, Force 7 is a near gale with winds of 28–33 knots.)

Later he goes on to describe Horn from west to east as a 'comparatively easy matter, for the prevailing winds are favourable and the current near Cabo de Hornos sets strongly to the east'. The advice given to masters under sail is not so encouraging or dogmatic: 'June and July are the best months for making a W-bound passage around Cabo de Hornos, as the wind is then often in the easterly quarter. The days are short, however, and the weather is cold.' Not surprising, since it is then midwinter in the southern hemisphere.

The appropriate volume of the *Admiralty Pilot* (South America vol. II) confirms the depressing advice given above, but adds that at least half of those winds over Force 7 are full gales or hurricane-strength winds. It also points out that, in typical winter conditions, in a 50–knot storm, ice will accumulate on the hull and rig at a rate of more than 1 inch each four-hour watch. 'When the air temperature is below the freezing point of sea-water and the ship is in heavy seas, considerable amounts of water will freeze on to the superstructure and those parts of the hull which are sufficiently above the waterline to escape being washed frequently by the sea. The amounts so frozen to surfaces exposed to the air will rapidly increase with falling temperatures, and might in extreme cases lead to the capsizing of the vessel.'

Another piece of advice to be borne in mind reads as follows: 'Should a vessel be wrecked or abandoned west of Cabo de Hornos, its boats should endeavour to reach Isla Grevy (30 miles NW of the Cape and protected from the west by Peninsula Hardy) where, by maintaining a fire, they may be able to attract the attention of the inhabitants of the islands to the north.'

It is not known whether this advice has survived from the 1832 first edition of the *Pilot*. Then it was of questionable value, since the inhabitants of those parts were short-tempered cannibals of the same tribe which killed four of Drake's men during his voyage of 1578 and frightened Lady Brassey when she cruised through the Straits of Magellan in her husband's 530-ton barque in 1876. There is further advice for those whose lifeboats get driven to the leeward of the passage leading to Isla Grevy: 'places where the grass is seen growing will almost certainly be found to indicate the vicinity of a sheep farm.'

The idea of green pastures in such wild terrain is hard to grasp until you realize that Cape Horn lies in latitude 56°S, the same distance from the equator as Edinbugh. Comparison of its climatic table with that for Ushuaia in the Beagle Channel and admittedly 60 miles north of the Cape, but the nearest point with authentic long-term weather records, suggests that Edinburgh may be less than 10°F warmer the year round, but suffers substantially more rainfall.

Another widespread misconception is that the Cape of Good Hope, the South Island of New Zealand and Cape Horn are roughly the same distance south. In fact, Cape Town is 1,200 miles nearer the equator and even Stewart Island off the southern extremity of New Zealand is 600 miles further north of Cabo de Hornos; hence circumnavigators being unable to sail a true Great Circle course (the shortest distance) across the Southern Pacific, because it would take them across the land mass of Antarctica, even if they survived the pack-ice protecting its shores.

When Drake sailed through from the Atlantic to the Pacific, he found out enough to be confident that there was open sea to the south of Tierra del Fuego. The gap between it and the South Shetland Islands is thus known to this day as Drake Passage. But the credit for discovering the dreaded Cape belongs to a Dutch explorer or pirate, Willem Corneliszoon Schouten, in 1611. He named it after his birthplace, Hoorn, a seaport of the western shore of the Ijsselmeer, now being shut in by land reclamation – the SW Polder.

It is fitting that the most thrilling account in modern times of making a west-east passage of the Horn should be by a fellow countryman, Cornelis van Rietschoten, on his way to winning the 1978 Whitbread Round-the-World Race in his 65 foot Sparkman and Stephens ketch *Flyer*. Here is how he recorded it at the time, without any danger of his spars icing up, for it was in midsummer:

The weather around the Horn where the grey-green waters of the Pacific mix with the brown Atlantic stream is almost always bad, blowing a full gale most days and a storm, that can build up to hurricane force for 3 days every 3 months or so, the rest. My first rounding in 1978 was a moment in life never to be forgotten and I wrote at the time:

'Three hours after sailing closehauled between Norta and Diego Islands we spotted the Horn – a sight we had sailed halfway round the world to see and one that none of us would easily forget.

'*Flyer* had beaten *Condor* round by 12 miles and it had all been straight forward sailing; I just couldn't believe our luck. But, just as if the Cape had read those thoughts, black clouds rolled across to mark another frontal passage. "More wind," I remarked at the time, rubbing my hands with glee, "that's what we need to keep pace with *Pen Duick*," but I didn't reckon on how much.

'The first squall to hit was a 50-knot blast, and swinging to a completely different angle, it caught us with all sail up and the boom lashed down on the opposite side. It hit with such ferocity that there was no time to think, and we went straight into a Chinese gybe. I was letting out the mizzen sheet at the time and just held on, suspended in mid air as the yacht lurched over. One crewman was thrown bodily across the deck to land in the scuppers, but everyone else managed to cling on somehow. For the first time *Flyer* lay trapped, pinned down by the weight of water in her sails and the wind that blasted in under the boom. Struggling to get a foothold back on deck, I caught a glimpse of the mainmast dipping beneath the waves. The navigator clambered up to release the preventer on the main

97

boom. Aedgard let slip the leeward running backstay and the sail crashed across smacking the water. The mizzen was also caught, the preventer jammed in its cleat by the strain on it, so I tore at the halyard and wrenched the sail down. *Flyer* twitched like a boxer out cold. We all wondered if she would be able to beat the count, for water was pouring below through the open hatch. But slowly she stirred, and swinging back up on her feet, unsteadily at first, shook herself down then waited patiently for us to gather our wits.

'The 2.2 oz spinnaker was in shreds; the pole had been wrenched from the mast, the slider broken, and sheets washed in all directions. Down below water was everywhere, soaking bedding, sails and clothes. Those off-watch who had been having dinner at the time found their food knocked into every corner, and ketchup spilt from a smashed bottle was splattered on the cabin ceiling. They retrieved their food and went on eating while we on deck pulled down the remnants of yet another blown spinnaker and re-set the sails. Within ten minutes we had *Flyer* thrusting forward again with a heavy reaching spinnaker set on the spare pole. Within twenty minutes all was ship shape on deck and we were pumping out.

'An hour later though and we were in big trouble again. Another squall ran up behind, this one at 40 knots, and though we were on the right gybe this time, it hit with such force that *Flyer* was driven right through the next wave. The strains on both hull and rig must have been enormous for the nose just buried and carried on down to leave 2 feet of water on deck. The boiling water was like a tidal wave and it tore down the deck prising hands free from their holds and bringing with it bodies, halyard sheets and anything else that was not well secured. *Flyer* was stopped completely. Another faint report from above, almost drowned out by the rush of water, signalled a second blown spinnaker. There was no time to think of consequences. Natural instincts were to fight for air, as *Flyer* staggered out of that watery grave to shake herself down and turn up into wind. Some picked themselves out of the scuppers, others had been thrown into the cockpit, but thankfully no one was washed overboard, it was quite incredible that we could survive two near disasters in less than an hour and come out of it all almost totally unscathed.

'The watch was ready to joist a third spinnaker, but I called out, "Folks, this is not our lucky day for spinnakers – pole out the blast reacher instead." Once the tattered pieces of spinnaker had been hauled down and the heavy reaching headsail set, we ran for the Strait de le Maire. I had had enough of Cape Horn'.

That reduction in sail was just as well, for in this deep cut between mainland and Staten Island where the bottom plunges down to 176 fathoms within metres of the shore there was such a steep sea running that we would almost certainly have lost yet another spinnaker. It was a wild run through the dark, *Flyer* pounding a path through the short waves and carrying a rooster tail of spray from her stern.

Conditions here four years later were like a millpond by comparison . . .

from *Blue Water Racing* by Cornelis van Rietschoten and Barry Pickthall

In November 1519, a century before Schouten rounded the Horn, Ferdinand Magellan led the three surviving ships of his original squadron of five out into the open sea 7 weeks after he had probed for a westwards passage from the Atlantic from Cape Virgines. He believed that the Spice Islands and the shores of Asia were then comparatively near at hand. This was the voyage that finally proved beyond doubt to the Flat Earth Society that they had got it all wrong, although Magellan himself did not survive to deliver the proof to the Emperor of Spain. In April 1521 he was hacked to death by natives in the Philippines.

The Captain-General had a proper sense of the occasion. As the keel of the *Trinidad* drove into these waters, touched for the first time by the timbers of a European vessel, his ships closed and the surviving priest in full vestments raised his crucifix from the poop deck of the *Trinidad* and every man knelt in prayer. He appealed for the favour of St. Andrew the Apostle, whose day it was, and bestowed a benediction both on this new ocean and on these who were about to sail across it. To the sound of the discharge of cannon, Magellan held aloft the great silk banner of his command which he had so long ago received from the hands of Emperor Charles, and prayed that the waters might always be as peaceful as they were that morning. In the hope that they might be, he pronounced that 'I shall name this sea the *Mar Pacifico*.'

Their prayers for pacific seas were answered and the winds and the currents remained favourable. But their worst sufferings still lay ahead. It was the vast distance they had to sail before reaching land that killed so many of them and crippled almost all with the scurvy. Contemporary cartographers always underestimated distances. According to the crude and speculative charts carried by Magellan, the West coast of America joined with the eastern extension of the Asian mainland at about 35 degrees south of the Equator. Magellan therefore steered north up the coast of Chile expecting soon to reach Asia, and a warmer climate for his men, before he gave up and changed course to the north-west. This only added further to the thousands of leagues he had to sail, and to their privations. 'We remained three months and twenty days without taking in provisions or other refreshments', recorded Pigafetta, 'and we only ate old biscuit reduced to powder, and full of grubs, and stinking from the dirt which the rats had made on it . . . and we drank water that was yellow and stinking.' Just as Magellan had feared. 'We also ate the ox hides which were under the main-yard . . .' first softening them in the ocean for several days.

from *The Blind Horn's Hate* by Richard Hough

In 1740, a century after Schouten had discovered the Horn, Commodore George Anson arrived on the scene from England with his squadron of six ships and 2,000 men. His experience was one of clawing his way round from east to west in ships which could not point better than six points off the wind and could not make any westing against contrary winds and currents.

Anson had based his hopes of being able to lead his squadron of eight ships safely through the Straits which separate Staten Island and Tierra del Fuego on earlier reports. It was certainly the shortest distance to Cape Horn. But the reality proved terrifyingly different, as his own account makes clear:

We had scarcely reached the southern extremity of the Streights of *Le Maire*, when our flattering hopes were instantly lost in the apprehensions of immediate destruction: For before the sternmost ships of the squadron were clear of the Streights, the serenity of the sky was suddenly changed, and gave us all the presages of an impending storm; and immediately the wind shifted to the southward, and blew in such violent squalls, that we were obliged to hand our top-sails, and reef our main-sail: The tide too, which had hitherto favoured us, now turned against us, and drove us to the eastward with prodigious rapidity, so that we were in great anxiety for the *Wager* and the *Anna Pink*, the two sternmost vessels, fearing they would be dashed to pieces against the shore of *Staten-land*; nor were our apprehensions without foundation, for it was with the utmost difficulty they escaped. And now the whole squadron, instead of pursuing their intended course to the S.W, were driven to the eastward by the united force of the storm, and of the currents; so that next day in the morning we found ourselves near seven leagues to the eastward of *Staten-land*, which then bore from us N.W. The violence of the current, which had set us with so much precipitation to the eastward, together with the force and constancy of the westerly winds, soon taught us to consider the doubling of Cape *Horn* as an enterprize, that might prove too mighty for our efforts, though some amongst us had lately treated the difficulties which former voyagers were said to have met with in this undertaking, as little better than chimerical, and had supposed them to arise rather from timidity and unskilfulness, than from the real embarrassments of the winds and seas; but we were now severely convinced, that these censures were rash and ill-grounded: For the distresses with which we struggled, during the three succeeding months, will not easily be paralleled in the relation of any former naval expedition.

*

It was on the 7th of *March*, as hath been already observed, that we passed Streights *Le Maire*, and were immediately afterwards driven to the eastward by a violent storm, and the force of the current which set that way. For the four or five succeeding days we had hard gales of wind from the same quarter, with a most prodigious swell; so that though we stood, during all that time, towards the S.W, yet we had no reason to imagine, we had made any way to the westward. In this interval we had frequent squalls of rain and snow, and shipped great quantities of water; after which, for three or four days, though the seas ran mountains high, yet the weather was rather more moderate: But, on the 18th, we had again strong gales of wind with extreme cold, and at midnight the main top-sail split, and one of the straps of the main dead eyes broke. From hence, to the 23d, the weather was more favourable, though often intermixed with rain and sleet, and some hard gales; but as the waves did not subside, the ship, by labouring in this lofty sea, was now grown so loose in her upper works, that she let in the water at every seam, so that every part within board was constantly exposed to the sea-water, and scarcely any of the Officers ever lay in dry beds. Indeed it was very rare, that two nights ever passed without many of them being driven from their beds, by the deluge of water than came upon them.

On the 23d, we had a most violent storm of wind, hail, and rain with a very great sea; and though we handed the main top-sail before the height of the squall, yet we found the yard sprung; and soon after the foot-rope of the main-sail breaking, the main-sail itself split instantly to rags, and, in spite of our endeavours to save it, much the greater part of it was blown over-board. On this, the Commodore made the signal for the squadron to bring to; and the storm at length flattening to a calm, we had an opportunity of getting down our main top-sail yard to put the Carpenters at work upon it, and of repairing our rigging; after which, having bent a new mainsail, we got under sail again with a moderate breeze; but in less than twenty-four hours we were attacked by another storm still more furious than the former; for it proved a perfect hurricane, and reduced us to the necessity of lying to under our bare poles.

From his own experience he reasoned that better conditions could be found as much as 300 miles south of the Cape. Certainly the adverse current would be less, but later navigators do not bear him out. The ferocity of the weather can be uniformly severe most of the way down to the Antarctic subcontinent.

But when the Spanish squadron of six ships under Don Joseph Pizarro in his sixty-six-gun flagship *Asia* set out to chase Anson, he had to cope with mutiny as well as all the other vicissitudes of weathering Cape Horn. The seventy-four-gun *Guipuscoa* with a crew of 700 men ended up as a dismasted hulk driven 250 miles by the persistent sou'westerly gales.

. . . when by the storms they met with off Cape *Horn*, their continuance at sea was prolonged a month or more beyond their expectation, they were thereby reduced to such infinite distress, that rats, when they could be caught, were sold for four dollars a-piece; and a sailor, who died on board, had his death concealed for some days by his brother, who, during that time, lay in the same hammock with the corpse, only to receive the dead man's allowance of provisions. In this dreadful situation they were alarmed (if their horrors were capable of augmentation) by the discovery of a conspiracy among the marines, on board the *Asia*, the Admiral's ship. This had taken its rise chiefly from the miseries they endured: For though no less was proposed by the conspirators than the massacring the officers and the whole crew, yet their motive for this bloody resolution seemed to be no more than their desire of relieving their hunger, by appropriating the whole ships provisions to themselves. But their designs were prevented, when just upon the point of execution, by means of one of their confessors, and three of their ringleaders were immediately put to death. However, though the conspiracy was suppressed, their other calamities admitted of no alleviation, but grew each day more and more destructive. So that by the complicated distress of fatigue, sickness and hunger, the three ships which escaped lost the greatest part of their men: The *Asia*, their Admiral's ship, arrived at *Monte Vedio* in the river of *Plate*, with half her crew only; the St. *Estevan* had lost in like manner half her hands, when she anchored in the bay of *Barragan*; the *Esperanza*, a fifty gun ship, was still more unfortunate, for of four hundred and fifty hands which she brought from *Spain*, only fifty-eight remained alive, and the whole regiment of foot perished except sixty men. But to give the reader a more distinct and particular idea of what they underwent upon this occasion, I shall lay before him a short account of the fare of the *Guipuscoa*, from a letter written by Don *Joseph Mendinuetta* her Captain, to a person of distinction at *Lima*; a copy of which fell into our hands afterwards in the *South-Seas*.

He mentions that he separated from the *Hermiona* and the *Esperanza* in a fog, on the 6th of *March*, being then, as I suppose, to the S.E. of *Staten-Land*, and plying to the westward; that in the night after, it blew a furious storm at N.W, which, at half an hour after ten, split his mainsail, and obliged him to bear away with his foresail; that the ship went ten knots an hour with a prodigious sea, and often ran her gangway under water; that he likewise sprung his main-mast; and the ship made so much water, that with four pumps and bailing he could not free her. That on the 19th it was calm, but the sea continued so high, that the ship in rolling opened all her upper works and seams, and started the butt ends of her planking and the greatest part of her top timbers, the bolts being drawn by the violence of her roll: That in this condition, with other additional disasters to the hull and rigging, they continued beating to the westward till the 12th: That they were then in sixty degrees of south latitude, in great want of provisions, numbers every day perishing by the fatigue of pumping, and those who survived, being quite dispirited by labour, hunger, and the severity of the weather, they having two spans of snow upon the decks: That then finding the wind fixed in the western quarter, and blowing strong, and consequently their passage to the westward impossible, they resolved to bear away for the river of *Plate*: That on the 22nd, they were obliged to throw overboard all the upper-deck guns, and an anchor, and to take six turns of the cable round the ship to prevent her opening: That on the 4th of *April*, it being calm but a very high sea, the ship rolled so much, that the main-mast came by the board, and in a few hours after she lost, in like manner, her fore-mast and her mizen-mast; and that, to accumulate their misfortunes, they were soon obliged to cut away their bowsprit, to diminish, if possible, the leakage at her head: That by this time he had lost two hundred and fifty men by hunger and fatigues; for those who were capable of working at the pumps, (at which every Officer without exception took his turn) were allowed only an ounce and half of biscuit *per diem*; and those were were so sick or so weak, that they could not assist in this necessary labour, had no more than an ounce of wheat; so that it was common for the men to fall down dead at the pumps.

from *Anson's Voyage Round the World in the Years 1740–44* by Richard Walter

When land was finally sighted seven weeks later, the crew refused to pump any more and obliged the captain to run her up on the beach, where she became a total loss. Surprisingly only 300 perished.

Early in 1896 the first man to sail alone around the world had worked his way through the Straits of Magellan, overcoming not only the williwaws (Cape Horn squalls), but the hostile intentions of the shaggy-haired Fuegian Indians. The story that he defended himself against unwelcome boarders at night by leaving carpet-tacks sprinkled around the upper deck is too good to deny, but is probably 'faction'. At last he cleared Cape Pillar at the western extremity of the Straits, confidently heading out into the Pacific in his tubby 36-foot shoal-draft yawl *Spray*. A century earlier she had been an oysterman in Delaware Bay, hence her 14-foot beam and draught of a little over 4 feet. Her overall length varied according to Captain Joshua Slocum's developing ideas of the sort of boat he needed to complete his voyage around the world. With a bumpkin added to sheet home the mizzen (or jigger, as he called it) and her considerable bowsprit, a marina berthing-master today would have charged her at 60-foot overall.

Slocum was not the first east–west sailor to be driven back by the greybeards of the Howling Fifties:

It was the 3rd of March when the *Spray* sailed from Port Tamar direct for Cape Pillar, with the wind from the northeast, which I fervently hoped might hold till she cleared the land; but there was no such good luck in store. It soon began to rain and thicken in the northwest, boding no good.

103

The *Spray* neared Cape Pillar rapidly, and, nothing loath, plunged into the Pacific Ocean at once, taking her first bath of it in the gathering storm. There was no turning back even had I wished to do so, for the land was now shut out by the darkness of night. The wind freshened, and I took in a third reef. The sea was confused and treacherous. In such a time as this the old fisherman prayed, 'Remember, Lord, my ship is so small and thy sea is so wide!' I saw now only the gleaming crests of waves. They showed white teeth while the sloop balanced over them. 'Everything for an offing,' I cried, and to this end I carried on all the sail she would bear. She ran all night with a free sheet, but on the morning of March 4 the wind shifted to southwest, then back suddenly to northwest, and blew with terrific force. The *Spray*, stripped of her sails, then bore off under bare poles. No ship in the world could have stood up against so violent a gale. Knowing that this storm might continue for many days, and that it would be impossible to work back to the westward along the coast outside of Tierra del Fuego, there seemed nothing to do but to keep on and go east about, after all. Anyhow, for my present safety the only course lay in keeping her before the wind. And so she drove southeast, as though about to round the Horn, while the waves rose and fell and bellowed their never-ending story of the sea; but the Hand that held these held also the *Spray*. She was running now with a reefed forestaysail, the sheets flat amidship. I paid out two long ropes to steady her course and to break combing seas astern, and I lashed the helm amidship. In this trim she ran before it, shipping never a sea. Even while the storm raged at its worst, my ship was wholesome and noble. My mind as to her seaworthiness was put to ease for aye.

When all had been done that I could do for the safety of the vessel, I got to the fore-scuttle, between seas, and prepared a pot of coffee over a wood fire, and made a good Irish stew. Then, as before and afterward on the *Spray*, I insisted on warm meals. In the tide-race off Cape Pillar, however, where the sea was marvellously high, uneven, and crooked, my appetite was slim, and for a time I postponed cooking. (Confidentially, I was seasick!)

The first day of the storm gave the *Spray* her actual test in the worst sea that Cape Horn or its wild regions could afford, and in no part of the world could a rougher sea be found than at this particular point, namely, off Cape Pillar, the grim sentinel of the Horn.

Farther offshore, while the sea was majestic, there was less apprehension of danger. There the *Spray* rode, now like a bird on the crest of a wave, and now like a waif deep down in the hollow between seas; and so she drove on. Whole days passed, counted as other days, but always a thrill – yes, of delight.

On the fourth day of the gale, rapidly nearing the pitch of Cape Horn, I inspected my chart and pricked off the course and distance to Port Stanley, in the Falkland Islands, where I might find my way and refit, when I saw through a rift in the clouds a high mountain, about seven leagues away on the port beam. The fierce edge of the gale by this time had blown off, and I had already bent a square-sail on the boom in place of the mainsail, which was torn to rags. I hauled in the trailing ropes, hoisted this awkward sail reefed, the forestaysail being already set, and under this sail brought her at once on the wind heading for the land, which appeard as an island in the sea. So it turned out to be, though not the one I had supposed.

I was exultant over the prospect of once more entering the Strait of Magellan and beating through again into the Pacific, for it was more than rough on the outside coast of Tierra del Fuego. It was indeed a mountainous sea. When the sloop was in the fiercest squalls, with only the reefed forestay-sail set, even that small sail shook her from keelson to truck when it shivered by the leech. Had I harboured the shadow of a doubt for her safety, it would have been that she might spring a leak in the garboard at the heel of the mast; but she never called me once to the pump. Under pressure of the smallest sail I could set she made for the land like a race-horse, and steering her over the crests of the waves so that she might not trip was nice work. I stood at the helm now and made the most of it . . . The sloop at last reached inside small islands that sheltered her in smooth water.

from *Sailing Alone Around the World* by Joshua Slocum

It took another seven weeks for Slocum to retrace his steps to the Pacific, this time through the Cockburn Channel. He repaired all the storm damage and re-rigged *Spray* as a yawl.

Although the records show that the worst seas and the heaviest winds are to be found WNW of the Horn, the Cape sometimes reserves its Sunday punch for those who have just rounded it in tolerable conditions and think their worries are behind them, as they shape up to the NE to clear Staten Island 150 miles along the route to the South Atlantic.

So it was in March 1967 for that great navigator Francis Chichester in his 53-foot ketch *Gipsy Moth IV*. Passing well north of Diego Ramirez Islands in relatively settled weather with a steady barometer he suddenly saw the Horn abeam to port, less than eight miles away, 'standing out like a black ice-cream cone'. He had already been sighted by the Antarctic patrol ship HMS *Protector* and by journalists in a Chilean Piper Apache, whose windscreen was obscured by spume blown off the waves 60 feet below. Chichester wrote:

Ten minutes after noon I logged: 'I tried to be too clever (as so often, I regret). I went out to try to coax *Gipsy Moth* to sail more across the wind; the motive being to get north into the lee of land.' I thought that if only I could make some northing, I would get protection in the lee of Horn Island, and the islands to the north of it. However, the seas did not like it when I started sailing across them, and a souser filled the cockpit half full when I was in it. As a result, I had to change all my clothes, and also put *Gipsy Moth* back on to her original heading. That kept me just on the edge of the wind shadow from Cape Horn, and that might have made for more turbulence.

However, the wind was backing slowly, so that I steadily approached the heading I wanted to Staten Island. Unfortunately, with the wind shifting into the south-west, I got no protection whatever from the land, and . . . the seas built up to some of the most vicious I had experienced on the voyage.

*

It had certainly been a rough sea before . . .; the cockpit had been filled five times up to then. It was an extraordinary sight to see the gear lever throttle control, and instruments of the motor which were placed half-way up the side of the cockpit, all under water. But that sea was kid's stuff compared to what was running three hours later. The biggest wind registered by the anemometer that I noticed was 55 knots. I was doubtful of the accuracy of this instrument in high winds, but even if it was only 55 knots that, added to the 8 knots of speed which *Gipsy Moth* was making, totted up to a 63-knot wind – Force 11. The seas were far more vicious than I should have expected from such a wind and they were frightening.

The self-steering gear seemed unable to control the heading so I went aft to inspect the gear. I found that the connection between the wind vane and the steering oar had come out of its socket again. I tried to replace its proper pin, but could not get it in by hand, so I fetched an ordinary split pin and used that.

I think that this particularly turbulent sea was due to being on the edge of soundings; a few miles to port the depth was only 50 fathoms, and a few miles to starboard it was 2,300 fathoms.

By 16.30, however, there had been one or two lulls, which cheered me enormously.

*

At 17.37 I logged:

'A definite lull, with wind not roaring or screaming, and wind speeds down to 25–30 knots. Long may it last! The trouble with these gales is that I lose my appetite just when plenty of food is needed, I am sure . . .'

I was headed north-east for the east point of Staten Island. *Gipsy Moth* was travelling fast, although she had only the storm jib set, and that was reefed so that the total area was only 60 square feet, which is not much for an 18-ton boat. The wind had swung round to south-west and I heard later than someone aboard *Protector* had said the wind was 100 miles an hour when she left *Gipsy Moth*. I think that was a misquote, but six hours later I was in an angry storm, as if the Horn was letting me know what it could do if it tried . . . I admit I was frightened for a while.

However, fear does not last. I turned in and went to sleep. I slept for about two hours, until an hour after midnight. I found that the speedometer batteries had run down and I changed them. Unfortunately I did not allow for the distance run being under-registered. This might have had serious consequences. I logged:

'The rolling is frightful. It is very difficult to stand in the cabin. The wind is pretty strong still, 23–33 knots in the quieter periods.'

The barometer had steadied. I ought to have realised that there was something wrong with the mileometer, because it registered only 8.8 miles run in three hours. All the morning I had been making good about 8 miles in one hour. I had run up the dead reckoning position at 22.00 using the distance recorded by the mileometer. I was on a heading of NE by E to pass close east of Staten Island. There seemed a good open space before me on the chart, with the east cape of Staten Island 85 miles ahead by the dead reckoning. The navigation looked so easy that I did not pay much attention to it.

At 04.40 in the morning I gybed, because *Gipsy Moth* had been forced up to a heading of NNE by the backing wind. I logged: 'My hands are numb and I have difficulty in hanging up my coat or in writing.' There was a strong wind still blowing, over 60 knots. I found that the long-suffering wind vane was catching up in the mizzen backstay, and I used a length of cord to prevent the backstay from fouling it. No wonder the self-steering gear had been eccentric in the gale! I had a hot rum to warm me up and wrote in the log:

'I now feel as tight as a coot, though I don't know how a coot could be tight. It was very good rum though. When we are going dead before the wind it seems as quiet as a church at times when the boat is not rolling. I think I am short of food – I have had only two square meals in two days, supplemented by snacks, mostly liquid like chocolate or honey and lemon. I am not sure that the paraffin stove is not upsetting me with carbon monoxide . . .'

There was nothing in sight at 05.30 and I had seen nothing while working for quite a while on the stern at daybreak. I felt hungry and started preparing breakfast. I chanced to look out of the window in the doghouse on the port side and I felt as if the roots of my hair all over my body had turned red. I was startled to the bone, when, on looking out of the hatch, I saw a vast craggy bulk of land less than 10 miles away, and we had nearly pased it. I expected Staten Island to be still 35 miles ahead. Had I been pushed in by the tide to close Tierra del Fuego in the night? If so I must be bearing down on Staten Island ahead as a lee shore in winds up to 40 knots. I took three bearings of a cape that *Gipsy Moth* was passing, from which I reckoned that we were 7 miles off it, and that the ground speed was 8.8 knots. As soon as I had sighted the land I had prised myself up in the companion and peered over the top of the hood above it. I was headed to pass a headland, leaving it 5 miles to port. I must establish my position. My breakfast, of course, had gone for a burton. Fortunately, the sun had risen nearly dead ahead; a sun observation would give me a position line which would decide how far up the coast I was. I hurriedly fished out the sextant and set to work. Meanwhile, the headland was rushing up fast. The hilly land rising to mountainous country behind it was moving up as fast as if I was passing in a train. I think I have seldom taken and worked out a sight quicker. At the same time I was taking it steadily, set on not making a mistake. I plotted the resultant position line. I was passing the East Cape of Staten Island. I could hardly believe it. I checked my working again – there was no mistake.

Although I could hardly believe it at the time, when I came to look at the chart and study the dead reckoning navigation, it all became simple. From my noon position near Cape Horn I had worked out the heading which would take me 5 miles past the easternmost cape of Staten Island. In fact, I passed 7 miles off it. The distance was 140 miles, and if I had worked out the time at the morning's ground speed of 7.4 knots my estimated time of arrival at the Cape would have been nineteen hours after leaving the noon position, i.e. at 07.00 on the Tuesday morning. In fact, I arrived there at one and a half minutes past 8. I took me longer, because the wind eased during the night, and *Gipsy Moth*, still with only the 60-foot spitfire set, slowed down. What I had forgotton to take into account was the fact that the speedometer batteries had run down, and had undoubtedly been under-registering; therefore I thought I was going much slower than in fact I was . . . I felt tired, strained and extremely lonely . . . On top of that I was seasick, and later in a Cape Horn grey-bearder storm, and so I neglected to take account of the mileometer under-reading.

Now Staten Island had rushed past, and already it was disappearing in the haze.

from *Gipsy Moth Circles the World* by Sir Francis Chichester

If the men who sailed the Cape Horners realized the risks they were taking to life and limb, they would not have been there – unless they had been delivered on board dead-drunk by a pimp in Port Talbot or Hamburg. Their indifference to hardship and danger was legendary, even amongst wooden ships and iron men.

One of Captain Miethe's outstanding qualities was his thoroughness. Once when the *Potosi* took a great sea – one of those murderous, nasty 'niners' which old-time Horn battlers reckoned snarled along at the rate of one in every nine big seas – right over the midships deck, the captain made a leap for the weather shrouds to get firm grip and not be washed away. But his hands found bights of running rigging, which gave. He did not let go, but the sea and the ship's tremendous roll to leeward spun him over end for end – pitched him a somersault, still clinging to the lines. His head struck the steel bar at the foot of the shrouds inboard where lead blocks were secured to get more purchase at the gear, and cleft it open about a foot. A kneecap was knocked adrift, and he had other injuries. There he was, a dreadful sight, flung on his beam ends, blood gushing from his wounded head (it looked far worse than it was), a collarbone broken, unable to stand because of the leg injury, loss of breath, and a bellyful of sea water. But he still had his grip. The mate helped him up. The ship was all right: the sea had done no particular damage. So Captain Miethe allowed himself to be helped to the little hospital down below.

Here he took command. The collarbone was no problem. The mate knew how to strap his shoulder up so that would mend.

'Knock it back,' he gave instructions for the shifted kneecap to be given a suitable tap with a wooden belaying pin. As for the broken head, it was only skin and such: there was no fracture of that hard headpiece.

from War with Cape Horn by Alan Villiers

The sailmaker cobbled the broken head together with twenty-four stitches.

The east–west passage around the Horn is the most daunting test of men and ships imaginable. The time-honoured advice is that midwinter is the best time to go. In spite of what *Ocean Passages* says, easterly winds are rare, but winds from the northerly quarter giving a comfortable reach around the Cape are a better than one-in-three chance, enabling most sailing ships to make light of the adverse ocean current of 1–1½ knots. But, as described at the start of this section, icing is an added danger, and in midwinter there are fifteen hours of darkness each day.

Commercial pressures and availability of cargoes sometimes dictated making the passage during historically unsuitable months for the voyage, especially once the competition of steamships loomed in the last quarter of the nineteenth century. So it was that the 1,800-ton square-rigger *Acamas*, commanded by the redoubtable Captain W. A. Nelson of Maryport, sailed at the end of August 1905 from Port Talbot with coal for Pisagua on the west coast of Chile. It was September – spring in the southern hemisphere – when she crossed the 50th parallel, the traditional starting-point for the treacherous 1,500 miles which have to be sailed before clearing the same latitude northbound in the blue Pacific.

All went well until we had just got through the Straits of Le Maire near Cape Horn. Standing to the southward under topsails in snow blizzards and a westerly gale, we were suddenly caught aback by a terrific squall from the S.S.W. Although the upper-topsail halyards were let go, the yards failed to come down owing to the pressure of the sails against the masts and the heavy list we had taken before gathering sternway. Fortunately we got round on the same tack again without getting dismasted – but it must have been a very near thing.

After that it blew so hard, with fierce snow and hail squalls, that we were forced to find shelter under Staten Island. There we remained for a few days, in company with one of Walmsley's barques, the *Lorton*, I think.

It was now towards the end of September 1905 and the Cape Horn weather seemed to be at its worst, very cold, and the gales ever from the Westward. We spent from two to three weeks off the pitch of the Horn, most of the time in company with the four-masted French ship *Tarapaca*, both ships always going about together on the various tacks. On one tack we got to nearly sixty degrees South trying to get a slant of wind.

One morning as we head-reached against the gale, we found the ship was down by the head and making heavy weather by shipping more water than usual forward. The force-pump pipe had got fractured in the fore peak – which had filled with water to sea level. It was fortunate that this break came when it did, and that we had the peak baled out and the fracture repaired with canvas and white lead, before the weather turned really bad.

About ten days later, just before dark, both the *Acamas* and the *Tarapaca* wore ship to the northward. While we were doing so the wind came away from the S.W. with hurricane force. The sea was mountainous, with a cross N.W. swell. The last we saw of the *Tarapaca* she was running across our bows in the twilight during a hail squall. She was rather too close for comfort, we thought, but she looked a wonderful sight as she sped before the gale under close-reefed topsails.

We ran to the northward all night all hands in the poop ready for any emergency. We had barely got in sufficient 'westing' so had to keep the wind well out on the port quarter. The two best helmsmen were kept at the wheel, getting a small tot of rum periodically to warm them.

A tub filled with straw was kept near the wheel in ordinary Cape Horn weather for the helmsman to stand in and keep his feet from being frost bitten, but that went missing on this terrible night as the ship pooped once or twice and everything moveable had been washed away. A high dangerous sea swept the main deck throughout the night as the ship staggered along about 12 knots under lower topsails.

When daylight came it revealed something of a mess. . .

The main hatch had been stove-in, the steel strong-back having snapped in half. Fortunately, the hatches had dropped down on the coal cargo instead of going overboard. The tarpaulins were in shreds, although still held in the cleats. A great deal of water must have gone down into the hold during the night. We also found the starboard bulwarks abreast of the main hatch had been bent outboard and several stanchions torn away from the waterways. The rivets had dropped out of the holes into the hold as the decks constantly flooded.

It was still blowing hard, with the decks awash, so the ship was hove-to. 'Chips' made a number of wooden plugs, after which a couple of the apprentices went into the hold, climbed over the coal and drove these plugs into the vacant rivet holes.

The big job was to secure the main hatch. But where to find the material to do it with? A sailing ship deep-loaded off the Horn has very little spare timber about the decks. Although all hands were by now very tired, there was no alternative but to send them down into No. 1. 'tween decks and to drag out as many 'shifting boards' as they could get. These boards were long 2 inch deals, lashed with rope yards in a fore-and-aft direction to the line of midship stanchions. It was no easy matter getting these out as they were buried in coal with only the forward ends of the planks exposed. The men, numbed with the cold, were dressed in oilskins with soul and body lashings.

Coal had to be shifted until the ropeyarn lashings holding the planks to the stanchions could be cut. And even after that, they took a lot of dragging out. However, by 4 p.m. there were sufficient planks available. But to get these along the deck was another job, as occasional heavy seas kept tumbling on board. So, a length of small rope was attached to the ends of each plank and secured to the belaying pins on the ship's rail whenever the sea came along.

By 5 p.m. we had the hatch covered with deals, lashed securely down to the ring-bolts in the hatch coamings, and before dark a new storm sail was spread over the lot and well lashed round the coamings. One watch was now sent below. The other watch got coal up to raise steam on the donkey. They also rigged the messenger chain from the winch to the main pumps as it was necessary to get the pumps working as soon as possible. There was about eight feet of water in the wells.

Fortunately, this was the last gale Cape Horn had in store for us. The wind gradually moderated to a fresh Southerly, and we soon got into fine, warm weather, where we could spread out our mildewed clothes in the sun for an airing.

Sailing into Pisagua Bay . . . we had made the passage out in 109 days, the longest passage I ever made to the West Coast. All the same, it was not so bad, comparatively speaking. Some of the ships which left about the same time as us took about 130 days or longer . . .

The French barque *Anne* arrived at Pisagua in 135 days, having sailed East About round the Cape of Good Hope and south of New Zealand. But the French ships got paid so much for every mile they sailed as a subsidy from their Government, therefore distance was no object.

from *Master of Cape Horn* by Hugh Falkus

Acamas was not the only full-rigged ship to take a pasting off the Horn during the awful southern weather of 1905. The record has it that 130 ships sailed from European ports for the Pacific coast of America during May, June and July. Only fifty-two of them reached their destinations without being reported overdue: thirty-two retired with severe storm damage, whilst four of them disappeared with all hands.

One that made it to Pisagua in Chile 139 days out with 3,600 tons of coal from Port Talbot was the 2,287-ton *British Isles*, launched from John Reid's Clydeside yard in 1884. She had a massive rig: the main truck was 180 feet above the waterline, whilst her main yard was 105 feet long. On passage through the South Atlantic her crew of only twenty seamen and four apprentices had to deal with a fire in one of her holds – a not unusual event after sailing through the tropics with a cargo of coal which had been loaded wet. It all had to be shovelled out and spread on deck until the source of the fire was exposed and dealt with. Luckily the weather remained fair.

She reached Cape Horn on the very day *Acamas* sailed from Port Talbot, 7,500 miles away.

[The *British Isles* passed] Staten Island with a fair and following *easterly* breeze and clear skies.

*

On 8th August, in the morning, we passed Cape Horn, well to the southward, in 57 degrees South, out of sight of land.

*

We had all sail set to the royals as we passed the meridian of the Cape. When a sight of the sun was taken at noon the officers for once made no secret of our position, and the word flew round that we had turned the famous Continental Corner-post.

During the pleasant run from Staten Island the Captain's wife and children had again appeared on deck, the lady looking pale and wan, but smiling bravely to share in the general elation.

Soon after noon the easterly wind dropped to a light breeze, and presently we were almost becalmed. At the same time the temperature dropped suddenly, the skies clouded, and snow began to fall. The air was now bitterly cold, and icicles formed in the rigging. The long oily-looking swell from the west took on a sinister look and feel as we breasted it. On the far western horizon dense masses of cloud loomed portentous.

Not having access to the barometer readings the crew did not know what was brewing, although the old hands could make a good guess.

But the Captain knew only too well, as the glass continued to fall, and he eyed the portents in the west. His wife and children returned to their quarters, out of sight.

Towards sunset the expected battle-cry rang out:
'All hands on deck!'

*

So, to the urge of bellowed commands, the creak of blocks, and the rhythm-ical chants of *Haul we Heigh we Ho*, by hard-driven men exerting themselves to the utmost in the oncoming darkness, all the sails were clewed up, except the foresail, the three lower topsails and a jib, to which we were reduced in good time.

The clewed-up sails had now to be furled. They lay in the buntlines in stiff folds, wet by the snow, which had solidified to ice in the fabric, but were fortunately not bellied out by a strong wind. Scrambling aloft, among the icicles on the rigging, I had my first experience of stowing frozen Number One canvas, working in the dark.

It was extremely uncomfortable with numbed fingers, in a temperature several degrees below freezing-point, to lay out with one's belly over a steel spar covered in ice, clutching and clawing at the ice-stiffened canvas to roll it up on the yard. This had not been my idea of a life at sea when I had donned the smart monkey-jacket of a brassbounder in my happy home, now so far away.

But I was learning fast . . .

By 10 p.m., everything was snugged down. I was in the watch on deck, standing by, as the Captain and Second Mate peered into the murk to the westward, from where the change of wind was expected. We had not long to wait, and by midnight a real Cape Horn Snorter was upon us.

*

Suddenly, in the wall of darkness to the westward, a line of vivid whiteness is glimpsed advancing relentlessly towards us. It is the surface of the water churned by the violence of the approaching storm, about a mile from us, so that it seethes as though boiling in a gigantic cauldron.

The oily swells are being transformed into dangerous running seas.

'Hard up the helm!' the Captain orders. 'Lee forebrace!'

The seamen move at the run and tail on to the lee braces, hauling the yards round on to the backstays, as, with a roar like the voices of ten thousand suddenly uncaged and ravenous lions, a squall of hurricane force drives down on the ship as though determined to tear her to pieces.

She shudders at the impact, and heels over until the lee rail is under, and the men there, bracing the yards up, are immersed to their waists in the icy-cold flood of water that pours in over the rail.

The black wall to windward bears down relentlessly on the labouring ship, with a deluge of hail and sleet as it expends its pent-up fury.

*

Squall follows squall in unremitting succession. The Cape Horn Snorter is shaking us in its teeth as a terrier shakes a rat. The drumming of the wind, the wild plunging and rolling of the ship in the cross sea, the masses of cloud hurtling past near the mastheads, the heavens opening to let loose

113

on us a deluge of snow, hail and sleet, would provide an awe-inspiring, perhaps terrifying, spectacle – if we had time to pause and ponder and observe them at leisure.

But, up to our waists in the water swirling across the deck as the ship rolls, we are preoccupied with holding on to the lifelines, to the belaying-pins, to the rail, to anything handy, as we unravel the tangle of ropes in the icy water, and secure them in the rigging beyond the reach of the sea. Like men in battle, we are too busy to have time to be frightened. Our minds are on the immediate tasks we have to do, but we know, without needing to be told, the penalty for failure to surmount the dangers which beset us, as we work on blindly in obedience to the exacting orders of those who have the responsibility of commanding us what to do.

Headed towards the frozen regions of Antarctica, we can make but little westing in the teeth of this gale. While it lasts, and the Master persists in trying to sail to the westward, the ship is little better than an unmanageable derelict, for she is drifting now, carried to leeward by the set of the current, the pressure of wind against the maze of rigging, and those mighty rollers pounding against her side. We are drifting sideways, drifting, drifting back east of the Cape we had so jubilantly sailed past 24 hours previously, the Continental Corner-post, the meeting-place of the oceans. The Greybeards of Cape Horn are laughing uproariously at us, in derision, because with our puny strength we have dared to challenge their supremacy and invade their solitudes.

In the dawn we are still drifting helplessly, with our wake streaming to windward at an angle of 60 degrees to our keel, and the storm shows no sign of abating.

An albatross appears out of the murk, to examine us in our plight. The gale is of hurricane force, but the bird sails serenely and unhurriedly through the air, within a few feet of the ship's rail, on the windward side.

Then it turns into the eye of the wind, and disappears in the murk – *westward* – without any discernible effort in its aerial gliding, while we are still drifting to leeward, incapable of emulating its brilliant defiance of the gusts.

Cape Horn was astern yesterday, but today it is again ahead of us. We have rounded the Cape twice – once going forward and once drifting back, and all in 24 hours! We have turned the Corner of the Continent, and have been turned back, willy-nilly.

We shall keep on trying, until the Greybeards relent, and let us through. Battling round the Horn, many a sailorman and many a ship, have perished; but the *British Isles* still floats; and even a Cape Horn Snorter must eventually abate its fury.

The *British Isles* was also handicapped through only carrying half the proper complement of seamen, an economy forced upon shipowners who were still trying to compete with steamships for cargoes. Inevitably there were casualties which further compounded her master's worries:

The ship took a terrible pounding. I do not know how she lived through it. At 6 p.m. came the climax of misfortune, as a mountainous ridge of water crested above us and crashed on the deck. Lashed to the rail, I, like the others, was submerged for a moment in waters swirling over my head, and emerged as the surge receded, gasping for air and half-drowned.

This was the limit. The ship was in chaos. In the relative 'smooth' for a few minutes that followed this monster sea, we saw that the Greek seaman, Hieronymos, was lying unconscious in the scuppers, face down in the water. His leg was jammed in a washport and held fast, with the heavy iron door pounding the leg to a pulp.

Three or four of us dragged him clear, and somehow dumped him, more dead than alive, into the forecastle, where the carpenter and steward tried to give him first aid.

His leg was more than broken. It was pulped to a horrible gory mash, but in the shuddering confusion that prevailed in every part of the ship, there was no time to pause and consider his plight.

The Captain and officers were hauling themselves by the lifelines through the wash on deck, in response to yells from forrard. The side of the port forecastle had been stove in by the crash of that gigantic sea, and the water was swirling breast-deep inside, where several men, incapacitated by frost-bite, were lying in the wreckage of the shattered bunks cursing and yelling for help.

They and their kits were transferred to the starboard forecastle.

Then somebody said, 'Where's Nielsen?'

He was a Dane, who had been the lookout man, standing between the boats housed on the top of the forward deck-house.

As we searched for him in the darkness on the deck-house, which had so recently been a haven of refuge for us also, when we braced up the fore-yards while wearing ship, we found that the top of the deck-house had been swept clean.

Not only had poor Nielsen gone overboard, but the two lifeboats also, to one of which he had lashed himself.

*

With the death of Nielsen and Davidson, the terrible injuries to Hieronymos and West, and ten men down with frost-bitten hands and feet, our crew now consisted of six worn-out seamen and four equally worn-out boys.

At length the weather relented and the *British Isles* was able to sail into warmer waters up the Chilean coast and deliver her outward cargo of coal to Pisagua and her seven sick seamen to hospital.

Operations were performed by the Chilean surgeons. None of these seven seamen returned to the ship. We heard eventually that two of them died in the hospital. One of these was John Witney, who had suffered the multiple fracture of his leg. One of the seamen suffering from severe frost-bite and gangrene also died, after an amputation of his leg.

The other seamen with severe frost-bite had his leg amputated, but survived the operation. The surgeons performed a second amputation of Jerry the Greek's leg, to arrest a further spread of gangrene, but he survived, and these two were eventually sent back to England, each with a wooden leg.

The other three in the hospital had minor amputations of their toes and eventually recovered.

Of the twenty seamen who had signed on for that tragic outward-bound voyage of the *British Isles*, three were lost overboard, three more died from injuries, two were permanently disabled, and three partially disabled – a heavy price to pay for delivering 3,600 tons of black diamonds to Pisagua.

from *The Cape Horn Breed* by Captain W. H. S. Jones

When the *British Isles* dropped anchor off Pisagua 139 days out she was over forty days overdue.

There are sheltered fjords between the mainland of South America and the Chilean archipelago of a thousand islands, linking the Atlantic and the Pacific oceans and bypassing Cape Horn. The Straits of Magellan were named after the Spanish explorer who first discovered them in 1520 when he entered from the east at Cabo Virgenes, 200 miles north of Cape Horn. Careful navigation for the next 2,000 miles through the southern equivalent of the Norwegian Leads will bring a ship out into the blue Pacific 600 miles further north at the Isla Chiloe.

Hal Roth and his wife Margaret had less than ten years' sailing experience behind them when they set out from San Diego, bound for the eastern seaboard of the USA. Sailing their 35-foot glass-fibre sloop *Whisper* they logged 2,438 miles between entering the waterway and emerging out through the Beagle Channel (named after the HMS *Beagle* which carried Charles Darwin on his expedition in 1831–6) and the Straits of Le Maire leading into the comparative safety of the South Atlantic.

Along the way they were frequently hit by flash squalls screaming down the mountainsides at up to 80 knots. One such katabatic wind – so-called because it blows downwards – hit them in the middle of the night when they lay at a secure anchorage just forty miles short of the Horn. Locally such sudden violent storms are known as a *panteoneros*, or cemetery winds. The boat was hurled bodily on to a rocky islet, well above the highwater mark. A Chilean Navy patrol boat found them after nine days in a makeshift tent. A hole the size of a tabletop had been torn out of her garboards. Nevertheless the resourceful Chileans jacked the boat upright and screwed on a plywood tingle, which enabled her to be relaunched and towed to the naval base of Punta Arenas for permanent repairs.

Three months later they finally rounded the Horn from east to west in midwinter on a benign day. Then they were on their way home. Hal Roth has neatly summarized the problems to be overcome on the inland waterways off Southern Chile, even if they don't include the awesome greybeards of the Southern Ocean.

Sailing in Cape Horn waters is like walking on a tightrope. As long as each of your steps is surefooted and in the right direction, all is perfection. In my view, small ship handling in the vicinity of the great Chilean mountains and glaciers is the most exciting sport in the world. Trouble lurks on all sides, however, and it takes only one slip to plunge into disaster.

The big problem is the wind, which can blow with violence that is hard for a distant reader to believe.

Cape Horn gales blow primarily from the west. As the depressions move eastward in the Southern Ocean at say 60° S, the wind to the northward blows first from the northwest, veers to the west, and finally blows hardest from the southwest. For more than one hundred twenty-five years, ship reports have verified that winds of at least Force 8 (34–40 knots) blow 23 percent of the time in the Cape Horn area. This means that you will find winds of thirty-seven knots and upward one day in four.

This is only part of the problem. Around mountains, the uneven heating and irregular topography introduce a turbulence factor of some 40 percent more and cause violent gustiness. Force 13 and 14 winds (72–89 knots) are no strangers to the Chilean channels, and Force 15 (90–99 knots) is more than casually known. A portion of the blame can be directed to the williwaw or Cape Horn squall:

The williwaw [according to the British *Pilot*], unlike most of the squalls which occur in tropical and temperate regions, depends largely, if not entirely, on the existence of strong winds or gales at sea at a height of several thousands of feet over the land. These strong winds generally prevail over an area of several thousand square miles. As they strike the rugged mountains of the archipelagos, they set up eddies of varying size and intensity . . . During the strongest williwaws, which occur most often westward of Cabo Froward and near the main coastline adjoining the stormiest region at sea, the wind almost certainly exceeds 100 knots.

For the fellow snug at home, such figures are mere numbers. Coming face to face with winds of these magnitudes in a small vessel, however, is an awesome test of man and boat.

Obviously no yacht or fishing boat or naval vessel or cargo ship goes sailing in hurricane winds by choice. You anchor in a sheltered place if possible and wait for better weather. In the channels there are many suitable bays, but ordinary anchoring techniques are quite useless when the wind begins to blow hard. In southern Chile all vessels – unless they are large enough to keep up steam and have crew to stand anchor watches – take lines ashore; otherwise they use radar and travel day and night.

Unfortunately, in the beginning you doubt the necessity of tying ashore. *My* anchors are better. *My* anchoring techniques are good enough. *My* judgement is adequate. Lines ashore? Mooring to trees? Humbug!

It is only after some months in the region, a careful reading of mariners' accounts, and discussions with other captains that you begin to get an idea of the scope of Cape Horn anchoring problems.

The strong winds blow from the west so you seek a bay or inlet that will protect you from westerly seas. Ideally, an anchorage should be on the east side of a long low finger of land that runs north and south or perhaps is a horseshoe open to the east. Low land to the west is preferred because the wind turbulence and resultant williwaws are less. Usually, however, a sheltered bay in the channel has mountains or steep hills on three sides. What you must do then is to try to predict where the westerly winds will funnel down, and to head the vessel in that direction. This means anchoring in front of a canyon or draw or low place in the hills that leads roughly westward. You sail up to such a place and creep as close to the shore as possible.

Sometimes a deep anchorage will allow you to go within a few feet of the shore; the water is often clear and you can watch the bottom come up. In addition the charts sometimes have detailed plans. Then you launch the dinghy and take lines to the land – generally two lines secured to separate strong points. If there are substaintial trees or logs, you can tie to them. Otherwise you carry anchors ashore and dig them into the beach or earth, or jam the flukes in cracks in the rock if you're near a stony shore . . . The noise may be wearisome and the heeling from the gusts may upset your nerves a little, but you and your vessel will be safe.

from *Two Against Cape Horn* by Hal Roth

Little had changed when Warren Brown from Bermuda went through the same waters in 1986 in his 65-foot sloop *War Baby*, formerly *Tenacious* when she was owned by Ted Turner and won the toughest Fastnet Race of all time in 1979. This voyage was different from the Roths', in that the boat was twice as big and correspondingly stronger. She was fully crewed by seasoned offshore sailors and had all modern navigation-aids. Nevertheless, it was no picnic:

The westerly howled and shrieked. For about six weeks we had been in the Chilean channels, exploring the glaciers visited by Tilman and Mason in days gone by, and now we were surfing in *War Baby* at ten knots through the Straits of Magellan. This gusty passage lived up to its reputation, as hurricane-force winds funnelled their way down between high mountains. With an apparent wind of sixty. I realized what the early explorers such as Magellan had to face, coming from the other direction. Using our radar, we clung to the mid-passage of the pitch black landscape; but out of the gloom, we could see snow-capped peaks rising on either side of us as we barrelled along.

It was quite a ride that night. Once we tried to find shelter, but as we approached the cliffs, the katabatic winds were even stronger, and we knew that even with two or three anchors out, we probably could not hold our position, and that we would run a great risk of being blown ashore, as had happened to Hal and Margaret Roth in *Whisper*. Therefore we pressed on, heading for Punta Arenas the following day. In the early hours of the morning, as we rounded Cape Froward, the winds decreased; but only for a short time, and soon we were beating in fifty-knot winds for the last fifty miles to Punta Arenas, which was to be our berth over the Christmas holidays.

We left Punta Arenas on January 9, and it was not long before we were hit by another storm – in fact we had a steady fifty knots apparent by the following evening. The shoreline through the eastern end of the Straits of Magellan is low, and with a hazy and overcast sky, visibility was poor.

Homeward-bound, we sailed past Smith Island, totally encased by glacier and allegedly never climbed by man. Ice on the way north was tricky, and one gale slowed us a bit. Also, a very unusual norther forced us to tack back and forth between the Atlantic and Pacific eight times. I don't know if that counts for one or eight roundings, but we made it to the Horn. In fact, we went ashore in two separate parties and climbed to the summit of Cabo de Hornos. One of the Chilean blue jackets on watch at the hut where we were served tea told me the weather forecast was northwest 15 kts. By the time all hands returned to the boat it was already blowing 30 kts. That was at sundown.

Later it blew 80 kts while we hove-to, east of the Wollastons. Houses ashore lost roofs, but *War Baby* took it in stride. After one day at Puerto Toro on Navarino Island, we sailed into the Beagle Channel and completed our voyage at Puerto Williams, the Chilean Naval Base.

from *Cruising Club of America News* (1987) by Warren Brown and E. Newbold-Smith

Choosing their moment, enterprising or even eccentric sailors have rounded the Horn in all manner of craft, although there is no record of anyone yet doing so on waterskis or a sailboard or in a bath-tub. In 1960, during a 41,500-mile circumnavigation in eighty-three days, all of them beneath the waves, Captain Edward L. Beach made the east–west passage in the nuclear submarine *Triton*. At 447 feet LOA and 7,750 tons submerged displacement, she was over twice the size of any of the thousands of Cape Horners that had gone before her under sail. He briefed his crew in the columns of the submarine's daily newspaper, *The Triton Eagle*:

It is not a usual thing for a sailor to round the Horn these days. Many spend a lifetime and never do. By far the majority of US Navy sailors have never done it. Quite obviously, if you ever brag about having been around the Horn, the next question will either be, 'Did you see it?' or 'What does it look like?'

We intend to take a picture and I think it will be possible to make enough copies for all hands. But more than this, I want every man aboard to be able to say he's seen it. Note: there will be no muster taken. If you don't want to see the Horn, no one will force you. But you'll wish you did later, because you'll probably never get the chance again.

And then, that morning, I let it be known that in the old days, when a sailor went around the Horn, he hoped not to see the fabled Cape. If anyone aboard an old sailing ship, bucking wind and tide to double the Cape, sighted the forbidding promontory looming through the haze, it was considered bad luck would follow very soon in the form of shipwreck on one of the most inhospitable coasts in the world.

More modern traditions, I announced, were different. A sailor who gazed upon Cape Horn deliberately would experience good luck for the rest of his seafaring career. Not only that, but all sailors who rounded the Horn automatically attained certain privileges denied ordinary mortals (one I did not recommend was that we might all have a pig tattooed on the calf of the right leg). Tradition has it also that sailors who have rounded the Horn may with impunity throw trash and slops to windward, and because of their great victory over the forces of the wind, none of it will ever be blown back into their faces. They also have the traditional right to wear their hats on the side of their heads instead of square above the eyebrows, as is required by Navy regulations (no one may wear it on the *back* of his head).

. . . Every man wanted a look, and it was necessary to go back and forth five times in front of the Cape before all hands had had their view.

Triton's Log for the passage may give some idea of the conditions the old-timers faced in the days of sail.

. . . We estimate the waves as 10 to 12 feet high and the wind about 25 knots from the west.

There are occasional rain squalls and the cloud coverage is rather low to the water. It is also noticed, after a few navigational cuts, that we are being set backwards, to the east, by a current of some 3 knots. Under such conditions it is easy to see how an old wind-jammer, trying to beat her way around the Cape, might find it almost impossible. Heavy winds and a strong current were both dead against her. Even a steamer would have her troubles at a time like this.

from *Around the World Submerged* by Captain Edward L. Beach, USN

The captain might have mentioned that the privilege of ditching garbage to windward extended to pissing over the weather side.

Disasters

The Apostle Paul was shipped out of Caesarea (on the coast north of modern Tel Aviv) as a prisoner of the centurion Julius, who was charged with delivering him and over two hundred others to Rome where they would stand trial. They sailed north coast-crawling as far as Turkey and thence to the south coast of Crete – a voyage of over 700 miles before setting out again on the last 500 miles to Italy.

They had no compass and were driven most of the way before a succession of north-easterly gales. Their landfall on the fifteenth day was not identified until they had been wrecked on a lee shore a few miles NW of Valletta in a bay now popular with water-skiers, appropriately called St Paul's Bay.

Near the end the crew panicked and prepared to abandon ship. They had already 'undergirded' her, a desperate measure intended to hold the structure of the hull together by passing chains or the heaviest warps under the keel and securing either end on deck. It remained part of the survival drill for seamen for at least another 1,500 years, for it crops up again in the days of Anson and Pizarro. Before the crew could cast themselves over the side, St Paul gave advice which might with advantage have been recalled during the 1979 Fastnet storm. The old biblical translation – 'Except these abide in the ship, ye cannot be saved.' – is more to the point than the words of the 1961 New English Bible:

When it was decided that we should sail for Italy, Paul and some other prisoners were handed over to a centurion named Julius, of the Augustan Cohort. We embarked in a ship of Adramyttium, bound for ports in the province of Asia, and put out to sea. In our party was Aristarchus, a Macedonian from Thessalonica. Next day we landed at Sidon; and Julius very considerately allowed Paul to go to his friends to be cared for. Leaving

121

Sidon we sailed under the lee of Cyprus because of the head-winds, then across the open sea off the coast of Cilicia and Pamphylia, and so reached Myra in Lycia.

There the centurion found an Alexandrian vessel bound for Italy and put us aboard. For a good many days we made little headway, and we were hard put to it to reach Cnidus. Then, as the wind continued against us, off Salmone we began to sail under the lee of Crete, and, hugging the coast, struggled on to a place called Fair Havens, not far from the town of Lasea.

By now much time had been lost, the Fast was already over, and it was risky to go on with the voyage. Paul therefore gave them this advice: 'I can see, gentlemen,' he said, 'that this voyage will be disastrous: it will mean grave loss, loss not only of ship and cargo but also of life.' But the centurion paid more attention to the captain and to the owner of the ship than to what Paul said; and as the harbour was unsuitable for wintering, the majority were in favour of putting out to sea, hoping, if they could get so far, to winter at Phoenix, a Cretan harbour exposed south-west and north-west. So when a southerly breeze sprang up, they thought that their purpose was as good as achieved, and, weighing anchor, they sailed along the coast of Crete hugging the land. But before very long a fierce wind, the 'North-easter' as they call it, tore down from the landward side. It caught the ship and, as it was impossible to keep head to wind, we had to give way and run before it. We ran under the lee of a small island called Cauda, and with a struggle managed to get the ship's boat under control. When they had hoisted it aboard, they made use of tackle and undergirded the ship. Then, because they were afraid of running on to the shallows of Syrtis, they lowered the mainsail and let her drive. Next day, as we were making very heavy weather, they began to lighten the ship; and on the third day they jettisoned the ship's gear with their own hands. For days on end there was no sign of either sun or stars, a great storm was raging, and our last hopes of coming through alive began to fade.

When they had gone for a long time without food, Paul stood up among them and said, 'You should have taken my advice, gentlemen, not to sail from Crete; then you would have avoided this damage and loss. But now I urge you not to lose heart; not a single life will be lost, only the ship. For last night there stood by me an angel of the God whose I am and whom I worship. "Do not be afraid, Paul," he said; "it is ordained that you shall appear before the Emperor; and, be assured, God has granted you the lives of all who are sailing with you." So keep up your courage: I trust in God that it will turn out as I have been told; though we have to be cast ashore on some island.'

The fourteenth night came and we were still drifting in the Sea of Adria. In the middle of the night the sailors felt that land was getting nearer. They sounded and found twenty fathoms. Sounding again after a short interval they found fifteen fathoms; and fearing that we might be cast ashore on a rugged coast they dropped four anchors from the stern and prayed for daylight to come. The sailors tried to abandon ship; they had already lowered the ship's boat, pretending they were going to lay out anchors from the bows, when Paul said to the centurion and the soldiers, 'Unless these men stay on board you can none of you come off safely.' So the soldiers cut the ropes of the boat and let her drop away.

Shortly before daybreak Paul urged them all to take some food. 'For the last fourteen days', he said, 'you have lived in suspense and gone hungry; you have eaten nothing whatever. So I beg you to have something to eat; your lives depend on it. Remember, not a hair of your heads will be lost.' With these words, he took bread, gave thanks to God in front of them all, broke it, and began eating. Then they all plucked up courage, and took food themselves. There were on board two hundred and seventy-six of us in all. When they had eaten as much as they wanted they lightened the ship by dumping the corn in the sea.

When day broke they could not recognize the land, but they noticed a bay with a sandy beach, on which they planned, if possible, to run the ship ashore. So they slipped the anchors and let them go; at the same time they loosened the lashings of the steering-paddles, set the foresail to the wind, and let her drive to the beach. But they found themselves caught between cross-currents and ran the ship aground, so that the bow stuck fast and remained immovable, while the stern was being pounded to pieces by the breakers. The soldiers thought they had better kill the prisoners for fear that any should swim away and escape; but the centurion wanted to bring Paul safely through and prevented them from carrying out their plan. He gave orders that those who could swim should jump overboard first and get to land; the rest were to follow, some on planks, some on parts of the ship. And thus it was that all came safely to land.

from the Acts of the Apostles, chapter 27

In the summer of 1889, Herbert Lightoller, aged fifteen, signed on for his second voyage, having already made the 30,000-mile round-trip to San Francisco as a brassbound apprentice – a euphemism for an officer-cadet, but actually employed as cheap labour in the sailing ships' losing battle against steam. This time he was bound to Calcutta for orders under the flamboyant Captain Jock Sutherland – the 'Most Daring Cracker-on out of Liverpool'. Their course took them halfway across the Southern Ocean to the vicinity of a small rocky outcrop, St Paul, where they would head north towards their destination. *Holt Hill* had already lost her fore and main topmasts in an earlier gale, whilst retaining a full sail-plan all the way up to the skysails on the mizzen. This made her a double handful to steer in big following seas, so sail had been reduced to balance the wheel.

. . . Nearing St Paul . . . another sailing ship of about the same size came rapidly up astern and overtook her. Jock was beside himself with rage.

'I've never let another ship pass me with any of my sails furled yet and I won't start now!' he fumed to his Chief Mate, James Williams. 'Set everything!'

The order was duly carried out and the *Holt Hill* began to surge forward heeling dangerously, almost broaching to while two men desperately fought with the helm to keep her steady and on course. Many times Lightoller thought she was going to go right over but for some reason she did not, as that four-masted barque that had the audacity to try and overtake Jock Sutherland and the *Holt Hill* was left far astern to become a dot on the horizon.

The *Holt Hill* was in no condition for cracking on and yet despite having made his point Jock refused to ease off and shorten sail. He just 'let her go' as he walked up and down the poop with the burly Cornishman Williams, a loyal Mate who always stood by Jock. Lightoller however got the impression that both men wanted to suggest shortening down right now but neither would give in to the other. Meanwhile the *Holt Hill* ploughed recklessly on into a steadily worsening gale.

*

The boys of the half-deck were turning in and about to put their lamp out when suddenly they heard the heavy clump of Mowatt's boots galloping across the deck above them followed by the dreaded cry, 'All hands on deck!'

Lightoller hurriedly got his clothes on and rushed up on deck in answer to the call. When he arrived it was not this time to be greeted with masts, spars and sails plummeting down to meet him. It was far more horrifying than that.

There before him stood a great rocky mass towering above the ship and they were racing straight towards it. The watch on deck had not seen it sooner because of the poor visibility in the rain squall. But then it had cleared revealing, to the Second Mate's horror, land dead ahead and at the speed the ship was moving, only minutes away.

He had panicked and ordered the helm 'hard down' in his desperate bid to steer clear of the obstruction, but as soon as Jock arrived on deck and sized up the situation he countermanded the order. 'Hard up!' he barked, realising that there was more sea-room if he turned the ship the other way. But either way it was already too late.

*

Meanwhile Lightoller just gaped transfixed at that evil mountain of rock looming closer and closer waiting to claim its prize. Then through the screaming gale he heard Jock give his command: 'Steady the helm. Put her straight at it. Steady as she goes. Belay everything.'

Not since the early days of his first voyage had Lightoller felt such fear inside him, but the boy was determined to hold himself together as the ship careered towards her doom.

The skipper and his thirty-two men and boys stared silently ahead at the gigantic black mass that was growing larger and larger in front of them. Nobody spoke, nobody moved; they just stood rooted to the deck of their doomed ship, clinging to the most secure thing that came to hand to steady themselves while she was picked up by the huge seas that were battering the base of those rocky cliffs.

Lightoller felt an eerie sensation during those brief and yet interminable moments when he waited to know what card it was that fate was to deal him. For most people death rarely ever gave them a chance to think about it. Even after a long illness the end, when it finally came, was sudden. But here he was, a mere youngster, facing up to a terrible reality that within the next few minutes he might be dead – and unbelievably, this was more than likely.

'Stand aft under the break of the poop!'

At the word from Jock everybody rushed aft to be in the safest place to be clear of falling gear when she hit. The experience of that earlier break-up, which all seemed such a long time ago, would be nothing compared to the avalanche of masts and running gear that might topple on them any moment now.

'Every man for himself!'

The last command of all. The suspense seemed to go on and on. For a moment it felt as though time was almost standing still. And then she finally struck.

The first contact was with an invisible outcrop of rock which she hit with such crushing force that the whole ship trembled. But the agony had just begun as the *Holt Hill* was driven on by the wind and sea over the deadly rocks which ripped through the plates of her keel, gouging the guts right out of her with a rending, grating sound that made the boy sick. It was a ghastly sensation to feel and hear the ship being torn apart beneath him.

The big question now was would she hold together sufficiently for them to have a chance of saving themselves, or would she immediately break up in pieces and throw them all to the mercy of the rocks and the vicious seas, in which case there could be no hope for anyone.

But the sea, even in its most ruthless moods, can have a way of inadvertently throwing out a lifeline. For the *Holt Hill* it came in the form of a huge wave which took hold of her, hoisted her up and carried her bodily towards the cliffs with such force that Lightoller thought for a moment she might sail right on up the cliff face. Instead, with almost uncanny precision, the *Holt Hill* came to a grinding and abrupt halt at the foot of the cliffs with her bows neatly planted in the pincer-like grip of two large pillars of rock which held her fast, and now prevented her from sliding back into the sea.

Only one man, the mate, lost his life, all the others having scrambled up the cliff-face. There they prepared themselves to endure months as castaways, living off penguin, wild rabbit and spring-water. They were familiar with the earlier misadventure of a leaking old steamship, the *Megaera*, which had beached herself there to avoid sinking. Her complement of 350 passengers and crew were on the island for four months before being rescued. *Holt Hill*'s survivors were luckier: they were taken off after just eight days and safely delivered to Adelaide.

Nearly a quarter of a century later 'Lights' joined the White Star flagship as second officer. He was relieved at midnight, just forty minutes before an iceberg tore a fatal slice underwater along almost the entire length of the world's largest and reputedly safest ocean-liner, the RMS *Titanic*. Had the iceberg appeared ahead whilst he was still on watch, would he have remembered Captain Sutherland's snap decision to belay everything and hold course 'steady as she goes'? Had he done so, it is unlikely that 1,500 lives would have been lost on a calm, clear but hazy night in the North Atlantic steamship lanes, even though she would have been going just as fast as *Holt Hill* was on impact, allowing for the berg having been sighted and Full Astern rung down two minutes before a head-on collision. As the senior surviving officer, Lightoller was the key witness at the series of inquiries held on both sides of the Atlantic. Yet there is no record of his ever having been asked to speculate on that point, nor did he volunteer his opinion. Turning to the events of 14 April 1912:

> Lightoller was coming to the end of his watch. He was perishing cold and beginning to think longingly of his warm bunk, but he remained stationed out in the open, in the position along the bridge he had chosen to get the best unobstructed view forward, every so often raising his glasses to his eyes and scanning the horizon carefully. He could see that visibility was still crystal clear with no sign of ice. He did not know that a message had just come in to the wireless room which would have told him instantly that a great mass of ice, including many large bergs, was sitting in the *Titanic*'s path and little more than 40 miles away.
>
> 'Lights' could not have been in a happier frame of mind. A happily married family man of 38 with a future that could hardly have looked more rosy. Another year or so and he would be promoted to Chief, if not in the *Titanic* perhaps the *Olympic*, or in the third of the big sisters still in the building, and then after another couple of years, perhaps three, his own command! A smaller ship of the line, no doubt, but she would be his. That would be a proud day for sure, not least for Sylvia, who was just as keen if not more so, for her husband to get on in his career as he was himself.

It was chilly on the bridge-wing, though. His mind went back to those horrendous seas of the Horn where, as a fourteen-year-old, he had found himself fighting his first life-and-death battle against the elements as he endured those endless, gruelling hours hanging on aloft. And then came that dark, moonless night when the storm just died away and the sea became an oily calm as the wind dropped with not so much as a breath of air to disturb the sails slatting idly at the yards. They were in amongst ice and in the worst conditions for seeing it; no wind, not even the slightest breeze, the sea as smooth as glass, and no moon – and never had the boy felt such cold . . .

'It's pretty cold!' said Murdoch as he arrived on the bridge, wrapped up in scarf and thick overcoat and flapping his arms about his body. Lightoller hardly needed reminding as he informed Murdoch the temperature had now fallen to freezing point. He had been rarely more grateful for the welcome sound of Four Bells and the end of his watch on that cold bridge.

The two of them stood together yarning for a spell gazing ahead while Murdoch got his night vision. Murdoch and Lightoller were old shipmates by now, having sailed together many times in the White Star mailboats . . .

They got on to more immediate matters, the ice reports and the weather conditions. The biting cold, apart from the discomfort it caused was equally insignificant to Murdoch who, like Lightoller, knew the temperature could fall to freezing at any time of the year in these waters, summer, winter or spring.

Lightoller mentioned the commander's earlier visit to the bridge and his discussion with him about the chances of encountering ice, but how he had seemed quite satisfied that visibility was clear enough to see it in plenty of time. There had been no apparent deterioration since, though the horizon did not seem to have quite the same marked definition that it had shown earlier.

The Sunday night revelry in the *Titanic* was drawing to a close. It was a night that many were agreed they would remember for a long time as they laughed and chatted their way to bed on the Grand Staircase under the gaze of the magnificent showpiece clock flanked by its two bronze figures symbolising 'Honour and Glory Crowning Time'. In the Palm Court the ship's versatile eight-piece orchestra under the leadership of Wallace Hartley was rounding off its concert with a selection from *The Tales of Hoffmann*, which many of the audience had seen and enjoyed at one of the celebrated opera houses of Europe during their travels. Hartley always knew just how to please the customers; whatever the mood, his little orchestra expertly catered for it. From Ragtime to Beethoven, it was always played to absolute perfection. There was a ripple of applause, Hartley bowed obligingly, Lightoller pressed on.

In the male-dominated smoking-room there were still a few scattered groups sitting around, some playing bridge, some just reading and others, over a final brandy and cigar, immersed in conversations ranging from amusing personal experiences to more weighty matters on the economic and political front. The coal strike, Lloyd George's budget and the Stock Exchange boom were the main talking points just now among the English passengers, while for the Americans the big sensation was Roosevelt's victory over Taft in the Pennsylvania primaries.

*

As Lightoller eventually surfaced on deck at the after end of the ship it would have been impossible for the men enduring that thick roasting atmosphere 60 feet below to believe how bitterly cold it was out in the open. Here on the poop he checked round to see that Quartermaster Rowe and his men were at their stations, and then with his rounds complete, hurriedly made his way back forward along the length of the liner to the officers' quarters behind the bridge and the warmth of his tiny cabin. He was never more thankful to roll himself up in the blankets and close his eyes at last.

It was just as he was nodding off in the quiet calm of his little room that suddenly he felt an ominous shudder run through the ship.

Of all the people who should have shared the blame for the disaster, 'Lights' was never suggested as one of them, even by the highest-priced lawyers acting for the interested parties in the official inquiries that followed. He could easily have put the spotlight on the guilty parties – the White Star Line, the ship's designer and the inadequate safety measures required by the government's regulatory authority. The price of a stateroom did not include a seat in a lifeboat, for there were not enough to go round. The ships were operated recklessly, with their timely arrival overriding all other considerations. Icebergs were only reported by ships which happened to miss them. Seventy-five years later the 1987 Zeebrugge ferry disaster showed that some of the lessons had still not been applied.

During the First World War, 'Lights' served in the Dover Patrol, winning a DSC for sinking a U-boat whilst commanding a destroyer. When peace came, he returned to the White Star Line, who soon made it obvious that they would never give him a command. After some years of frustration he was driven to resign. Nowadays it would have been called constructive dismissal, and a tribunal would have awarded him a handsome payout. As it was, he simply stopped drawing £38 a month as chief officer of *Celtic*.

But if Lightoller had been harbouring any second thoughts about his decision to leave the White Star Line, the company he had served with unwavering loyalty since the day he joined them over twenty years previously, these were at once dispelled when, at the end of his last voyage from New York, he arrived at head office to 'await the pleasure' of the managers. His letter of resignation had already been briefly acknowledged without a word of regret, and as he entered the room the man at the head of the table looked up and simply said with a wave of the hand: 'Oh, you're leaving us are you? Oh well, goodbye.' With that the door was held open for him, he was out, and that was the end of it.

from *Lights* by Patrick Stenson

Before the next war broke out, Naval Intelligence had the good sense to recruit this great sailor to carry out clandestine surveys of the Friesian Islands and the coastline of the Low Countries in his converted naval pinnace, *Sundowner*. At the age of sixty-six he took her across to Dunkirk and brought back 130 soldiers from the encircled beaches. For the next six years he was in the Admiralty Ferry Service, delivering new ships from their builders' yards to their operators. He was seventy-two when he finally retired as a lieutenant-commander, RNR, with a bar added to his DSC.

Captain Frederick Marryat's prodigious output of yarns about the sea was based on his own career in the Royal Navy during the early part of the nineteenth century. His other claim to fame is that he devised a flag signal code which formed the basis of the International Code of Signals. His service under the flamboyant Lord Cochrane during the blockade of the enemy fleet off Toulon was the background for his most successful novel, *Mr Midshipman Easy*.

In it, HMS *Aurora* was giving chase to a convoy of small enemy ships close inshore near Cap Sicie – the rocky headland which guards the south-west approaches to the naval base at Toulon – when there was an abrupt change in the weather, typical of those parts to this day. Heavy squalls were accompanied by poor visibility. The first order given in the extract below may seem contradictory, but it was to have the mainsail brailed up and furled on its own cross-yard.

Considering the vulnerability of all ships with tall rigs to being struck by lightning, it is surprising that the scene he vividly described was not commonplace, yet is a rare misfortune.

'Captain Wilson, if you please, we are very close in,' said the master; 'don't you think we had better go about?'

'Yes, Mr Jones – Hands about ship – and – yes, by heavens we must! – up mainsail.'

The mainsail was taken off, and the frigate appeared to be immediately relieved. She no longer jerked and plunged as before.

'We're very near the land, Captain Wilson; thick as it is, I think I can make out the loom of it – shall we wear round, sir?' continued the master.

'Yes, hands wear ship – put the helm up.'

It was but just in time, for as the frigate flew round, describing a circle, as she payed off before the wind, they could perceive the breakers lashing the precipitous coast, not two cables' length from them.

'I had no idea we were so near,' observed the captain, compressing his lips; 'can they see anything of those vessels?'

'I have not seen them this quarter of an hour, sir,' replied the signalman, protecting his glass from the rain under his jacket.

'How's her head now, quarter-master?'

'South south-east, sir.'

The sky now assumed a different appearance – the white clouds had been exchanged for others dark and murky, the wind roared at intervals, and the rain came down in torrents. Captain Wilson went down into the cabin to examine the barometer.

'The barometer has risen,' said he, on his return on deck. 'Is the wind steady?'

'No, sir, she's up and off three points.'

'This will end in a south-wester.'

The wet and heavy sails now flapped from the shifting of the wind.

'Up with the helm, quarter-master.'

'Up it is – she's off to the south-by-west.'

The wind lulled, the rain came down in a deluge – for a minute it was quite calm, and the frigate was on an even keel.

'Man the braces. We shall be taken aback directly, depend upon it.'

The braces were hardly stretched along before this was the case. The wind flew round to the south-west with a loud roar, and it was fortunate that they were prepared – the yards were braced round, and the master asked the captain what course they were to steer.

'We must give it up,' observed Captain Wilson, holding on by the belaying pin. 'Shape our course for Cape Sicie, Mr Jones.'

And the *Aurora* flew before the gale, under her foresail and topsails close reefed. The weather was now so thick that nothing could be observed twenty yards from the vessel; the thunder pealed, and the lightning darted in every direction over the dark expanse. The watch was called as soon as the sails were trimmed, and all who could went below, wet, uncomfortable and disappointed.

'What an old Jonah you are, Martin,' said Gascoigne.

'Yes, I am,' replied he; 'but we have the worst to come yet, in my opinion. I recollect, not two hundred miles from where we are now, we had just such a gale in the *Favourite*, and we as nearly went down, when –'

At this moment a tremendous noise was heard above, a shock was felt throughout the whole ship, which trembled fore and aft as if it was about to fall into pieces; loud shrieks were followed by plaintive cries, the lower deck was filled with smoke, and the frigate was down on her beam ends. Without exchanging a word, the whole of the occupants of the berth flew out, and were up the hatchway, not knowing what to think, but convinced that some dreadful accident had taken place.

On their gaining the deck it was at once explained; the foremast of the frigate had been struck by lightning, had been riven into several pieces, and had fallen over the larboard bow, carrying with it the main topmast and jib-boom. The jagged stump of the foremast was in flames, and burnt brightly, notwithstanding the rain fell in torrents. The ship, as soon as the foremast and main topmast had gone overboard, broached-to furiously, throwing the men over the wheel and dashing them senseless against the carronades; the forecastle, the forepart of the main deck, and even the lower deck, were spread with men, either killed or seriously wounded, or insensible from the electric shock. The frigate was on her beam ends, and the sea broke furiously over her; all was dark as pitch, except the light from the blazing stump of the foremast, appearing like a torch held up by the wild demons of the storm, or when occasionally the gleaming lightning cast a momentary glare, threatening every moment to repeat its attack upon the vessel, while the deafening thunder burst almost on their devoted heads. All was dismay and confusion for a minute or two; at last Captain Wilson, who had himself lost his sight for a short time, called for the carpenter and axes. They climbed up, that is, two or three of them, and he pointed to the mizenmast; the master was also there, and he cut loose the axes for the seamen to use; in a few minutes the mizenmast fell over the quarter, and the helm being put hard up, the frigate payed off and slowly righted. But the horror of the scene was not yet over. The boatswain, who had been on the forecastle, had been let below, for his vision was gone for ever. The men who lay scattered about had been examined, and they were assisting them down to the care of the surgeon, when the cry of 'Fire!' issued from the lower deck. The ship had taken fire at the coal-hole and carpenter's store-room and the smoke that now ascended was intense.

'Call the drummer,' said Captain Wilson, 'And let him beat to quarters – all hands to their stations – let the pumps be rigged and the buckets passed along. Mr Martin, see that the wounded men are taken down below. Where's Mr Haswell? Mr Pottyfar, station the men to pass the water on by hand on the lower deck. I will go there myself. Mr Jones, take charge of the ship.'

Pottyfar, who actually had taken his hands out of his pockets, hastened down to comply with the captain's orders on the main deck, as Captain Wilson descended to the deck below.

'I say, Jack, this is very different from this morning,' observed Gascoigne.

'Yes,' replied Jack, 'so it is, but I say, Gascoigne, what's the best thing to do? – when the chimney's on fire on shore, they put a wet blanket over it.'

'Yes,' replied Gascoigne, 'but when the coal-hole's on fire on board, they will not find that sufficient.'

'At all events, wet blankets must be a good thing, Ned, so let us pull out the hammocks; cut the landyards and get some out – we can but offer them, you know, and if they do no good, at least it will show our zeal.'

'Yes Jack, and I think when they turn in again, those whose blankets you take will agree with you, that zeal makes the service very uncomfortable. However, I think you are right.'

The two midshipmen collected three or four hands, and in a very short time they had more blankets than they could carry – there was no trouble in wetting them, for the main deck was afloat – and followed by the men they had collected, Easy and Gascoigne went down with large bundles in their arms to where Captain Wilson was giving directions to the men.

'Excellent, Mr Easy, excellent Mr Gascoigne!' said Captain Wilson. 'Come my lads, throw them over now, and stamp upon them well'; the men's jackets and the captain's coat had already been sacrificed to the same object.

Easy called the other midshipmen, and they went up for a further supply; but there was no occasion, the fire had been smothered; still the danger had been so great that the fore magazine had been floated. During all this, which lasted perhaps a quarter of an hour, the frigate had rolled gunwale under, and many were the accidents which occurred. At last all danger from fire had ceased, and the men were ordered to return to their quarters, when three officers and forty-seven men were found absent – seven of them were dead, most of them were already under the care of the surgeon, but some were still lying in the scuppers.

*

. . . Jack was interrupted in his third glass, by somebody telling him the captain wanted to speak with Mr Hawkins and with him.

Jack went up, and found the captain on the quarter-deck with the officers.

'Mr Easy,' said Captain Wilson, 'I have sent for you, Mr Hawkins, and Mr Gascoigne, to thank you on the quarter-deck, for your exertions and presence of mind on this trying occasion.' Mr Hawkins made a bow. Gascoigne said nothing, but he thought of having extra leave when they arrived at Malta. Jack felt inclined to make a speech, and began something about when there was danger that it levelled every one to an equality even on board of a man-of-war.

'By no means, Mr Easy,' replied Captain Wilson; 'it does the very contrary; for it proves which is the best man, and those who are the best raise themselves at once above the rest.'

from *Mr Midshipman Easy* by Captain Frederick Marryat

In 1745 Pizarro was coming to the end of his commission in the South Atlantic pursuing Anson when he was obliged to press a number of local Indians in Montevideo to make up his ship's company for the voyage home. He noticed that they were skilled in the use of *bolos*. Their chief was a villain named Orellana, who was brutally beaten up by one of the ship's officers:

It was about nine in the evening, when many of the principal Officers were on quarter-deck, indulging in the freshness of the night air; the waste of the ship was filled with live cattle, and the forecastle was manned with its customary watch. *Orellana* and his companions, under cover of the night, having prepared their weapons, and thrown off their trouzers and the more cumbrous part of their dress, came all together on the quarter-deck, and drew towards the door of the great cabbin. The Boatswain immediately reprimanded them, and ordered them to begone. On this *Orellana* spoke to his followers in his native language, when four of them drew off, two towards each gangway, and the Chief and the six remaining *Indians* seemed to be slowly quitting the quarter-deck. When the detached *Indians* had taken possession of the gangway, *Orellana* placed his hands hollow to his mouth, and bellowed out the war-cry used by those savages, which is said to be the harshest and most terrifying sound known in nature. This hideous yell was the signal for beginning the massacre: For on this they all drew their knives, and brandished their prepared double-headed shot, and the six with their Chief, which remained on the quarter-deck, immediately fell on the *Spaniards*, who were intermingled with them, and laid near forty of them at their feet, of which above twenty were killed on the spot, and the rest disabled. Many of the Officers, in the beginning of the tumult, pushed into the great cabbin, where they put out the lights, and barricadoed the door. And of the others, who had avoided the first fury of the *Indians*, some endeavoured to escape along the gangways into the forecastle, but the *Indians*, placed there on purpose, stabbed the greatest part of them, as they attempted to pass by, or forced them off the gangways into the waste. Others threw themselves voluntarily over the barricadoes into the waste, and thought themselves happy to lie concealed amongst the cattle; but the greatest part escaped up the main shrouds, and sheltered themselves either in the tops or rigging. And though the *Indians* attacked only the quarter-deck, yet the watch in the forecastle finding their communication cut off, and being terrified by the wounds of the few, who not being killed on the spot, had strength sufficient to force their passage along the gangways, and not knowing either who their enemies were, or what were their numbers, they likewise gave all over for lost, and in great confusion ran up into the rigging of the fore-mast and bowsprit.

Thus these eleven *Indians*, with a resolution perhaps without example, possessed themselves almost in an instant of the quarter-deck of a ship mounting sixty-six guns, with a crew of near five hundred men, and continued in peaceable possession of this post a considerable time.

*

However, when the *Indians* had entirely cleared the quarter-deck, the tumult

133

in a great measure subsided; for those, who had escaped, were kept silent by their fears, and the *Indians* were incapable of pursuing them to renew the disorder. *Orellana,* when he saw himself master of the quarter-deck, broke open the arm-chest, which, on a slight suspicion of mutiny, had been ordered there a few days before, as to a place of the greatest security. Here he took it for granted, he should find cutlasses sufficient for himself and his companions, in the use of which weapon they were all extremely skilful, and with these, it was imagined, they proposed to have forced the great cabbin: But on opening the chest, there appeared nothing but fire-arms, which to them were of no use. There were indeed cutlasses in the chest, but they were hid by the fire-arms being laid over them. This was a sensible disappointment to them, and by this time *Pizarro* and his companions in the great cabbin were capable of conversing aloud, through the cabbin windows and port-holes, with those in the gun-room and between decks, and from hence they learnt, that the *English* (whom they principally suspected) were all safe below, and had not intermedled in this mutiny; and by other particulars they at last discovered, that none were concerned in it but *Orellana* and his people. On this *Pizarro* and the Officers resolved to attack them on the quarter-deck, before any of the discontented on board should so far recover their first surprize, as to reflect on the facility and certainty of seizing the ship by a junction with the *Indians* in the present emergency. With this view *Pizarro* got together what arms were in the cabbin, and distributed them to those who were with him: But there were no other fire-arms to be met with but pistols, and for these they had neither powder nor ball. However, having now settled a correspondence with the gun-room, they lowered down a bucket out of the cabbin-window, into which the gunner, out of one of the gun-room ports, put a quantity of pistol cartridges. When they had thus procured ammunition, and had loaded their pistols, they set the cabbin-door partly open, and fired some shot amongst the *Indians* on the quarter-deck, at first without effect. But at last *Mindinuetta,* whom we have often mentioned, had the good fortune to shoot *Orellana* dead on the spot; on which his faithful companions abandoning all thoughts of farther resistance, instantly leaped into the sea, where they every man perished. Thus was this insurrection quelled, and the possession of the quarter-deck regained, after it had been full two hours in the power of this great and daring Chief, and his gallant and unhappy countrymen.

Pizarro having escaped this imminent peril steered for *Europe,* and arrived safe on the coast of *Galicia* in the beginning of the year 1746, after having been absent between four and five years, and having, by his attendance on our expedition, diminished the naval power of *Spain* by above three thousand hands, (the flower of their sailors) and by four considerable ships of war and a Patache.

from *Anson's Voyage Round the World in the Years 1740–44* by Richard Walter

Gales

Many writers about ships and the sea focus attention on the different ways in which captains drove their ships. Some held on until the sails were one by one blown to ribbons – just as modern ocean-racing skippers are prone to do. Others shortened sail at dusk or at the first sign of a blow. In the Cape Horners sailors particularly disliked the practice of tying down a full reef on each sail before furling it, so that it could be spread again with a reduced area as the wind eased off. The late Alasdair Garrett, for many years editor of the Royal Cruising Club's annual *Roving Commissions*, spelled out the attributes needed by a blue-water skipper under sail:

'Any fool can carry sail on a ship –' burst out the master, indignant at the officer of the watch failing to order sail to be shortened. But the words were spoken a century ago in the Golden Age of seafaring before mechanical propulsion drove sail from the face of the great oceans. Indeed, the ship-master often found himself between the devil and the deep blue sea. On the one hand, his owners expected as fast a passage as the ship was capable of; on the other, a voyage account which included a long list of items of heavy weather damage – spars, sails and cordage carried away – was likely to incur the owners' displeasure and they were often not slow to make the master aware of it. Yet one cannot fail to draw inspiration from their achievements in an age when radio, weather forecasts and all the other aids to the safe conduct of a vessel of today were unknown. Of course, the sea exacted its toll and there were casualties. Ships were posted overdue and later, after weeks of anxiety, as lost without trace. All too often the reason for their being overwhelmed remained a matter for conjecture.

The middle decades of the present century have seen the regeneration of sail and its reappearance on the oceans is now commonplace. The great square-rigger of yesterday with its towering masts and spread of canvas and a ship's company of two score men or more has given way to tiny vessels, some with less canvas than would make a belltent and manned by only four or five souls and often fewer. Although for the most part they are amateur sailors, they are the living heirs to a noble tradition of sail, and it therefore behoves them to acquire the skills of a seaman in order to be worthy of their inheritance. It is true that science and the ingenuity of man have made great advances. Our knowledge of the behaviour patterns of wind and sea has increased immeasurably and with it the means of placing this knowledge at the disposal of the seafarer a thousand miles or more from the land. But still the might of wind and sea remains unsubdued, ready to exact a toll of those who treat them lightly.

Indeed, the sea demands definite qualities in the seafarer – certain attitudes of mind and character. Humility, prudence and a recognition that there is no end to learning and to the acquisition of experience. Humility I put first, for who would dare be other than humble in the presence of two great elements – of sea and sky and all the uncertainties which they hold for us? Prudence comes second – it is the ingrained characteristic of the professional seaman – and I would define it as the ability to distinguish between the risk which can reasonably be accepted having regard to prevailing conditions and the risk which must be rejected as unacceptable. Lastly, learn by your own experience and by the experience of others, for there is never an end to your learning.

He summed up the creed of the shipmasters during the Golden Age of sail as follows:

'Like all true art, the general conduct of a ship and her handling in particular cases had a technique which could be discussed with delight and pleasure by men who found in their work, not bread alone, but an outlet for the peculiarities of their temperament. To get the best and truest effect from the infinitely varying moods of sky and sea, not pictorially, but in the spirit of their calling, was their vocation, one and all; and they recognized this with as much sincerity, and drew as much inspiration from this reality, as any man who ever put brush to canvas. The diversity of temperaments was immense amongst those masters of the fine art.'

from *Heavy Weather Sailing* by K. Adlard Coles

The English Channel has more than its share of gales and dangerous seas at almost any time of the year. Recently oceanographers announced that the seas encountered in these waters are now up to 25 per cent bigger than they were when records were first begun. The most recent hurricane-strength blow was in October 1987, which did untold damage ashore and in harbours, yet claimed few lives at sea, partly because it hit in the middle of the night after the end of the normal sailing season. Claud Worth has left us an account of what seems to have been a similar storm which he survived during a passage from Falmouth to the Thames Estuary at the time of the 1896 September equinox. He set out with one hired hand ('obese and alcoholic-looking') whom he picked up in a pub to help him sail his 28-foot 6½-ton gaff cutter *Tern*. Both her long bowsprit and topmast could be housed in heavy weather, since he described her as being over-canvassed. She had the pilot cutter's traditional square stem, long overhang aft and low freeboard amidships.

I had a week for the trip. After that there was no possibility of my joining the yacht, even for a day, until the following April. I was therefore prepared, if necessary, to put up with rather more than I usually care for in the matter of weather, in order to get the vessel home. But, it need scarcely be said, if I had foreseen what was coming, she would have had to remain at Falmouth. Having fortunately come safely out of it, I am glad to have had this experience of what a small vessel can live through. In its prolonged violence and in the havoc which it wrought at sea, I think that this gale must be the worst which has occurred in the 'yachting season' within the memory of most of us.

*

Monday, September 21st. – S.S.W., moderate. Started with whole mainsail. Wind freshened off Dodman. Tied up one reef and furled staysail. My A.B. turned out to be no sailor and was quite useless to me. So put into Plymouth and anchored in Catwater at 6.30 p.m. Fired out my 'A.B.' Much wind and rain in night.

Tuesday, September 22nd. – Fine and strong wind. Single-handed, got topmast on deck and coiled away topmast gear; reefed bowsprit. Bought sixteen small mutton chops and had them cooked ashore, as I do not expect to have much time for cooking.

Got away at about midday. Two reefs in mainsail, reefed staysail and third jib. Wind strong W.S.W. Very heavy sea between Bolt Tail and Start. Three or four heavy seas broke over the starboard quarter, and once she nearly broached-to, but no harm was done. Brought up in south-west corner of Torbay, off a little sandy beach. Bower and about forty fathoms chain. It took about twenty minutes' pumping to clear ship of water. Blowing hard, so tied up third reef in case of a shift of wind.

Wednesday, September 23rd. – Wind and rain in night, but slept securely knowing that I was prepared. Wind W., breezing up again harder than yesterday. Must be back by Monday, and cannot leave the ship anywhere, as I shall not be able to fetch her; so shall start this afternoon, so as to get to Needles in daylight to-morrow.

*

Lit binnacle lamps and tied canvas round. Lit riding light and put it in well. Started with three reefs in mainsail, single reef in staysail, and spitfire jib, at about 6 p.m. Wind W., blowing hard, with rain. Determined to get well to southward while I could, as if I found sea very bad I might have to run her off before it very often. (This turned out to be fortunate.) Course S.E., therefore. As I drew away from the land I found the sea very heavy and as much wind as I wanted for my three reefs. Binnacle lamps went out, but I had the Start light and an occasional look at compass to guide me, as riding light burned all right. About an hour after dark wind increased so much that she would not have any more, so watched my chance and hove her to on starboard tack and hauled down my fourth reef – very heavy work. Wind inclined to back. Stood away on course again, very often dead before it, but getting to southward when I could. Rain. No lights visible.

Thursday, September 24th. – She dished up several small seas with her long low counter, but soon after midnight sea was so heavy and irregular that she was almost out of hand. While I was waiting for a chance to heave her to, a great sea came over the taffrail, completely burying the vessel. I was nearly taken overboard, and the cockpit was filled to the coamings. She broached-to, and I expected that the next sea would finish her. But luckily it only partly broke on board, and then there was a smooth during which I got in the slack of the mainsheet and all fast before she began to pay off again. Headsails were already aback, so I lashed helm a-lee, and she lay fairly quiet. Pumped ship. Had brandy, bread and a chop, and felt better for it. About 3.30 a.m. crawled along deck and furled staysail. The steering and pumping had kept me warm, but now, sitting in the well – of course, soaked to the skin – the cold wind seemed to blow clean through me.

Just as the first streaks of dawn began to appear wind backed S.W. and blew harder than ever, and she would not lie any more, at one moment all shaking, next fell off and lay over, until I thought sometimes that the mast would go. Sea-anchor and warp were all ready, so led warp through hawsepipe, bent on drogue, and put it over. Tried to take in jib, but it flogged itself to rags as soon as I started the halyard. Let go throat halyard and got throat down, so that gaff was nearly up-and-down the mast. Got boom amidships. Slacked peak halyards, and sail flogged horribly. Paid out drogue warp as she gathered sternway, slacked topping-lifts, and got boom on deck and mainsheet fast. Then gradually got sail off without accident. Slowly paid out the whole forty fathoms of warp.

After she was once fairly astream of her drogue she shipped no more heavy water. She stood first on one end, then on the other, but climbed each sea safely. The wind tore off the tops of the seas, and the spray came in sheets, everything white as far as one could see. Daylight; no land visible. At about 11 a.m. wind suddenly veered to W., and blew – I don't want to pile on superlatives, but I have been in a pampero off the Plate, and a heavy gale of wind in the South Pacific, and I have never known the wind so strong or the seas so steep and so near breaking. A large barque, the *Rose Ellen* of Wilmington, passed quite close, running up Channel under bare poles. Managed to change my clothes and to feed. About 2 p.m. wind moderated a little. By 6 p.m. blowing only a moderate gale, but still too much wind and sea for me to make sail single-handed.

Tried to fix riding light to runner, but finally gave it up as it would not keep alight. About 9.30 p.m. lay down on cabin floor and slept until midnight.

Friday, September 25th. – Less wind and sea now, but judged it best to ride to my drogue a few hours longer. Several times from the top of the sea caught sight of Portland lights bearing about N.N.E., distant perhaps ten miles (?). Glad to know approximately my position. At dawn blowing a hard breeze only, and less sea. Shook out close reef, hoisted treble-reefed mainsail, got drogue on board, hoisted reefed staysail, and away.

*

Sunday, September 27th. – Beachy Head 4 a.m.; 7 a.m. hove-to and shook out reef. Lit coke stove, had breakfast, and stood away on course again. Nice breeze, W. About 11 a.m. passed Dungeness. About 4.30 p.m. anchored about a mile north of Deal pier.

Monday, September 28th. – A slice of luck. Wind at first W.S.W. After I rounded the Longnose it backed S.S.W., and allowed me to lay all through overland channel. A nice whole-sail breeze. Some showers. Moored off Queensborough about 2 p.m.

The strength of the wind may be gauged by the fact that though we had been out in some very hard breezes, we had only twice before used the third reef and never the fourth. *Tern's* failure to lie-to during this gale was due to the fact that she was unable to stand up to the close-reefed mainsail. To set the trysail in place of the mainsail would have been a heavier task than I could have managed single-handed. I have often wondered whether she would have lain-to safely under trysail. I think she would, but am not sure.

The sea-anchor was the ordinary conical bag of very stout canvas, stopped to a strong iron hoop thirty-eight inches in diameter. The fact that the windage of *Tern's* mast and boom was little, if at all, forward of her centre of lateral resistance undoubtedly had much to do with her riding so well to the drogue. Her drift was about a mile an hour as nearly as I could guess. A vessel with cut-away forefoot and mast far forward would require a very large drogue and some sort of riding sail aft to keep her head up to the wind.

No one who was interested in maritime affairs in 1896 is likely to forget this gale and the enormous destruction it wrought among shipping on our south and west coasts. Large numbers of fishing vessels and coasters and literally hundreds of lives were lost. Several of the Havre fishermen, in running for shelter, were lost with all hands in the broken water of the estuary. [Later the Met. Office reported sustained winds Force 9 at Portland.]

from *Yacht Cruising* by Claud Worth

The following account of the sort of weather regularly encountered by Russian convoys is fiction, but no one ever painted a truer picture of what it was like in reality in a 'River' Class frigate.

Huge waves, a mile from crest to crest, roared down upon the pigmies that were to be their prey; sometimes the entire surface of the water would be blown bodily away, and any ship that stood in the path of the onslaught shook and staggered as tons of green sea smote her upper deck and raced in a torrent down her whole length. Boats were smashed, funnels were buckled, bridges and deck-houses were crushed out of shape: men disappeared overboard without trace and without a cry, sponged out of life like figures wiped from a blackboard at a single imperious stroke. Even when the green seas withheld their blows for a moment, the wind, screaming and clawing at the rigging, struck fear into every heart; for if deck-gear and canvas screens could vanish, perhaps even men could be whipped away by its furious strength . . . For the crew of *Saltash*, there was no convoy, and no other ships save their own; and she, and they, were caught in a mesh of fearful days and nights, which might defeat them by their sheer brutal force. Normally a good sea boat, *Saltash* had ridden out many storms and had often had strength to spare for other ships that might be in difficulties; now, entirely on her own, she laboured to stay afloat, wearily performing, for hour after hour and day after day, the ugly antics of a ship which refused, under the most desperate compulsion, to stand on her head.

Throughout it all, the ship's relay-loudspeaker system, monotonously fed by a satirical hand, boomed out a tune called *Someone's Rocking My Dreamboat*.

Each of them in the wardroom had problems of a special sort of cope with, over and above the ones they shared with the rest of the crew – the problem of eating without having food flung in their faces, of sleeping without being thrown out of their bunks, of getting warm and dry again after the misery of a four-hour watch: above all, the problem of staying unhurt.

Scott-Brown, the doctor, was kept busy with this human wreckage of the storm, treating from hour to hour the cuts, the cracked ribs, the seasickness that could exhaust a man beyond the wish to live. His worst casualty, the one which would have needed all his skill and patience even if he had been able to deal with it in a quiet, fully-equipped operating-theatre ashore, was a man who, thrown bodily from one side of the mess-deck to the other, had landed on his knee-cap and smashed it into a dozen bloody fragments.

Johnson, the engineer officer, had a problem calling for endless watchfulness – the drunken movements of the ship, which brought her stern high out of the water with every second wave, and could set the screws racing and tearing the shaft to bits unless the throttle were clamped down straight away.

Raikes, in charge of navigation, was confronted by a truly hopeless job. For days on end there had been no sun to shoot, no stars to be seen, no set speed to give him even a rough D.R. position: where *Saltash* had got to, after five days and nights of chaos, was a matter of pure guess-work which any second-class stoker, pin in hand, could have done just as well as he. Ill-balanced on the Arctic Circle, sixty-something North by nothing West – that was the nearest he could get to it: *Saltash* lay somewhere inside these ragged limits, drifting slowly backwards within the wild triangle of Iceland, Jan Meyen Island and Norway.

*

Ericson . . . was fulfilling once more his traditional rôle of holding the whole thing together. After five days and nights of storm, he was so exhausted that the feeling of exhaustion had virtually disappeared: anchored to the deck by lead-like legs and soaked sea-boots, clamped to the bridge rail by weary half-frozen arms, he seemed to have become a part of the ship herself – a fixed pair of eyes, a watchful brain welded into the fabric of *Saltash*. All the way north to Murmansk he had had to perform the mental acrobatics necessary to the control of twenty escorts and the repelling of three or four different kinds of attack: now the physical harassing of this monstrous gale was battering at his body in turn, sapping at a life-time's endurance which had never had so testing a call made upon it, had never had to cope with an ordeal on this scale.

Assaulted by noise, bruised and punished by frenzied movement, thrown about endlessly, he had to watch and feel the same things happening to his ship.

The scene from the bridge of *Saltash* never lost an outline of senseless violence. By day it showed a square mile of tormented water, with huge waves flooding in like mountains sliding down the surface of the earth: with a haze of spray and spume scudding across it continually: with gulfs opening before the ship as if the whole ocean was avid to swallow her. Outlined against a livid sky, the mast plunged and rocked through a wild arc of space, flinging the aerials and the signal halyards about as if to whip the sea for its wickedness. Night added the terrible unknown; night was pitch-black, unpierceable to the eye, inhabited by fearful noises and sudden treacherous surprises: by waves that crashed down from nowhere, by stinging spray that tore into a man's face and eyes before he could duck for shelter. Isolated in the blackness, *Saltash* suffered every assault: she pitched, she rolled, she laboured: she met the shock of a breaking wave with a jar that shook her from end to end, she dived shuddering into a deep trough, shipping tons of water with a noise like a collapsing house, and then rose with infinite slowness, infinite pain, to shoulder the mass of water aside, and shake herself free, and prepare herself for the next blow.

Ericson watched and suffered with her, and felt it all in his own body: felt especially the agony of that slow rise under the crushing weight of the sea, felt often the enormous doubt as to whether she would rise at all. Ships had foundered without trace in this sort of weather: ships could give up, and lie down under punishment, just as could human beings: here, in this high corner of the world where the weather had started to scream insanely and the sea to boil, here could be murder: here, where some of *Compass Rose*'s corpses might still be wandering, here he might join them, with yet another ship's company in his train.

He stayed where he was on the bridge, and waited for it to happen, or not to happen. He was a pair of red eyes, inflamed by wind and salt water: he was a brain, tired, fluttering, but forced into a channel of watchfulness: he was sometimes a voice, shouting to the helmsman below to prepare for another threatening blow from the sea. He was a core of fear and of control, clipped small and tight into a body he had first ill-treated, and then begun, perforce, to disregard.

*

The weather was still wild; but with the convoy intact and the main chaos retrieved, the hours ahead seemed bearable and hopeful, and above all suitable for oblivion.

from *The Cruel Sea* by Nicholas Monsarrat

Captain H. K. Oram may best be remembered as the captain of the submarine flotilla for which the new T-Class *Thetis* from Cammell Laird's was destined in 1939 when she sank in Liverpool Bay during her acceptance trials, with the loss of all but four of her company. Captain Oram was one who escaped. He did so to supervise the salvage of the stricken submarine and rescue of her crew. But it all went sadly awry and marked the end of his career.

He had begun in happier circumstances as a cadet in the training-ship *Worcester*. Leaving her in 1911 he signed on to learn his trade in earnest in the wool-clipper *Port Jackson*, a 2,300-ton four-masted barque and one of the swiftest on the Australian run.

South of the Cape of Good Hope she flew before a succession of westerly gales. The new cadet (a first-voyager) was not competent to be a full-blown helmsman, but stood his trick as leewheel, helping the third-voyager who was in charge. The sight of the following seas threatening to poop the barque or, worse still, cause her to broach was so awesome that many ships rigged a screen abaft the helmsmen so that they could not be distracted by fear. Oram takes up the story as the two of them wrestled with the lively wheel:

In the brightness of the night it was fascinating to look aloft at the straining sails and sense the whims of the labouring ship under our hands. With the compass jumping about in its gimbals it was difficult to read the card in the dim light of the binnacle lamp and we were steering on a star just clear of the fore t'gallant. It was not too easy to hold the ship on a steady course but I soon found myself instinctively anticipating the need for helm to check the yaw, and I was indulging in mild confidence when my mate was sent forrard on a job and I was told to take over the wheel. Flattered by this trust I moved over to the weather side and, grasping the spokes with determination, sang 'Blow the man down' to myself in the exhilaration of the moment.

For a time all went well, and I was just thinking that under my expert helmsmanship the decks were dry, when fate took a hand. A squall blew up and without warning the wind backed four points, a black cloud masked my guiding star and, in a sudden gust, the binnacle lamp blew out. This combination was too much and, sensing the ship sheering off course, I frantically struggled to put the helm down to check the swing. But I was too late – with the great swell now on the beam the ship rolled heavily and a green sea flooded the deck amidships. The Third Mate, thrusting me roughly aside, took over and yanking the helm down regained control. In scorching words I was roundly cursed for being a useless 'sodger' and told to get to hell out of it. My cup of misery overflowed – but worse was to come. The green sea that had flooded the deck to bulwark level took time to drain away through the washports and, under the lift of the bow, tons of spent water surged aft and, flooding through a door left carelessly open, well nigh washed the Mate out of his bunk. With rasping sarcasm the wet and angry blue-nose blew such remnants of pride that I still carried out of their bolt ropes and I spent the rest of my watch, and half my watch below, with bucket and swab dolefully mopping up the aftermath of my unwitting lapse from grace.

This foretaste of the Roaring Forties was typical of many wet and dreary days to follow as we ran eastwards. It was not all bad; there were days of relatively fair weather and, even when careering before a westerly, our hardship was compensated by the comforting knowledge that we were covering 200 miles or more towards the end of the voyage. But always, fair or foul, the great swell rolled on, the ship groaned and creaked in constant violent movement, the southern spring was lamentably cold and, despite careful helmsmen, heavy seas crashed on board all too frequently. Life deteriorated into an endurance trial against discomfort and weariness. Food, at best of times unattractive, was even more so when the cook's galley fire was dowsed by a sea and our hot meal dowsed with it.

Later, *Port Jackson* left Sydney homeward-bound with a full cargo of wheat. Seven days out a vicious easterly headed her, and both watches went aloft in the middle of the night to furl sails on her masts which were only a few feet shorter than Nelson's column. When the morning watch was mustered at 0400 the chief cadet was missing, having fallen off the rigging unnoticed in the rising gale.

I had been yarning to Bazalgette the previous evening and it seemed beyond the bounds of credibility that he had gone from our company.

The Captain held an enquiry next morning but little tangible evidence was forthcoming. Those who had been reefing the fores'l reported that Bazalgette had been seen on the lee yard arm and that he was probably the last man down. Nobody had actually seen him come off the yard and it was assumed that he had either slipped off the footrope and dropped into the sea or that he had come down the lee rigging and that the fierce wind had torn away his handhold and blasted him overboard. Though his ultimate cry had been heard there would have been no hope of rescue on such a dark tempestuous night.

Later that morning we were called aft for a memorial service. This was the first occasion on which the Captain had suffered the loss of a cadet and he was visibly distressed. As we listened to the sombre words of committal

I looked out at the streaked turbulence of the angry sea and, imagining Bazalgette's loneliness, took comfort in the thought that his dark ending must have been mercifully swift.

One hundred miles or so to the south of New Zealand we steadied up on the 50th parallel of latitude for our long run to the east and for the next three weeks experienced typical westerlies alternating with brief days of contrary winds.

*

I had good reason to remember that . . . day. I was busy with Molly Morgan on a splicing job and, as the fore-deck was awash most of the time with seas breaking on board, we took our work on to the top of the half-deck where it was comparatively dry. Settling down in the lee of the hen-coop we braced ourselves against the violent movement of the ship which, wallowing in the heavy swell, was rolling a full 30° each way. The sun was shining and we were agreeing that this was not at all a bad way to spend our afternoon when our attention was roused by maternal cluckings within the coop. Molly, who always kept an ear cocked for a quick chance, thought that a fresh egg would go down well with our tea and told me off to investigate. Taking a look round to check that the Second Mate was not in a position to witness our abstraction I cased the joint and got on with the job. I had just thrust my hand under the protesting mum when, without warning, as if in retribution for felony, a bloody great sea reared up and with an almighty rush swept clean over the scene of the crime. The next few seconds were hectic and confused and I had not got over my surprise when I found myself lying on my back holding on like grim death to the keel of the starboard lifeboat which had been lifted out of its chocks by the now receding sea. Molly had been equally lucky and had fetched up wrapped round a stanchion. But the fowls, and our egg, had gone overboard leaving no trace of their habitation except the wire rope that had formerly lashed them to the deck.

By this time we had become accustomed to accepting general hardship as our way of life but as time went on work on deck was made painful for most of us by nagging sea-cuts – cracks on the palms of the hands which, under the aggravation of constant hauling on salt soaked ropes, stubbornly refused to heal.

A month out from Australia, two thirds of our way across the Pacific, we began to work to the southward to round Cape Horn. This took us into the Fifties and a tearing westerly gale during which we logged eleven knots under three tops'ls and fores'l and made good 250 miles in 24 hours – the best day's run of the voyage. Though it was a grim day of lowering clouds and blinding squalls the dark threat of the weather was lightened by the ship's exultant speed.

Cape Horn has a legendary, and well deserved, reputation for harsh treatment of ships and sailors.

*

At the best of times the west-bound ships had a bitter struggle to claw their way round – at worst they were stressed to the limits of endurance, and many, dismasted, had to limp back to the Falklands under jury rig. Through the centuries a tragic number of battered vessels succumbed and foundered without trace.

With such a long history of battle and disaster it is not surprising that the term 'Cape Horner' epitomises the ultimate in hard seagoing.

In comparison with the trials of west-bounders the passage from west to east presented relatively few hazards. Helped by prevailing winds, and carried on their way by a favourable east-going current, Atlantic-bound ships customarily rounded the Horn with no more difficulties than they had experienced while running their easting down across the Pacific. In bad weather and poor visibility the Masters of east-bound ships, always anxious about their longitude, were naturally on edge at the prospect of making a landfall on such a treacherous lee shore but, unless the weather had been exceptionally cloudy, they had confidence in their latitude and kept well to the southward and clear of danger.

This applied in our case and with a strong wind under our tail we ran into the South Atlantic without sighting the dreaded Cape Stiff.

It had taken us five and a half weeks to sail 6,130 miles across the Pacific at an average speed of 6½ knots. A log of daily distances run shows that we covered 200 miles or more on no less than thirteen days of this 38-day passage from Sydney to the Horn which, though by no means a record, was not bad going.

Having rounded this significant corner we really felt that we were on the homeward stretch and wisecrackers cautioned the look-out to keep his eyes skinned for the smoke of a tug on the northern horizon. In reality we were still a week short of the half way mark and still had to sail the best part of 8,000 miles before we could hope to pick up soundings to the west of Land's End.

Six weeks in the roaring forties had given us a bellyfull of heavy going and it was a relief to sail in relatively moderate seas under the lee of the Falklands. We happened to strike lucky winds and covered 2,000 miles to the northward in a week and a half. It grew warmer day by day, the ship dried out and almost before we had realized our good fortune we were coming up to Capricorn and the south-east Trades with our salt-caked sea-boots stowed away and the rigours of the Southern Ocean all but forgotten.

from *Ready for Sea* by Captain H. K. Oram

The same Herbert Lightoller who was the senior surviving officer in the *Titanic* has also left us a graphic account of his first experience of a cyclone, in the Indian Ocean. On return to Britain as a survivor from the wreck of *Holt Hill* on St Paul island, he immediately shipped in her sister-ship *Primrose Hill* on a voyage to Calcutta. They got caught in a cyclone in the Bay of Bengal.

They were in the Bay of Bengal when they had their first inkling that trouble was imminent. First the barometer fell dramatically and then, away to the south-east, the sky could be seen getting duller and thicker. Captain Wilson knew what was coming and the call went up for all hands on deck to take in sail.

In was the height of the cyclone season and they were about to meet one.

*

And then suddenly it was upon them, a storm of such spite Lightoller never thought could be possible, even after experiencing the seas round Cape Horn. This time nobody would have stood a chance on deck, let alone aloft, as the crew scurried for the nearest protection in the ship. Some made for the galley, others for the fo'c's'le and the rest for the whaleback at the stern, and then prayed for the terror to pass and for their lives to be spared.

The seas rose up and burst all over the ship from all angles; over bows and stern, from starboard and port. Then came the lightning, fierce and violent, flashing all around them, making holes in the water big enough to drop in a small boat. The sound was deafening so that a man might yell at the top of his voice right next to you and he would not be heard.

Lightoller had been amazed how the *Primrose Hill* survived the winter seas of the Horn but now she was surely being driven beyond her limit as the sea plummeted on top of the ship filling her up 'rail on rail'. It was a case of willing her to lift to it before the next sea came crashing down on top of her, trying to force her further under.

The storm continued to blast at them harder and then above the banshee scream of the wind came a crack like the sound of a cannon firing. Lightoller looked aloft to see one of the topsails being carried away leaving behind just a few tattered shreds on the yard. Then there was another crack as another sail went, and then another and another.

The seas began leaping frantically straight up in the air. The *Primrose Hill* leapt with them. It was a sign that their worst fears had materialised. The ship was right in the centre of the cyclone. They were in dire trouble and there was now only one chance of saving themselves, and that was for the yards carrying what canvas remained to be hauled round on the opposite tack to meet the imminent change in the direction of this treacherous, revolving wind.

Despite the terrible dangers of being on deck at the height of such a storm no one needed second bidding to follow the cry to man the halliards and get the ship on a new tack before she was caught 'aback'. There might have been a heavy risk of being washed overboard but it would be the end for all of them anyway if they did not quickly get those yards hauled round.

In those vital minutes both men and boys found a strength and purpose

146

they never thought they possessed. The job was completed in time and as the wind returned once again in full force, but now blowing in the reverse direction, the *Primrose Hill* was prepared. It came with a vengeance as though trying to make up for having failed to drown the ship at the first attempt. But the *Primrose Hill* could take everything which that crazy sea threw at her.

And then it was passed and gone, and the ship was left tossing dizzily around in the heavy gale that followed in the wake of the cyclone. They were clear of the worst of it. The skipper and many of the hands who had experienced the sea in its most brutal moods had never been in anything quite like it. The *Primrose Hill* had performed miracles in the way she had survived. Few other ships, they all agreed, could have taken such punishment and survived.

But now came the job of putting the damage to rights as Lightoller found himself back in that situation of working non-stop aloft hour after hour clearing up the wreckage, replacing the remnants of ripped sails with fresh canvas and disentangling the hundreds of feet of rope that had got twisted around the masts and spars and knotted up with shreds of sail. Even though the worst of the danger had passed, the sea continued to thunder aboard and no man could afford to relax as the threat was always there of being caught unawares by a sudden torrent of water over the rail and being tossed overboard.

On reflection Lightoller decided that he would settle for a full blown gale round Cape Horn any time sooner than face a cyclone.

from *Lights* by Patrick Stenson

On her voyage from Madras to Canton the East Indiaman *Plassey* had to endure a typhoon – or 'tuffoon' as it was called in the 1780s . . .

After spending four days very agreeably at Malacca, where we found much to see and entertain us, we returned to the *Plassey* and proceeded on our way to China, still accompanied by the *Triton*, but the additional water she had taken in so altered her sailing for the worse that on the second day we ran away and left her. Having cleared the Straits, our daily conversation was the probability of encountering a Tuffoon, or violent gale of wind so called, frequently happening in the China Seas towards the latter part of the year. Captain Waddell, in jocularity, used to desire me to keep a good look out of an evening, and if the sun set, as seamen phrase it, *angrily*, casting a copper tint all over the sky, attended with a thick heavy atmosphere, we might expect a puff in a few hours. Four days after the captain had mentioned these symptoms to me, I was sure from his conversation with the officers at breakfast, and the orders he gave, that he expected bad weather. It was then blowing fresh, and by the hour of dinner the wind so increased that the top sails were close reefed.

The sun that evening did set as he had described, the appearance being quite horrible; the thick and heavy clouds were of a dismal deep orange colour and the sea became extremely agitated. The top gallant masts and yards were lowered upon deck and every preparation made for encountering a tempest. By eight in the evening it blew so tremendously that every sail was taken in and we ran under bare poles. At nine, in an instant, the wind shifted almost to the opposite point. So sudden and violent was it that had a single yard of canvas been out the consequences might have been serious. As it was, we immediately hove to. We lay tumbling about sadly, and had a dismal night, shipping heavy seas, which swept away every thing they came against. The gale was accompanied by excessively vivid lightning and thunder as if the artillery of the world had all been discharged at once. This was the first storm I had ever been in, and greatly did the effects of it surprize me. The *Plassey* was one of the best sea boats that ever swam, behaving, as the seamen said, wonderfully well, yet the motion was so quick and violent that every timber and plank seemed to shake. All attempts to keep my legs being useless, I retired to my cot, which every moment struck the deck on one side or the other. Day light made no favourable change. About eleven in the morning I got up, and being young and active I managed to get upon deck, where the grandeur of the scene, terrific as it was, greatly surprized me. I fastened myself with a rope upon the quarter deck by the advice of the Doctor, who had scarcely given it when the ship, taking a deep and desperate lee lurch, he lost his hold, and away he flew like a shot to leeward, falling with great force against the ship's side, his head striking within two inches of the aftermost port out of which every body upon deck thought he must have gone. He had a narrow escape from a watery grave, and was dreadfully bruised from the violence of the fall.

Our cargo from Madras being cotton, the ship was so crank that she sometimes lay for half an hour at a time in a manner water logged, her gunwale being completely enveloped in the sea, so that I frequently thought she never would right again. The gale continued all the second day and night, but towards morning of the third moderated and soon after fell calm. The sea being enormously high and confused, the ship rolled and pitched to such a degree that the masts were every moment expected to go over her side. So serious a disaster fortunately for us did not happen, and after several hours terrible tumbling about in all directions, a fresh breeze and from the right quarter, sprung up; we made sail, which steadied the ship, and the following day saw the Grand Ladrones, a cluster of Islands off the coast of China.

from the *Memoirs of William Hickey* ed. by Alfred Spencer

Even the most powerful steamships can encounter conditions at sea that severely limit their freedom of action or may ultimately overwhelm them. There were occasions during Murmansk convoys when converted deep-sea trawlers acting as escorts on the screen were sunk by stress of weather. As far as the Escort Force commander knew, they simply disappeared off the radar. The Pacific typhoon which caught Admiral Halsey's Carrier Task Force 38 in December 1944 was another victory for the seas, exacerbated by the formation maintaining for too long the course ordered for replenishment which was unsuitable and dangerous in the circumstances. Three destroyers were sunk by stress of weather, with the loss of over 750 officers and men. Herman Wouk's novel describes the terrifying conditions which all but claimed the old four-stacker *Caine*.

A steamship, not being a slave to the wind like a sailing vessel, is superior to ordinary difficulties of storms. A warship is a special kind of steamship, built not for capaciousness and economy, but for power. Even the mine-sweeper *Caine* could oppose to the gale a force of some thirty thousand horsepower; energy enough to move a weight of half a million tons one foot in one minute. The ship itself weighed little more than a thousand tons. It was a grey old bantam bursting with strength for emergencies.

But surprising things happen when nature puts on a freak show like a typhoon, with wind gusts up to a hundred and fifty miles per hour or more. The rudder, for instance, can become useless. It works by dragging against the water through which it is passing; but if the wind is behind the ship, and blows hard enough, the water may start piling along as fast as the rudder so that there is no drag at all. Then the ship will yaw or even broach to. Or the sea may push one way on the hull, and the wind another, and the rudder a third, so that the resultant of the forces is very erratic response of the ship to the helm, varying from minute to minute, or from second to second.

It is also theoretically possible that while the captain may want to turn his ship in one direction, the wind will be pushing so hard in the other direction that the full force of the engines will not suffice to bring the ship's head around. In that case the vessel will wallow, broadside to, in very bad shape indeed. But it is unlikely. A modern warship, functioning properly and handled with wisdom, can probably ride out any typhoon.

The storm's best recourse in the contest for the ship's life is old-fashioned bogyman terror. It makes ghastly noises and horrible faces and shakes up the captain to distract him from doing the sensible thing in tight moments. If the wind can toss the ship sideways long enough it can probably damage the engines or kill them – and then it wins. Because above all the ship must be kept steaming under control. It suffers under one disadvantage as a drifting hulk, compared to the old wooden sailing ship: iron doesn't float. A destroyer deprived of its engines in a typhoon is almost certain to capsize, or else fill up and sink.

When things get really bad, the books say, the best idea is to turn the ship's head into the wind and sea and ride out the blow that way. But even on this the authorities are not all agreed. None of the authorities have experienced the worst of enough typhoons to make airtight generalizations. None of the authorities, moreover, are anxious to acquire the experience.

from *The Caine Mutiny* by Herman Wouk

The reality of the typhoon on 18 December 1944 which briefly saved the Japanese in Luzon from being blasted by Task Force 38 was that it formed and hit the fleet with little or no early warning. There was no oceanwide meteorological organization from which reliable forecasts might have been made. Commanders at all levels had no previous experience of ship-handling in a typhoon, and Buys Ballot's Law did not enter into the tactical reckoning of Admiral Halsey. His overriding priority was to hit Mindoro. But first it was urgent to refuel his force of fifty screening destroyers in formation around his fleet of fourteen strike carriers, eight battleships and fifteen cruisers, not counting the fleet train of twelve tankers and five escort carriers carrying replacement aircraft. They were called upon as soon as the typhoon had passed to replace 146 aircraft lost overboard or destroyed on the flightdecks – the same number claimed to have been shot down by the Royal Air Force on Battle of Britain Day four years earlier.

This typhoon was comparatively small; but, owing to the fact that a number of deballasted destroyers ran smack into it, more damage was inflicted on the Navy than by any other storm since the famous hurricane at Apia, Samoa, in March 1889. Three destroyers capsized and six or seven other ships were seriously damaged, with the loss of almost 800 officers and men. As Admiral Nimitz said, this was the greatest uncompensated loss that the Navy had taken since the Battle of Savo Island.

*

. . . this tight, young, wicked little typhoon came whirling along undetected toward waters where Third Fleet was trying to fuel. The sea was making up all day 17 December but the waves came from the same direction as the northerly wind (which was not above Force 8 – 30 to 40 knots), and that gave no indication of a typhoon. Wind and sea, however, had already rendered fueling difficult. Destroyer *Maddox*, a new 2200-tonner, required three hours' work to obtain 7093 gallons from oiler *Manatee*. The hose then parted and she had to cut the towline, narrowly avoiding a collision. Two hoses parted on *New Jersey* when she tried to fuel destroyers *Hunt* and *Spence*. Escort carrier *Kwajalein* (Captain Robert L. Warrack), one of the replacement-plane CVEs that belonged to an oiler group, was unable to transfer pilots by breeches buoy, and canceled air operations at noon. Her deck crews then concentrated on respotting and relashing planes, which were secured three ways with steel cables, the air having been let out of the F6F landing gears. It was too rough for escort carriers to recover C.A.P.

Two planes still aloft at 1500 were flagged off from their respective flattops and the pilots were ordered to turn their planes upside down and bail out. They were rescued by a destroyer.

*

At 1345 Admiral Halsey issued a typhoon warning, to alert Fleet Weather Central to what was going on. This was the first reference to the storm as a typhoon in any official message. Unknown to Command Third Fleet, three of his destroyers had already gone down.

*

By the afternoon of 18 December, Task Force 38 and its attendant fueling groups were scattered over a space estimated at 50 by 60 miles. Except in the case of the battleships, all semblance of formation had been lost. Every ship was laboring heavily; hardly any two were in visual contact; many lay dead, rolling in the trough of the sea; planes were crashing and burning on the light carriers. From the islands of the carriers and the pilothouses of destroyers sailors peered out on such a scene as they had never witnessed before, and hoped never to see again.

Still acting on incomplete or inaccurate data about the track of the typhoon, Admiral Halsey in his flagship *New Jersey* tried three different fuelling rendezvous in the hope of finding easier conditions. But, until the final signal was made for all units to act independently (and save their ships), this massive fleet was being manoeuvred across the path of the oncoming storm. Some found themselves briefly in the classic 'still centre', with blue skies overhead. It was the larger fleet destroyers which suffered most. They could only survive by ballasting their empty fuel tanks with water or by reducing their top-hamper. Some were saved by the force of the seas wiping out fixtures which contributed to their instability:

At about 1100 on the 18th, Commander F. J. Ilsemann, the unit commander in *Monongahela*, ordered a change of course to 140°. While this maneuver was being executed the wind increased to over 100 knots. As *Hull's* fuel tanks were 70 per cent full she did not take in salt-water ballast; events proved that it would have been well to have done so. When proceeding to her new station incident to the change of course, her helm failed to respond to any combination of rudder and engines. She lay in irons in the trough of the sea with the north wind on her port beam, yawing between courses 80° and 100°. The whaleboat, the depth charges and almost everything else on deck were swept off as she rolled 50 degrees to leeward, and before eight bells the rolls increased to 70 degrees. From two or three of them she recovered, but a gust estimated to be of 110-knot velocity pinned her down on her beam ends. Sea flooded the pilothouse and poured down the stacks, and at a few minutes after noon she went down. Of her complement of 18 officers and 246 men, only 7 officers and 55 men were ultimately rescued.

Only one of the three destroyers that were overwhelmed and sank was dangerously low on fuel. Nevertheless the Court of Enquiry held that even they should have water-ballasted sooner.

Even worse was to come. At 1210 *Dewey* rolled 65 degrees to starboard, recovered, rolled 75 degrees and hung there. The barometer needle went off the scale at 27 and kept dropping; Captain Mercer believes that it reached 26.60. A lurch caused the skipper to lose his footing on the weather wing of the almost perpendicular bridge deck; he grasped a stanchion, and, before the astonished eyes of his quartermaster, hung there as on a trapeze. He was preparing to order the destroyer's mast to be cut away with an acetylene torch when No. 1 stack pulled out at boat-deck level and fell 'thwart ship, completely flattened; and although this loss caused flarebacks in No. 1 fire room and let in more sea water, it reduced the ship's 'sail area' so that stability improved. Engineers maintained boiler pressure so that all pumps were soon working. By 1300 the center of the storm had passed, and by 1800 *Dewey* had full way on and was able very cautiously to wear around to a westerly course.

*

Monaghan (Lieutenant Commander F. Bruce Garrett) was another *Farragut*-class destroyer that failed to stay afloat. She was operating independently of the task force at the height of the typhoon, with fuel tanks 76 per cent full. The skipper reported to Captain Acuff at 0925 December 18 that he was unable to steer the base course, and was then heading about 330° with the wind on starboard bow. Apparently he wore ship later, which took his destroyer as near to the track of the typhoon's center as *Hull*. At about 1100 her skipper attempted to ballast her weather side. *Monaghan's* senior survivor, Water Tender 2nd Class Joseph C. McCrane USNR, testified that he and his helper with great difficulty opened the ballast valves to the after tanks, but it was then too late to save her. Electric power and steering engine failed at about 1130. The engine and fire rooms' overheads began to rip loose from the bulkheads. *Monaghan* made several heavy rolls to starboard, hung there for a time, and shortly before noon foundered. Of her entire company only six enlisted men survived.

Spence (Lieutenant Commander J. P. Andrea), a 2100-tonner of *Fletcher* class, larger, newer and more stable than the others, formed part of Admiral Sherman's Task Group 38.3. Her fuel was down to 15 per cent capacity on 17 December. After an unsuccessful attempt to fuel from *New Jersey*, she was sent at 0800 December 18 to Captain Acuff's group in the hope of fueling at the first opportunity, since by that time she had only enough oil for 24 hours' steaming at 8 knots. The commanding officer began water-ballasting too late, after breakfast on the 18th, and Condition 'Affirm' was never set. On a course heading southwesterly, she began rolling heavily to

152

port. Water entered through ventilators and sloshed around below, short-circuiting the distribution board. The rudder jammed at hard rght. At 1110 *Spence* took a deep roll to port, hung there a moment, recovered, rolled again, and then was swallowed up by the sea. Only one officer and 23 enlisted men were rescued.

Fleet-Admiral Chester Nimitz, Commander-in-Chief Pacific, was perhaps less than fair to Admiral Halsey who saw it all from the enclosed bridge of the largest battleship in the world. His covering letter to the report of the Court of Inquiry was a timely reminder that the sea will always win against those who do not respect it. The last three sentences – the same length as the Lord's Prayer – should be overprinted on every Master's ticket and watchkeeping certificate:

A hundred years ago, a ship's survival depended almost solely on the competence of her master and on his consant alertness to every hint of change in the weather. To be taken aback or caught with full sail on by even a passing squall might mean the loss of spars or canvas; and to come close to the center of a genuine hurricane or typhoon was synonymous with disaster. While to be taken by surprise was thus serious, the facilities for avoiding it were meager. Each master was dependent wholly on himself for detecting the first symptoms of bad weather, for predicting its serious-ness and movement, and for taking the appropriate measures, to evade it if possible and to battle through it if it passed near to him. There was no radio by which weather data could be collected from over all the oceans and the resulting forecasts by expert aërologists broadcasted to him and to all afloat. There was no one to tell him that the time had now come to strike his light sails and spars, and snug her down under close reefs or storm trysails. His own barometer, the force and direction of the wind, and the appearance of sea and sky were all that he had for information. Cease-less vigilance in watching and interpreting signs, plus a philosophy of taking no risk in which there was little to gain and much to be lost, was what enabled him to survive.

*

The safety of a ship against perils from storm, as well as from those of navigation and maneuvering, is always the responsibility of her commanding officer; but this responsibility is also shared by his immediate superiors in operational command, since by the very fact of such command the individual commanding officer is not free to do at any time what his own judgment might indicate . . .

It is most definitely part of the senior officer's responsibility to think in terms of the smallest ship and most inexperienced commanding officer under him. He cannot take them for granted, give them tasks and stations, and assume either that they will be able to keep up and come through any weather that his own big ship can; or that they will be wise enough to gauge the exact moment when their task must be abandoned in order for them to keep afloat . . .

In conclusion, both seniors and juniors must realize that in bad weather, as in most other situations, safety and fatal hazard are not separated by any sharp boundary line, but shade gradually from one into the other. There is no little red light which is going to flash on and inform commanding officers or higher commanders that from then on there is extreme danger from the weather, and that measures for ships' safety must now take precedence over further efforts to keep up with the formation or to execute the assigned task. This time will always be a matter of personal judgment. Naturally no commander is going to cut thin the margin between staying afloat and foundering, but he may nevertheless unwittingly pass the danger point even though no ship is yet *in extremis*. Ships that keep on going as long as the severity of wind and sea had not yet come close in capsizing them or breaking them in two, may nevertheless become helpless to avoid these catastrophes later if things get worse. By then they may be unable to steer any heading but in the trough of the sea, or may have their steering control, lighting, communications and main propulsion disabled or may be helpless to secure things on deck or to jettison topside weights. *The time for taking all measures for a ship's safety is while still able to do so. Nothing is more dangerous than for a seaman to be grudging in taking precautions lest they turn out to have been unnecessary. Safety at sea for a thousand years has depended on exactly the opposite philosophy* [editor's italics].

from *History of United States Naval Operations in World War II*,
volume XIII, by Samuel Eliot Morison

Even the chaplains in the Task Force could have been forgiven for suffering moments of doubting whether the happy ending of Psalm 107 could be depended upon:

They that go down to the sea in ships, that do business in great waters;
These see the works of the Lord, and his wonders in the deep.
For he commandeth, and raiseth the stormy wind, which lifteth up the waves thereof.
They mount up to the heaven, they go down again to the depths: their soul is melted because of trouble.
They reel to and fro, and stagger like a drunken man, and are at their wits end.
Then they cry unto the Lord in their trouble, and he bringeth them out of their distresses.
He maketh the storm a calm, so that the waves thereof are still.
Then they are glad because they be quiet; so he bringeth them unto their desired haven.

Psalm 107, verses 23–30

The great story-teller Joseph Conrad was born in Poland in 1857. After twenty years at sea under sail and steam he married and settled in Kent, becoming a naturalized Englishman. Most of his prolific output was autobiographical; some was based on yarns he had heard during his seafaring days all over the world. The story of the freighter *Nan Shan* caught in a typhoon in the South China Sea is typical. She had her for'ard hold filled with 200 coolies and their accumulated baggage being shipped back to Foochow after completing seven years' contract labour in Malaya.

As the steamer plugged onwards all the signs of an impending typhoon were there. The barometer had plummeted, but there was little wind. Only a massive swell building up on one beam. The mate Jukes was apprehensive and reported to the captain in the bridge charthouse:

'Swell getting worse, sir.'

'Noticed that in here,' muttered Captain MacWhirr. 'Anything wrong?'

Jukes, inwardly disconcerted by the seriousness of the eyes looking at him over the top of the book, produced an embarrassed grin.

'Rolling like old boots,' he said, sheepishly.

'Aye! Very heavy – very heavy. What do you want?'

At this Jukes lost his footing and began to flounder.

'I was thinking of our passengers,' he said, in the manner of a man clutching at a straw.

'Passengers?' wondered the Captain, gravely. 'What passengers?'

'Why, the Chinamen, sir,' explained Jukes, very sick of this conversation.

'The Chinamen! Why don't you speak plainly? Couldn't tell what you meant. Never heard a lot of coolies spoken of as passengers before. Passengers, indeed! What's come to you?'

Captain MacWhirr, closing the book on his forefinger, lowered his arm and looked completely mystified. 'Why are you thinking of the Chinamen, Mr. Jukes?' he inquired.

Jukes took a plunge, like a man driven to it. 'She's rolling her decks full of water, sir. Thought you might put her head on perhaps – for a while. Till this goes down a bit – very soon, I dare say. Head to the eastward. I never knew a ship roll like this.'

He held on in the doorway, and Captain MacWhirr, feeling his grip on the shelf inadequate, made up his mind to let go in a hurry, and fell heavily on the couch.

'Head to the eastward?' he said, struggling to sit up. 'That's more than four points off her course.'

'Yes sir. Fifty degrees . . . Would just bring her head far enough round to meet this . . . .'

Captain MacWhirr was now sitting up. He had not dropped the book, and he had not lost his place.

'To the eastward?' he repeated, with dawning astonishment. 'To the . . . Where do you think we are bound to? You want me to haul a full-powered steamship four points off her course to make the Chinamen comfortable! Now, I've heard more than enough of mad things done in the world – but this . . . If I didn't know you, Jukes, I would think you were in liquor. Steer four points off . . . And what afterwards? Steer four points over the other way, I suppose, to make the course good. What put it into your head that I would start to tack a steamer as if she were a sailing-ship?'

'Jolly good thing she isn't,' threw in Jukes, with bitter readiness. 'She would have rolled every blessed stick out of her this afternoon.'

'Aye! And you just would have had to stand and see them go,' said Captain MacWhirr, showing a certain animation. 'It's a dead calm, isn't it?'

'It is, sir. But there's something out of the common coming, for sure.'

'Maybe. I suppose you have a notion I should be getting out of the way of that dirt,' said Captain MacWhirr, speaking with the utmost simplicity of manner and tone, and fixing the oilcloth on the floor with a heavy stare. Thus he noticed neither Jukes' discomfiture nor the mixture of vexation and astonished respect on his face.

'Now, here's this book,' he continued with deliberation, slapping his thigh with the closed volume. 'I've been reading the chapter on the storms there.'

This was true. He had been reading the chapter on the storms. When he had entered the chart-room, it was with no intention of taking the book down. Some influence in the air – the same influence, probably, that caused the steward to bring without orders the Captain's sea-boots and oilskin coat up to the chart-room – had as it were guided his hand to the shelf; and without taking the time to sit down he had waded with a conscious effort into the terminology of the subject. He lost himself amongst advancing semi-circles, left- and right-hand quadrants, the curves of the tracks, the probable bearing of the centre, the shifts of wind and the readings of barometer. He tried to bring all these things into a definite relation to himself, and ended by becoming contemptuously angry with such a lot of words and with so much advice, all head-work and supposition, without a glimmer of certitude.

'It's the damnedest thing, Jukes,' he said. 'If a fellow was to believe all that's in there, he would be running most of his time all over the sea trying to get behind the weather.'

But the captain could not contemplate having to explain the fuel bills if he sailed several hundred miles extra to avoid the worst of the storm or to make life bearable for the coolies trapped below and being thrown from side to side, fighting each other for the contents of their burst camphor-wood chests.

156

The motion of the ship was extravagant. Her lurches had an appalling helplessness: she pitched as if taking a header into a void, and seemed to find a wall to hit every time. When she rolled she fell on her side headlong, and she would be righted back by such a demolishing blow that Jukes felt her reeling as a clubbed man reels before he collapses. The gale howled and scuffled about gigantically in the darkness, as though the entire world were one black gully. At certain moments the air streamed against the ship as if sucked through a tunnel with a concentrated solid force of impact that seemed to lift her clean out of the water and keep her up for an instant with only a quiver running through her from end to end. And then she would begin her tumbling again as if dropped back into a boiling cauldron. Jukes tried hard to compose his mind and judge things coolly.

The sea, flattened down in the heavier gusts, would uprise and over-whelm both ends of the *Nan-Shan* in snowy rushes of foam, expanding wide, beyond both rails, into the night. And on this dazzling sheet, spread under the blackness of the clouds and emitting a bluish glow, Captain MacWhirr could catch a desolate glimpse of a few tiny specks black as ebony, the tops of the hatches, the battened companions, the heads of the covered winches, the foot of a mast. This was all he could see of his ship. Her middle structure, covered by the bridge which bore him, his mate, the closed wheelhouse where a man was steering shut up with the fear of being swept overboard together with the whole thing in one great crash – her middle structure was like a half-tide rock awash upon a coast. It was like an outlying rock with the water boiling up, streaming over, pouring off, beating round – like a rock in the surf to which shipwrecked people cling before they let go – only it rose, it sank, it rolled continuously, without respite and rest . . .

The *Nan-Shan* was being looted by the storm with a senseless, destructive fury: trysails torn out of the extra gaskets, double-lashed awnings blown away, bridge swept clean, weather-cloths burst, rails twisted, light-screens smashed – and two of the boats had gone already. They had gone unheard and unseen, melting, as it were, in the shock and smother of the wave. It was only later, when upon the white flash of another high sea hurling itself amidships, Jukes had a vision of two pairs of davits leaping black and empty out of the solid blackness, with one overhauled fall flying and an iron-bound block capering in the air, that he became aware of what had happened within about three yards of his back.

He poked his head forward, groping for the ear of his commander. His lips touched it – big, fleshy, very wet. He cried in an agitated tone, 'Our boats are going now, sir.'

*

A dull conviction seized upon Jukes that there was nothing to be done. If the steering-gear did not give way, if the immense volumes of water did not burst the deck in or smash one of the hatches, if the engines did not give up, if way could be kept on the ship against this terrific wind, and she did not bury herself in one of these awful seas, of whose white crests alone, topping high above her bows, he could now and then get a sickening glimpse – then there was a chance of her coming out of it. Something within him seemed to turn over, bringing uppermost the feeling that the *Nan-Shan* was lost.

'She's done for,' he said to himself, with a surprising mental agitation, as though he had discovered an unexpected meaning in this thought. One of these things was bound to happen. Nothing could be prevented now, and nothing could be remedied. The men on board did not count, and the ship could not last. This weather was too impossible.

After many hours they reached the still eye of the typhoon. The wind dropped. Briefly there were stars overhead. The captain braced himself to face the worst quarter of the typhoon about to hit his battered ship. He felt obliged to brief the mate in case he found himself alone on the bridge:

'Now for it!' muttered Captain MacWhirr. 'Mr. Jukes.'

'Here, sir.'

The two men were growing indistinct to each other.

'We must trust her to go through it and come out on the other side. That's plain and straight. There's no room for Captain Wilson's storm-strategy here.'

'No, sir.'

'She will be smothered and swept again for hours.' mumbled the Captain. 'There's not much left by this time above deck for the sea to take away – unless you or me.'

'Both, sir,' whispered Jukes, breathlessly.

'You are always meeting trouble half way, Jukes.' Captain MacWhirr remonstrated quaintly. 'Though it's a fact that the second mate is no good. D'ye hear, Mr. Jukes? You would be left alone if . . .'

Captain MacWhirr interrupted himself, and Jukes, glancing on all sides, remained silent.

'Don't you be put out by anything,' the Captain continued, mumbling rather fast. 'Keep her facing it. They may say what they like, but the heaviest seas run with the wind. Facing it – always facing it – that's the way to get through. You are a young sailor. Face it. That's enough for any man. Keep a cool head.'

'Yes, sir,' said Jukes, with a flutter of the heart.

*

The ship laboured without intermission amongst the black hills of water, paying with this hard tumbling the price of her life. She rumbled in her depths, shaking a white plummet of steam into the night, and Jukes' thought skimmed like a bird through the engine-room, where Mr. Rout – good man – was ready. When the rumbling ceased it seemed to him that there was a pause of every sound, a dead pause in which Captain MacWhirr's voice rang out startlingly.

'What's that? A puff of wind?' – it spoke much louder than Jukes had ever heard it before – 'On the bow. That's right. She may come out of it yet.'

The mutter of the winds drew near apace. In the forefront could be distinguished a drowsy waking plaint passing on, and far off the growth of a multiple clamour, marching and expanding. There was the throb as of many drums in it, a vicious rushing note, and like the chant of a tramping multitude.

Jukes could no longer see his captain distinctly. The darkness was absolutely piling itself upon the ship. At most he made out movements, a hint of elbows spread out, of a head thrown up.

Captain MacWhirr was trying to do up the top button of his oilskin coat with unwonted haste. The hurricane, with its power to madden the seas, to sink ships, to uproot trees, to overturn strong walls and dash the very birds of the air to the ground, had found this taciturn man in its path, and, doing its utmost, had managed to wring out a few words. Before the renewed wrath of winds swooped on his ship, Captain MacWhirr was moved to declare, in a tone of vexation, as it were: 'I wouldn't like to lose her.'

He was spared that annoyance.

*

On a bright sunshiny day, with the breeze chasing her smoke far ahead, the *Nan-Shan* came into Fu-chau. Her arrival was at once noticed on shore, and the seamen in harbour said: 'Look! Look at that steamer. What's that? Siamese – isn't she? Just look at her!'

She seemed, indeed, to have been used as a running target for the secondary batteries of a cruiser. A hail of minor shells could not have given her upper works a more broken, torn, and devastated aspect: and she had about her the worn, weary air of ships coming from the far ends of the world – and indeed with truth, for in her short passage she had been very far; sighting, verily, even the coast of the Great Beyond, whence no ship ever returns to give up her crew to the dust of the earth. She was incrusted and gray with salt to the trucks of her masts and to the top of her funnel; as though (as some facetious seaman said) 'the crowd on board had fished her out somewhere from the bottom of the sea and brought her in here for salvage.' And further, excited by the felicity of his own wit, he offered to give five pounds for her – 'as she stands.'

from *Typhoon* by Joseph Conrad

Survival

Ernest Shackleton was already an Antarctic explorer when Captain Scott was pipped at the post by the Norwegian Roald Amundsen becoming the first man to reach the South Pole by a margin of a few days in December 1911. Shackleton then determined to bring home for Britain the last great achievement in the Antarctic, that of crossing the Polar Continent from the Weddell Sea via the Pole to the Ross Sea, a little matter of 1,800 miles.

He led the expedition from the 350-ton barquentine-rigged steamer *Endurance*, stoutly built in Sanderfjord south of Oslo, home of so many Norwegian sealers and whaling ships. By the time she was ready to leave from Plymouth, war with Germany had broken out, but Winston Churchill declined the offer of all her fifty-six officers and men to form the crew of an HM ship and join the fleet. Shackleton received a laconic telegram from the Admiralty saying simply: 'Proceed.'

Endurance sailed from Grytviken on South Georgia for the Weddell Sea on the day Admiral von Spee and his victorious squadron from the Battle of Coronel cleared the Magellan Straits 1,000 miles to the west on their way to the Falklands, where a superior force of Royal Navy battlecruisers exacted a terrible revenge on them. After making good progress south through pack-ice for six weeks, Shackleton's ship had crossed latitude 76° South when his log entry carried the awesome word 'beset'. The ship was held fast in the grip of massive, grinding ice-packs. She was carried 570 miles to the north at an average speed of two miles per day until 27 October, when the ice finally crushed her to matchwood and she sank.

For the next six months the survivors continued to drift northwards, finally having to shoot and eat the last of their dogs just as they reached the open sea. There they launched *Endurance*'s three ship's boats for the sixty-mile sail to Elephant Island, 600 miles SE of Cape Horn. With southern winter upon them, Shackleton wasted no time. With five companions he forthwith set out in the 20-foot open whaler *James Caird* to sail 820 miles across the Southern Ocean to seek help from South Georgia. Some protection was provided by canvas tarpaulins laid over a makeshift half-deck extending most of the way aft, but that did little to alleviate the plight of the crew of the smallest boat ever to take on those terrifying seas.

The tale of the next sixteen days is one of supreme strife amid heaving waters. The sub-Antarctic Ocean lived up to its evil winter reputation. I decided to run north for at least two days while the wind held and so get into warmer weather before turning to the east and laying a course for South Georgia. We took two-hourly spells at the tiller. The men who were not on watch crawled into the sodden sleeping-bags and tried to forget their troubles for a period; but there was no comfort in the boat. The bags and cases seemed to be alive in the unfailing knack of presenting their most uncomfortable angles to our rest-seeking bodies. A man might imagine for a moment that he had found a position of ease, but always discovered quickly that some unyielding point was impinging on muscle or bone. The first night aboard the boat was one of acute discomfort for us all, and we were heartily glad when the dawn came and we could set about the preparation of a hot breakfast.

*

A severe south-westerly gale on the fourth day out forced us to heave to. I would have liked to have run before the wind, but the sea was very high and the *James Caird* was in danger of broaching to and swamping. The delay was vexatious, since up to that time we had been making sixty or seventy miles a day; good going with our limited sail area. We hove to under double-reefed mainsail and our little jigger, and waited for the gale to blow itself out. During that afternoon we saw bits of wreckage, the remains probably of some unfortunate vessel that had failed to weather the strong gales south of Cape Horn. The weather conditions did not improve, and on the fifth day out the gale was so fierce that we were compelled to take in the double-reefed mainsail and hoist our small jib instead. We put out a sea-anchor to keep the *James Caird's* head up to the sea. This anchor consisted of a triangular canvas bag fastened to the end of the painter and allowed to stream out from the bows. The boat was high enough to catch the wind, and, as she drifted to leeward, the drag of the anchor kept her head to windward. Thus our boat took most of the seas more or less end on. Even then the crests of the waves often would curl right over us and we shipped a great deal of water, which necessitated unceasing baling and pumping. Looking out abeam, we would see a hollow like a tunnel formed as the crest of a big wave toppled over on to the swelling body of water. A thousand times it appeared as though the *James Caird* must be engulfed; but the boat lived. The south-westerly gale had its birthplace above the Antarctic Continent, and its freezing breath lowered the temperature far towards zero.

*

About 11 a.m. the boat suddenly fell off into the trough of the sea. The painter had parted and the sea-anchor had gone. This was serious. The *James Caird* went away to leeward, and we had no chance at all of recovering the anchor and our valuable rope, which had been our only means of keeping the boat's head up to the seas without the risk of hoisting sail in a gale. Now we had to set the sail and trust to its holding. While the *James Caird* rolled heavily in the trough, we beat the frozen canvas until the bulk of the ice had cracked off it and then hoisted it. The frozen gear worked protestingly, but after a struggle our little craft came up to the wind again, and we breathed more freely. Skin frost-bites were troubling us, and we had developed large blisters on our fingers and hands.

The landfall was somewhere on the unhospitable south coast with a full westerly gale threatening to wreck her on a lee shore.

We stood in towards the shore to look for a landing-place, and presently we could see the green tussock-grass on the ledges above the surf-beaten rocks. Ahead of us and to the south, blind rollers showed the presence of uncharted reefs along the coast. Here and there the hungry rocks were close to the surface, and over them the great waves broke, swirling viciously and spouting thirty and forty feet into the air. The rocky coast appeared to descend sheer to the sea. Our need of water and rest was wellnigh desperate, but to have attempted a landing at that time would have been suicidal. Night was drawing near, and the weather indications were not favourable. There was nothing for it but to haul off till the following morning, so we stood away on the starboard tack until we had made what appeared to be a safe offing. Then we hove to in the high westerly swell. The hours passed slowly as we waited the dawn, which would herald, we fondly hoped, the last stage of our journey. Our thirst was a torment and we could scarcely touch our food; the cold seemed to strike right through our weakened bodies. At 5 a.m. the wind shifted to the north-west and quickly increased to one of the worst hurricanes any of us had ever experienced. A great cross-sea was running, and the wind simply shrieked as it tore the tops off the waves and converted the whole seascape into a haze of driving spray. Down into valleys, up to tossing heights, straining until her seams opened, swung our little boat, brave still but labouring heavily. We knew that the wind and set of the sea was driving us ashore, but we could do nothing. The dawn showed us a storm-torn ocean, and the morning passed without bringing us a sight of the land; but at 1 p.m., through a rift in the flying mists, we got a glimpse of the huge crags of the island and realized that our position had become desperate. We were on a dead lee shore, and we could gauge our approach to the unseen cliffs by the roar of the breakers against the sheer walls of rock.

*

The chance of surviving the night, with the driving gale and the implacable sea forcing us on to the lee shore, seemed small. I think most of us had a feeling that the end was very near. Just after 6 p.m., in the dark, as the boat was in the yeasty backwash from the seas flung from this iron-bound coast, then, just when things looked their worst, they changed for the best. I have marvelled often at the thin line that divides success from failure and the sudden turn that leads from apparently certain disaster to comparative safety. The wind suddenly shifted, and we were free once more to make an offing.

from *South* by Sir Ernest Shackleton

At last they found a gap in the reefs and sailed into the shelter of what turned out to be King Haakon's Bay, the only safe anchorage on the south side of the island. The next thirty-six hours it took Shackleton and two of his crew to cross a succession of glaciers and 2,500-foot mountain ranges were as testing as any they had spent in the open whaler.

The twenty-two men left behind on Elephant Island were not recovered until over four months later. Three early attempts were thwarted by impenetrable ice. Shackleton finally delivered them back to civilization at Punta Arenas in Chile on 3 September 1916. By then British casualties on the Western Front alone had exceeded 850,000. All the survivors saw active service on their return, many of them in minesweepers. Three of them were killed.

Shackleton was commissioned as a major and ended the war in North Russia in charge of Arctic equipment and transport.

In 1925 Richard England ran away to sea and shipped as ship's boy in the coastal trading schooner *Via*. During a spell when she was laid up for refit, he should have sailed in the much smaller ketch *Excel* from Poole. He missed her, which was just as well:

At 3 p.m. Friday, 28 October, 1927, the Moelfre, Anglesey, pulling and sailing lifeboat *Charles & Eliza Laura* was called out in the teeth of a sou'-westerly gale and heavy seas, to search for a vessel reported in distress off Carmel Point. The vessel hadn't been located when darkness set in; the weather was rapidly getting worse and it seemed hopeless to continue to look for her. Just as the search was about to be called off, the wreck was sighted.

As the lifeboat soared on the crests of the big seas, her crew saw a little ketch, low in the water, half her bulwarks gone and her sails in ribbons, wallowing helplessly. Through the spray and spindrift, three men could be seen on her signalling to be taken off. The wreck was awash with the angry waves piling over her and it was obvious she might founder any moment.

Second Coxswain William Roberts, prompted by Captain Owen Jones with the approval of all the crew, decided to sail the lifeboat directly on top of the ketch amidships, hoping a big wave would carry her aboard, as it seemed impossible to get alongside in time to make a rescue.

William Roberts steered on the crest of a huge wave straight at the wreck and the lifeboat struck the mainhatch coamings of the *Excel* with terrific force, 'grounding' on her deck. For a few moments the lifeboat lay on top

163

of the wreck, just long enough for the three men to be hauled into her. One of the rescued men had a small dog in his arms as he was being pulled into the lifeboat but the animal struggled free and was swept away. When the waterlogged ketch dropped sickeningly into a trough, the *Charles & Eliza Laura*, badly holed in three places, slid clear.

The gale increased to hurricane force and it was hopeless to attempt sailing back to Moelfre. Throughout a long, dark night, the damaged lifeboat beat about in the raging seas. She was full of water and had lost most of her buoyancy. The waves broke over her continuously. Rescuers and rescued alike had to hold on grimly to the lifelines to save themselves from being washed overboard.

Sixty-five-year-old William Roberts, who, like his mates had been tumbled aft time and time again by the seas, had injured his head and was getting very feeble. He was washed right out of the boat on one occasion but still had the presence of mind to retain his grip on a lifeline. Two of his mates hauled him back aboard but he became very weak. The incessant battering of the waves, as the small craft plunged through, rather than over them; the blinding, choking brine in eyes, throat and nostrils and the stupefying effects of constant immersion in the icy water was as much as the strongest man could bear. Will Roberts died during the night. He talked to his friend Tom Williams right to the end. His last words were a request for a chew of tobacco.

from *Schoonerman* by Captain Richard England

Captain James P. Barker was only thirty-one years old when he commanded one of the crack Cape Horners of them all, the *British Isles*, as she fought for survival during the terrible winter of 1905. When one of his best seamen was catapulted overboard from the mizzen topsail yard he had to take a hard decision:

On 14th August – the sixth day of the storm – the mizzen topsail was split in a squall of hurricane force. As I was in the watch on deck, I went aloft with the men to furl the torn sail, after it had been clewed up.

We lay out on both sides of the yard, and began a two-hours' struggle with the frozen Number One canvas, which was bellied out by the terrific force of the wind to a rigidity which, for a long time, defied our efforts to make even a crease in it, to secure us a hold.

During a lull betweeen squalls, we managed to gather the canvas in, and lay over it, on the yard, to hold it down with the weight and pressure of our bodies and arms, while the gaskets were passed around it.

A seaman named Davidson – a fine fellow, quiet-mannered and good at his work – was at the centre, reaching over to catch the bunt-gasket, which was being thrown up to him by a man crouching on the foot-rope below the yard.

At this moment another squall struck the ship. The blast ripped the canvas from the grip of the men at the weather end of the yard. With a noise like a clap of thunder the whole sail bellied out. Davidson, leaning far over the yard, could not scramble back to a foothold.

We saw him hurtled forward over the bellied sail, as though thrown from a catapult, with arms and legs grotesquely flailing the air, and his oilskin coat ballooning, as he fell 40 feet sheer into the raging seas, while the ship lay down with her lee rail in the water under the impact of the squall.

'Man overboard!' roared Paddy Furlong, the first to collect his wits.

'Man overboard! Man overboard!' we all yelled at the top of our voices as, following Paddy's example, we let the sail go, to blow itself to ribbons, and scrambled down to the poop-deck as best we could, while the force of the wind pressed our bodies against the rigging and made every step down a laborious effort.

'Man overboard! Man overboard!' The hoarse voices of men with staring eyes and blanched faces were carried away in the roaring wind. Huddled under the weather-cloth on the poop, we were joined there almost immediately by the Captain, the Mate, and men of the watch below, all peering at the black spot astern, which showed where Davidson was making a desperate and futile struggle for life.

We saw that by some miracle he had caught hold of a rope trailing in the water. His voice came faintly:

'Help! Help! For God's sake, help!'

It could be only a matter of minutes, perhaps seconds, before his numbed fingers would have to let go of the rope in the icy water. Every man on the poop had but one thought. No lifeboat could be got into or out of the water in the tremendous sea that was running. . . .

The Captain called for volunteers to man a lifeboat. There was no answer from the half-frozen men huddled under the weather-cloth.

The alternative of ordering a boat to be launched was the Captain's prerogative, and his alone. Faced with this awful situation, he would not give the order, as he knew no lifeboat could live in those terrible seas. The agony of mind he endured in those fateful moments, as Davidson clung to that trailing rope, will never be known; but, by his decision, he emerged from the ordeal to fill a place among the giants of the Cape Horn breed, whose unerring instincts, in times of crisis, were a measure of their seaman-like quality.

The crew stood bewildered, muttering among themselves. Paddy Furlong, Hans Hansen, Otto Schmidt and the other old hands shook their heads, knowing full well, as the Captain did, that the attempted launch of a boat would result in the loss of perhaps another half-dozen lives.

Poor Davidson was doomed, and every man knew it. They were no curs, but the odds were impossible. As they hesitated, another huge sea and squall struck the ship, which shuddered and heeled over, awash from stem to stern, as all hands braced themselves and grabbed at the poop-rail, while the ship shook herself like a wet spaniel as she wallowed in the trough and laboriously righted herself to breast the next precipitous crest.

When the flying spray permitted another glimpse aft, Davidson had disappeared.

'Jaysus have mercy on his soul, the poor fella,' murmured Paddy Furlong, crossing himself. 'He's gone, and nothing can divvil a one of us do to help him now.'

The others stood silent, with white faces and grief in their eyes, as Paddy's pious sentiments voiced the feelings of all.

As though this tragedy were not enough for one day, another fine seaman, named West, when going forward, after the watch was relieved, was caught on the main deck by a heavy sea breaking on board, and, dashed into the scuppers, was knocked unconscious and lay there rolling helplessly.

A chain-gang of men rescued him and dragged him aft, where he was placed on the cabin-table for first aid. His skull was stove in with a gaping cut about five inches long, which was bleeding profusely. Only an operation, by highly skilled surgeons, could save his life. He was breathing stertorously, with occasional heavy groans, as the Captain and the carpenter swabbed the wound, shaved his head, and strapped the injury with plaster and bandages, to the best of their ability.

Then he was carried, still unconscious, to the spare cabin and lashed into a bunk, well tommed off, in company with Witney, the man with the broken leg, who was in the other bunk.

By these casualties the services of three seamen – as it happened, all English – had been lost, a considerable reduction in our meagre complement for working the ship.

from *The Cape Horn Breed* by Captain W. H. S. Jones

Dr David Lewis, a New Zealander with an insatiable compulsion for sailing to the furthest frontiers of human experience, left Sydney in October 1972 aiming to become the first yachtsman to circumnavigate Antarctica. He must have known that his boat was too small, but the 32-foot steel-hulled *Ice Bird* was more than he could afford. After a brief stop at Stewart Island off Otago to sort out problems he had in trying to maintain sufficient power to keep in radio contact with his sponsors, he sailed eastwards along the 60th parallel – destination the US Antarctic base at Palmer, so called after the sealer Nathaniel Palmer who touched down there in November 1820, just ten months after the Royal Navy's Edward Bransfield had discovered Antarctica. The base was on the north-west shore of the Antarctic Peninsula, about 400 miles south of Cape Horn on the opposite side of Drake's Passage.

Before sailing, his research included Soviet charts and publications, which led him to expect waves up to 35 feet high. Then he looked closely:

they were recorded in metres (so not 35 feet but 115 feet!), a daunting thought in a boat the size of a Half-Tonner. He was fully aware of the risks of being capsized and lists eight experienced sailors who have lived to tell the tale, some of them without going near the Southern Ocean. Nevertheless, until the 1979 Fastnet Race, most offshore sailors in North Atlantic waters discounted the possibility of being rolled clean over in a well-found keelboat. During the night of 13 August 1979, there were confused seas up to 40 feet high and winds gusting to 60 knots. One rescue helicopter pilot reported needing 70 knots airspeed to hover over a disabled yacht. No less than seventy-seven boats were rolled either right over or until their masts were substantially below the horizontal. Nearly all of them were boats of less than 38 feet overall. *Ice Bird*'s dimensions and general design characteristics strongly suggest that she would have suffered the same fate on the Continental Shelf less than 100 miles from the holiday beaches of Cornwall, let alone 3,500 miles WSW of Cape Horn.

David Lewis had all the right ideas of riding out ultimate storms with mountainous, breaking seas. He kept the waves fine on the quarter to reduce the risk of being pitchpoled end-for-end. His problems were twofold: he got becalmed in the deep troughs, lost steerage way and tended to be lying dangerously close to beam-on when hit by the next runaway monster; this problem became critical when his self-steering gear was wiped out.

> . . . this storm was something altogether new. By evening the estimated wind speed was over sixty knots; the seas were conservatively forty feet high and growing taller – great hollow rollers, whose wind-torn crests thundered over and broke with awful violence. The air was thick with driving spray.
>
> *Ice Bird* was running down wind on the starboard gybe (the wind on the starboard quarter), with storm jib sheeted flat as before. Once again I adjusted the wind-vane to hold the yacht steering at a small angle to a dead run, and laid out the tiller lines where they could be grasped instantaneously to assist the vane. This strategy had served me well in the gale just past, as it had Dumas and Moitessier. But would it be effective against this fearful storm? Had any other precautions been neglected? The Beaufort inflatable life raft's retaining strops had been reinforced by a criss-cross of extra lashings across the cockpit. Everything movable, I thought, was securely battened down; the washboards were snugly in place in the companionway; the hatches were all secured. No, I could not think of anything else that could usefully be done.
>
> Came a roar, as of an approaching express train. Higher yet tilted the

stern; *Ice Bird* picked up speed and hurtled forward surfing on her nose, then slewed violently to starboard, totally unresponsive to my hauling at the tiller lines with all my strength. A moment later the tottering breaker exploded right over us, smashing the yacht down on to her port side. The galley shelves tore loose from their fastenings and crashed down in a cascade of jars, mugs, frying pan and splintered wood. I have no recollection of where I myself was flung – presumably backwards on to the port bunk. I only recall clawing my way up the companionway and staring aft through the dome.

The invaluable self-steering vane had disappeared and I found, when I scrambled out on deck, that its vital gearing was shattered beyond repair – stainless steel shafts twisted and cog wheels and worm gear gone altogether. The stout canvas dodger round the cockpit was hanging in tatters. The jib was torn, though I am not sure whether it had split right across from luff to clew then or later. My recollections are too confused and most of that day's log entries were subsequently destroyed.

I do know that I lowered the sail, slackening the halyard, hauling down the jib and securing it, repeatedly unseated from the jerking foredeck, half blinded by stinging spray and sleet, having to turn away my head to gulp for the air being sucked past me by the screaming wind. Then lying on my stomach and grasping handholds like a rock climber, I inched my way back to the companionway and thankfully pulled the hatch to after me.

I crouched forward on the edge of the starboard bunk doing my best to persuade *Ice Bird* to run off before the wind under bare poles. She answered the helm, at best erratically, possibly because she was virtually becalmed in the deep canyons between the waves; so that more often than not the little yacht wallowed broadside on, port beam to the sea, while I struggled with the tiller lines, trying vainly to achieve steerage way and control.

And still the wind kept on increasing. It rose until, for the first time in all my years of seagoing, I heard the awful high scream of force thirteen hurricane winds rising beyond 70 knots.

*

The intolerable present became too intrusive to be ignored; the past faded into the background. Veritable cascades of white water were now thundering past on either side, more like breakers monstrously enlarged to perhaps forty-five feet, crashing down on a surf beach. Sooner or later one must burst fairly over us. What then?

I wedged myself more securely on the lee bunk, clutching the tiller lines, my stomach hollow with fear. The short sub-Antarctic night was over; it was now about 2 a.m.

My heart stopped. My whole world reared up, plucked by an irresistible force, to spin through giddy darkness, then to smash down into daylight again. Daylight, I saw with horror, as I pushed aside the cabin table that had come down on my head (the ceiling insulation was scored deeply where it had struck the deck head) . . . daylight was streaming through the now gaping opening where the forehatch had been! Water slopped about my knees. The remains of the Tilley lamp hung askew above my head. The stove remained upside down, wedged in its twisted gymballs.

Ice Bird had been rolled completely over to starboard through a full 360° and had righted herself thanks to her heavy lead keel – all in about a second. In that one second the snug cabin had become a shambles. What of the really vital structures? Above all, what of the mast?

I splashed forward, the first thought in my mind to close that yawning fore hatchway. My second – oh, God – the mast. I stumbled over rolling cans, felt the parallel rules crunch underfoot and pushed aside the flotsam of clothes, mattresses, sleeping bag, splintered wood fragments and charts (British charts floated better than Chilean, I noted – one up to the Admiralty). Sure enough the lower seven feet of the mast, broken free of the mast step, leaned drunkenly over the starboard bow and the top twenty-nine feet tilted steeply across the ruptured guard wires and far down into the water, pounding and screeching as the hulk wallowed.

The forehatch had been wrenched open by a shroud as the mast fell. Its hinges had sprung, though they were not broken off and its wooden securing batten had snapped. I forced it as nearly closed as I could with the bent hinges and bowsed it down with the block and tackle from the bosun's chair.

Then I stumbled back aft to observe, incredulously, for the first time that eight feet of the starboard side of the raised cabin trunk had been dented in, longitudinally, as if by a steam hammer. A six-inch vertical split between the windows spurted water at every roll (it was noteworthy, and in keeping with the experience of others, that it had been the lee or downwind side, the side underneath as the boat capsized, that had sustained damage, not the weather side where the wave had struck).

What unimaginable force could have done that to eighth-inch steel? The answer was plain. Water. The breaking crest, which had picked up the seven-ton yacht like a matchbox, would have been hurtling forward at something like fifty miles an hour. When it slammed her over, the impact would have been equivalent to dumping her on to concrete. The underside had given way.

Everything had changed in that moment of capsize on 29 November at 60° 04′S., 135° 35′W., six weeks and 3,600 miles out from Sydney, 2,500 miles from the Antarctic Peninsula. Not only were things changed; everything was probably coming to an end. The proud yacht of a moment before had become a wreck: high adventure had given place to an apparently foredoomed struggle to survive.

Two weeks later *Ice Bird* was capsized again, before the last of her sails disintegrated. By this time Lewis's hands were frostbitten, making emergency repairs and continual bailing with the toilet bucket painful and laborious. But finally, at the end of January 1973 he made it to the hospitable and well-organized American base at Palmer, just 1,500 miles from the South Pole. The boat wintered there and was refitted within the capabilities of the base. After leaving there in December 1973 he threaded his way through ice-floes past hundreds of bergs the size of container ships, heading for the Signy base in South Orkney. Much of the trip was through thick fog, so an intermittent lookout had to be kept through the Perspex dome in the main hatch, whilst David Lewis steered from below using an ice-axe jury-rigged as a whipstaff. The thickness of the fog governed how long he could read his current paperback between looks, a 'two-page fog' being poor visibility. Seven weeks later, *Ice Bird* was once again in trouble:

The first intimation that something right out of the ordinary was on its way was the plummeting of the barometer on the evening of 23 February. Before the 24th was an hour old, the severe northerly gale, which accompanied the warm front of a deep cyclonic depression, was upon us, bringing fog and stinging rain. By 3 a.m. it was at its full force nine fury. By 6.30 a.m. there was not a breath of wind at all. I was terror-struck.

This was the dread eye of the storm; the deceptively quiet hurricane vortex, whence few small boats had emerged. The night's strong northerly gale would be as nothing compared with what must abruptly terminate the temporary lull – the 'dangerous semicircle' cold front coming in on the wings of a gale of unimaginable ferocity from the opposite quarter.

The huge waves, released from the weight of the wind, reared skyward in toppling pyramids that almost stood *Ice Bird* on end. The stillness was uncanny. I made sure that the sea anchor warp was free and that the storm jib was hard-sheeted. Then I waited.

At half-past eight the expected line squall screamed out of the south-west at an initial velocity of 50 knots, or force 10. An hour and a half later it was blowing a consistent 70 knots (force 12) and gusting to 80 knots – nearly 100 miles an hour (force 13), the top of the anemometer scale. Force 12 is a hurricane.

'Fear and dread. God help us,' I wrote, and put the log away.

The glass began to rise and the sky to clear, but this was simply a cold-front feature. The hurricane continued unabated. The anemometer needle came hard up against the 80-knot stop more frequently than ever until the wind broke the instrument around noon. The seas grew steadily higher and broke ever more furiously. I crouched over the whipstaff, my eyes glued to the strip of vibrating sailcloth outside the dome that was my wind direction indicator. We were running down-wind at an angle to the enormous, heavily breaking seas. Twice during the afternoon the yacht was knocked down flat. Both times she recovered, but this was the writing on the wall. Even should the hurricane wind moderate soon, the waves would not, and forty-

170

foot monsters all around were now tumbling into surf. Ironically, around 4 p.m. the wind did start slackening.

Crash! My world was submerged in roaring chaos as a mighty hand rolled *Ice Bird* over, not ungently, upside down. I slithered round the side of the cabin as she went, and ended up in a heap on the ceiling. Then, just as smoothly, the yacht righted herself by rolling back upright the same way and I slid back with her. It was 4.15 p.m.

I could see from below that the backstays had gone; there was little doubt as to what I should find on deck. The mast had broken midway between the foot and the spreaders, and the pieces were floating alongside . . .

*

Lying in my sleeping bag, I worked out the main points. Once the yacht was jury rigged, her initial course should be due north, lest the westerlies sweep her right past Africa. The rig itself would need to have sufficient windward ability to cope with the Cape of Good Hope's unpredictable weather. Somewhat cheered at having made a small beginning, I was able to relax and sleep reasonably soundly.

The dismasted yacht was tossing wildly enough to make one's footing precarious when I dragged myself from my bunk in the morning and, dubiously fortified with cold coffee, resolutely put behind me lost hopes and set to work. The broken mast was stripped and the rigging disentangled and coiled, a physically exhausting task which extended well into the afternoon. Next came the jury mast. The boom was again the basis, but this time (to enable more sail to be carried), it was extended three feet by the gaff. The overlapping spars were clamped firmly together with oversized jubilee clips (hose clamps) supplied by the *Geographic* for camera clamps, reinforced by rope seizing and a fixed halyard to prevent slipping. At this stage the wind increased and it became too rough to continue working. I went below, uncertain if worse was to come and expressed my dread, 'God grant this isn't another gale.'

To my relief, 26 February brought much calmer weather. Even so, it took from 7 a.m. to half-past four in the afternoon to equip mast and 'topmast' with ten stays and three halyards between them. Then came the moment of truth. Could I raise the mast?

from *Ice Bird* by Dr David Lewis

He did, but realized that he would have to put into Cape Town for repairs. He made it three weeks later, where he had to leave the boat to meet other commitments. His son Barry took over and made the 6,000-mile voyage to Sydney in eighty-six days.

Possibly because of his long career in submarines, Commander Bill King had his entry for the 1969 Golden Globe Single-handed Round-the-

World Race, *Galway Blazer*, built with similar attention to watertight integrity. Angus Primrose designed her 42 feet overall, 30 feet on the waterline, yet displacing only 4½ tons. She had a fully battened junk-rig on two unstayed masts, with all her running rigging led back to one main hatch aft. Once clear of the Doldrums she showed her paces and was making swift progress towards the 50th parallel at a point 250 miles SSE of Tristan da Cunha when her skipper suddenly faced as great danger as any he had endured in command of submarines throughout the Second World War. He was not far short of his sixtieth birthday when he braced himself for another bare-knuckle fight with the odds heavily stacked against him.

For three days I had no time to take up my pen. The worst storm I have ever encountered during half a lifetime spent at sea, suddenly erupted. It was the afternoon of October 30th when the roar of the wind increased to hurricane force. How can I describe the huge procession of mammoth waves generated by that limitless power-house of the Roaring Forties? I had seen storms from the tiny platform of submarines or on sailing boats all over the world; but no mental picture ever occurred to me of the typhoon tumult which now battered *Galway Blazer*.

How high were the waves? There were no waves. A sea top erupting into pointed mountain peaks would suddenly be pressed down into flatness, blown off by wind-scream, mercifully shutting out the grey-green light, so that only the immediate streaky shoulders of sea hills could be seen. The air might clear to reveal a quarter of a mile of racked, spume-laden ocean, but not far enough to let me see the origin of the immediate threatening tumble. Although shut off from the furious orchestration by my hurricane hatches, I could not insulate the shriek of Nature's insane ravings. The patent *Dorade* ventilators became organ pipes, and their eerie drone added a new, artificial note to the cacophony.

For twenty-four hours I remained standing in the cockpit, under the hatches, watching and attempting to steer. There was no opportunity to eat; nor, in such conditions, while spellbound by the terrible heaving world outside, did I grow particularly hungry.

This was the ultimate storm. Elemental Force could cook up no more destructive tumult in open seas.

The cataclysm was racing down from the northward, and my sea room lay towards the ice-bound Polar land mass two thousand miles to the southward. At least there was no danger of being driven on to a lee shore.

Braced in the cockpit I felt my indestructible little boat's hull lift and heave, now flung violently sideways, now pointed almost vertically downward into a sea trench, the pit of which could not be glimpsed.

All through the end of one day and a whole night and then another day, *Galway Blazer* danced to the ocean's furious outcry.

In the very midst of the hurricane, the sky cleared, and I saw a full moon flaming coldly, detached from the awful scene.

There was little difference between day and night in the light outside. During the second day, I noticed the witch's cauldron of sea was growing less colossal, and the winds abating. I realized that such a storm should not have been expected in these regions. We were out of the hurricane area, but once in a lifetime one of these typhoon-tropic storms can blow up out of place, and out of season. Such a one had found me.

In the past Fate had dealt me a huge round of lucky cards. After six years of warfare I emerged from incessant submarine patrols, during which enemy bombs, depth charges, shells, bullets and ramming bows passed close aside.

Fair enough. I had picked up an unlucky hand, and this smashing tempest roared across my little boat for twenty-four hours. She had stuck it all bravely, and suffered no damage.

Towards the evening of October 31st – Hallowe'en, the witches' big night! – I felt the storm centre had passed.

The wind started to die down. At about force 9 I decided to go out on deck. I took the hurricane hatches off and went aft to look at the vane-steering. I tried to discover the reason it had been locking, but I could not. Then, as if led by a guardian angel, I returned to the enclosed cockpit for a piece of rope to secure the foresail before sailing on under bare poles again. I was sitting jambed into place under the open hatches, coiling down the rope, when the cockpit became a cocktail shaker.

Over she went to 90°. The boat was now lying right over on her side. Hurled by the elemental forces of the breaking peak of a rogue sea mountain, she was using her side as a surfer would his board, to speed and accelerate down the face of the wave. The masts must still have been in air, their proper element, and I had time to think, 'She will come back again; that great lead keel will swing her upright.'

Even as the thought crossed my mind, a vast new force started to act upon us. In those confused seas there was no proper pattern. Some cross-riding protuberance of foam-lashed water rode across the trough in which we might have recovered. Into this obstacle our mast tops now buried themselves, driven by the frightful impetus of our sideways rush. The leverage of a new element, imposed on our mastheads, now started the action of the mariner's most dreaded catastrophe: a complete roll over, upside-down.

I had a rapid change of mind. 'She will come back again' became 'No, she won't'; and, indeed, she did not.

I was on my shoulders pressed against the deckhead, which was normally above me, my head pointing to the sea bottom, fifteen thousand feet below, looking at the green water pouring up through both hatches.

Curiously, I felt no fear at that moment. There was nothing I could do, except cling on to my wedged-in position.

I knew she would quickly right herself by the down-swing of the two-ton lead keel. The boat had been specifically designed to withstand a disaster of this nature, without hull damage. I felt, perhaps, a pained surprise that I should have been defeated by the aftermath of the tempest, after riding out its fury. I stared, perhaps stupidly, at the inrushing columns of water, and then looked away. Similarly, if one sustains some frightful injury, one does not like to look at the wound and the distortion of one's limbs; then, with a mighty flick, up she came.

The cockpit was full of green water up to the top of the half door, perhaps three tons of it. My eyes flickered over the mess below deck and focused on the gymballed stove, hanging upside down. Irrationally it held my gaze while I pulled myself together for action; action there had to be, as we lay helpless and battered in the raging seas.

I could not tell, during those brief, upside-down moments, in what direction our recovery took place – whether we came up the same side as we went down, or on the opposite side. Did we also take a violent nose-dive and nearly pitchpole end over end? Later, I examined the evidence of damage and displaced articles below, and formed various theoretical ideas. If, as I think, she took a tremendous nose-dive as well as rolling over, that must have helped my gravitational attachment to the boat, as my back was against the forward bulkhead of the cockpit.

What mattered, and what then pleased me, was that I had survived undamaged, and so apparently had the hull. If it had happened sixty seconds later, I would have been out on deck under the capsized boat and under the broken foremast.

It happened so quickly. I had to realize later what had occurred and, when I had closed the hatches and pumped out the water, I pulled myself on deck, to meet a scene of devastation. The foremast had snapped off about twelve feet up. The main was still miraculously standing, but bent over to starboard at a drunken angle, the vane lay shattered in a tangle of twisted metal shaft.

from *Capsize* by Commander W. D. King

Galway Blazer limped along on her jury bipod mast after the disaster, with nearly 1,000 miles to go to Cape Town. For the last 200 miles she was towed in by a friendly yachtsman who came out and made a rendezvous with her. Later Bill King sailed on, only to be rammed and all but sunk by a Great White shark. The hole was underwater near her garboards. Flooding could only be controlled by sailing well heeled over on one tack whilst the hole was patched over. In the process he sailed three days towards Antarctica and away from safety, which lay in Fremantle, Western Australia. He finally completed his solo circumnavigation in 1973.

During Joseph Conrad's first voyage in the Far East he was the junior officer in the barque *Judea*. Somewhere south of Java he found himself in his first command – the 14-foot dinghy to which he had taken after the barque caught fire.

The skipper lingered disconsolately, and we left him to commune alone for a while with his first command. Then I went up again and brought him away at last. It was time. The ironwork on the poop was hot to the touch.

Then the painter of the long-boat was cut, and the three boats, tied together, drifted clear of the ship. It was just sixteen hours after the explosion when we abandoned her. Mahon had charge of the second boat, and I had the smallest – the 14-foot thing. The long-boat would have taken the lot of us; but the skipper said we must save as much property as we could – for the underwriters – and so I got my first command. I had two men with me, a bag of biscuits, a few tins of meat, and a breaker of water. I was ordered to keep close to the long-boat, that in case of bad weather we might be taken into her.

*

But we did not make a start at once. We must see the last of the ship. And so the boats drifted about that night, heaving and setting on the swell. The men dozed, waked, sighed, groaned. I looked at the burning ship.

*

At daylight she was only a charred shell, floating still under a cloud of smoke and bearing a glowing mass of coal within.

Then the oars were got out, and the boats forming in a line moved round her remains as if in procession – the long-boat leading. As we pulled across her stern a slim dart of fire shot out viciously at us, and suddenly she went down, head first, in a great hiss of steam. The unconsumed stern was the last to sink; but the paint had gone, had cracked, had peeled off, and there were no letters, there was no word, no stubborn device that was like her soul, to flash at the rising sun her creed and her name.

We made our way north. A breeze sprang up, and about noon all the boats came together for the last time. I had no mast or sail in mine, but I made a mast out of a square oar and hoisted a boat-awning for a sail, with a boat-hook for a yard. She was certainly over-masted, but I had the satisfaction of knowing that with the wind aft I could beat the other two. I had to wait for them. Then we all had a look at the captain's chart, and, after a sociable meal of hard bread and water, got our last instructions. These were simple: steer north, and keep together as much as possible.

*

Before sunset a thick rain-squall passed over the two boats, which were far astern, and that was the last I saw of them for a time. Next day I sat steering my cockle-shell – my first command – with nothing but water and sky around me. I did sight in the afternoon the upper sails of the ship far away, but said nothing, and my men did not notice her. You see I was afraid she might be homeward bound, and I had no mind to turn back from the portals of the East. I was steering for Java – another blessed name – like Bankok, you know. I steered many days.

I need not tell you what it is to be knocking about in an open boat. I remember nights and days of calm when we pulled, we pulled, and the boat seemed to stand still, as if bewitched within the circle of the sea horizon. I remember the heat, the deluge of rain-squalls that kept us baling for dear life (but filled our water-cask), and I remember sixteen hours on end with a mouth dry as a cinder and a steering-oar over the stern to keep my first command head on to a breaking sea. I did not know how good a man I was till then. I remember the drawn faces, the dejected figures of my two men, and I remember my youth and the feeling that will never come back any more – the feeling that I could last for ever, outlast the sea, the earth, and all men; the deceitful feeling that lures us on to joys, to perils, to love, to vain effort – to death; the triumphant conviction of strength, the heat of life in the handful of dust, the glow in the heart that with every year grows dim, grows cold, grows small, and expires – and expires, too soon, too soon – before life itself.

And this is how I see the East. I have seen its secret places and have looked into its very soul; but now I see it always from a small boat, a high outline of mountains, blue and afar in the morning; like faint mist at noon; a jagged wall of purple at sunset. I have the feel of the oar in my hand, the vision of a scorching blue sea in my eyes. And I see a bay, a wide bay, smooth as glass and polished like ice, shimmering in the dark. A red light burns far off upon the gloom of the land, and the night is soft and warm. We drag at the oars with aching arms, and suddenly a puff of wind, a puff faint and tepid and laden with strange odours of blossoms, of aromatic wood, comes out of the still night – the first sigh of the East on my face. That I can never forget. It was impalpable and enslaving, like a charm, like a whispered promise of mysterious delight.

We had been pulling this finishing spell for eleven hours. Two pulled, and he whose turn it was to rest sat at the tiller. We had made out the red light in that bay and steered for it, guessing it must mark some small coasting port. We passed two vessels, outlandish and high-sterned, sleeping at anchor, and, approaching the light, now very dim, ran the boat's nose against the end of a jutting wharf. We were blind with fatigue. My men dropped the oars and fell off the thwarts as if dead. I made fast to a pile. A current rippled softly. The scented obscurity of the shore was grouped into vast masses, a density of colossal clumps of vegetation, probably – mute and fantastic shapes. And at their foot the semicircle of beach gleamed faintly, like an illusion. There was not a light, not a stir, not a sound. The mysterious East faced me, perfumed like a flower, silent like death, dark like a grave.

And I sat weary beyond expression, exulting like a conqueror, sleepless and entranced as if before a profound, a fateful enigma.

A splashing of oars, a measured dip reverberating on the level of water, intensified by the silence of the shore into loud claps, made me jump up. A boat, a European boat, was coming in. I invoked the name of the dead; I hailed: *Judea* ahoy. A thin shout answered.

It was the captain. I had beaten the flagship by three hours, and I was glad to hear the old man's voice again, tremulous and tired. 'Is it you, Marlow?' 'Mind the end of that jetty, sir,' I cried.

He approached cautiously, and brought up with the deep-sea lead-line which we had saved – for the underwriters. I eased my painter and fell alongside. He sat, a broken figure at the stern, wet with dew, his hands clasped in his lap. His men were asleep already. 'I had a terrible time of it,' he murmured.

from *Youth* by Joseph Conrad

Jimmy Colet had to make a hasty departure from his twenty-year humdrum life as a clerk in a City shipping office. At the end of a bitter row he hit his despotic old boss and found he had killed him. He shipped as a purser in a leaky old tramp steamer heading for the Far East and Chinese owners. On the fringe of a cyclone in the Indian Ocean some rusty plates near her forepeak opened up. She lost her rudder and was left helplessly rolling her bridge-ends under. As transverse bulkheads buckled and split she slowly settled by the head. Captain Hale gave the orders for the two serviceable lifeboats to be lowered and then remained to go down with his ship. They set double-reefed sails in the dying storm and headed towards known steamship lanes.

The boat was rather crowded; there was a great variety of heads and caps forward. One fellow rejoiced to recognise a pal in the bows.

"'Ullo, Percy, I see you. Coming for a nice sail?'

There was a long silence; nothing was to be heard but the shrill swish and flight of the waters along the gunwale, and the creaking of the boat. When she mounted a sea and was exposed to the wind, she heeled and jammed into the broad round of the hill-top. Collins sat mute and observant, but occasionally made a request to a man:

'Keep watch by the halyards there.'

Presently Gillespie spoke to him:

'You and Sinclair agreed about it?'

'Yes, the old man gave us our orders. The only thing to do. We ought to be picked up, on this course.'

They heard, breaking another long interval of quiet, a plaintive voice in the crowd forward.

'Alf, 'ave you noticed where the gentlemen's room is in this ship?'

It grew hot, but there was no shelter from the glare. They must keep still, and ache. They could not ease away from the white fire. Colet, like his fellows, watched the seas. There was no more singing. They had begun already to peer beyond intently for the chance which would take them out of this huddled discomfort. Their narrow foothold was as lively as a bubble, flinching from every minor torment of the ascent and the dive. The inclines of the ocean were mesmeric with the horror of bulk whelming in unrest. The waters never paused. Respite was not there, and Colet found himself sighing for an outlook that would keep straight and still, and let him have his thoughts in peace. The sun continued its fire from a cloudless sky on the shelterless and silent boatful; but, whenever they were superior on a summit, and could see beyond the shifting and translucent parapets of their prison, only Sinclair and his crowd were in sight. And Sinclair's boat looked overladen and trifling. The inconsequence of their neighbour, when she was sighted below, as if fixed in a spacious hollow, was a warning to themselves; they, too, were like that. Colet spied Sinclair's charge with relief, if it were but the top of her mast above an intervening ridge. All right, so far. Sinclair was still there.

Gillespie sat noting the pursuit of the following seas. He exclaimed to the helmsman:

'Look out, Collins. Here's a beauty coming.'

Collins smiled, but kept this back to whatever was after them astern. The boat went squattering on the running hill till it found the wind at the top of it, and the hill was swinging ahead from under them. Not that time. Gillespie shook his head with dislike of it; but his eyes went again up their wake to look for the next attack.

The seas quivered in their mass with the original eagerness of that impulse which first sent them rolling round the globe. They would never stop. Their glassy inclines were fretted with lesser waves and hurrying cornices. They were flanged by outliers which deceived with hidden valleys, and the boat, rising briefly, dropped unexpectedly under the shadow of the superior headlong hill.

'Look out!' The startled watcher beside the steersman was compelled then to an involuntary shout of warning.

'It could be worse,' said Collins. 'She's not bad to steer, but it makes me sleepy. Here Wilson. Take a turn at it.'

Collins then superintended the distribution of some rations. A little water, a very little water, and some biscuits went round.

'And listen, you men,' he called out; 'if you don't want to go balmy, leave the sea-water alone. Bear that in mind to-morrow. All loonies will be put overside.'

'Good for you, sir. We'll watch it. But chase the cook along with the ham and eggs.'

*

The group aft, about Wilson, murmured a conversation, in which Wilson learned the name of the star which was in the general direction of their course, and how he should use it. They continued some speculation among the stars, whispering their attempts at mysteries, while the navigator gave names, haunting and occult names, to the glittering points of night.

'We shall have to keep this man awake,' said Collins. 'I was not quite all there all the time I was steering.'

Their gossip went back to the ship. They guessed at where her plates had parted. They spoke of their old ship, but they did not name her master. Collins explained his hopes of the course they were on, and they wondered how long it would be before a ship was sighted. Frequently they glanced to the spark which showed where Sinclair was in the night. Then Gillespie was left to keep the steersman company, and to call Colet at midnight to sit with the second officer.

Colet tried to sleep, but he had no sooner forgotten the cramp and the cold than the boat kicked him awake again. He turned about, to try the other side, and so got a memory of Wilson's head bent forward, a presiding head, austere and calm, isolated in the gloom. A fellow at the other end was retching. The hours stood still. He thought he would never sleep; but then again the boat jolted him into full consciousness of the cold, and in surprise he saw over them the dark wing of the sail. He turned back again. The bench was hard and wet, and gave nowhere. He could feel the slight timber vibrating under his arm; she was as giddy as an air-ball. Impossible to sleep, while listening to the fall of waters in the dark. When Gillespie gently pressed his knee, he sat up abruptly as if he had been dreaming of a crisis. Collins was taking Wilson's place.

'Eight bells,' said Gillespie, 'and all's well. Change over.'

Colet's teeth chattered on their own account. They got into full speed before they were checked. And nobody would have guessed that night itself could be so dark, when there was nothing in it but the sound of unseen waters in flight, and the thin protests of their frail security as it was hurled along through nothing.

from *Gallion's Reach* by H. M. Tomlinson

After many days of diminishing hope they were picked up by a passenger liner and put ashore in Rangoon. Months later, Colet met his old ship-mate Sinclair in Penang and shipped home with him.

Before Singapore fell in February 1942, Lieutenant Geoffrey Brooke, along with the other survivors from *Repulse* and *Prince of Wales*, had spent the two months after their ships were sunk by Japanese torpedo-bombers doing whatever they could to help in the hopeless cause of defending Malaya. Amongst other fire-brigade duties, he ran a ferry from Penang after the local crew had deserted, then withdrew to Singapore for the every-man-for-himself evacuation. Brooke made it to Sumatra in a junk after being sunk in a Chinese river-steamer amongst the Sinkep Islands.

Eighteen of them then sailed 1,660 miles in six weeks from Padang in SW Sumatra to within sight of Ceylon. Their boat was a ketch-rigged *prauw*, 45 feet on the waterline, with a 16-foot beam and a draught of only 4 feet, there being no keel, so windward progress was out of the question. Her name was *Sederhana Djohanis* (Lucky John).

Another limitation, somewhat basic under the cirucmstances, that had dawned on a few of us was that *Djohanis* was not meant to go out of sight of land! With her huge sail area and flattish bottom she was designed for shore breezes and the traditional Malay 'tidak apa' (swing it till Monday) philosophy. An inability to sail close-hauled had already been appreciated but yet another serious weakness was clearly demonstrated at 04:30 when sail was made to an easterly wind. Probably we were clumsy in the half light, but the mainsail tore on something, drawing attention to the shocking state of the canvas and rigging. To begin with the sails were made of very thin, cheap canvas, now rotting, that tore if poked hard with the finger! At night stars could be seen through the mainsail, which was the worst though closely contested offender. Much of the cordage was on its last legs; it was four-stranded and corresponded to tarred sisal. There was hardly any spare. Only the 'essential services' such as throat halliards boasted real blocks (these being rough native affairs), other locations having merely a piece of wood with a hole in it. The resulting wear and tear was appalling.

*

'Tore a large hole while lowering, through catching in wire strand on starboard runner. Mended this. Hoisted again. Tore a large hole through catching under boom. Repaired this. Finally hoisted 10:30 by which time no wind. Onshore breeze began 11:30. A bloody night and a bloody morning. Seriously worried re sails and gear. May make for Nias and see what we can do.'

This proved to be typical of the conditions until we cleared the area of *sumatras*, as these vicious squalls were called. Though clearly related in devilment to the *gregale* of Malta, its twin at Gib (which would sweep down the Rock to flatten unsuspecting naval whalers) and Portland's speciality, *sumatras* took the palm for surprise. In the middle of a sultry calm a long black shadow would suddenly appear, racing towards us over the water; seconds later the boat would heel right over as if struck and go tearing off, usually to the accompaniment of ripping canvas. Sometimes the squalls would veer 360° and then die as suddenly as they had come.

*

Striking west for Ceylon (about 1,000 miles as the seagull flies) contact with terra firma was severed for the last time at 17:00 (on March 12), nor did *Sederhana Djohanis* ever drop anchor again.

Not long after this a fresh south-westerly breeze came off the land and showed signs of blowing up strong. The mainsail was already down, being patched where the topping-lift had rent it in two places, and we sacrificed the mizzen. In spite of preparation, the jib downhaul jammed when the storm arrived with a rush to tear the sail right down one cloth. The foresail was soon lowered too, the wind reaching about force seven. In two and a half hours we covered 26 miles under bare poles.

*

At last, on March 28 a steady breeze arrived. The north-east monsoon at last? And then from the heights of hope we were shot to the depths of gloom. 'Aircraft!' We dived below and Jamal took the tiller as usual. The bomber approached slowly from astern but with any luck . . . *Ratatat . . . ratatatatat!*

The bullets crackled on the water, on the hull and penthouse roof, and a few smacked around inside. There was a pause while we got to our feet, swearing volubly, and quickly piled any useful material against the side. Then someone remembered Jamal and Soon and called them in. They had sat still at the tiller while bullets sent wood slivvers flying and lashed the surrounding water for seconds. 'Jaga biak! Tuan, dia balek!' And sure enough, it was back again. We got down feeling bloody. To have to lie and take it like this was infuriating as well as frightening, and one was much tempted to be up and doing.

He circled the boat three times, giving us in all five long burst

At last they believed they were approaching Ceylon . . .

The distinct rumble and crump of gunfire and bombs was heard, just over the horizon. It went on for an appreciable time. Obviously a naval battle was in progress, perhaps the prelude to invasion.

*

More troubled weather brought surprise squalls, but though pretty weak – everyone had lost several stone – we were well drilled by this time and bungling would produce a bellow from the helmsman. Waterspouts towered up on the horizon, after which the wind blew steadily and the boat skimmed before it. This period of a few days ending on April 11 was the only one which could boast the north-east monsoon in the steady form expected. Had we not been favoured with this dying effort, the story might even then have ended very differently.

And then something happened.

It was pronounced as one might expect by the lookout screaming 'Land!' with a hysterical bellow, or someone croaking the magic word through parched and swollen lips. Gorham, who had been scanning the horizon through glasses for some time, said, 'I don't think you'll all be disappointed if you come up here and see what I see.'

from *Alarm Starboard!* by Geoffrey Brooke

They were picked up by a passing tanker and taken to Colombo, after the *prauw* had been sunk by gunfire. Brooke then went on to the relative comfort of Russian convoys in a cruiser, ending his war as a flight-deck officer in one of the carriers in the British Pacific Fleet coping with kamikazes diving into the deck-park of Corsairs and Avengers.

THE LIGHTER SIDE

One of the best temporary cures for pride and affectation is seasickness; a man who wants to vomit never puts on airs.

Henry Wheeler Show

How holy people look when they are seasick.

Samuel Butler

This is a disappointingly short chapter, for humorous writing about the sea before the turn of this century takes some finding. Perhaps it was because there was nothing to laugh about in the lives of sailors in earlier times.

Captain William Ebbs, MBE, was master of the Pole Star freighter *Martin Luther*, which he had recommended to her parsimonious owners as being no longer fit for the conveyance of cargo, animals or sailors. He was ordered to head office in Leadenhall Street by the direct descendant of the eighteenth-century founder of the line, a red-headed Orkney sea-captain who had 'roared his way round the China coast for forty years and by not troubling overmuch about working men and ships to death sailed himself into a fortune'. To his surprise Ebbs was not sacked, but instead offered immediate command of a passenger liner about to sail for Australia. The first person he met inside his new cabin, which was designed for the entertainment of passengers and resembled the tea-lounge of a residential hotel, was the purser . . .

He heard a cough behind him.

'Ah, Purser!' Ebbs recognized the white bands on his visitor's cuff.

'Good morning, sir. My name is Prittlewell. Herbert Prittlewell. I hope the cabin is satisfactory?'

'Perfectly, thank you.'

'I had your predecessor's gear removed as soon as I heard of his indisposition, sir.'

'Very sad, very sad,' Ebbs said, becoming solemn again. 'I have – ah, of course, sent some flowers and grapes and so forth.'

'I'm sure you have, sir.'

Prittlewell looked at Ebbs shrewdly. As the *Charlemagne*'s hotel manager he spent his life assessing people, separating the ones who were genuinely important, wealthy, honest, or married from those taking advantage of the isolation of the sea to pretend they were. He was a tall grey handsome man with a monocle, like a cartoon Admiral, and he had a graceful manner that might have flowered first in Dartmouth, an older public school, or at least South Kensington. But Prittlewell had been to none of these places. He had begun as a fourteen-year-old bell-boy aboard a Pole Star liner, where he found that packages of soap, butter, tea, and cutlery could be safely smuggled ashore in a gutted copy of a Mission Bible and sold handsomely to the neighbours in his native Stepney. This spirit had quickly projected him through the lower ranks of stewards, but he soon became dissatisfied with such trivial scrounging and set himself to acquire book-keeping, good manners, and a wardroom accent, in order to achieve control of the dozen silent percentages and score of unmentioned favours that bring power and profit to the purser of a large liner.

185

'I've brought your own gear up, sir,' he said, as two stewards struggled in with the loaf-shaped leather trunk and dozen paper parcels in which Ebbs moved his possessions.

'Thank you, Purser.'

'This is your first command of a passenger ship, I believe, sir?' Prittlewell had speculated more sharply than anyone on board about Ebbs's accession to the *Charlemagne*, as his income depended largely on keeping the Captain's eyes from his account books.

'I really can't see why that is of any importance,' Ebbs told him. 'To the sailor all ships are the same. They float on the water, they contain machinery, they feed you and sleep you. It is only the people inside them who matter. I should like you to remember that, please.'

'Certainly, sir.'

Ebbs sat down in his pink desk chair. 'I gather we have a full ship for the voyage?'

'Yes, sir. Not a spare shed.'

'I beg your pardon?'

'No unoccupied cabins, sir. Perhaps you would like to see the passenger list?'

'Ah, thank you!' Ebbs eagerly took a bundle of type-written flimsy. 'Nothing like starting work at once, eh? Well, well!' he murmured, flicking over the smudgy sheets. 'Remarkable, isn't it? Here are these people, whom I couldn't tell from Adam and Eve, and by the end of the voyage we'll all be firm friends and know each other inside out.'

'Most remarkable, sir.'

'If you will kindly give me half an hour,' Ebbs went on, 'I shall prepare a list of people I wish to sit at my table. A somewhat chancy selection, I think? Like picking horses. However, from the ages and occupations so thoughtfully provided by the head office, I should be able to gather some congenial company. I don't want any young women —'

'The Company have already sent me a list of passengers who will be sitting at your table, sir.'

'You mean I have no say in the matter at all?'

'None whatever, sir.'

The new master turned to his servant for advice on how to handle the social side of his command.

'You have been Tiger to a good many Captains, I believe?'

Burtweed smiled benevolently. 'My twenty-fourth, sir. And as nice a bunch of gentlemen as you could expect to meet,' he continued modestly, as if talking of his own successful children.

'Quite. I'll admit that I'm becoming a little uneasy about entertaining for dinner to-night nine complete strangers, one of whom has already sent me an extremely offensive letter.'

186

'It takes all sorts to make a passenger list, sir,' said Burtweed generously, starting to clear away the dishes.

'I wondered if you had any – ah, advice, any experience of former Captains to draw upon, as it were?' Ebbs asked him. 'What did Captain Buckle say to the passengers, for instance? Surely he had some sort of small talk up his sleeve?'

'I am proper glad you asked, sir,' Burtweed said with feeling. 'Really I am, sir. Very difficult it can be sometimes at table, and I – I —' He stared at his feet and swallowed. 'I *do* want you to be a success, sir. Not being able to offer advice unasked —'

'You are asked, Burtweed, you are asked.'

'Thank you, sir. Well, sir. The first thing, you must tell a funny story.'

Ebbs rubbed his chin. 'I don't think I know any funny stories.'

'Captain Buckle only had one, sir. He told it every voyage.'

'You remember it, Burtweed?'

'Bless us, yes sir! Fifty times I must have heard it, regular twice a voyage. It was a real scream, sir.'

'Perhaps you could repeat it to me?'

'With the greatest of pleasure, sir. It was about a Captain and a Chief Engineer —'

'Perfectly proper, I hope?' Ebbs asked severely.

'Oh, perfectly, sir! Never bring a blush to a cheek, Captain Buckle wouldn't. You see, this Captain, sir, was – with great respect – one of the old school, sir, and always heaved the lead when his ship was coming into port, like in the old days before echo-sounders and all that, sir. Well, this Captain prided himself he could tell what port they was in just by looking at the lead, sir, and seeing the mud what was brought up from the sea bottom. But one day the Chief Engineer grabs the lead, sir, on its way to the bridge, takes it to his cabin, and wipes his best boots on it. The Captain takes one look at it, you see, sir, and says to the mates: "Gentlemen," he says, "I have the honour to inform you that the ship is now situated at the corner of Sauchiehall Street and Argyll Street." '

There was silence.

'I see,' Ebbs said. He thought deeply, scratching his ear. 'Not a bad tale.'

'Had the passengers in fits sometimes, sir. Captain Buckle called it his ice-breaker.'

Needless to say, the Tiger's story never got a fair hearing at the captain's table, but Ebbs was on surer ground when it was time for the first church service on the long voyage . . .

'Let us pray,' said Canon Swingle.

Ebbs reverently lowered his head, and began keenly inspecting the rows of passengers under his eyebrows.

*

As Ebbs's only acquaintance with the prayer-book in the past twenty-five years had been on the disposal of his dead shipmates, he had deputed command of the *Charlemagne*'s spiritual navigation to Canon Swingle. The Canon now stood between himself and Shawe-Wilson at a flag-draped table in the first-class lounge, giving the service the professional polish of his practised monotone. He was a lean, vague man of the type often found desiccating in English cathedrals, and had been stimulated by his surroundings and large captive congregation to decorate his supplications with the rich hand of a Victorian architect.

'Like this so fragile bark which bears us all,' he insisted, 'we uncertainly navigate the currents of this life. We barely miss the perilous headland and rocky cape, we foolishly scrape shoal and sandbank, and we lay helpless in storm and tempest, fearful for our brittle hull and feeble decks. We are blind to the lighthouse and deaf to the foghorn, lost, unable to steer, searching for the miracle of the joyous harbour . . .'

This idiot doesn't say much for my navigation, Ebbs thought, folding his arms.

They rose to sing *For Those in Peril on the Sea* (Ebbs had vetoed *Nearer My God to Thee* as traditionally reserved for the ship disappearing beneath them) while Mutt and Jeff passed round cocktail salvers for the collection with their special Sunday expressions of piety. Church is always well attended by ship's passengers, less from a resort to religion because of the insecure environment than the lack of alternative amusements on Sunday mornings and the impossibility of staying in bed.

Towards the end of the voyage there was the inevitable ship's concert . . .

Mrs Judd, sitting in the front row of deck-chairs with Ebbs, touched him on the hand and whispered: 'Do you think we can escape?'

Ebbs nodded. They guiltily slipped from their places while Broster was noisily arranging his larynx for the next song.

'I'd much rather be talking to you, William,' she said, smiling up at him as they walked gently forward along the deserted deck. 'So much rather.'

'Dear Edith,' Ebbs said solemnly. 'How very sincerely I feel the same.' He blew his nose loudly.

For the past few days Ebbs had been weathering an invigorating emotional storm. A ship in hot weather is a fine incubator for intimacies, and within an hour of first settling herself with a Green Chartreuse in his cabin Mrs Judd had revealed that her name was Edith, that she was a widow, her husband had grown tobacco in Rhodesia, she was going to stay with a sister in Sydney whom she hadn't seen for fifeen years, she was fond of Sealyhams and long walks, couldn't stand bananas, preferred the cold but was subject to chilblains, and thought T. S. Eliot was terrific. At the same time she discovered that Ebbs was passionately fond of sherry trifle, was frightened of bats, had a brother who came to a bad end in Canada, and wanted to find a way of making white collars last longer at sea.

The next day Ebbs was amazed how coincidence repeatedly thrust them together. Whenever he appeared on deck he either stumbled across her steamer chair or happened to find her taking the air on the rail outside his cabin. By the following night he had learned that she married her husband a week after meeting him, was thirty-two last birthday, slept in bed-socks in winter, had an operation for appendicitis when she was twelve, thought Ebbs was the most lovable man she had ever seen, and wore her stockings rolled below her knees in hot weather. She simultaneously found that Ebbs had an ingrowing toenail, was once almost engaged to a New Zealand girl who abandoned him for an Auckland pork-butcher, felt depressed in the tropics, thought she was the most sympathetic woman in the world, used to play the flute, and hated onions.

'How awful that we'll soon have to part!' she sighed. They were leaning on the rail where Priscilla had thrown the red lead at Ebbs. From aft came faint sounds of the latest assault on Gilbert and Sullivan.

'But I trust not for ever, my dear,' Ebbs said wistfully. 'After all, the end of the voyage is by no means the end of the world.'

from *The Captain's Table* by Richard Gordon

The same author's previous book was a classic in its own right, but may best be remembered for the film later made from it, *Doctor at Sea*, in which Brigitte Bardot made her début. It tells the story of the freighter *Lotus* under her formidable master, Captain Vincent Hogg. The ship is described as being accident-prone, like a big awkward schoolgirl. She had lost her propeller on her maiden voyage. When war came, she soon proved the effectiveness of the magnetic mine, only to have her stern blown off twenty minutes into her next voyage after repairs. Returning to trading in peacetime, she embarked a newly qualified doctor for the round trip to South America . . .

Sunday was recognizable, as it was the only occasion when we flew the flag at sea. From eight to midday the red ensign waved from the gaff on the mainmast, to convince the Almighty that we had not forgotten him – for there was no one else but ourselves to see it. The appearance of the flag that symbolized the Sabbath was greeted warmly by all hands, not through reverence but because, under Ministry of Transport regulations, we all got an extra half-day's pay.

Sunday was also marked by the ceremony of full inspection. This was ordered by Captain Hogg's copy of *Instructions for Masters*, the manual through which the Fathom Steamship Company directed and advised their commanders, which contained in its yellow pages regulations designed to right such nautical disasters as mutiny, epidemics of smallpox, lost anchor, and imminent shipwreck. At eleven o'clock the four of us fell in behind the Captain, who indicated the exceptional occasion by carrying a torch and a walking-stick. On the poop the ship's company was lined up ready for us – deckhands under the charge of the Bos'n on the port side, firemen and greasers to starboard, and catering staff, in fresh white jackets, standing nervously athwartships. Captain Hogg passed down the ranks scowling into each face like a vengeful but short-sighted victim at an identification parade, then we marched in and out of the little, green-painted crews' cabins that each smelt of feet and hair-oil. They had been cleaned and tidied so that nothing in the slightest degree disturbing could fall into the Captain's visual fields. The decks were scrubbed, the blankets folded ostentatiously, and the owners' possessions – varying from a guitar to a caged canary – were set in unnaturally tidy piles. Captain Hogg shone his torch beneath the bunks, inspected the undersurfaces of tables and chairs, and thrust the crook of his walking-stick into every inviting orifice. Usually his rummaging produced nothing more than a cloud of dust and an empty beer-tin, but occasionally he would drag out a saloon plate, a silver coffee-pot, a mildewed loaf, a pair of underpants, or the crumpled photograph of an inconstant girl friend.

The captain did not always stick to routine for evolutions . . .

I sat up and switched on the light. Seven short rings, meaning 'Boat Stations.' Someone on the bridge had obviously leant on the alarm button. I was wondering what to do when the whistle blew 'Abandon Ship.'

'Christ!' I said. I jumped from my bunk like a sprinter off the mark. I fell over the hot-water can, picked myself up, and threw open the cabin door. Trail lived opposite me, and had just come off watch. He was looking disturbed.

'What's up?' I asked anxiously.

'It's abandon ship.'

'I know! But why?'

'Search me, Doc. She was all right when I came off the bridge. We'd better get up top.'

I hitched up my pyjama trousers and started for the companionway.

'Your life-jacket, you fool!' Trail shouted at me.

'Oh lord! I forgot.'

I ran back to my cabin, pulled on my life-jacket, and started tying it. It occurred to me I should make an attempt to save some of my possessions, so I picked up my empty sponge-bag and stuffed one or two handy articles into it. I later discovered I had preserved from the deep a shoehorn, two empty cigarette tins, a roll of film, and a copy of *Teach Yourself Spanish*. Grabbing a tin of morphine from the locker, I hurried towards the boatdeck.

The crew of the *Lotus* had boat drill at four-thirty every Friday afternoon, as prescribed by the Ministry of Transport, and this was always carried out efficiently, with calmness, and in an atmosphere of polite co-operation.

There are, however, certain factors that complicate boat drill in earnest which are not operative during its harmless rehearsals. In the first place, it is usually night-time, there is a cold wind blowing, and it is raining. A strong sea is running, which makes it difficult to swing the boats out without smashing them. Everyone has been woken up from a deep sleep and is bad tempered. The Bos'n has forgotten where he put the handle to one of the davits. The Third has lost the roll-call. All hands are perplexed and naturally worried about saving themselves as well as giving whole-hearted enthusiasm to preserving their shipmates. Also, all the lights are out.

I slipped over the wet deck, now alive with hurrying sailors, and found my way to the huddle of men round my own boat. They were cutting away the strings holding the canvas cover, under the directions of the Third.

'My God, what a lash-up!' the Third said. 'All right, Bos'n. Stand-by to swing.'

'Swing out all boats!' Captain Hogg's voice came through the loud hailer.

'Swing out!' the Third repeated.'

Three men swung on each davit handle with an energy usually shown at sea only when arriving in port ten minutes before the pubs shut.

'Swing out, there!' Captain Hogg repeated. 'The ship is going down!'

A rocket flew into the air and exploded into gently falling coloured stars.

'Get a move on, you men!' he shouted.

'Come on, come on!' Trail ordered impatiently. 'Stand-by the falls, there!'

'Excuse my interrupting,' I said. 'But if we're sinking we don't seem to have much of a list on.'

'Cut it out, Doc! Right, lower away there! Steady forrard!'

Hornbeam, in his life-jacket and underpants, came breathlessly over to us.

'What's up?' I asked.

'Search me. The Old Man started it. I went up to the bridge and he kicked me off.'

Suddenly the deck lights snapped on. We all paused and looked at one another.

'Right!' came from the loud hailer. 'That was the poorest exhibition I've seen in all my years at sea. That was boat drill, see? As it should be done. None of this Friday afternoon tea-party stuff. You're the most inefficient crew I've ever had the misfortune to sail with. Swing 'em in again and dismiss.'

To a chorus of groans and ingenious profanity the boats were swung in and made fast.

from *Doctor at Sea* by Richard Gordon

Cartoonists were the first to focus on the foibles and eccentricities of yachting's Top People, the members of the Royal Yacht Squadron at

Cowes and those who sought to emulate them. But, since the 1950s, sailing has been adopted with enthusiasm by hundreds of thousands of aspirants from all walks of life who flock to the London Boat Show each January. Many characters have become folklore in our time . . .

. . . the uncappable story, of course, goes to the Grandad of Cowes racing, F. Ratsey, who in later life started to be beaten by some of the upstarts like young Uffa Fox. Whilst sometimes over-taken on boat speed he was never beaten with guile. He had the reputation of knowing the ground so well that he could short-tack up the coast to keep out of the tide in a rock-dodging way which invariably ended up grounding the followers. He particularly wanted to win one race in Cowes Week, and for several previous races the fleet noticed that Mrs Ratsey was to be seen bathing in her striped costume on the beach by the hardest piece of tide. Mr Ratsey was heard to say that he had arranged for her to be an early sort of depth finder as he knew he could always sail up to her when the water came to the bottom of the red stripe on her costume. He won his race: most of the competition went aground. Mrs Ratsey had been on the crucial station, with the water up to the red stripe on her costume, boats piled up all round her, swearing, pushing and puffing, trying to get off. Then she stood up.

Buying a competitive ocean-racer at the Boat Show is one thing, but getting a reliable crew to campaign her is quite another. In the sidestreets of Roo Valley (Earls Court) there seems to be a neverending supply of foredeck fodder in the shape of unattached Australian boat-bums. Here's how you enlist them . . .

You need a couple of heavies who will pull and wind without too much argument, and these can be supplied at short notice by our old Australian foredeck hand Bruce Leadfoot O'Riley. Leadfoot does not sail himself these days, but has settled down in some comfort to live in England just off Eaton Place. He likes to think he is still a dinkum boy by keeping company with the ever-present crowd of Australian Rule rugby players who are over in the old country and also know that Leadfoot may fit them up with either a bird or a bit of sailing for the weekend. Leadfoot's organization is known as 'Rentastrine' and all you have to do is to let him know where, when, and how many. He trips over to the bar where his current supply is waiting; details the two nearest the door who are also sober enough to be playing two-up and can follow his instructions.

Though the Rentastrine process may seem casual, you will invariably get first class hands from him, but the two adopted will keep you guessing by arriving seconds before your departure and have the minutest bag of sailing kit you have ever seen (which they share between them) and a case of Fosters each. If you are lucky one will be able to understand you and vice versa, the other will understand you not and vice versa. Both of them, incidentally, will be called Bruce.

You will have to get Bruce No. 1 to translate to Bruce No. 2. 'Bruce, would you mind asking the other Bruce if he could kindly set up the downhaul on the main boom.'

'EARBRUCESKIPWANSYERTOWACKRUPAKICKERANDSOCK ERDOWNYEBOOMVANGMATE.'

Surprisingly, this will work far more effectively than you could ever get the same chore organized in English.

All Bruces will be strong, so strong in fact that if told to start pulling or winding something they should also be told to stop before the handle bends or they pull the head of the sail through the block or the track out of the deck.

They will prove great fun and you might think that they should be invited to join the crew on a regular basis. They will accept your offer willingly, but the contact number will turn out to be a pay telephone on the landing of a large Edwardian house in Earls Court. The charming New Zealand girl who answers this will tell you she does know several Bruces, but she thinks they were the Bruces who went off last Wednesday in a converted London taxi to the Munich Bierfest.

You replace Bruce and Bruce as required by going back to Leadfoot for another Bruce and Bruce. Your new Bruces will have just come back from a cultural tour of Europe which took in a conducted trip round 119 breweries and the Munich Bierfest.

Owners of cruising yachts have different problems to contend with. Often their crews are strangers to life in a small yacht in the Channel when the going gets tough. Domestic trouble usually starts in the smallest compartment in the boat . . .

. . . the only unpleasant job you have to do yourself is to unblock the loo when inevitably it becomes blocked. Claud Worth's galvanized bucket might have left its mark, but like the catheads of sailing ships or the high poop of a Chinese junk, was a practical answer to the problem. Since we decided to get decent we have to defy the hydraulic laws, and there have been more attempts to build a good marine loo than patents on nutcrackers.

They all leak, and block. An American friend came close to solving the problem with a notice which in its way made the point - 'Nothin' down here you ain't ate'. Whilst that was clever, he kept the old one too long, and it bust into a lot of pieces of porcelain. The crew didn't mind too much, but his wife who had been sitting on it when it bust in the middle of the Channel Race is said to have finished the race in a very low state of morale. With thirty more hours beating to windward she was lucky not to have suffered the most unlikely accident in the history of ocean racing.

I know your chemical contraption works at Chertsey. For God's sake don't put it in *Lassitude*, you will have enough trouble when you do a really good broach without having a downward-pointing chemical toilet. Leave the one you have got, put some new rubber washers on it, and keep it well swilled with that disinfectant supplied in plenty outside the hull.

Further advice to this owner came by letter from a friend . . .

You will be better off leaving Girl Friends ashore. At your age I do not expect you to take that advice. When they come to use the head do not expect them to understand the technology. Even if your mission in life were teaching Zambians to fly Concorde you will get beat on this one.

'Look Celia, first turn the big gate valve with the handle pointing forward, then put your hand under the stand and turn the valve on. When you have finished pump with the lever and control the flow with the little silver valve, then turn the gate valve off and the handle back pointing aft.'

If you try it, you will either have a tearful lady squeaking at you after half an hour that 'your loo' doesn't work, or worse she will come up with the little silver lever which came off in her hands. You will find it easier to bow to the inevitable at the outset and tell her to use the white thing up at the front and then ask Henry nicely to pump it all out when she has done her worst. If you must take them to sea for a long passage Henry will enjoy giving a protracted lesson before you start. It won't make any difference, but Henry enjoys that demonstration very much.

In either case never tell girls that in practical use the boat falling off a good wave will create a surge effect in the pan. That is a marine experience they are better left to discover themselves.

from *Sod's Law of the Sea* by Bill Lucas and Andrew Spedding

Early in the eighteenth century the sailor's acceptance of his lot afloat expressed itself in the grim irony of cartoons with elaborate captions and one-liners in balloons, still to be found as faded lithos in old waterfront taverns. One writer at the time, Edward (Ned) Ward, has left us a series of derisive portraits of his shipmates from the captain downwards, showing little respect for any – the stuff of ships' concerts or Crossing-the-Line ceremonies. He leads off with his view of the captain, over-looking the admiral because he presumably never served in a flagship . . .

The great Cabin is the *Sanctum Sanctorum* he inhabits; from this all Mortals are excluded by a Marine, with a brandish'd Sword, who guards this Bird of Paradise as watchfully as the Centries do the Geese in *St. James's Park*.

Sometimes a humble Supplicant is admitted to the threshold, usher'd in by the Barber, the Master of his ceremonies; and while this poor Mendicant addresses him with Fear and Trembling, this Son of *Boreas* (that it might not daunt the Creature too much) looks round, and turns his Sternpost directly upon him.

It must be a great Change of Weather indeed, when he deigns to walk the Quarter-deck, for such a Prostitution of his Presence, he thinks, weakens his Authority, and makes his Worship less reverenced by the Ship's crew.

Here he is easily distinguished from all besides; for his Steps bear Proportion with the Height of his Post, moving along with grave State, like the Ghost.

Upon his first popping up, the Lieutenants sheer off to one other Side, as if he was a Ghost indeed; for 'tis impudence for any to approach him within the Length of a Boat-hook.

By this servile Obeisance, one would fancy him to be a Constellation dropt from the Clouds, or that at least he was Monarch of far more Territories, than ever he touched at in all his Voyagings.

He fulfils to a tittle the never-failing Proverb, *Set a Beggar on Horseback, and He'll ride to Peg Crancum's*; for being once mounted his wooden Steed, there is no stopping his Career, for he makes every thing sheer before him.

He is an everlasting Admirer of that old Saying, *Familiarity breeds Contempt*; which he takes in so extensive a Sense, that he allows no Distinction betwixt an Officer and a Swabber; exacting infinitely more Ceremony from his Lieutenant, than he will allow to God Almighty.

In fine, looking all around, and seeing his Spot of Territory incircled with Salt-water, he fancies himself as Great a Prince as the Prince of *Great Britain*.

This Pride of his is the only Sea-sickness that he is plagued with, and which intoxicates him to that degree, that he neither knows himself or others; but it holds him no longer than while he's aboard. Remove him ashore once, and his Brains grow settled, and he becomes your humble Servant in an instant.

His Lieutenants are his great Eye-sore, because they alone lay Pretensions to Gentility, a Thing that alarms him more than a lighted Pipe in a Powder-Room. He uses them with much stricter Severity, considering their Station, than he does the lousy Crew; he tops upon them like a Yard-arm, to depress them the lower on the other Side.

The plain Truth is, 'tis somewhat better being his Dog, or his Monkey, than his Subaltern, for he makes a hail Fellow of these upon his Quarter-deck, whilst he keeps all besides at a surly Distance.

*

A great Politician he must needs be, for he sails with every Shift of Wind; and when the Gale of good Fortune shrinks, he alters his Course, and reaches his Port by the traverse Rules of Injustice and Oppression.

If the Wind and Tide of Affairs prove too violent, he then certainly trims about, and bears away for any Place, 'tis no matter what Port, whether *Turk* or Infidel; for against Wind and Tide too, there is no Working.

Ned Ward next turns his attention to the lieutenants. In those days they held the rank from the day they were selected for promotion from midshipman, which could well be in middle age, until being appointed in command of a ship.

He is no Hypocrite as to his Vices, that is certain; for he'll tell you a hundred times over without asking, what a notable lewd Fellow he is, and has been in his Generation, and values himself not a little upon the Reputation of it.

He'll swear to you, he has made more Cuckolds than Bowls of Punch; and believes there is no more Sin in taking a Spell with a Whore, than in pumping a leaky Vessel.

The Surgeon makes much more of his Debauchery, than his Courage, and always takes care to patch him up with Speed, to have the better Customer of him.

But yet, after all, if you won't believe he is very often guilty of Lying, you'll wrong him; for he is not altogether so very a Miscreant as he would pass for, fathering many more wicked Pranks than ever he had Force or Courage to be guilty of. Lord! what a Number of fine Women he has overset; and how many lusty Fellows has he made look pale, whom he never once saw or dream'd of.

Not but that he has made many Attempts of both Kinds, and with the like Success, as seldom coming off from the one without a Clap, as from the other without a Beating: When he has got his Belly-full of both, he puts aboard again, and one Summer's Voyage buries all in Oblivion.

When he's out at Sea, he is in a strange Pickle, and oft looks around him, with as pensive a Phiz, as a Horse penn'd up in a Pinfold. Lord, cries he, who but a Madman would go Sea to fish for Bread! Ads Death, there is no living like a Christian but upon *Terra firma*.

But as there is no Place so wretched, as to want its Comforts, he weans by Degrees his Longings after the Flesh-pots of *Sodom*, and in lieu of Whores, makes Cards and Dice his serious Entertainment. He tempers his bad Throws with good Punch, for the Box and Glass go Hand in Hand together. By the Time he has unloaded his Pockets, he is floated off his Legs, and then drives upon the Coast of *Bedfordshire*, and there he sticks fast till next Morning.

He as little thinks of going to Heaven as to *Jamaica*: He cannot, he says, find any fixed Pole-Star, or mathematical Rules to trust to in that Voyage; so he shapes his Course after his Captain, without observing any Latitude in his Doings.

Next, it is the turn of the chaplain . . .

The plain Truth is, he is much better at composing a Bowl of Punch than a Sermon.

He seldom molests a poor dying Soul with his Visits, because he wisely considers, that a Sailor is a Man of no ceremony; he verily creates far more Peace of Conscience to the Ship's Company by his Practice than his Preaching; for he is the great Exemplar they walk by.

*

He reckons a sober Chaplain in the Navy to be a downright Nonconformist, and thinks himself obliged in Conscience to keep aloof from him to avoid being tainted with so damnable a Heresy.

He's an equal Enemy to Popery and *Calvinism*, and manifests it thoroughly in his Zeal for a Sirloin in *Lent*, and minc'd Pyes at *Christmas*.

There's no Hell to him like living eternally on salt Provisions; Fire and Brimstone is but a Fool to it.

Of all Ceremonies, he likes well that of a Cushion in Praying; yet, to shew his Excess of Loyalty, he will drink the King's Health on his Knees without one.

He drinks and prays with much the like Fervour. He turns up his Glass and the Whites of his Eyes together, and in the Sincerity of his Heart drinks it off most canonically.

He abominates all Slurring upon friendly Society, and had much rather chuse to drink twice, than be once suspected of baulking his Neighbour.

To shew his abundant Humility, he will sometimes drink Flip with the Midshipmen; and to prevent the Fall of a weak Brother, he will oft be so charitable as to drink for him.

It would seem that Ned was not too impressed by the professional skills of the surgeon on board . . .

If he has a smattering in Chemistry, he is a toping Spark indeed, and gabbles about the Intrails of Nature, like any Heathen Philosopher: But of all his Knowables, *Alkali* and *Acid* he esteems to be the very *Ne plus ultra* of physical Discoveries.

The Mystery of his Art and Science, consists in a long List of Fustian Words and Phrases, whose true Sense he is more puzzl'd to lay, than to anatomise the Body of a fat Capon: And as for his Performance upon Legs and Arms, he does it after a Way, 'tis true; but, betwixt you and me, the Slaughter-house on *Tower-hill*, would scarce grant him there Journeyman's Wages.

He's too lazy and proud to visit common Sailors; and they are not sick enough, he thinks, who are able to come and tell him their Ailments. And hence 'tis plain, that he may with Justice boast, that very few die under his Hands, which is as much as *Ratcliff* himself could pretend to.

The poorest Patients are sure to fare best where he is, because he leaves them to Nature, the less dangerous Doctor of the two. But an Officer with a Purse, must be sure to part with it, as a Badger with his Stones, if ever he hopes to bring off his Carcass.

He's unalterably convinced, that almost all our Distempers proceed from an over Repletion; and therefore his first Intention in all Cures, is to empty your Pockets; which strikes at the very Root of all Intemperance.

197

Nowadays cooks at sea are properly trained professionals, with the finest raw materials that can be obtained and refrigerated. They offer a standard and choice of fare which are rarely bettered ashore. Not so in Ned Ward's day . . .

His Knowledge extends not to half a Dozen Dishes; but he's so pretty a Fellow at what he undertakes, that the bare Sight of his Cookery gives you a Belly-full.

He cooks by the Hour Glass, as the Parsons preach Sermons; and will no more surpass one Puncto of Time, than a scrupulous *Virtuoso* in the Concoction of his Stomach, or an Alchymist in the cooking of his grand Elixir.

All his Science is contained within the Cover of a Sea-Kettle. The composing of a Minc'd-pye, is Metaphysicks to him; and the roasting of a Pig as puzzling as the squaring of a Circle.

Not but that he has an admirable Hand in squeezing of Silver from Beef-fat; which he does with as much Dexterity as a Quack does Gold from a Dog's Turd; and though the Extraction be very gross, it's yet so well refined, that it does not, in the least, smell of the Kettle.

He has sent the Fellow a thousand times to the Devil that first invented Lobscouse; but, for that lewd Way of wasting Grease, he had grown as fat in Purse as a *Portsmouth* Alderman, and made his Son seven Years ago a downright Gentleman.

He's never so hungry as to lick his own Fingers, nor such a Fool, as to wipe them on his Breeches; but he sweeps off the luscious Stuff as cleverly as a Dairy-Maid does her Butter, and firkins it too up as carefully.

The Purser (when at a low Ebb for Butter) helps out his Stock by a dexterous Mixture with the Cook's Ware; and as for Candles, he can never be in the Dark, so long as the Cook has any Fat about him, with which he makes Lights to lighten the Gentiles, to the Glory of his saving Invention.

Tho' salt Water's the Element that supports him, yet he can no more live without Fire than a Salamander: Were this once extinguished, *Old Nick* and he might return to *Terra firma*, and go a grazing for a Subsistence.

He's an excellent Mess-mate for a Bear, being the only two-legg'd Brute that lives by his own Grease; but tho' he be no lean Scab, yet he's very rarely pursy; and no Wonder, for there's near as much Stuff drops from his Carcase every Day, as would tallow the Ship's Bottom.

When it comes to describing his own kind, the seaman, he is preoccupied by his exploits ashore during the brief time it takes the waterfront publican and the doxies to separate him from the money he has saved during a three-year commission in distant waters . . .

Nothing makes him droop, like an empty Brandy-bottle; whilst there's anything in it, he sticks by't as close as the Load-stone does to cold Iron:

Plenty of this, and a *Mediterranean* Sun, makes him as dry and huskish in one Summer, as a toasted Bisket, to the great Discomfort of his disappointed Doxy, who finds him more sapless than a squeezed Lemon, and as unpalatable to her as chop'd Straw in *Spain* is to an *English* Mare.

Let him rise never so early, his Stomach is sure to rise with him. His common Breakfast is a salt Mouthful, a dry Dram, and a Pipe of Tobacco. Fortify'd with this infernal Recipe, he's as insensible of our *Northern* Blasts, as a Gun, or a Knighthead. –

*

. . . when he does get ashore, he pays it off with a Vengeance; for knowing his Time to be but short, he crowds much in a little Room, and lives as fast as possible.

His first Care is, to truck some old cumbersome Coat or other, for a good warm Lining to his Belly; and then to be sure his Courage is up, and he must have a Brush with some Vessel of Iniquity or other. He's sure to board the very first he sees, and carries her streight, without Expence of Shot or Powder; but unlucky *Fortune*, that should favour the Bold, leaves him in the Lurch; for, instead of meeting with a Purchase, he finds himself grappled to a Fireship, who sets him in such a Flame in a Twinkling, that all the Water-Grewel in the Universe can't save him.

He's so often us'd to reeling at Sea, that when he's reeling drunk ashore, he takes it for granted to be a Storm abroad, and falls to throwing every thing out at the Windows, to save the Vessel of a Bawdy-house.

His Furlow is commonly but a Night or so; and it is well for him it is no longer, for he needs but a Week to spend a Twelvemonth's Pay in Reversion. If he has a Reversion clear of Incumbrances, it is a Wonder, and makes him think upon Pay-day much oftener than the Day of Judgment.

from *The Wooden World* by Edward Ward

To this day the boats' crews who serve the occupant of the cuddy are a source of gossip for the Lower Deck about what goes on there. This irreverent tit-bit from George III's reign is typical:

When the *Glasgow* was stationed in the Mediterranean, her commander, the Honorable Captain A. Maitland, an officer of handsome private fortune, maintained when at Malta, Leghorn, and Naples, a sumptuous table, at which not only British officers, but ladies and foreigners of distinction, were received with a liberality and urbanity which reflected the highest credit on their munificent host. On one of these occasions, when guests of no ordinary importance were invited, a sailor belonging to the crew of the barge employed in bringing forward the several dishes to the captain's cabin, rolling his eyes and licking his lips in anticipation of a regale on the remnants, as the several dainties, both foreign and British, passed in rapid succession through his hands, exclaimed to the coxswain, 'My eyes and limbs! the skipper tucks in a precious lot of good things under his belt!'

199

'Why not?' replied the coxswain. 'Did you never know that the captain was a reg'lar-built epicure?' 'Epicure! epicure! what the devil's that?' demanded our innocent lambkin. 'Why, you know-nothing lubber!' cried his intelligent instructor, with a look of ineffable contempt, 'an epicure's a fellow as can *eat any thing*, to be sure!'

from *Naval Sketch-book* by Captain W. N. Glascock

'Talking of birthdays,' resumed Winstanley, 'we had a notorious fellow on board the *Hippopotamus*, when I was in his Majesty's service . . .'

'Curse the *Hippopotamus*, are you going to give us another long yarn about her?' growled his messmate.

The other did not notice, but said, 'This man was an incorrigible drunkard, and could not be kept from intoxication. Flogging and every species of punishment had been tried in vain. He was brought aft upon the old charge, and was at the time scarcely able to stand upon his legs. 'How comes it, you scoundrel, that I again see you in this disgraceful situation?' demanded the officer.

'Please, Sir, it is my birthday,' answered the sailor.

'Your birthday,' angrily retorted the officer, 'why, you told me the very same thing a week ago, and, if it were your birthday, is that an excuse for drinking until you become a beast?'

'No, Sir,' said the culprit, 'it's no excuse, it's only a custom.'

'How many more birthdays shall you have this year, you good-for-nothing drunkard?'

'It's very hard to say, Sir,' stammered the sot in reply. 'I make it a point to keep those of all my family, and I have a great many brothers and sisters, besides uncles, aunts, cousins, and distant relations.'

from *The Saucy Jack* by a Blue-Jacket

One of the earliest contemporary writers who exploited the humorous side of life at sea was the prolific W. W. Jacobs at the turn of the century. Not surprisingly, few of his sit-coms concerned the hairshirt life during distant offshore voyages in undermanned, overpressed tall ships fighting for commercial survival against steamships. His world and its characters were mostly in trading barques engaged in the coastal trade, slipping away at the turn of the tide from moorings near a pub in Wapping or Greenhithe, with orders for South Wales.

His humour was pre-H. M. Bateman or custard-pie slapstick but of the genre in which cartoon caption-writers often ended with: '. . . collapse of stout party'. In one story all but two of the crew – a Roman Catholic and a Seventh Day Adventist – had been recruited into the Salvation

Army and at the start of a voyage were down below praying for guidance
to reach the hard heart of the lost lamb – the skipper himself:

The climax was reached at tea-time, when an anonymous hand was thrust
between the skylight, and a full-bodied tract fluttered wildly down and
upset his tea.

'That's the last straw!' he roared, fishing out the tract and throwing it
on the floor. 'I'll read them chaps a lesson they won't forget in a hurry
and put a little money into my pocket at the same time.'

*

'Well,' said Captain Bowers, with a wink at the mate, 'I'm going to give
you chaps a little self-denial week all to yourselves. If you all live on biscuit
and water till we get to port, and don' touch nothing else, I'll jine you and
become a Salvationist.'

*

Three days passed, and the men stood firm, and, realising that they were
slowly undermining the skipper's convictions, made no effort to carry him
by direct assault. The mate made no attempt to conceal his opinion of his
superior's peril, and in gloomy terms strove to put the full horror of his
position before him.

'What your missus'll say the first time she sees you prancing up an'
down the road tapping a tambourine, I can't think,' said he.

'I shan't have no tambourine,' said Captain Bowers cheerfully.

'It'll also be your painful dooty to stand outside your father-in-law's pub
and try an' persuade customers not to go in,' continued Bob. 'Nice thing
that for a quiet family!'

The skipper smiled knowingly, and rolling a cigar in his mouth, leaned
back in his seat and cocked his eye at the skylight.

'Don't you worry, my lad,' said he, 'don't you worry. I'm in this job and
I'm coming out on top. When men forget what's due to their betters, and
preach to 'em, they've got to be taught what's what. If the wind keeps fair,
we ought to be home by Sunday night or Monday morning.'

The other nodded.

'Now, you keep your eyes open,' said the skipper; and, going to his stateroom, he returned with three bottles of rum and a corkscrew, all of which
with an air of great mystery, he placed on the table and then smiled at the
mate. The mate smiled too.

'What's this?' inquired the skipper, drawing the cork and holding a bottle
under the other's nose.

'It smells like rum,' said the mate, glancing round, possibly for a glass.

'It's for the men,' said the skipper, 'but you may take a drop.'

The mate, taking down a glass, helped himself liberally and, having
made sure of it, sympathetically but politely expressed his firm opinion
that the men would not touch it under any conditions whatever.

*

'Will anybody have a drop?' asked the owner, waving the bottle to and fro (in front of the Salvationists on the poop).

As he spoke a grimy paw shot out from behind him, and, before he quite realised the situation, the cook had accepted the invitation and was hurriedly making the most of it.

'Not you,' growled the skipper, snatching the bottle from him; 'I didn't mean you. Well, my lads, if you won't have it neat you shall have it watered.'

Before anyone could guess his intention he walked to the water-cask and, removing the cover, poured in the rum. In the midst of a profound silence he emptied the three bottles.

The ploy failed because one of the Salvationists had a secret supply of unadulterated drinking water in bottles so they could not be tricked into breaking their pledge. The story tails off without the reader knowing how the skipper adapted himself to his new way of life.

Another of W. W. Jacobs's yarns was about the sailing-barge *Osprey* due to sail from the London River to Ipswich. At 0545 the mate was waiting for her master, overdue from having slept ashore. When he appeared, hobbling painfully, he was accompanied by his daughter Maggie Cringle, a pretty girl of twenty. Then he informed the mate that she would take over command for the voyage.

'Cast off,' said she, in a business-like manner, as she seized a boat-hook and pushed off from the jetty. 'Ta ta, Dad, and go straight home, mind; the cab's waiting.'

'Ay, ay, my dear,' said the proud father, his eye moistening with paternal pride as his daughter, throwing off her jacket, ran and assisted the mate with the sail. 'Lord, what a fine boy she would have made!'

He watched the barge until she was well under way, and then, waving his hand to his daughter, crawled slowly back to the cab; and, being to a certain extent a believer in homœopathy, treated his complaint with a glass of rum.

'I'm sorry your father's so bad, miss,' said the mate, who was still somewhat dazed by the recent proceedings, as the girl came up and took the wheel from him. 'He was complaining a goodish bit all the way up.'

*

'Look here, my lad,' said the new skipper grimly, 'if you think you can steer better than me, you'd better keep it to yourself, that's all. Now suppose you see about your bedding, as I said.'

The mate went, albeit he was rather suprised at himself for doing so, and hid his annoyance and confusion beneath the mattress which he brought up on his head. His job completed, he came aft again, and, sitting on the hatches, lit his pipe.

'This is just the weather for a pleasant cruise,' he said amiably, after a few whiffs. 'You've chosen a nice time for it.'

'I don't mind the weather,' said the girl, who fancied that there was a little latent sarcasm somewhere. 'I think you'd better wash the decks now.'

'Washed 'em last night,' said the mate, without moving.

'Ah, after dark, perhaps,' said the girl. 'Well, I think I'll have them done again.'

The mate sat pondering rebelliously for a few minutes, then he removed his jacket, put on in honour of the new skipper, and, fetching the bucket and mop, silently obeyed orders.

*

'Perhaps you'd better let me take the wheel a bit,' said the mate, not without a little malice in his voice.

'No; you can go an' keep a look-out in the bows,' said the girl serenely. 'It'll prevent misunderstandings, too. Better take the potatoes with you and peel them for dinner.'

Osprey cleared the estuary and made her way northwards through the night.

'I'm going to turn in,' said she; 'call me at two o'clock. Good-night.'

'Good-night,' said the other, and the girl vanished.

. . . It is possible that the fatigues of the day had been too much for her, for when she awoke, and consulted the little silver watch that hung by her bunk, it was past five o'clock, and the red glow of the sun was flooding the cabin as she arose and hastily dressed.

The deck was drying in white patches as she went above, and the mate was sitting yawning at the wheel, his eyelids red for want of sleep.

'Didn't I tell you to call me at two o'clock?' she demanded, confronting him.

'It's all right,' said the mate. 'I thought when you woke would be soon enough. You looked tired.'

'I think you'd better go when we get to Ipswich,' said the girl, tightening her lips. 'I'll ship somebody who'll obey orders.'

'I'll go when we get back to London,' said the mate. 'I'll hand this barge over to the cap'n, and nobody else.'

'Well, we'll see,' said the girl, as she took the wheel. '*I* think you'll go at Ipswich.'

*

'I'd rather go back to London with you,' he said slowly.

'I daresay,' said the girl. 'As a matter of fact I wasn't really meaning for you to go, but when you said you wouldn't I thought we'd see who was master. I've shipped another mate, so you see I haven't lost much time.'

'Who is he,' inquired the mate.

'Man named Charlie Lee,' replied the girl; 'the foreman here told me of him.'

'He'd no business to,' said the mate, frowning; 'he's a loose fish; take my advice now and ship somebody else. He's not at all the sort of chap I'd choose for you to sail with.'

'You'd choose,' said the girl scornfully; 'dear me, what a pity you didn't tell me before.'

'He's a public-house loafer,' said the mate, meeting her eye angrily, 'and about as bad as they make 'em; but I s'pose you'll have your own way.'

'He won't frighten me,' said the girl. 'I'm quite capable of taking care of myself, thank you. Good evening.'

The mate stepped ashore with a small bundle, leaving the remainder of his possessions to go back to London with the barge. The girl watched his well-knit figure as it strode up the quay until it was out of sight, and then, inwardly piqued because he had not turned round for a parting glance, gave a little sigh, and went below to tea.

*

'Well, you do know how to handle a craft,' said Lee admiringly, as they passed down the river. 'The old boat seems to know it's got a pretty young lady in charge.'

'Don't talk rubbish,' said the girl austerely.

The new mate carefully adjusted his red necktie and smiled indulgently.

'Well, you're the prettiest cap'n I've ever sailed under,' he said. 'What do they call that red cap you've got on? Tam-o'-Shanter is it?'

'I don't know,' said the girl shortly.

'You mean you won't tell me,' said the other, with a look of anger in his soft dark eyes.

'Just as you like,' said she, and Lee, whistling softly, turned on his heel and began to busy himself with some small matter forward.

The rest of the day passed quietly, though there was a freedom in the new mate's manner which made the redoubtable skipper of the *Osprey* regret her change of crew, and to treat him with more civility than her proud spirit quite approved of. There was but little wind, and the barge merely crawled along as the captain and mate, with surreptitious glances, took each other's measure.

'This is the nicest trip I've ever had,' said Lee, as he came up from an unduly prolonged tea, with a strong-smelling cigar in his mouth. 'I've brought your jacket up.'

'I don't want it, thank you,' said the girl.

'Better have it,' said Lee, holding it up for her.

'When I want my jacket I'll put it on myself,' said the girl.

'All right, no offence,' said the other airily. 'What an obstinate little devil you are.'

'Have you got any drink down there,' inquired the girl, eyeing him sternly.

'Just a drop o' whiskey, my dear, for the spasms,' said Lee facetiously. 'Will you have a drop?'

'I won't have any drinking here,' said she sharply. 'If you want to drink, wait till you get ashore.'

'*You* won't have any drinking!' said the other, opening his eyes, and with a quiet chuckle he dived below and brought up a bottle and a glass. 'Here's wishing a better temper to you, my dear,' he said amiably, as he tossed off a glass. 'Come, you'd better have a drop. It'll put a little colour in your cheeks.'

'Put it away now, there's a good fellow,' said the captain timidly, as she looked anxiously at the nearest sail, some two miles distant.

'It's the only friend I've got,' said Lee, sprawling gracefully on the hatches, and replenishing his glass. 'Look here. Are you on for a bargain?'

'What do you mean?' inquired the girl.

'Give me a kiss, little spitfire, and I won't take another drop to-night,' said the new mate tenderly. 'Come, I won't tell.'

'You may drink yourself to death before I'll do that,' said the girl, striving to speak calmly. 'Don't talk that nonsense to me again.'

She stooped over as she spoke and made a sudden grab at the bottle, but the new mate was too quick for her, and, snatching it up jeeringly, dared her to come for it.

'Come on, come and fight for it,' said he; 'hit me if you like, I don't mind; your little fist won't hurt.'

No answer being vouchsafed to this invitation he applied himself to his only friend again, while the girl, now thoroughly frightened, steered in silence.

'Better get the sidelights out,' said she at length.

'Plenty o' time,' said Lee.

'Take the helm, then, while I do it,' said the girl, biting her lips.

The fellow rose and came towards her, and, as she made way for him, threw his arm round her waist and tried to detain her. Her heart beating quickly, she walked forward, and, not without a hesitating glance at the drunken figure at the wheel, descended into the fo'c'sle for the lamps.

The next moment, with a gasping little cry, she sank down on a locker as the dark figure of a man rose and stood by her.

'Don't be frightened,' it said quietly.

'Jack?' said the girl.

'That's me,' said the figure. 'You didn't expect to see me, did you? I thought perhaps you didn't know what was good for you, so I stowed myself away last night, and here I am.'

'Have you heard what that fellow has been saying to me?' demanded Miss Cringle, with a spice of the old temper leavening her voice once more.

'Every word,' said the mate cheerfully.

The new mate continued to call out for the skipper . . .

'I'll knock his head off,' said the mate; 'you stay down here.'

'Mag-*gie!*' came the voice again, '*Mag* – HULLO!'

'Were you calling me, my lad?' said the mate, with dangerous politeness, as he stepped aft. 'Ain't you afraid of straining that sweet voice o' yours? Leave go o' that tiller.'

The other let go, and the mate's fist took him heavily in the face and sent him sprawling on the deck. He rose with a scream of rage and rushed at his opponent, but the mate's temper, which had suffered badly through his treatment of the last few days, was up, and he sent him heavily down again.

'There's a little dark dingy hole forward,' said the mate, after waiting some time for him to rise again, 'just the place for you to go and think over your sins in. If I see you come out of it until we get to London, I'll hurt you. Now clear.'

The other cleared, and, carefully avoiding the girl, who was standing close by, disappeared below.

'You've hurt him,' said the girl, coming up to the mate and laying her hand on his arm. 'What a horrid temper you've got.'

'It was him asking you to kiss him that upset me,' said the mate apologetically.

'He put his arm round my waist,' said Miss Cringle, blushing.

'*What!*' said the mate, stuttering, 'put his – put his arm – round – your waist – like —'

His courage suddenly forsook him.

'Like what?' inquired the girl, with superb innocence.

'Like *that*,' said the mate manfully.

'That'll do,' said Miss Cringle softly, 'that'll do. You're as bad as he is, only the worst of it is there is nobody here to prevent you.'

from *Many Cargoes* by W. W. Jacobs

Much of the laughter around the bar in a yacht club concerns boats which have gone aground, preferably on a well-known hazard. This quote relates to an incident during the Round-the-Island Race, somewhere along the south shore of the Isle of Wight between Freshwater and St Catherine's Point:

Uffa Fox often frightened me by urging Max Aitken to take his big wishbone schooner *Lumberjack* ever closer inshore on a foul tide. At one spot his confidence was based on having ridden his mare, Frantic, off the beach and out of her depth at that point. Suddenly we came up all-standing at 10 knots. 'We must draw more than sixteen hands,' was Max's historic comment.

from *The Shell Guide to Yacht Navigation* by Captain John Coote

Sailors within visual signalling range of each other at sea have long shown a talent for pithy one-liners ranging from the laconic to the ridiculous. Their brevity stems from the days when messages by flag signal were confined to a vocabulary of 1,000 words; all of this before the days of incessant chatter on radio telephones. Captain Jack Broome who commanded the destroyer screen on the catastrophic Russian convoy PQ17 in 1942 was himself a lively wit with a keen sense of the absurd. He put together *Make a Signal*, a history of signalling at sea throughout the ages, illustrated by his own cartoons which sometimes appeared in *Punch*. He observed how signals have survived as part of our maritime tapestry, from Nelson's 'England expects that every man will do his duty' to one from another Commander-in-Chief Mediterranean – Admiral Sir Andrew Cunningham, generally reckoned to be a dry and uncommunicative man without any evident sense of humour. However, when Admiral Sir James Somerville, Commander Force 'H', a powerful striking group operating in his area, was made a Knight Commander of the Order of Bath on top of the KBE he already held, he congratulated him as follows:

'Fancy, twice a Knight at your age.'

During the First World War an admiral who had invited a lady to lunch in his flagship found that he had to go to sea at short notice. So he signalled the captain of a ship which was known to be remaining at anchor as follows:

'I invited Lady A. to lunch today but as we are sailing unexpectedly I would be glad if you would give her luncheon instead. I am leaving my barge behind with orders to report to you. This may make it easier for you to look after Lady A. Please make whatever use of her you like.'

This exchange took place some time earlier when Lord Charles Beresford as C.-in-C. Mediterranean was at anchor off Corfu, where the German Emperor was in residence in his summer palace, which was near a nunnery. Some British midshipmen who had landed for a picnic were obliged to swim back to the flagship when her boat did not come ashore to recover them at the expected time:

His Imperial Majesty to C.-in-C.: 'I am sorry to inform you that the nuns have been shocked by the attire of some of your young officers this afternoon.'

C.-in-C. to the Kaiser: 'The incident is greatly regretted but Your Majesty is misinformed on one point. The young gentlemen in question had no attire.'

In later days, a fussy destroyer flotilla leader called a ship about to go to sea on exercises: 'How long do you expect to be after leaving harbour?'

Reply: '310 feet as usual.'

On arrival at a foreign port the admiral's flag lieutenant signalled the senior officer ashore: 'Who do you recommend for Admiral's woman?'

Whilst the man on shore was trying to work that out, an amendment arrived: 'Reference my signal. Please insert washer between Admiral and woman.'

During a fleet review when ships were to man the side and cheer the monarch as she passed, one captain asked how many 'hips' precede 'Hooray': 'Interrogative 2 hips or 3.' Reply: '2 as in Marilyn Monroe.'

During the war the local flag officer at Gibraltar signalled: 'Small round object sighted 180 degrees 5 miles from Europa Point. Probably mine.' The flag officer Force 'H' which happened to be in the area replied: 'Certainly not mine.'

from *Make a Signal* by Captain Jack Broome

It is surprising that the scriptwriters of 'The Goon Show' or the Marx Brothers should have overlooked Stephen Leacock's great parody of the romantic adventure novel featuring pirates, buried treasure and the hero being marooned on a desert island. *Soaked in Seaweed* was written by a professor at McGill University in Canada. His lectures must have been well attended.

It was in August in 1867 that I stepped on board the deck of the *Saucy Sally*, lying in dock at Gravesend, to fill the berth of second mate.

Let me first say a word about myself.

I was a tall, handsome young fellow, squarely and powerfully built, bronzed by the sun and the moon (and even copper-coloured in spots from the effect of the stars), and with a face in which honesty, intelligence, and exceptional brain power were combined with Christianity, simplicity, and modesty.

As I stepped on the deck I could not help a slight feeling of triumph, as I caught sight of my sailor-like features reflected in a tar-barrel that stood beside the mast, while a little later I could scarcely repress a sense of gratification as I noticed them reflected again in a bucket of bilge water.

'Welcome on board, Mr. Blowhard,' called out Captain Bilge, stepping out of the binnacle and shaking hands across the taffrail.

I saw before me a fine sailor-like man of from thirty to sixty, clean-shaven, except for an enormous pair of whiskers, a heavy beard, and a thick moustache, powerful in build, and carrying his beam well aft, in a pair of broad duck trousers across the back of which there would have been room to write a history of the British Navy.

Beside him were the first and third mates, both of them being quiet men of poor stature, who looked at Captain Bilge with what seemed to me an apprehensive expression in their eyes.

The vessel was on the eve of departure. Her deck presented that scene of bustle and alacrity dear to the sailor's heart. Men were busy nailing up the masts, hanging the bowsprit over the side, varnishing the lee-scuppers and pouring hot tar down the companion-way.

Captain Bilge, with a megaphone to his lips, kept calling out to the men in his rough sailor fashion:

'Now, then, don't over-exert yourselves, gentlemen. Remember, please, that we have plenty of time. Keep out of the sun as much as you can. Step carefully in the rigging there, Jones; I fear it's just a little high for you. Tut, tut, Williams, don't get yourself so dirty with that tar, you won't look fit to be seen.'

*

Next morning with a fair wind astern we had buzzed around the corner of England and were running down the Channel.

On the third morning Captain Bilge descended to my cabin.

'Mr. Blowhard,' he said, 'I must ask you to stand double watches.'

'What is the matter?' I inquired.

'The two other mates have fallen overboard,' he said uneasily, and avoiding my eye.

I contented myself with saying, 'Very good, sir,' but I could not help thinking it a trifle odd that both the mates should have fallen overboard in the same night.

Surely there was some mystery in this.

Two mornings later the Captain appeared at the breakfast-table with the same shifting and uneasy look in his eye.

'Anything wrong, sir?' I asked.

'Yes,' he answered, trying to appear at ease and twisting a fried egg to and fro between his fingers with such nervous force as almost to break it in two – 'I regret to say that we have lost the bosun.'

'The bosun!' I cried.

'Yes,' said Captain Bilge more quietly, 'he is overboard. I blame myself for it, partly. It was early this morning. I was holding him up in my arms to look at an iceberg, and, quite accidentally I assure you – I dropped him overboard.'

Three more members of the crew disappeared before Mr Blowhard became suspicious, after he had witnessed the captain throwing the cabin-boy overboard during the night. So he tackled him on the matter:

'You threw that boy overboard!'

'I did,' said Captain Bilge, grown suddenly quiet, 'I threw them all over and intend to throw the rest. Listen, Blowhard, you are young, ambitious, and trustworthy. I will confide in you.'

Perfectly calm now, he stepped to a locker, rummaged in it a moment, and drew out a faded piece of yellow parchment, which he spread on the table. It was a map or chart. In the centre of it was a circle. In the middle of the circle was a small dot and a letter T, while at one side of the map was a letter N, and against it on the other side a letter S.

'What is this?' I asked.

'Can you not guess?' queried Captain Bilge. 'It is a desert island.'

'Ah!' I rejoined with a sudden flash of intuition, 'and N is for North and S is for South.'

'Blowhard,' said the Captain, striking the table with such force as to cause a loaf of ship's bread to bounce up and down three or four times, 'you've struck it. That part of it had not yet occurred to me.'

'And the letter T?' I asked.

'The treasure, the buried treasure,' said the Captain, and turning the map over he read from the back of it – 'The point T indicates the spot where the treasure is buried under the sand; it consists of half a million Spanish dollars, and is buried in a brown leather dress-suit case.'

'And where is the island?' I inquired, mad with excitement.

'That I do not know,' said the Captain. 'I intend to sail up and down the parallels of latitude until I find it.'

Mr Blowhard readily agreed to join the captain in his scheme. He reported that the men were on the point of mutiny because they were uneasy about the disappearance of so many of their company. So the bosun's mate was sent for:

'Tompkins,' said the Captain as the bosun's mate entered, 'be good enough to stand on the locker and stick your head through the stern port-hole, and tell me what you think of the weather.'

'Aye, aye, sir,' replied the tar with a simplicity which caused us to exchange a quiet smile.

Tompkins stood on the locker and put his head and shoulders out of the port.

Taking a leg each we pushed him through. We heard him plump into the sea.

'Tompkins was easy,' said Captain Bilge. 'Excuse me as I enter his death in the log.'

*

'Meantime, Mr. Blowhard,' he said, rising, 'if you can continue to drop overboard one or two more each week, I shall feel extremely grateful.'

Three days later we rounded the Cape of Good Hope and entered upon the inky waters of the Indian Ocean. Our course lay now in zigzags and, the weather being favourable, we sailed up and down at a furious rate over a sea as calm as glass.

On the fourth day a pirate ship appeared. Reader, I do not know if you have ever seen a pirate ship. The sight was one to appal the stoutest heart. The entire ship was painted black, a black flag hung at the masthead, the sails were black, and on the deck people dressed all in black walked up and down arm-in-arm. The words 'Pirate Ship' were painted in white letters on the bow. At the sight of it our crew were visibly cowed. It was a spectacle that would have cowed a dog.

The pirate ship lay alongside and fierce hand-to-hand fighting ensued 'with fifteen minutes off for lunch'.

At the end of two hours, by mutual consent, the fight was declared a draw. The points standing at sixty-one and a half against sixty-two.

The ships were unlashed, and with three cheers from each crew, were headed on their way.

'Now, then,' said the Captain to me aside, 'let us see how many of the crew are sufficiently exhausted to be thrown overboard.'

He went below. In a few minutes he reappeared, his face deadly pale. 'Blowhard,' he said, 'the ship is sinking. One of the pirates (sheer accident, of course, I blame no one) has kicked a hole in the side. Let us sound the well.'

We put our ear to the ship's well. It sounded like water.

The men were put to the pumps and worked with the frenzied effort which only those who have been drowned in a sinking ship can understand.

*

'The ship is bound to sink,' he said, 'in fact, Blowhard, she is sinking. I can prove it. It may be six months or it may take years, but if she goes on like this, sink she must. There is nothing for it but to abandon her.'

That night, in the dead of darkness, while the crew were busy at the pumps, the Captain and I built a raft.

Unobserved we cut down the masts, chopped them into suitable lengths, laid them crosswise in a pile and lashed them tightly together with bootlaces.

Hastily we threw on board a couple of boxes of food and bottles of drinking fluid, a sextant, a chronometer, a gas-meter, a bicycle pump and a few other scientific instruments. Then taking advantage of a roll in the motion of the ship, we launched the raft, lowered ourselves upon a line, and under cover of the heavy dark of a tropical night, we paddled away from the doomed vessel.

The break of day found us a tiny speck on the Indian Ocean. We looked about as big as this (.).

In the morning, after dressing, and shaving as best we could, we opened our box of food and drink.

There were fifty-two tins of bully beef and fifty-two bottles of lager with crown-tops, but nothing with which to open them.

We awoke to find ourselves still a mere speck upon the ocean. We felt even smaller than before.

Over us was the burnished copper sky of the tropics. The heavy, leaden sea lapped the sides of the raft. All about us was a litter of corn beef cans and lager beer bottles. Our sufferings in the ensuing days were indescribable. We beat and thumped at the cans with our fists. Even at the risk of spoiling the tins for ever we hammered them fiercely against the raft. We stamped on them, bit at them and swore at them. We pulled and clawed at the bottles with our hands, and chipped and knocked them against the cans, regardless even of breaking the glass and ruining the bottles.

It was futile.

On the tenth day the Captain broke silence.

'Get ready the lots, Blowhard,' he said. 'It's got to come to that.'

'Yes,' I answered drearily, 'we're getting thinner every day.'

I prepared the lots and held them to the Captain. He drew the longer one.

'Which does that mean,' he asked, trembling between hope and despair. 'Do I win?'

'No, Bilge,' I said sadly, 'you lose.'

*

But I mustn't dwell on the days that followed – the long quiet days of lazy dreaming on the raft, during which I slowly built up my strength, which had been shattered by privation.

*

It was on the fifth day after that I was awakened from a sound sleep by the bumping of the raft against the shore . . .

In a fever of haste I rushed to the centre of the island. What was the sight that confronted me? A great hollow scooped in the sand, an empty dress-suit case lying beside it, and on a ship's plank driven deep into the sand, the legend, '*Saucy Sally*, October, 1867.' So! the miscreants had made good the vessel, headed it for the island of whose existence they must have learned from the chart we so carelessly left upon the cabin table, and had plundered poor Bilge and me of our well-earned treasure!

Sick with the sense of human ingratitude I sank upon the sand.

The island became my home.

There I eked out a miserable existence, feeding on sand and gravel and dressing myself in cactus plants. Years passed. Eating sand and mud slowly undermined my robust constitution. I fell ill. I died. I buried myself.

Would that others who write sea stories would do as much.

from Soaked in Seaweed by Stephen Leacock

FAR HORIZONS

Exploration

Around 750 BC the Greek poet Homer proclaimed two epic poems following the siege of Troy, which ended with stormtroopers debouching from the famous wooden horse. A century later they were put in writing by others after having been handed down by word of mouth. Odysseus, better remembered by his Latin name of Ulysses, sailed from Troy on a long series of misadventures compounded by violent storms and navigational errors, over which scholars have argued for a thousand years. Each generation has sought to separate myth from reality and to identify the names of places whose names have no positive equivalent on Admiralty charts. One thing is certain: Homer wrote the first epic sea-story and inspired the whole Greek nation in the belief that it was a mighty sea-power. Reading a straightforward translation made early this century, one is not greatly enlightened:

So soon as early Dawn shone forth, the rosy-fingered, anon Odysseus put on him a mantle and doublet, and the nymph clad her in a great shining robe, light of woof and gracious, and about her waist she cast a fair golden girdle, and a veil withal upon her head. Then she considered of the sending of Odysseus, the great-hearted. She gave him a great axe, fitted to his grasp, an axe of bronze double-edged, and with a goodly handle of olive wood fastened well. Next she gave him a polished adze, and she led the way to the border of the isle where tall trees grew, alder and poplar, and pine that reacheth unto heaven, seasoned long since and sere, that might lightly float for him. Now after she had shown him where the tall trees grew, Calypso, the fair goddess, departed homeward.

And he set to cutting timber, and his work went busily. Twenty trees in all he felled, and then trimmed them with the axe of bronze, and deftly smoothed them, and over them made straight the line. Meanwhile Calypso, the fair goddess, brought him augers, so he bored each piece and jointed them together, and then made all fast with trenails and dowels. Wide as is the floor of a broad ship of burden, which some man well skilled in carpentry may trace him out, of such beam did Odysseus fashion his broad raft. And thereat he wrought, and set up the deckings, fitting them to the close-set uprights, and finished them off with long gunwales, and therein he set a mast, and a yard-arm fitted thereto, and moreover he made him a rudder to guide the craft. And he fenced it with wattled osier withies from stem to stern, to be a bulwark against the wave, and piled up wood to back them. Meanwhile Calypso, the fair goddess, brought him web of cloth to make him sails; and these too he fashioned very skilfully. And he made fast therein braces and halyards and sheets, and at last he pushed the raft with levers down to the fair salt sea.

It was the fourth day when he had accomplished all. And, lo, on the fifth, the fair Calypso sent him on his way from the island, when she had bathed him and clad him in fragrant attire. Moreover, the goddess placed on board the ship two skins, one of dark wine, and another, a great one, of water, and corn too in a wallet, and she set therein a store of dainties to his heart's desire, and sent forth a warm and gentle wind to blow. And goodly Odysseus rejoiced as he set his sails to the breeze. So he sate and cunningly guided the craft with the helm, nor did sleep fall upon his eyelids, as he viewed the Pleiads and Boötes, that setteth late, and the Bear, which they likewise call the Wain, which turneth ever in one place, and keepeth watch upon Orion, and alone hath no part in the baths of Ocean. This star, Calypso, the fair goddess, bade him to keep ever on the left as he traversed the deep. Ten days and seven he sailed traversing the deep, and on the eighteenth day appeared the shadowy hills of the land of the Phæacians, at the point where it lay nearest to him; and it showed like a shield in the misty deep.

Now the lord, the shaker of the earth, on his way from the Ethiopians, espied him afar off from the mountains of the Solymi: even thence he saw Odysseus as he sailed over the deep; and he was mightily angered in spirit, and shaking his head he communed with his own heart. 'Lo now, it must be that the gods at the last have changed their purpose concerning Odysseus, while I was away among the Ethiopians. And now he is nigh to the Phæacian land, where it is ordained that he escape the great issues of the woe which hath come upon him. But, methinks, that even yet I will drive him far enough in the path of suffering.'

*

Even as he spake, the great wave smote down upon him, driving on in terrible wise, that the raft reeled again. And far therefrom he fell, and lost the helm from his hand; and the fierce blast of the jostling winds came and brake his mast in the midst, and sail and yard-arm fell afar into the deep. Long time the water kept him under, nor could he speedily rise from beneath the rush of the mighty wave: for the garments hung heavy which fair Calypso gave him. But late and at length he came up, and spat forth from his mouth the bitter salt water, which ran down in streams from his head. Yet even so forgat he not his raft, for all his wretched plight, but made a spring after it in the waves, and clutched it to him, and sat in the midst thereof, avoiding the issues of death; and the great wave swept it hither and thither along the stream. And as the North Wind in the harvest tide sweeps the thistle down along the plain, and close the tufts cling each to other, even so the winds bare the raft hither and thither along the main. Now the South would toss it to the North to carry, and now again the East would yield it to the West to chase.

*

And Athene, daughter of Zeus, turned to new thoughts. Behold, she bound up the courses of the other winds, and charged them all to cease and be still; but she roused the swift North and brake the waves before him, that so Odysseus, of the seed of Zeus, might mingle with the Phæacians, lovers of the oar, avoiding death and the fates.

So for two nights and two days he was wandering in the swell of the sea, and much his heart boded of death. But when at last the fair-tressed Dawn brought the full light of the third day, thereafter the breeze fell, and lo, there was a breathless calm, and with a quick glance ahead, (he being upborne on a great wave,) he saw the land very near. And even as when most welcome to his children is the sight of a father's life, who lies in sickness and strong pains long wasting away, some angry god assailing him; and to their delight the gods have loosed him from his trouble; so welcome to Odysseus showed land and wood; and he swam onward being eager to set foot on the strand. But when he was within earshot of the shore, and heard now the thunder of the sea against the reefs – for the great wave crashed against the dry land belching in terrible wise, and all was covered with foam of the sea – for there were no harbours for ships nor shelters, but jutting headlands and reefs and cliffs; then at last the knees of Odysseus were loosened and his heart melted, and in heaviness he spake to his own brave spirit:

'Ah me! now that beyond all hope Zeus hath given me sight of land, and withal I have cloven my way through this gulf of the sea, here there is no place to land on from out of the grey water. For without are sharp crags, and round them the wave roars surging, and sheer the smooth rock rises, and the sea is deep thereby, so that in no wise may I find firm foothold and escape my bane, for as I fain would go ashore, the great wave may haply snatch and dash me on the jagged rock – and a wretched endeavour that would be. But if I swim yet further along the coast to find, if I may, spits that take the waves aslant and havens of the sea, I fear lest the storm-winds catch me again and bear me over the teeming deep, making heavy moan; or else some god may even send forth against me a monster from out of the shore water; and many such pastureth the renowned Amphitrite. For I know how wroth against me hath been the great Shaker of the Earth.'

Whilst yet he pondered these things in his heart and mind, a great wave bore him to the rugged shore. There would he have been stript of his skin and all his bones been broken, but that the goddess, grey-eyed Athene, put a thought into his heart. He rushed in, and with both his hands clutched the rock, whereto he clung till the great wave went by. So he escaped that peril, but again with backward wash it leapt on him and smote him and cast him forth into the deep. And as when the cuttlefish is dragged forth from his chamber, the many pebbles clinging to his suckers, even so was the skin stript from his strong hand against the rocks, and the great wave closed over him. There of a truth would luckless Odysseus have perished beyond that which was ordained, had not grey-eyed Athene given him sure counsel. He rose from the line of the breakers that belch upon the shore, and swam outside, ever looking landwards, to find, if he might, spits that take the waves aslant and havens of the sea. But when he came in his swimming over against the mouth of a fair-flowing river, whereby the place seemed best in his eyes, smooth of rocks, and withal there was a covert from the wind, Odysseus felt the river running, and prayed to him in his heart:

'Hear me, O king, whosoever thou art; unto thee am I come, as to one to whom prayer is made, while I flee the rebukes of Poseidon from the deep. Yea, reverend even to the deathless gods is that man who comes as a wanderer, even as I now have come to thy stream and to thy knees after much travail. Nay pity me, O king; for I avow myself thy suppliant.'

So spake he, and the god straightway stayed his stream and withheld his waves, and made the water smooth before him, and brought him safely to the mouths of the river. And his knees bowed and his stout hands fell, for his heart was broken by the brine. And his flesh was all swollen and a great stream of sea water gushed up through his mouth and nostrils. So he lay without breath or speech, swooning, such terrible weariness came upon him. But when now his breath returned and his spirit came to him again, he loosed from off him the veil of the goddess, and let it fall into the salt flowing river. And the great wave bare it back down the stream, and lightly Ino caught it in her hands. Then Odysseus turned from the river, and fell back in the reeds, and kissed earth, the grain-giver.

from *The Odyssey* by Homer

In 1941 Ernle Bradford was a nineteen-year-old able seaman on a run ashore from his ship in Alexandria when he met Andreas, a native of Ithaca who, against the odds, contrived to make a living in wartime Egypt. From the outset he spoke of Ulysses as a real person, not a character in a fable. He was 'the Artful Dodger . . . the shopkeeper with his thumb on the scales . . . an eye for the girls, handy with a knife in a dark alley . . . yet capable of honesty on most of the major issues . . .'

The war over, Ernle Bradford returned to the Mediterranean and spent twenty years cruising around in small yachts. In between writing a succession of successful books with a Mediterranean background, he identified the places Ulysses visited and authenticated his voyages in a manner that has convinced many leading scholars.

In the extract that follows, he covers the same episodes in the early translation above. He was convinced that Calypso's island was Malta, although not necessarily the small island off its north-west coast, Gozo, where to this day guides show tourists the genuine site of her grotto. Many other local tourist boards have their own versions.

After seven years of exile he was saved by his ancestor Hermes, who had been despatched by Zeus to order Calypso to let Ulysses return home. Calypso's meeting with the Messenger of the Gods gives us some indication of Homer's real feelings about the immoral immortals. 'When Hermes had spoken, Calypso answered with feeling: "How cruel you are, you gods, and how unparalleled for jealousy! You cannot bear to see a goddess sleeping with a man, even if she does it without any concealment and after having made him her legitimate husband"!'

Calypso is nevertheless constrained to obey the dictates of almighty Zeus. Although she protests that she has no ship in which to send Ulysses on his way, she is forced to promise that she will give him the means to sail home, and 'such directions as will carry him safe and sound to Ithaca.' After Hermes has gone, she makes her way to the seashore where she knows that she will find Ulysses. He has long given up any pretence of being happy in her island. One might describe his behaviour as ungallant in the extreme: 'His eyes, as always, were wet with weeping. All the sweetness of life was flowing away in the tears he shed for his lost home. It was a long time since the Nymph had brought him any pleasure. True, at night he had to sleep with her under the roof of her cavern, but he was no more than a cold lover with a passionate woman. Always the daytime found him sitting on the rocky strand, gazing with tearful eyes across the wastes of water, tormenting himself with sighs and groans of anguish . . .' It is not difficult to feel some sympathy with Calypso, and under the circumstances she behaves extremely well.

Without reproaching Ulysses for his ingratitude, she at once gives him the necessary directions to make his escape. Suspicious to the last, Ulysses does not hesitate to say that in suggesting he makes a raft and embarks on the high seas, the goddess may have something other than his survival in mind. His suspicion of her motives only confirms him in her affections. Anyone who has ever lived in the Levant will recognize the respect that is everywhere accorded to guile and craftiness. The qualities which are supposedly embodied in King Arthur, Charlemagne, or Abe Lincoln, are not those which are held in the greatest reverence in the eastern Mediterranean. Some of Ulysses' actions which may seem to us despicable rather than admirable, would have been viewed quite differently by Homer's audience – or, indeed, by a group of Aegean islanders to this day.

Calypso now proceeds to show Ulysses to a corner of the island where trees are growing which are suitable for shipbuilding. There are alders, poplars, and firs and – although the poet does not tell us so – I am fairly sure that it was the firs which Ulysses felled first with the 'double-bladed bronze axe' that Calypso so thoughtfully provided. He cut down twenty trees and then, with the adze and augers which Calypso had also given him, proceeded to build himself a raft. The Homeric account of the raft-building is as factual and accurate as an extract from a manual on the subject. 'Twenty trees in all he felled, and lopped their branches with his axe; then trimmed them in a workmanlike manner and trued them to the line. Presently Calypso brought him augers. With these he drilled through all his planks, cut them to fit across each other, and fixed this flooring together by means of dowels driven through the interlocking joints, giving the same width to his boat as a skilled shipwright would choose in designing the hull for a broad-bottomed trading vessel. He next put up the decking, which he fitted to ribs at short intervals, finishing off with long gunwales down the sides. He made a mast to go in the boat, with a yard-arm fitted to it; and a steering oar too, to keep her on her course. And from stem to stern he fenced her sides with plaited osier twigs and a plentiful backing of brushwood, as some protection against the heavy sea.' With cloth which Calypso provided he then made a sail. After which he stepped and rigged the mast, and arranged the sheet-leads.

*

The raft described by Homer is very akin in construction, although on a miniature scale, to the barges still used on the Nile. It is perfectly possible that the poet may have heard of such vessels from Greek sea-raiders who had been down to Egypt. Rafts of a somewhat similar type have also been used on the Euphrates since time immemorial, and the Phoenicians will certainly have been acquainted with such sailing-rafts long before the Greeks.

*

Many of the 19th- and early 20th-century objections to the plausibility of the voyage of Ulysses were based on ignorance. Scholars of those days had little idea what the human being can endure and survive. Just as there is nothing unseamanlike about the raft of Ulysses, so there is nothing in all his adventures on the sea which seems incredible to the survivors of our own century.

It is noticeable that the author of the *Odyssey* does not ignore those important details so often forgotten in poetry – food and drink. No sooner had Ulysses got his raft ready and dragged it down on rollers to the sea, than Calypso was at hand with his victuals. She put into his boat two leather skins, one full of wine the other of water. Here again one notices the practical touch – 'It was the larger one that was full of water.' Exactly! For stimulating and pleasant though wine is, it is no thirst-quencher, and a man embarking on a long raft-voyage would rather have plenty of water than plenty of wine. Calypso also gave him a leather sack full of corn, and plenty of 'appetizing meats'. Sensible, like all the women in the *Odyssey*, she had also given him a good bath beforehand and a new set of robes.

Clean, and in fresh clothes, with plenty of provisions, water, and some wine – Ulysses was ready to leave. He had everything that a man could want who was setting out on a long, single-handed voyage.

It was most probably summer when Ulysses left Calypso's island. It would not be too hazardous an undertaking to attempt to cross the Mediterranean on a well-built pine-log raft at that time of the year. I have sailed round Malta in an open dinghy in July, and have known of a crossing from Sicily made by two young men in a folding canvas canoe.

Calypso, true to her promise, not only enabled him to make his craft but also gave him his sailing directions. After the long and complicated instructions given him by Circe, these were simplicity itself. There was no reason why they should not have been, for all that the sailor has to do to reach Greece from Malta is to sail east. Any course between east and northeast will bring him out somewhere on the western coast of Greece, and once Ulysses reached the west coast – whether it was off the Peloponnese or further north by the islands – he knew his way home. The west coast of Greece was his native sea, and he had sailed all round the Peloponnese on his way to the Trojan war some nineteen years before. There were no Siren Rocks, no dangerous volcanoes, and no whirlpools to warn him against. Between Malta and Greece the deep Ionian holds no hazards, except the normal ones of wind and weather.

Calypso's instructions to Ulysses were that he should keep the Great Bear, or the Plough, 'on his left hand as he made his way across the open sea.' So long as he kept this constellation, 'the only one that never bathes in Ocean's Stream,' to port, or on the left of his line of advance, he would reach his home. This was absolutely true, and if one were to set off from Malta to Greece today in a small boat without any compass this is exactly what one would do. By keeping the constellation of the Plough on one's left hand, one would automatically be sailing east.

*

So Ulysses left the island. Taking a general direction from the sun by day, and a fairly accurate direction from the Plough at night, he headed out across the Ionian Sea. Calypso, one may presume, having concealed her grief at his departure, returned to her sacred grotto where her handmaids were awaiting her. There, no doubt, two or even three small half-Greek boys playing about in the sand.

It was with a 'warm and gentle breeze,' Calypso's final gift, that Ulysses left the island and 'with a happy heart he set his sail to catch the wind.' The wind is more than likely to have been a westerly, for the highest percentage of winds off Malta blow from this quarter in summer. A westerly will have been ideal for the course he had to sail, giving him either a quartering or a stern wind. The voyage passed uneventfully, and one must assume that for long periods of time, most probably during the day, Ulysses lashed the steering oar while he had a sleep. At night it was essential for him to keep awake in order to steer by the Plough. But so long as the westerly held, he could have hauled down his sail while he took a rest, for there are no real currents in the central Ionian except those set up by wind action. These local currents can be quite strong if the wind has been in one quarter for a number of days, so he could easily have slept while the gentle easterly drift eased him on his way towards Greece. Homer, in fact, says that 'he never slept,' but kept his eyes on the stars and particularly the Great Bear. But I take this as confirmation that he did his real sailing at night when he could navigate more accurately. No man could keep awake for seventeen days and nights, and that was the length of time which it took Ulysses to reach the western shores of Greece from Malta. '. . . For seventeen days he held his way, and on the eighteenth there came into view the shadowy mountains of the Phaeacians' country.'

I am confident that the land of the Phaeacians was Corcyra, or Corfu as it is now better known. Just assuming for the moment this to be so, let us look at the raft voyage in terms of wind, weather, and the distance from Malta to Corfu. Now the direct course for the voyage is north-east from Grand Harbour, Malta, to a point off the north-western coast of Corfu. The distance is 330 sea miles. Clearly one cannot calculate the speed of a raft for which one has no hull – or sail – dimensions, no knowledge of exactly what courses were steered, and no information as to the wind-strength and direction. But, on the limited data available – the length of time taken by Ulysses on the voyage, and the distance between Malta and Corfu – then a seventeen-day voyage for a course of 330 miles gives a distance made good of a little under twenty miles per day. That is to say, Ulysses' raft has an average speed for the whole voyage of about three-quarters of a knot.

This is slow, but perfectly reasonable, for a small raft with one man on board, and one somewhat inefficient sail. Clearly there must have been times when the raft was making two knots or more, while at other times it may well have been almost stopped, or even losing ground. If Calypso had instructed Ulysses to keep the Great Bear on his *right* hand, or to steer straight for it, then one could indeed have said that 'all this takes place in fairyland.' It would have been absurd if Ulysses had made the voyage in five days. It would have been most improbable that he could have taken as long as fifty – even if a small raft could have accommodated enough water and stores for so long a voyage. But seventeen days is highly likely from every point of view.

'The land looked like a shield laid on the misty sea . . .' – a miraculous description of Corfu as one approaches it. But no sooner did Ulysses get within sight of the Ionian islands than, as before, the weather broke.

*

Poseidon, we are told, had been on a visit to the Ethiopians and was returning to Olympus, when he saw Ulysses on his raft drawing near to the land of the Phaeacians. The Sea God knew that this was the place where Ulysses was 'destined to bring to an end his long ordeal,' so he immediately raised a great storm. 'East Wind and South Wind and the violent West all combined together . . .' – So much, perhaps, for poetic licence. But the line 'From the North came a white squall, rolling before it a huge sea' returns us to probability. The most dangerous wind in this part of the Ionian is the Bora, the north wind that blows all the way down the Adriatic from Trieste (where I have known them rig safety-lines in the city streets to prevent people being blown off their feet).

In the confusion, a mountainous wave sweeps down on the raft of Ulysses, the steering-oar is torn from his hands, the mast, yard-arm, and sail go overboard, and he himself is swept into the sea. He swims frantically after his raft and it is fortunate for him that the sail has gone, or he would have known the horror of watching his one chance of salvation disappearing away from him down-wind. But he manages to regain the raft and crouches there, 'squatting amidships where he felt safe from immediate death.' He is now at the mercy of the wind and the waves, but luckily he is still within sight of the coast.

At this point in the story Ulysses is saved by the intervention of Leucothea, the White Goddess, a marine divinity possibly associated with the flashing 'white' of the wave crests when the sea runs high. 'Strip off your clothes,' she tells him, 'and take this veil and wind it round your waist. Then swim for the shore.' The goddess appropriately enough appears in the disguise of a sea-mew. Having given him her veil and her advice, she dives back again into the sea – just as a gull seems to do when the lift of a wave carries it out of one's sight. Although the magic veil is no more than a poetic touch, the White Goddess's advice is sound enough by any standards. The shore is in sight, his raft will soon break up, and the best thing for Ulysses to do is to take off his heavy robes. They have already been described as 'weighing him down' when he was washed off the raft. Ulysses, it seems quite clear, has decided that he had better get out of his waterlogged clothes and swim for the shore.

He is just on the point of doing this when he has second thoughts and, considering how far away the land looks, decides to remain on his raft as long as possible. He will stay with it until it begins to break up, naturally hoping that before this happens he will have been carried a little closer to the coast. But only a few minutes later a huge wave rears itself over his raft and bursts aboard. Under the impact of the collapsing water, the dowels and joints which hold the planks together give way. As the raft disintegrates Ulysses throws off his robes, winds the veil around him, and lays fast hold on one of the planks.

The initial violence of the storm is over. The confused seas subside, and the wind comes steady from the north. For two days and nights Ulysses drifts before it on his plank. 'But on the morning of the third day there was a beautiful dawn, the wind dropped, and a dead calm fell on the sea.' Now he will have known the wonderful sensation of the sun warm upon his back, and of his water-crinkled skin reviving as the salt dried white on his body. Even so his troubles were not at an end, for the land towards which the swell was driving him was steep-to and rocky. There was no beach or cove where he could land.

The heavy swell left over by the gale was thundering against an iron-bound coast. Explosions of spray threw drifting mist veils into the air, and ahead he could see jagged rocks fringing a sheer cliff. He was already getting into the boom-and-sizzle of the surf, feeling the undertow plucking beneath him. A bursting roller lifted him forward and he was carried in towards the rocks. Striking out on his own (presumably having abandoned his plank) he managed to break clear of the wave, and to lay hold of a large rock which jutted out into the sea a little beyond the shoreline. A few seconds later, as the greater roller swept back from the coast, he was torn from the rock and carried seaward by the undertow. 'Pieces of skin stripped from his strong hands were left sticking to the rock, like the pebbles that stick to the suckers of an octopus when he is hauled from his hole in the rocks . . .'

The backwash of the roller carried Ulysses well clear of the breakers. Wisely deciding to avoid this treacherous part of the land he swam down the coast, always keeping to seaward of the heaving surf. Presently he saw a change in the surface of the sea ahead of him – a different feeling, no doubt, in the water on his body. It was the coolness of a stream flowing out into the sea. Now wherever a river runs into the sea there is a clean entrance to the land; and wherever a river enters the sea, its current will flatten the waves round about.

Ulysses swam landwards into the mouth of the sweet, freshwater stream. He was safe at last. After nineteen years he set foot once more on one of the Ionian islands.

from *Ulysses Found* by Ernle Bradford

The earliest voyage recorded in the Bible was the twelve months spent by the Ark under the command of her most experienced Captain. He was just past his six-hundredth birthday when he closed the hatches on his precious cargo of those whom God had preselected to repopulate the earth after the great flood.

The precise design parameters were handed down from on high. In those days there were no naval architects to question her 6:1 beam-to-length ratio, which optimized accommodation space within her three-deck layout. Given that a cubit was the length of a forearm (a little over 18 inches), she worked out about the size of a cross-Channel ferry. Another famous houseboat, although not as beamy, which has similar key dimensions but a different operational mission, is HMS *Britannia*.

The Ark had no propulsion, and there is no record of how far she drifted, but her draught must also have been about the same as the Royal Yacht's, for God only arranged a least depth of 22 feet over the highest mountain peaks.

This is the story of Noah. Noah was a righteous man, the one blameless man of his time; he walked with God. He had three sons, Shem, Ham and

Japheth. Now God saw that the whole world was corrupt and full of violence. In his sight the world had become corrupted, for all men had lived corrupt lives on earth. God said to Noah, 'The loathsomeness of all mankind has become plain to me, for through them the earth is full of violence. I intend to destroy them, and the earth with them. Make yourself an ark with ribs of cypress; cover it with reeds and coat it inside and out with pitch. This is to be its plan: the length of the ark shall be three hundred cubits, its breadth fifty cubits, and its height thirty cubits. You shall make a roof for the ark, giving it a fall of one cubit when complete; and put a door in the side of the ark, and build three decks, upper, middle, and lower. I intend to bring the waters of the flood over the earth to destroy every human being under heaven that has the spirit of life; everything on earth shall perish. But with you I will make a covenant, and you shall go into the ark, you and your sons, your wife and your sons' wives with you. And you shall bring living creatures of every kind into the ark to keep them alive with you, two of each kind, a male and a female; two of every kind of bird, beast, and reptile, shall come to you to be kept alive. See that you take and store every kind of food that can be eaten; this shall be food for your and for them.' Exactly as God had commanded him, so Noah did.

The LORD said to Noah, 'Go into the ark, you and all your household; for I have seen that you alone are righteous before me in this generation. Take with you seven pairs, male and female, of all beasts that are ritually clean, and one pair, male and female, of all beasts that are not clean; also seven pairs, male and female, of every bird – to ensure that life continues on earth. In seven days' time I will send rain over the earth for forty days and forty nights, and I will wipe off the face of the earth every living thing that I have made.' Noah did all that the LORD had commanded him. He was six hundred years old when the waters of the flood came upon the earth.

And so, to escape the waters of the flood, Noah went into the ark with his sons, his wife, and his sons' wives. And into the ark with Noah went one pair, male and female, of all beasts, clean and unclean, of birds and of everything that crawls on the ground, two by two, as God had commanded. Towards the end of the seven days the waters of the flood came upon the earth. In the year when Noah was six hundred years old, on the seventeenth day of the second month, on that very day, all the springs of the great abyss broke through, the windows of the sky were opened, and rain fell on the earth for forty days and forty nights. On that very day Noah entered the ark with his sons, Shem, Ham and Japheth, his own wife, and his three sons' wives. Wild animals of every kind, cattle of every kind, reptiles of every kind that move upon the ground, and birds of every kind – all came to Noah in the ark, two by two of all creatures that had life in them. Those which came were one male and one female of all living things; they came in as God had commanded Noah, and the LORD closed the door on him. The flood continued upon the earth for forty days, and the waters swelled and lifted up the ark so that it rose high above the ground. They swelled and increased over the earth, and the ark floated on the surface of the waters. More and more the waters increased over the earth until they covered all the high mountains everywhere under heaven. The waters increased and the mountains were covered to a depth of fifteen cubits. Every living creature that moves on earth perished, birds, cattle, wild animals, all reptiles, and all mankind. Everything died that had the breath of life in its nostrils, everything on dry land. God wiped out every living thing that existed on earth, man and beast, reptile and bird; they were all wiped out over the whole earth, and only Noah and his company in the ark survived.

When the waters had increased over the earth for a hundred and fifty days, God thought of Noah and all the wild animals and the cattle with him in the ark, and he made a wind pass over the earth, and the waters began to subside. The springs of the abyss were stopped up, and so were the windows of the sky; the downpour from the skies was checked. The water gradually receded from the earth, and by the end of a hundred and fifty days it had disappeared. On the seventeenth day of the seventh month the ark grounded on a mountain in Ararat. The water continued to recede until the tenth month, and on the first day of the tenth month the tops of the mountains could be seen.

After forty days Noah opened the trap-door that he had made in the ark, and released a raven to see whether the water had subsided, but the bird continued flying to and fro until the water on the earth had dried up. Noah waited for seven days, and then he released a dove from the ark to see whether the water on the earth had subsided further. But the dove found no place where she could settle, and so she came back to him in the ark, because there was water over the whole surface of the earth. Noah stretched out his hand, caught her and took her into the ark. He waited another seven days and again released the dove from the ark. She came back to him towards evening with a newly plucked olive leaf in her beak. Then Noah knew for certain that the water on the earth had subsided still further. He waited yet another seven days and released the dove, but she never came back. And so it came about that, on the first day of the first month of his six hundred and first year, the water had dried up on the earth, and Noah removed the hatch and looked out of the ark. The surface of the ground was dry.

By the twenty-seventh day of the second month the whole earth was dry. And God said to Noah, 'Come out of the ark, you and your wife, your sons and their wives. Bring out every living creature that is with you, live things of every kind, bird and beast and every reptile that moves on the ground, and let them swarm over the earth and be fruitful and increase there.' So Noah came out with his sons, his wife . . .

from Genesis, chapter 7

Ever since the voyage of the Kon-Tiki raft caught the attention of the public there has been a succession of sailor-scholars seeking to test the credibility of legendary explorers' voyages in ancient times. Except for movie-makers, no one has yet checked out Noah's story or tried to recreate St Paul's calamitous landfall on Malta.

But many besides the descendants of the Aztecs have sought to shake the widely held belief that Columbus discovered America in 1492. They say that Norsemen made it in their longboats 500 years earlier all the way to the Great Lakes – hence those Viking artefacts turning up in Minnesota. After historian Tim Severin graduated from Cambridge and married an expert on medieval texts from Harvard they sailed with their three-year-old daughter as far afield as Turkey and became convinced that St Brendan and his Irish monks reached North America a thousand years before the Genoese nagivator sighted San Salvador in the Caribbean.

He had a replica built of the sort of corracle which might have been seen off Kerry in the sixth century. Colin Mudie designed her: 36 feet long with 8-foot beam, displacing 5 tons fully laden with crew and provisions needed to sail across the North Atlantic. Only such materials and tools available to St Brendan at the time were used on her construction. So her frames and stringers were of ash, covered by oxhide skins tanned with oak-bark and greased with tallow and oils from sheepskin. Two miles of leather thongs were used to fasten the whole banana-shaped hull together. On that was stepped two masts with square-sails, 140 and 60 square feet. They ran into a gale as soon as they set sail:

Why on earth, then, were my crew and I sailing such an improbable vessel in the face of a rising gale? The answer lay in the name of our strange craft: she was called *Brendan* in honor of the great Irish missionary, Saint Brendan, who had lived in the sixth century. Tradition said that Saint Brendan had made a voyage to America, and this astonishing claim was not just a wild fairy tale, but a recurrent theme based on authentic and well-researched Latin texts dating back at least to A.D. 800. These texts told how Saint Brendan and a party of monks had sailed to a land far across the ocean in a boat made of oxhides. Of course, if the claim was true, then Saint Brendan would have reached America almost a thousand years before Columbus and four hundred years before the Vikings. Such a notion, declared the skeptics, was harebrained. To suggest that anyone could have crossed the Atlantic in a boat made of animal skin was unthinkable, impossible, a mere fantasy, and the idea of a leather boat proved it. But the Latin texts were absolutely positive about the boat being made of leather, and they even explained how Saint Brendan and his party of monks had built this vessel. The obvious way of checking the truth of this remarkable story was to build a boat in similar fashion and then see if it would sail the Atlantic. So there we were, my crew and I, out in the ocean to test whether Saint Brendan and the Irish monks could have made an ocean voyage in a boat of leather.

Before getting thus far, Severin had researched the project thoroughly, mostly in the British Museum Library:

But it was the *Navigatio Sancti Brendani Abbatis*, more usually known as the *Navigatio* or *Voyage of Brendan*, that sealed his reputation. This was the text which my wife and I had both read as students and remembered as something remarkable. It had been written in Latin, and it described how Saint Brendan, living in the west of Ireland, had been visited by another Irish priest who described to him a beautiful land far in the West over the ocean where the word of God ruled supreme. The priest advised Brendan to see this place for himself, and so Brendan built a boat specially for the voyage, making a framework of wood on which he stretched oxhides for the hull. Then he loaded ample stores, spare oxhides and fat to dress the hides, and set sail with seventeen monks to find this Promised Land. They had a long, hard journey. They wandered from one island to another and had many adventures until they finally won through to their destination, and managed to explore the fringe of the Promised Land before setting sail once again for Ireland. Some of their adventures were obviously fabulous.

On 17 May 1976, Severin rowed out of Brandon Creek with four companions, set sail and reached Reykjavik in Iceland via the Faeroes two months later. There he laid up and refitted until the following summer. On 7 May they sailed across the Denmark Strait, heading for Cape Farewell and Newfoundland in a boat which could not sail at all to windward, yet planned to get there against the prevailing winds.

Halfway to Greenland they encountered a south-westerly storm which threatened to drive them all the way into the Arctic ice. Then they might have remembered the words of one Kerryman watching their departure: 'Sure they'll make it – but they'll need a miracle.'

Soon, for the third time in as many days, the wind turned against us, and picked up strength. Our spirits fell with the barometer. For three days now we'd been struggling in circles, covering the same patch of ocean with no progress. It was very disheartening. Enhanced by the almost constant rain, the sea took on a permanently hostile look. From one point of view the huge swells were impressive. They came as great marching hills of water, heaped up by the wind blowing counter to the main ocean current. They were grand monuments to the power of Nature. But seen from a small open boat, they depressed the spirit. It was difficult to judge their height, but whenever *Brendan* sank into the troughs, the swells were far higher than her mainmast . . .

At 6:20 A.M. on May 20, we picked up a faint signal from the Prins Christianssund which gave the weather forecast I had been dreading: we were due for a southwest gale, force 8 rising to force 9 of about forty-five miles an hour, precisely from the direction in which we were headed. We scarcely needed the warning. The ugly look of the cloudy wrack ahead of us was enough to advise us that we were in for heavy weather. Sure enough, within an hour, we were struggling first to reef the mainsail, then to lower it altogether and lash it down. Only the tiny headsail was left up to draw us away downwind and give the helmsman a chance to jockey the boat among the ever-larger seas which now began to tumble and break around us . . .

Then it was time to pay out the main warps in loops from the stern to slow *Brendan* down. I was fearful that she would somersault or slew sideways and roll clean over if she went too fast down the face of a wave. Finally we poured whale oil into our oil bag, pricked holes in the canvas, and dangled the bag from a short stern line. The oil bag left a streak of oil in our wake which partly quenched the worse of the wave crests directly behind us, but it was all the helmsman could do to keep *Brendan* running directly downwind of the slick where it would do any good. Each wave swung the little boat out of control; she threatened to broach and spill, until the trailing rope loops took hold with a thump that shook the steering frame, and literally hauled her straight. Looking back one could see the tremendous strain on the ropes, literally tearing across the surface of the sea under pressure, the spray rising from them like smoke. In this fashion we fought the gale, and in the next five hours of flight we squandered every mile of hard-earned progress from the previous day. And there was no end in sight for the gale.

*

Boom! Again a heavy wave came toppling over the stern, smashed aside the shelter door and poured in, slopping over my face as I lay head-to-stern. We sprang up and tried to save the sleeping bags from the flood. But it was too late. In a split second the situation had returned to exactly where it had been before. Water was everywhere. The bilges were full, and the cabin was awash. *Brendan* was near-stationary before the breaking seas, and George and I were wading around the cabin floor with icy water soaking through our stockinged feet.

Once again it was back to the pumps for an hour, rocking back and forth at the pump handles, hoping silently that another wave would not add to the damage while *Brendan* was handicapped. Then back to the same chore of stripping out the cabin contents, squeezing out the sodden items, mopping up and returning everything to its place.

It was clear that the open cockpit aft had to be covered. Severin then remembered Roman legionaries using leather shields to protect them against missiles thrown from the enemy ramparts.

I shoved the leather sheets out of the cabin door. They were stiff and unwieldy in the cold. So much the better, I thought, they will be like armor plate.

Quickly I pointed out to Trondur what needed to be done. Immediately he grasped the principle, nodded his understanding, and gave a quick grin of approval.

Then he was off, knife in hand, scrambling up onto *Brendan*'s unprotected stern where the waves washed over the camber of the stern deck. It was a very treacherous spot, but it was the only place where the job could be done properly. With one hand Trondur held onto his perch, and with the other he worked on the leather sheets we passed up to him. Every now and then, the roar of an oncoming breaker warned him to drop his work, and hold on with both hands while *Brendan* bucked and shuddered and the wave crest swirled over the stern . . .

In less than fifteen minutes the job was done. A leather apron covered the larger part of *Brendan*'s open stern, leaving just enough room for the helmsman to stand upright, his torso projecting up through the tortoise. Leather cheek plates guarded the flanks.

Boom! Another breaker crashed over the stern, but this time caromed safely off the tortoise and poured harmlessly back into the Atlantic; only in one spot did it penetrate in quantity, where I had plugged a gap beneath the leather apron with my spare oilskin trousers. So great was the force of the water that the trousers shot out from the gap, flying across the cockpit on the head of a spout of water.

But it was worth it. Even if we were losing the distance we had made and were being blown back in our tracks, we had survived the encounter with our first major Greenland gale. We had made *Brendan* seaworthy to face the unusual conditions of those hostile seas, and we had done so with our own ingenuity and skills. Above all, we had succeeded by using the same basic materials which had been available to Saint Brendan and the Irish seagoing monks. It was cause for genuine satisfaction.

from *The Brendan Voyage* by Tim Severin

On 26 June 1976, six weeks out from Iceland, they reached Newfoundland. No one has yet proved that St Brendan had not done so, 1,400 years previously.

On being demobilized from the Norwegian Army at the end of the Second World War, Thor Heyerdahl set out to prove that the Polynesians who populated the islands of the South Pacific originated from Peru, having been driven across from their homeland by the South Equatorial Current and the trade winds. He built a raft following the design and materials known to have existed in the days of the Incas. Its hull consisted of the trunks of nine balsa trees hewn in the jungles of Ecuador. The longest of them was 45 feet. Nine athwartships logs each 18 feet long were laid across them. They were all lashed together by 1¼-inch hemp. A bamboo and matting superstructure was built on top with a single 250 sq. ft square-sail set from a crossyard on a tripod mast. Steering was by a 19-foot oar between tholes and by adjusting solid fir daggerboards driven down in the gaps between the planks. Obviously there could be no thought of making ground to windward with such a rig, but they did clock up days' runs of over 80 miles once they were pointed in the right direction.

From Callao the raft with its crew of six was towed 50 miles offshore to clear the inshore arm of the Humboldt Current which might have swept them northwards towards the Doldrums, before they were cast off on the edge of the South-East Trades.

Experts predicted that the balsa logs would get waterlogged and lose their buoyancy within three weeks, while their constant movement in any kind of a seaway would soon chafe through the hemp lashings. Neither was borne out by events, but their first taste of bad weather was an anxious time:

By the late afternoon the trade wind was already blowing at full strength. It quickly stirred up the ocean into roaring seas which swept against us from astern. Now we fully realised for the first time that here was the sea itself come to meet us; it was bitter earnest now, our communications were cut. Whether things went well now would depend entirely on the balsa raft's good qualities in the open sea. We knew that from now onwards we should never get another on-shore wind or chance of turning back. We had got into the real trade wind, and every day would carry us farther and farther out to sea. The only thing to do was to go ahead under full sail; if we tried to turn homewards we should only drift farther out to sea stern first. There was only one possible course, to sail before the wind with our bows towards the sunset. And, after all, that was just the object of our voyage, to follow the sun in its path, as we thought Kon-Tiki and the old sun-worshippers must have done when they were chased out to sea from Peru.

We noted with triumph and relief how the wooden raft rose up over the first threatening wave-crests that came foaming towards us. But it was impossible for the steersman to hold the oar steady when the roaring seas rolled towards him and lifted the oar out of the thole-pins, or swept it to one side so that the steersman was swung round like a helpless acrobat.

Not even two men at once could hold the oar steady when the seas rose against us and poured down over the steersman aft. We hit on the idea of running ropes from the oar-blade to each side of the raft, and, with other ropes holding the oar in place in the thole-pins, it obtained a limited freedom of movement and could defy the worst seas if only we ourselves could hold on.

As the troughs of the sea gradually grew deeper it became clear that we had got into the swiftest part of the Humboldt Current. This sea was obviously caused by a current and not simply raised by the wind. The water was green and cold and everywhere about us; the jagged mountains of Peru had vanished into the dense cloud-banks astern. When darkness crept over the sea our first duel with the elements began. We were still not sure of the sea; it was still uncertain whether it would show itself a friend or an enemy in the intimate proximity we ourselves had sought.

*

Two men at a time took turns as steering watch, and, side by side, they had to put all their strength into the fight with the leaping oar, whilst the others tried to snatch a little sleep inside the open bamboo cabin. When a really big sea came, the men at the helm left the steering to the ropes and jumped up and hung on to a bamboo pole from the cabin roof, while the masses of water thundered in over them from astern and disappeared between the logs or over the side of the raft. Then they had to fling themselves at the oar again before the raft could turn round and the sail thrash about. For if the raft took the seas at an angle the waves could easily pour right into the bamboo cabin. When they came on board from astern they disappeared between the projecting logs at once, and seldom came so far forward as the cabin wall. The round logs astern let the water pass as if through the prongs of a fork. The advantage of a raft was obviously this: the more leaks the better – through the gaps in our floor the water ran out, but never in.

*

The next night was still worse; the seas grew higher instead of going down. Two hours on end of struggling with the steering oar was too long; a man was not much use in the second half of his watch, and the seas got the better of us and hurled us round and sideways, while the water poured on board. Then we changed over to one hour at the helm and an hour and a half's rest. So the first sixty hours passed, in one continuous struggle against a chaos of waves that rushed upon us, one after another, without cessation. High waves and low waves, pointed waves and round waves, slanting waves and waves on the top of other waves. The one of us who suffered the worst was Knut. He was let off steering watch, but to compensate for this he had to sacrifice to Neptune and suffered silent agonies in a corner of the cabin. The parrot sat sulkily in its cage and hung on with its beak and flapped its wings every time the raft gave an unexpected pitch and the sea splashed against the wall from astern. The *Kon-Tiki* did not roll so excessively. She

232

took the seas more steadily than any boat of the same dimensions, but it was impossible to predict which way the deck would lean next time, and we never learned the art of moving about the raft easily, for she pitched as much as she rolled.

The crew's confidence in their craft was complete when they first met a real storm.

Two days later we had our first storm. It started by the trade wind dying away completely, and the feather white trade wind clouds which were drifting over our heads up in the topmost blue being suddenly invaded by a thick black cloud-bank which rolled up over the horizon from southward. Then there came gusts of wind from the most unexpected directions, so that it was impossible for the steering watch to keep control. As quickly as we got our stern turned to the new direction of the wind, so that the sail bellied out stiff and safe, just as quickly the gusts came at us from another quarter, squeezed the proud bulge out of the sail, and made it swing round and thrash about to the peril of both crew and cargo. But then the wind suddenly set in to blow straight from the quarter whence the bad weather came, and as the black clouds rolled over us the breeze increased to a fresh wind which worked itself up into a real storm.

In the course of an incredibly short time the seas round about us were flung up to a height of fifteen feet, while single crests were hissing twenty and twenty-five feet above the trough of the sea, so that we had them on a level with our masthead when we ourselves were down in the trough. All hands had to scramble about on deck bent double, while the wind shook the bamboo wall and whistled and howled in all the rigging.

To protect the wireless corner we stretched canvas over the aftermost wall and port side of the cabin. All loose cargo was lashed securely, and the sail was hauled down and made fast round the bamboo yard. When the sky clouded over the sea grew dark and threatening, and in every direction it was white-crested with breaking waves. Long tracks of dead foam lay like stripes to windward down the backs of the long seas, and everywhere where the wave-ridges had broken and plunged down, green patches, like wounds, lay frothing for a long time in the blue-black sea. The crests blew away as they broke, and the spray stood like salt rain over the sea. When the tropical rain poured over us in horizontal squalls and whipped the surface of the sea, invisible all round us, the water that ran from our hair and beards tasted brackish, while we stumbled about the deck bent double, naked and frozen, seeing that all the gear was in order to weather the storm.

Ninety-four days out they sighted land, Puka-Puka, one of the Tuamotu archipelago lying 250 miles south-west of the Marquesas islands. The raft was still seaworthy after logging 4,000 miles across the Pacific. But they were swept past it and headed for clouds on the western horizon which they knew to be Angatau island. This time they made a perfect landfall, but could not find a gap in the reefs, even with the help of local canoes.

So they drifted on. Three days later their voyage came to an abrupt end. They found a line of coral reefs girdling a string of atolls including Raroia stretched across their path. There was no way of avoiding them, so *Kon-Tiki* was flung on to the reef of an uninhabited island. Their distress call on a wartime saboteur's set with a hand-cranked generator was picked up by a ham in Colorado. Local canoes from the next island took the whole crew off and entertained them round the clock until a schooner from Tahiti took them and the remains of the raft back to civilization.

We must have hit the reef that time. I myself felt only the strain on the stay, which seemed to bend and slacken jerkily. But whether the bumps came from above or below I could not tell, hanging there. The whole submersion lasted only seconds, but it demanded more strength than we usually have in our bodies. There is greater strength in the human mechanism than that of the muscles alone. I determined that if I was to die, I would die in this position, like a knot on the stay. The sea thundered on, over and past, and as it roared by it revealed a hideous sight. The *Kon-Tiki* was wholly changed, as by the stroke of a magic wand. The vessel we knew from weeks and months at sea was no more; in a few seconds our pleasant world had become a shattered wreck.

I saw only one man on board besides myself. He lay pressed flat across the ridge of the cabin roof, face downwards, with his arms stretched out on both sides, while the cabin itself was crushed in like a house of cards, towards the stern and towards the starboard side. The motionless figure was Herman. There was no other sign of life, while the hill of water thundered by, in across the reef. The hardwood mast on the starboard side was broken like a match, and the upper stump, in its fall, had smashed right through the cabin roof, so that the mast and all its gear slanted at a low angle over the reef on the starboard side. Astern, the steering block was twisted round lengthways and the crossbeam broken, while the steering oar was smashed to splinters. The splashboards at the bows were broken like cigar boxes, and the whole deck was torn up and pasted like wet paper against the forward wall of the cabin, along with boxes, cans, canvas and other cargo. Bamboo sticks and rope-ends stuck up everywhere, and the general impression was of complete chaos.

*

All this happened in the course of a few seconds, while the *Kon-Tiki* was being drawn out of the witches' kitchen by the backwash, and a fresh sea came rolling over her. For the last time I bellowed 'hang on!' at the pitch of my lungs amid the uproar, and that was all I myself did; I hung on and disappeared in the masses of water which rushed over and past in those endless two or three seconds. That was enough for me. I saw the ends of the logs knocking and bumping against a sharp step in the coral reef without going over it. Then we were sucked out again. I also saw the two men who lay stretched out across the ridge of the cabin roof, but none of us smiled any longer. Behind the chaos of bamboo I heard a calm voice call out:

'This won't do.'

And I myself felt equally discouraged. As the masthead sank farther and farther out over the starboard side I found myself hanging on to a slack line outside the raft. The next sea came. When it had gone by I was dead tired, and my only thought was to get up on to the logs and lie behind the barricade. When the backwash retreated, I saw for the first time the rugged red reef naked beneath us, and perceived Torstein standing bent double on gleaming red corals, holding on to a bunch of ropes' ends from the mast. Knut, standing aft, was about to jump. I shouted that we must all keep on the logs, and Torstein, who had been washed overboard by the pressure of water, sprang up again like a cat.

Two or three more seas rolled over us with diminishing force, and what happened then I do not remember, except that water foamed in and out, and I myself sank lower and lower towards the red reef over which we were being lifted in. Then only crests of foam full of salt spray came whirling in, and I was able to work my way in on to the raft, where we all made for the after end of the logs, which was highest up on the reef.

*

The reef stretched like a half-submerged fortress wall up to the north and down to the south. In the extreme south was a long island densely covered with palm forest. And just above us to the north, only 600 or 700 yards away, lay another but considerably smaller palm island. It lay inside the reef, with palm-tops rising into the sky and snow-white sandy beaches running out into the still lagoon. The whole island looked like a bulging green basket of flowers, or a little bit of concentrated paradise.

This island we chose.

*

I was completely overwhelmed. I sank down on my knees and thrust my fingers deep down into the dry warm sand.

The voyage was over. We were all alive.

from *The Kon-Tiki Expedition* by Thor Heyerdahl

In early Victorian days the dream of British explorers, encouraged by the Admiralty, was to find a navigable route from the Atlantic to the Pacific – the North-West Passage. Sir John Franklin had commanded two earlier expeditions to the Canadian Arctic before he was appointed a colonial governor in Australia. Upon his return at the age of fifty-nine, this veteran of Copenhagen and Trafalgar persuaded the First Lord of the Admiralty to give him command of another expedition.

Franklin left on 18 May 1845, in a bomb vessel of 370 tons, the *Erebus*, accompanied by Captain Fitzjames as his second-in-command. In a slightly smaller vessel, the *Terror*, was Captain Crozier, who had served under Parry and James Ross. The ships carried 139 officers and men with provisions for three years. Franklin's original intention was to sail westwards through Lancaster Sound and Barrow Sound, after which he expected to find enough sea-room south of Banks Land to allow him to reach Bering Strait. He shared Sir John Barrow's belief that Banks Land was probably an island of no great size. However, if he found that his way to the west was barred, he would turn north along Wellington Channel looking, as he went, for a break out to the west. His orders from the First Lord were to push along Barrow Strait without wasting any time on exploring openings on either hand. When he reached Cape Walker at the western end of the Strait, he was to keep to the south and west, as far as ice or undiscovered land permitted. If he could make no headway there, he could seek an anchorage in Wellington Channel until spring brought new opportunities.

Three weeks to Stromness in Orkney, four weeks to Disco Bay in Greenland – Franklin had plenty of time on the voyage to catch up with his reading of Arctic literature. He observed that the explorers who had gone before him painted a picture of his task that was somewhat less simple than Sir John Barrow's fervent prose had suggested: 'I am inclined to think,' Franklin wrote to Parry, 'that there exists much land between Woolaston and Banks Lands, which I hope may be separated into islands.' Sobered by what he read in the works of those who had preceded him, Franklin set off from Disco on 13 July, northward along the Greenland coast where, in Melville Bay, just north of the seventy-fourth Parallel, he fell in with a whaler, the *Prince of Wales*. The whaler's log noted that all Franklin's men were well, in good spirits and confident that they would finish the job in good time. It was the last time that the crews of the *Erebus* and *Terror* were seen alive.

By the autumn of the following year, September 1846, nobody had heard anything from Franklin and his men. But then, nobody expected to.

In January 1850, two ships sailed from England in search of Franklin. Commander Robert McClure in HMS *Investigator* passed through the Straits of Magellan to the Pacific and then approached the problem from the Bering Sea. He very nearly made it, but was forced by scurvy to decide upon abandoning his ship and head for home, rather than face a fourth winter beset in the ice. As far as the Admiralty was concerned, McClure's name had now been added to the growing roll of lost sailors in the Arctic. In 1852 a flotilla of four ships set out to find him. Just before McClure had dispersed his sailors in groups on different routes towards safety, a lone officer from HMS *Resolute*, Lieutenant Pym, appeared, having made a twenty-eight-day sledge journey from the east where his ship was also in the grip of the ice, with Captain Kellett on board.

The day after Pym's arrival at the ship, McClure left to meet Captain Kellett at Dealy Island, which he did twelve days later. He meant to make arrangements to send his sick men back to England. He had no intention of going there himself. He had seen the North-west Passage and he was determined, if he could, to sail his ship through it! At the worst, he would wait through another winter and then go eastwards on foot to a place on the coast of North Somerset where he knew that ample supplies existed. From there, with luck, he would pick up a whaler that would take him home or, failing that, he would wait for a new relief expedition to come. He drafted a letter to the Admiralty announcing that, among other things, he had discovered 'the accurate knowledge of that Passage between the Atlantic and Pacific Oceans, which for so many hundred years has baffled maritime Europe.' He would sail through the channel he had found. Captain Kellett, however, took a different view. He saw the ravages of scurvy among the sick men from the *Investigator* and ordered a medical inspection of all the crew. The doctors found that all but two of them showed symptoms of the disease. With bitterness in his heart, McClure was forced to abandon his plan. The stores of the *Investigator* were put ashore, in the hope that they would be useful to the lost Captain Collinson should he pass that way. The colours were nailed to the ship's masthead. Then she was abandoned.

By the time McClure returned to England at the end of September, the public was informed that he had found the North-west Passage. He was promoted to Captain and given a knighthood. There was, however, another question. Should he be given the reward which Parliament had earmarked for the discoverer of the Passage? The bodies of four white men had been found near the mouth of the Great Fish River (the Back River) four years earlier. They must have belonged to Franklin's expedition. In that case, they must have completed the circle of sea communication between Barrow Strait and the open waters along the mainland coast which overland explorers had found. Should not their families be given the prizes? Lady Franklin, whose opinion in these matters was heard with deep respect, said she thought that her husband had found another, and more navigable, channel than McClure's, but that McClure was the first who had made his individual way from one ocean to the other. This, she said, might not be the object which had 'engaged the attention of the civilized world for centuries' but it was a distinction of which any man might be proud. After this nicely balanced verdict, Parliament voted McClure £10,000. So the riddle of the centuries had at last been solved – or had it? For, after all, the first explorers had gone out to find a commercially viable route.

Apparently it did not exist. Later, they had searched for a navigable passage. And, so far, nobody had navigated it!

The first real clue to the fate of Franklin came in a report to the Admiralty by Dr John Rae who was, like so many servants of the Hudson's Bay Company, an Orkney man and, like Franklin's old friend, Sir John Richardson, was a surgeon trained in Edinburgh. He had been in the service of the Company since 1833. When Richardson led an overland expedition to look for Franklin, Rae went with him. In 1851, now aged 38, he set off again on a sledge journey which took him from Great Bear Lake 1,100 miles along the coast of the Wollaston Peninsula. Immediately afterwards, he made a survey by boat of the south and east coasts of Victoria Island. After that, turning south, Rae and two companions journeyed up the Coppermine River. After eight months, Rae had travelled 5,380 miles. This vigorous explorer was leading an expedition for the Hudson's Bay Company on a survey of the western coast of Boothia when he came on the traces of Franklin. At Pelly Bay in 1854, Rae fell in with an Eskimo who repeated to him a story he had heard. According to it, four years before, white men had been seen by Eskimos making their way to the south over the ice off King William Island. It appeared that their ships had been crushed in the ice. Now, with food running short, they were hoping to find game on the Canadian mainland. Later on, these Eskimos came on the bodies of thirty-five of the men. They also found a telescope, a gun and ammunition. But the white men had found no game and it was apparent to the Eskimos that they had tried to stave off death by cannibalism. The Eskimo who told this grim story to Dr Rae was able to produce some evidence to support it, table goods which had been found at the white men's camp including a small silver plate inscribed 'Sir John Franklin, K.C.H.' Rae went at once to York Factory on Hudson's Bay and sent his news to the Secretary of the Admiralty. It reached London soon after the return of the McClure expedition.

Next year, 1855, the Admiralty, by this time fully occupied with managing the naval part of the Crimean War, asked the Hudson's Bay Company to send an expedition to the mouth of the Back River in the hope of coming on more clues to Franklin's fate. There, in Eskimo huts, between Lake Franklin and the estuary, the search party found tent poles, oars, tools, etc. which the Eskimos said came from a boat belonging to white men who had starved to death some years before. On Montreal Island in the estuary itself, other relics were found, including a stick on which somebody had carved the name 'Terror'.

from *The North-West Passage* by George Malcolm Thomson

It was not until 1903 that Roald Amundsen and six young Norwegians did a midnight flit from their creditors in Oslo in the 72-foot auxiliary cutter *Gjoa* – vintage 1882 with an engine developing all of 15 b.h.p.

Ostensibly their mission was to locate the magnetic North Pole, which presented few problems. When the compass went berserk, they had reached the spot. Spending two winters in the ice, they finally threaded their way through tortuous and uncharted narrow channels to reach the Bering Sea, and so to San Francisco. In the process, Amundsen had to head 400 miles south after leaving Baffin Bay on the eastern threshold before turning westwards and coast-crawling along the northern shores of mainland Canada.

That was the secret which had eluded explorers since Frobisher's expedition three centuries earlier.

In 1977, when he was in his eightieth year, Bill Tilman was flattered by being invited by his twenty-four-year-old protégé Simon Richardson to sail as one of his crew in a voyage to the Antarctic. It was no ordinary trip, for it was another milestone in the development of the form of exploration first indulged in by this ex-Himalayan mountaineer – to sail to a hitherto unconquered peak as far away from the equator as possible and then climb it. On this occasion it was to be Smith Island in the South Shetlands group, 500 miles south of Cape Horn.

The chosen vessel was as unorthodox as the austere old lovable curmudgeon himself, a Rotterdam harbour tug converted on a shoestring to a gaff cutter with a heavy unwieldy rig. She was named *En Avant*, which roughly translates as 'Press On'.

On passage from Rio to the Falklands the sea claimed them all.

It can be argued that Tilman went to the well once too often in boats which would be better left parked as exhibits in a maritime museum, but he would have had it no other way. He sailed to the Southern Ocean and the length of both coasts of Greenland before his veteran pilot-cutter *Mischief* sank under tow after having hit a rock off Jan Mayen Island north of the 70th parallel; the old hull had been strained and softened up by constant grinding in pack-ice. Here he tells us about the boat and his method of crew selection:

Is your journey really necessary? became the question. Why attempt to drag five other misguided men half-way across the world when it is obvious that most of our present-day troubles come from men not staying quietly in their room at home? But upon visiting *Mischief* to see how things are going, such weak thoughts are speedily banished. She and her kind were never built so that men should stay quietly at home. She breathes sturdy, eager confidence, a living embodiment of the truth that the sea is for sailing, that strenuousness is the immortal path and sloth the way of death.

A few words about *Mischief*, the chief figure in this account. She was originally a Bristol Channel Pilot cutter built at Cardiff in 1906; in length 45ft., beam 13ft., drawing 7ft. 6ins. aft, and of 29 tons Thames Measurement. Her gaff rig is still the same but she now has an auxiliary petrol engine. With full tanks the range is less than 300 miles, so that her motive power is essentially sail. The first Cardiff pilot to own her was a Mr William Morgan, known throughout the Bristol Channel as 'Billy the Mischief'. When the individual competitive pilot service came to an end in 1912, she was taken over along with sixty-seven other cutters by the Cardiff Steam Pilot Service, an event which marked the end of those stirring days in the Bristol Channel, when each pilot in his own boat strove to be the first to board an incoming ship.

*

'Hand (man) wanted for long voyage in small boat. No pay, no prospects, not much pleasure.' Thus ran the advertisement I inserted in the Personal Column of *The Times* about a month before the day I hoped to sail. In planning a second and, fortunately, more successful voyage to the Crozet islands in the Southern Ocean, I had run into the usual difficulty of finding a crew. A minimum of four were needed, five would be better, of whom one at least must be a mountaineer or at any rate capable of moving freely and looking after himself on easy rock, ice or snow. Ideally, of course, all should have had some sailing experience. One of them, I hoped, would have an invincible stomach and a turn for cooking on paraffin stoves in cramped quarters in a stuffy, unstable galley; and another should have some knowledge of small marine engines and the numbing effect upon them of sea air and salt water. All must be of cheerful, equable temper, long-suffering, patient in adversity, tolerant of the whims and uncouth manners or habits of others, neat and cleanly, adaptable, unselfish, loyal – in fact, possessed of most of the qualities in which the majority of men, including myself, are notably deficient.

Whatever sensations his crews might have enjoyed in *Mischief*, fast passages under sail were seldom among them, as this description of her homeward trip through the Mediterranean makes plain. His 'comparatively fast' homeward leg from Gibraltar to Lymington averaged under 2½ knots along the rhumb line.

> . . . having sailed up the Red Sea we passed through the Canal out into the Mediterranean, where, traversing it, we spent two solid months of light, fickle, and contrary winds. So that ships which passed us homeward bound passed us again two or three weeks later when they were once more outward bound, saluting us as they went as an old but rather slow-moving acquaintance. We understood why in the old days galley-slaves were an essential form of propulsion in the Mediterranean. From Gibraltar the passage was comparatively fast, taking only twenty days. The usual

summer gale blew us up Channel and we tied up at Lymington thirteen months after leaving it, thus ending a fruitless voyage of 22,000 miles.

She exceeded that speed only with a gale of wind behind her and, as occurred during the leg from Bermuda on the way home from Patagonia, when the Gulf Stream added another knot.

By great circle course the distance from Bermuda to the Scillies is 3,353 miles. We did it in thirty-two days and for most of the way we had generous gales of wind and usually from a favourable direction. The passage was marked by a number of minor mishaps, attributable sometimes to our own folly or laziness and sometimes to the wearing out of the running rigging on the last few thousand miles of a twenty thousand mile voyage. The first, which might have been more serious, occurred a few days out early one morning in my watch. We had been running all night with whole mainsail and a twin boomed out. When I took over she was rolling and yawing wildly, but probably no more than she had been doing during the night. At length the gybe which I was beginning to fear happened. For a moment the wire boom guy held the boom high in the air; then it broke, and the boom crashed over wrapping the main sheet round the horse and breaking the back-stay tackle. The staysail was flat aback as well, so that when the crew tumbled up in response to my yell they were not a little startled by my new arrangements. With the mainsheet round the horse it was impossible for us to haul the boom in-board so that the sail could then be lowered. Taking a horribly rash decision I told them to stand by for another gybe. Back the boom came with a sickening crash, the main sheet unwound itself in a flash, and all was well. We then handed the mainsail, hoisted the twins, and felt much safer.

Next morning in a wild squall and at the inconvenient time of just before breakfast the sheet of one of the twins parted, and a few seconds later the cranse iron at the outer end of the other boom came adrift. We now had both sails streaming out ahead of the ship like washing on a line. We tamed them after a fierce struggle and fortunately before anything had been torn. The wind then moderated and a period of wet, misty weather succeeded these alarms. . .

Another depression soon caught up with us and for two days we sped – everything reefed down – before a southerly gale. I judged we were doing 'twelve knots and a Chinaman', as the saying goes. Anyhow we ran 350 miles (by sights) in two days while the great following seas took *Mischief* in their arms and hurled her forwards. In our enthusiasm we began shortening the passage by days or even weeks, but I deprecated too much optimism by enumerating all the accidents which might happen to us, including even the breaking of the boom. Sure enough the next day it did break.

That night the barometer dropped very steeply and at three in the morning it was blowing very hard and raining. As usual we had left the mainsail up for too long and no one fancied taking it down in such wild conditions in the dark. As she was going too fast for safety we streamed over the counter the bights of two of our heaviest warps to slow her down and then prayed for dawn. By morning – it was Midsummer Day – the wind moderated and shifted to north-west. A big sea was running and the boom, which should have been hauled in and pinned amidships – for now there was scarcely enough wind to fill it – was slamming about. It had already broken the rope tail of its wire guy when I took over after breakfast. I at once noticed that it had a slight curve. Suspecting that it was sprung I was about to call all hands when it broke, fairly in the middle. We had not yet taken out the reefs, that is there were four or five rolls of canvas round the boom. Having got it inboard we managed to straighten the boom by means of the throat halyards, but unrolling the sail with the boom lying on the deck was quite a job. We cut off a couple of feet at each end of the boom where the fittings were attached and threw the rest overboard.

*

Towards the end of June there began a spell of dirty weather which was to last almost to the Scillies. Rain, high winds, and rough seas combined to make life wet and wearing. The companion way was boarded up, the hatch cover closed, the skylight battened down – but nevertheless water managed to find its way below. Although the helmsman was partly protected by the dodger rigged round the cockpit he still had the benefit of enough spray and solid water to keep him awake; and even the briefest of visits to the cockpit to survey the weather compelled one to be fully clothed. As one stood at the foot of the companion struggling into wet oilskins before going on watch, one would call hopefully to the helmsman for some words of comfort, for the least hint of a change for the better. But seldom were they forthcoming . . . The night of 29 June was particularly bad. The glass having fallen had apparently steadied. We had the trysail up and a twin boomed out. During the night the glass slumped to 29.2in. and at four in the morning, when we must have been doing seven knots, we had to hand the sails and run under storm jib alone. When daylight broke on a grey wilderness of white-capped waves we successfully experimented with a couple of oil bags trailing from either quarter. We found that even the finest film of oil had a remarkably soothing effect when angry waves tried to break close to our counter.

*

Discomfort can more easily be borne when one is being driven homewards with such vigour. Every day we ran our hundred miles or more, whether under storm jib alone or with the trysail and a twin. Opportunities for taking sights had to be promptly seized. They were not common and on two consecutive days we could not take any at all. However, on 5 July, in improving weather, we found ourselves only 60 miles from the Bishop rock. That night we picked up the light and by breakfast time on a lovely summer morning we were off St Mary's. A year and a day after leaving we passed

Falmouth, but by now we were enveloped in a dense fog. For three days as we groped our way up Channel the fog persisted. Because of the tide we anchored in home waters for the first time in Swanage bay, but at last on 9 July we entered Lymington river and tied up at the yard where we had fitted out.

. . . [On the voyage] tempers strained to breaking-point when cooped up in a small ship together. 'Ships are all right – it's the men in them' was, I suspect, the thought of each one of us on many occasions . . . the same idea was openly and more pointedly expressed. It was loyalty to the ship that held the crew together . . .

from *Mischief in Patagonia* by H. W. Tilman

Lone Sailors

Robin Knox-Johnston, a twenty-nine-year-old Merchant Navy officer, set sail from Falmouth in Cornwall on 14 June 1968 in a tubby 44-foot (including bowsprit) double-ended Bermudan ketch built by himself two years previously in Bombay. Three hundred and thirteen days later, he replied to the Falmouth customs launch's traditional hail of 'Where from?' with 'Falmouth'. He had thus sailed into the history books as the the first man to circumnavigate the globe without stopping.

Six weeks out he had time to reflect, having spent half that time laboriously ghosting across the Doldrums. He still had 27,000 miles to go.

As usual after a radio contact I felt the loneliness of my situation and sought comfort in my books:

'I had a most unsatisfactory day. I always do when I have been in radio contact. I get excited by getting through and then the feeling of anti-climax follows, and I feel depressed. I spent a lot of time lying on a bunk reading and finished *Erewhon and Erewhon Revisited* by Samuel Butler. I cannot think why I have never heard of this book before.'

and on another occasion

'Finished *War and Peace* by Tolstoy today. I know that good books like good wine should be taken of sparingly, but I could not stop myself in this case.'

But in the evenings I could put my tape recorder on and soon cheer up:

'I repaired the Gilbert and Sullivan tape cassette . . . and had a wonderful evening. I joined in sitting at the table in the homely light of the cabin light. It is not cold enough yet for clothes, just pleasant . . . I think I'll have a nip of Grant's. I can think of no one with whom I'd trade my lot at present. Intelligent, attractive and interesting female company is all that I require to make the situation quite perfect. Not that I am feeling romantic at present, but if I had female company I expect I would!'

Some of the problems associated with loneliness and having to do absolutely everything for oneself were beginning to appear. Normally, when I have a number of jobs that need to be done, I take the one that most suits my mood at the time. This just would not do now; I had to do things at once or when the weather was favourable regardless of my mood. Then, too, if there was nothing urgent to be done, and no job that could occupy my time, I found myself getting bored and books would act only as a temporary stopgap. I would get restless and long for the voyage to be over, and it was not until October that I found I had come to accept at all philosophically that I was to spend perhaps a year of my life in this way.

Cooking was becoming a chore, and as for thinking up new menus from the limited selection of food available, my imagination was running dry.

'I had some difficulty deciding what to have for dinner. If one had to put as much mental effort and imagination into the reproduction of the human race, it would have died out long ago. Eventually I decided on an omelette, but the four eggs I broke were all bad so then I made a cheese sauce and threw a tin of carrots and some parsley into it. Not bad; too much flour in the sauce, though.'

This, I think, was the second period of my adjustment. When I had got over the initial problems and doubts, a short period of acceptance of the new environment arrived. This was followed by a second, longer stage of deeper and more serious doubts. Surviving this, I had my second wind, and was able to settle down to things. I got through it by forcing myself to do some mental as well as physical work.

Not long afterwards he had serious thoughts of giving up when he was in the South-East Trades half-way between Rio and St Helena. His main halyard winch brake had failed, dumping the mainsail down in a hurry, and the boom gooseneck fitting attaching to the mast was about to fracture. Both defects were indicative of the low-budget gear with which the boat was equipped, promising more serious trouble in the Roaring Forties. The inspiration for continuing the voyage came not from any thoughts of the *Sunday Times* race he was taking part in, but from motives of which Rudyard Kipling and Baden-Powell would have thoroughly approved.

'But the point that is at present worrying me is whether I should go on knowing this and other weaknesses. None of them is disastrous taken by itself but the combination could be, and if the mainsail dropped, or the gooseneck gave at the wrong moment I could be in real trouble. I won't make any decision as yet, I'll wait until I get the opportunity to have a closer look at everything, and I don't think I'll mention any of these troubles in my report . . . as there is no point in alarming people. If I make Australia O.K. then all this will, upon reflection, just appear as a localized panic. If I decide to pull in, the reasons will be obvious to all. I don't fancy pulling in somehow, not having come this far . . .

'*1830*. I have wedged the tape recorder and have G. & S. on again; it always cheers me up, but I would have liked a tape of stirring patriotic stuff – the thought of generations of Britons and their achievements always encourages me, a reminder of traditions which spurred them on. Most nations have a bookful of heroes but, and of course I'm prejudiced, I always feel that Britain has a greater share than most. After all, in my circumstances would a Drake, Frobisher, Grenville, Anson, Nelson, Scott or Vian (note – all seamen!) have thought of giving up? It's a great encouragement to think of countrymen like these looking down on one, even if this little voyage can never come close to their achievements. In its own small way, though, it is a continuation of the same traditions – and notice how it is mostly Britons who have responded to the challenge . . .

*

'I feel lonely tonight. Listening to L. M. [Laurenço Marques radio] has brought back memories of South Africa, and although human nature being what it is one always remembers the good times and forgets the bad, on the whole we had many more good memories in S. A. It's Saturday night and I can remember the parties all too well. People were much more social and seemed to enjoy themselves more there than in the U.K. I still regret not settling there at times. This sudden contact with a world that I have missed for two years is not the most settling of sensations. Still it's pleasant here, the sea is flat calm and the sheets are rattling in unison with the sound of water lapping the hull. The moon has just risen and it's not yet got cold. I have just made a mug of cocoa and am sitting drinking it as I write this. A short while back I was shaking to Little Richard who has apparently come back into fashion with the re-emergence of Rock 'n Roll. It's as well I am on my own as my 'Shaking' is very graceless. Despite what I have written, I do not allow myself to get maudlin when I am alone. Ah, that's better – Ella Fitzgerald – from Paraguay. This music is making me romantic, or rather longing to be. There's nothing to beat dancing under a tropical moon, Latin-American music for preference.'

Three weeks later he had crossed the 40th parallel and was into the Southern Ocean riding out his first big westerly blow. For a while *Suhaili* seemed happy flying along with the self-steering gear (the Admiral, as he called it) working beautifully. Then it happened:

The next thing I remember is being jerked awake by a combination of a mass of heavy objects falling on me and the knowledge that my world had turned on its side. I lay for a moment trying to gather my wits to see what was wrong, but as it was pitch black outside and the lantern I kept hanging in the cabin had gone out, I had to rely on my senses to tell me what had happened. I started to try to climb out of my bunk, but the canvas which I had pulled over me for warmth was so weighted down that this was far from easy.

As I got clear *Suhaili* lurched upright and I was thrown off balance and cannoned over to the other side of the cabin, accompanied by a mass of boxes, tools, tins and clothing which seemed to think it was their duty to stay close to me. I got up again and climbed through the debris and out onto the deck, half expecting that the masts would be missing and that I should have to spend the rest of the night fighting to keep the boat afloat. So convinced was I that this would be the case that I had to look twice before I could believe that the masts were still in place. It was then that I came across the first serious damage. The Admiral's port vane had been forced right over, so far in fact that when I tried to move it I found that the stanchion was completely buckled and the ⅝-inch marine plywood of the vane had been split down about 10 inches on the mizzen cap shroud. The whole thing was completely jammed. Fortunately I was using the starboard vane at the time, because I could not hope to try and effect repairs until I could see, and the time was 2.50 a.m. It would not be light for another four hours. *Suhaili* was back on course and seemed to be comfortable and I could not make out anything else wrong; however, I worked my way carefully forward, feeling for each piece of rigging and checking it was still there and tight. I had almost gone completely round the boat when another wave came smashing in and I had to hang on for my life whilst the water boiled over me. This is what must have happened before. Although the whole surface of the sea was confused as a result of the cross-sea, now and again a larger than ordinary wave would break through and knock my poor little boat right over. I decided to alter course slightly so that the seas would be coming from each quarter and we would no longer have one coming in from the side, and went aft to adjust the Admiral accordingly.

Having checked round the deck and rigging, and set *Suhaili* steering more comfortably, I went below and lit the lantern again. The cabin was in an indescribable mess. Almost the entire contents of the two starboard bunks had been thrown across onto the port side and the deck was hidden by stores that had fallen back when the boat came upright. Water seemed to be everywhere. I was sloshing around it it between the galley and the radio as I surveyed the mess and I could hear it crashing around in the engine-room each time *Suhaili* rolled. That seemed to give me my first job and I rigged up the pump and pumped out the bilges.

from *A World of My Own* by Robin Knox-Johnston

Then he discovered that there was a major leak all around the base of the cabin-top, with water pouring in as each wave rolled over the boat. If the weakened superstructure was washed away, he would be left with a gaping hole 6 feet by 12 feet, to all intents then in an open boat 700 miles south of Cape Town. He was later able to reinforce the cabin-top fastenings with long bolts and nuts, which stood up to the steady succession of gales which were to be *Suhaili*'s lot for the next weeks crossing the Indian Ocean.

On 11 June 1978 a twenty-eight-year-old New Zealand sheep-farmer's daughter, Naomi James, became the first woman to circumnavigate the globe alone when she sailed past Kingswear Castle into the River Dart and home after what was then a record 273 days. That included unscheduled stops of three days each for emergency repairs at Cape Town and Port Stanley. Her husband Rob, a professional yacht skipper, was in the crew of *Great Britain II* on the Whitbread Round-the-World Race whilst his young bride Naomi was sailing alone along the same route.

When she set out she would not have been eligible to take part in the *Observer* Single-handed Race across the North Atlantic, let alone make a non-stop voyage around the world, for she had less than two years' total sailing experience, mostly as cook. She learnt navigation as she went along, making all the classic mistakes, like applying magnetic variation the wrong way and measuring off distances along the longitude scale of the chart. Her 53-foot masthead cutter was a stock Van de Stadt glassfibre hull, a robust well-found boat which took all that the Southern Ocean could dish out. One knockdown tore both shrouds away from their point of attachment aloft. Repairing them involved climbing the mast in violent weather several times.

The crunch came 2,000 miles WNW of Cape Horn:

On the 27th, that which I had always dreaded happened. Hours later I wrote in my log:

I capsized at 0500 this morning. I was only half awake at the time, but suddenly aware that the wind had increased even beyond the prevailing force ten. It was just daylight, and I was trying to make up my mind whether to get up and try steering when I heard the deafening roar of an approaching wave. I felt the shock, a mountain of water crashed against *Crusader's* hull, and over she went. An avalanche of bits and pieces descended on me as she went under, and I put up my arms to protect my face. After a long and agonizing pause she lurched up again. I don't recall the act of climbing out of my bunk or even my sleeping bag, but I found myself well and truly free of them both.

As far as I remember, my first move was to look through the skylight at the rigging. It scarcely registered that the mast was still standing. I could hear water running into the bilges, so I quickly started to pump. For a terrible moment I felt that she was sinking, but as I pumped I could see the level going down. I pumped in a frenzy for a few minutes and then jumped on deck to see if the mast and rigging were really all right.

I noticed one spinnaker pole had gone and the other was broken. The sails which had been lashed along the guard rails were dragging in the water. I hauled them aboard somehow and re-tied them to the rails. The radio aerial was flying loose, and the deck fitting from which it had been torn was now letting in water. As a temporary measure I plugged it with an old T-shirt and returned below to continue pumping the bilges. There was a strong smell of paraffin and milk. All the stores on the top bunk had been hurled out and the lee-cloth hung in shreds. My main concern was that she might go over again, so I left things below as they were, dug out some thick socks, gloves, hat and oilskins (all wet) and went to the helm to steer.

I secured my safety harness to the compass binnacle and faced the waves so that I could see them coming. The vision scared me stiff. The waves were gigantic, a combination of twenty-foot swells with twenty- to thirty-foot waves on top. One crashed near by, and it didn't need any imagination to realize what would happen if one of these monsters fell on me.

Suddenly *Crusader* started to surf, and I gripped the wheel desperately to keep the stern directly on to the wave and hold her straight. The next wave picked her up like a toy and wrenched all control from me.

*

I steered on devoid of thought and incapable of feeling. At 10.30 a.m. I detected a lull, followed half an hour later by another. At last I began to feel better, and when on a trip below I saw a bottle of port rolling in a corner and took a swig. I also grabbed some water biscuits and ate them at the wheel.

At 11.30 the wind was down to force eight, but I kept steering until 2 p.m., by which time the wind had reduced to intermittent heavy squalls. It now seemed safe, so I left her lying-a-hull. The radio was drenched but it worked, and after an hour of concentrated cleaning up the interior was almost back to normal. However, there seemed to be a curious itinerary of missing items, including my fountain pen, the can opener, hairbrush and kettle. Most of my crockery was broken. A bad moment was finding my Salalite transistor quite dead; that meant no more time signals to check the error of my chronometer. Still, the clock was quartz and kept very good time, and there was no reason to think it might suddenly become erratic.

My bed was sopping wet, but fortunately I had a spare sleeping bag stowed away in a plastic bag. I hauled it out in triumph – bone dry! The cabin heater soon dried out my pillow. I had no dry footwear and on the floor was a slippery mixture of milk, paraffin and bilge water.

After clearing up I made myself a cup of tea and heated some tomato soup. I then slept for an hour but only fitfully as I could hear water dripping into the bilges. I finally stirred myself and found that the water was coming from the hole in the deck where the insulator had been. The best I could do was to fill it with more rags until the weather improved. At 5 p.m. the wind strength was force eight again, but the seas were settling down, and within two hours the barometer had begun to climb. The weather might have improved but I still felt very shaky.

*

I awoke the following morning feeling sore and lethargic. I was still heading due north, but making a mere two knots. I didn't dare risk a bigger sail – not yet anyway. With the previous day's decision to sail back to New Zealand still in my mind, I studied the chart and felt an overwhelming depression. All those miles for nothing. Everything I had achieved so far would go to waste. It all seemed so wrong. I sat down and once again wrote out my arguments for giving up, or rather for not going on. The awful indecision was back. As *Crusader* was still in one piece after the previous day's storm, I wasn't sure that my earlier doubts about her seaworthiness in bad weather could still be used as reasons for abandoning my course to Cape Horn. I suddenly began to question my true motives for turning back, and all at once realized that that decision had been caused by fear. How then could I reconsider going on? The answer was that at this precise moment I also realized that by surmounting the storm I had almost totally eliminated the fear that had been dogging me for so long.

In my log I wrote:

a) If that rig can stand a capsize without the proper shrouds, then it should withstand ordinary bad weather when I fit a decent replacement; b) it's 2800 miles to the Falklands as opposed to 3000 to New Zealand against the current and head winds; c) surely there are not likely to be too many severe storms in the next three to four weeks.

Having written down these considerations the decision I had to make became clear: I turned around once more and set course for the Horn. My mood changed rapidly from depression to positive optimism – I was on my way again. I wrote down the priorities for the day:

> Fix the hole in the deck where the aerial has broken off. Make a replacement hatch-cover for the cockpit bin which is open and letting in water. Fix the shrouds. Yippee! We're off!

At midnight on 14 March the starboard shrouds collapsed again. I jogged along under shortened sail until morning and then went aloft to inspect the damage. Fortunately, it wasn't too bad. Unable to get the shroud plates over the bolt as originally intended, I had linked them to the bolt with a shackle and a large steel ring. It was the steel ring, gripped by the bolt, which had suffered. The strain must have been immense, for the ring had straightened into an oblong shape before finally parting. I replaced it with a heavy shackle and within half an hour I was on my way again. By midday I was 500 miles from the Horn.

*

Early on the 19th the wind fell away completely and I managed a few hours' sleep, getting up at 2 a.m. when it suddenly blew strongly from the WSW. I kept the mainsail set until 6 a.m., then hauled it down in the increasing wind, disconnected the Sailomat and began to steer. I had planned to pass within fifteen miles to the south (windward) side of Diego Ramirez Islands which lie sixty miles to the west of Cape Horn, but didn't think I would see them unless the visibility improved. It was very cold and it rained all the time. And yet despite the misery I was not too worried about the gale, as I was keyed up for the final battle, and I felt I could tackle anything!

At 4 p.m. I wrote:

> I've steered all day. The wind shows no signs of dropping yet and visibility is still poor, but I must be past the islands by now. I am going to stay on this course until I reckon that I am well past the Horn; then I shall gybe and head for Illa Los Estados on the eastern side. I only hope the wind doesn't force me further south and into the ice. My planned course will take me as much as fifty to sixty miles south of the Horn and that is below the ice limit for this year. The sea pattern has changed, and the waves are now much shorter and steeper which indicates shallower water. *Crusader* is bouncing around like a cork. I'm glad it's no more than just gale force.

In the late evening I gybed towards Illa Los Estados, having estimated I had finally passed Cape Horn, the focal point of all my fears and apprehensions of the previous four months. Then I went to bed at 11.30 and slept for four hours, my longest uninterrupted sleep for six months. When I woke I found myself heading south and hurriedly changed course to the northeast.

*

250

At mid-morning the wind increased so I was forced to lie-a-hull; by the afternoon the wind had backed to the SW. Then I continued steering under bare poles for the rest of the afternoon. The wind force was eight with heavy squalls, but by 8 p.m. it had moderated sufficiently for me to put up the storm jib and reconnect the self-steering. I went back to my bunk feeling very tired and absolutely no elation at having passed the Horn.

*

In attempting this voyage I risked losing a life that had at last become fulfilling; but in carrying it out I experienced a second life, a life so separate and complete it appeared to have little relation to the old one that went before. I feel I am still much the same person now, but I know that the total accumulation of hours and days on this voyage have enriched my life immeasurably.

from *At One with the Sea* by Naomi James

Cruising

The Victorian aristocracy were unexpectedly adventurous sailors. Discounting Lord Cardigan dining in the luxurious saloon of his private steam-yacht moored off the Crimea whilst the troopers of his Light Brigade froze in tents ashore, there were some remarkable voyages made under sail. Elsewhere I have touched on the 37,000-mile circumnavigation in 1876–7 by Lord and Lady Brassey in their three-masted 582-ton auxiliary schooner *Sunbeam*. But twenty years before that Lord Dufferin had cruised his 85-ton schooner *Foam* to Jan Mayen Island and Spitzbergen, not far short of latitude 80°N and only 630 miles short of the Pole. His log of that voyage was a best-seller. Whilst the owner did not suffer from seasickness and treasured the time spent below in his cosy, well-furnished stateroom, his friend Fitz was prostrated. The steward, Wilson, was not much help:

> For the last ten days we have been leading the life of the 'Flying Dutchman'! Never do I remember having had such a dusting: foul winds, gales and calms – or rather breathing spaces, which the gale took occasionally to muster up fresh energies for a blow – with a heavy head sea that prevented our sailing even when we got a slant. On the afternoon of the day we quitted Stornoway I got a notion how it was going to be; the sun went angrily down behind a bank of solid grey cloud, and by the time we were

up with the Butt of Lewis the whole sky was in tatters and the mercury nowhere, with a heavy swell from the north-west.

As, two years before, I had spent a week in trying to beat through the Roost of Sumburgh under double-reefed trysails, I was at home in the weather; and guessing we were in for it, sent down the topmasts, stowed the boats on board, handed the foresail, rove the ridge-ropes and reefed all down. By midnight it blew a gale, which continued without intermission until the day we sighted Iceland; sometimes increasing to a hurricane, but broken now and then by sudden lulls which used to leave us for a couple of hours at a time tumbling about on the top of the great Atlantic rollers – or Spanish waves, as they are called – until I thought the ship would roll the masts out of her. Why they should be called Spanish waves no one seems to know; but I had always heard the seas were heavier here than in any other part of the world, and certainly they did not belie their character. The little ship behaved beautifully, and many a vessel twice her size would have been less comfortable. Indeed, few people can have any notion of the cosiness of a yacht's cabin under such circumstances. After having remained for several hours on deck in the presence of the tempest – peering through the darkness at those black liquid walls of water, mounting above you in ceaseless agitation or tumbling over in cataracts of gleaming foam – the wind roaring through the rigging – timbers creaking as if the ship would break its heart – the spray and rain beating in your face – everything around in tumult – suddenly to descend into the quiet of a snug, well-lighted little cabin, with the firelight dancing on the white rosebud chintz, the well-furnished bookshelves, and all the innumerable knick-knacks that decorate its walls – little Edith's portrait looking so serene – everything about you as bright and fresh as a lady's boudoir in Mayfair – the certainty of being a good three hundred miles from any troublesome shore – all combine to inspire a feeling of comfort and security difficult to describe.

These pleasures, indeed, for the first days of our voyage, the Icelander had pretty much to himself. I was laid up with a severe bout of illness I had long felt coming on, and Fitz was seasick. I must say, however, I never saw anyone behave with more pluck and resolution; and when we return, the first thing you do must be to thank him for his kindness to me on that occasion. Though himself almost prostrate, he looked after me as indefatigably as if he had already found his sea legs; and, sitting down on the cabin floor, with a basin on one side of him and pestle and mortar on the other, used to manufacture my pills, between the paroxysms of his malady, with a decorous pertinacity that could not be too much admired.

Strangely enough, too, his state of unhappiness lasted a few days longer than the eight-and-forty hours which are generally sufficient to set people on their feet again. I tried to console him by representing what an occasion it was for observing the phenomena of seasickness from a scientific point of view; and I must say he set to work most conscientiously to discover some remedy. Brandy, prussic acid, opium, champagne, ginger, mutton chops, and tumblers of salt water were successively exhibited; but I regret to say, after a few minutes, each in turn *re*-exhibited itself with monotonous punctuality. Indeed, at one time we thought he would never get over it; and the following conversation, which I overheard one morning between him and my servant, did not brighten his hopes of recovery.

This person's name is Wilson, and of all men I ever met he is the most desponding. Whatever is to be done, he is sure to see a lion in the path. Life in his eyes is a perpetual filling of leaky buckets and a rolling of stones uphill. He is amazed when the bucket holds water or the stone perches on the summit. He professes but a limited belief in his star – and success with him is almost a disappointment. His countenance corresponds with the prevailing character of his thoughts, always hopelessly chapfallen; his voice is as of the tomb. He brushes my clothes, lays the cloth, opens the champagne, with the air of one advancing to his execution. I have never seen him smile but once, when he came to report to me that a sea had nearly swept his colleague, the steward, overboard. The son of a gardener at Chiswick, he first took to horticulture, than emigrated as a settler to the Cape, where he acquired his present complexion, which is of a grass-green; and finally served as a steward on board an Australian steam packet.

Thinking to draw consolation from his professional experiences, I heard Fitz's voice, now very weak, say in a tone of coaxing cheerfulness, 'Well, Wilson, I suppose this kind of thing does not last long?'

The Voice, as of the tomb – 'I don't know, sir.'

Fitz – 'But you must have often seen passengers sick.'

The Voice – 'Often, sir; *very* sick.'

Fitz – 'Well, and on an average, how soon did they recover?'

The Voice – 'Some of them didn't recover sir.'

Fitz – 'Well, but those that did?'

The Voice – 'I know'd a clergyman and his wife as were ill all the voyage; five months, sir.'

Fitz – (Quite silent.)

The Voice; now become sepulchral – 'They sometimes dies, sir.'

Fitz – 'Ugh!'

Before the end of the voyage, however, this Job's comforter himself fell ill, and the doctor amply revenged himself by prescribing for him.

At last, on the morning of the eighth day, we began to look out for land. The weather had greatly improved during the night; and, for the first time since leaving the Hebrides, the sun had got the better of the clouds and driven them in confusion before his face. The sea, losing its dead leaden colour, had become quite crisp and burnished, darkling into a deep sapphire blue against the horizon, beyond which, at about nine o'clock, there suddenly shot up towards the zenith a pale gold aureole, such as precedes the appearance of the good fairy at a pantomime farce; then, gradually lifting its huge back above the water, rose a silver pyramid of snow, which

I knew must be the cone of an ice mountain, miles away in the interior of the island.

from *Letters from High Latitudes* by Lord Dufferin

Frank Cowper pioneered single-handed cruising in small open boats in the latter part of the nineteenth century, when most attention was focused on big yachts racing with a dozen or more paid hands. He took a 16-foot dayboat down to the Bay of Biscay to explore the Morbihan, then graduated to *Undine*, a 22-foot fishing cutter. He wrote extensively for the only yachting magazine of the day, *Hunt's*, whist compiling a five-volume series of pilotage books for amateur yachtsmen covering the British Isles and Brittany. In those days the creeks and harbours around the Solent rarely had more than one yacht berthed in each of them, whereas today they are home for over 30,000 boats.

But he noted that changes were on the way, for example at Bembridge . . .

Sailing out of Portsmouth at slack water one may go east or west as the breeze decides. Bembridge is a very favourite little cruise, only now it is next to impossible to find a clear berth inside the harbour unless one is lucky in being put on some vacant moorings. It was to Bembridge I first went in 1872 from Emsworth, and next year I brought over my Breton boat, the year after buying *Undine I.*, née *Blazer*. The little harbour was at that time the *beau ideal* of a single-handed cruiser's port. Everyone was civil. No one grudged me enjoying my sport in my own way. I never heard an offensive remark. No one ever dreamed of casting anyone else's dinghy adrift or filling it with cinders or dirt, experiences I have recently enjoyed at Harwich and Burnham. All odd jobs were readily undertaken, and I never heard any grumbling at the amount of the 'tips.' The few of 'The Quality' who boated did it as simply as myself, and everybody knew everybody else, thinking none the worse of them if they were richer or poorer than the other.

But Bembridge has seen changes. A golf club, a sailing club, a large hotel, and a reclaimed harbour have arisen since those days, and Bembridge is, for me, no longer the little haven under the wooded slope, where a few wooden cottages nestled on the edge of a sandy 'Duvver' and a church spire above admired its own reflection in the still water below.

There were no buoys or beacons in those days other than a few withies on the port hand going in, the outer one of which rejoiced in the name of 'Anthony.'

An old housewife expected her husband back from lifting his lobster pots. As he did not come, the old lady became anxious. To fortify herself she had recourse to her husband's consolation, and then sallied forth to the sands. The tide was out, the breeze strong, and the fumes of her potation were stronger. She sighted the last perch, and calling, 'Anthony. Oh, Anthony, is that you?' fell into its withered arms, mistaking the perch for her husband. There he found her, and ever after the boom went by the name of Anthony – at least, so I was told. A black and white buoy marks the place now.

Bembridge wives no longer go on the sands to look for their wandering husbands, or mistake withered sticks for the adored ones they seek, or if they do they are not found by their husbands. The proper title of this inlet in old days was Brading (or St. Helen's) Haven.

Towards the end of the century when Frank Cowper started doing the fieldwork for his pilotage books in earnest, he needed and bought a bigger boat, the 48-foot ex-Dover fishing lugger *Lady Harvey*. His account of visiting Weymouth bears retelling:

Weymouth is a place that can only be enjoyed with winds that blow down or across the harbour. Winds that blow in make it very uncomfortable. The first time I ever went in it was blowing a fresh E. wind. I let go where the harbour-master told me, but I had little room to round up head to wind, as several large steam yachts were lying on the mooring-buoys, narrowing the channel considerably. The inner harbour alongside the quays is always crowded with colliers and coasters, and there is not much water. If one wants to lay up a yacht in the Backwater the charge for opening the bridge is 15s., so the bridge-openers are not over-worked.

Weymouth Sands are perfect for bathing. Here the first bathing machine ever seen in England was made for Squire Allen, the Somersetshire squire whom Fielding took as a type for Squire Allworthy in the inimitable 'Tom Jones,' and here the Duke of Gloucester, son of George III., used to come for sea baths. He even persuaded his Royal parent to try a dip.

The news got abroad. Weymouth, or rather Melcombe, rose to the occasion. As the Royal machine rumbled down to the sea another machine accompanied it. It was mysterious, suspicious. A dull clang was heard inside, like that awsome groan which issued from the fatal horse which Troy invited to her own undoing.

The machine pauses a little behind the Royal box. Presently the door of Royalty opens, and, with such dignity as it is possible for a shivering, podgy old gentleman, of very commonplace appearance, to assume, the King of Great Britain, France, and Ireland descends the chilly steps.

Suddenly a crash of music is heard, and to the too zealous strains of 'God Save the Queen' his Majesty hastily takes refuge in the waves. What would happen if Royalty were now to take a dip publicly on the beach at Worthing or Brighton I shudder to think. Excursion trains would be run from all over the kingdom, and the beach would be black for miles along with Kodaks and Brownies, not to speak of the flotilla of boats covering the sea before the Royal bathing machine. In the days of George III, people were less curious and more polite.

255

Proceeding westwards from Weymouth, Frank Cowper recorded his experience of being sucked into the race off Portland Bill, which could just as easily have been written nearly a century later.

I shall not soon forget my experience of Portland Race. It was about half-past three when I weighed anchor one October morning to catch the ebb off the Bill. I knew nothing about the conditions prevailing, and it had been blowing hard from the S.W. the day before.

Dawn broke just as I sighted the Beacon. The wind was light and foul. I did not notice I was being swept out from the land, when suddenly I saw a great white wall ahead. I went about, but in another minute I was pitched into it, neck and crop. In spite of having tackle on both sides of the tiller, I could not possibly hold it. I was hurled about the deck, holding on to the tiller all the time. The seas came on board fore and aft. I had no steerage way, and could get no command over the boat. In this way *Lady Harvey* was carried through, helpless as a turtle on its back, pirouetting as a coryphée, and sluiced from stem to stern as a warship after coaling. There may have been danger, probably there was, but I was far too battered and hustled to think about it. All I could give heed to was how to get the giddy old thing to steer; but not until she had enjoyed a quarter of an hour's romp was I able to bring her to her senses. Then we were about a mile or more W. of the Bill and heading for Bridport.

Since then I have never been carried into the thick of the Race, but I have had it very bad once or twice, and the last time but one when I came E. was obliged to gybe on the top of a thundering snorter. It was broken water everywhere, and I had no choice unless I ran on the Beacon.

Once across Lyme Bay, he sailed into Dartmouth before going west to the Scillies and back. It was on homeward passage near Bolt Head and Prawle Point on either side of the entrance to Salcombe that he had a spot of bother with his dinghy whilst it was under tow:

I well remember the Prawle, for it was here I had to go ashore to the Coastguard Station to recover my dinghy that had broken adrift off Bolt Head. I sailed round from Salcombe and anchored close in shore on the E. side of the head. A small rock just awash lay off the point, sheltering me slightly from the swell, but the landing was a little wet, as it had been blowing fresh from the W. for some days. It was a steep climb up to the Coastguard Barracks, but when I reached the platform on which they stand I was rewarded by a most magnificent view. I think Prawle is the loveliest spot I know for a Coastguard Station; but the men did not like it, in spite of the S. aspect and sunny situation, sheltered from the N. and E. by steep hills. Their wives complained it was very inconvenient for shopping. This aspect had not occurred to me. My boat I found all right, and I took her away. The oars and rowlocks, however, were lost, but, in view of the narrow escape from drowning I myself had experienced, this was only a small matter.

The accident came about through towing the dinghy from Fowey. As I intended putting into Plymouth I did not trouble to take the boat on board, as I mostly did when making a passage. Off Plymouth, however, I had reason to change my mind, and kept on for Salcombe. Across Bigbury Bay the sea was bad, and as I neared Bolt Head it became worse, for the ebb was coming out strong from Salcombe. Several severe jerks made me anxious for the safety of the boat. I told the boy to get another rope to put on, and was preparing to luff up to make it fast when the painter parted and the boat broke adrift.

The sea was short and steep. I rounded up and tried to get hold of the boat, but lost a boathook in two attempts, and at last, growing desperate, I resolved to jump over and row the boat alongside. My first idea was to jump into it, but, as very likely I should do some damage, I stripped and dived into the water as the yacht luffed up. When I got hold of the dinghy it was full of water, and turned over directly I caught hold of it. The oars and rowlocks parted company at once – so did *Lady Harvey*. I tried to get the water out, and turned the boat over again, but, of course, it was useless – every sea washed over the submerged boat and me. Then I found I was losing my breath and getting cold, so I gave up all attempts, which only exhausted me, and, holding on to the keel of the boat, I raised myself to look for *Lady Harvey*. She had disappeared! I was now very cold, and the breaking seas knocked the breath out of me. I began to realise that I was face to face with 'the Great Perhaps,' and soberly regarded my chances. Bolt Head was about a mile to leeward. It was quite steep-to, even if I could have reached it, and the tide was setting me seawards. That was not encouraging. Then I saw a mast. It was a fishing boat, but, like the Levite, it passed by on the other side. I raised myself and shouted, but without result. Then, just when I gave up all hope, there, cresting the waves to windward, came *Lady Harvey*. The boy was steering, or rather standing by the quarter, looking everywhere for me. In the short hollow waves he could not see me. I saw it was neck or nothing, so, leaving the dinghy, I swam to *Lady Harvey*. Fortunately, she was hove-to nearly – at least, the foresail was flapping. She had no steerage way. Then suddenly the boy saw me. He threw a rope. It missed me and sank. I swam for the channels, but the yacht rose on a wave and I was left at least 8ft. below. I gave up all hope as the boat slowly passed by. Then I saw the jigger boom under the mizen. It had wire stays each side. I swam under the stern, and at that moment *Lady Harvey* plunged and rose again. I seized the chance. With an effort I wriggled out of the water high enough to grasp the wire stays, and with a supreme struggle got on board. I had been in the water three-quarters of an hour and was cold. The boy saw my plight. He got me my oilskins. I preferred warmer material next my skin, but had no time for luxuries. In another half hour we were in Salcombe, and the boat went drifting about until picked up by a Prawle fisherman and recovered by me three days afterwards.

from *Sailing Tours* by Frank Cowper

Cruising in small yachts with amateur crews dates back to mid-Victorian days, usually in converted fishing boats or pilot cutters better suited to being caught out in a gale the wrong side of Berry Head than in making ground to windward in fickle light airs. Sea anchors, storm trysails and oil bags were important parts of their inventory.

Claud Worth, a distinguished Harley Street eye surgeon, was one of the first to whet others sailors' appetites by accounts of his remarkably adventurous cruises from 1888 onwards. The seven boats he owned were most around 35 feet overall, 25 feet on the waterline and drawing over 6 feet. Accounts of his cruises from the Orkneys to the Bay of Biscay originally appeared in *Yachting Monthly*. In 1910 they were brought together in his classic book *Yacht Cruising*, a forerunner of John Illingworth's *Offshore*, although hardly speaking the same language. In his own profession he was better known for having written the standard textbook on squinting. In 1889 he first cruised to Ireland, ending in the beautiful harbour of Glandore, near the Old Head of Kinsale in West Cork. His log recalls the voyage home:

Monday, June 3rd. At 8.30 a.m. we left Glandore Harbour homeward bound (six weeks after having set sail from *Foam's* home port of Grays in Essex). A fine day, a smooth sea and a nice little SW'ly breeze. Set course SE¾S [I make that 142½° magnetic – Ed.] for the Longships, 156 miles away.

We felt very sad as this beautiful country slowly faded from view. Surely there can be no finer cruising ground. A strong tidal stream runs around the headlands, but a mile or two outside them the tides are quite slack, in fact we never worried about the tides at all. There were many passing showers, but not one day of persistent rain. It is true that this coast is exposed to the whole drift of the Atlantic, but there is always a snug retreat to run for if the weather should prove too bad. And, unless the wind is due west, one generally has plenty of sheltered water to sail in. In any case, to be weather-bound in one of these harbours is far less irksome that to be imprisoned in such a place as Penzance or Newhaven.

We never quite understood the people of this S.W. coast. At first they seemed sullen, but if we spoke to any of them they returned out salutation heartily. A conversation was usually followed by a request for whisky, old rope, or anything else they happened to think of – an unpleasing contrast to the sturdy independence of the fishermen of Cornwall and Devon. But

I believe that this arose from a frank and simple nature; like children, they just asked for what they wanted, and were as ready to give as to receive.

It took just over three days to reach the Longships north of Land's End. It must have been frustrating for the owner, who did not like to hang about:

> When we cruising men say that we care little for speed we deceive ourselves. It troubles us not at all when we are passed in smooth water by a racer, or a so-called 'fast cruiser,' or by any vessel merely by virtue of a large sailspread. But in a fresh breeze in open water, more especially in a peg to windward, to be beaten by a yacht of one's own size is a hateful experience. Therefore I like to have the most effective rig which I can comfortably handle without professional assistance. As a rule one could raise among one's friends a sufficient crew for a very big vessel, and even one man with no previous sea experience may be of great assistance so long as he is not sea-sick. But if no suitable companion is available it is necessary to be able to handle the yacht absolutely alone. My preference, therefore, is for the cutter rig up to 7 or 8 tons, a snug cutter or yawl up to about 15 tons, and the ketch for larger boats.
>
> My objection to paid hands in a small yacht is due, not to any dearth of willing, honest and reliable sailormen, but to the fact that in a vessel under about 40 tons there is scarcely room for proper sanitary arrangements for the crew and for a galley separate from the fo'c's'le. It is not pleasant to have one's food prepared in the apartment in which the men sleep and in which they perform their toilet.

To this day the heads are a source of trouble, although the most modern ones all have the single lever for pumping and flushing to which Claud Worth took such objection. He also noted that blockages are mostly caused by people carelessly using the heads as an all-purpose garbage disposal unit. Bill Snaith of *Figaro* fame had a pointed notice outside the heads door: 'Do not put anything into the pan which has not first been swallowed.'

> In many vessels the W.C. gives trouble. In some yachts which are in other respects well kept, one becomes aware of its presence as soon as one opens the door of the compartment in which it is situated. But by strict observance of simple rules all bother may with certainty be avoided. Have nothing to do with a fitting which pumps water in and pumps it out again by means of the same lever. Under ordinary conditions it does not give enough water to properly flush the pipe. But if it should become temporarily blocked, one pumps water in without pumping it out. Sea water should be admitted by a cock and pumped out by a separate lever. A plumber, experienced in yacht work, tells me that the things which most frequently cause the valves to hang up are matches, hair-pins, hair, and bits of string. After use, let

the pan fill with water, then pump it dry. Repeat this six times. The last time give an extra stroke to pump air through the syphon. This will prevent the possibility of water syphoning back into the vessel in case the valves should be defective. Chemicals are not needed during a cruise. Sea water is the best possible disinfectant if one uses enough of it. But before leaving the yacht at moorings it is well to pour a little carbolic acid into the pan. Once in two or three years the W.C. should be taken out and the pump releathered.

In one respect Claud Worth had the advantage over today's cruising yachtsmen. He was never faced with a bill for £8 or more just to lie alongside for the night in a marina. Not everyone would agree with his choice of the three best artificial harbours in the British Isles.

Wednesday to Saturday, July 15th to July 18th. – It rained almost incessantly the whole time, and blew most of a gale from S.W. If we had been pressed for time we could have turned down to the Land's End in a couple of days, but, having time to spare, we preferred to wait for more cheerful weather. The crew visited places of interest in the neighbourhood, and enjoyed the hospitality of the Royal Irish and Royal St. George Yacht Clubs.

The question of harbour dues is not an important one for yachts, and no one would object to contributing to the upkeep of the harbours he uses. But it is a curious fact that the amount of dues charged to yachts at different harbours is in inverse proportion to the accommodation afforded. For instance, at Kingstown, Lowestoft, and Blyth, the three most comfortable artificial harbours in the British Isles, no dues are demanded from yachts, while at such places as Penzance, Shoreham, and Ramsgate the dues are higher than anywhere else.

The Kingstown he refers to is now the port of Dublin and called Dun Laoghaire.

By 1908 Mrs Worth joined the crew, when her husband finally gave way and had a motor fitted to his 42-footer of 21 tons, Thames *Maud*, designed and built by William Fife in 1899.

Just before starting on our cruise we had a Seal paraffin motor of 2½ h.p. fitted. Every sailorman will naturally feel that the presence of that motor requires some explanation. It is seldom that we can find time for a long cruise. Usually we have to be content with week-ends, with trains to catch in order that appointments may be kept on Monday. That little motor relieved one of all anxiety about getting back to moorings on a calm Sunday evening. Of course, we had no use for the motor while there was any wind. We wanted something which would move the vessel in a flat calm just a little faster than two men with sweeps. We would not spoil the sail-room, so the motor and silencer must go in the paint locker, under the sail-room floor. We would not bore the sternpost or cut the rudder or deadwoods;

we therefore put the motor on port-side of the paint locker and the propeller under the port quarter, the aft end of the stern tube being supported by a V-shaped gunmental bracket. The two little propeller-blades feathered fore and aft for sailing. A comparison of log readings before and after fitting the motor shewed that it did not detract from the vessel's speed under sail.

from *Yacht Cruising* by Claud Worth

At thirty-six, Weston Martyr threw up his job in a New York shipping office and persuaded a friend to do likewise. Together they sank every cent they could muster into building a 42-foot schooner to his design in a family boatyard in Sheldon, Nova Scotia. Here the traditional skills of shipwrights with adzes survived, fashioning each strake and timber out of carefully selected seasoned wood. When mere carpenters and cabinet-makers tried to emulate them the results were discouraging:

And here I want to tell you a story about a ship that was made during the war. She was a steamer, and she was built of wood – good wood; and the men who designed and made her were good and able craftsmen too. As soon as this ship was completed she steamed a few miles down a river and commenced to load a full cargo of coal. For at that time ships were being murdered at sea by the dozen each day, and the coal was worth its weight in copper on the other side of the ocean. When the ship felt the first weight of her cargo she began to squeak, and then she cried out in pain. But the coal, as I have said, was badly wanted, so the stevedores, and even the ship's own men, pretended not to hear the ship's complaint, but just went ahead trimming in the cargo through four hatches at the rate of 200 tons an hour. And when a thousand tons or so were lying heavy within her the ship stopped crying out aloud, for by then she was in so much pain that she could only groan. She groaned dreadfully, though, for I heard her myself and she frightened me – and this is a true tale.

But the men still went ahead loading the coal, until, with only 300 tons more needed to bring her down to her marks, the poor ship gave such a sudden loud scream that the master stevedore jumped and turned pale, and blew his whistle to stop all work at once. For a while he scratched his head and looked troubled as he spat reflectively down the main hatch. Then, 'There's a war on,' said he, 'so we've got to give her the rest, I guess. We're breaking her heart, though, poor thing; but it's her back we'll break if we ain't careful. Put the hatches on Nos. 1 and 4, boys, and we'll try and finish her off amidships. And if she won't take it all, there, we'll leave it – for I'd sooner get fired than break a ship in half!'

So they finished her off amidships, and sent her out to sea.

It was a fine day, calm and hazy, as she steamed out into deep water, and she moved now without a sound, as if her teeth were clenched – and she trembled. She went along like a man who carries too heavy a burden, and presently she tripped and stumbled (it was only a little ground swell)

261

– and she opened out and fell apart like a flimsy old crate that some one had stepped on. In five seconds there was nothing there at all except a floating scum of coal dust, with some timbers and an odd man or two bobbing about in the middle of it.

Choosing a name for their boat led to a disagreement with his partner:

Jane is a good name, and there is no fancy nonsense about it. It is a pretty name too – for a girl. But I never can see a ship as a lady at all. I know it is unusual to feel like this about ships, and that a ship is a 'she' all the world over. I call ships 'shes' myself; but inside me I always think of a vessel as a man. And I think this feeling of mine is due to the fact that, although I am a seaman, I do not love the sea. I love to sail a ship; but I fear the sea, and all the while I am sailing on it I feel that I am safe solely because of the strength and courage of my ship – and *in spite* of the sea. I have feared the sea at times with a very great fear indeed; and I regard a ship, whose brave business it is to fight all its life against a remorseless, implacable and terrible enemy, as a warrior and not as a woman. So I put my foot down on George's *Jane*, and would have none of her.

Every detail of the new boat's design was determined by Martyr's experience of running away to sea in 1900 and spending the years before the First World War roaming around the Pacific in all manner of craft.

The *Southseaman's* insides are, I suppose, a little unusual, and this is due to the fact that, when I planned them, I imagined myself down below there, trying to get comfortable while a lot of wet and dirty weather outside was doing it best to thwart my desires. I have had to pass a considerable portion of my life aboard small craft of various kinds, and after a long and mixed experience of the life, I have come to two very definite conclusions concerning it. One is, that life on a small boat in fine weather is the only kind of life worth living. The other is that, in bad weather, it's just plain hell.

from *The Southseaman* by Weston Martyr

Hilaire Belloc was eighty-three when he died in 1953, acclaimed as a prolific poet, historian and essayist. His constant fascination was with the sea, which he sailed in two ancient pilot-cutters, neither of them designed or equipped beyond the standards prevailing in the latter part of the nineteenth century. His own skills as a sailor and navigator were painfully but never wholly achieved. In his first book about his experiences afloat he wrote of the challenge of sailing *Nona* alone across the Channel for the first time . . .

Certainly every man that goes to sea in a little boat of this kind learns terror and salvation, happy living, air, danger, exultation, glory and repose at the end; and they are not words to him but, on the contrary, realities which will afterwards throughout his life give the mere words a full meaning. And for this experiment there lies at our feet, I say, the Channel.

It is the most marvellous sea in the world – the most suited for these little adventures; it is crammed with strange towns, differing one from the other; it has two opposite people upon either side, and hills and varying climates, and the hundred shapes and colours of the earth, here rocks, there sand, there cliffs and there marshy shores. It is a little world. And what is more, it is a kind of inland sea.

*

The sea being calm, and the wind hot, uncertain and light from the east, leaving oily gaps on the water and continually dying down, I drifted one morning in the strong ebb to the South Goodwin Lightship, wondering what to do. There was a haze over the land and over the sea, and through the haze great ships a long way off showed, one or two of them, like oblong targets which one fires at with guns. They hardly moved in spite of all their canvas set, there was so little breeze. So I drifted in the slow ebb past the South Goodwin, and I thought: 'What is all this drifting and doing nothing? Let us play the fool and see if there are no adventures left.'

So I put my little boat about until the wind took her from forward, such as it was, and she crawled out the sea.

It was a dull, uneasy morning, hot and silent, and the wind, I say, was hardly a wind, and most of the time the sails flapped uselessly.

But after eleven o'clock the wind first rose, and then shifted a little, and then blew light but steady; and then at last she heeled and the water spoke under her bows, and still she heeled and ran, until in the haze I could see no more land; but ever so far out there were no seas, for the light full breeze was with the tide, the tide ebbing out as strong and silent as a man in anger, down the hidden parallel valleys of the narrow sea. And I held this little wind till about two o'clock, when I drank wine and ate bread and meat at the tiller, for I had them by me, and just afterwards, still through a thick haze of heat, I saw Gris-Nez, a huge ghost, right up against and above me; and I wondered, for I had crossed the Channel, now for the first time, and knew now what it felt like to see new land.

Though I knew nothing of the place, I had this much sense, that I said to myself: 'The tide is right down Channel, racing through the hidden valleys under the narrow sea, so it will all go down together and all come up together, and the flood will come on this foreign side much at the same hour that it does on the home side.' My boat lay to the east and the ebb tide held her down, and I lit a pipe and looked at the French hills and thought about them and the people in them, and England which I had left behind, and I was delighted with the loneliness of the sea; and still I waited for the flood.

But in a little while the chain made a rattling noise, and she lay quite slack and swung oddly; and then there were little boiling and eddying places in the water, and the water seemed to come up from underneath sometimes, and altogether it behaved very strangely, and this was the turn of the tide. Then the wind dropped also, and for a moment she lolloped about, till at last, after I had gone below and straightened things, I came on deck to see that she had turned completely round, and that the tide at last was making up my way, towards Calais, and her chain was taut and her nose pointed down Channel, and a little westerly breeze, a little draught of air, came up cool along the tide.

When this came I was very glad, for I saw that I could end my adventure before night. So I pulled up the anchor and fished it, and then turned with the tide under me and the slight half-felt breeze just barely filling the mainsail (the sheet was slack, so powerless was the wind), and I ran up along that high coast, watching eagerly every new thing; but I kept some way out for fear of shoals, till after three good hours under the reclining sun of afternoon, which glorified the mist, I saw, far off, the roofs and spires of a town and low piers running well out to sea, and I knew that it must be Calais. And I ran for these piers, careless of how I went, for it was already half of the spring flood tide, and everything was surely well covered for so small a boat, and I ran up the fairway in between the piers and saw Frenchmen walking about and a great gun peeping up over its earthwork, and plenty of clean new masonry. And a man came along and showed me where I could lie; but I was so strange to the place that I would not take a berth but lay that night moored to an English ship.

And when I had eaten and drunk and everything was stowed away and darkness had fallen, I went on deck, and for a long time sat silent, smoking a pipe and watching the enormous lighthouse of Calais, which is built right in the town, and which turns round and round above one all night long.

And I thought: 'Here is a wonderful thing! I have crossed the Channel in this little boat, and I know now what the sea means that separates France from England. I have strained my eyes for shore through a haze. I have seen new lands, and I feel as men do who have dreamed dreams.'

from *The Hills and the Sea* by Hilaire Belloc

Uffa Fox, maverick tearaway ex-choirboy, the terror of Isle of Wight women and policemen alike, built his fame on a succession of unbeatable International 14-foot dinghies turned out from his makeshift yard on a converted chain-ferry parked in the mud of the Medina River in Cowes. He hit upon the lines of a dinghy that was so easily driven that it would plane (surf) on the crest of even a moderate wave. But his genius was founded on earlier experiences as a blue-water sailor, making three transatlantic crossings in yachts long before they became commonplace. One was in 1923 in the Grand Banks schooner *Diablesse*, 46 feet on the waterline. In her he learned a lot about sea-kindly hulls, a strong rig and dependable shipmates, as the following passage from his autobiography makes clear:

On this night our way lay through the Nantucket Shoals which called for exact navigation and careful steering on the various compass bearings if we were to survive and not break up on the ever shifting, sandy shoals. It was a dark, wild night, with a great wind and flashing phosphorescent seas, and Bill Kelly as navigator read off the different courses and distances on the charts, while I steered them and trimmed our sails to suit. We swept through small, steep seas at terrific speed under all four lowers, driving hard through this early stage of an autumn gale, as this meant that the tide would have less effect on us through all these channels.

Throughout the night *Diablesse* tore along at her top speed under perfect control. It was tremendous fun, with every minute packed with thrills. Because of this great excitement, the night passed swiftly, although it was a long night as far as hours went, because it was near the autumnal equinox with twelve hours of daylight and twelve hours of darkness. We had sailed so fast that when daylight came we were well clear of all the shoals.

As now both Bill and I were tired out from sailing all the day before, and the excitement and energy we had expended through the night, we decided to lay *Diablesse* to. We took in all her sails except the foresail and eased the sheet of this a little, and now our perfect ship lay with her head tucked under her wing. She rode out this gale in her usual robust manner, throwing up the spray on either hand, and taking very little water on deck as she forged quietly ahead, hardly making any leeway. We were glad that we had a ship under us able to take care of herself and us when we were tired. She enabled us to rest, eat, and regain the energy we had expended in the previous twenty-four hours.

Diablesse now bowed and curtsied to the great sweeping seas, for she was hove to, and as her speed through the water was down to about one knot, her motion was far less than through the night when we were going between nine and eleven knots. The speed at which you travel is a measure of your discomfort. Going to windward our speed was seven knots and now hove to only one knot, and as you encounter seven times as many seas in the same space of time, it follows that at the speed of seven knots you strike every wave with seven times the power, as well as seven times as many waves, so therefore your motion is seven times more violent.

This is the reason why being hove to is so restful.

Through all that memorable night, as well as watching the flashing seas, I also spent a lot of time looking at the mast and sails as they danced to and fro across the night sky. Now that we were peacefully hove to I realised how much I had enjoyed the wild, reckless drive through the night, as had Bill Kelly and his schooner, which had already carried us safely some 5,000 miles across the Atlantic during the summer by way of Madeira and the

Bermudas. The three of us knew, understood, and had confidence each in the other.

from *The Joys of Life* by Uffa Fox

Like Bill Snaith (see p. 66) Carleton Mitchell is an enormously experienced offshore yachtsman who is also a naturally gifted writer. He will be remembered for ever as the outright winner of three consecutive Bermuda Races in his centreboard yawl *Finisterre*. Unusually for such a competitive racing skipper, he has also cruised all over the world. His observant eye has left us with a priceless collection of memorable pen-pictures. One critic described him as the writer-philosopher of the beat-to-windward generation. Unlike most cruising men, he is soon bored by calms and slow progress, as his description of a frustrating passage from Plymouth to Cowes makes clear:

It says in all the books that the English Channel is a windy place . . . with the peculiar and disagreeable steepness of sea produced by strong tidal currents. Yet when we left Plymouth (after 3000 miles racing at snail's pace across the Atlantic in a freak high pressure system) the dread Channel lay as smooth as the lake in Central Park.

I was proceeding on the simple meteorological premise that it had to blow when it hadn't for so long. We dropped lines from the floating quay, shouted over to *Janabel*, our French competitor, dipped a limp ensign at a corvette anchored in the inner harbor, and powered bravely past the breakwater with almost empty fuel tanks. The marina, that peculiarly American institution where yachtsmen may take aboard the necessities of life afloat – water, ice, gasoline or diesel oil, beer – did not exist. So out we went. After all, *Caribbee* was an ocean racing yawl, and easily driven hull 57 feet overall driven by 1585 square feet of working sail, with plenty more light stuff to hang aloft. And it simply had to blow.

Over the hill where Drake had bowled as the Spanish Armada approached carrying a breeze made famous by history, great cumulus clouds towered; not the clouds of wind, but of a lazy summer day along the shore, with bees droning in gardens and little boys splashing happily in ponds . . .

Our appreciation of nature began to fade in the afternoon off Bolt Head, a bold promontory. The tide turned foul and the wind trailed off to a whisper, barely enough to bend rising smoke from a cigarette. The genoa sheet sagged. Reluctantly we started the engine, running it slowly to conserve fuel.

At ten a gentle warm breeze and a new moon appeared astern together. Gratefully, thinking of the compensations of a sailor's life, we turned off the engine and set a spinnaker. It was a perfect night: now the breeze is striking in, we assured ourselves as little ripples began to feather along the track of the moon, now we will carry this on to Cowes and be in London in plenty of time . . . Optimism springs eternal in the sailor's breast. The log records with what little foundation:

Midnight. Jibed spinnaker.
0100. Becalmed after one hour reaching on port tack.
0115. No steerageway. Log line almost vertical.
0200. Log line tending aft. Regained bare steerageway.
0300. Wind since midnight has come from all directions except ahead. Now ahead. Spinnaker down, genoa up.
0420. Sighted Portland Bill light. On engine. Course altered for light.
0700. Hazy ahead. Mirror calm.

The fearsome English Channel lay as docile as a mountain pool. Pushed along by the engine, *Caribbee*'s bow wave ran out to form a perfectly smooth V which trailed far astern, unmarred. Piled clouds reflected with mirror clarity.

By nine o'clock we had almost had it: sounding revealed a bare spit of oil in one tank, a thin line scarcely dampening the stick in the other. Inshore, steep curling waves began to lift into the Race of Portland. Even with the engine turning, we were barely holding our own against the ebbing tide.

In desperation I studied the chart. Behind the Bill of Portland, a slim peninsula, I saw there was a buoyed channel into the fishing village of Weymouth. To reach it we would have to pass the fortified breakwater of Portland Naval Base, but I reasoned that as long as we gave the sacrosanct harbor a good berth we would not be molested. At Weymouth I was certain we would be able to find fuel. If we could make it.

Caribbee turned the corner and headed north, out of the worst of the tide. We soon could see the breakwater of the naval base, and the forts at the entrances which had protected inner installations from sorties by the Germans. Behind loomed the silhouettes of large vessels of the Royal Navy. Only a couple of miles to go . . .

But Gene Nichols, in charge of mechanical problems, who hovered over the tanks like a doctor administering a blood transfusion, suddenly looked up and said, 'We won't make it. Getting pretty low.'

'Haven't we anything? How about kerosene?'

He considered. 'I think there's a little left in the can. I'll see.'

While he burrowed into the lazarette I surreptitiously poured into the tank a large tin of salad oil from the galley, having once read how hero saved ship and girl by making port on the cargo of coconut oil. That was in the South Pacific, of course, and was in one of those magazines you buy while waiting for a train, but anyway I thought it worth a try. Gene added the kerosene. A peculiar smell arose, and from under our counter appeared a vapor plume not unlike a jet airplane at low altitude, but the engine didn't miss a beat.

The breakwater came closer, came abeam. Although the outer fortresses were unmanned, there was plenty of activity inside the harbor. A large aircraft carrier swung to a mooring. Nearby were a pair of cruisers and coveys of destroyers and lesser craft. Small boats darted back and forth.

The exhaust changed its steady rhythm. 'About empty,' announced Gene.

'How about the spare running lights and cabin lamp?'

'Okay,' he replied, and decanted a pitiful few drops from the fonts into the starboard tank.

We were exactly opposite the East Ship Channel of Her Majesty's Naval Operating Base. It looked battle scarred and formidable. Having served as lieutenant, junior grade, in a navy on the other side of the world, I knew people didn't go barging into combat establishments with pleasure vessels. It simply isn't done, and damn the reason. In a moment of panic I visualized whistles blowing and loudspeakers blaring if an admiral looked out of a window at Brooklyn or Norfolk to see a little boat barging in.

Yet I found myself swinging the wheel hard left. There are fates worse than a cleanly drilled death, and broiling windless, iceless and beerless in the English Channel seemed one of them. *Caribbee* passed beyond the sacred portals. Nobody paid the slightest attention. Diffidently we crept by frowning turrets and gaping muzzles without a challenge, but then could find no place to go. Quays were lined solid with ships in various stages of commission. Between them there were no gaps. Anchoring seemed unwise. The engine began to miss. I slipped out the clutch and *Caribbee* drifted to bare steerageway.

We came to a stop off what seemed to be the worst possible place to pick in a foreign navy yard, the submarine dock. Sleek grey monsters lay snout to tail, bristling with devices I was sure were on the top secret list. Aboard the nearest, an officer in fatigue uniform looked up from supervising a working party. He was the first person who had seemed aware of our existence. This is it, I thought, sunk without a trace far from home for illegal entry with intent to spy . . .

'I say,' called the officer. 'Would you chaps like to tie alongside?'

On the last gasp from our fuel we made it. The working party moved across the submarine's deck to take our lines. There was not the slightest flicker of curiosity on a single face. Obviously small yachts flying the American flag appeared out of the haze every hour on the hour at Her Majesty's Portland Marina.

'Hot today, what?' said the officer casually as we tried to adjust fenders to the rounded topsides.

'Certainly is.'

'Calm, too. Very calm lately,' said the officer.

'That's our trouble,' I answered, sensing an opening. 'We couldn't sail. No wind. We're out of fuel, and have to be in Cowes this afternoon.' I paused, gulped, and took the final plunge. 'Any place here where we can buy some diesel oil?'

He shook his head. 'I'm afraid not. But come aboard. We'll go see the CO.'

*

The captain became brisk. 'Biggs, tell the Supply Officer of *Caribbee*'s requirement. Bring me the forms. Keep them simple. I'll sign whatever necessary.' He turned back to me and smiled: 'A spot of reverse lend-lease, what?'

The Supply Officer arrived with a sheaf of papers. Captain Boord signed. The Supply Officer signed. They were handed over for me to sign.

Pen poised, I looked up. 'Twenty *tons?*' I queried feebly.

'Correct,' the Supply Officer said efficiently. 'Twenty tons of diesel oil. Present these in triplicate to the fueling depot and they'll pump it aboard.' He turned to the captain. 'We'll work it in on our generating allowance report. Cut the red tape.'

'But twenty tons!'

He looked at me. 'Isn't that what you want?'

'No. Twenty gallons.'

'Twenty *gallons?*' he repeated in horror. 'There is no way I can make out a requisition for twenty *gallons!*'

There was a long pause while the navy tried to conn through a sea of regulations. Lt. Squires saved the day. 'Pardon me, captain. But I could let him have it from the ship, with your permission, sir.'

We went back to the quay. Two men from the working party undogged a small circular hatch on the after deck of H.M.S. *Ambush* and disappeared. We bent a line on *Caribbee*'s deck bucket and lowered it into the depths of the submarine. A muffled shout arose, the bucket was hauled up, passed across, and poured into our funnel. Slowly we filled one tank.

from *The Wind Knows No Boundaries* by Carleton Mitchell

Navigation

The magnetic compass did not exist before the twelfth century. Until then ocean navigators relied on many other aids, from the stars to sighting birds on known flight paths and the behaviour of ocean swells relative to nearby islands. The temperature of the seawater and cloud patterns also provided useful pointers. In the broad wastes of the Pacific there were many astonishing long voyages made without charts or instruments of any kind. Dr David Lewis of *Ice Bird* fame in Antarctica has researched the methods of these early navigators by sailing along their tracks between islands hundreds of miles apart, using as navigators some of the descendants of the great Polynesian pilots, whose status in the islands was as great as any king's. Ramfe in Tikopia in the Reef Islands to the east of the Solomons described how he made one of his classic landfalls:

Ramfe kept the south-east trade wind abeam to port, and set course by holding the sinking Southern Cross over the tip of the outrigger.

After the Cross, *Rua Tangata*, had set, he used the stars that followed it in succession towards the south-western horizon. (It is noteworthy that Ramfe, untaught as he was, had no difficulty at all in steering by a constellation a good 30° from the actual guiding 'star' for the New Hebrides – the setting Scorpio.)

After daybreak the adventurers held course by the ever-changing bearings of the sun and by the feel of the swells that swept up from the southeast and passed beneath the canoe, lifting it up and rolling it over to starboard without any pitching motion at all.

'Steering by the seat of your pants,' I suggested.

'No,' Ramfe corrected me, 'by him,' and he gestured beneath his loin cloth towards his testicles.

Another night of light winds and they made land. They had been at sea 37 hours in all.

*

[Next] time Ramfe let Orion's Belt set on the port bow and then till dawn used a *kavenga*, or succession of stars that one after another followed it down over the western horizon. Once again sun and swells were his references by day. Birds were seen, but these were only, said Ramfe, 'birds of the "middle sea" ' – shearwaters probably, that range the open ocean disdaining land, and hence are no help in locating it.

'Birds are a nagivator's very best friends,' Teeta of Kuria was to tell me later, but those that he pointed to were terns, noddies and boobies, all species that roost ashore and fly out daily to their offshore fishing grounds. At first light, when they fly out from land and at dusk when they return, their flight path is an infallible signpost for the seaman. For the rest of the day the birds are interested only in shoals of fish, not in homing. The terns and noddies fish in mixed flocks 20–25 miles from shore; the boobies in smaller groups 30–35 miles out. This may not seem very far, but the sight range of a Pacific atoll from a canoe platform to the tops of the coconut palms is 10 miles, so birds more than treble a voyager's target.

Night fell over the little crew of Tikopians and the precisely ordered stars once more appeared. 'The compass may go wrong, the stars never,' a Tongan captain once remarked and, indeed, the stars do provide a small boat skipper, with far more exact alignments than does the gyrating card of a magnetic compass.

In the last hour before dawn Ramfe felt the canoe begin to check in its stride. The trade wind swell continued to sweep under it and hurry it forward but now it would hesitate momentarily to the slap of returning waves reflected back from land. Daylight revealed the land to be the mountainous Vanikoro, still some 30–35 miles away. The wind fell light and fickle, so it was late afternoon before the canoe glided through the reef pass into still water.

Ramfe's use of reflected waves set me feverishly re-examining accepted doctrine, which was that locating land by wave patterns was the exclusive preserve of the Micronesian Marshall Islanders. Now the technique had turned up in identical form in Polynesian Tikopia 1,100 miles to the south. Was this coincidence? It was not long before Ramfe's compatriot, Tupuai, provided the answer. He drew me the diagram . . . of reflected waves and how to use their angle as a guide towards land. The Tikopian and Marshallese wave analyses were identical. The Marshallese innovation was to represent wave or swell patterns, for teaching purposes, by means of 'stick charts'. These have nothing in common with Western charts. Rather, they are made to demonstrate, by curved coconut ribs and cowrie shells, the manner in which swells are bent and are reflected back by islands, and how, by 'reading' their junction lines, a seafarer may come safely to land.

I was to find land swell patterns to be a way of 'expanding' the target that was practised from one end of the Pacific to the other. Far from being confined to the Marshalls, it was part of the stock in trade of navigators on every group we visited. The only difference was how far offshore the phenomena were detected, and this appeared to be a function of the size of an island's underwater pediment rather than of the navigator's skill.

An even more exciting revelation was in store.

I must digress for a moment. The path each star traces from east to west across the sky remains much the same, at any rate, for centuries. At the zenith of its arc it passes right above points on the earth whose latitude equals the star's declination or celestial latitude.

It follows that an observer who notes that a particular star passes directly above his head will know his latitude to be the same as the celestial latitude of that star. For instance, if he has learned, as Hawaiian legend puts it, which stars 'are suspended severally over various lands, such as *Hokule‘a* [Arcturus] in the Hawaiian islands,' and he recognizes the star in the zenith to be *Hokule‘a* he knows he is in Hawaii's latitude. Similarly, if Sirius (declination 17°S.) passes right overhead, he must be in the latitude of Tahiti (17°S.) and also of Fiji (17°S.), for zenith stars indicate latitude (distance north or south) but not longitude (distance east or west).

The determination by zenith stars of what amounts, in our terms, to latitude, has long been postulated as a Polynesian navigational method, but on largely circumstantial evidence. Judge then my feelings when Ramfe broke off from pointing out *kavenga* stars, that touched the horizon round the points of the compass, to gesture casually above his head.

'The star on top is not the same as an island's guiding star (*kavenga*),' he said. 'It is a different thing. The star on top is no use for steering by. The star on top for Tikopia, Anuta and Vanikoro is *Manu*,' He indicated Rigel. 'When *Manu* is on top we know that Tikopia or Anuta or Vanikoro are nearby.'

'Nearby,' would, of course, only be applicable if the voyager was near the appropriate longitude. The three islands mentioned are all within 40 miles of latitude. Other lands, like the New Hebrides, Sikaiana and Rennell had different 'on top' stars, Ramfe continued. His grandfather had known them but he himself, did not.

This intelligence was later repeated independently, almost word for word, by Samoa and Tupuai at Nukufera.

The Tikopians' unexpected revelation would have been more significant, were it not for the fact that Rigel, whose declination is 8°15'S., does *not* pass over Tikopia, whose latitude is 12°17'S., but 240 miles north of the island. Even in A.D. 1000, when Rigel's declination was 9°25'S., the descrepancy was still 145 miles.

One possible explanation is that Tikopian zenith star observations may have been made by sighting up the sail. Throughout the south-east trade wind season, which is favourable for Tikopian voyaging, the wind would incline the sail north of the vertical, regardless of the tack it was on. The angle of heel in a moderate breeze would be 3° or 4°, so that Rigel would, in fact, be above the line of the masthead when the canoe was in the latitude of Tikopia.

*

Night fell. Tevake interrupted my thoughts by drawing my attention to the way our guide stars were sinking obliquely towards the north-west horizon and cautioning me that each one could only be used for a very short while. He himself was so well oriented by these awkwardly slanting stars that he was able to tell me confidently that the wind had backed 10°. I seriously doubted that such accuracy was attainable until Canopus rising dead astern confirmed that we were exactly on course and that the wind *had* changed precisely as Tevake had said.

As *Isbjorn* pitched and wallowed along beneath the supremely indifferent tropic stars, Tevake stood thoughtfully by the rail.

'Of course,' he said rather hesitatingly, looking back at me over his shoulder, 'you must know all about *te lapa*.' I truthfully denied knowing anything about it at all.

'Then look.' Tevake pointed over the side. 'No, not on top, deep down. You see him all same underwater lightning.' The phrase was apt. Streaks, flashes, and momentarily glowing plaques of light kept appearing a fathom below the surface. Tevake explained that *te lapa* streaks dart out from directions in which islands lie. The phenomenon is best seen eighty to a hundred miles out and disappears by the time a low atoll is well in sight. He stressed that it was quite different from ordinary surface luminescence. Tevake told me it was customary to steer by it on overcast nights.

*

A few months after I returned to Australia, Tevake wrote to ask if I was setting down all that he had taught me, adding that he was beginning to feel very old and was rapidly becoming weaker. I replied immediately, reassuring him.

Months later I heard the sequel. The spirit of Tevake, the dying tropic bird, could not be confined but must soar one more time to ultimate freedom. The veteran navigator had bade formal farewell to his family and lifetime friends on Nufilole and, seating himself in a one-man canoe, had paddled out into the ocean he loved on a voyage of no return. The seafarers of the world are diminished by his passing.

*

The origin of the Tuita clan is lost in time . . .

It was the blind Tuita, Kaho Mo Vailahi who, centuries later, thrust the family into the limelight. The story goes that a royal flotilla was returning to Tonga from Samoa where the king, as custom dictated, had gone to have his pants area tattooed (a king who flouted this convention is till remembered as Mataele 'Usitea – Mataele of the White Bottom). Akau'ola, assisted by Ula, was piloting the one-hundred-foot royal *kalia*, while the blind Tuita and his son Po'oi were in charge of a smaller double canoe. Time passed but land failed to materialize, until at last it was apparent that the unthinkable had happened, the High Navigator was lost. As a last resort the Tuita's *kalia* was summoned alongside and the undistinguished old man was called into consultation.

Blind Kaho bade his son Po'oi indicate where certain stars would appear and had him luff the *kalia* into a breaking wave, that he might feel and taste the spray in his face. Then he dipped his arm down into the sea.

'This is not Tongan water but Fijian,' he announced. 'The waves are from the Fiji Lau group near Lakemba island. Let us alter course to the westward.' Next morning they duly sighted Lakemba.

from *The Voyaging Stars* by Dr David Lewis

Writing thirty years earlier than David Lewis, Thor Heyerdahl, the leader of the Kon-Tiki expedition when five Norwegians sailed from Peru to the South Pacific islands on a raft, commented on the skill of the ancient Polynesians who blazed the same trail. He discounts the theories about swells and water temperature, but acknowledges their familiarity with the stars.

The old Polynesians were great navigators. They took bearings by the sun by day and the stars by night. Their knowldege of the heavenly bodies was astonishing. They knew that the earth was round, and had names for such abstruse conceptions as the equator and the northern and southern tropics. In Hawaii they cut charts of the ocean on the shells of round bottle gourds, and on certain other islands they made detailed maps of plaited boughs to which shells were attached to mark the islands, while the twigs marked particular currents. The Polynesians knew five planets, which they called wandering stars, and distinguished them from the fixed stars, for which they had nearly two hundred different names. A good navigator in old Polynesia knew well in what part of the sky the different stars would rise, and where they would be at different times of the night and at different times of the year. They knew which stars culminated over the different islands, and there were cases in which an island was named after the star which culminated over it night after night and year after year.

Apart from the fact that the starry sky lay like a glittering giant compass revolving from east to west, they understood that the different stars right over their heads always showed them how far north of south they were. When the Polynesians had explored and brought under their sway their present domain, which is the whole of the sea nearest to America, they maintained traffic between some of the islands for many generations to come. Historical traditions relate that when the chiefs from Tahiti visited Hawaii, which lay more than 2,000 sea miles farther north and several degrees farther west, the helmsman steered first due north by sun and stars, till the stars right above their heads told them that they were on the latitude of Hawaii. Then they turned at a right angle and steered due west till they came so near that birds and clouds told them where the group of islands lay.

Whence had the Polynesians obtained their vast astronomical knowledge, and their calendar, which was calculated with astonishing thoroughness? Certainly not from Melanesian or Malayan peoples to the westward. But the same old vanished civilised race, the 'white and bearded men' who had taught Aztecs, Mayas and Incas their amazing culture in America, had evolved a curiously similar calendar and a similar astronomical knowledge which Europe in those times could not match.

In Polynesia, as in Peru, the calendar year had been so arranged as to begin on the particular day of the year when the constellation of the Pleiades first appeared above the horizon, and in both areas this constellation was considered the patron of agriculture.

In Peru, where the continent slopes down towards the Pacific, there stand to this day in the desert sand the ruins of an astronomical observatory of great antiquity, a relic of the same mysterious civilised people which carved stone colossi, erected pyramids, cultivated sweet potatoes and bottle gourds, and began their year with the rising of the Pleiades. Kon-Tiki knew the stars when he set sail upon the Pacific ocean.

from *The Kon-Tiki Expedition* by Thor Heyerdahl

In 1892 the Revd J. J. Curling was vicar of Hamble. Few parishioners realized that in his previous mission he had given lectures on coastal navigation to the fishermen of the Bay of Islands in Newfoundland until he wrote a manual on the subject which became a standard work. Besides being an ordained priest, he had been commissioned in the Royal Engineers, which is, no doubt, where he became interested in navigation, as so many sappers have to this day. He also held a Board of Trade Certificate to command his own yacht.

It is hard to realize that even then there was no better way of estimating a ship's speed through the water than using a sand-glass to time a knotted line as it was streamed over the taffrail. Once there was an unfortunate sailor in a crack clipper ship holding the reel from which the log-line ran out as though it had just hooked a sailfish. The line came up all-standing at 12 knots with such violence that it jerked the sailor overboard to an untimely end. He happened to be Chinese, and was there and then immortalized by the expression '12 knots and a Chinaman' referring to speeds past the stops, somewhere over that speed. In the Golden Age of Sail that might well be 20 knots.

Measurent of Distance at Sea – Distance at sea is measured by means of a Patent Log, or by a log-line and log-ship with a 14 sec. or 28 sec. sand-glass, or by a watch with a seconds hand.

Patent Log – A patent log is towed continually from the quarter with line enough to clear the eddies in the ship's wake; it consists of a rotator, to which vanes are attached to make it rotate as it is towed through the water; these vanes are fitted at such an angle with the axis of the rotator that the revolutions made by the log in passing through a certain distance correspond with the distance registered by three dials contained in the log itself. These dials measure tenths, or quarters, units, and tens of miles respectively, up to 100 miles.

Common Log – The common log consists of a flat piece of wood called the log-ship, made in the shape of a quadrant, the circular edge being loaded with sufficient lead to make it float upright in the water; one side of the quadrant should be about 6 in. long. Sometimes a conical canvas bag, about 4 in. diameter in the mouth, and 9 in. or 10 in. in length, is used instead of the wooden log-ship. The log-line is attached to the log-ship by three legs of line, each 3 ft. long, so that the log-ship may offer a little resistance and so keep its position in the water. One of these legs is fastened to the log-ship by a bone peg, that readily comes out through the pressure of the water against the log-ship, when it is hauled in board after the rate of sailing has been determined. When used, the log and some portion of the line known as the 'stray-line' is thrown over the stern; the log, soon losing the impetus or speed of the vessel, remains stationary in the water, and the line is permitted to run out freely as the ship sails onward for an interval of time marked by the sand-glass.

Log-line – In order to measure the ship's rate of sailing in sea miles per hour, the length of a knot on the log-line must bear the same proportion to a sea mile that the seconds of the sand-glass bear to an hour.

Now in 1 hour there are 3600 sec. And in one sea mile there are 6080 feet; therefore to calculate the length of a knot on the log-line:

3600 sec. : 28 sec. :: 6080 ft. : required length = 47.3 feet.

If a 14 sec. glass be employed, the number of knots read from a log-line constructed with knots of 47.3 ft. each must be doubled.

The log-line is marked with a piece of bunting at the end of the stray line, which should be 12 fathoms long.

One knot at every half knot.

A piece of leather at the first knot.

Two knots at two knots.

Three knots at three knots, and so on.

The log-line should be wetted before being marked, and the lengths of each knot frequently measured to insure the constant correctness of the log-line; it is wound on a reel, from which it can be readily paid out without checks. The tenths of a knot can be easily reckoned by hand, when the log is hauled in.

from *Coastal Navigation* by Revd J. J. Curling

Weston Martyr and his friend George set sail from Sheldon, Nova Scotia, with the intention of sailing their new 42-foot schooner *Southseaman* to Bermuda before taking her to New York, where circumstances would oblige them to sell her to the first serious bidder. Crossing the Gulf Stream they encountered violent local storms and spent some time hove-to with sea anchors streamed. Unpredictable eddies carried them far off course and they had no radio aids, so it is not surprising that they missed the island altogether. It is not until much later in his narrative that he acknowledges that his homecoming landfall at Montauk Point at the eastern end of Long Island was due to their having sailed into a fleet of rum-running schooners at anchor fifteen miles off shore awaiting transhipment of their bootleg cargoes to high-speed motorboats.

When we set out we intended to reach New York by way of the Bermudas; but, as you shall see, we could not find those elusive isles, so we voyaged on, fifteen hundred miles from Sheldon, to the south and eastward, until we reached the western fringe of the Sargasso Sea in 60 W. and 25 N. Then we turned round and sailed for New York; and we covered close on three thousand miles in all without seeing a sign of any land between Cape Sable, our departure, and Montauk Point, our landfall. Most landsmen to whom I have talked about this cruise appeared to think it must have been a very terrible and wearying experience; but all men who love the sea will know better. To doubters and scoffers I like to tell the story of the New Bedford whaler who returned to his home port with an empty ship after a long, long whaling voyage. His friends were very sorry for him, and commiserated with him to such an extent that finally he blew up. 'See here,' said he, 'we've been out three years, and we never seen a whale; but, by Gee! I'll tell the world *we had one hell of a fine sail.*' Well – so did George and I.

His views on finding one's way across the oceans still command respect, as they would have done amongst early Polynesian navigators:

I think this is a good place to tell you about our methods of navigation. Nine days before we sailed from Sheldon neither George nor I could have found our position by an astronomical observation if our very lives had depended on it; and, now that we were out of sight of land and our lives *did* more or less depend upon our knowledge of nautical astronomy, I personally could not have recognised the First Point of Aries from a hole in the ground. But George could – or said he could. George had taken eight short and hectic lessons in navigation from Old Cap. Jennings, and he was now the proud owner of an old sextant, a chronometer watch older still, and a collection of tables, text-books, and almanacs through which he could not as yet find his way, but which he hoped to master before we made our next landfall. I hoped so too.

Judging from what I have just written, it might appear that George and I were looking for trouble – with every prospect of finding it. Knowing next to nothing about scientific navigation, we were setting out on a long voyage with the certainty before us of having to make some very difficult landfalls. However, we did know a thing or two, and we had a very clear idea of what we were up against, so that we were not really a couple of such innocent and unsophisticated babes in the wood as might appear. For one thing, George, who once upon a time had been a banker, was a great hand at figures, and he was confident that, with study, practice, and luck, he would be able to find the reefs off Bermuda before they found us. And if George failed, then – that was where I came in. I – But this will not do. I see that my particular brand of navigation requires a paragraph or two to itself.

There are two methods of finding a ship's position on the face of the waters: (1) by scientific calculation; (2) by empirical guess; and, though no scientist or certificated navigator will ever admit it, there are points about No. 2 which mark it as superior in many respects to No. 1, and which seem to indicate that the empirical guessing scheme is the one for the small boat sailorman to follow if he wishes to find his way in safety across the seas.

*

Once, during those dreadful years when I was slave to a down-town New York broker, I went in for a course of navigation. It was a course run by a correspondence school that advertised extensively and fiercely. . . . I took that course seriously, I can tell you. It turned out to be an extremely good and thorough course – in spite of those flamboyant advertisements – and I worked hard at it. I used to fancy myself greatly as a seaman in those days, and I actually believed there was very little about seamanship anybody could tell me. And after five weeks of my course I began to see myself a navigator as well! Before that time I had always carried about with me a secret shame. I could splice wire and sail a ship to wind'ard; but I could not shoot the sun or work out a sight. Another few weeks of this course, said I to myself, and I'll be able to look the Astronomer-Royal in the eye without blushing. I was a proud man, I assure you. Then along came the next week's lesson, and it was all about spherical triangles. Before I read that lesson I had no idea there were such things in the world as spherical triangles, and when I had read my lesson once I still could not see how a triangle could be spherical anyway . . .

The spherical triangles completely defeated me – and they do still. I gave up. I gave up my course. I gave up the spherical triangles. I gave up the hope of ever being a scientific navigator.

However, I was not, after all, very much cast down by that business. I thought of all those old-time sailors who explored the seas of this world – most unscientifically, but most successfully. These old gentlemen sailed about the oceans with no instrument except a compass to guide them; but all the same they seem to have managed very well. I thought of my old skipper, Captain Bloody Webb, who sailed his schooner safely for years and years all over the North and South Pacific with nothing but a battered old quadrant, which he *never* used, and a locked mahogany chronometer case – in which he kept the ship's money. He may have kept a chronometer there too, but he certainly never wound it. I thought, too, of those Banks schooner skippers, who sometimes never see the land for six months on end, but who navigate from spot to spot with precision, by instinct, I think, and their sense of smell. I remembered also some voyages of my own: a seven hundred mile passage, for instance, through ten days of gale and calm, head winds and fog, when, navigating by the empirical guessing system, I made my desired landfall dead ahead. This may have been luck, and the successful termination of some other long passages may have been luck too. But I do not think so. I think I must just be a natural born empirical guesser.

*

. . . Let the Celestial Bodies withdraw themselves demurely behind a veil of cloud, and the scientific navigator is immediately ruined. It is no fun being a scientific navigator, running, for instance, under an obscured sky before a gale of wind to a port situated somewhere ahead upon a perilous lee shore. At a time like that a ship is fortunate if there be an empirical guesser aboard, for *he* will be the man to guide her safely into harbour. The blotting out of the sun, or a moon or two, or all the stars cannot prevent a master of that fine art known as dead reckoning from fixing the position of his ship.

Any one can learn to shoot the sun; but to be able, *at any time*, to put a finger on the chart and say, with confidence, 'We are *here*,' one must first be a seaman of long experience, skilled in the art of guessing right, with a power of reasoning out the effect of all the forces of wind and tide and sea, and have a sense within one that is akin to the instinct of the homing bird. *This* is a fine art, as I said before.

from The Southseaman by Weston Martyr

It has to be said that not only did Weston Martyr sail past Bermuda without sighting the island during his shake-down cruise, but he repeated the trick next year. *Southseaman* had been bought by an inexperienced owner for the 1923 Bermuda Race on the condition that he and George took charge. But for doing so, they might well have won instead of suffering the humiliation of crossing the line after the race committee had packed up and gone home, thirty-six hours after the boat ahead.

Notwithstanding this setback, he so fired the enthusiasm of a number of likeminded cruising men in Britain with the idea of racing offshore that he was responsible for initiating the Fastnet Race in 1925, which led to the formation of the Royal Ocean Racing Club. Not everyone shared his enthusiasm. Many pundits, including the cruising guru Claud Worth, pronounced the venture unseamanlike. The Royal Yacht Squadron denied the fleet of seven starters the use of their line for the start.

The author of the following passage, written in 1987, had not read Weston Martyr's book at the time. All that has happened in the intervening sixty years relevant to the point at issue is that quartz-crystal movements for clocks and watches has greatly diminished the chronometer as being a prime source of major navigational errors.

I rate simultaneous star shots at morning or evening twilight as not worth the bother. In ideal conditions – so rarely found in a yacht – a set of stars with Polaris (the feeble but easily found North Star) and three other correctly identified stars will give you an instant fix of potentially high reliability; but typically you find yourself cold and wet on deck at night with five-eighths cloud and only fleeting glimpses of your preselected stars between douches of cold seawater.

Naturally the quality of the horizon degenerates quickly at dusk, while the stars themselves melt away at dawn. The whole business of sitting around waiting to fire from the hip is tedious not only for the navigator but also for his chosen timekeeper. Then follows the chore of working it all out. Robin Knox-Johnston sailed 27,000 miles around the world in 313 days without taking a star sight except on rare occasions for fun or to pass the time.

from *The Shell Guide to Yacht Navigation* by Captain John Coote

Since Weston Martyr wrote, Dr Marvin Creamer has completed a solo circumnavigation without any instruments whatever, not even a wristwatch or a clock. Also Commander Bill King of *Galway Blazer* fame made all three of his long-distance passages including one around the world without taking star sights.

Most of the epic single-handed voyages were undertaken with insufficient funds to back them, which manifests itself in yachts being less than properly equipped for tackling huge distances offshore. In Robin Knox-Johnston's case his ketch *Suhaili* was distinctly short of many navigation aids. For example he only carried seventeen charts to see him round the world, and one of them was rubber-stamped 'Not to be used for navigation'. It is interesting that he never took star sights except in especially benign weather, and then just to pass the time. The reason for relying entirely on sun sights is that the quality of the horizon at dawn or dusk as seen from the deck of a wildly heaving yacht is likely to lead to unreliable results.

The charts I took were sufficient as I did not plan to put in anywhere, but the Admiralty ice chart would have been a useful addition. A larger-scale chart of Foveaux Strait would have been useful as things turned out and since I planned to go through there from the start I should have taken one. I had more charts than I needed for Cape Horn, but better safe than sorry. In retrospect, a large-scale chart of Otago Harbour might also have saved me from some embarrassment!

For fixing my position at sea out of sight of land I used my ageing Plath sextant, and an old but reliable chronometer. I gave up using my patent log with its 100 foot log line as it proved inaccurate, and once the log line became covered with gooseneck barnacles it was nothing but a drag to our progress. I had no electronic navigational aids because I could not afford them before I set out, but a Direction Finder and Echo Sounder would have been useful. As a general rule I took one sight only at a time instead of the more usual three from which you can get an average position, but I took some care over this one. My reasoning was that as it took me well over a minute to get below, take the chronometer time, write down the readings and scramble back on deck, an average of sights taken over a period of 2 to 3 minutes would be of little greater use than one sight taken with care. As a rule I took one sight early in the morning to obtain the longitude, and the Meridian Altitude at noon for the latitude. If approaching land I would take another sight in the afternoon, and although I was always prepared to take star sights I never found it necessary. On the occasions I managed to check my navigation I was usually within a mile or so of where I expected.

As far as Pilots, Tide Tables and Light lists are concerned, I had all I wanted.

from *A World of My Own* by Robin Knox-Johnston

The coastwise trade in schooners during the inter-war years was carried out with minimal aids to navigation.

In my first schooners I rarely saw a chart. Occasionally, I glimpsed one of the 'blue backs', published by Imray, Laurie, Norie & Wilson, which were the most popular, being easy to read and covering a large area of the coast.

When I was 'boy' in the *Via*, her old captain once proudly showed me his one and only chart. It was of the Irish Sea and was the oldest chart I've ever set eyes on, outside of museums. Tattered, yellow with age and so stained and mildewed it was almost unreadable, it reminded me of the one in the story of the old shipmaster and his mate poring over their chart and the captain, with his spectacles perched on the end of his nose, stubbing his thumb at a mark on the chart, saying: 'Is this 'ere a buoy, Bill, or is it just another bit of fly muck?'

Light lists were not much in evidence, either. I can only remember once seeing an out-dated Reed's Home Trade, opened at the light list, during my early schoonering.

. . . Even barometers and cabin clocks were considered luxuries.

I gradually picked up the arts of a schoonerman in the time-honoured way: by keeping my eyes and ears open. I soon realised our greatest danger was the land and the prime factor in navigating a sailing vessel was to give her a safe offing under every condition of weather. Our captains had the most intimate knowledge of the sailing qualities of their commands and, making due allowances for tidal set and leeway, they were able to make the most astonishingly accurate estimates of our progress. Headlands and seamarks always materialised as predicted. I doubt if a mechanical log could have measured our erratic progress with such accuracy. It certainly couldn't have compensated for tide and leeway.

from *Schoonerman* by Captain Richard England

SWEETHEARTS AND WIVES

In every mess I find a friend, in every port a wife
But the standing toast, that pleased the most,
Was the wind that blows, the ship that goes,
And the lass that loves a sailor.

Charles Dibdin

Jack's Molls – 'Wives' Afloat

Not all women on board ships in Nelson's day were whores.There were a few wives entered on the books, some of them carrying marriage lines to prove it. Their survival depended on each captain's own attitude in these matters. Some of the ladies afloat were of the stuff of Hollywood legends, like the Irish daughter of a lawyer who went out to the West Indies, Anne Bonny. She married the pirate John Rackham, better known as Calico Jack, and fought alongside him until his capture in 1720. Before he met his end after trial in Jamaica she said her adieus, ending with a quote worthy of her namesake in later American folklore: 'If you had fought like a man, there would be no need to hang like a dog.' She was acquitted because she was pregnant. For women determined to go to sea it was easy enough to buy sailors' clothes in the Dockyard ports. How long they survived undetected on board was a matter of luck:

Conspicuous among women who threw the dust of successful deception in the eyes of masters and shipmates is Mary Anne Talbot. Taking to the sea as a girl in order to 'follow the fortunes' of a young naval officer for whom she had conceived a violent but unrequited affection, she was known afloat as John Taylor. In stature tall, angular and singularly lacking in the physical graces so characteristic of the average woman, she passed for years as a true shellback, her sex unsuspected and unquestioned. Accident at length revealed her secret. Wounded in an engagement, she was admitted to hospital in consequence of a shattered knee, and under the operating knife the identity of John Taylor merged into that of Mary Anne Talbot.

It is said, perhaps none too kindly or truthfully, that the lady doctor of the present day no sooner sets up in practice than she incontinently marries the medical man around the corner, and in many instances the sailor-girl of former days brought her career on the ocean wave to an equally romantic conclusion. However skilled in the art of navigation she might become, she experienced a constitutional difficulty in steering clear of matrimony. Maybe she steered for it.

A romance of this description that occasioned no little stir in its day is associated with a name at one time famous in the West-India trade. Through bankruptcy the name suffered eclipse, and the unfortunate possessor of it retired to a remote neighbourhood, taking with him his two daughters, his sole remaining family. There he presently sank under his misfortunes. Left alone in the world, with scarce a penny-piece to call their own, the daughters resolved on a daring departure from the conventional paths of poverty.

Making their way to Portsmouth, they there dressed themselves as sailors and in that capacity entered on board a man-o'-war bound for the West Indies. At the first reduction of Curaçoa, in 1798, as in subsequent naval engagements, both acquitted themselves like men. No suspicion of the part they were playing, and playing with such success, appears to have been aroused till a year or two later, when one of them, in a brush with the enemy, was wounded in the side. The surgeon's report terminated her career as a seaman.

Meanwhile the other sister contracted tropical fever, and whilst lying ill was visited by one of the junior officers of the ship. Believing herself to be dying, she told him her secret, doubtless with a view to averting its discovery after death. He confessed that the news was no surprise to him. In fact, not only had he suspected her sex, he had so far persuaded himself of the truth of his suspicions as to fall in love with one of his own crew. The tonic effect of such avowals is well known. The fever-stricken patient recovered, and on the return of the ship to home waters the officer in question made his late foremast hand his wife.

from *The Press Gang* by J. R. Hutchinson

The superstition amongst sailors that women on board spell bad trouble may have receded, but was certainly not taken seriously in Nelson's day, when HM ships had them on board in considerable numbers with the tacit approval of their commanding officers, even if the Regulations explicitly outlawed them.

Captain Robert Wauchope was an exception. He accepted an appointment as flag captain on the condition that prostitutes should not be allowed on board. For his pains he was hauled before the First Sea Lord – none other than Nelson's Hardy – and informed that his objection was contrary to the wishes of the Admiralty and he must therefore give up his commission. It was touch and go for Captain Wauchope, who had to appeal over the First Sea Lord's head to remain on the active list. He went on to become an Admiral.

Admiral Hardy would have been well aware that women fought alongside their lovers and protectors at the Nile and Trafalgar. He may have had a hand denying three of them their claims to be awarded the campaign medals struck after those victories. But, like it or not, they were always there in the foetid bilges and liable to appear at unexpected moments:

In May, 1815, the *Horatio* struck on a needle rock, and the sea came flooding in at the rate of eight inches a minute. All hands were turned to the pumps; after a quarter-hour of frantic exertions an attempt was made to build up a rim of water-resistant oakum around the gash, press a sail down over it, and seal its edges with more oakum. This process was called *thrumming*. But thrumming on this scale took time and sufficient helpers, all hands were needed at the pumps, and the situation was of desperate extremity.

All at once five women appeared on the scene. Only one of them was known to the officer relating the episode; she was the boatswain's wife. By his manner of reference to the others he had never set eyes of any of them, which points to the reasonable inference that they were stowaways. Quickly they took over at the lethal break, releasing the men who were needed at the pumps, and 'rendered essential service in thrumming the sail'. The moment they succeeded in sticking it down firmly, 'a change was felt at the pumps', says the narrator, and one hears the great breath of relief. The rate of pumping, a singularly terrible exertion, is specified in Admiralty papers: 500 to 800 strokes a minute for serious emergency, or eight to twelve strokes a second respectively. The ship being saved, the four unknown apparitions melted away again into their secret holes.

Yet, if only to one person, and by implication rather than relation, the narrative seems infinitely moving. The lieutenant knew nothing, or seemed to know nothing, of the four stowaways; the boatswain's wife, on the other hand, must have known all about them. How otherwise could she have recruited her working team from the hold as quickly as she did? But her knowledge she had kept to herself, till faced by the threat of the ship's going down with all hands. Was her earlier silence through mere silent partisanship of sex? through obscure compassion for those fallen into the nethermost pit, whose lot she would not make harder by betrayal? Had her connivance even extended to leaving food where it could be spirited away with least risk of observation?

Such considerations, if they existed, never found their way into official records. But what we do know is that, having considerably helped to save the ship, they received no word of thanks, and equally, of course, no reward.

In earlier days there had been an even more bizarre discovery that women were secreted and maintained on board in the darkest corners of those unlit ships:

On July 10, 1763, 'a Woman was found dead and sewed up in a Hammacoe in the Bread Room on board of His Majesty's Ship *Defiance*'. A week later, 'a Court Martial assembled on board His Majesty's ship *Essex*, for inquiry into the cause [case], and for trying' several men 'for being the Cause of her Death'.

*

Henry Dearing, late Master-at-Arms of the *Defiance*, sworn:

I heard in the month of May last while the Ship was at Sea, rumoured among the People between Decks that there was a dead Woman in the Ship abaft down below. I know no more of it.

It turned out that she had been secretly attended by the surgeon's mate during her last illness, when he'd 'bled her, given her a Vomit and then a grain of Opium'. The court martial acquitted those involved and ruled that the prostitute's death had been due to natural causes.

The problem came to a head in 1822 with the publication of an anonymous pamphlet, which laid it on the line:

A STATEMENT OF CERTAIN IMMORAL PRACTICES IN H.M.'S NAVY, thrust the problem into broad daylight and made no bones about it.

This STATEMENT was a pamphlet of some sixty pages setting forth the experiences of the writer, and of four other Naval officers like himself, on H.M. ships in port unreservedly yielded up, by time-honoured custom, to the waterfront prostitute.

It is frequently the case that men take two prostitutes on board at a time, so that sometimes there are more women than men on board. The lower deck is already much crowded by the ship's own company; you may figure . . . the intolerable confusion and filth . . . when an addition of as many women as men is made to this crowd. Men and women are turned by hundreds into one large compartment, and in sight and hearing of each other shamelessly and unblushingly couple like dogs.

The pamphlet touches on the situation of the families of married seamen who wish to pay a visit while the ship is in port:

Wives and families, sometimes comprising daughters from 10 to 15 years of age, are forced either to witness these scenes, or to forego altogether the society of their husbands and parents. For all inhabit the same deck, huddled together whatever be their age or sex or character, eating, drinking and sleeping without any screen or separation between, and with every licentious propensity being unrestrainedly indulged.

Parents know nothing, he continues, of what they plunge their boys into when permitting them to enter the Naval Service:

The same abominations are going on in the midshipmen's births [sic]. A mid of 14 or 15 who had come on board only the day before, was thrust into bed with a prostitute by one of the lieutenants. It was the practice of the younger mids and boys to 'row guard' (as the expression was) between decks, seeking a connection with the superfluous women. Moreover they are ridiculed if they have not yet entered what God emphatically calls 'the paths of hell'.

The author now dares to mention, in this pamphlet accessible to the general public, the most cruel of the damaging effects:

The consequence is that two of the midshipmen contracted a foul disease, as well as many of the boys.

Allusion to the forbidden term conducts to the unexpected revelation that some commanders are attempting preventive measures; such attempts, though clearly sporadic, seem to indicate a state of modern medical practice already past its dawn:

Before the seaman is allowed to take his prostitute on the lower deck, IN MANY SHIPS *it is insisted to get her examined by the assistant surgeon; if she is infected, she is sent out of the ship. But in one vessel, after every precaution was taken, one of these poor creatures died on board, of the venereal disease.*

The response of Naval surgeons to this new duty illustrates a corresponding ambivalence of medical attitudes:

It must be mentioned, to the honour of the assistant surgeons in the Navy, that SOME *of them have resisted the order of their captains, and have chosen to brave the consequences rather than submit to actions so degrading.*

The pamphlet ends by entreating some official and permanent regulation to deal with the abuse misnamed 'the indulgence'.

It was catch-22 for those in command. Shore leave could not be risked for ships' companies made up mainly of pressed men who were kept on board for years. Even though ships reaching port moored a long way off shore – to discourage swimmers – the necessary solace for sex-starved Jack Tars was soon delivered alongside in full view of the officer of the watch and the master-at-arms.

'After having moored our ship, swarms of boats came around us, a great many of them freighted with a cargo of ladies: a sight truly gratifying, for our crew of 600 had seen but one woman in 18 months. So soon as these boats came alongside, the seamen flocked down pretty quick and brought their choice up, so that we had about 450 aboard.'

Here is one example where his natural kindness betrays him.

'Of all the human race, these poor young creatures are the most pitiable; the ill-usage and degradation they are driven to submit to, are indescribable; but from habit they become callous, and so totally lost to all sense of shame, that they seem to retain no quality which belongs to a woman, but the shape and name. On the arrival of any man-o-war in port these girls flock down to the shore, where boats are always ready.'

But others beside the girls have a money-stake in the game.

'As they approach the boat, the boatman surveys them from stem to stern; and carefully culls out the best-looking, and the most dashingly dressed, observing to one that she is *too old*; to another, she is *too ugly*; he will not be able to sell them, and he'll be damned if he has his trouble for nothing.'

Jack explains this selectiveness in terms of percentage. The boatman, beside his regular fare, gets three shillings of what the girl gets, and on a good day his takings may be five pounds. But if the cargo is too unattractive, 'officers have been known to lean over the rail and tell the boatman to push off with his lot of ugly devils; he will not allow his men to have them. The girls,' he adds 'are not sparing of their epithets on such occasions'.

The Queen's Regulations and Admiralty Instructions on the subject were not enforceable until after 1861, when shore leave became a matter of routine. For the next hundred years the prohibition against women in warships was rigorously enforced. The skipper of a US nuclear submarine was summarily relieved of his command on the direct orders of Admiral Rickover because pictures appeared in a local Florida newspaper showing that go-go girls had been on the upper deck during a brief harbour movement from one berth to another.

Now both the Russians and the Americans have women officers at sea, but fulfilling different roles from those which gave rise to the time-honoured toast on Saturday nights in all wardrooms: 'To sweethearts and wives . . . may they never meet.'

from *The Hidden Navy* by Evelyn Berckman

In the middle of the eighteenth century, when the press-gangs were most active, there were many stories of imposters who rounded up men and then sold them to crimps whose business it was to find the crews for merchantmen. It had its lighter moments. The hangers referred to in this extract were cudgels:

> The most successful sham gang ever organised was perhaps that said to have been got together by a trio of mischievous Somerset girls. The scene of the exploit was the Denny-Bowl quarry, near Taunton. The quarrymen there were a hard-bitten set and great braggarts, openly boasting that no gang dare attack them, and threatening, in the event of so unlikely a contingency, to knock the gangsmen on the head and bury them in the rubbish of the pit. There happened to be in the neighbouring town 'three merry maids,' who heard of this tall talk and secretly determined to put the vaunted courage of the quarrymen to the test. They accordingly dressed themselves in men's clothing, stuck cockades in their hats, and with hangers under their arms stealthily approached the pit. Sixty men were at work there; but no sooner did they catch sight of the supposed gang than they one and all threw down their tools and ran for their lives.

from *The Press Gang* by J. R. Hutchinson

Piracy was never so profitable as it was along the south-east coast of China in the early days of the nineteenth century. One group of 800 large pirate-junks and 1,000 auxiliaries was led by Ching Yih, who ran his organization along strict naval lines – indeed he was adressed as 'Chief Admiral'.

> One of the most successful pirates of that time was a very young man named Chang Paoa who was attached to the Red Squadron. He came from

Sin Huy, to the south-west of Canton, and was fishing with his father when they were captured by Ching Yih and forced into piracy. He was made captain of one of the pirate-junks and became the favourite of Mrs. Ching.

In 1807 Ching Yih lost his life when his junk foundered in a typhoon, but his wife, Ching Yih Saoa, survived. She took over command of all the squadrons and sailed in Chang Paoa's junk, promoting him to the command of the red squadron. It would appear that these lady pirates were great lovers as well as being cruel and bloodthirsty fighters. Chang Paoa was young and handsome, and there is little doubt that his ability to make love, as well as his prowess in battle, was a deciding factor in Mrs. Ching living on board his junk. Aku, a helper of pirates who had her American paramour, and Lai Choi San, a most bloodthirsty woman pirate – they will both be mentioned later – were also known to combine promiscuity with piracy.

Mrs. Ching made three regulations for her pirate fleet and insisted that Chang saw they were carried out:

(1) If any man goes privately on shore, or what is called transgressing the bars, he shall be taken and his ears perforated in the presence of the whole fleet; repeating the same act he shall suffer death.

(2) Not the least thing shall be taken from the stolen and plundered goods. All shall be registered and the pirate receive for himself out of ten parts only two, eight parts belonging to the storehouse called the general fund; taking anything out of this general fund, without permission, shall be death.

(3) No person shall debauch at his pleasure captive women taken in the villages and open places and brought on board a ship (junk), he must first request the ship's purser for permission, and then go aside in the ship's hold. To use violence against any woman or to wed her without permission, shall be punished with death.

On Mrs. Ching's instructions Chang ordered that wine, rice, and other goods obtain from the villagers should be paid for, and capital punishment meted out to pirates who took these goods by force without paying for them. For this reason the pirates were never in want of provisions, gunpowder and other necessities for carrying on their activities. This strong discipline was introduced in 1807 by Mrs. Ching, but it seems that it was only a practice in theory and had to be altered following the action taken by the Chinese Government.

Mrs. Ching insisted on every transaction being carried out by written application. The pirates called the purser 'the ink and writing master' and plunder became known as 'a transhipping of goods'. If the captain of a pirate-junk left the line of battle when engaged with the enemy he could be charged with desertion, and, if found guilty, beheaded. Mrs. Ching did nothing by halves.

The after-end of these pirate-junks was restricted to accommodating the captain and his wives – he usually had five or six – and his family. No pirate was allowed to have a woman on board unless married to her according to their law, and with regard to this it seems that Mrs. Ching would say: 'Do as I tell you, not as I do!'

The accommodation for the crew was said to be a small berth, about 4 ft square, for a man, his wife and family. This seems not only fantastically small but impossible, and could only be carried out in the aggregate. To say the pirate-junks were overcrowded would be an understatement. There is no doubt that they swarmed with vermin; rats in particular, for the crews encouraged them to breed and ate them as a delicacy. In fact there were few creatures they would not eat. One favourite dish was caterpillars and boiled rice. The pirate crews were fond of gambling and spent all their leisure hours card-playing or smoking opium.

from *Pirates of the Eastern Seas* by Captain A. G. Course

In his diaries William Hickey described the lives of women living in sampans off Canton during the closing days of the eighteenth century, as they continued to do for the next two centuries . . .

Whole families reside entirely in their sampans, not going on shore once in six months. They carry on their respective trades or businesses upon the water, buying and selling precisely the same as in a market; the butchers, bakers, &c., having each a fixed station, so that everyone knows exactly where to go for what he wants.

The females of the higher order are entirely secluded, take no part in domestic arrangements, nor ever mix in society, or are even seen except by their nearest relations, living in indolence and luxury, whilst the poor women in humble life are made to execute the most laborious and menial services of the house or sampan. These are frequently seen tugging at an oar, having one infant receiving its nourishment at the breast and another slung behind her. Each child has a vegetable substance, somewhat resembling a gourd or pumpkin, fastened to its back, which, being of a buoyant nature, if the infant falls overboard floats it until picked up by its parents or any other sampan that happens to be near. The plant that thus floats the child, has the number and station of the sampan to which it belongs cut in Chinese characters upon it, by which the child is at once ascertained, otherwise in such a multitude of boats great confusion would arise. It scarcely ever happens that any one is drowned. The women who are not doomed to slave for bread, have in early infancy shoes of iron, or some equally hard substance, put upon their feet, which confine them so closely as to prevent the growth. The pain consequent of so strange a custom must be dreadful, yet custom that operates alike in all countries and upon all persons enables them to endure it. They are of course cripples, and can scarce walk.

Young Hickey also had an opportunity to observe white women in the East at the time . . .

About the middle of April, 1778, Commodore Price and his squadron sailed for Madras, and proved of important service to the Admiral. Soon after the departure of the *Resolution* and *Royal Charlotte*, Commodore Richardson gave a splendid fête on board the *Britannia* to the whole gentry of Calcutta. The ship was fitted up for the occasion with the greatest taste, no expence being spared. The sole error committed was not having a fixed accommodation ladder, from the want of which the ladies were obliged to be hoisted in by the common coarse method of a chair. There was in Calcutta at that time a Mrs. Wood, wife to a gentleman of rank in the Company's service. This good lady was of a most unwieldy form, her size being immense. Being one of the guests invited, upon coming alongside the *Britannia* she was placed in the chair, and the four men stationed at the halliards directed to hoist away. They accordingly started, but making no progress imagined the rope had jammed in the block. Finding upon examination that not to be the case, the boatswain looked from the deck into the boat, when seeing the enormous figure in the chair he exclaimed, 'Oh, damn my eyes, but I don't wonder, my lads, you could not budge. There's a cargo nothing short of all hands can move, so clap on, clap on, I say, my lads,' and he put half a dozen more men to the halliards, when they set out with a loud huzza, actually running the chair with Mrs. Wood in it almost up to the main yard-arm. Although all who saw it felt the great impropriety and insolence of the act, the scene was so irresistibly ridiculous as to excite a general laugh. The officers, of course, interfered and procured the lowering and release of the terrified lady, whose husband was loud in his calls for having the delinquents punished. For some minutes we feared this untoward circumstance would have interrupted the harmony of the day, but Mrs. Wood with great good nature interceded for the culprits, who were suffered to escape with a severe reprimand from Captain Hicks, who was the next officer to Commodore Richardson.

After a most magnificent dinner, at which were present one hundred and fifty ladies and gentlemen, arranged between decks, the bulkhead of the great cabin having been removed so as to make a space sufficient for the tables, an excellent band of martial music played a variety of favourite tunes. The meal being finished, the ladies adjourned to the quarter-deck and round-house, where after coffee, tea, and all the usual accompaniments, dancing commenced under a spacious awning, brilliantly illuminated by many hundred coloured lamps, the effect of which was beautiful. A party of men who preferred sacrificing at the shrine of Bacchus to that of joining the damsels in the merry dance remained below, swilling burgundy, champagne, and claret, all rendered most palatable by being cooled in ice.

But life was not always thus for wives and girlfriends of the officers of the East India Company, as the sad story of an actress, who gave up the theatre to accompany her unlucky lover, reminds us . . .

This unfortunate *Nancy* upon the doing away of the Bengal marine scheme by orders for that purpose from the Court of Directors was sent from Bombay to Europe as a packet, under the command of Captain Haldane, whom the public prints too truly termed 'the child of misfortune,' he having been once cast away when mate of an Indiaman, losing everything he possessed. He afterwards got the command of the *Fairford*, a noble vessel of the Company's which upon her first voyage was destroyed by fire in the harbour of Bombay, he again losing all but life. Mr. Hornby, the Governor at the time, feeling for the heavy loss Captain Haldane thus sustained, with the humane intention of assisting him, fitted out the *Nancy* as a packet, giving him the command and also lending him a considerable sum of money to purchase an investment.

Captain Haldane had taken out in the *Fairford* the famous actress, Mrs. Cargill, who was greatly atttached to him, so much so as to relinquish the stage on which she had attained much celebrity, to follow his fortunes. This beautiful and accomplished woman embarked with him in the *Nancy* for England. After a remarkable fine passage they reached the British soundings, when a tremendous tempest arose. It being in the depth of winter, and they being (as was supposed) mistaken in their reckoning, ran ashore upon the rocks off the Islands of Scilly, where every soul on board perished. The corpse of Mrs. Cargill, with a child clasped in her arms, was washed on shore upon one of the Islands, where both were buried.

from the *Memoirs of William Hickey* ed. by Alfred Spencer

A Victorian Hostess Sails Around the World

On 6 July 1876 the 531-ton three-masted gaff topsail schooner *Sunbeam* saluted the Commodore of the Royal Yacht Squadron at Cowes as she set off on a circumnavigation of the globe. Wind and tide were favourable, so she was able to bank her fires, lower the funnel and feather the propeller. It was probably the first such extended cruise to be undertaken solely for pleasure. The natives of Tahiti were nonplussed by their visitors. 'No sell brandy?' – 'No.' 'No stealy men?' – 'No.' 'No do what then?'

Under the command of her owner Tom Brassey, MP for Hastings, she had a complement of forty-three, including a lady's maid for his remarkable wife Annie, a nanny for her four young children, a stewardess, four stewards and three cooks. A doctor and four guests made up the afterguard. There were also two dogs, three birds and a kitten which disappeared on the first day out, presumed to have gone down the hawse-pipe, although the children hoped she might have been packed away amongst the new sails. Nothing escaped the observant Lady Brassey, who has left us a remarkable account of the voyage seen through the eyes of a Victorian society hostess.

Heading for the Straits of Magellan from the River Plate, she reported an unusual encounter with the barque *Monkhaven*, which was flying signals to indicate that she was on fire. Her crew of fifteen were taken on board *Sunbeam*, from whose rigging they watched their ship burn to the waterline.

For two hours we could see the smoke pouring from various portions of the ill-fated barque. Our men, who had brought off the last of her crew, reported that, as they left her, flames were just beginning to burst from the fore-hatchway; and it was therefore certain that the rescue had not taken place an hour too soon. Whilst we were at dinner, Powell called us up on deck to look at her again, when we found that she was blazing like a tar-barrel. The captain was anxious to stay by and see the last of her, but Tom was unwilling to incur the delay which this would have involved.

We accordingly got up steam, and at 9 p.m. steamed round the *Monk-shaven*, as close as it was deemed prudent to go. No flames were visible then; only dense volumes of smoke and sparks, issuing from the hatches. The heat, however, was intense, and could be plainly felt, even in the cold night air, as we passed some distance to leeward. All hands were clustered in our rigging, on the deck-house or on the bridge, to see the last of the poor *Monkshaven*, as she was slowly being burnt down to the water's edge.

She was a large and nearly new (three years old) composite ship, built and found by her owners, Messrs. Smales, of Whitby, of 657 tons burden, and classed A1 for ten years at Lloyd's. Her cargo, which consisted of coal for smelting purposes, was a very dangerous one; so much so that Messrs. Nicholas, of Sunderland, from whose mines the coal is procured, have great difficulty in chartering vessels to carry it, and are therefore in the habit of building and using their own ships for the purpose. At Buenos Ayres we were told that, of every three ships carrying this cargo round to Valparaiso or Callao, one catches fire, though the danger is frequently discovered in time to prevent much damage to the vessel or loss of life.

The crew of the *Monkshaven* – Danes, Norwegians, Swedes, Scotch, and Welsh – appear to be quiet, respectable men. This is fortunate, as an incursion of fifteen rough lawless spirits on board our little vessel would have been rather a serious matter. In their hurry and fright, however, they left all their provisions behind them, and it is no joke to have to provide food for fifteen extra hungry mouths for a week or ten days, with no shops at hand from which to replenish our stores. The sufficiency of the water supply, too, is a matter for serious consideration. We have all been put on half-allowance, and sea-water only is to be used for washing purposes.

Some account of the disaster, as gathered from the lips of various members of the crew at different times, may perhaps be interesting. It seems that, early on Monday morning, the day following that on which the fire was discovered, another barque, the *Robert Hinds*, of Liverpool, was spoken. The captain of that vessel offered to stand by them or do anything in his power to help them; but at that time they had a fair wind for Monte Video, only 120 miles distant, and they therefore determined to run for that port, and do their best to save the ship, and possibly some of the cargo. In the course of the night, however, a terrible gale sprang up, the same, no doubt, as the one of which we had felt the effects on first leaving the River Plate. They were driven hither and thither, the sea constantly breaking over them and sweeping the decks, though fortunately without washing any of them overboard. After forty-eight hours of this rough usage the men were all exhausted, while the fire was gradually increasing in strength beneath their feet, and they knew not at what moment it might burst through the decks and envelope the whole ship in flames . . . But our captain, who is very good to his crew, and a religious man too, said, 'There is One above who looks after us all.' That was true enough, for, about ten minutes afterwards, as I was talking to the cook, and telling him it was all over with us, I saw a sail to leeward, and informed the captain.

Luckily this ship turned out to be *Sunbeam*, although her wearing a white ensign yet having no visible armament puzzled the captain of *Monkshaven*. Sailing ships continued to carry smelting coal to the west coast of Chile beyond the turn of this century, and the incidence of self-ignited fires deep within the holds was almost a matter of routine.

When *Sunbeam* suffered her own fire it was in the Sea of Japan and fortunately extinguished by her own resources. It was none the less a frightening experience, as Lady Brassey wrote:

At 2.30 a.m. I was awakened by a great noise and a loud cry of 'The ship is on fire!', followed by Mr. Bingham rushing into our cabin to arouse us. At first I could hardly realise where we were, or what was happening, as I was half stupid with chloral, pain and smoke, which was issuing from each side of the staircase in dense volumes. My first thought was for the children, but I found they had not been forgotten. Rolled up in blankets, they were already in transit to the deck-house. In the meantime Mr. Bingham had drenched the flames with every available jug of water, and Tom had roused the crew and made them screw the hose on to the pump. They were afraid to open the hatches to discover where the fire was, until the hose and *extincteurs* were ready to work, as they did not know whether or not the hold was on fire, and the whole ship might burst into a blaze the moment the air was admitted. Allen soon appeared with an *extincteur* on his back, and the mate with the hose. Then the cupboard in Mr. Bingham's room was opened, and burning cloaks, dresses, boxes of curios, portmanteaus, &c., were hauled out, and, by a chain of men, sent on deck, where they were drenched with sea-water or thrown overboard. Moving these things caused the flames to increase in vigour and the *extincteur* was used freely, and with the greatest success. It is an invaluable invention, especially for a yacht, where there are so many holes and corners which it would be impossible to reach by ordinary means. All this time the smoke was pouring in volumes from the cupboard on the other side, and from under the nursery fireplace. The floors were pulled up, and the partitions were pulled down, until at last the flames were got under. The holds were next examined. No damage had been done there; but the cabin floor was completely burnt through and the lead from the nursery fireplace was running about, melted by the heat.

The explanation of the cause of the fire is very simple. Being a bitterly cold night, a roaring fire had been made up in the nursery, but about half-past ten the servants thought it looked rather dangerous and raked it out. The ashpan was not large enough, however, to hold the hot embers, which soon made the tiles red-hot. The woodwork caught fire, and had been smouldering for hours, when the nurse fortunately woke and discovered the state of affairs. She tried to rouse the other maids, but they were stupefied with the smoke, and so she rushed off at once to the doctor and Mr. Bingham. The former seized a child under each arm, wrapped them in blankets, and carried them off to the deck-house, Mabelle and the maids following, with more blankets and rugs, hastily snatched up. The children were as good as possible. They never cried nor made the least fuss, but composed themselves in the deck-house to sleep for the remainder of the night, as if it were all a matter of course. When I went to see them, little Muriel remarked: 'If the yacht is on fire, mamma, had not Baby and I better get our ulsters, and go with Emma in the boat to the hotel, to be out of the way?' It is the third time in their short lives that they have been picked out of bed in the middle of the night and carried off in blankets away from a fire, so I suppose they are getting quite used to it.

By half-past three all danger was past, and we began to settle down again, though it took a long time to get rid of the smoke.

There were many happier times on the cruise. In the South Seas, Lady Brassey became the first lady to be sent aloft in a boatswain's chair:

At 1.30 p.m. land was sighted from the mast-head, and at two o'clock I saw from the deck what looked like plumes of dark ostrich feathers rising from the sea. This was the island of Tatakotoroa – also known as Narcissus, or Clarke Island – to the eastward of the Paumotu or Low Archipelago of the South Seas . . .

After lunch, Tom had me hoisted up to the foretopmasthead in a 'boat-swain's chair,' which is simply a small plank, suspended by ropes at the four corners, and used by the men to sit on when they scrape the masts. I was very carefully secured with a rope tied round my petticoats, and, knocking against the various ropes on my way, was then gently hoisted up to what seemed at first a giddy height; but when once I got accustomed to the smallness of the seat, the airiness of my perch, and the increased roll of the vessel, I found my position by no means an unpleasant one. Tom climbed up the rigging and joined me shortly afterwards. From our elevated post we could see plainly the formation of the island, and the lagoon in the centre, encircled by a bank of coral, in some places white, bare, and narrow, in others wide and covered with palm trees and rich vegetation: it was moreover possible to understand better the theory of the formation of these coral islands. I was so happy up aloft that I did not care to descend; and it was almost as interesting to observe what a strange and disproportioned appearance everything and everybody on board the yacht presented from my novel position, as it was to examine the island we were passing. The two younger children and the dogs took the greatest interest in my aërial expedition, and never ceased calling to me and barking, until I was once more let down safely into their midst. As soon as we had seen all we could of the island, fires were banked, and we proceeded under sail throughout the evening and night.

On 26 May *Sunbeam* dropped anchor off Hastings after logging 37,000 miles, and the travellers were ferried ashore by local boats, before a triumphant return to their home at Battle. Lady Brassey signed off her journal with a poem in the style of a Victorian hymn-writer:

> I travell'd among unknown men,
> In lands beyond the sea,
> Nor, England did I know till then
> What love I bore to thee.

from *A Voyage in the Sunbeam* by Lady Brassey

A Honeymoon Cruise in a 24-ft Ocean-Racer

Anita Leslie, the historian and biographer of Jenny Jerome, may have been a blood relation of Winston Churchill's and thus game for anything, but had little idea of what she was letting herself in for when she flew out to Antigua with her six-month-old son to meet her husband. After a long war in command of submarines he became an ocean-racing freak of the hairshirt fraternity, shipping as navigator to John Illingworth in the all-conquering *Myth of Malham*. After that he sailed his own 24-foot RNSA one-design *Galway Blazer* across to English Harbour with only a cripple as crew. On being reunited with his young wife he planned a leisurely cruise down to the Grenadines and back. But first he had to teach her to sail. It could only be in the trade winds funnelling between Antigua and Guadeloupe at a steady 25 knots.

It was a brilliant sunny day, perfect for a sail, I thought, despite Bill's repeated suggestions to give it up if I felt inclined, for the clouds were racing overhead. But nothing had ever seemed more exhilarating than the speed of my little home. Standing at the tiller obeying Bill's directions as we tacked into the outer bay, the delights of sun and sea and wind were such that I could not imagine why we had wasted so much time in harbour. I thought I was a good sailor. I thought I liked it rough. The wind, the spray, the salty champagne air, all went to my head.

The entrance of English Harbour is almost invisible in its wall of cliff. You sail out and look back on a high solid shoreline which gives no inkling of the deep inlet behind. 'How will we ever find our way home?' I shouted. Bill murmured something about compass and bearings, and I realized, not for the first time in this life, how impossible it is for me to learn anything out of a book. My brain won't hold theory, it must have been made the wrong shape. I can only grasp that which my eyes see and my hands do. *The Elements of Navigation* was a tome I had been forced to lay down at the fourth page as hopelessly beyond my comprehension.

*

'It's really blowing too hard to put up the mizzen,' said Bill thoughtfully, 'I think we'll keep straight out to sea. It's not the sort of day to explore a coast. Say when you've had enough.'

But I could never have enough of this!

And seeing Bill go below to prepare himself lunch I insisted on eating a cucumber and a packet of biscuits.

We had been sailing for over an hour and Bill was explaining wind-angles and canvas-tension when it began to grow really rough. The little boat took her buffeting well, but each wave seemed to hit her with concentrated fury and even in the small space of the cockpit I kept getting knocked about.

'I've always loved these light displacement boats!' cried Bill, elated. 'She can ride out a storm like a cork!'

Occasionally waves swept right over us, and having neglected Bill's advice to tie a towel around my neck inside the oilskin I was soon soaked. Then a tired feeling crept over me accompanied by an aching desire to close my eyes and not look at those huge dark blue waves towering over the hull. I began to think of my baby and wish I was back there rocking his cradle – or whatever it was he had.

'Think I want to go to sleep,' I presently remarked.

'I don't advise you to go below,' said Bill, but having eaten a good lunch (he always ate far more at sea than on land) he took over the tiller while I crept down to change my wet shirt. It was rather warm in the cabin and the sight of my bunk grew irresistible. I felt I simply must have a little snooze. Lying down I tried to pull up the canvas lee board to hold me in, but the boat now pitched with such force I could not get the bar to catch. In an unguarded moment a crashing wave hurled me out on to the floor with my legs caught around the mast. I began to grow weak from the buffetting and feared my leg might be broken. The motion was so violent I could not even *try* to crawl back into my bunk. Irritation, exhaustion, hopelessness, deathly sickness succeeded each other in rapid succession. Bill, unaware of my predicament, sat happily in the roaring wind at the tiller, watching the canvas and occasionally altering course. When he finally looked down the hatch a sorry sight met his eyes.

'Why are you lying on the floor? Come up and get some air. People often feel sick below.'

'Turn round,' I wailed.

'What's that?'

'Go back!'

'Can't hear.'

'Home!' I put my last strength into a shriek that beat the wind's shriek.

'All right. Going about now.'

Happily the floor space was small, so having discovered my leg bones were intact I could get wedged there during the battering that followed. Keeping my eyes tight-shut I cheered myself with the thought that there was such a thing as death. 'Honey, I did say it would be rough,' came from the hatch. 'Do put on your oilskin and come up. It's getting calmer now. We will soon be in the lee of the island.'

But Honey refused to budge. Not until we were approaching the harbour entrance did I clamber to my feet, grabbing on to the rails for dear life, wrap up warm in the first sweaters to hand and reappear in the cockpit. Then suddenly in the silver-blue world of flying-fish I felt all right and rather ashamed . . .

At last came the moment when they left the relative peace of English Harbour.

The trade winds caught us hard so that the little ship strained and bounded away from Antigua, her bow smashing through wide sapphire troughs of Atlantic breakers while the silver bodies of flying fish streaked arrow-like on every side. With mizzen and jib and mainsail pulling hard in a reaching wind the boat was at her shivering best, and at seven knots we knew the height of sailing bliss, as with lee rail submerged, *Galway Blazer* reached her highest possible speed and spray embellished her hull with new jewelled wings.

I spent eight hours glued to the compass, for concentration on steering which makes some people sick has the opposite effect on me, and with *two* men aboard to whom sea-sickness was unknown it would have been unbearably humiliating to succumb. I looked at Bill revelling in the wind's violence and heard occasional sleepy chortles from Tarka when the buffeting sea roused him from sleep. Their laughter would be unendurable.

Naturally I did not *want* Bill or the baby to be sick, but there was something very aggravating about having to take such care when I was the person who had the idea of a sailing boat in the first place.

Determination to remain out in the cockpit all day and to concentrate on steering the course preserved me from all but the fear of disaster. Bill scrambled about the heaving deck, altering sails and maintaining his balance on one toe while exhorting me to steer slightly more to windward or continuing my technical training by shouting in my ear questions such as: 'If I fell overboard now what would you do?'

'Turn into the wind or jibe?'

My terrorized mind slowed to crawling pace by the pounding waves and fear of nausea would frantically try to calculate how to jibe in one's tracks. We passed one ship, a trading schooner coming up from the south.

'Who gives way?' shouted Bill.

'We do.'

'Why?'

'Because the wind is coming from over there.'

'Say it properly.'

'*They* are on the starboard tack.'

And so I learnt.

*

Only when sailing can the mind leap to quite such intense extremes, from such rapture to the depths of pusillanimous misery. A heavy swell with little wind drives even those who are immune to sickness to despair, making them swear that never will they set to sea again, but within a few minutes unbearable hell turns to heaven and smiles show on every face. Morbid thoughts, grey-green gloom, longings for death change almost instantaneously to a sensation of excitement and speed. The sea is no longer the enemy, but foam-capped and lovely. Rainbow-tinted spray flies around and you know the elation on tearing through your own bejewelled paradise, free of all mankind.

The cruise was not a total success. The boat had no auxiliary engine, so that many crossings from one island to the next ended under the lee of their destination as the wind fell right away at dusk. Recovering the anchor without a windlass in steep-to anchorages became a major evolution. Their main problems were in finding someone to launder the sailbag full of dirty baby linen they always arrived with and, unbelievably, being able to buy fresh fruit or fish, for the islanders ate all that they could not sell to merchants. Finally time ran out, with *Galway Blazer* due to sail 1,200 miles north and prepare herself for the Newport–Bermuda Race. Anita watched her husband leave Antigua with no more worries about shopping, or finding the transport has not turned up or the bank has just shut. All the decisions had been made, for good or for bad.

It was a hot blue day with a few strips of cloud racing by in a fair wind. I sat out on the gun turret beneath the washing-line and let Tarka pat Nelson's cannons. Out in the harbour small figures were moving on *Galway Blazer*. Then the mainsail was hoisted, she turned slowly in the breeze and moved towards the harbour entrance. As jib and mizzen went up I longed to be aboard, going through the kindergarten routine that five months of scoldings had taught me. Long before reaching the cliffs the sails filled and she darted towards St. James' Fort with the sudden speed of a cheetah.

She had heeled right over with wings of spray each side of her bows, when she passed beneath the Fort, so close we could shout good-byes. Then she rounded the point and the trade winds took her off into the open sea, bellying her canvas and driving her fast over the bright choppy waves. Climbing up beside the harbour light we waved and waved while the little boat sped away, her sails becoming a mere white fleck that finally vanished into the vast blue horizon.

When the sun set in golden flames behind Antigua and dusk crept over the deep, I was still staring northwards, pacing up and down the old brick gun platform, half-seeing that speck of a sail charging on through the night, hankering to be with her. But it's no good sighing for adventure when your heart has got chained down by the firmest anchor in all the world – a fat, rosy baby.

from *Love in a Nutshell* by Anita Leslie

The Captain's Lightning Courtship

In 1927 Captain Andrew B. Cunningham was in command of the cruiser-flagship of the America and West Indies Squadron, HMS *Calcutta*. On one cruise they visited Trinidad and stayed ashore with the governor, Sir Horace Byatt, and his sister Nora. In his autobiography he tells of the consequence of that visit in his own clipped manner:

> It was during a Course (at the Imperial Defence College in 1929) that I renewed my acquaintance with Miss Nora Byatt, home from Trinidad with her brother Sir Horace, who had been relieved as Governor . . . I was appointed in command of HMS *Rodney* in the Atlantic Fleet in mid-December. We decided to get married about the same time . . . I had many complimentary messages on my courage in taking on a wife and the largest battleship in the Navy at the same time.
>
> We were married on December 21st.

> from *A Sailor's Odyssey* by Admiral of the Fleet, Viscount Cunningham of Hyndhope

TRADE IN PEACETIME

Immigrant Ships

The *Star of Hope* was a smart 600-ton full-rigged ship reduced to a role she was never designed for – carrying immigrants across the North Atlantic in the years following the great potato famine in Ireland. Captain Killick found that he had inherited an iron-fisted bucko mate in Bonser, along with Dave, stowaway-turned-cabinboy. Ashore in Liverpool, streetside agents outside the pubs were selling 'safe, short, easy passages' to New York for three guineas or less. Once on board, the hapless passengers, most of whom had never been to sea before, were battened down between decks in conditions of indescribable squalor. Dave was put in charge of them and had to sleep in their midst.

The captain, as he went off, was judging the possibilities of his voyage. He had no time to give to the beauty of her lines. Four hundred emigrants, and his ship was sure to be loaded beyond capacity. More than enough. She would provide water for them, and that was all. They would have to feed themselves. Bonser, who appeared to know his work, and had talked to a few of them, was delighted because they supposed America is just out of sight. Only out of sight. One day on the water and they would be there. They think food enough for a picnic will see them across.

The ship's stores he had inspected couldn't keep them alive, if the usual westerly winds muzzled the ship all the way over. And that could happen.

*

That medicine chest, though; that was another thing. He must keep it in mind. It had been carried about for years, evidently, and never replenished. The bottles that were not stale or broken were empty, and the mess stank like the poisonous accident it was. The ship's surgeon had not complained about it, and that was a bad sign – one of those surgeons, very likely, who have to look up the difference between sternum and cranium. Ship-fever was bound to come, more or less, to the miserable wretches in those crowded alleyways below, battened down when the decks were awash; and he had heard of worse sickness in these ships, and more than once.

If this trip wasn't going to be a nice basinful for him, then he could thank his lucky stars. What was it that blackbeard of a mate said just before he came away? 'What's a corpse or two? The fishes could have the lot of us, and no questions asked.' That man Bonser had the cut of one who had served under the Jolly Roger. All the better if he had. He would know the use of discipline.

Finally the time came to sail down the Mersey. The crew was delivered on board that morning and did nothing for the captain's confidence . . .

The sailors were slack and lazy. They were brought aboard that morning

with their sea-chests and canvas bolsters, some of them as helpless as dead men, and had to be dragged forward along the deck out of it. Packet rats, the second mate called them. Several of the brutes cheered just now, when a rope tautened and flung a passenger head over heels, and knocked him out. Captain Killick stood above at the break of the poop, and didn't seem to have much to do with it. The emigrants, who came aboard in a great mob just before the ship moved, lumbered the deck, like stacks of dummies, and did not speak . . .

Between decks, Dave did his best to explain the standing orders affecting the passengers. He found a man smoking a pipe . . .

Dave hesitated, then bent down. 'No smoking allowed below deck, sir,' he said.

The man leaned leisurely on his elbow. 'An' who'll stop it?' he asked. He then went on to tell Dave of the frightful things that happened to anyone who tried to stop him from doing what he liked. A woman laughed.

Dave moved on. That fellow hadn't met the mate yet, but a meeting would come about pretty soon. Bonser had given strict orders about his duties below. He had to watch it that there were no naked lights, and no smoking. No lights, even when all was battened down in hard weather and it was dark as the inside of a black cow. But a glim was to be kept at the main hatchway after sunset, only that.

'If it'll burn,' Bonser had remarked. 'Usually it won't, or only burn blue when the weather lasts, and the hatches can't be lifted. When it comes to that, Commodore, you'll have to choke with the rest, to save the ship from foundering. That's the proper thing to do. All the same, wet or fine, middle watch or dog watch, no fighting down here, and no gambling, which is the same as fighting, and no lovemaking, which is worse than gambling for shindies. Stop it, boy. Pull 'em adrift.

'And another thing. The passengers are to sweep all alleyways clean before breakfast. Clean, mind, if they are sick, and sick most of 'em will be till we lift the land, and after that. No litter, no dead infants to be left about for more than a day. For me, I'd sooner berth with the cables than turn in with your crowd. And they must carry up their dirt, and cast it overboard, to loo'ard. Show 'em which is loo'ard before they let go. What blows inboard you'll eat, for learn you must, somehow. But I'll say you are coming along handsome.

'Though mind this again. When you come across him, and you'll do it, a passenger dying isn't so much odds as a man smoking. A dying man can wait till the sailmaker isn't too busy to measure him, but I'll be down at the word, and I'll strangle the man who won't put out his pipe when ordered. . . Do you want to die?'

As it turned out, the difficulties were not as hard as Dave thought they would be. Most of the trouble disappeared after Bonser had been down to persuade sense into that passenger who always had his pipe alight. The

man began to argue. He said he'd do what he liked, he'd paid his money, he wasn't a nigger or a sailor, he was a free Englishman.

Bonser didn't talk. He moved at once. As he twisted the pipe out of the man's mouth it popped like a cork. The furious passenger started to scramble out of his bunk, but he was helped out, and faster than he could have moved by himself. To save the kicks Bonser held the man off at arm's length by the throttle, and for so long that the kicking died down. The women began to scream at Bonser for a murderous bully, and the men threatened, but he took no notice. The smoker fell limp and was bundled into his bunk again. He didn't move much then.

The passengers' lot was relieved by yarns spun by the shipwright Chips . . .

The ship heeled, and a toddler fell against Chips. The audience clutched one another for support. The sudden complaining of the timbers was noticeable. 'She's talking to us,' said Chips.

'Why, can a ship talk? I thought it was only the boards moving,' said a girl. 'I listened to them last night.'

Chips regarded the child gravely. 'Some men I know say of their ship, they say it of this one because they like her, that she can do anything but talk. I heard one say it only yesterday. That's because they don't know. They live with her but she's laughing at them. Of course she can talk. She has a lot to say, from the kelson to the tops. Why, there was an admiral I sailed with, when he didn't know what canvas to carry, would go to the mainmast and whisper to it. Then the ship told him what he had better do, and she was always right, was that ship. So that admiral never lost a spar till he went to another ship that was either dumb or wicked. He lost that one and serve her right. She never said anything. Now what do you think of that?'

'A wicked ship? I've never heard of it. This ship isn't wicked, is she?'

'Our ship? She's nearly as good as you. She's so good she falls off her course if there's gambling or bad language on a Sunday . . .'

A man laughed. 'Did you ever hear the like of it! Go on now, say a ship has a soul to be saved, same as parson says we've got, and we've only to try.'

'Stow that,' said Chips, as if he were going to be angry. 'Don't mention parsons here, mister, no black coats, not if you want to see land. That's the sure way to call up dirt. The weather backs into the wrong quarter when you monkey with words aboard ship. She didn't hear you then, or she'd have shivered her timbers at a mistake. That shows whether she's got a soul or not. Live long enough, and don't get pride in your parts, and you'll learn better. You'll know then of the bad ship, the one with a bit of gibbet post about her somewhere. She's the devil's own, that one. You can't get anything right with her no matter how you try. It's always a headwind with that ship. She's the ship with footropes that break when they're new, and you're done. Keep off a ship like that, or you'll be cast away on Coffin Island among landcrabs and no water. Why, if ships haven't got souls, how do you account for ghost ships, tell me that?'

'I don't account . . .'

Inevitably the *Star of Hope* ran into a storm during which all the immigrants despaired of ever seeing the next sunrise, let alone the Manhattan skyline. When the weather eased up, there was a familiar ceremony on deck . . .

It was then eight bells, the morning watch. There was a muster amidships, crew and passengers. The Red Ensign was run up halfway to the gaff, and the main yards backed. Way was taken off her. She rolled in the long swell, without progress.

It was mid-ocean. To larboard, quite close abeam, a Mother Carey's chicken drifted up the long hills of water, then scooted down the valleys, dragging its toes just off the rippled glass, a tiny mite to be there alone. The ship rolled, and the spars complained sadly. The undertone of the wind was in the rigging. All stood to attention, and she rolled.

Seven figures were laid out in a row on the deck, sewn up in old sailcloth, their feet towards the water where the bulwarks had gone, on the lee side. The sailmaker and Chips had been busy fixing them up. Bonser whispered that the stout party this end in a canvas overcoat was the surgeon, but who was that ha'porth at the other end?

Dave knew, but he didn't say. He couldn't say. It seemed such a pity now that she never had that drink. Captain Killick came forward, a book in his hand, and with him were Mr. Cree and the tall young lady they said was Mrs. Cree. The captain tucked his cap under his arm. The men uncovered. A block swung and creaked overhead, and the surge of the ocean sighed as it met her; but when the captain began to read his voice had command of all other sounds. At last he lowered his voice, and came to it. 'We therefore commit these bodies to the deep . . .'

The men lifted each canvas bundle to the sliding board, tilted it, and the shape dived off; one after another they plunged. The last to go was the small one. The waters swelled all alive to the deck level as it went, and met it. The splash it made jumped in Dave's throat; the waters took it and vanished. Mrs. Cree was weeping. The group stood without moving, though it was all over. That block was beginning to whine again.

The captain slapped on his cap and walked quickly aft, but stopped and turned his head.

'Why don't you fill away that mainyard, Mister?' he called out sharply. 'Away now.'

from *Morning Light* by H. M. Tomlinson

The Golden Age of Sail

My fascination with the men and ships who raced each other round the world during the Golden Age of Sail at speeds undreamed of by contemporary steamships dates back to my childhood in Tientsin, North China, during the early 1930s. A gentle old lady regularly came as babysitter when my parents dined out. She regaled me with stories of how she had been born to the captain's wife and spent her early years aboard one of the smartest clippers afloat. Indeed she was named after the flyer from Robert Steele's yard in Greenock – *Serica*.

She was on board in 1863 when she fetched up at the London River on the same tide as her two great rivals, *Aeriel* and *Taeping*, each ninety-nine days out from Foochow.

The most famous of them all, because she has been restored to her original state and now attracts hundreds of thousands of visitors each year to her berth at Greenwich, is *Cutty Sark*, named after the mini-dress worn by the witch in Robert Burns's poem 'Tam O'Shanter'. Her figurehead depicts the witch Nannie with one arm outstretched as she tried to catch the tail of the grey mare on which a young farmer she fancied was fleeing.

She was launched in Dumbarton in 1869, expressly designed to challenge the supremacy of the Aberdeen-built *Thermopylae*, an 1868 model which claimed to be the fastest sailing ship afloat. They were almost of identical size, 212 feet long on a beam of 36 feet and of just under 1,000 gross tonnage.

Inevitably they met in a match-race from Shanghai to London. By the time they were approaching the Cape of Good Hope fifty-six days out, *Cutty Sark* had worked out a lead of over 400 miles, when disaster struck. She lost her rudder. For six days she was hove-to out of control whilst a jury rig could be assembled and shipped in ugly seas. By the time she had regained steerage, her rival was nearly 500 miles ahead. She was further hampered by only being controllable at speeds up to 8 knots, yet she still reached the Downs less than a week behind her rival.

A great duel was arranged in 1872 between *Cutty Sark* and *Thermopylæ*. Both vessels left Shanghai on the same day and within an hour or two of each other. They were, however, some time in getting clear away owing to fresh gales and thick fogs in which it was impossible to proceed, and *Cutty Sark* did not drop her pilot until 21st June.

They were then held up by calms and fogs until 2 A.M. on the 23rd, when the N. E. monsoon began to blow strong and soon freshened to a gale, which split the *Cutty Sark's* fore top-gallant sail to pieces.

The monsoon held until the 26th when at 1 A.M., in lat. 20° 27′ N., long. 114° 43′ E., the two racers were in sight of each other, *Cutty Sark* being in the lead.

On the 28th June they were again together, this time with *Thermopylæ* 6 miles to windward of her opponent, the wind being fresh from the S. W. with heavy squalls, but they did not meet again until approaching Gaspar Straits. The weather continued boisterous until the 1st July, up to which date *Cutty Sark* had only had one observation since leaving port.

On the Cochin China Coast the usual land and sea breezes were worked but crossing to the Natunas fresh gales and squalls and split sails were the experience of both clippers.

On 15th July in 108° 18′ E. on the equator, *Thermopylæ* sighted *Cutty Sark* about eight miles ahead, but gradually fell astern, and on the following morning *Cutty Sark* could only just be seen from the fore topsail yard bearing S. E. At 10 A.M. on 17th July *Cutty Sark* led *Thermopylæ* through Stolzes Channel, but on the 18th some unfriendly waterspouts compelled the former to bear up out of her course and take in sail and this let *Thermopylæ* up. At 6 A.M. on the 19th both ships arrived off Anjer, *Thermopylæ* now having a lead of 1½ miles. Here *Cutty Sark* was hove to for a couple of hours whilst Captain Moodie went ashore with letters. At noon on the 20th, *Thermopylæ* was three miles W. by S. of *Cutty Sark*, both vessels being hung up by calms and baffling airs. And it was not until the 26th, with Keeling Cocos Island in sight to the nor'rard, that there was any strength in the S. E. trade; from this point, however, the wind came fresh from the E. S. E. and stunsail booms began to crack like carrots.

This was the sort of weather that *Cutty Sark* revelled in, and she went flying to the front with three consecutive runs of 340, 327 and 320 miles. She carried the trades until 7th August, when at 1 P.M. the wind suddenly took off as if cut by a knife, and remained calm and baffling until the 9th when it commenced to breeze up rapidly from the S. W.

The 11th August found *Cutty Sark* battling with a strong westerly gale, but with a good lead of *Thermopylæ*. From this date, however, the weather fought for the latter, and the following quotations from Captain Moodie's private log will show the bad luck which attended *Cutty Sark* in losing her rudder.

August 15. Lat. 34° 26′ S. long. 28° 1′ E. At 6.30 A.M. a heavy sea struck the rudder and carried it away from the trunk downwards. Noon, wind more moderate, tried a spar over the stern but would not steer the ship. Thereupon began construction of a jury rudder, with a spare spar 70 feet long.

August 20. 34° 38′ S., 27° 36′ E. Light wind from westward. Noon, strong westerly breeze and clear. About 2 P.M. shipped jury rudder and sternpost, a difficult job as there was a good deal of sea on. [It will be noticed that whilst *Cutty Sark* lay hove to, with her crew working night and day on the jury rudder, fine fair winds, which carried *Thermopylæ* round the Cape, were blowing, but no sooner was the rudder ready for shipping into place than the wind chopped round into the west and began to blow up for a further series of head gales.]

August. 21. 34° 19′ S. 26° 58′ E. Distance 36 miles. Strong westerly gale.

August 23. 35° 49′ S., 20° 58′ E. Distance 194 miles. Stiff breeze from south to E. N. E. and sharp head sea. Midnight, wind hauled to N. W. Rounded Cape Agulhas. [On this day *Thermopylæ* was in 31° 43′ S., 13° E., 490 miles ahead.]

Cutty Sark next had a succession of heavy head gales, which did not let up until the 31st, and sorely tested the capabilities of the jury rudder. The awning stanchions which connected the steering chains to the back of the rudder were carried away, and several of the eye-bolts which held the rudder to the post were broken, but they managed to steer with two wire rope pennants shackled to an eye-bolt placed in the back of the rudder in case of accident to the chains.

The jury rudder, however, carried *Cutty Sark* to 7° 28′ N., 20° 37′ W., without further accident. The ship was found to steer very well with the wind right aft, but with strong beam winds and when going anything over 10 knots the rudder was not nearly so efficient, and it was often necessary to reduce sail to keep the ship down to about eight knots.

On 1st September in 30° 44′ S., 12° 24′ E., the succession of fierce northerly gales at last grew tired of buffeting the lame duck and the normal weather for running down to St Helena set in. The island was passed at 9 A.M. on 9th September, and on the 15th *Cutty Sark* crossed the line. Her best runs between 1st September and this date were 210, 211, 214, 226, 227, 221, and 207, pretty good work for a ship which was not allowed to do more than eight knots.

All this time, however, the jury rudder was gradually breaking its fastenings and on the 20th September the last of the eye-bolts holding the rudder to the post gave way and the whole contrivance had to be hoisted up for repairs. Captain Moodie was now so short of material that he had to shape flat pieces of iron so that they would work on the iron stanchions instead of the eye-bolts. The repairs were smartly done and on the following day the jury rudder was once more ready for lowering. On the first occasion a kedge anchor of 5½ cwt. had been used to sink it into place, but owing to the bad sea running this had been lost. On 21st September Moodie determined to fix the post and rudder in place without using any weight to sink it. When all was ready the sails were filled and the ship given a little headway, the rudder and post were then lowered and streamed right astern, the rudder was then hauled close to the trunk and the sails laid back. As the ship lost headway the weight of the chains partially sank the rudder, then as the ship slowly gathered sternway and the slack of the guys was hauled in, the heel of the rudder sank and allowed the head to be easily hauled up through the trunk. This operation is very easy to write about, but in its proper execution it required such seamanship as is hardly known nowadays.

Cutty Sark had fine strong N. E. trades to within a day of the Western Islands, but, unfortunately, had to be kept down to a speed of 200 miles a day, as beyond that her jury rudder could not control her.

On the last lap of the passage she unfortunately met with strong winds and gales from the nor'rard and eastward, and on 12th October, the day that *Thermopylæ* arrived in the Downs, she was battling against a fresh N. N. E. gale in 45° 37' N., 13° 26' W. This gale lasted until *Cutty Sark* also reached the Downs on 18th October, less than a week behind her rival, for which fine performance Captain Moodie received great praise in shipping circles. Indeed, though *Thermopylæ* arrived first, all the honours of the race belonged to *Cutty Sark*, for she was hove to for more than six days whilst the jury rudder was being made. And between the day on which she lost her rudder and that of her arrival, she wasted eleven days making 139 miles, added to which, when she had a chance to go ahead, her speed had to be reduced to eight knots or half of what she was capable of doing. It therefore seemed pretty certain that, but for her accident, *Cutty Sark* must have beaten *Thermopylæ* by several days.

from *The China Clippers* by Basil Lubbock

Cutty Sark made eight voyages in the tea trade before the opening of the Suez Canal stacked the odds in favour of steamships. From 1883 she spent eleven years on the wool trade with Australia. She made one voyage from Newcastle in New South Wales to the Lizard in sixty-nine days, whilst her rival clocked an outward run to Melbourne of fifty-nine days, a record which stands.

It is not surprising that these graceful thoroughbreds of the oceans and their hard-driving crews should have inspired some great writers to give of their best. In 1933 John Masefield wrote a novel based on those epic races betwen the tea clippers, which has rightly become a classic. The *Bird of Dawning*, known to all sailors of the time as *The Cock*, was a warm favourite to win the annual race from Foochow, driven by her religious maniac master, Captain Miserden, who sought divine inspiration to govern his tactics all the way home.

One of her opponents was *Blackgauntlet*, a thinly disguised version of *Cutty Sark*, driven in his third tea race by the young, aloof martinet, Captain Duntisbourne. Early in the passage the mate had been felled by a solid block falling from aloft and killed instantly. That left the second mate, Cruiser Trewsbury, to share the after-cabin alone with the master. It was not a happy arrangement, for Cruiser had made one voyage in a steamship, which put him beyond the pale. In thick fog to the west of the Azores the captain overruled his orders to sound the foghorn and *Blackgauntlet* was promptly run down and sunk by a steamer which did not stop for survivors. Cruiser got away in one boat with sixteen survivors, but the captain's longboat failed to disengage from its falls and went down with *Blackgauntlet*.

They were now dropped astern of the sinking ship. As they rested on their oars, Cruiser put by the tiller, and lit another red flare. Up above them, only a few fathoms away, was the ellipse of the ship's stern, with the black gauntlet carved in high relief over the words –

Blackgauntlet
London
Ever First

'She's down by the head already,' James Fairford said.
'She's going to dive,' Cruiser said. 'Give way together. What's wrong with the long-boat?'

*

'My God,' Cruiser said, 'why don't they lower?'
It may have been that he saw more than they did, as a looker-on will; it may have been that the fall had jammed in the forward sheave again; or that Captain Duntisbourne had had some fancy of his own. Cruiser shouted with all his strength, 'Lower away the long-boat falls there.'
Even as he shouted, the after end of the long-boat dropped a little, and a man slid down a life-line into her. On the same instant the ship bowed suddenly forward, as in a big 'scend: a spray lifted high along her rail as she dipped to it. She lifted her bows a few feet, dipped them again in what seemed slow time: and then with horrible speed flung herself over on the lowering boat.

Two days later Cruiser came across a clipper ship lying hove-to with her yards backed and both sets of boat-falls hanging unattached from their davit-heads, evident sign that the crew had abandoned ship. It was the *Bird of Dawning*.

She had 3 feet of water in her hold, but it was not gaining. Cruiser soon found evidence of sabotage: a water inlet pipe had been sawn through, the main pump suction was clogged by tea-leaves and its piston immobilized by wire lashings. The reason for her master's precipitate decision to take to the boats was found amongst his personal papers. It was bizarre:

The second drawer contained a row of books, placed backs upward along the drawer so as to chock each other. These books had seen a good deal of service, they were much used, and had been more than once in salt water. Cruiser took out the first volume which came to hand: it had not been thrust well home into the row and seemed indeed to be offering itself to his hand. It was a mean sort of book in a bad binding and ill print. He opened it at the title page and read.

Habakkuk Unveiled

Mudde.

On the flyleaf was the Captain's signature, in a bold, flowing, well-formed sea-hand – R. Miserden, Capt. 1857 – with a note below, in fainter ink:

'I bought this Book for my Eternal Salvation at the house of the Prophet, 27, Seacole Lane, Millwall, on my 35th Birthday - R. M.'

On the title page, the purpose of the book was declared.

Habakkuk Unveiled
being an Interpretation of the Prophecies
Concerning the Destruction of the World
Now shortly to happen
The whole being a Revelation of the Prophet's
Mission
granted in Vision to the Prophet's Follower.
Ebenezer Mudde
of the First church of Habakkuk. The year of
Wrath, 1853.

He glanced at the book, which contained a fiery doctrine about the coming end of the world. Miserden had read it very carefully, with ejaculations pencilled in the margin, such as: 'Lord grant it.' 'O that I may see it.' 'Hark to truth,' etc. Under one fiery passage at a chapter ending he had written: 'This light is too blinding.' Cruiser looked at the light according to Ebenezer Mudde. He read: 'Already the brimstone is prepared, the tow teased and the powder of blasting mealed. The first trumpet has blown, the second is about to blow. At the third, the flame shall be put to the heap, and then too late the wretches of this world will hold their hands to Habakkuk, who will answer them with fearful justice, "Too late." '

The next book was The Form of Prayer to be used at the Visitations of the Fire in the gatherings of the First Church of Habakkuk, as Revealed to the Prophet's Follower, Ebenezer Mudde. Towards the end of this book were printed metrical versions of the Book of Habakkuk arranged to be sung to well-known tunes, and at the end some blank pages, into which Captain Miserden had entered jottings of Ebenezer Mudde's sermons: – 'E. M. spoke with much Fire on H. III, 7, searching words, wh. convinced F. of being in the Prophet's Wrath.'

316

'F. fasted till she was conscious of Fire.'

'Very conscious of Fire.'

'Comfortable sermon from E. M. on the second Trumpet.'

'E. M. on the supping up of the East Wind. O that such words should not be in every sinful heart.'

'F. and I fasted and put on white raiment expecting the Second Trumpet this day.'

The next book was called:

Habakkuk Takes Horse
For a Ride of Denunciation through the Land of Dagon, being England.
A Word of the Preparation for
The Second Trumpet
Now about to blow.
by
Ebenezer Mudde, F. P. (follower of the Prophet).
The 7th year of the wrath of Habakkuk.

The next was a printed account of the Revelation of Habakkuk to his handmaid, Fraterna Miserden, who after long being the devoted wife of Roger Miserden, sea captain, and a faulty follower of the Prophet, received by Visitation Revelation of the Prophet, and put aside carnal life that she might persuade others to the eternal truth of the fire. It was a slim little book with a ghastly engraving of Fraterna woodenly persuading others.

The next books were note-books containing jottings by Captain Miserden over a term of years.

'Called on the Prophet who at last vouchsafed the South East trades.'

'Habakkuk bade me stand in with the land, against my carnal judgement; on standing in, lo, I had the landwind, which brought us clear of the Swatows.'

'All hands scraping paintwork, this being the Prophet's Direct Command to me R. M.'

'The prophet directed me to tack ship against my carnal judgment. Lo, within three hours, Mr. Todd desired more doctrine and spoke of promptings of the Fire. Finished the poop with a second coat of oil.'

'The Prophet vouchsafed such wind as makes me hope we may win yet. Scourged against carnal man. Drank one half pint of Dr. Gubbins's Mixture against the same. The *Thermopylæ* hull down astern.'

The last book in the drawer was a photograph album, with a thickly-embossed cover, clasped with a brass clip. Cruiser opened it. There were a few photographs in it of Fraterna Miserden, and of her parents, all looking stiff and grim in their best clothes. Later in the book were photographs of a strange-looking man, with long grey hair and beard. From his look, Cruiser judged that he had some narrow intensity but small intelligence, he had the look of sect and of authority. Somehow Cruiser seemed to have seen the face leaning over some small counter, selling grocery. The figure was dressed to the waist in the black of Sunday coat and waistcoat. Over his trousers he wore something between a Masonic apron and a kilt. There was a figure painted or embroidered upon this robe: it represented Habakkuk brandishing three arrows with his right hand, while with his left he offered a scroll to a little kneeling man. Underneath this portrait was written, 'Ebenezer Mudde, F. P., to his Brother in the Fire, Roger Miserden.'

*

'That is as much as I'm likely to know,' Cruiser thought, 'but there may be more somewhere. If the Prophet directed him to cut through the intake pipe and choke the pump and persuade all hands to abandon ship, he would certainly have done it. That seems the likeliest explanation yet.'

from *The Bird of Dawning* by John Masefield

Cruiser had her pumped dry in short order and with his depleted crew set all sail and drove for the English Channel with a westerly gale behind her. The finish of the race in Masefield's novel was even more dramatic than the real thing between *Serica, Aeriel* and *Taeping* had been in 1863. Three ships converged together in the Downs north of Dover. Bloody Bill China, hard-drinking skipper of *Fukien*, sailed through the *Bird of Dawning*'s lee, giving his customary salute to a rival thus outsailed by hoisting a bottle of brandy to the crojack yard and shooting it down – then issuing grog all round. Luffing up to cross *Bird of Dawning*'s bows, she was caught by a sudden squall which ripped the top-gallant masts out of her.

Passing the Nab the previous day Cruiser had floated a message off on a lifebuoy to an inward-bound smack, which ensured that she was met by tugs from Dover and towed up-river to a triumphant homecoming, showered with honours and salvage money.

Captain Miserden and his crew had been rescued and returned to England, where he was put under restraint for two years before being released and joining the ministry of Ebenezer Mudde.

Fishing on the Grand Banks

The shallow Grand Banks which lie to the south-east of Newfoundland are renowned for fog and icebergs which drift down from Greenland on the Labrador Current until they melt in the warm Gulf Stream which passes through on its Great Circle course to Europe. Ever since Cabot's day in the fifteenth century they have also provided a rich and easily gathered harvest of codfish, which boats collected from as far afield as Dieppe and Vigo.

Before the days of ocean-going steam trawlers, fishermen on the Banks earned their living by sailing great distances, at the end of which they put their nest of sixteen small dories over the side to haul in the catch by hook and line. Each night the fish were gutted and packed down in salt in the ample hold of their mother-ship. When full, up to 200 tons of cod were then sailed back to home ports like Gloucester or Marblehead in Massachusetts. Since they were over 800 miles from the Banks, the schooners engaged on this trade remained on station until they had a full hold. Allowing for the passage out and back and interruption by gales, each voyage might last up to three months.

The Grand Banks schooners were all of sturdy construction and built to recognizably similar designs, with sweet sheerlines, low freeboards and long overhangs. They were amongst the most sea-kindly sailing craft ever built. Typically they were about 140 feet long, had a draught of 15 feet and carried 10,000 square feet of sail, mostly in the huge mainsail on its long overhanging boom.

Rudyard Kipling immortalized them in his book *Captains Courageous*. It later provided Spencer Tracy with arguably his greatest screen role as Manuel, the Portuguese line-fisherman who rescued the only son of an American tycoon when he fell over the stern of a passing eastbound transatlantic steamship, due to a combination of seasickness and smoking a strong cigar at the age of fifteen.

Manuel delivered his sodden catch back to the schooner *We're Here* from Gloucester. There young Harvey Cheyne demanded to be taken back to New York without delay, where his papa would amply reward them all. But the owner-skipper, Disko Troop, had other ideas and put his uninvited crew on a salary of $10 a month, alongside his son Dan as another dogsbody on board. At the end of the voyage Harvey was a man. He even hesitated to pick up his inheritance and old way of privileged life. On being reunited with his father, who had long since given him up for dead, he had much to tell. There was the memorable encounter with Uncle Abishai's doomed schooner, which the whole fleet sought to avoid as a notorious Jonah:

'It's blowed clear,' Disko cried, and all the foc'sle tumbled up for a bit of fresh air. The fog had gone, but a sullen sea ran in great rollers behind it. The *We're Here* slid, as it were, into long, sunk avenues and ditches which felt quite sheltered and homelike if they would only stay still; but they changed without rest or mercy, and flung up the schooner to crown one peak of a thousand gray hills, while the wind hooted through her rigging as she zigzagged down the slopes. Far away a sea would burst in a sheet of foam, and the others would follow suit as at a signal, till Harvey's eyes swam with the vision of interlacing whites and grays. Four or five Mother Carey's chickens stormed round in circles, shrieking as they swept past the bows. A rain-squall or two strayed aimlessly over the hopeless waste, ran down wind and back again, and melted away.

'Seems to me I saw somethin' flicker jest naow over yonder,' said Uncle Salters, pointing to the north-east.

'Can't be any of the fleet,' said Disko, peering under his eyebrows, a hand on the foc'sle gangway as the solid bows hatcheted into the troughs. 'Sea's oilin' over dretful fast. Danny, don't you want to skip up a piece an' see how aour trawl-buoy lays?'

Danny, in his big boots, trotted rather than climbed up the main rigging (this consumed Harvey with envy), hitched himself around the reeling crosstrees, and let his eye rove till it caught the tiny black buoy-flag on the shoulder of a mile-away swell.

'She's all right,' he hailed. 'Sail O! Dead to the no'th'ard, comin' down like smoke! Schooner she be, too.'

They waited yet another half-hour, the sky clearing in patches, with a flicker of sickly sun from time to time, that made patches of olive-green water. Then a stump-foremast lifted, ducked, and disappeared, to be followed on the next wave by a high stern with old-fashioned wooden snail's-horn davits. The sails were red tanned.

'Frenchman!' shouted Dan. 'No, 'taint neither. Da-ad!'

'That's no French,' said Disko. 'Salters, your blame luck holds tighter'n a screw in a keg-head.'

'I've eyes. It's Uncle Abishai.'

'You can't nowise tell fer sure.'

'The head-king of all Jonahs,' groaned Tom Platt. 'Oh, Salters, Salters, why wasn't you abed an' asleep?'

'How could I tell?' said poor Salters, as the schooner swung up.

She might have been the very *Flying Dutchman*, so foul, draggled, and umkempt was every rope and stick aboard. Her old-style quarter-deck was some four or five feet high, and her rigging flew knotted and tangled like weed at a wharf-end. She was running before the wind – yawing frightfully

– her staysail let down to act as a sort of extra foresail, – 'scandalised,' they call it, – and her foreboom guyed out over the side. Her bowsprit cocked up like an old-fashioned frigate's; her jib-boom had been fished and spliced and nailed and clamped beyond further repair; and as she hove herself forward, and sat down on her broad tail, she looked for all the world like a blouzy, frouzy, bad old woman sneering at a decent girl.

'That's Abishai,' said Salters. 'Full o' gin an' Judique men, an' the judgments o' Providence layin' fer him an' never takin' good holt. He's run in to bait, Miquelon way.'

'He'll run her under,' said Long Jack. 'That's no rig fer this weather.'

'Not he, 'r he'd 'a done it long ago,' Disko replied. 'Looks's if he cal'lated to run *us* under. Ain't she daown by the head more'n natural, Tom Platt?'

'Ef it's his style o' loadin' her she ain't safe,' said the sailor slowly. 'Ef she's spewed her oakum he'd better git to his pumps mighty quick.'

The creature threshed up, wore round with a clatter and rattle, and lay head to wind within earshot.

A gray-beard wagged over the bulwark, and a thick voice yelled something Harvey could not understand. But Disko's face darkened. 'He'd resk every stick he hez to carry bad news. Says we're in fer a shift o' wind. He's in fer worse. Abishai! Abi*shai!*' He waved his arm up and down with the gesture of a man at the pumps, and pointed forward. The crew mocked him and laughed.

'Jounce ye, an' strip ye, an' trip ye!' yelled Uncle Abishai. 'A livin' gale – a livin' gale. Yah! Cast up fer your last trip, all you Gloucester haddocks. *You* won't see Gloucester no more, no more!'

'Crazy full – as usual,' said Tom Platt. 'Wish he hadn't spied us, though.'

She drifted out of hearing while the gray-head yelled something about a dance at the Bay of Bulls and a dead man in the foc'sle. Harvey shuddered. He had seen the sloven tilled decks and the savage-eyed crew.

'An' that's a fine little floatin' hell fer her draught,' said Long Jack. 'I wondher what mischief he's been at ashore.'

'He's a trawler,' Dan explained to Harvey, 'an' he runs in fer bait all along the coast. Oh no, not home, he don't go. He deals along the south an' east shore up yonder.' He nodded in the direction of the pitiless Newfoundland beaches. 'Dad won't never take me ashore there. They're a mighty tough crowd – an' Abishai's the toughest. You saw his boat? Well, she's nigh seventy year old, they say; the last o' the old Marblehead heel-tappers. They don't make them quarter-decks any more. Abishai don't use Marblehead, though. He ain't wanted there. He jes' drif's araound, in debt, trawlin' an' cussin' like you've heard. Bin a Jonah fer years an' years, he hez. Gits liquor frum the Feecamp boats fer makin' spells an' selling winds an' such truck. Crazy, I guess.'

The dishevelled 'heel-tapper' danced drunkenly down wind, and all eyes followed her. Suddenly the cook cried in his phonograph voice: 'It wass his own death made him speak so! He iss fey – fey, I tell you! Look! She sailed into a patch of watery sunshine three or four miles distant. The patch dulled and faded out, and even as the light passed so did the schooner. She dropped into a hollow and – was not.

'Run under, by the Great Hook-Block!' shouted Disko, jumping aft. 'Drunk or sober, we've got to help 'em. Heave short and break her out! Smart!'

Harvey was thrown on the deck by the shock that followed the setting of the jib and foresail, for they hove short on the cable, and to save time, jerked the anchor bodily from the bottom, heaving in as they moved away. This is a bit of brute force seldom resorted to except in matters of life and death, and the little *We're Here* complained like a human. They ran down to where Abishai's craft had vanished; found two or three trawl-tubs, a gin-bottle, and a stove-in dory, but nothing more. 'Let 'em go,' said Disko, though no one had hinted at picking them up. 'I wouldn't hev a match that belonged to Abishai aboard. Guess she run clear under. Must ha' been spewin' her oakum fer a week, an' they never thought to pump her. That's one more boat gone along o' leavin' port all hands drunk.'

from *Captains Courageous* by Rudyard Kipling

Trading under Sail

Richard Henry Dana took two years off his law studies at Harvard to ship as a deckhand in a brig on a round trip from Boston to the Pacific coast. The freshness of his narrative style makes it hard to believe that the published account of his voyage was written 150 years ago by a nineteen-year-old making his first trip. The excitement of clearing the bar at the harbour entrance, with every sail set and drawing to send the *Alert* scudding on her way, is clearly evoked. Note how the author had to stay aloft to furl and unfurl the fore royals on command from down below to get the most out of her.

The *California* had finished discharging her cargo, and was to get under way at the same time with us. Having washed down decks and got breakfast, the two vessels lay side by side, in complete readiness for sea, our ensigns hanging from the peaks, and our tall spars reflected from the glassy surface of the river, which, since sunrise, had been unbroken by a ripple. At length a few whiffs came across the water, and by eleven o'clock the regular northwest wind set steadily in. There was no need of calling all hands, for we had all been hanging about the forecastle the whole forenoon, and were ready for a start upon the first sign of a breeze. Often we turned our eyes aft upon the captain, who was walking the deck, with every now and then a look to windward. He made a sign to the mate, who came forward, took his station deliberately between the knight-heads, cast a glance aloft, and called out, 'All hands, lay aloft and loose the sails!' We were half in the rigging before the order came, and never since we left Boston were the gaskets off the yards, and the rigging over-hauled, in shorter time. 'All ready forward, sir!' – 'All ready the main!' – 'Cross-jack yards all ready, sir!' – 'Lay down, all hands but one on each yard!' The yard-arm and bunt gaskets were cast off; and each sail hung by the jigger, with one man standing by the tie to let it go. At the same moment that we sprang aloft, a dozen hands sprang into the rigging of the *California*, and in an instant were all over her yards; and her sails, too, were ready to be dropped at the word. In the mean time our bow gun had been loaded and run out, and its discharge was to be the signal for dropping the sails. A cloud of smoke came out of our bows; the echoes of the gun rattled our farewell among the hills of California, and the two ships were covered, from head to foot, with their white canvas. For a few minutes all was uproar and apparent confusion; men jumping about like monkeys in the rigging; ropes and blocks flying, orders given and answered amid the confused noises of men singing out at the ropes. The topsails came to the mast-heads with 'Cheerily men!' and, in a few minutes, every sail was set, for the wind was light. The head sails were backed, the windlass came round 'slip-slap' to the cry of the sailors; – 'Hove short, sir,' said the mate; 'Up with him!' – 'Aye, aye, sir.' A few hearty and long heaves, and the anchor showed its head. 'Hook cat!' The fall was stretched along the decks; all hands laid hold; – 'Hurrah, for the last time,' said the mate; and the anchor came to the cat-head to the tune of 'Time for us to go,' with a rollicking chorus. Everything was done quick, as though it *was* for the last time. The head yards were filled away, and our ship began to move through the water on her homeward-bound course.

The *California* had got under way at the same moment, and we sailed down the narrow bay abreast, and were just off the mouth, and, gradually drawing ahead of her, were on the point of giving her three parting cheers, when suddenly we found ourselves stopped short, and the *California* ranging fast ahead of us. A bar stretches across the mouth of the harbour, with water enough to float common vessels, but, being low in the water, and having kept well to leeward, as we were bound to the southward, we had stuck fast, while the *California*, being light, had floated over.

We kept all sail on, in the hope of forcing over, but, failing in this, we hove aback, and lay waiting for the tide, which was on the flood, to take us back into the channel. This was something of a damper to us, and the captain looked not a little mortified and vexed. 'This is the same place where the *Rosa* got ashore, sir,' observed our red-headed second mate, most *mal à propos*. A malediction on the *Rosa* and him too was all the answer he got, and he slunk off to leeward. In a few minutes the force of the wind and the rising of the tide backed us into the stream, and we were on our way to our old anchoring-place, the tide setting swiftly up, and the ship barely manageable in the light breeze. We came-to in our old berth opposite the hide-house, whose inmates were not a little surprised to see us return. We felt as though we were tied to California; and some of the crew swore that they never should get clear of the *bloody* coast.

In about half an hour, which was near high water, the order was given to man the windlass, and again the anchor was catted; but there was no song, and not a word was said about the last time. The *California* had come back on finding that we had returned, and was hove-to, waiting for us, off the point. This time we pased the bar safely, and were soon up with the *California*, who filled away, and kept us company. She seemed desirous of a trial of speed, and our captain accepted the challenge, although we were loaded down to the bolts of our chain-plates, as deep as a sand-barge, and bound so taut with our cargo that we were no more fit for a race than a man in fetters; while our antagonist was in her best trim. Being clear of the point, the breeze became stiff, and the royal-masts bent under our sails, but we would not take them in until we saw three boys spring aloft into the rigging of the *California*, when they were all furled at once, but with orders to our boys to stay aloft at the top-gallant mast-heads and loose them again at the word. It was my duty to furl the fore royal; and, while standing by to loose it again, I had a fine view of the scene. From where I stood, the two vessels seemed nothing but spars and sails, while their narrow decks, far below, slanting over by the force of the wind aloft, appeared hardly capable of supporting the great fabrics raised upon them. The *California* was to windward of us, and had every advantage; yet, while the breeze was stiff, we held our own. As soon as it began to slacken, she ranged a little ahead, and the order was given to loose the royals. In an instant the gaskets were off and the bunt dropped. 'Sheet home the fore royal! – Weather sheet's home!' – 'Lee sheet's home!' – 'Hoist away, sir!' is bawled from aloft. 'Overhaul your clew-lines!' shouts the mate. 'Aye, aye, sir! all clear!' – 'Taut leech! belay! Well the lee brace; haul taut to windward,' – and the royals are set. These brought us up again; but, the wind continuing light, the *California* set hers, and it was soon evident that she was walking away from us. Our captain then hailed, and said that he should keep off to his course; adding, 'She isn't the *Alert* now. If I had her in your trim she would have been out of sight by this time.' This was good-naturedly answered from the *California*, and she braced sharp up, and stood close upon the wind up the coast; while we squared away our yards, and stood before the wind to the south-southwest. The *California's* crew manned her weather-rigging, waved their hats in the air, and gave us three hearty cheers, which we answered as heartily, and the customary single cheer came back to us from over the water. She stood on her way, doomed to eighteen months' or two years' hard service upon that hated coast, while we were making our way to our home . . .

from *Two Years Before the Mast* by Richard Henry Dana

Captain Richard England served nearly fifteen years in the home trade under sail before the Second World War. During the early 1930s there was still a substantial amount of cargo carried between the lesser ports under sail. In 1930 there were over 600 ships listed under the British Sailing Ship Owners' Association, and they excluded Irish and unregistered craft. Their viability was already threatened by small coastal motor vessels, many of them Dutch. Nevertheless, when Captain England was demobbed from his wartime service with 40 Commando, Royal Marines, he set about finding a trading schooner as a home for his family and a means of providing for them by carrying cargoes. The double topsail schooner *Nellie Bywater* had been built in Millom, Cumberland, in 1873. She was 98 feet overall on a 22-foot beam and drew 11 feet 5 inches. When he acquired her in 1945, he became only her third owner in seventy-two years. From the start it was a losing battle:

January, February and March 1947, were the coldest three months I can ever remember on the British coast. Blizzard followed blizzard without a break and temperatures were so low the sea froze solid in little-used estuaries. Throughout this trying spell of bad weather we were trading across the Irish Sea; Connah's Quay to Belfast with bricks and tiles, and scrap metal back to Summer's Steelworks, Shotton. Freight rates for both commodities were so poor that to be weatherbound inevitably meant a loss, yet the weather became increasingly severe each passage, and life was hard in the *Nellie Bywater*. The icing-up of rigging and sails was a constant worry and we were forever freeing frozen running gear blocks and shovelling snow overboard.

The arctic weather had obviously come to stay, so we sent the children ashore to some relatives for the duration of the freeze. We were very thankful for the fine, safe port of Belfast at one end of our Irish Sea crossings as Chester River was truly a desolate spot in such bad weather.

*

Connah's Quay had been a very prosperous sailing ship port. At the turn of the century, Ferguson & Baird built fine schooners in a yard at the seaward end of the long, piled quay, and there were four schooner owners in the town, Reney, Foulkes, Royle and Coppack.

The *Useful*, owner-master Captain John Wynne, was the sole survivor of the former large, local schooner fleet, and her master the last of the hardcase Chester Rivermen. Short, broad, with a face like wrinkled leather, Johnny Wynne was in a very truculent and critical mood when he came to inspect the rival *Nellie Bywater* during our second visit to the Quay.

In colourful language, with frequent pauses to hawk and spit on our clean deck, he informed the mate of his poor opinion of our schooner. Nothing about the *Nellie Bywater* met with his approval.

*

The *Useful*, loaded with bricks and tiles for Belfast, was anchored off Mostyn, and a few hours after visiting us Captain Wynne was outward bound. During the night there was another blizzard in the Irish Sea and the *Useful* was driven ashore at the base of the lofty cliffs near Douglas, Isle of Man. Distress signals from the stricken schooner were unseen.

The heavy seas began to break up the little vessel but her crew managed to jump to a narrow ledge near the bottom of the cliff. In pitch darkness, and blinded by driving snow and spindrift, the exhausted men, nearly paralyzed with cold, struggled inch by inch up the ice-coated cliff face. The mate, Captain Wynne's son, carried the ship's dog which his father had refused to leave to drown. With unbelievable endurance they all succeeded in reaching the cliff top, but fifty yards or so beyond the edge of the precipice they collapsed in the deep snow and would have died there from exposure had it not been for the little dog they'd saved.

A sheep farmer in search of stock trapped in snow drifts heard its whinning. He found the unconscious men nearly buried under the snow and summoned help from his farm. The frozen schoonermen were carried to the farm where, with care and attention, they recovered and even made light of their ordeal.

Sometimes competing with motor vessels spurred Captain England beyond prudent limits. Having been weatherbound in the Chester River and seen a competitor set out under power a day earlier, he finally took off in pursuit for Belfast. *Nellie Bywater* nearly met her end on the Chicken Rocks south-west of the Isle of Man:

Twenty-four hours later there was a break in the heavy clouds to wind'ard and the barometer had risen slightly. Although there was still plenty of wind the wireless forecast gave an improvement for weather in the Irish Sea.

'Let's go, Colin!' I said to the mate.

The anchor was hove up in record time. When the sails were hoisted, great lumps of ice fell out of their folds . . .

*

The short day ended and through a wild, black night we drove the schooner as hard as she could go. We'd failed to sight a single ship since leaving Chester River as so often happens in bad weather.

I mustered the two lads to tackle the mains'l but as I did so, the rhythm of the schooner's movements altered to a wild, disordered tumble and she began to take solid water over both rails.

Without sufficient experience, Jack and the boy were not much help in the frightening conditions, with the boarding seas sweeping them off their feet. The sail, when half lowered, was pinned against the backstays by the wind and stubbornly refused to come down. Gazing aloft, waiting for one of the violent rolls to ease the sail, I suffered a shock. Almost overhead in the thick haze there appeared a pale incandescence for a few seconds, then it vanished. I saw it again and automatically began counting. The thirty-seconds interval was enough . . . it was the Chicken Rock light.

I clawed my way to the wheelhouse to warn Colin of our close proximity to the Rock and told him to make as much southing as possible.

The next hour was a nightmare. Caught between the run of the steep seas and the backwash off the Chicken Rock, the *Nellie Bywater* was tossed about like a chip of wood. Great dollops of water leaped over the rails from every direction. The racket was indescribable, but above all the other sounds I could hear the ominous metallic clinking of the tiles in the hold. The partially lowered mainsail made the schooner almost unmanageable and it had to come down.

Groping blindly for the peak downhaul, I received a sharp blow in the face, then my neck was encircled in a vicelike grip and I soared aloft, caught in a bight of the downhaul whipped about by the flailing gaff. I knew no more until I hit the deck with a jarring shock and was in such pain I thought my right arm and shoulder had been badly broken. A boarding sea swept me against the wheelhouse and left me at the mate's feet. Before I could tell him what had happened another sea washed me for'ard and deposited me in the waterways.

I think I went temporarily crazy after that . . . picked myself up and muzzled the heavy mainsail practically unaided, for I remember securing the last gasket on a roughly furled sail, although in a state of shock.

Eased by the reduction of canvas, the *Nellie Bywater* gradually crept around the invisible Chicken Rock under the ghostly beam of the lighthouse. The fog-gun kept sounding, the reports coming from every point of the compass with varied volume and distinct echoes at times. I never trusted a fog-gun after that demonstration. Still in a daze, I wondered if the lightkeepers in their lofty eyrie could see us through the fog.

The bearing of the light altered with painful slowness but eventually we gained sufficient offing to scrape around the Chicken.

Later, when we'd gained a lee from the Isle of Man, we reset the mainsail and with much less sea clipped along for the Copelands with the fog left behind us.

*

The *Nellie Bywater* arrived at her usual berth in the Clarendon Dock, Belfast on the evening's tide. There was no sign or news of the rival motor vessel but I'd lost interest in her whereabouts. My sole concern was the state of our cargo, for I fully expected a rubble of broken pipes and tiles after hearing the racket from the hold off the Chickens.

But all was well. The cargo was safely unloaded five days later, when the motor-ship from Chester berthed astern. She had been sheltering in the Menai Straits for nearly a week.

The weather was not *Nellie Bywater*'s only enemy. Bureaucracy on both sides of the Irish Sea precluded her from carrying some lucrative and available cargoes. The Ministry of Fuel blocked off coal, which had been a regular pre-war cargo for trading schooners. The Ministry of Food would not issue permits for potatoes, which were rationed in England. Finally the enterprising owner's wife, Bill, loaded a ton of contraband potatoes in full view of the inspectors. They showed a greater profit on the voyage than the 160 tons of scrap they carried at a take-it-or-leave-it rate.

Soon cargoes became scarcer and less profitable, so an offer to do a charter for the film *The Elusive Pimpernel* was snapped up. From St Malo, where some of the French scenes were shot, Captain England was taken by taxi to reconnoitre the Bay of Mont St Michel. He knew what was coming next, but it would have to await a big spring tide, not due for another month.

> Gazing intently across the bay, I noticed a narrow ribbon of white appear, extending the full width of the inlet. It began travelling towards us at an incredible speed, a monstrous, foam-topped tidal wave. Soon it was audible as a low murmur which rapidly increased to a roar. Sweeping forward at a devastating rate, the huge wave struck the island with an explosive boom, dissolving in spray on the rocks below us. Mont St Michel was again a true islet of the sea.
>
> Statistics of the remarkable phenomena I'd just witnessed state that the sea withdraws as far as ten miles at certain periods, leaving some 100,000 acres of the bay dry, sometimes for as long as two weeks. When the tide again covers the seabed, it races in at the extraordinary speed of 210 metres a minute.

When the day for shooting came, all went well in spite of a local pilot who panicked. Captain England later wrote: 'It was an anxious time for me with only a few inches below the schooner's keel, and I could feel her smelling the bottom.' To ground on the highest tide of the year could be the end of *Nellie Bywater*. The French pilot had been drowning his anxiety in cognac throughout, but that did not stop him boasting to the dockmaster at St Malo that he had taken the schooner right to the ramparts of Mont St Michel and back. He was not believed. Later Captain England saw the movie in Plymouth and was disappointed to find that most of the sequences he had risked his ship for had been left on the cutting-room floor. Nevertheless a future in the film industry seemed assured, until the production company and its studios were abruptly shut down. There were a few odd jobs, such as escorting a Channel swimmer, but hope for the future now rested on getting charter work in the Caribbean.

Nellie Bywater set sail from Falmouth a few days before Christmas. At first the weather was kind, but Christmas Day found *Nellie Bywater* off Ushant at the beginning of the end.

Reports of further casualties were pouring into Lloyds. The Panamanian steamer *Buccaneer*, 7,256 tons, had lost her propeller 150 miles west of Brest and needed immediate assistance; the American steamer *Flying Enterprise*, 6,711 tons, had split her deck and topsides and was listing over to 30 degrees, west of Brest; the Panamanian *Panamante*, 7,176 tons, was in severe weather sou'-west of Ushant, with her steering gear out of action . . .

Wednesday, 26 December
About 9 a.m., with Ushant on our lee about 12 miles distant, we wore ship during a lull. She required a scrap of headsail to help her round and two sails blew to shreds before we could get one to stand. In coming to the port tack, this one also blew away but we were on the desired tack heading about nor' by west in an effort to reach a West Country port.

*

Friday, 28 December
By dawn, the wind had eased off a great deal until it was about Force 8 and the sea wasn't nearly so bad. Prawle Point and the Start were ahead and for a time I hoped we could round these headlands to find a lee. But, the wind backed quickly to sou'-sou'-west, preventing us weathering them. At last, the cunning, treacherous sea had trapped the crippled *Nellie Bywater* on a dangerous lee shore, a situation I'd been dreading. We altered course for Plymouth as there was still a faint possibility of scraping past Bolt Head and Tail. Salcombe lay tantalisingly off our starboard beam, yet inaccessible owing to the state of the bar.

We hoisted the NC code flags and ungriped our lifeboat. Shortly afterwards a large tanker came up astern and by semaphore, we requested her master to radio Plymouth for a tug and in the meantime stand by us. The time was 9 a.m. The vessel was the British Tanker Company's M. T. *British Birch* of 8,000 tons, light and rolling heavily in the big sea.

*

We weathered Bolt Tail but were setting down on the land. The *British Birch* signalled he would try to tow us. I instructed the mate to reply: 'Keep away or you'll sink us!'

I was unable to read what was sent but the tanker continued to close our lee side. Thoroughly alarmed, I yelled to the mate to repeat his warning signal.

The tanker still approached us, enormous and lethal, rolling like a cockle-

329

shell. She was being magnificently handled but in the heavy sea anything could happen.

Bill and little Inga were with me in the wheelhouse and Jo was a few yards away in the shelter of the cabin companionway. They watched the tanker closing us, wide-eyed and apprehensive.

Dangerously near and paralled to the battered, jury-rigged little schooner, the *British Birch* fired her line-throwing gun. A rocket with its attached line arced over the *Nellie Bywater*'s after deck. The tanker steamed clear and lay hove-to, blowing to loo'ard and paying out a very big new hawser which my crew hauled aboard the schooner.

The *British Birch* steamed to wind'ard across our bows, in an attempt to straighten the towrope which lay as a great semi-circle in the sea off our lee bow. I stationed the mate with a sharp axe near the taut hawser, ready to cut it adrift if necessary.

The towrope resisted the efforts to straighten it but the immense power of the tanker was transmitted through the hawser, listing our little vessel over in the most alarming way; the strain was too much for any wooden ship. I signalled the mate to cut but before he could do so, the hawser apparently parted. With incredible speed, the *Nellie Bywater* rolled over to port, throwing me over the wheel and dipping the weather foreyardarm into the sea. Then, even more violently, she rolled back to starboard and I felt a dreadful shudder passing through her timbers – the convulsive paroxysm of a stricken ship as the holding-down bolts of engines, water and fuel tanks sheared and everything, including the ballast, thundered to starboard.

The wheelhouse was instantly submerged, trapping all inside below the sea. Swirled about like a chip of wood, my sense of direction gone, I tried desperately to find my wife and daughter. With lungs nearly bursting, I touched someone's clothing and instinctively knew it was little Inga. Groping blindly, I found a window opening and pushed the child through it. I was nearly done for but the fear of losing my wife spurred me on. With a last frantic effort, I found her trapped under the wheel spindle and, with difficulty, got her through the window, her lifejacket nearly foiling me.

It was my last recollection of being in the submerged wheelhouse. I must have lost consciousness and the structure, battered by the seas, probably broke up and released me, for when I came to again I was on the surface.

The *Nellie Bywater* lay capsized on her starboard side, the masts level with the water . . .

I was rapidly weakening and being without a lifejacket myself, my heavy clothing and seaboots were weighing us down. Several times I'd struggled to rid myself of the boots and outer garments but was unable to do so. Gradually my lungs were being clogged with choking brine. Numbed by exposure and exhaustion, we were both immune to further suffering and it seemed best to let the sea take us. On the point of giving up, I saw a big, ocean-going tug not more than fifty yards away and summoned up a final effort.

The tug was rolling violently, alternately exposing her bottom to the keel and then plunging her heavy beltings below the waves. A line of lifebuoys hung along her side. Reaching the vessel, I waited for the dangerous belting to hit the water and then thrust my free arm through one of the buoys. The tug rolled away from us, nearly pulling my arm from its socket and I blacked out.

I came to briefly aboard the tug. I was lying on her saloon sole, two burly seamen pumping salt water out of me. Around me were members of my crew, huddled in blankets.

Struggling to a sitting position, I asked for my wife. Someone said she was in the Chief Engineer's quarters with Inga and the nurse. Still in the throes of a nightmare, I checked the survivors. John Divers and my eldest daughter Jo were not with them.

Fearfully, I asked where they were, although I already knew the answer. The silence confirmed that they were both lost.

The shock was too much to bear and, mercifully, I lost consciousness again and knew nothing for several hours.

from *Schoonerman* by Captain Richard England

Life did not treat the Englands kindly over the next thirty years. He set up in business as a sailmaker of the old school, only to have his expertise overtaken by computer-operated machines. They ended up in a caravan near Swindon. There he took three years to write his book. It won the 'Best Book of the Sea' Award in 1981.

Smuggling

The traffic in contraband around the British Isles dates back to the reign of Charles II when the 'owlers' smuggled raw wool out of England to the garment-makers of Europe. The better-remembered trade in the other direction did not flourish until the beginning of the eighteenth century, after which it became a major industry until the middle of Queen Victoria's reign. Much romantic folklore has attached itself to the Free Traders, depicting them as swashbuckling, hard-living, courageous seamen engaged in a freemasonry which indulged in the technical offence of evading duty on certain imports.

Public sympathy was behind them, few juries along the south coast would convict them, a fair number of the Preventive Officers were in collusion with them or only too ready to avoid confrontation, West Country parsons (up to the advent of Charles Wesley) were persuaded by their churchwardens to look the other way if duty-free brandy was temporarily hidden in the crypt or even the font. So the legends persist, some apocryphal but many based on fact. If not an honourable profession, it was certainly a respected one amongst seaside communities, as the following tale from Hastings in 1832 shows:

> . . . one of the most noted of the local fraternity was a fat, good-natured fellow called Raper, who commanded a remarkably fast-sailing lugger, called the *Little Anne*. Though an inveterate free-trader, so far from assailing the 'Warriors' with taunts and abuse, like the rest of his comrades, Raper conducted himself with undeviating civility. On being asked by an officer, once, why he did not quit smuggling and turn fisherman, he replied 'What! would you have me sit bobbing an eel all day, to catch sixpen'orth of whiting? No! I was born a smuggler, I was bred a smuggler, and I shall die a smuggler; but I have no wish to see my children tread in the same footsteps. If either of my boys gets into a boat, I'll either break his legs or make him a linen-draper, sooner than he shall larn all the trouble that his father has experienced.'

> from *The Smugglers* by Shore and Harper

The reality is closer to Dr Johnson's definition of a smuggler: 'A wretch who, in defiance of the laws, imports and exports goods without payment of the customs'. They were ruthless, desperate men who thought nothing of killing an informer in public by slow torture or gunning down a soldier or sailor who threatened to thwart their plans. Large areas of Kent and Sussex became no-go areas for the law.

In 1747 the notorious Hawkhurst Gang, extending its sphere of operations far to the west of its home territory, broke into the Customs House at Poole to recover 2 tons of tea and thirty-nine casks of brandy which a revenue cutter had seized offshore. Passing through Fordingbridge on their way back, one of the smugglers happened to speak to an acquaintance called Chater, who later mentioned the matter. When some of the gang were arrested and about to stand their trial at Chichester, Chater was ordered to make his way to the local magistrate there, accompanied by a customs officer from Southampton. The landlady of the White Hart at Rowlands Castle gave them away. Then the heavy mob moved in. The customs man was tortured and buried alive at the Red Lion in Rake

on the Portsmouth road. The other one was worked over with a knife.
Expecting to die, he knelt and began to

say the Lord's Prayer. One of the villains got behind and kicked him, and
after Chater had asked what they had done to Galley, the man who was
confronting him drew his knife across the poor man's face, cut his nose
through, and almost cut both his eyes out. And, a moment later, gashed
him terribly across the forehead. They then proceeded to conduct him to
a well. It was now the dead of night, and the well was about thirty feet
deep, but without water, being surrounded with pales at the top to prevent
cattle from falling in. They compelled him to get over, and not through
these pales, and a rope was placed round his neck, the other end being
made fast to the paling. They then pushed him into the well, but as the
rope was short they then untied him, and threw him head foremost into
the former, and, finally, to stop his groanings, hurled down rails and
gateposts and large stones.

I have omitted the oaths and some of the worst features of the incident,
but the above outline is more than adequate to suggest the barbarism of a
lot of men bent on lawlessness and revenge. Drunk with their own success,
the gang now went about with even greater desperation. Everybody stood
in terror of them; Custom officers were so frightened that they hardly
dared to perform their duties, and the magistrates themselves were equally
frightened to convict smugglers.

Up to the time of Trafalgar they confidently reckoned to overcome
whatever forces the law deployed against them at sea or on land by force
or sheer weight of numbers. They could outsail or outgun most revenue
ships; for good measure, they hijacked some of them for their own
purpose. Once landed, they could muster up to 200 men to run the
contraband in from the beach to a safe warehouse or distribution centre.
Afloat they doubled as pirates, ashore as highwaymen. They went to
some lengths to maintain their cover as innocent fishermen . . .

. . . these cutter and smacks . . . put to sea from whatever port to which
they belonged – London, Dover, Rye, Folkestone, or wherever it might be
– having on board a small number of hands, their professed object being
to fish. Having stood some distance away from the land, they would be
met during the night by a number of smaller craft, and under cover of
darkness would take on board from the latter large crews, much merchandise, and a considerable amount of money. The smaller craft rowed or
sailed back to the beach before daylight, and the bigger craft, now well
supplied with men, money, and merchandise, stood on their course for
some Dutch or French port. There they purchased such goods as they
required, disposed of those which they had brought, and again set sail for
home. The vessel was again met at a convenient distance from the English

shore by smaller boats if a favourable signal had been flashed from the land; and, using the darkness of the night, once more both the cargo and the supernumerary men were put into the boats, after which the latter ran the stuff ashore in casks already slung and in bales, while the smack headed for her harbour whence she had set out. As she had just the same crew as before, no suspicions were aroused, and it was presumed she had been out fishing . . .

Even when confronted with a revenue cutter, the smuggler often got the better of it, sometimes by little more than the threat of force. The famous North Sea smuggler 'Smoker' not only frightened the revenue cutter *Swallow* out of his area, but followed her into the bay where she was anchored, and crashed into her quarter to enforce the cutter to cut her anchor warp and sail right out of the area. In 1778 off St Albans Head, 'Smoker' met his match in a more resolute revenue cutter, *Kite*.

After a time the lugger hauled up a point, so that she was heading S. E. by S., the wind being moderate S. W. During the chase the lugger did her best to get away from the cutter, and set her main topsail. The cutter at the time was reefed, but when she saw the lugger's topsail going up she shook out her reefs and set her gaff topsail. It was some little time before the *Kite* had made up her mind that she was a smuggler, for at first she was thought to be one of the few Revenue luggers which were employed in the service. About 11 o'clock, then, the *Kite* was fast overhauling her, notwithstanding that the lugger, by luffing up that extra point, came more on the wind and so increased her pace. It was at first a cloudy night – and perhaps that may have made the *Kite's* skipper a little nervous, for he could hardly need to be reefed in a moderate breeze – but presently the sky cleared.

As the *Kite* approached she hoisted her signals and fired a musket shot . . . But in spite of these signals, which every seafaring man of that time knew very well meant that the pursued vessel was to heave-to, the lugger still held on and took no notice. After that the *Kite* continued to fire several times from her swivel guns. Later still, as the *Kite* came yet closer, the latter hailed her and requested her to lower her sails, informing her at the same time that she was a King's cutter. Still the lugger paid no heed, so the cutter now fired at her from mukskets. It was only after this that the lugger, seeing her chance of escape was gone, gave up, lowered sail, wore round, and came under the *Kite's* stern. The cutter hoisted out a boat, the midshipman already mentioned was sent aboard the lugger, and the latter's master was brought to the *Kite*, when whom should they find to be their prisoner but David Browning, better known as 'Smoker,' of North Sea fame?

. . . The lugger was then put in charge of the midshipman and a prize crew from the cutter, the prisoners being of course taken on board the *Kite*.

Both lugger and cutter then let draw their sails, and set a course N. E. for the Isle of Wight anchor in Spithead. Browning in due time appeared in Court, and a verdict was given for the King, so that at last this celebrated smuggler had been caught after many an exciting chase.

It was not always as simple as that. Shots were often fired in anger on both sides, and the revenue cutters' crews had to have their resolve stiffened by cash payments for disabilities suffered in these actions and all their medical expenses ashore guaranteed. The Deal smugglers were especially tough customers, and plans were made for the local Army garrison to come to the aid of revenue men caught in a one-sided contest, as happened in February 1805, when the cutter *Tartar*, in the service of the

Customs, and the Excise cutter *Lively* were at 10 P.M. cruising close to Dungeness on the look-out for smuggling craft. At the time mentioned they saw a large decked lugger which seemed to them indeed to be a smuggler. It stood on its course and eventually must run its nose ashore. Thereupon a boat's crew, consisting of men from the *Tartar* and the *Lively*, got out their oars and rowed to the spot where the lugger was evidently about to land her cargo. They brought their boat right alongside the lugger just as the latter took the ground. But the lugger's crew, as soon as they saw the Revenue boat come up to her, promptly forsook her and scrambled on to the beach hurriedly. It was noticed that her name was *Diana*, and the Revenue officers had from the first been pretty sure that she was no innocent fishing-vessel, for they had espied flashes from the shore immediately before the *Diana* grazed her keel on to the beach.

Led by one of the two captains out of the cutters, the Revenue men got on board the smuggler and seized her, when she was found to contain a cargo of 665 casks of brandy, 118 casks of rum, and 237 casks of Geneva. Besides these, she had four casks, one case and one basket of wine, 119 bags of tobacco, and 43 lbs. of tea – truly a very fine and valuable cargo. But the officers had not been in possession of the lugger and her cargo more than three-quarters of an hour before a great crowd of infuriated people came down to the beach, armed with firearms and wicked-looking bludgeons. For the lugger's crew had evidently rushed to their shore friends and told them of their bad luck. Some members of this mob were on horseback, others on foot, but on they came with oaths and threats to where the lugger and her captors were remaining. 'We're going to rescue the lugger and her goods,' exclaimed the smugglers, as they stood round the bows of the *Diana* in the darkness of the night. The Revenue men warned them that they had better keep off, or violence would have to be used to prevent such threats being carried out.

But it was impossible to expect reason from an uncontrolled mob raging with fury and indignation.

A pitched battle ensued, with cutlasses and pistols drawn on both sides. The customs were getting the worst of it, especially when most of their guns were silenced through having wet powder. The sergeant and his guard were scrambled from the nearby barracks of the Lancashire Militia, who finally drove the smugglers off. In spite of a reward of £200 being offered, no eyewitnesses came forward for eight years. Then the two ringleaders were put on trial – and found not guilty.

After 1815, when Britain need no longer maintain strong naval forces to contain Bonaparte, the forces of the law were enhanced, with forty-four revenue cutters deployed, backed by a greater number of warships:

> . . . whilst the age of smuggling by violence and force took a long time to die out, yet it reached its zenith about the middle or the last quarter of the eighteenth century. Right till the end of the grand period of smuggling violence was certainly used, but the year 1815 inaugurated a period that was characterised less by force and armed resistance than by artfulness, ingenuity, and all the inventiveness which it is possible to employ on a smuggling craft. 'Smugglers,' says Marryat in one of his novels, 'do not arm now – the service is too dangerous; they effect their purpose by cunning, not by force. Nevertheless, it requires that smugglers should be good seamen, smart, active fellows, and keen-witted, or they can do nothing . . . All they ask is a heavy gale or a thick fog, and they trust to themselves for success.' It was especially after the year 1816, when, as we shall see presently, the Admiralty reorganised the service of cruisers and the Land-guard was tightened up, that the smugglers distinguished them-selves by their great skill and resource, their enterprise and their ability to hoodwink the Revenue men.

These included not only the now-familiar devices of false bottoms and high-value contraband like silks being stowed under an innocent cargo, but many more ingenious ruses. In Flanders it was possible to buy four-stranded rope of which the core was made of twisted tobacco. Sometimes casks of spirits were moored offshore for later collection. High marks must go to the genius who thought up this one:

> A . . . trick which sprang up . . . about 1815, was that of having the casks of spirits fastened, the one behind the other, in line on a warp. One end of this rope would be passed through a hole at the aftermost end of the keel, where it would be made fast. As the vessel sailed along she would thus tow a whole string of barrels like the tail of a kite, but in order to keep the casks from bobbing above water, sinkers were fastened. Normally, of course, these casks would be kept on board, for the resistance of these objects was very considerable, and lessened the vessel's way. Any one who has trailed even a fairly thick warp astern from a small sailing craft must have been surprised at the difference it made to the speed of the vessel.

But so soon as the Revenue cutter began to loom big, overboard went this string of casks towing merrily below the water-line. The cutter would run down to her, and order her to heave-to, which she could afford to do quite willingly. She would be boarded and rummaged, but the officer would to his surprise find nothing at all and be compelled to release her. Away would go the cruiser to chase some other craft, and as soon as she was out of the range of the commander's spy-glass, in would come the tubs again and be stowed dripping in the hold. This trick was played many a time with success, but at last the cruisers got to hear of the device and the smugglers were badly caught.

from *King's Cutters and Smugglers* by E. Keble Chatterton

With the reduction of duty and the increasing vigilance of the Excise, smuggling became less and less profitable. Chatterton concludes that the age of evading customs with bulk cargoes was over. He did not live to see the ex-landing-craft enter Cherbourg in 1945 just after the end of the Second World War, flying the White Ensign. Her skipper said he had been ordered to stock up the battleship *Vanguard*'s wines for the forthcoming Royal Cruise to South Africa. The whole cargo was safely landed near Poole and sold on the black market in London. At the next attempt one of the crew squealed and the skipper ended up in prison.

He was an American who had served in the RNVR, briefly as a wartime submariner. During that time he often discussed the possibility of acquiring an old H-Class boat (vintage 1916) and using it to intercept a Union-Castle liner bringing bullion home from the Cape. No one took him seriously.

WAR AT SEA

Anti-Submarine Warfare

One often wonders how the authors of *Mr Roberts* and *The Caine Mutiny* could ever persuade their readers of the authenticity of the unlikely bunch of oddballs they portrayed as their crews, all in the same ship.

Marcus Goodrich led the way for all of them in his novel *Delilah*, also written against a background of the US Navy policing the Southern Pacific, but in his case just before the outbreak of the First World War. His description of an early coal-burning destroyer and her unconventional crew in the Philippines has to be preserved:

> She was very slim and light. She was always tense, often a-tremble, and never failed to give the impression of being a mass of almost terrible power wrapped in a thin and fragile blue-grey skin. The materials that went into the making of her complete being were more curious and varied than those that went to compose her creator, Man – for Man himself formed part of her bowels, heart, and nerve centres. She ate great quantities of hunked black food, and vented streams of grey debris. Through her coiled veins pumped vaporous, superheated blood at terrific pressure. She inhaled noisily and violently through four huge nostrils, sent her hot breath pouring out through four handsome mouths, and sweated delicate, evanescent, white mist. Her function in existence was to carry blasting destruction at high speed to floating islands of men; and her intended destiny, at the opposite pole from that of the male bee, was to die in this act of impregnating her enemy with death. It was, perhaps, for this reason that she carried her distinctly feminine bow, which was high and very sharp, with graceful arrogance and some slight vindictiveness, after the manner of a perfectly controlled martyr selected for spectacular and aristocratic sacrifice. Her name was *Delilah*.

> from *Delilah* by Marcus Goodrich

After two and a half years of unremitting convoy escort duty, with danger, boredom and acute discomfort dished out to her crew in equal measure, the corvette *Compass Rose* under command of Lieutenant-Commander Ericson finally scored a kill. She blew a U-boat to the surface with depth-charges and then dispatched it by gunfire.

> A final explosion from below drove a cascade of oily water upwards: then there was silence. 'Cease fire,' said Ericson, when the sea began to close in again and the surface flattened under a spreading film of oil. 'Wheel amidships. Stop engines. And stand by with those scrambling-nets.'
> The wonderful moment was over.
> For one man aboard *Compass Rose* it had been over for some little time.

A young seaman, one of the victorious pom-pom's crew, had been killed outright by the lone machine-gunner on the U-boat; the small group of men bending over his body, in compassion and concern, was out of sight behind the gun-mounting, but they made a private world of grief none the less authentic for being completely at variance with the rest of the ship. They were, however, truly private: no one else could see them: and no one else had eyes for anything but the remnants of the U-boat's crew as they swam towards the safety of *Compass Rose*. Many of these, in an extremity of fear or exhaustion, were gasping and crying for help: still exalted by their triumph, the men aboard *Compass Rose* began to cheer them ironically, unable to take seriously the plight of people whom they knew instinctively had been, a few minutes before, staunch apostles of total warfare. . . . 'These are my favourite kind of survivors,' said Morell suddenly, to no one in particular: 'they invented the whole idea themselves. I want to see how they perform.'

They performed as did all the other survivors whom *Compass Rose* had picked out of the water: some cried for help, some swam in sensible silence towards their rescuers, some sank before they could be reached. There was one exception, a notable individualist who might well have sabotaged the whole affair. This was a man who, swimming strongly towards the scrambling-net which hung down over the ship's side, suddenly looked up at his rescuers, raised his right arm, and roared out: 'Heil Hitler!' There was a swift and immediate growl of rage from aboard *Compass Rose*, and a sudden disinclination to put any heart into the heaving and hauling which was necessary to bring the survivors on board. 'Cocky lot of bastards,' said Wainwright, the torpedo-man, sullenly: 'we ought to leave them in to soak. . . .'

Lockhart, who was standing on the iron deck overseeing the rescue-work, felt a sudden spurt of rage as he watched the incident. He felt like agreeing with Wainwright, out loud: he felt that the Captain would be justified in ringing 'Full ahead' and leaving these men to splash around until they sank. But that was only a single impulse of emotion. 'Hurry up!' he called out, affecting not to notice the mood of the men round him. 'We haven't got all day. . . .' One by one the swimmers were hauled out of the water: the man who had shouted was the last to be lifted out, and he had his bare foot so severely trodden on by Leading-Seaman Tonbridge, not a light-treading character, that he now gave a shout of a very different sort.

'Less noise there!' said Lockhart curtly, his face expressionless. 'You're out of danger now. . . . Fall them in,' he added to Tonbridge, and the prisoners were marshalled into an untidy line. There were fourteen of them, with one dead man lying at their feet: the crew of *Compass Rose* stood around in a rough semicircle, staring at their captives. They seemed an insignificant and unexciting lot . . .

*

Ericson had ordered the German captain, who was among the prisoners, to be put in his own cabin, with a sentry on the door as a formal precaution; and later that morning, when they were within sight of the convoy and steaming up to report to *Viperous*, he went below to meet his opposite number. That was how he phrased it, in his mood of triumph and satisfaction . . .

The meeting was an unhappy one, with the U-boat commander opening with a 'Heil Hitler!' and ending by complaining about the captain's cabin being unsuitable accommodation for an officer in the German Navy. 'You're a bastard in any language,' Ericson replied, and left orders for the sentry to shoot him if he gave any trouble. 'I'm not particularly interested in getting you back to England. We could bury you this afternoon if I felt like it.' When he left, Ericson wondered why he did not feel ashamed of himself.

Not long afterwards, *Compass Rose* was sunk by a torpedo. The pathetic handful of survivors was gathered together on two Carley rafts.

Eleven men, on the two rafts; no others were left alive by morning.

It reminded Lockhart of the way a party ashore gradually thinned out and died away, as time and quarrelling and stupor and sleepiness took their toll. At one stage it had been almost a manageable affair: the two Carleys, with their load of a dozen men each and their cluster of hangers-on, had paddled towards each other across the oily heaving sea, and he had taken some kind of rough roll-call, and found that there were over thirty men still alive. But that had been a lot earlier on, when the party was a comparative success . . . As the long endless night progressed, men slipped out of life without warning, shivering and freezing to death almost between sentences: the strict account of dead and living got out of hand, lost its authority and became meaningless. Indeed, the score was hardly worth the keeping, when within a little while – unless the night ended and the sun came up to warm them – it might add up to total disaster.

On the rafts, in the whispering misery of the night that would not end, men were either voices or silences: if they were silences for too many minutes, it meant that they need no longer be counted in, and their places might be taken by others who still had a margin of life and warmth in their bodies.

from *The Cruel Sea* by Nicholas Monsarrat

The next day, eight survivors, including Ericson, were picked up by the Escort Force commander's ship.

The Battle of the Atlantic (1940–45) went through many phases, with first one side gaining a tactical edge, only to have the other regain the upper hand with new weapons or equipment. Centimetric radar got into the battle before U-boats were fitted with intercept receivers on compatible frequencies. This enabled the RAF's maritime aircraft to jump on surfaced U-boats in vital areas, for example those crossing the Bay of Biscay between their French bases and distant patrol areas. The Type XXI snorkel-fitted U-boat with 18-knot submerged speed came on the scene too late. Most of the battle was fought by Type VIIC 750-ton U-boats capable of 17 knots on the surface but only 9 knots submerged in short bursts. During the early years they had relied for their invulnerability on their low profile on the surface and their ability to be able to dive below the deepest setting available for detonating depth-charges.

They were opposed by escort groups, consisting mainly of sloops or corvettes with little margin of speed over a surfaced enemy. But they were led by some tenacious and skilful captains. Given reasonable sonar conditions, they could, in the end, outwit the average U-boat skipper, who was unlikely to have had much combat experience. The most famous and successful Escort Force commander was F. J. Walker in HMS *Starling* leading the Second Support Group, consisting of five others of the same class. They often detected surfaced U-boats first by intercepting their frequent tactical radio traffic in the course of setting up a concerted wolf-pack attack with other boats threatening the same convoy. They could be pinpointed by cross-bearings using VHF radio direction-finding gear. Once they had a U-boat in firm contact without any thermal layers to hide under, its end was only a matter of time. On one mission in 1944 he accounted for six U-boats, bringing his tally to twenty kills.

His encounter with the twenty-seven-year-old Kapitan-Lieutenant Poser in U-202 in June 1942 was typical. The first maximum pattern did no more than throw some of the U-boat's crew off their feet and smash a lot of auxiliary fittings. The Kapitan then ordered her down to 400 feet (in reality the U-boat's depth would have been shown in metres):

During *Starling's* working-up trials, Walker had devised a depth-charge barrage attack for use against U-boats believed to be hugging extreme depths for safety. The plan, known as 'Operation Plaster,' called for three ships in close line abreast to drop depth charges set to 550 feet at five-second intervals.

Now he signalled *Wild Goose* and *Kite* to close in on either side of *Starling* and the three ships steamed forwards over the 'pinged' position of the U-boat dropping a continuous stream of depth charges. It was the naval equivalent of the artillery barrage that precedes an infantry attack. The sea heaved and boiled under the non-stop impact of the explosions.

Twisting and turning and always leaving a trail of charges, the ships 'plastered' the area of U-202. In three minutes a total of seventy-six depth charges had rocked and shaken the attacking ships almost as much as it had the U-boat.

Poser, hearing the first of the barrage explode beneath him, at first thought his hunters outwitted. After minutes of continuous shuddering blasts threatening to blow out every rivet, he decided to dive as deep as U-202 could go. He gave his orders calmly, while the sweat streamed down his face.

'Slow ahead both engines' . . .

'Diving' . . .

'Take her down slowly. . . .'

Tautly the control room crew watched the depth gauge. How far down would she go; and could they get below the rolling roar of depth charges? The engineer officer called out the reading:

'Five hundred . . . 550 . . . 600 . . . 650 . . . 700.' That was the limit she had taken on exercises. Much more, and she would crack under the tremendous pressure.

'Seven hundred and fifty feet. . . .'

The first lieutenant muttered hoarsely into the silence.

'For heaven's sake, Sir, she won't take any more. Let's stay here or surface and fight it out. She'll break up at any moment if we go further.'

Poser ignored the plea and went on staring rigidly at the controls, his mind concentrating on the creaks and groans reverberating through the boat from the straining hull.

'Seven hundred and eighty . . . 800. . . .' Now it was the engineer's turn to plead with his captain.

'With the weight of water on top now, Sir, she probably won't go up. For the love of God, no further.'

Still there was silence from Poser. Above they could hear the dull explosions of the depth charges cushioned by a gap of 300 feet of ocean. It was not the depth charges that would worry them now: only that the U-boat would hold together.

'Eight hundred and twenty feet, Sir.'

Poser snapped out a command.

'Level off and keep her trimmed at 820. Steer due north with revolutions for three knots.'

He left the control room abruptly and the amazed crew saw him take off his jacket, collapse on his bunk and begin reading. He called out to the first lieutenant.

'Warn the crew to use as little energy as possible and to talk only when necessary. The more we conserve our air the longer we can stay down. The enemy might leave us alone or lose us in a few hours.'

There was little hope of that. Above, Walker took Starling in for a second attack with charges set at 300 feet. When this had little effect, he called in

Wild Goose and *Kite* again and the three ships set off on a second barrage attack. The only damage inflicted was to blow *Kite's* gyro compass out of action, and Walker sent her into the outfield, bringing in *Woodpecker* to take her place.

Woodpecker carried out a single attack also without result and Walker turned to the officers on *Starling's* bridge. 'Now we have established that he isn't too shallow, we can only assume he must be deeper than we thought.'

He made several test runs on asdic bearing and found he was losing echo each time at a range of seven hundred yards. This meant the U-boat was deeper than 500 feet. 'What I wouldn't give,' he exclaimed to all and sundry, 'for a good and large charge capable of being set to 700 feet.' He had no idea at that time – neither had the Admiralty – that U-boats could withstand the pressure of water more than 800 feet.

*

'The U-boat,' Walker wrote later, 'was sitting pretty well out of reach and all our antics only made him discharge the wretched S.B.T.s ['submarine bubble targets' used as decoys]. It was all most maddening, but the laugh was very much on our side because not only were asdic conditions perfect and the enemy could easily be held up to a mile, but I could afford to wait for two days while Fritz obviously could not. In any event, it was merely childish of him to try and palm off S.B.T.s on my asdic team and myself. I decided that as he was obviously staying out of reach, I would wait until he had either exhausted his patience, his batteries or his high pressure air.'

By 8 p.m. Poser had taken several evasive turns quite fruitlessly and attempted to distract his tormentors with more S.B.T.s. But Walker was still in contact, with the remainder of the Group patrolling round two miles away, ready to take over contact should *Starling* lose it.

He told Impey and Burn: 'We will sit it out. I estimate this chap will surface about midnight. Either his air or his batteries will run out by then.'

At two minutes past midnight on June 2nd, the air gave out in *U-202* and Poser ordered: 'Take her to the surface.'

Above, only the faint swish of water round the sloops disturbed the penetrating silence as they waited. Without any audible warning, the U-boat rose fast through the water and surfaced with her bows high in the air where they hung momentarily before falling back into the water. The crew leapt through the conning tower hatch to man the guns, and Poser shouted for full speed in the hope of outrunning the hunters.

On *Starling's* bridge, the tiny silver conning tower and the wash of water was just visible in the moonlight as the U-boat broke surface.

'Starshell . . . commence.'

One turret spread the heavens with light, then came the crash and flash of the Group's first broadside laying a barrage of shells round the small target.

*

Three high explosive shells had torn great holes in *U-202's* foredeck, more hits had sliced jaggedly through her conning tower and fifteen of her crew lay dead or dying at their action stations. Poser clutched the periscope column, pulled a revolver from his pocket and gave his last order.

'Abandon ship . . . abandon ship.'

The cry was taken up and passed through the U-boat. Poser turned to say good-bye to his officers. Rather than be captured he was prepared to take his own life. But two of his officers had panicked under the hail of shellfire and, anticipating his order, were already swimming fast from the danger area with a group of sailors who were all crying out for help.

Furiously, Poser threw away his revolver and cursing under his breath decided to be taken prisoner so that one day, when Germany had won the war, he could have the satisfaction of seeing his two defecting officers court-martialled.

By 12.30 a.m. the battle was over and the survivors picked up, two officers and sixteen men in *Starling*, two officers and ten men in *Wild Goose*. The first three to scramble up the nets dangling over *Starling's* side were stopped when they reached the guard rail and asked the name of their captain and the number of the U-boat. They refused to answer. When this was reported to Walker, he said:

'Don't let them come aboard, Number One. And tell them they cannot be picked up until they have given the information we want.'

The three survivors were ordered back into the water where they shouted and screamed for mercy while Filleul, who was in charge of rescue operations, shrugged and repeated the questions. *Starling* was moving slowly away until one lost his nerve and cried out:

'Kapitan Poser, U-boat *202*.'

He was still sobbing out the reply when they were picked up again, blue with cold. Fifteen minutes later, the scuttling charges in *U-202* exploded . . .

from *Walker, R.N.* by Lieutenant Terence Robertson

Two years later Captain Walker died of exhaustion at the age of forty-eight, having fought his enemy and himself to a standstill. But by now there were dozens of escort groups, manned by younger men who had profited from his example and tactical know-how.

The Battle of the Atlantic was as good as won.

Submarines

That submarines are now taken for granted as decisive, front-line weapons, manned by an élite corps of laid-back deadpan professionals has only reluctantly been accepted by military leaders within the past generation. When the first British boats crept out of Haslar Creek from their base at Fort Blockhouse at the beginning of this century, few admirals of any nationality had any idea of their potential. They were 'damned un-English', manned by scruffy, eccentric characters with a jargon and discipline of their own. If captured in war it was widely held that they should be treated as pirates and hanged.

Yet within a few weeks of the outbreak of the First World War in 1914, Otto Weddingen in *U-9* sank the armoured cruisers *Hogue*, *Cressy* and *Aboukir* with the loss of nearly 1,500 lives, more than our total casualties at Trafalgar. Three years later a handful of these sneaky craft had run rings round our bow-and-arrow anti-submarine defences and come within an ace of winning the war by cutting our North Atlantic lifeline. They nearly did it again in 1942–3. Meanwhile the Royal Navy's infant submarine fleet notched up its own battle-honours in the Baltic, the Sea of Marmara and the North Sea.

In the inter-war years an active acoustic detection device (then called asdic, but now sonar), with a notional range of 2,500 yards in perfect conditions, seemed to give the depth-charge crews a better chance. The battlefleet, with its beautifully orchestrated broadsides of 16-inch guns and growing aircraft-carrier arm, was held to be more secure than ever in playing its role in undisputed command of the seas. This precept was varied from 1942 onwards when the US Navy's strike carriers became the capital ships of the day and dominated naval strategy until the nuclear submarines appeared on the scene, so to speak, since they often conceal their presence for months on end.

Life for Royal Navy submariners in the 1930s was wrapped up in set-piece exercises with the battlefleets, with little chance to develop the flair and initiative with which they kept at the Axis jugular in the central Mediterranean when they were the main offensive naval forces at Britain's disposal.

There was no shortage of crews from the regular ranks, so members of the Volunteer Reserve were not recruited until after the losses of the 1940 Norwegian campaign had to be made good. One of the first was

Sub-Lieutenant Edward Young, RNVR, a young book publisher who had never set foot in a submarine before. He ended the war in command of HM Submarine *Storm*, having won a DSO and two DSCs. His modest account of his war became a runaway best-seller. It remains one of the best first-person records of submarine warfare in any language.

Its introduction evokes all the doubts and unspoken fears which crossed the mind of any sailor as he walked over the plank to report on board the fore-casing of his first submarine. Few ever regretted it.

The average man's almost superstitious horror of submarines is surely due to ignorance of how they work and of what the life is like. One of my reasons for writing this book was to try to remove that ignorance and to show what a fascinating life it is. Some people genuinely suffer from claustrophobia; others imagine they would do so inside a submarine, yet cheerfully travel in aeroplanes and underground trains. It is, I suppose, a matter of temperament. In spite of its uncomfortable moments I found wartime life in a submarine preferable to being shelled in a trench knee-deep in mud, or being shut up in the belly of a tank in the heat of a desert battle, or bombing Germany night after night, or working down in the engine-room of any large surface ship.

I once heard a junior submarine officer, in the presence of his commanding officer, refer to submarine pay as 'danger money.' 'DANGER?' roared the C.O. 'Danger! What you get extra pay for, my boy, is skill and responsibility. What the hell do you mean, *danger?*'

In times of peace submarines rarely hit the newspaper headlines unless something goes wrong and one of them is sunk; and then every man who has never been to sea is ready with suggestions for raising her off the bottom and getting the men out. Unfortunately this aspect of the submarine service has acquired a grossly exaggerated importance in the public eye, and every time there is a disaster we hear on all sides well-meaning people demanding more safety devices and better methods of escape. These demands never come from submariners themselves. A submarine is a war machine, and though reasonable safety devices are essential, and indeed are continually being improved, they must take second place to fighting efficiency. Fatal railway accidents could be abolished if all trains were limited to a speed of five miles an hour, and the safest submarine in peacetime (but not in wartime!) would be one that could not dive at all. The submarine service prefers to concentrate rather on making its ships and its men so efficient that the chances of an accident are reduced to the minimum. And though submarines travel thousands of miles every year, surfaced and submerged, fatal accidents are in fact remarkably rare.

from *One of Our Submarines* by Edward Young

As it happened, Edward Young survived such an accident in his first operational submarine, the 500-ton HMS *Umpire*. Leaving her builder's yard at Chatham, she was heading north in convoy when she fell behind station due to an engine defect. An anti-submarine trawler escorting a southbound convoy along the narrow east coast swept channel known as 'E-boat Alley' made a chance encounter and promptly sank her by ramming. All but two of her ship's company of forty went down to the bottom, where the submarine settled in 60 feet of water. Young was one of four to escape from the conning tower without any escape apparatus. Most of the remainder got out from the engine-room hatch using the Davis escape breathing gear (DSEA), on which generations of submariners had been trained from the shallow escape tank at Fort Blockhouse.

It was not until after the war that it was found that the DSEA gear's use of pure oxygen was lethal if inhaled under pressure at depths much below 40 feet. This danger was not exposed sooner, since from 1942 onwards submarines clipped all their hatches except the conning tower and gun tower shut from the outside as well, to reduce the incidence of them being sprung open by depth-charging.

Thereafter DSEA sets were mostly used in harbour on Saturday mornings, since their slim charging bottles known as 'oxlets' were believed to dispense an instant cure for hangovers. Later, the charioteers, those who rode two-man torpedoes with similar breathing sets, could be identified in West End nightclubs by their habit of taking a whiff from their oxlets, before the band packed up their instruments and caught the 5 a.m. tram from Kingsway to Streatham with the printers from Fleet Street.

There were other aspects of peacetime training which bore little relevance to wartime. One was that torpedoes were definitely not expendable, as Bill King found out when he was torpedo officer in a glossy submarine on the China station. The incident which he describes below in his autobiography *The Stick and the Stars* should have marked him down as being richly endowed with that special attribute found only in the most successful wartime commanders – luck. Perhaps it would then have surprised no one to learn that he was alone in surviving command of an operational submarine throughout the Second World War.

After this particular morning's exercise one of *Orpheus'* torpedos could not be found. All day long we combed the ocean in squares, hoping to sight the 15-ft. long metal shape bobbing on the waves. In vain. Eventually we returned at nightfall with everyone's temper high and an official enquiry looming.

Asked if I had, as my duty demanded, seen the stop-valves open [if shut, the compressed air would never reach the torpedo's engine], I had to answer no. I had merely accepted the T.G.M.'s word. Therefore I alone was to blame, and a more crestfallen young officer seldom crept off a submarine.

The sea had been choppy at the time and I thought we might well find it later, but the repeated searches, which to everyone's annoyance had to be made, yielded no result.

Two months later, however, rumours reached our flotilla. Some weird totem had been washed up on the seashore 180 miles away and the local Chinese peasants had carried it in jubilation to their inland village, there to be placed in a special temple. A naval expedition hurried forth to investigate, and, behold, there beneath its own little roof of woven palm leaves sat *my* torpedo. It had been set up in the middle of the village as an object of veneration and delight! A torpedo weighs nearly two tons, so it seemed incredible that these primitive folk could have carried it several miles inland, but they showed how they managed it – slinging it from bamboo poles with twelve men a side. Quite how the Navy explained a torpedo to them I don't know, but amidst huge merriment my 'fish', which the Chinese had hoped to be a portent from the Fertility Goddess, was carried back to the seashore and eventually towed out to an awaiting ship. Somewhat rusted after its spell of deification the torpedo went in for a 'refit', and as far as I know it later did its duty in the war. I never again failed to examine each valve myself.

At the outbreak of war, Bill King was commanding HMS *Snapper*, one of a flotilla operating from Harwich which patrolled the Skagerrak throughout the endless summer of 1940, when Hitler scooped up Norway and overran Europe. There were not enough hours of darkness in which to surface undetected for recharging batteries. The seas were calm, shallow and heavily mined. Successes against the enemy were bought at a frightening price. Finally *Snapper* was recalled for a dockyard overhaul. Doenitz realized the importance of such opportunities to revitalize his U-boat crews by relaxing them in surroundings of unlimited luxury and licence. The British simply gave local leave, taken how and where each member of the crew found possible. Here's how Bill King saw it during his refit time in the autumn of 1940.

Back in Scotland I discovered a surprising change. Six months previously I had been the most junior lieutenant in command. Now losses had taken such a toll that I suddenly found myself Senior Submarine Officer in the flotilla. Before I had time to taste the grandeur of this situation it was time to go south for a refit. *Snapper* wobbled down the Scottish coast in November with her steering at its last gasp.

I had good friends in Northumberland who made me free of their lovely house and their best hunters. Was it I, the clean-shaven, spruced-up individual, who strolled down to a fresh hunting breakfast in the firelit dining-room, gazed out of the tall windows at green lawns, and made leisurely comments about sporting events? The same I who, a week before, had crept bearded and unwashed and short of sleep out of *Snapper*'s conning-tower? We have so many selves and it is important to try out a number of them or one may get rusted into one shape. My nights ashore had been getting increasingly bad, I dreamt incessantly of horrible submarine problems and awoke soaked with sweat, trying to work out how to deal with a caved-in submarine or one stuck on the sea floor or, worst of all, for some unaccountable reason how to halt my submarine from diving *into the earth*. Now dreaming only of persuading horses over stone walls and ditches, I awoke with a smile of anticipation as the chintz curtains were pulled to let the silvery dawn of a crisp January day stream into the quiet room. Ah, the silence of those winter nights and the slow waking into silence. The days spent chasing foxes over the romantic Braes of Derwent country. The tiny triumph of reaching the end of a two-hour run alone with the huntsman (on someone else's best horse!) and being given the brush of the largest fox ever killed there.

After the battle of perplexities we had encountered in the North Sea it gave one great confidence to learn that our authorities, presumably anxious that no German spies should be given the opportunity of galloping around after hounds, had ruled that Naval officers on horseback were not to be allowed the disguise of top hat or bowler. I had to go hunting in my uniform jacket and Naval cap (hardly designed to give protection to gentlemen landing on their heads) . . .

At intervals of pulling off hunting-boots, soaking in hot baths and enjoying that best-meal-in-the-world, an after-hunting dinner, I busied myself seeing how *Snapper*'s crew had been looked after. I found them dismally billeted in an old mens' consumptive home and thinking this poor treatment for returned warriors, I embarked on a blazing row with various authorities. At length my men were given lodging allowances and told to make themselves comfortable wherever they chose. Within a week one had got into trouble with his landlady's daughter and another had to be most expensively disentangled from a singer. As the Chinese say, the wisest man fusses least.

In mid-January, just when *Snapper* had completed her refit and was ready to re-emerge into the fray, I went sick and retired to hospital. I thought I would be fit for her next patrol, but when the date came I still lay in bed and she sailed under a charming young man, Lieutenant Jimmy Prowse. It was his first patrol as commanding officer, and the area he had to cover was the Bay of Biscay. It was very rough weather at the time and I fretted. At night, when the winter wind and rain beat against the hospital windows, I would awake and think of the small steel ship and wonder how she fared.

The fortnight seemed long – longer still the day when she was overdue.

Snapper did not return from that patrol. The enemy made no claim, and we never knew what happened to her.

There were other interludes during the war. Operational commanding officers were pulled out of their submarines for a breather, just as aircrews were stood down after a certain number of combat sorties. In the darkest days of the 10th Flotilla's campaign during 1942, Bill King found himself for a few weeks as Staff Officer Operations in the shore base on Manoel Island. He found it anything but relaxing:

When our submarines had all left harbour I turned wearily to my task. For three weeks I slept beside the chart-table and spent most of the day and night crouched over it attending to the flood of incessant signals. It was rather horrible knowing what was happening and not being in it. I never went out except to climb on the roof at the hour scheduled for a submarine's return. From that flat mediaeval roof of honey-coloured sandstone I could see the rendezvous for submarines at the end of the patrol. Anxiously pacing the fortifications, watching the dawn light up the green or violet sea, I would know the bitter, nervous wondering, the heart-searching of a staff officer who may have made a mistake. When no grey conning-tower hove into sight I returned leaden-hearted to the office and tried to work out what our inadequacies might have been. It was cruel work.

Immediately Operation Torch had been launched, our submarines, manned by exhausted commanding officers, some nearly at the end of their nervous endurance, went out to sink the inevitable convoys of reinforcements to Tunisia. While an immense curtain of aircraft shadowed and chased them they blew holes in the enemy's sea-line. Many were hunted to death, depth-bombed and crushed, deep under the water. Those who returned flew the Jolly Roger with a bar across it for each ship sunk, an idea which had been started to give the crews a bit of fun!

My job, which had never before consisted of being 'the one who waits', began to play on my nerves. When sick with anxiety I went up to the roof to see my friends return and had to note the blanks, I realized for the first time what Captain Ruck-Keene must have gone through when he waited for us to come back from the North Sea and over and over again had to record the ominous 'an hour overdue', 'a day overdue' and then 'a week overdue – presumed lost'. That was all one ever knew.

Submarine losses were small in the Mediterranean compared to the North Sea, but the old sweats were getting tired. I can remember talking to a submarine captain in our command and sensing suddenly that he was at the end of his tether. I knew that he ought to be pulled out. But we had no qualified commanding officer to replace him. It would have meant withholding a submarine from action.

The accuracy of a psychic bid is so important when one has command.

When a man is fighting against his own inner convictions that he is burnt out, his leaders must sense it and act. I let him go to sea *just once more*. His ship did not return. Too late I realized that I had, like him, known it and felt powerless to speak.

from *The Stick and the Stars* by Commander W. D. King

Here it is appropriate to interject a word about our boats which failed to return from patrols in the Mediterranean. Of seventy-seven British submarines sunk in the Second World War, forty-four went down in the Mediterranean, hardly 'small losses'. The Norwegian campaign cost us nine boats, admittedly from fewer which were operationally available.

If there are relatively few autobiographical books about submarines of lasting merit, there is a wealth of fiction, starting with that classic pacesetter of science fiction, Jules Verne. In 1870, when the French Navy was still building warships with sails as their primary means of propulsion, his *Twenty Thousand Leagues Under the Sea* foretold with uncanny accuracy the submarines which would dominate the seas a century later. It was no coincidence that in 1955 the world's first nuclear submarine should be named *Nautilus* after Captain Nemo's legendary craft.

Although her dimensions were those of a post-Second-World-War Fleet submarine, her performance closely matched those of today's latest nuclear boats, with her 19-foot diameter single-screw propulsion giving her 40 knots submerged and extreme diving depth. Here Captain Nemo briefs his unwitting prisoner Arronax:

'There is a powerful agent, obedient, rapid, easy, which conforms to every use, and reigns supreme on board my vessel. Everything is done my means of it. It lights it, warms it, and is the soul of my mechanical apparatus. This agent is electricity.'

'Electricity?' I cried in surprise.

'Yes, sir.'

'Nevertheless, Captain, you possess an extreme rapidity of movement, which does not agree well with the power of electricity. Until now, its dynamic force has remained under restraint, and has only been able to produce a small amount of power.'

'Professor,' said Captain Nemo, 'my electricity is not everybody's. You know what sea water is composed of. In a thousand grammes are found 96½ per cent of water, and about 2⅔ per cent of chloride of sodium; then, in a smaller quantity, chlorides of magnesium and of potassium, bromide of magnesium, sulphate of magnesia, sulphate and carbonate of lime. You see, then, that chloride of sodium forms a large part of it. So it is this sodium that I extract from sea water, and of which I compose my ingredients, I

354

owe all to the ocean; it produces electricity, and electricity gives heat, light, motion and, in a word, life to the *Nautilus*.'

'But not the air you breathe?'

'Oh, I could manufacture the air necessary for my consumption, but it is useless, because I go up to the surface of the water when I please. However, if electricity does not furnish me with air to breathe, it works at least the powerful pumps that are stored in spacious reservoirs, and which enable me to prolong at need, and as long as I will, my stay in the depths of the sea. It gives a uniform and unintermittent light, which the sun does not. Now look at this clock; it is electrical, and goes with a regularity that defies the best chronometers. I have divided it into twenty-four hours, like the Italian clocks, because for me there is neither night nor day, sun nor moon, but only that factitious light that I take with me to the bottom of the sea. Look, just now, it is ten o'clock in the morning.'

'Exactly.'

'Another application of electricity. This dial hanging in front of us indicates the speed of the *Nautilus*. An electic thread puts it in communication with the screw, and the needle indicates the real speed. Look, now we are spinning along with a uniform speed of fifteen miles an hour.'

Arronax is then taken on a tour of the ship:

A door opened, and I found myself in the compartment where Captain Nemo – certainly an engineer of a very high order – had arranged his locomotive machinery. This engine-room, clearly lighted, did not measure less than sixty-five feet in length. It was divided into two parts; the first contained the materials for producing electricity, and the second the machinery that connected it with the screw. I examined it with great interest, in order to understand the machinery of the *Nautilus*.

'You see,' said the Captain, 'I use Bunsen's contrivances, not Ruhmkorff's. Those would not have been powerful enough. Bunsen's are fewer in number, but strong and large, which experience proves to be the best. The electricity produced passes forward, where it works, by electro-magnets of great size, on a system of levers and cog-wheels that transmit the movement to the axle of the screw. This one, the diameter of which is nineteen feet, and the thread twenty-three feet, performs about a hundred and twenty revolutions in a second.'

'And you get then?'

'A speed of fifty miles an hour.'

Captain Nemo described her double-hull construction and methods of control underwater:

'The *Nautilus* is composed of two hulls, one inside, the other outside, joined by T-shaped irons, which render it very strong. Indeed, owing to this cellular arrangment it resists like a block, as if it were solid. Its sides cannot yield; it coheres spontaneously, and not by the closeness of its rivets; and the homogeneity of its construction, due to the perfect union of the materials, enables it to defy the roughest seas.

'These two hulls are composed of steel plates, whose density is from .7 to .8 that of water. The first is not less than two inches and a half thick, and weighs 394 tons. The second envelope, the keel, twenty inches high and ten thick, weighs alone sixty-two tons. The engine, the ballast, the several accessories and apparatus appendages, the partitions and bulkheads, weigh 961.62 tons. Do you follow all this?'

*

'To steer this boat to starboard or port, to turn, in a word, following a horizontal plane, I use an ordinary rudder fixed on the back of the sternpost, and with one wheel and some tackle to steer by. But I can also make the *Nautilus* rise and sink, and sink and rise, by vertical movement by means of two inclined planes fastened to its sides, opposite the centre of flotation, planes that move in every direction, and that are worked by powerful levers from the interior. If the planes are kept parallel with the boat, it moves horizontally. If slanted, the *Nautilus*, according to this inclination, and under the influence of the screw, either sinks diagonally or rises diagonally as it suits me. And even if I wish to rise more quickly to the surface, I ship the screw, and the pressure of the water causes the *Nautilus* to rise vertically like a balloon filled with hydrogen.'

from *Twenty Thousand Leagues Under the Sea* by Jules Verne

Nautilus cost £200,000 (£70 million today) including the pictures and other works of art used to furnish her. Her owner modestly admitted to being able to afford to pay off the entire national debt of France without missing it.

In peace and war submarine crews have faced death in terrifying circumstances, ranging from carbon-monoxide poisoning to a catastrophic implosion of the hull as the depth-gauge needle passes the point of pressure-hull collapse – a figure known to all on board within 5 per cent accuracy. In Tom Clancy's *Hunt for Red October* the Soviet nuclear attack submarine *E. S. Politovskiy* shares both fates. It is worth noting that in all his novels Tom Clancy's grasp of technical detail on ships, weapons and tactics are acknowledged by the top brass in the Pentagon to be uncomfortably near the truth.

The scene is set with the third Alfa Class running deep at 42.3 knots – 110 per cent power – as she had been for over four days racing for the eastern seaboard of North America. Most of the monitor gauges were showing on their red limits when the primary high-pressure reactor

356

cooling pipe started to vibrate ominously. A request to slow down for repairs was angrily overruled by the Political Officer.

A *michman* at the forward end of the compartment heard it first, a low buzz coming through the bulkhead. At first he thought it was feedback noise from the PA speaker, and he waited too long to check it. The clapper broke free and dropped out of the valve nozzle. It was not very large, only ten centimetres in diameter and five millimetres thick. This type of fitting is called a butterfly valve, and the clapper looked just like a butterfly, suspended and twirling in the water flow. If it had been made of stainless steel it would have been heavy enough to fall to the bottom of the vessel. But it was made of titanium, which was both stronger than steel and very much lighter. The coolant flow moved it up, towards the exhaust pipe.

The outward-moving water carried the clapper into the pipe, which had a fifteen-centimetre inside diameter. The pipe was made of stainless steel, two-metre sections welded together for easy replacement in the cramped quarters. The clapper was borne along rapidly towards the heat exchanger. Here the pipe took a forty-five-degree downward turn and the clapper jammed momentarily. This blocked half of the pipe's channel, and before the surge of pressure could dislodge the clapper too many things happened. The moving water had it own momentum. On being blocked, it generated a back-pressure wave within the pipe. Total pressure jumped momentarily to thirty-four hundred pounds. This caused the pipe to flex a few millimetres. The increased pressure, lateral displacement of a weld joint, and cumulative effect of years of high-temperature erosion of the steel damaged the joint. A hole the size of a pencil point opened. The escaping water flashed instantly into steam setting off alarms in the reactor compartment and neighbouring spaces. It ate at the remainder of the weld, rapidly expanding the failure until reactor coolant was erupting as though from a horizontal fountain. One jet of steam demolished the adjacent reactor-control wiring conduits.

What had just begun was a catastrophic loss-of-coolant accident.

The reactor was full depressurized within three seconds. Its many gallons of coolant exploded into steam, seeking release into the surrounding compartment. A dozen alarms sounded at once on the master control board, and in the blink of an eye Vladimir Petchukocov faced his ultimate nightmare. The engineer's automatic trained reaction was to jam his finger on the SCRAM switch, but the steam in the reactor vessel had disabled the rod control system, and there wasn't time to solve the problem. In an instant, Petchukocov knew that his ship was doomed. Next he opened the emergency coolant controls, admitting seawater into the reactor vessel. This automatically set off alarms throughout the hull.

In the control room forward, the captain grasped the nature of the emergency at once. The *Politovskiy* was running at one hundred fifty metres.

He had to get her to the surface immediately, and he shouted orders to blow all ballast and made full rise on the diving planes.

*

In the control room power was lost to the electrically controlled trim tabs on the trailing edge of the diving planes, which automatically switched back to electrohydraulic control. This powered not just the small trim tabs but the diving planes as well. The control assemblies moved instantly to a fifteen-degree up-angle – and she was still moving at thirty-nine knots. With all her ballast tanks now blasted free of water by compressed air, the submarine was very light, and she rose like a climbing aircraft. In seconds the astonished control room crew felt their boat rise to an up-angle that was forty-five degrees and getting worse. A moment later they were too busy trying to stand to come to grips with the problem. Now the *Alfa* was climbing almost vertically at thirty miles per hour. Every man and unsecured item aboard fell sternward.

*

In the *Politovskiy's* reactor, the runaway fission reaction had virtually annihilated both the incoming seawater and the uranium fuel rods. Their debris settled on the after wall of the reactor vessel. In a minute there was a metre-wide puddle of radioactive slag, enough to form its own critical mass. The reaction continued unabated, this time directly attacking the tough stainless steel of the vessel. Nothing man made could long withstand five thousand degrees of direct heat. In ten seconds the vessel wall failed. The uranium mass dropped free, against the aft bulkhead.

Petchukocov knew he was dead. He saw the paint on the forward bulkhead turn black, and his last impression was of a dark mass surrounded with a blue glow. The engineer's body vaporized an instant later, and the mass of slag dropped to the next bulkhead aft.

Forward, the submarine's nearly vertical angle in the water eased. The high-pressure air in the ballast tanks spilled out of the bottom floods and the tanks filled with water, dropping the angle of the boat and submerging her. In the forward part of the submarine men were screaming. The captain struggled to his feet, ignoring his broken leg, trying to get control, to get his men organised and out of the submarine before it was too late . . .

In the engine room, the changing angle dropped the melted core to the deck. The hot mass attacked the steel deck first, burning through that, then the titanium of the hull. Five seconds later the engine room was vented to the sea. The *Politovskiy's* largest compartment filled rapidly with water. This destroyed what little reserve buoyancy the ship had, and the acute down-angle returned. The *Alfa* began her last dive.

The stern dropped just as the captain began to get his control room crew to react to orders again. His head struck an instrument console. What slim hopes his crew had died with him. The *Politovskiy* was falling backwards, her propeller windmilling the wrong way as she slid to the bottom of the sea.

It took nine minutes for the *Politovskiy* to fall the two thousand feet to the ocean floor. She impacted savagely on the hard sand bottom at the edge of the continental shelf. It was a tribute to her builders that her interior bulkheads held. All the compartments from the reactor room aft were flooded and half the crew killed in them, but the forward compartments were dry. Even this was more curse than blessing. With the aft air storage banks unusable and only emergency battery power to run the complex environmental control systems, the forty men had only a limited supply of air. They were spared a rapid death from the crushing North Atlantic only to face a slower one from asphyxiation.

from *The Hunt for Red October* by Tom Clancy

The final two extracts in this chapter give an inkling of the quality of leadership and morale needed by the German U-boat arm during the Second World War. The first describes the odds against breaking through the Straits of Gibraltar into the Western Mediterranean, only seven miles wide and patrolled around the clock by destroyers and maritime patrol aircraft. This Type VIIC U-boat pushed her luck on the surface too far.

One-eight-zero – due south. We were heading straight for the African coast, buy why?

Somebody yelled: 'The port engine's packed up!' That crazy racket – could it really be the product of a single engine?

A sudden glare from the conning-tower drew my gaze upwards. Beside me, the Chief also stared up at the dazzling magnesium light.

'Star-shells!' he shouted.

The engine noise was driving me insane. I wanted to plug my ears against the almost palpable flow of sound. Better still, I opened my mouth like a gunner. The next explosion might erupt at any moment.

I heard myself counting. Superimposed on the murmured succession of numbers, a new cry of panic from the stern: 'Motor-room bilge rising fast . . .'

I'd never swum wearing escape gear, not even in practice. The patrol ships – how far away were they? Far too dark, nobody would spot us in the water. And the current . . . A lot of power behind it – the Old Man had said so himself. It would scatter us in minutes. If we had to swim for it, we were lost. The surface current flowed out of the Mediterranean – in other words, into the Atlantic. Nobody would find us in the Atlantic. Nonsense, I'd got it all wrong: it would carry us into the Mediterranean. Surface current, undercurrent . . . Keep counting! Seagulls, slashing beaks, gelatinous corpses, bare white skulls coated with slime . . .

Three hundred and seventy-nine, three hundred and eighty . . .

'Dive dive dive!'

The main vents snapped open. This time the U-boat was bow-down within seconds.

The Captain descended the ladder. Left foot, right foot – normality itself, unlike his voice. 'Bloody star-shells! It's like the Chinese New Year up there . . .' The tremor vanished. 'I could have read a newspaper.'

What now? Weren't we abandoning ship after all? Nothing could be inferred from the Captain's dimly lit face. Lowered lids, deep creases above the bridge of his nose. He didn't seem to register the reports from aft.

Our bow-down angle pressed me hard against the forward bulkhead. I could feel the paintwork cold and clammy against my palms. Was I wrong, or were we going down faster than usual? All hell broke loose. Men reeled into the control-room, slithering, falling headlong. One of them butted my stomach with his head as he fell. I pulled him to his feet but failed to recognize who it was. Had I missed an 'All hands forward!' in the general hubbub?

The depth-gauge! The needle was still turning, though we were trimmed for 30 metres. It should have slowed down long ago. Staring at it, I became aware of a blue haze. Smoke was drifting forward into the control-room.

The Chief glanced round. For a fraction of a second, consternation showed in his face.

He gave a plane order designed to trim the boat dynamically. The waterstream from the screws should have forced our bow up, but were the motors developing full power? I couldn't hear their familiar hum. Were they running at all?

Everything was drowned by the scuff and slither of boots on deck-plates – whimpering, too. Who could it be? The meagre light made it hard to identify anyone.

'Foreplane jammed!' one of the planesmen called without looking round.

The Chief kept his torch on the depth-gauge. In spite of the smoke, I saw the needle swing rapidly from 50 metres to 60. When it passed 70, the Captain shouted 'Blow!' The sharp hiss of HP air soothed my jangling nerves. Thank God for some buoyancy at last!

But the needle continued to revolve. Of course, nothing abnormal in that. It would go on turning until the downward tendency was reversed. There was bound to be a time-lag.

Now, though – now it simply had to stop. My eyelids gave an involuntary flutter. I wrenched them open, forced myself not to blink and peered intently at the dial. The needle showed no sign of slowing, still less stopping. It passed the 80-metre mark, then the 90.

I stared with every ounce of energy I had, trying by sheer will-power to arrest the thin black strip of metal that rotated so inexorably in the beam from the Chief's torch. No use. It passed the 100–metre mark and crept onwards.

'I can't hold her,' whispered the Chief.

Can't hold her, can't hold her . . . Why not? Insufficient buoyancy to

360

offset the weight of the water we had taken in? Had we simply become too heavy? Was this the end? At what depth would the pressure hull collapse? When would the steel skin bulge inwards between the frames and burst?

The needle brushed past the 120-metre mark, still turning steadily. My eyes flinched away from the dial. I stood up, plastered against the bulkhead. One of the Chief's lessons flashed through my mind: at greater depths, water-pressure reduces a submarine's volume, thereby reducing the volume of the water she displaces. In other words, the greater the compression, the smaller the upthrust of displaced water and the greater the boat's relative weight. No more buoyancy, just the earth's attraction and an accelerating rate of descent . . .

'190,' the Chief reported, '200 – 210 . . .'

And deeper still.

The figure reverberated inside my skull: 210!

I stopped breathing. The noise of rending metal could come any time now – and the green cataract.

Where first?

The whole boat creaked and groaned. There was a sharp crack like a pistol-shot, then a muffled whine which pierced me through and through.

The whine grew shriller until it resembled the scream of a circular saw rotating at full speed.

Another sharp report, more creaks and groans.

'260 and still falling,' called an unfamiliar voice. I found myself toiling up the incline. My feet slipped. I just managed to save myself by the hoisting wire of the search periscope, which cut painfully into my palm.

Steel bands encircled my chest.

The needle was about to pass the 270-metre mark. Another whiplash. Rivet-heads must be snapping. No rivets or welded joints could withstand such pressure.

A voice was intoning: 'Yea, though I walk through the valley of the shadow of death . . .' The Vicar? Figures thronged the control-room, groping and fumbling in the gloom.

A sudden impact knocked my legs from under me. I rolled across the deck and fetched up against a figure in a leather jacket. My hands clutched at a dim face. A many-voiced cry issued from the forward bulkhead. Like an answering echo, other shouts came from the stern. The deck-plates rattled and clanged as they jumped in their beds. There was a prolonged tinkle of glass, like a Christmas-tree falling over. The hull reverberated under another violent shock, and another. A moment later my body was sawn clean across by a strident screech. The boat juddered insanely and was smitten by a series of dull blows, as if we were bumping across a gravel-bed. From outside came the throaty trumpeting of some prehistoric monster, the squeal of a thousand pigs, two more blows on a mighty gong – and then, quite suddenly, the tumult died. All that remained was a high singing note.

'We're there.' The words were clearly articulated but the voice seemed to come from behind a locked door. It belonged to the Captain.

The torch-lit gloom persisted. I wondered why nobody had switched on the emergency lighting. My ears registered a gurgling sound. The bilge? Water from outboard wouldn't have gurgled like that.

I tried to distinguish and locate various sounds: cries, whispers, murmurs, voices edgy with panic.

'Damage reports!' I heard the Captain say. Imperiously, a moment later: 'I must have accurate damage reports!'

Light at last – of a sort. What were all those men doing there? I blinked hard, narrowed my eyes to slits and tried to penetrate the semidarkness. Shouts and disconnected words impinged on my consciousness. Most of the noise came from aft.

My gaze was drawn alternately by two faces, the Captain's and the Chief's. I caught fragments of damage reports, sometimes a whole sentence, sometimes the odd word. Men hurried aft, wide-eyed with terror. One of them barged into me and almost knocked me down.

A shovelful of sand . . . Who had said that? The Captain, naturally. 'At least there's a shovelful of sand under the keel.'

I struggled to understand what had happened. It was dark up top – not pitch-dark, admittedly, but not flooded with moonlight either. No flyer could have spotted us in that gloom. Bomb a submarine at night? It wasn't a practical proposition. Perhaps it had been a shell after all. Ship's gun, shore battery? But the Old Man had yelled something about a plane. And what of the crescendo of sound immediately before the explosion?

The Chief scuttled to and fro, barking orders.

And then? 'We're there!' The gravel-bed, the pressure hull . . . We carried as little armour-plating as an addled egg. The crazy squealing, the tram rounding a bend . . . It was obvious: we had run full tilt into the rocky bottom – what else? Full ahead both and bow-down. To think that the boat had survived, when her steel skin was already compressed to the point of collapse. And then that impact, that shock, that collision . . .

from U-boat by Lothar-Gunther Buchheim

It was the beginning of a nightmare lasting over forty-eight hours. The depth-charging was almost continuous, what little breathable air remained was polluted by chlorine gas from seawater getting into smashed main battery cells and neither boat nor her crew were in any state to fight. They struggled to the surface. The anti-submarine forces had already chalked up their kill and resumed patrolling elsewhere, just long enough for the U-boat to creep past Cape Spartel, put into the Atlantic and, incredibly, get safely back to La Pallice on the Bay of Biscay. It was sunk by low-level air-attack just after securing in the entrance lock to the impregnable U-boat shelter.

The following account of another Type VIIC vividly describes her two worst enemies: the weather in the North Atlantic in midwinter and the growing strength and technical superiority of British escort forces.

The weather showed its most unfriendly side: sky dark, water as grey as lead. Not for nothing does the loading line 'Winter North Atlantic' on the sides of merchant ships allow for lighter loading than in the peaceful summer. But the U-boat was up to the neck in it and had to take everything as it came, including the heavy storm that dragged on without ceasing for over a week, during which the wind backed and veered between SW and NW, screaming and howling up to hurricane strength. Within a few hours on 8 January an enormous sea developed which threatened to smash everything, and we met squalls which tore the combs from the wave tops. Visibility closed in, rain alternated with snow, sleet and hail. As far as the eye could see there were only rolling hills with strips of foam coursing down their sides like the veins in marble. On the surface, the U-boat literally climbed the mountainous seas, plunged through the wave crests, hung for a moment with its stem in the empty air and plunged down the other side into the trough of the waves. When it buried it nose, the screws in the stern seemed to be revolving in air. Then the stern dropped down, the screws disppeared in the maelstrom and the exhaust broke off with a gurgle. In the hard thumps U 333 shuddered in every frame-member like a steel spring. Striking high up in front against the conning tower and from behind into the open bridge screen, the seas smothered us and we had to shut the conning-tower hatch for a while to prevent foundering.

Wet to the skin despite oilskins and sea-boots, the bridge watch were scarcely able to hold the heavy binoculars with their clammy hands. Wedged between periscope supports and bridge casing, they all hung on by safety belts and swivels, which did not prevent the sea tearing away a look-out during the continuing storm and hurling him to the deck, with serious injury to his eye.

*

Wind Force 8 was the least, then the storm rose to Force 10, and in breathtaking squalls reached a full 11 to 12: a hurricane! The Beaufort scale ends at 12: wind speeds of over 65 knots, air filled with foam and spray, sea completely white, all distant visibility ceases, wave lengths 300 metres and more . . .

The inside of the boat was like a dice cup with everything whirling about. Those who had something to do groped from support to support. Sleeping was hardly possible, one just dozed.

After the season of long nights and great storms is over, the U-boat is in greater danger of detection in calm seas and good visibility.

Glowing hot, sunny days alternated with shining star-lit nights and made us forget the war for while until, east of the Bermudas and outside the customary steamer routes, it unexpectedly appeared over the horizon in the shape of two mast-heads. The fair illusion was destroyed and reality drained the Atlantic dream of its magic ... After the masts the funnel appeared. I made do with this scanty picture and on account of the mirror-smooth sea kept my distance so as not to be spotted. I tried to intercept her on the surface, although that was not easy. As it later transpired, she was the *British Prestige*, a motor ship of the British Tanker Co., London, of 11,000 tons laden. What she was laden with will presently be told. Alone and unprotected, the ship was clearly bound for Europe, her continual and confusing zig-zags notwithstanding.

Slowly stalking closer, I pursued the tanker into the afternoon without her noticing us. Perhaps she was blinded by the setting sun, but it was not until twilight that I succeeded in starting the attack. The range was down to 1,200 metres. Everything seemed set for a copybook performance. So – 'Tube 3 – Stand by to fire.'

'Tube 3 – Fire!'

The stop-watch ticked and nothing happened. The seconds became longer and longer – as did my face. Damnation! – missed. The next tube ...

There seemed to be a jinx. The second torpedo missed as well. How could these two failures be explained? For the time being I disappeared from the surface, had the tubes reloaded under water, surfaced again and set off after the tanker, which had not been standing still either. Just as I had caught up with her and was intending to start the third attack, she performed one of her incalculable zig-zags and everything had to begin all over again. The moon, meanwhile, had risen and was lighting up U 333 in every detail. We had no option but to submerge – and particularly as in these very minutes the tanker laid herself wide open. It was now or never. Stand by to attack!

Down periscope, briefly, feed in the firing data, up periscope again. It was the shorter aerial search periscope, the one with the wider field of vision. The dark form of the tanker stood in the blinding moonlight, totally exposed on the silver sea. A splendid target, close enough to touch! But then, quite suddenly, the scene was wiped out and through the lens I saw nothing but blackness. The gigantic side of the tanker, as tall as a house, was coming straight towards us, so close that it was too late for evasion. There were grinding and crashing noises which sounded as though a goods train was passing over us ...

As the captain of *British Prestige*, Ernest W. Hill from Canterbury, later described it, he had just ordered another change of course of 90 degrees and was about to sit at his desk to write to his wife when the tanker was shaken from stem to stern by a massive shock, as though she had run at full speed over a reef. In a flash he was back on the bridge where the first officer shouted to him: 'Torpedo track to starboard!' But the captain guessed right and said: 'That will be the U-boat we rammed when turning, and now pressed down under our keel.' Later, they thought they spotted a long shadow in the moonlight and made off at maximum speed.

In U 333 we had been hurled to and fro. In the control room we stood in a fountain of water, jets coming from everywhere. Water was pouring from the periscope well and from the ventilation ducting. This heavy break-in of water pointed to a gash in the pressure hull. There was only one thing to do: surface!

The conning-tower hatch refused to open so we had to climb out through the galley hatch and clear the conning-tower hatch from outside. Then we saw the extent of the damage: the tanker had first hit us at the bow, twisted our nose to port and then, with the turning of her screws acting like a chopper, shaved off the bridge and mangled our 'three little fishes'. The watertight stem was torn open, the forward net-cutter had gone and something was also missing from the stern one. The steel casing of the conning tower was dented, the periscope snapped, the D/F set and torpedo aiming sight destroyed. The bow caps of tubes two and four were jammed and could not be opened. So much for our damage.

In spite of her damage, U-333 lived to fight again, as the odds against the U-boats steadily lengthened. At the height of the battle, U-333 intercepted and attacked a heavily escorted homeward-bound Gib–UK convoy. The captain dived to attack. His periscope was sighted and a pattern of ten depth-charges dropped right over his boat.

The effect was terrible and is hard to describe. Suddenly everything went black and everything stopped, even the motors. In the whirl of the shock waves the rudderless boat was seized like a cork and thrust upwards. There was a cracking and creaking noise, the world seemed to have come to an end, then crashes and thuds as the boat was thrown onto its side and everything loose came adrift. I managed to grab the steel strop on the periscope, then my legs were pulled from under me. We had collided with the frigate's bottom which was now thrusting away above us, steel against steel. Certainly the British were no less shaken than we, seeing that 'just before the first charge exploded, the ratings on watch in the boiler room heard the periscope scrape down the side' (Precis of Attack by HMS *Exe*. Reference A.U.D. 861/43).

Seconds later, the periscope broke off. The swaying boat reared up, struck the hull of the *Exe* with its conning tower and the control room and listening compartment immediately flooded. The water quickly rose above the floor plates. The light of a torch lying on the chart table showed a picture of devastation. All the indicator gear was hanging loose, the glass was splintered, light bulbs had burst. Cable ends spread in bundles through the control room, the emergency lighting accumulators had torn free. Before I even got to the depth-keeping controls the boat was again shaken by the heaviest depth charges. Like a stone we slipped backwards towards the ocean bed which here lay 5,000 metres below.

From the engine room the hydrostatic external pressure, indicating depth, was passed on from mouth to mouth and the fall of the boat stopped by blowing the tanks with compressed air. It rose slowly, then faster and faster until it had to be flooded again so as not to shoot out of the water like an arrow. Beams from the torches flicked over the walls glistening with moisture. It trickled and poured. As none of the pumps was working the water that had come in was transferred in buckets from hand to hand from the lower lying stern – where it was already above the coaming of the alleyway hatch – into the central bilge. Gradually the boat swung back from the slanting position to the horizontal.

Fortunately the switchboard was still dry, there was no short-circuit. We could put back the knife switches which had fallen out and in feverish haste got the electric motors working. Though the noise of the port propeller shaft showed that damage had been caused, its turning again was music in our ears.

My log says: 'Decide to hold the boat by all possible means and slowly go deeper. Damage very great and cannot yet be assessed.' From the British viewpoint we were 'in the centre of the (first) pattern when it exploded' and 'the first attack must certainly have damaged the U-boat so severely that it was unable to surface.' When an oil patch was sighted at 1156 and a sample was collected it was believed we had sunk.

But in fact we had let ourselves drop from 60 to 140 metres. Meanwhile the entire convoy in its whole length went thumping past us overhead. In such a situation that is about the safest place for a stricken U-boat, particularly as any hydrophone contact is lost in propeller wash. Nothing can touch one, unless perhaps a ship is torpedoed and falls on one's head.

But hardly was the mass of the ships past than we were overwhelmed with a drum-fire such as I had never yet experienced. And that is saying a lot. It began at mid-day and went on till 2055 like a continuous thunder storm, now close, now further away, the heavy-sounding depth charges and the lighter Hedgehogs. And each time we thought, 'Now there'll be a direct hit,' but in fact the explosions detonated further away, we had to wipe the cold sweat from our faces. So-called heroism has much to do with it. And when finally the torture ended and the great silence began we refused to believe it, but stood there wide-eyed, gasping and struggling for breath, waiting for the next series.

Luckily we had little time for reflection. There was too much to do. The worst damage had to be repaired. Damage to instruments (speed and trim indicators, water and pressure gauges, depth recorder) belonged to the lesser evils. Broken telephones and radio could be accepted. Even a destroyed fire-control panel lost significance for survival, particularly as the heads of all the torpedoes in the tubes had been dented, not to mention the plastic cap of my acoustic torpedo which I had thought so important.

From the seepage of water in the boat runnels were formed which could be pumped out more or less.

But the starboard diesel had been thrust sideways and fallen from its base, and this was more than problematical. Now by the sweat of our brow we had to wedge and support it with beams. And hardly less serious was the port propeller shaft, which had been bent and was hammering loudly. To complete our misfortune, the radio installation was so badly damaged that despite trying three times I was only able to send a short mutilated signal.

Air was running out. Our bodily exertions had used it up quicker than usual, and it had to be improved with potash cartridges and oxygen . . . After nine hours of depth-charging which had thoroughly shaken the boat and repeated blowing tanks to maintain depth, there was hardly any compressed air left.

from *U-333* by Peter Cremer

One hour after the last depth-charge, U-333 was forced to surface. The damage was appalling. Both periscopes were wiped off. The upper hatch was blocked by a propeller blade wrenched off from the frigate as she rammed. Luckily there was a big sea running, and U-333 made good her escape on the surface. Her captain, Peter Cremer, had already won the Knight's Cross to his Iron Cross, for sinking three ships off Florida after most of her bridge superstructure had been wiped off when she was rammed on her first patrol. He ended the war in the bunker in Berlin.

Surface Battles

The defeat of the Spanish Armada just 400 years ago was not, as most schoolboys believe, another set-piece battle, like Trafalgar. Its consequences were of crucial importance to Elizabeth I and her subjects, since it lifted for ever the threat of invasion by the all-conquering Catholic monarch, Philip II of Spain. His armies already controlled much of continental Europe, including the Low Countries, where his nephew, the Prince of Parma, had assembled an invasion army ready to force a Channel crossing. But, as a sea-battle, victory over the Spaniards owed more to the weather and the tides than to close combat.

Initially there was a series of skirmishes during the eight days it took the Duke of Medina Sidonia's 130 ships to head up-Channel from the Lizard for his rendezvous off Calais with Parma's armies.

Francis Drake, the great circumnavigator, had not long before returned laden with Spanish booty after his successful raid on Cadiz. He was appointed second-in-command to Lord Howard of Effingham with his ninety-five ships based on Plymouth, whilst Lord Henry Seymour waited off Dover with a fleet about one-third that number. Folklore has it that the cool buccaneer Drake insisted on finishing his game of bowls on The Hoe overlooking Plymouth Sound before sailing to deal with the approaching Armada. The truth of the matter is that he and his ships had to wait for the next ebb tide before they could clear the harbour.

The first decisive move came when Howard loosed fireships into the anchorage off Calais, where the enemy fleet lay against a lee shore with no way of battling their way out except by running to the eastward and risking all the sandbanks which protect the Netherlands coast like a series of coral reefs.

The English admirals, lying off Calais, had not been prepared to stake their country's safety on any chance of weather or connivance of the Dutch. They faced across the water, only two musket shots away, a fleet that was still unbroken in order and unbeaten in battle. The Armada might have been punished, how badly they did not know, but, since the accidents of the first day's engagement, it had not lost a single ship. And this, after a squandering of ammunition such as nobody – Drake alone excepted – had foreseen, was deeply discouraging.

On Sunday morning (7 August) the commanders met in Howard's stately cabin in the *Ark Royal*. It was clear to all of them that, short of some extraneous help, a tactical device was needed to break up the close defensive order of the Armada. It was now or never, for at any hour the two Dukes might join forces. What was to be done? Fireships might be used, as Sir William Wynter had mentioned five days earlier and for which, at that moment, the provident Walsingham was collecting pitch and faggots at Dover. But there was no time to wait for fuel from England. The fleet must improvise its own fireships. Drake at once offered a ship of his own, the *Thomas* (200 tons); Hawkins put in the *Bark Bond* (150 tons); another two ships were taken from Drake's westward squadron – altogether there were eight vessels totalling 1,240 tons which during one feverish day were crammed with every kind of combustible. During the afternoon, Drake changed the position of his squadron so that its new anchorage was directly to windward of the Spanish fleet. That night when the ships and the crews of volunteers were ready, they weather became the ally of the English Navy. The tide at midnight set towards the Spanish anchorage and a fresh wind sprang up from the west. The eight fireships were set off on their course together, with results that surpassed all reasonable expectations.

*

The Spanish look-out men in Calais Road saw eight black shapes approaching on the wind; each shape showed a spark of red fire which, in a matter of minutes, swelled into a mass of flames so that eight floating furnaces were bearing down on the anchored galleons. Worse still, the loaded cannon aboard these mysterious vessels fired their shot as the flames reached their charges. Instantly, a frenzy seized on the Spaniards. The fireships had a mile and a half to cover and wind and current to help them. The Armada had ten minutes to get clear. Cables were cut. A hundred and fifty anchors were abandoned in Calais Sands. Sails were set to catch the wind. Every ship made off as best she could, so as to put as much sea-room as possible between her and the dreaded mine machines (*maquinas de minas*).

After this moment of panic, Medina Sidonia steadied his scattered fleet and sought to bring it into a coherent fighting formation off Gravelines. There the British fell upon them and quickly destroyed three of their most powerful warships. The wind and tide were now threatening to throw most of the Armada on to the same beaches across which soldiers of the British Expeditionary Force made their escape from the advancing Nazis 350 years later. It then became the scene of another miracle, when the wind abruptly backed to the south-east and enabled the Spaniards to make their escape into the North Sea and thence find their way home by going west-about the British Isles.

The distance alone to their nearest safe refuge – 2,300 miles – must have set the chaplains in the fleet to intercede for another divine intervention, like a fresh northerly gale on rounding Cape Wrath. But it was not to be.

Drake was confident that, in the state to which the Armada had been reduced by the fighting, it would be sure to suffer losses on the long voyage back to Spain. Even so, he can hardly have counted on the toll being as grievous as in fact it was. In time, news of the sufferings of those Spaniards leaked back to Madrid and was seized on avidly by the Venetian ambassador – 'I am very hungry and thirsty,' wrote one unfortunate from Scalloway in Shetland. 'One pint of wine a day. You cannot drink the water. It stinks.' Three ships were lost on the Scottish coast and seventeen on the Irish. There are doubts about some items in the casualty list; but on the whole it seems that the reefs and shoals of western Ireland accounted for most of King Philip's losses, 'dissevered on the high seas and to a great number of them driven into divers dangerous bays and upon rocks and there cast away'. Some were driven to seek succour among the 'wild Irish';

369

others, even less fortunate, fell into the clutches of the Lord Deputy and his minions and without any ado had their throats cut, saving only those who, 'by their apparel, seemed to be persons of great distinction' and good for a profitable ransom.

Don Alonzo de Leyva, who held in Spanish eyes a position comparable with that of Sir Philip Sidney in English, the flower of the nation's youth and chivalry, adored by king and people alike, lost his ship off Achill Island and seized a deserted galleon, the *Gerona*, which he found in Donegal Bay. With him was an adventurous company of young men recruited from the best families in Spain. These bright paladins patched up the *Gerona* as best they could and set sail for home. Alas, the galleon struck a rock and went down with all of them. In the respect that death came quickly, they were not the least fortunate of the victims of that homeward voyage. Sir Richard Bingham, Governor of Connaught, and only a shade less bloodthirsty than the Lord Deputy in Dublin, reported complacently to the Queen that 'the cruel and bloody hands of Your Highness's enemies, overthrown through the wonderful handiwork of Almighty God, by great and horrible shipwrecks upon the coasts of this realm . . . did all perish in the sea save the number of 1,100 or upwards which we put to the sword.'

Not all those Spaniards who survived the seven weeks' voyage with 'never good night or day' while it lasted, found happiness at the end of it. The Duke of Florence's galleon, which had been in the thick of the fighting, crawled into port, unfit for repair. The *Santa Ana* reached San Sebastian. There she was burnt, on the same day that her admiral, Oquendo, died – of shame, as they said. Soon, too, Recalde, sick and sorrowful, would be dead.

On the whole, the Spanish royal navy came out of the ordeal better than the auxiliary vessels – only seven King's ships were lost while the Armada as a whole had lost fifty-one.

from *Sir Francis Drake* by George Malcolm Thomson

Over 20,000 officers and men of the Armada, which had set sail with such high hopes in May, perished, mostly in shipwrecks.

One of the most celebrated frigate actions of all time was that fought at point-blank range outside Boston on 1 June 1813. The fifteen-minute action turned on the state of training of the opposing ships' companies and the characters of their commanding officers.

Captain Philip Bowes Vere Broke, of his Majesty's frigate *Shannon*, was all that an officer ought to be, and had brought his crew to a state of proficiency in the use of the broadsword, pike, musket, and great guns which was most unusual in the British navy. To his lot it fell in the spring of 1813 to guard the coast east of Cape Cod with the *Shannon* and the *Tenedos*, and blockade the four American frigates *Congress, President, Chesapeake,* and *Constitution,* then in the harbour of Boston. But blockading was too tame a duty, and more than once he endeavoured to persuade some one of them to come out and fight. For a time he was not successful, and Commodore Rodgers, declining the challenge, ran out on the night of April thirteenth with the *President* and *Congress.* Greatly disappointed, Broke thereupon sent away the *Tenedos,* and formally challenged Lawrence to meet him in the *Chesapeake.*

The Yankee James Lawrence had joined the US Navy at the age of seventeen in 1781 and saw service in the Mediterranean before returning to the West Indies. There he commanded USS *Hornet* when she intercepted and sank the brig HMS *Peacock.* For this exploit he was awarded command of the thirty-six-gun frigate USS *Chesapeake.* The omens were not good, for she had struck to the frigate HMS *Leopard* a year before off Hampton Roads. She lived to fight again only because the victor contented himself with removing British deserters found on board – a not uncommon source of recruitment for the young US Navy in those days.

From the day when she struck to the *Leopard* the *Chesapeake* had been looked on by both officers and men as a most unlucky ship, a superstition which no event in her career ever tended to dispel. On her return to port, April 9th, after an unsuccessful cruise, her old crew left her, to seek for better fortune in some more lucky ship, and such new men as could be secured had been enlisted to fill their places. Some were British, a few were Portuguese; others had never yet seen service on an armed ship. All were unknown to each other and to their officers, and, having never been to sea together, they were without discipline or training. Indeed, it was not till the anchor was about to be weighed that the last draft came aboard, and these still had their hammocks and bags stowed in the boats that brought them when the *Chesapeake* surrendered.

The *Shannon,* on the other hand, was commanded by an officer as courageous, as skilful, and as energetic as Lawrence, and manned by a well-disciplined and well-practised crew. Every day in the forenoon the men were exercised at training the guns, and in the afternoon in the use of the broadsword, the musket, and the pike. Twice each week the crew fired at targets with great guns and musketry, and on such occasions the man who hit the bull's-eye received a pound of tobacco. At times Broke would order a cask thrown overboard and then suddenly command some particular gun to be manned to sink it, a practice more than once witnessed by the American officers at the Charlestown Navy Yard. Save in discipline and number of men (for the *Chesapeake* had forty-nine more than the *Shannon*), the two frigates were not ill matched, as in length, breadth of beam, in guns, and weight of metal they were almost exactly equal.

Considering the *Chesapeake* to be a fair match for the *Shannon* Broke had

371

been most anxious to meet her. Accordingly, on June 1st, seeing the *Chesapeake* riding at anchor below Fort Independence as if waiting to put to sea, Broke ran into the harbour and raised his flag. Lawrence immediately fired a gun and displayed his colours, mustered his crew, told them he intended to fight, and when the tide turned went down the harbour under a press of sail.

*

. . . *Chesapeake*, having rounded the Boston Light, bore off to the eastward, and with the *Shannon* was soon lost to sight. The guns were heard, but almost three weeks passed before it was finally known how the fight ended. The pilot who left the *Chesapeake* at five in the afternoon reported to Commodore Bainbridge that the firing began at six; that in twelve minutes both ships were laying alongside each other as if for boarding; that at this moment a dreadful explosion occurred on the *Chesapeake*, and that when the smoke had blown away the British flag was seen flying over the American. His story was strictly true. But the people could not believe it, even when a boat belonging to the *Chesapeake* was picked up at sea.

*

At last, June 18th, Halifax newspapers with a long account of the funeral honours paid to Lawrence and Ludlow reached Boston, and all doubt was removed.

It then appeared that after passing the lighthouse at one o'clock the *Chesapeake* followed her enemy till five, when the *Shannon* luffed and waited for her to come up. The wind blowing fresh from the west, Lawrence might easily have chosen his position. But he threw away this advantage, came down on the *Shannon*'s quarter, luffed, and ranged up some fifty yards from her starboard side. At ten minutes before six the firing began, and for seven minutes the frigates ran on side by side. Then, some shot from the *Shannon* having crippled the sails of the *Chesapeake*, she came up into the wind and was taken aback, and drifted slowly stern foremost toward the enemy. Every gun on the *Shannon*'s broadside swept her from stem to stern. Man after man was shot down at the wheel. A hand grenade blew up the arms chest, and the stern of the *Chesapeake*, drifting helplessly, struck the *Shannon* amidships. A fluke of the *Shannon*'s anchor caught in a port of the *Chesapeake*. A boatswain rushed forward to lash the ships, and Broke, calling up his boarders, stepped on the muzzle of one of *Chesapeake*'s guns and leaped over the bulwark to her quarter-deck. Just at this moment Captain Lawrence fell, mortally wounded, and was carried below, crying out, 'Don't give up the ship!' 'Keep the guns going!' 'Fight her till she sinks!' Obedient to his orders, a few men on the quarter-deck made a desperate resistance. In all, some fifty men followed Broke, and, as they came forward, not a live man was on the quarter-deck and not an officer on the spar-deck. Lawrence and Ludlow, his first lieutenant, had been mortally wounded and carried to the cock-pit. The second lieutenant was stationed below. The third lieutenant fled; whereupon the foreigners and raw sailors, seeing the British on the spar-deck, deserted their quarters, and a Portuguese boatswain, having removed the gratings of the berth-deck, the men rushed headlong down the after-ladders. Then was it that Lawrence, hearing the men come down, cried out repeatedly, 'Don't give up the ship! Blow her up!' But he was helpless. Broke was in possession of the spar-deck. Still the English captain might have been beaten, for at this moment the two frigates parted, leaving fifty Englishmen on the *Chesapeake*'s deck. Seeing this, a few Americans of spirit made a desperate attack, in the course of which Broke almost lost his life. But resistance was useless. The guns ceased firing, the flag came down, and without any formal surrender the *Chesapeake* passed into British hands for the second time, and was taken into Halifax a prize. There Lawrence and Ludlow, having died of their wounds on the way in, were buried with military honours on the 6th of June. Their bodies were not, however, destined to rest long in foreign soil. Deeply as their countrymen felt the humiliation of the defeat, they did not forget the patriotism, the devotion, the inspiring death of Lawrence. They put on mourning. They made of the injunction 'Don't give up the ship!' a war cry which has never since been forgotten, and ten of them, all masters of vessels, under the lead of George Crowninshield Jr, having obtained a flag of truce, brought back the bodies of Lawrence and Ludlow a few weeks later to Salem, whence they were carried by land to New York city and laid with all the honours of war in the yard of Trinity Church.

From Halifax news of the capture was carried to England by a brig which reached Plymouth on July 7th, and the next night the glad tidings were announced in Parliament, and received with boundless joy. So important was the victory in English eyes that the Tower guns were fired, and in time Captain Broke was made a baronet and a knight commander of the Bath, and received from London a sword and the freedom of the city. Concerning the fate of the frigate, whose history is bound up with so much that is shameful and so much that is heroic in our annals, it is worth while to recall that she was taken to England, and in 1820 was condemned and sold. Neither our Government nor our people had patriotism enough to buy her, and her shot-marked, blood-stained timbers were bought by a miller of Wickham, Hants, and were used to build a flour-mill, which is still standing.

from *A History of the People of the United States* by John B. McMaster

The sober view of naval historians is that, had he not died, Lawrence should have been court-martialled for recklessly underestimating the odds in favour of his better trained and more skilful opponent – and, incidentally, for sailing in defiance of his superior's orders.

The encounter was as bloody as it was brief: USS *Chesapeake* lost 146 men killed and wounded to her opponent's eighty-five.

The history of naval warfare has been punctuated by a few decisive victories which have settled the balance of power between nations for generations. The Greeks wiped out the Persians at Salamis in 480 BC. Muhammadan sea-power in the Mediterranean was extinguished by the Christians under Don John of Austria only a few years before the Spanish Armada sailed on its last voyage in 1588. Its fate was settled by the combined hostility of Elizabeth's sea-captains and the cruel weather that has always been Britain's best defence against invasion.

In October 1805 Nelson overwhelmed the combined French and Spanish fleets off Trafalgar, leaving the Royal Navy unchallenged, at least in European waters.

Nearly a hundred years later in the narrow straits between Japan and Korea, the young Japanese Navy, created in the age of steam and armoured gun-turrets without any preconceived notions about fighting under sail, intercepted and wiped out what was left of Tsar Nicholas's Navy. A year earlier, in 1904, the First Russian Pacific Squadron had been humiliated by Admiral Togo and his modern striking fleet. Admiral Vitheft in his flagship *Tsesarevich* was killed outright, and his squadron scattered in disarray. Those who made it to the refuge of Port Arthur were soon sunk at their moorings by Japanese artillery.

A punitive force was quickly formed in the Baltic under the Tsar's favourite admiral, the vain, inflexible martinet, Rozhestvensky, who neither sought nor heeded anyone's advice. All tactical decisions were his alone, to be followed without question. During the seven long months it took the squadron of thirty-eight combatant ships and its attendant transports, tugs and hospital ships to reach the Japanese via the Cape of Good Hope, there were many long delays waiting for colliers or the co-operation of local authorities. At no time did the admiral explain his course of action even to his own staff, let alone the other flag officers or captains in the fleet.

Revolutionary elements emerged, even amongst the officers. They did little to sustain morale. All were convinced that they would never reach Vladivostok, let alone return safely home.

On 14 May 1905 they steamed straight into the waiting Japanese fleet, led by nineteen armoured battleships and cruisers, with forty destroyers and torpedo boats in support. On paper the two sides were not unevenly matched. Rozhestvensky could call on the same number of ships with 12-inch guns and had a slight numerical superiority in secondary armament. There the comparison ended. The Japanese fleet was trained and led to a high pitch of efficiency, and they alone had the benefit of recent combat experience. Their gunnery control systems were greatly superior. The few hits scored by the Russians were nullified by defective shells, each carrying 80 per cent less explosive content than the same-calibre enemy projectile. They did not know it, but the odds had been further loaded against the Second Pacific Squadron by a bureaucratic decision in Moscow to double the moisture content in their pyroxlin explosive for the long voyage through the tropics. Thus few of them exploded on impact, whereas the Japanese shells not only burst on hitting but had an added incendiary effect which proved decisive. Here is how the critical phase of the battle was later recalled by Supply Assistant Novikoff-Priboy. His action station was in the sick-bay, which soon looked more like an abattoir given over to ritual slaughter, but he seems to have left it for the upper deck. The scene on the admiral's bridge was chaotic:

> Terror made the chiefs crouch on the deck where they were shielded by the armour-plate wall of the tower. Only the bluejackets remained at their posts – the men at the steering-wheel, rangefinders, speaking-tubes, and telephones – obeying the call of duty, while their officers squatted or knelt. Even the stubborn and imperious Rozhestvensky stooped lower and lower to avoid the hail of splinters. At length, like all the officers, he was on his knees. In fact, he set a pusillanimous example. In this humiliating posture, his head drawn down upon his chest, he looked more like an intimidated passenger than the commander of a squadron. From time to time one of the junior officers ventured to raise his head and glance through the port-holes. Several of them had already been slightly wounded.
>
> Captain Ignatsius, at this juncture, said to the admiral:
>
> 'Your Excellency, the enemy seems to have got our range very well. May we change our course?'
>
> 'All right,' answered Rozhestvensky immediately.
>
> At 2.05 p.m., therefore, the *Suvoroff* payed off two points to starboard. Thereupon the hits slackened for a while. Soon, however, the Japanese having readjusted their aim, matters became as bad as before. A 6-inch shell struck the conning-tower. It did not do any serious damage, but gave all within a bad shake and stopped the chronometer.
>
> On the poop, on the spar-deck, and in the admiral's cabin a series of conflagrations broke out. The fire-fighting brigade was called into action. But it was impossible for the men to keep afoot on the open deck, where incendiary shells were continually bursting. The men of the fire-party were struck down, singly or by groups; the hoses were severed. Little by little the separate fires fused into a roaring furnace extending from the fore-bridge to the stern-bridge.
>
> Vladimirsky, the senior artillery lieutenant, who was in the conning-tower, was severely wounded. The port range-finder was smashed; and since it was from the port side that our fire was directed towards the

Japanese, the starboard instrument was transferred to port. Artillery Flag-Lieutenant Berseneff, a very tall and lean man, had just taken his place at the Barr-Stroud in order to ascertain the range, when he was hit by a shell-splinter and killed on the spot. The two steersmen were also killed. The reserve steersmen were summoned, but meanwhile two flag officers, Lieutenants Sverbeeff and Krzhizhanovsky, took the wheel. The spokes were splashed with the blood of the slaughtered men.

The *Suvoroff* now resumed her previous course, N. 23° E.

The news which reached the conning-tower from various parts of the ship was far from cheering. The sick-bay on the main deck had been hit, and a place already full of wounded men had been transformed into a shambles. A shell had made a serious leak close to the port under-water torpedo-tube. A message came by telephone:

'Large-calibre shells have struck the stern 12-inch turret and have put it out of action.'

By this time half the guns of the ironclad had become ineffective.

The admiral, though wounded by a shell-splinter, remained in the conning-tower. But his presence there was futile, since it was no longer possible for him to retain command of the squadron.

So insistent was the enemy fire that no one could reach the connecting bridge to hoist signals. Any who attempted to do so were instantly struck down. Furthermore, the halyards had been swept away, and the box containing the flags used in signalling had been devoured by the flames. The mainmast, severed by shells, had fallen overboard. The lower yard-arm of the mizen had likewise been shot away.

Rozhestvensky, powerless and passive, stayed at his post, hoping for a shot which would relieve him of the burden of command.

*

In the conning-tower the second range-finder was knocked to pieces by flying splinters. The admiral turned his face, convulsed with anguish, in the direction of the noise; and, through his clenched teeth, uttered the one word:

'Damnable!'

But how to save the situation? How to inform the other units of the fleet that their last resource must lie in bold independent action, since the flagship had borne the brunt of the enemy fire and was no longer in a condition to lead? The trouble was that Rozhestvensky had accustomed them to act as sheep following their shepherd, and without the shepherd they were helpless. All still relied upon the will of the admiral, who was kneeling in the conning-tower of the *Suvoroff*.

The Japanese, taking advantage of their superior speed, swiftly enveloped the head of our column, the Russian flagship being at the centre of the arc formed by their vessels. At 2.25 p.m. the *Mikaza*, then about forty cable-lengths distant, was directly barring our line of advance. Hitherto only five or six of our foremost warships had been able to participate in the action.

An officer pointed this out to the admiral. He ordered the course to be changed four points to starboard, in order to bring our column into some sort of parallelism with the attacking force and thus introduce our rearmost units to the fight.

It was just when the change of course was being effected that a large-calibre shell burst close to the conning-tower. Some of the occupants were killed outright. The others were wounded, including the admiral, whose forehead was lacerated by a splinter. The men at the wheel having been struck down, and the helm having been starboarded, the *Suvoroff* began to turn in a circle. The unguided flagship got out of line. The tragedy of the *Tsesarevich* at Port Arthur was repeated.

Thenceforward the column followed what had been the second ironclad, the *Alexander III*. To begin with, this vessel steered in the wake of the aberrant *Suvoroff*, but resumed her original course as soon as her captain realized that the flagship had been definitely put out of action. Temporarily she drew the enemy fire upon herself and thus saved the *Suvoroff* from a further battering with big guns.

On the flagship a conflagration broke out close to the conning-tower. Flag-Lieutenant Sverbeeff took command of a fire-fighting party, which had, of course, to work in the open. Being wounded in the back, the lieutenant sought surgical aid. In the conning-tower the admiral remained seated with hanging head. There was no possibility of conveying him below across the open deck, where fires were raging and on which the Japanese machine-guns were still playing. His control of the squadron of thirty-eight units was at an end. Flat-Lieutenant Filippovsky, though his wounds were bleeding freely, endeavoured to steer the *Suvoroff*, but the steering-gear had been so badly damaged that the ship would not answer her helm, wobbling alternately from port to starboard and from starboard to port.

A few minutes later, another shell hit the conning-tower, and numerous splinters flew in through the loopholes. The admiral was wounded again, this time on the foot. The captain of the *Suvoroff*, struck down at first, soon struggled back into a kneeling posture, looking savagely about him and clasping his bald head, where blood was spouting from a scalp-wound. He was carried below for treatment. Flag-Lieuteant Krzhizhanovsky, whose hands had been badly torn by tiny splinters, made an attempt to get the steering-gear in order again. All the appliances in the conning-tower had been shattered, and communication between the tower and other parts of the ship had been cut off.

By three o'clock in the afternoon the conflagration had extended to the fore-bridge and the chart-room. Most of those in the conning-tower were dead, the only survivors being four in number, badly wounded: Admiral Rozhestvensky, Staff-Captain Clapier de Colongue, Flag-Lieutenant Filippovsky, and one of the quartermasters. They were in danger of a horrible fate, for they might either be stifled by smoke or roasted to death. Since it was impossible to escape by way of the burning bridge, the only exit was through the central post in the bowels of the ship, close to the keel. Thrusting the corpses aside, the four men opened the trapdoor, and made their way down the tube by the ladder of cramps. The others were afraid that the admiral might lose his grip and fall headlong, but he managed to retain hand and foot holds, and reached the bottom without further mishap.

The *Suvoroff* had had such a gruelling as to have become irrecognizable. The mainmast and the after-funnel had been shot away, the after-bridge and the spurs demolished, the upper deck was in flames, the hull had been pierced in several places; nothing was left to recall the trim flagship. Looming through the clouds of black smoke, with only the truncated mizen-mast and the fore-funnel projecting above the deck, her silhouette recalled that of the Japanese cruisers of the *Matsushima* type. After the *Alexander III*'s frustrated endeavour to make for the north behind the tail of the enemy fleet, the *Suvoroff*, astray upon the field of action, crossed the Russian line near its middle and wandered vaguely between the contending fleets. Our rear vessels, not aware of the circumstances in which the flagship had left the head of the line, took her for a Japanese vessel in distress and opened fire upon her, hoping to finish her off!

*

The flagship was being directed from the central post. Of all the staff, only Flag-Lieutenant Filippovsky remained there in a fit state to take charge. The others had disappeared, including the admiral. Disregarded by everyone, Rozhestvensky wandered for a time in the depths of the ironclad, limping as he went, and stopping now and again as if to reflect. He wanted to make his way into one of the still intact turrets, but his route was blocked by flames. He issued no orders. The bluejackets, who were carrying on as best they might, paid no heed to him. He had become a superfluous passenger.

*

At this juncture Flag-Captain Clapier de Colongue, having recovered from the insensibility brought on by shock or loss of blood, was running hither and thither throughout the ship to ask everyone he encountered:

'Where is the admiral?'

Perhaps never before, in a sea-fight or a land-action, has a chief of staff been thus in search of an admiral or a generalissimo.

'He passed this way,' answered some of those questioned.

'His Excellency was making for the upper deck,' declared others.

At length an officer was found who could give precise information. Rozhestvensky was in the middle starboard turret.

When the battle had lasted for four hours, the *Suvoroff* was once more between our lines and the enemy's, and again the Japanese concentrated their attack on her. The second funnel was shot away, the conflagration was renewed, and the deck spouted flames like a volcano. Those on board the other Russian vessels which passed near her were heartbroken to witness this spectacle of devastation and death.

*

The *Suvoroff*, zigzagging as she went, made slow progress. The upper deck, bending in the heat of the flames, collapsed upon the battery deck. The stokers were choked by the fumes which came down into the stoke-hole through the ventilating shafts. The armour-plating on the hull along the water-line crumpled up under the heat, and many leaks were sprung. Still, the flagship continued obstinately afloat.

from *Tsushima* by A. Novikoff-Priboy

The admiral and his staff were transferred from his crippled flagship to a destroyer which then surrendered to the Japanese the following day.

Vice-Admiral Rozhestvensky recovered from his wounds and returned to face a court-martial in Moscow. He was acquitted, mainly it seems to discourage further investigations into why the once-proud Russian fleet was so heavily outclassed by the beardless, myopic Japanese.

Only one ship in the squadron – an auxiliary – reached Vladivostok. The rest were either sunk or captured by the enemy, who only lost two front-line ships and 115 men killed, whereas over 5,000 Russian sailors never reached port.

Japanese naval supremacy went unchecked in the Pacific until the Battle of Midway in 1942, whilst Russia ceased to exist as a naval power until Admiral Gorshkov created the Red Fleet half a century later.

At this distance in time it is hard to realize how little interest was shown by most British people during 1914–18 in the war at sea. Their attention was focused on the ever-lengthening lists of casualties in France published in the daily newspapers and those crowded trains delivering the wounded to Victoria from Dover, in exchange for raw recruits heading for the trenches, with a life-expectation measured in weeks.

The widely read humorous weekly *Punch* concerned itself mainly with Haig's armies and their supporting cast in Westminster, whilst Jellicoe's Grand Fleet was a forgotten asset swinging round its moorings in Scapa Flow. References to naval operations were few and far between, as often as not dealing with the steadfastness of the fishermen who manned the naval auxiliary forces, especially the minesweepers. In November 1917, the editor felt obliged to remind his readers that all was well with the Silent Service:

If we were to believe some critics, the British Navy is directed by a set of doddering old gentlemen who are afraid to let it go at the Germans, and cannot even safeguard it from attack. The truth, as expounded by the First Lord, Sir Eric Geddes, in his maiden speech, is quite different. Despite

379

the Jeremiads of superannuated sailors and political longshoremen, the Admiralty is not going to Davy Jones's locker, but under its present chiefs, who have, with very few exceptions, seen service in this War, maintains and supplements its glorious record.

Save for an occasional game of 'tip and run,' as with the North Sea convoy, enemy vessels have disappeared on the surface of the ocean; and the long arm of the British Navy is now stretching down into the depths and up into the skies in successful pursuit of them. If the nation hardly realises what it owes to the men of the Fleet and their splendid comrades of the Auxiliary Services, it is because this work is done with such thoroughness and so little fuss, and, as Mr. Asquith puts it, 'in the twilight and not in the limelight.'

The report of the greatest naval engagement of all time is brief but shows a real insight into the significance of the battle. The comment which follows was written within days of Hipper and Scheer's ships regaining the safety of their bases:

June, 1916.

At last the long vigil in the North Sea has ended in the glorious if indecisive battle of Jutland, the greatest sea fight since Trafalgar. Yet was it indecisive? After the momentary dismay caused by the first Admiralty *communiqué* with its over-estimate of our losses, public confidence, shaken where it was strongest, has been restored by further information and by the admissions of the enemy. We have to mourn the loss of many ships, still more the loss of splendid ships' companies and their heroic captains. We can sympathise with the cruel disappointment of those who, after bearing the brunt of the action, were robbed of the opportunity of overwhelming their enemy by failing light and the exigencies of a strategy governed in the last resort by political caution. But look at the sequel. The German Fleet, badly battered, retires to port; and despite the pæans of exultation from their Admirals, Kaiser, and Imperial Chancellor, remains there throughout the month. Will it ever come out again? Meanwhile, Wilhelmshaven is closed indefinitely, and nobody is allowed to see those sheep in Wolff's clothing – the 'victorious fleet.' The true verdict, so far as we can judge, may be expressed in homely phrase: The British navy has taken a knock but given a harder one. We can stand it and they can't.

from *Mr Punch's History of the Great War*

Others, notably Winston Churchill, wrote at greater length and probed deeper into why the encounter off Jutland was not the decisive victory everyone confidently expected. It largely turned on the personalities and preconceived tactical ideas of the opposing Commanders-in-Chief. Jellicoe's inflexible creed is neatly stated:

380

... there was no reason to doubt that thirty minutes' firing within ten thousand yards between two parallel lines of battle would achieve a complete victory.

Therefore for years Jellicoe's mind had been focussed upon the simplest form of naval battle: the single line and the parallel course; a long-range artillery conflict; and defensive action against torpedo attack. Everything beyond this opening phase was speculative and complicated. If the opening phase were satisfactory, everything else would probably follow from it. The Admiralty could not look beyond providing their Commander-in-Chief with an ample superiority in ships of every kind. The method and moment of joining battle and its tactical conduct could be ruled by him alone. It is now argued that it would have been better if, instead of riveting all attention and endeavour upon a long-range artillery duel by the two fleets in line on roughly parallel courses, the much more flexible system of engaging by divisions, of using the fastest battle-ships apart from the slower, and of dealing with each situation according to the needs of the moment, had been employed. It may well be so; and had there been several battles or even encounters between the British and German fleets in the war, there is no doubt that a far higher system of battle tactics would have developed. But nothing like this particular event had ever happened before, and nothing like it was ever to happen again.

*

Jellicoe did not know. Nobody knew. All he knew was that a complete victory would not improve decisively an already favourable naval situation, and that a total defeat would lose the war. He was prepared to accept battle on his own terms; he was not prepared to force one at a serious hazard. The battle was to be fought as he wished it or left unfought.

But while we may justify on broad grounds of national policy the general attitude of the Commander-in-Chief towards the conditions upon which alone a decisive battle should be fought, neither admiration nor agreement can adhere to the system of command and training which he had developed in the Fleet. Everything was centralized in the Flagship, and all initiative except in avoiding torpedo attack was denied to the leaders of squadrons and divisions. A ceaseless stream of signals from the Flagship was therefore required to regulate the movement of the Fleet and the distribution of the fire. These signals prescribed the course and speed of every ship as well as every manœuvring turn. In exercises such a centralization may have produced a better drill. But in the smoke, confusion and uncertainty of battle the process was far too elaborate ...

Let us now take the position of Admiral Scheer. He had no intention of fighting a battle against the whole British Fleet. He was under no illusions about the relative strength of the rival batteries. Nothing could be more clownish than to draw up his fleet on parallel courses with an opponent firing twice his weight of metal and manned by a personnel whose science, seamanship and fortitude commanded his sincere respect. He had not come out with any idea of fighting a pitched battle. He had never intended to fight at a hopeless disadvantage. If he met weaker forces or equal forces, or any forces which gave a fair or sporting chance of victory, he would fight with all the martial skill and courage inseparable from the German name. But from the moment he knew that he was in the presence of the united Grand Fleet and saw the whole horizon bristling with its might, his only aim was to free himself as quickly as possible without dishonour from a fatal trap. In this he was entirely successful.

However, the first serious action of the day did not involve Jellicoe, but a leader of a very different stamp – the flamboyant, fox-hunting Vice-Admiral David Beatty in HMS *Lion* with six battlecruisers, supported on his disengaged quarter by the five modern heavily armoured battleships of Rear-Admiral Evan-Thomas's 5th Battle Squadron. Immediately on sighting Admiral Hipper's five battlecruisers, Beatty did not wait to concentrate his forces but charged straight at the enemy at full speed. Fire was opened at 14,000 yards. Within half an hour two of his battlecruisers had been destroyed by plunging salvoes which exploded within their lightly protected magazines. HMS *Indefatigable* and *Queen Mary* took nearly 2,000 men down with them. The flagship would have gone the same way, but for the 'sublime act of personal courage' by Major Hervey of the Royal Marine Artillery, who ordered the magazine of his stricken turret to be shut down and flooded just before a cordite charge exploded above it.

At this moment the Vice-Admiral turned to his flag captain and remarked in the understatement of a lifetime, 'There seems to be something wrong with our bloody ships today. Turn two points to port,' thus closing the enemy further. (What was wrong had not been properly understood and acted upon a quarter of a century later, when the battleship *Bismarck* wiped out the 42,000-ton HMS *Hood* in exactly similar fashion.)

Beatty's battlecruisers and the 5th Battle Squadron now started to gain the ascendancy over Hipper's squadron. But the arrival on the scene of von Scheer's High Seas Fleet caused Beatty to wheel his forces and draw the enemy towards Jellicoe's Grand Fleet, then closing from about forty miles to the NNW. Soon Jellicoe was forced to make his first tactical decision, how to deploy his twenty-four battleships into line of battle. He could only think of forming line ahead, a ponderous manoeuvre taking over twenty minutes to execute. Churchill was highly critical of Jellicoe's decision:

But there was surely a third course open to Sir John Jellicoe which had none of the disadvantages of these hard alternatives. Although it involved a complicated evolution, it was in principle a very simple course. In fact it was the simplest and most primitive of all courses. He could have deployed on his centre and taken the lead himself.

*

Equally it did not occur to him to take an obvious precaution against the escape of the enemy which could not have risked the safety of his Fleet. His cautious deployment on the outer wing made it the more imperative to make sure the enemy was brought to battle. To do this he had only to tell the four *Queen Elizabeths* of the 5th Battle Squadron, instead of falling tamely in at the tail of the line and thus wasting all their unique combination of speed and power, to attack separately the disengaged side of the enemy. These ships would not have been in any danger of being overwhelmed by the numbers of the enemy. They were eight or nine knots faster than Scheer's Fleet as long as it remained united. They could at any moment, if too hard pressed, break off the action. Thus assured, what could be easier than for them to swoop round upon the old *Deutschland* squadron and cripple or destroy two or three of these ships in a few minutes? It would have been almost obligatory for Scheer to stop and rescue them; and taken between two fires, he would have been irrevocably committed to battle. This was exactly the kind of situation for which the division of fast super-Dreadnoughts, combining speed, guns and armour in an equal degree, had been constructed at such huge expense and trouble as one of the main acts of my administration of the Admiralty. But neither the Commander-in-Chief nor their own Admiral could think of any better use for them than to let them steam uselessly along in the rear of the Fleet at seventeen knots, their own speed being over twenty-four.

Therefore at 6.15 p.m. precisely the order was given by signal and wireless to deploy on the port wing. The fateful flags fluttered in the breeze, and were hauled down. The order became operative, and five-sixths of the immense line of British battleships turned away and began to increase their distance from the enemy. The first move of the Battle Fleet at Jutland had been made.

*

Meanwhile Hood with the 3rd Battle Cruiser Squadron had been engaging Hipper's battle-cruisers with good effect. But at 6.31 a salvo from the *Derfflinger* smote the *Invincible*. In the words of the Official Narrative,

'Several big explosions took place in rapid succession; masses of coal dust issued from the riven hull; great tongues of flame played over the ship; the masts collapsed; the ship broke in two, and an enormous pall of black smoke ascended to the sky. As it cleared away the bow and stern could be seen standing up out of the water as if to mark the place where an Admiral lay.'

Of her crew of 1,026 officers and men, six only survived.

Visual contact between the two main forces lasted a little over two hours. Scheer broke off the action behind a series of torpedo attacks, from which Jellicoe took avoiding action by turning away. 'The range opened, the Fleets separated, and Scheer vanished again from Jellicoe's view – this time for ever.'

> Night had now come on, and by nine o'clock darkness had fallen on the sea. Thereupon the conditions of naval warfare underwent profound changes. The rights of the stronger fleet faded into a grey equality. The far-ranging cruisers were blinded. The friendly destroyers became a danger to the ships they guarded. The great guns lost their range. Now, if ever, the reign of the torpedo would begin. The rival Navies, no more than six miles apart, steamed onwards through the darkness, silent and invisible, able to turn about in five minutes or less in any direction, no man knowing what the other would do or what might happen next.
>
> But Admiral Scheer had made up his mind, and his course, though perilous, was plain.

It was to head for the barn. Although the Admiralty intercepted and decoded German wireless traffic making it apparent that the High Seas Fleet was already steaming towards their swept channel near the Horn Reef to the south-east, Jellicoe did not trust the information when it was handed to him at 23.30 and maintained his southerly – and opening – course through the night. There was a chance encounter between British destroyers and the battleship *Pommern*, which was quickly dispatched with her company of 700 men.

The final tally of British losses was three battlecruisers, three armoured cruisers and eight destroyers, against the Germans' one battleship, one battlecruiser, four light cruisers and five destroyers. Six thousand officers and men of the Royal Navy perished that day, mostly entombed in ships lost due to design deficiencies.

> So ended the Battle of Jutland. The Germans loudly proclaimed a victory. There was no victory for anyone; but they had good reason to be content with their young Navy. It had fought skilfully and well. It had made its escape from the grip of overwhelming forces, and in so doing had inflicted heavier loss in ships and men than it had itself received. The British Battle Fleet was never seriously in action. Only one ship, the *Colossus*, was struck by an enemy shell, and out of more than 20,000 men in the battle ships only two were killed and five wounded. To this supreme instrument had been devoted the best of all that Britain could give for many years. It was vastly superior to its opponent in numbers, tonnage, speed, and above all gun power, and was at least its equal in discipline, individual skill and courage. The disappointment of all ranks was deep; and immediately there

384

arose reproaches and recriminations, continued to this day, through which this account has sought to steer a faithful and impartial passage. All hoped that another opportunity would be granted them, and eagerly sought to profit by the lessons of the battle. The chance of an annihilating victory had been perhaps offered at the moment of deployment, had been offered again an hour later when Scheer made his great miscalculation, and for the third time when a little before midnight the Commander-in-Chief decided to reject the evidence of the Admiralty message. Three times is a lot.

*

The ponderous, poignant responsibilities borne successfully, if not triumphantly, by Sir John Jellicoe during two years of faithful command, constitute unanswerable claims to the lasting respect of the nation. But the Royal Navy must find in other personalities and other episodes the golden links which carried forward through the Great War the audacious and conquering traditions of the past; and it is to Beatty and the battle-cruisers, to Keyes at Zeebrugge, to Tyrwhitt and his Harwich striking force, to the destroyer and submarine flotillas out in all weathers and against all foes, to the wild adventures of the Q-ships, to the steadfast resolution of the British Merchant Service, that the eyes of rising generations will turn.

from *The World Crisis 1911–1918* by Winston S. Churchill

Geoffrey Brooke, nephew of the great reacehorse trainer Atty Persse and an Olympic Modern Pentathlon competitor, had other claims to being out of the run of typical naval officers during his twenty-four-year career. He had to admit to being incurably seasick, so he was posted from one big ship to another, which would hardly be the pattern for one who was almost continually in action throughout the war. In the new battleship *Prince of Wales* he was an appalled eyewitness to the abrupt destruction of two of our smartest battlecruisers, thought to epitomize Britain's naval supremacy.

The first was soon after 05.00 on 22 May 1941 when they engaged the German battleship *Bismarck* and her consort, the heavy cruiser *Prinz Eugen* as they broke out from the Denmark Straits heading for our convoy lanes. Brooke's action station was to spot the fall of shot of their own salvos from a point high above the superstructure in the after main armament director, which afforded him a grandstand view of what turned out to be a brief encounter. HMS *Hood* was just 800 yards ahead, steaming at 27 knots, when the ship's public address system clicked on:

'This is your Captain speaking. The two enemy ships are in sight and we shall be opening fire any minute now. Good luck to you all.'
   I could see nothing except the unbroken straight line of the horizon. The

records say the time was 0538. The loudspeaker came on again. 'This is the padre speaking. I am going to read a short prayer.' This he did. Though by no means irreligious, I must admit I found this distracting. But not for long. Something suddenly came up over the horizon to grow slowly but distinctly; the top of a mast. Then a little to the left something else. I shall never forget the thrill of that moment. A squate grey lump on a stalk, with bars protruding each side – the *Bismarck*'s main armament director. 'Director target,' said Mr White evenly. It grew by the second like a serpent rearing up, while our rangetaker spun his wheel, trying to converge his two half-images in the face of driving spume . . .

*

'Ready to open fire Sir!' This was to the Captain and one could not hear the reply. Surely it was yes and why weren't we firing? The whole of the *Bismarck* was now visible and I could not restrain a gasp of admiration, tinged with awe. Long and rakish with undeniably majestic lines, she was a fawnish grey, not bluish like our ships – or it may just have been the light. I noticed with a pang that all her 15-inch guns were pointing in our direction.

There was a *boom* from not far off. The *Hood* had opened fire. Seconds later, 'Shoot' said Guns. Ting-ting went the fire gong and I shut my eyes. *BAROOM!* The *Prince of Wales'* first salvo was away from 'A' and 'B' turrets. The slight concussion and the brown smoke that drifted aft (the wind dispersed it fairly quickly) brought welcome relief from inaction. My fingers moved up and down the three knobs. Suddenly a rippling yellow flash played in front of the *Bismarck*, followed by a dark cloud that, nearly blotting her out, hung for an appreciable time. She had fired. At whom? The range was 25,600 yards (nearly 13 miles) and it would take almost a minute to find out. There was a hoarse croak from a box on the bulkhead, heralding the fall of our shot, and a cluster of white columns rose to form a wall behind the *Bismarck* (and I think to the right, but that was B-C's pigeon). I pressed 'over'. *BAROOM!* went another salvo, following one from the *Hood*. Another flash from the *Bismarck*. More smoke. Wait. Croak. Splash. Press for another 'over'. *BAROOM!* Flash. On it went, Guns ordering corrections ('Left one. Down ladder shoot') in a level voice as each salvo landed, each time nearer. So far nothing seen of the enemy's shells. Presumably she was firing at the *Hood*. (The cruiser was also firing at the *Hood* but she was so far to the left that I could not see her without taking my glasses off the *Bismarck* and after the initial scrutiny I never saw her again during the action.)

Prince of Wales altered course to bring her after turret to bear . . .

The ship steadied up and then began to come back to port. Dick Beckwith said 'My God! The *Hood*'s gone!'

I shot a glance up at him. He was staring horrified over his left shoulder, through his rear port. We both looked back into our glasses. Though I

386

heard the words quite distinctly they meant nothing at that moment. It was if that part of my brain not concerned with the long grey shape that belched flame and smoke simply was not working. I could have stood up and had a quick look (afterwards wishing I had) but it did not occur to me.

In less than two minutes the 42,000-ton flagship had taken all but three of her company to the bottom. *Prince of Wales* was soon under concentrated fire of both enemy ships and was obliged to break off the action and retire under cover of a smoke-screen.

Six months later she was in Singapore when the USN Pacific Fleet was decimated at Pearl Harbor. With the old battlecruiser *Repulse* and two destroyers she sailed to intercept Japanese invasion forces landing in northern Malaya. The aircraft-carrier which was to have given this aptly named 'Force Z' some sort of air cover was on the other side of the world being patched up after an unfortunate grounding in the Caribbean. There were some RAF fighters based in Singapore, but they were not scrambled in time to intervene in the last act. *Prince of Wales* had taken a lucky but crippling torpedo hit early on which left her with little power of manoeuvre. Geoffrey Brooke's account starts with the final 'Alarm Starboard!'

On tin hat for another attack, but they were not concerned with us this time. No doubt the enemy had seen we were crippled and could wait while they concentrated on the indomitable *Repulse*.

We were then subjected to a ringside view of the end of that gallant ship. There can be no more dreadful sight than that of a large vessel, full of one's own kith and kin, being hounded to the bottom. The seemingly inexhaustible supply of aircraft with which this was accomplished indicated to the impotent watchers what could be in store for us too.

This time her tormentors came in individually from all directions. It was agonising to watch the gallant battlecruiser, squirming and twisting her way through what we knew was a web of crossing torpedo tracks, guns banging and crackling defiance. One plane flew between the two ships from aft on a parallel course to the *Repulse*. She hit it just before it came in line with us and a fire started at the tail. The flames ate their way towards the cockpit and the machine began to porpoise as the tail lost directional control. Although it was clear the men inside had only seconds to live I watched with undiluted pleasure. The plane slowed, its whole fuselage a torch, and then the blazing mass dived into the sea. A cloud of smoke went up and we all cheered. Turning back to the *Repulse* I was just in time to see another plume shoot up from her port quarter. Her port screws and rudder must be damaged and this, one knew, was the beginning of the end. Even as the thought registered there were three more hits in quick succession, two on this side of her and one on the other. As the last aircraft pulled up and away the *Repulse* had a severe list and her speed was right down.

She was now about four miles away. The sea was calm and grey, as was the sky. At the end she was steaming slowly at right angles to our line of sight, from right to left. She was still making headway when her bow began to go under like an enormous submarine and terrible to see. As the waves came aft along her fo'c's'le – tilted towards us – and then engulfed the great 15-inch turrets, still fore and aft, she listed further and remained so for a time. Then she rolled right over, upperworks, mast, funnels and all splashing on to the surface of the sea. She lay on her side for a few seconds – perhaps longer – stopped at last. Then her keel came uppermost and she began to sink by the stern. The last thing I saw was the sharp bow, pointing skywards, disappearing slowly in a ring of troubled water.

from *Alarm Starboard!* by Geoffrey Brooke

See pp.180–1 for the author's subsequent escape from the shambles of the fall of Singapore in a 45-foot native coastal *prauw*.

In March 1942, the Allied situation at sea in the Mediterranean theatre was desperate. Crete had been abandoned with heavy losses, whilst our beleaguered army at Tobruk had only been sustained by cruel losses of men and ships. There was no aircraft-carrier east of Gibraltar, and only two battleships remained under Admiral Cunningham's command after HMS *Barham* had been sunk by a U-boat with the loss of over 850 men. The two surviving capital ships were hardly at short notice for sea, since each of them rested awash but on the bottom of Alexandria harbour after the Italian Lieutenant de la Penne had coolly penetrated the boom defences with his three chariots (human torpedoes) and fixed charges to their bottoms.

It was at this moment that the Commander-in-Chief was reminded by Churchill that it was imperative to get a convoy through to Malta. The odds were stacked against Rear-Admiral Vian getting any of the four supply ships through if the Italian battlefleet should intervene. His force consisted of an obsolete AA-cruiser and four light cruisers armed with 5.25-inch twin turrets, ten fleet destroyers and six destroyer-escorts. How they withstood the ceaseless massed attacks by the Luftwaffe and drove off the 15-inch battleship *Littorio*, three heavy cruisers and eight fleet destroyers must go down as one of the most brilliant sea-fights of the war, even though Vian's ships only achieved one hit by gunfire and missed with all their torpedoes. The victory was won by audacity and a high level of seamanship in vile weather, during which their well-rehearsed smoke-screens protected the convoy from the enemy gunsights. It must have been the last naval action in which smoke-screens played a decisive role, before the advent of centimetric radar made them irrelevant.

The convoy sailed from Alexandria at 7 a.m. on March 20th, escorted by the *Carlisle*, Captain D. M. L. Neame, and six destroyers, the *Sikh*, *Zulu*, *Lively*, *Hero*, *Havock* and *Hasty*. Rear-Admiral Vian, in the *Cleopatra*, with the cruisers *Dido* and *Euryalus*, and the *Jervis*, *Kipling*, *Kelvin* and *Kingston*, left harbour at 6 p.m. It had been arranged that 'Hunt' class destroyers should carry out an anti-submarine sweep between Alexandria and Tobruk the night before the convoy sailed and during daylight on the 20th, after which they were to fuel at Tobruk and join the convoy during the forenoon of the 21st. At 11 a.m. on the 20th, while engaged on the anti-submarine sweep, the *Heythrop* was torpedoed by a U-boat. Taken in tow by the *Eridge*, she sank at 4 p.m. with a loss of fifteen killed or missing. Vian's force and the convoy, which had been joined by five of the six 'Hunts' from Tobruk, met about seventy miles north of Tobruk during the morning of the 21st, and proceeded westward at 12 knots with relays of fighters overhead. A sixth 'Hunt' from Tobruk, delayed by a fouled propeller, joined up in the evening. These six ships – the *Southwold*, *Beaufort*, *Dulverton*, *Hurworth*, *Avon Vale* and *Eridge* – each with their six 4-inch guns – provided a most valuable addition to the anti-aircraft defence of the convoy.

The *Penelope* and *Legion* from Malta joined Vian at 8 a.m. next morning, the 22nd, so the force was complete, well on its way and within about two hundred and fifty miles of Malta. It had already passed the dangerous area between Crete and the hump of Cyrenaica to the southward without attack. This was largely attributable to the successful shelling by the Army of the airfield at Martuba and their threat against Tmimi, some sixty miles west of Tobruk.

But Vian's peaceful progress was soon to be interrupted. On the evening of the 21st the convoy had been reported by German transport aircraft passing from Cyrenaica to Crete, and soon after 5 a.m. on the 22nd, Vian had a report, timed about four hours earlier, from Submarine P.36 to the effect that destroyers and heavier ships were leaving Taranto. This indicated that air attacks might start at any moment, while enemy battleships and cruisers might appear a few hours later. Because of the continual and heavy bombing attacks upon Malta, the air reconnaissance from the island was very thin and the further movements of enemy surface forces were not reported.

The air attacks upon Vian's force and the convoy started at 9.30 a.m. on the 22nd, half an hour after the last fighter patrol had had to leave, and continued with increasing intensity until dusk. In all some one hundred and fifty aircraft were used, torpedo and high-level bombers, shadowers and spotters. The attacks during the morning, confined to a few torpedo shots at long range by Italian aircraft, were not particularly dangerous. The convoy being well protected by an inner screen of cruisers and destroyers, with more destroyers about two miles ahead, the Italians were beaten off by heavy gunfire. It was later in the day, when the German aircraft came into action, that the convoy and escort were hard put to avoid damage.

Vian was determined that come what might the convoy would not turn back; but should, in his own words, 'proceed to Malta even if enemy surface forces made contact.' The general plan which had been evolved and practised was for the four cruisers and eleven 'Fleet' destroyers to be organized in five divisions. Working semi-independently, they would lay smoke between the enemy and the convoy, and then turn and attack with torpedoes under cover of the smoke-screen if the enemy attempted to break through it. At the same time the anti-aircraft cruiser *Carlisle* and one 'Hunt' class destroyer would lay a smoke-screen across the wake of the convoy, while the remaining five 'Hunts' formed a close escort to the convoy against air attack.

At 12.30 p.m. Vian assumed his organization to fight a surface action on the lines planned, and an hour later, when a shadowing aircraft dropped four red flares ahead of the convoy, he had his first intimation that enemy ships were probably in the vicinity. They were not expected to make contact until 4.30 or 5 p.m. However, at 2.10 p.m. the *Euryalus* reported smoke to the northward, while seventeen minutes later both the *Euryalus* and *Legion* reported ships in that direction, much earlier than expected. Originally thought to be three battleships they were, in fact, two 8-inch cruisers and one 6-inch cruiser with four destroyers. Their range was about twelve miles. It was blowing a strong breeze from the south-east, which was rapidly freshening, with a rough sea and moderate swell.

The Rear-Admiral at once led out to the northward, concentrating by divisions, while the convoy and close escort turned away to the southward. Once clear of the convoy Vian's divisions turned eastward to lay their smoke-screen. The enemy opened fire at 2.36 at very long range, and as they had now been recognized as cruisers, Vian swung round towards them, still making smoke. At 2.56 the *Cleopatra* and *Euryalus* opened fire on a heavy cruiser at a range of about twenty thousand yards; but the enemy turned northward after five minutes and finally drew out of range. One of the Italian cruisers turned back for a few minutes for a sharp exchange of fire with our two cruisers; but turned away at 3.15 to rejoin her consorts. The enemy having gone, Vian steered to rejoin the convoy, and at 3.35 made me a signal saying 'Enemy driven off'.

We were, of course, intercepting all his signals at Alexandria. So far all was well.

*

A few Italian high-level bombers had harmlessly attacked Vian's striking force during the short engagement. The whole venom of the German J.U.

88's had been concentrated on the convoy, which made high-level and dive-bombing attacks from 9,000 feet. Thanks to the good shooting of the escort and the excellent handling of the convoy their attacks achieved nothing except to cause a great expenditure of ammunition on our part. The *Carlisle* had already expended one-third of her outfit, while the *Southwold*, one of the 'Hunt' class, reported – 'Nine attacks so far. Forty per cent 4-inch ammunition remaining.' In the heavy sea and the rising wind the destroyers had been fighting their guns in the most difficult conditions, with their gun crews drenched. The ships were washing down forward and aft. Even the bridges and director towers of the cruisers were swept by heavy spray when they steamed to windward.

Hardly had the Rear-Admiral overhauled the convoy when the *Zulu*, at 4.37, again reported four ships to the north-eastward. At 4.48 we heard Vian's report of one enemy battleship and four cruisers, and at 5.8 he reported that the enemy battleship was accompanied by cruisers and destroyers. The enemy was in two groups, and as we know now the nearest, about nine miles away, consisted of two 8-inch cruisers with a 6-inch cruiser and four destroyers, and the second, at a distance of 15 miles, of the battleship *Littorio*, and four destroyers. They were all steering south-west at high speed to cut off the convoy from Malta.

*

The pall of thick smoke laid by our ships, and constantly added to, spread like a thick blanket over the surface of the sea as it drifted to the north-westward with the wind. The enemy consistently tried to move round this smoke-screen to the westward to get at the convoy to the south. Our ships, dodging out and in of the frayed and tattered edges of the smoke cloud like a pack of snapping terriers, determinedly prevented the Italian movement by engaging with guns and torpedoes as opportunity offered.

No enemy destroyers seem to have taken part in the action. The Italian force engaged consisted of the battleship *Littorio*, with her 15-inch guns, two 8-inch cruisers and one 6-inch cruiser; ours of four weak cruisers and eleven destroyers. Out-gunned though they were, our ships did not hesitate to engage at the moderate ranges of 10,000 to 14,000 yards, or to close in to 6,000 yards to fire torpedoes. We had some casualties. Hit by a 6-inch shell on the bridge, the *Cleopatra*, Vian's flagship, was damaged and sustained some casualties. The *Havock*, near missed by a 15-inch shell, had a boiler badly damaged which reduced her speed to 16 knots. Another 15-inch shell crippled the *Kingston* as she turned to fire torpedoes at a range of 6,000 yards, though she was able to reach Malta under her own steam. The *Euryalus* and *Lively* were hit by shell splinters, though their damage was not serious. The only hit sustained by the Italians was by a medium-sized shell which burst aft in the *Littorio*. Our expenditure of ammunition was heavy; but much of the gunfire was inevitably ineffective, the range being uncertain and the shell splashes being invisible because of smoke, the wild weather and the long range at which most of the action was fought.

391

Exceptionally fine work was done by Captain Micklethwait and his four destroyers which held off the enemy without other support for nearly half-an-hour, described by Vian as 'a remarkable feat'; while Captain Poland, with his four destroyers and the *Legion*, was responsible for the determined and courageous torpedo attack at 6,000 yards which finally caused the enemy to turn back. From the Italian accounts we know that many torpedoes crossed the enemy line, though none hit. The threat was enough.

Our relief at Alexandria was indescribable when we heard that the Italians were withdrawing. To try and take some of the responsibility off Vian I signalled to him that doubtless he had considered dispersing the convoy and letting them make their way to Malta as fast as they could steam. He had anticipated my thoughts and had already done so. At 7.40 p.m. with darkness fast approaching and the convoy not being in sight, he had decided to turn back to Alexandria and to send the convoy on. It was known that the Italians were retiring to the northward, and having failed to make contact with the convoy by day, being driven off, it was unlikely that they would risk a night attack. 'The weather was strong south-easterly to east-south-easterly gale, with a rising sea and swell,' Vian wrote in his despatch. 'Fuel in the "K" class and "Hunt" class destroyers was insufficient to allow an extra day to be spent in the central basin off Benghazi, so it was necessary to get as far east as possible through bomb alley by daylight.'

*

The two Malta ships, the *Penelope* and *Legion*, joined the convoy after dark, as did the damaged *Havock* and *Kingston*. The *Carlisle* and the six 'Hunt' destroyers also remained in company. At 7 p.m. Captain Hutchison, of H.M.S. *Breconshire*, the convoy Commodore, had obeyed the operation orders on his own initiative, and had dispersed his four ships on diverging courses to make the best of their way to Malta at full speed, each with a destroyer or two as escort. It was intended that they should reach the island at daylight on the 23rd; but the enforced detour to the south during the action gave the enemy bombers another chance. In spite of the gregale, and a thick and lowering dawn, aircraft appeared at daylight. The ships had to run the gauntlet of the aircraft attacks all the way to the entrance to the Grand Harbour, with the escorts, perilously short of ammunition, opening fire only when immediate danger threatened. Our fighters did good work, though greatly hampered by the weather and the damage caused to the airfields by continual bombing.

The Norwegian *Talabot* and the *Pampas* passed through the breakwater entrance soon after 9 a.m., each accompanied by a destroyer. Both ships had had narrow escapes two hours before, the *Pampas* actually being hit by bombs which failed to explode.

The *Clan Campbell* was sunk fifty miles south of Malta and the supply ship *Breconshire* mortally wounded, although later towed into Grand

Harbour and most of her cargo of fuel unloaded through pipes driven into her exposed bottom. Apart from the fuel only 5,000 of the 26,000 tons of cargo which had been embarked was safely landed at Malta, after the *Talabot* with her vital cargo of ammunition had to be flooded and sunk in harbour, in case the whole lot exploded.

Vian had a difficult passage back to Alexandria in the teeth of the gale, though his ships suffered no damage beyond that caused by the bad weather. He had started off at 22 knots; but soon had to reduce to 18 and then to 15 knots. By dawn on the 23rd only one destroyer, the *Sikh*, was still in company, all the others having dropped astern through the bad weather in which most of them had sustained damage. R.A.F. fighters were over the force throughout most of the day, though working at very long distances from their bases. Enemy shadowers appeared during the morning; but no attacks developed until 4.10 p.m., when eight J.U. 87's came in, concentrating largely upon the damaged *Lively*, which was a mile or so astern because of her action and weather damage. Until dusk sporadic attacks were made by J.U. 88's and torpedo-bombers, though no ships were hit. Speed was increased when the weather moderated, and the *Lively*, unable to steam more than 17 knots, was detached to Tobruk.

Vian, with the rest of the force, was able to increase to 26 knots at dawn on the 24th, and after an early morning attack by two enemy torpedo-bombers which achieved nothing, he arrived at Alexandria at 12.30 p.m. – 'honoured', as he says, 'to receive the great demonstration that then ensued.' Indeed, they had a wonderful reception, being enthusiastically cheered by the crews of all the warships and merchant vessels in the harbour.

*

The determination and team-work of all the ships engaged more than fulfilled the high standard expected of them. This, combined with the fine leadership and masterly handling of his force by Philip Vian, produced a heartening and thoroughly deserved victory from a situation in which, had the roles been reversed, it is unthinkable that the convoy or much of its escort would not have been destroyed.

from *A Sailor's Odyssey* by Admiral of the Fleet, Viscount Cunningham of
Hyndhope

Sources

Anon, *Cavendish, or the Patrician at Sea*,

Anon, *The Life of a Sailor*,

Anon, *The Saucy Jack*, R. Bentley, 1832

Beach, Captain Edward, L., *Around the World Submerged*, Hodder and Stoughton, 1965

Belloc, Hilaire, *The Hills and the Sea*, Methuen, 1906

Berckman, Evelyn, *The Hidden Navy*, Hamish Hamilton, 1976

Bradford, Ernle, *Ulysses Found*, Hodder and Stoughton, 1963

Brassey, Lady, *A Voyage in the Sunbeam*, Longman's Green, 1878

Brooke, Geoffrey, *Alarm Starboard!*, Patrick Stephens, 1982

Broome, Captain Jack, *Make a Signal*, Putnam, 1955

Brown, Warren and Newbold-Smith, E., extract from *CCA News*, 1987

Buchheim, Lothar-Gunther, *U-boat*, Collins, 1974

Burland, Charles, *The Ship's Captain's Medical Guide*, HMSO, 1918

Carson, Rachel, *The Sea Around Us*, Staples, 1951

Chalmers, W. S., *The Life and Letters of David, Earl Beatty*, Hodder and Stoughton, 1951

Chamier, Captain F., *Ben Brace, The Last of Nelson's Agamemnons*, R. Bentley, 1836

Chatterton, E. Keble, *King's Cutters and Smugglers*, George Allen, 1912

Chichester, Sir Francis, *Gipsy Moth Circles the World*, Hodder and Stoughton, 1967

Churchill, Winston S., *The World Crisis, 1911–1918*, Odhams, 1938

Clancy, Tom, *The Hunt for Red October*, Collins, 1985

Coles, K. Adlard, *Heavy Weather Sailing*, Grafton, 1988

Conrad, Joseph, *Typhoon*, J. M. Dent, 1902

——, *Youth*, J. M. Dent, 1902

Coote, Captain John, *The Shell Guide to Yacht Navigation*, Faber and Faber, 1987

Cowper, Frank, *Sailing Tours*, Upton Gill, 1893

Course, Captain A. G., *Pirates of the Eastern Seas*, Frederick Muller, 1966

Cremer, Peter, *U-333*, The Bodley Head, 1982

Cunningham, Admiral of the Fleet Viscount, *A Sailor's Odyssey*, Hutchinson, 1951

Curling, Revd J. J., *Coastal Navigation*, Simpkin and Marshall, 1892

Dana, Richard Henry, *Two Years Before the Mast*, 1869

Darwin, Charles, *The Voyage of the Beagle*, J. M. Dent, 1959

Dufferin, Lord, *Letters from High Latitudes*, John Murray, 1857

England, Richard, *Schoonerman*, Hollis and Carter, 1981

Falkus, Hugh, *Master of Cape Horn*, Victor Gollancz, 1982

Forrester, C. S., *Mr Midshipman Hornblower*, Michael Joseph, 1950

Fox, Uffa, *The Joys of Life*, Newnes, 1966

Glascock, Captain W. N., *Naval Sketch-book*, Simpkin and Marshall, 1826

Goodrich, Marcus, *Delilah*, J. M. Dent, 1941
Gordon, Richard, *The Captain's Table*, Michael Joseph, 1954
——, *Doctor at Sea*, Michael Joseph, 1953
Heyerdahl, Thor, *The Kon-Tiki Expedition*, Allen and Unwin, 1950
Homer, *The Odyssey*, translated by Butcher and Lang, Penguin
Hough, Richard, *The Blind Horn's Hate*, Hutchinson, 1971
Hutchinson, J. R., *The Press Gang*, Eveleigh Nash, 1913
Jacobs, W. W., *Many Cargoes*, Methuen, 1900
James, Naomi, *At One with the Sea*, Hutchinson, 1979
Jones, W. H. Sidney, *The Cape Horn Breed*, Andrew Melrose, 1956
Kahre, George, *The Last Tall Ships*, Conway, 1978
King, Commander W. D., *Capsize*, Nautical, 1969
——, *The Stick and the Stars*, Hutchinson, 1958
Kipling, Rudyard, *Captains Courageous*, Macmillan, 1897
Knox-Johnston, Robin, *A World of My Own*, Grafton, 1988
Koelbel, William H., *The Seas and the Oceans*, Motorboating Magazine, [1930s]
Kusche, Lawrence D., *The Bermuda Triangle Mystery – Solved*, Harper and Row, 1975
Leacock, Stephen, *Nonsense Novels ('Soaked in Seaweed')*, Bodley Head, 1918
Leslie, Anita, *Love in a Nutshell*, Hutchinson, 1952
Lewis, David, *Ice Bird*, Collins, 1975
——, *The Voyaging Stars*, Collins, 1978
Lloyd, Christopher, *The British Seaman*, Collins, 1968
Lubbock, Basil, *The China Clippers*, Glasgow, Brown, 1914
Lucas, Bill and Spedding, Andrew, *Sod's Law of the Sea*, Stanford Maritime, 1977
McMaster, John B., *A History of the People of the United States*, Farrar, Straus and Giroux, 1964
Marryat, Captain Frederick, *The King's Own*, Saunders and Otley, 1830
——, *Mr Midshipman Easy*, Richard Bentley, 1836
Martyr, Weston, *The Southseaman*, Blackwood, 1926
Masefield, John, *The Bird of Dawning*, Heinemann, 1933
Mitchell, Carleton, *The Wind's Call*, Scribners, 1971, (published UK as *The Wind Knows No Boundaries*), Nautical, 1972
Monsarrat, Nicholas, *The Cruel Sea*, Cassell, 1951
Morgan, Charles, *The Gunroom*, Chatto and Windus, 1919
Morison, Samuel Eliot, *History of US Naval Operations in World War II*, vol. XIII, Little Brown, 1959
New English Bible, Oxford University Press and Cambridge University Press, 1967
Newby, Eric, *The Last Grain Race*, Secker and Warburg, 1956
Novikoff-Priby, A., *Tsushima*, trans. Eden and Cedar Paul, Allen and Unwin, 1936
Oman, Carola, *Nelson*, Hodder and Stoughton, 1947
Oram, Captain H. K., *Ready for Sea*, Seeley Service, 1974
Pope, Dudley, *Life in Nelson's Navy*, Allen and Unwin, 1981

Punch (ed.), *Mr Punch's History of the Great War*, Cassell, 1919

Raleigh, Professor Walter, *Hakluyt's Voyages*, James Maclehose, 1904

Randier, Jean, *Men and Ships around Cape Horn*, Arthur Barker, 1969

Rietschoten, Cornelis van and Pickthall, Barry, *Blue Water Racing*, Nautical, 1985

Robertson, Terence, *Walker, R. N.*, White Lion, 1975

Robinson, C. N., *The British Tar in Fact and Fiction*, Harper and Bros, 1909

Roth, Hal, *Two Against Cape Horn*, Stanford Maritime, 1979

Severin, Tim, *The Brendan Voyage*, Hutchinson, 1978

Shackleton, Sir Ernest, *South*, Heinemann, 1919

Shore and Harper, *The Smugglers*, Cecil Palmer, 1928

Slocum, Joshua, *Sailing Alone Around the World*, Rupert Hart-Davis, new ed. 1948

Smyth, H. Warington, *Mast and Sail*, John Murray, 1906

Snaith, William, *On the Wind's Way*, Putnam, 1973

Spencer, Alfred (ed.), *Memoirs of William Hickey*, Hurst and Blackett, 1918

Stenson, Patrick, *Lights: The Odyssey of C. H. Lightoller*, Bodley Head, 1984

Thomson, George Malcolm, *Sir Francis Drake*, Secker and Warburg, 1972

——, *The North-West Passage*, Secker and Warburg, 1975

Tilman, H. W., *Mischief in Patagonia*, Cambridge University Press, 1957

Tomlinson, H. M., *Gallion's Reach*, Harper and Row, 1927

——, *Morning Light*, Hodder and Stoughton, 1946

Verne, Jules, *Twenty Thousand Leagues Under the Sea*, James Nisbet, (1869)

Villiers, Alan, *War with Cape Horn*, Hodder and Stoughton, 1971

Walter, Richard, *Anson's Voyage Round the World in the Years 1740–44*, Martin Hopkinson, 1928

Ward, Edward, *The Wooden World*, Edwin Chappell, 1907

Worth, Claud, *Yacht Cruising*, J. D. Potter, 1910

Wouk, Herman, *The Caine Mutiny*, Jonathan Cape, 1951

Young, Edward, *One of Our Submarines*, Rupert Hart-Davis, 1952

Ziegler, Philip, *Mountbatten*, Collins, 1985

Acknowledgements

For permission to reprint copyright material the publishers gratefully acknowledge the following. Where the copyright-holder is other than the original publisher, the latter's name is given in brackets. The name of the US rights controller follows that of the UK and Commonwealth copyright-holder. One name only denotes world rights. Faber and Faber apologizes for any errors or omissions in this list and would be grateful to be notified of any corrections that should be incorporated in any future reprint of this volume. Sources are listed alphabetically by author.

Around the World Submerged by Capt. Edward L. Beach (Hodder and Stoughton, 1963), Laurence Pollinger Ltd and Holt Rinehart and Winston Inc.; *The Hills and the Sea* by Hilaire Belloc (Methuen), A. D. Peters and Co Ltd; *The Hidden Navy* by Evelyn Berckman (1976), Hamish Hamilton Ltd; *Ulysses Found* by Ernle Bradford (Hodder and Stoughton, 1963), A. M. Heath for the Estate of Ernle Bradford; *Alarm Starboard!* by Geoffrey Brooke (Patrick Stephens, 1982), Thorsons Publishing Group Ltd; *Make a Signal* by Capt. Jack Broome (Putnam, 1955), A. M. Heath for the Estate of Jack Broome; Extract from *CCA News*, 1987, by Warren Brown and E. Newbold-Smith, the Cruising Club of America; *U-boat* by Lothar-Gunther Buchheim (1974), Collins Publishers; *The Sea Around Us* by Rachel Carson (Staples, 1951), Laurence Pollinger Ltd and Oxford University Press, New York, for the Estate of Rachel Carson; *Gipsy Moth Circles the World* by Sir Francis Chichester (1967), Hodder and Stoughton Ltd and John Farquharson Ltd; *The World Crisis 1911–1918* by Winston S. Churchill (Odhams, 1938), Curtis Brown on behalf of the Churchill Estate; *The Hunt for Red October* by Tom Clancy (Collins, 1985), the Putnam Publishing Group and Tom Clancy; *Heavy Weather Sailing* by K. Adlard Coles, Grafton Books, a division of the Collins Publishing Group, Mrs Mamie Coles and John De Graaf Inc.; *The Shell Guide to Yacht Navigation* by Capt. J. Coote (1988), Faber and Faber Ltd and Capt. J. Coote; *A Sailor's Odyssey* by Admiral of the Fleet Viscount Cunningham (Hutchinson, 1951), Mrs H. M. B. McKendrick; *Schoonerman* by Richard England (Hollis and Carter, 1981), The Bodley Head; *Master of Cape Horn* by Hugh Falkus (1982), Victor Gollancz Ltd; *Mr Midshipman Hornblower* by C. S. Forrester (Michael Joseph, 1950), A. D. Peters and Co. Ltd; *The Joys of Life* by Uffa Fox (Newnes, 1966), The Hamlyn Publishing Group Ltd; *The Captain's Table* (1954) and *Doctor at Sea* by Richard Gordon (1953), Michael Joseph Ltd and Richard Gordon; *The Kon-Tiki Expedition* by Thor Heyerdahl (Allen and Unwin, 1950), Unwin Hyman Ltd and Simon and Schuster Inc. (1984); *The Blind Horn's Hate* by Richard Hough (Hutchinson, 1971), London Management and Richard Hough; *At One with the Sea* by Naomi James (1979), Century Hutchinson Publishing Group Ltd; *The Stick and the Stars* (Hutchinson, 1958) and *Capsize* (Nautical, 1971) by Bill King, Commander W. D. King; *A World of My Own* by Robin Knox-Johnston (Grafton, 1988), Grafton Books (a division of the Collins Publishing Group) and John

Farquharson Ltd; *The Bermuda Triangle Mystery – Solved* by Lawrence D. Kusche (Harper and Row, 1975), L. D. Kusche; *Nonsense Novels ('Soaked in Seaweed')* by Stephen Leacock (Bodley Head, 1918), the Estate of Stephen Leacock, Dodd, Mead and Co. Inc. (USA), and McClelland and Stewart (Canada); *Love in a Nutshell* by Anita Leslie (Hutchinson, 1952), Century Hutchinson and Commander W. D. King; *Ice Bird* (Collins, 1975) and *The Voyaging Stars* (Collins, 1978) by David Lewis, Curtis Brown (Pty) Australia Ltd; *Sod's Law of the Sea* by Bill Lucas and Andrew Spedding (Stanford Maritime, 1977), George Philip Ltd; *The Bird of Dawning* by John Masefield (Heinemann, 1933), the Society of Authors as the Literary Representatives of the Estate of John Masefield; *The Wind's Call* (Scribners, 1971, and, under the title *The Wind Knows No Boundaries*, Nautical, 1972), by Carleton Mitchell, Charles Scribner's Sons, an imprint of Macmillan Publishing Company; *The Cruel Sea* by Nicholas Monsarrat (Cassell, 1951/ Penguin), Mrs Ann Monsarrat for the Estate of Nicholas Monsarrat, 1951, and Alfred A. Knopf Inc.; *History of US Naval Operations in World War II*, Vol. XIII, *The Liberation of the Philippines: Luzon-Mindanao, the Visayas, 1944–1945* by Samuel Eliot Morison (1959), Little, Brown and Company; *The Last Grain Race* by Eric Newby (1956), Martin Secker and Warburg Ltd; *Nelson* by Carola Oman (Hodder and Stoughton, 1947), the Estate of Carola Oman; *Life in Nelson's Navy* by Dudley Pope (Allen and Unwin, 1981), Campbell Thomson and McLaughlin Ltd. for Dudley Pope and Naval Institute Press; *Two Against Cape Horn* by Hal Roth (Stanford Maritime, 1978), Hal Roth and W. W. Norton Inc.; *The Brendan Voyage* by Tim Severin (1978), Century Hutchinson Publishing Group and Anthony Sheil Ltd; *Mast and Sail* by H. Warington Smyth (John Murray, 1906), Nigel Warington Smyth; *On the Wind's Way* by William Snaith (Secker and Warburg, 1972, Putnam, 1973), Raymond Lowey Inc. and the Putnam Publishing Group; *Lights: The Odyssey of C. H. Lightoller* by Patrick Stenson (Bodley Head, 1984), C. H. Lightoller and W. W. Norton Inc.; *Sir Francis Drake* (Secker and Warburg, 1972) and *The North-West Passage* by George Malcolm Thomson (Secker and Warburg, 1975), David Higham Ltd; *Mischief in Patagonia* by H. W. Tilman (Cambridge University Press, 1957), the Executors of H. W. Tilman; *Gallion's Reach* (Harper and Row, 1927) and *Morning Light* (Hodder and Stoughton, 1946) by H. M. Tomlinson, Mrs Dorothy Tomlinson; *War with Cape Horn*, by Alan Villiers (Hodder and Stoughton, 1971), Laurence Pollinger Ltd for the Estate of Alan Villiers; *The Caine Mutiny* by Herman Wouk (1951), Jonathan Cape and Doubleday and Co; *One of our Submarines* by Edward Young (Rupert Hart-Davis, 1952), Edward Young; *Mountbatten* by Philip Ziegler (Collins, 1985), Collins Publishers and Alfred A. Knopf Inc.

The extract from the *New English Bible* (1970) is reproduced by permission of Oxford and Cambridge University Presses.

Index